An Introduction to Language

An Introduction to Language

SEVENTH EDITION

Victoria Fromkin

University of California, Los Angeles (Deceased)

Robert Rodman

North Carolina State University, Raleigh

Nina Hyams

University of California, Los Angeles

THOMSON
™
WADSWORTH

Australia   Canada   Mexico   Singapore   Spain   United Kingdom   United States

An Introduction to Language,
Seventh Edition

Victoria Fromkin, Robert Rodman, Nina Hyams

Publisher: *Michael Rosenberg*
Acquisitions Editor: *Stephen Dalphin*
Developmental Editor: *Amanda Robinson*
Production Editor: *Lianne Ames*
Director of HED Marketing: *Lisa Kimball*
Executive Marketing Manager: *Ken Kasee*
Marketing Manager: *Katrina Byrd*
Manufacturing Coordinator: *Marcia Locke*

Compositor, Text Designer: *Publishers' Design and Production Services*
Project Manager: *Gail Farrar*
Copyeditor: *Joan Flaherty*
Cover Illustration: © *Artville/Getty*
Cover Designer: *Ha Nguyen*
Printer: *Maple Vail Printers*

Printed in the United States
   3 4 5 6 7 8 9 10   07 06 05 04

For more information contact Wadsworth,
25 Thomson Place, Boston, Massachusetts 02210 USA,
or you can visit our Internet site at
http://www.wadsworth.com

For permission to use material from this text or product contact us:

Tel	1-800-730-2214
Fax	1-800-730-2215
Web	www.thomsonrights.com

**Library of Congress
Cataloging-in Publication Data**

Fromkin, Victoria
   An introduction to language / Victoria Fromkin, Robert Rodman, Nina Hyams.—7th ed.
      p. cm.
   Includes biographical references and index.
   ISBN 0-15-508481-X
   1. Language and languages. 2. Linguistics.   I. Rodman, Robert.   II. Hyams, Nina M.   III. Title
P107 .F76 2002
410—dc21

                                    2002069080

To the memory of Victoria Fromkin

About the Authors

Victoria Fromkin received her bachelor's degree in economics from the University of California, Berkeley, in 1944 and her M.A. and Ph.D. in linguistics from the University of California, Los Angeles, in 1963 and 1965, respectively. She was a member of the faculty of the UCLA Department of Linguistics from 1966 until her death in 2000, and served as its chair from 1972 to 1976. From 1979 to 1989 she served as the UCLA Graduate Dean and Vice Chancellor of Graduate Programs. She was a visiting professor at the Universities of Stockholm, Cambridge, and Oxford. Dr. Fromkin served as president of the Linguistics Society of America in 1985, president of the Association of Graduate Schools in 1988, and chair of the Board of Governors of the Academy of Aphasia. She received the UCLA Distinguished Teaching Award and the Professional Achievement Award, and served as the U.S. Delegate and a member of the Executive Committee of the International Permanent Committee of Linguistics (CIPL). She was an elected Fellow of the American Academy of Arts and Sciences, the American Association for the Advancement of Science, the New York Academy of Science, the American Psychological Society, and the Acoustical Society of America, and in 1996 was elected to membership in the National Academy of Sciences. She published more than one hundred books, monographs, and papers on topics concerned with phonetics, phonology, tone languages, African languages, speech errors, processing models, aphasia, and the brain/mind/language interface — all research areas in which she worked. Professor Fromkin passed away on January 19, 2000, at the age of 76.

Robert Rodman received his bachelor's degree in mathematics from UCLA in 1961, a master's degree in mathematics in 1965, a master's degree in linguistics in 1971, and his Ph.D. in linguistics in 1973. He has been on the faculties of the University of California at Santa Cruz, the University of North Carolina at Chapel Hill, Kyoto Industrial College in Japan, and North Carolina State University, where he is a professor of computer science. His current areas of interest are computer speech processing, and in particular, lip synchronization — animating a face to speech; and voice recognition — computer identification of persons by voice alone. Professor Rodman resides in Raleigh, North Carolina, with his wife, Helen, and their two dogs.

Nina Hyams received her bachelor's degree in journalism from Boston University in 1973 and her M.A. and Ph.D. degrees in linguistics from the Graduate Center of the City University of New York in 1981 and 1983, respectively. She joined the UCLA faculty in 1983, where she is currently professor of linguistics and co-director of the UCLA

Psycholinguistics Laboratory and the UCLA Infant Language Laboratory. Her main areas of research are childhood language development and syntax. She is author of the book *Language Acquisition and the Theory of Parameters* (D. Reidel Publishers, 1986), a milestone in language acquisition research. She has also published numerous articles on the development of syntax and morphology in children. She has been a visiting scholar at the University of Utrecht and the University of Leiden in the Netherlands and has given numerous lectures throughout Europe and Japan. Professor Hyams resides in Los Angeles with her son, Michael, and their two dogs, Pete and Max.

Preface

Well, this bit which I am writing, called Introduction, is
really the er-h'r'm of the book, and I have put it in, partly
so as not to take you by surprise, and partly because I
can't do without it now. There are some very clever
writers who say that it is quite easy not to have an
er-h'r'm, but I don't agree with them. I think it is much
easier not to have all the rest of the book.

A. A. Milne

The seventh edition of *An Introduction to Language* is dedicated to the memory of our
friend, colleague, mentor, and coauthor, Victoria Fromkin. Vicki loved language,
and she loved to tell people about it. She found linguistics fun and fascinating, and she
wanted every student and every teacher to think so, too. Though this edition is completely rewritten for improved clarity and currency, we have nevertheless preserved
Vicki's lighthearted, personal approach to a complex topic, including humorous and
pithy quotations from noted authors (A. A. Milne was one of Vicki's favorites). We hope
we have kept the spirit of Vicki's love for teaching about language alive in the pages of
this book.

The first six editions of *An Introduction to Language* succeeded, with the help of
dedicated teachers, in introducing the nature of human language to tens of thousands
of students. This is a book that students enjoy and understand, and that professors find
effective and thorough. Not only have majors in linguistics benefited from the book's
easy-to-read yet comprehensive presentation, majors in fields as diverse as teaching
English as a second language, foreign language studies, general education, psychology,
sociology, and anthropology have enjoyed learning about language from this book.

This edition includes new developments in linguistics and related fields that will
strengthen its appeal to a wider audience. Much of this information will enable students
to gain insight and understanding about linguistic issues and debates appearing in the

national media, and will help professors and students stay current with important linguistic research. We hope that it may also dispel certain common misconceptions that people have about language and language use.

The second chapter, "Brain and Language," retains its forward placement in the book because we believe that one can learn about the brain through language, and about the nature of the human being through the brain. This chapter may be read and appreciated without technical knowledge of linguistics. When the centrality of language to human nature is appreciated, students will be motivated to learn more about human language, and about linguistics, because they will be learning more about themselves. As in the previous edition, highly detailed illustrations of MRI and PET scans of the brain are included, and this chapter highlights some of the new results and tremendous progress in the study of neurolinguistics over the past few years. The arguments for the autonomy of language in the human brain are carefully presented so that the student sees how experimental evidence is applied to support scientific theories.

Chapters 3 and 4, morphology and syntax, have been substantially revised to reflect current thinking on how words and sentences are structured, in particular, with regard to the concept of *head*. Comparison of languages is intended to enhance the student's understanding of the differences among languages as well as the universal aspects of grammar. Nevertheless, the introductory spirit of these chapters is not sacrificed, and students gain a deep understanding of word and phrase structure with a minimum of formalisms, and a maximum of insightful examples and explanations, as always supplemented by quotes, poetry, and humor.

Chapter 7, phonology, is also substantially revised to reflect current paradigms, yet with a greater emphasis on insights through linguistic data accompanied by small amounts of well explicated formalisms, so that the student can appreciate the need for formal theories without experiencing the burdensome details. In this chapter as well as the chapters on morphology and syntax, "how to" sections on language analysis give students the opportunity for hands-on linguistic study. Exercises, many of them new, further increase the student's understanding of how language works.

The most significant revisions and additions to the seventh edition occur in Part 3, "The Psychology of Language." Chapter 8, "Language Acquisition," is rewritten "from the bottom up" to reflect the tremendous progress in our knowledge of how children learn language. Material on the acquisition of non-English languages supplements the generous amount of data already present on English acquisition. Bilingualism is taken up in detail with much new data, as is L2—the learning of a second language. The arguments for innateness and Universal Grammar that language acquisition provides are exploited to show the student how scientific theories of great import are discovered and supported through observation, experiment, and reason. As in most chapters, American Sign Language (ASL) is discussed and its important role in understanding the biological foundations of language emphasized.

In chapter 9, the section on psycholinguistics is updated to conform to recent discoveries, and the section on computational linguistics has been entirely renovated to reflect progress in machine translation, speech synthesis, speech recognition, and language understanding.

Part 4 is concerned with language in society, including sociolinguistics and historical linguistics. Chapter 10 includes material on language variation and the study of ethnic minority and social dialects. Attitudes toward language and how they reflect the views and mores of society are included in this chapter. We establish the scientific basis for discussing such topics as Ebonics (a popular term for dialects of African-American English) and so-called "standard" languages. Another section on language and sexism reflects a growing concern with this topic.

Chapter 11 on language change includes a greatly expanded section on language extinction, the reasons for it, and what may be done about it. The chapter has also been restructured to improve clarity, and is supplemented with additional exercises and examples of the comparative method.

Chapter 12 on writing systems has additional discussions on writing communication via the Internet, which has a flavor of its own. This chapter should be read by those interested in the teaching of reading, and offers some reasons as to "why Johnny can't read."

Terms that appear bold in the text are defined in the revised glossary in the appendix. The glossary has been expanded and improved with more than 600 entries.

The order of presentation of chapters 3 through 7 was once thought to be nontraditional. Our experience, backed by previous editions of the book and the recommendations of colleagues throughout the world, have convinced us that it is easier for the novice to approach the structural aspects of language by first looking at morphology (the structure of the most familiar linguistic unit, the word). This is followed by syntax, the structure of sentences, which is also familiar to many students, as are numerous semantic concepts. We then proceed to the more novel (to students) phonetics and phonology, which students often find daunting. However, the book is written so that individual instructors can present material in the traditional order of phonetics, phonology, morphology, syntax, and semantics (chapters 6, 7, 3, 4, and 5) without confusion, if they wish.

As in previous editions, the primary concern has been with basic ideas rather than detailed expositions. This book assumes no previous knowledge on the part of the reader. A list of references at the end of each chapter is included to accommodate any reader who wishes to pursue a subject in more depth. Each chapter concludes with a summary and exercises to enhance the student's interest in and comprehension of the textual material.

We are deeply grateful to the individuals who have sent us suggestions, corrections, criticisms, cartoons, language data, and exercises, all of which we have tried to incorporate in this new edition. We owe special thanks to colleagues who reviewed the manuscript in progress: Jennifer Cole and Rajka Smiljanic, University of Illinois at Urbana-Champaign; Molly Diesing, Cornell University; Genevieve Escure, University of Minnesota; Patrick Farrell, University of California-Davis; Elly van Gelderen, Arizona State University; Maurice Holder, University of New Brunswick; Bruce C. Johnson, University of Northern Colorado; Jane Kaplan, Ithaca College; Chin W. Kim, University of Illinois at Urbana-Champaign; Elisabeth Kuhn, Virginia Commonwealth University; Seung-Jae Moon, University of Wisconsin, Milwaukee; William C. Ritchie, Syracuse University; Michael B. Smith, Oakland University; Tully J. Thibeau, University of Montana; and Thomas E. Young, Purdue University North Central.

Others who have helped us are (and if we have omitted any of the many, please forgive us): Jon Hareide Aarbakke, Susan Ballance, Paul Baltes, Merry Bullock, Lyle Campbell, Richard S. Cervin, Don Churma, Billy Clark, Charles J. Coker, Susie Curtiss,

Roy Dace, J. Day, Kamil Ud Deen, David Deterding, Anthony Diller, Gregoire Dunant, M. Therese Gallegos, Mary Ghaleb, Jill Gilkerson, Lila R. Gleitman, Mark Hansell, Eric Hyman, Herbert Immenga, Olaf Jäkel, Yan Jiang, Kyle Johnson, Irina Kalika, Rachel Lagunoff, Yonata Levy, Monica Macaulay, Peggy MacEachern, Marcyliena Morgan, Pamela Munro, Jihwan Myeong, JaeHo Myung, Almerinda Ojeda, Gunter Radden, Willem J. deReuse, Otto Santa Ana, Carson Schütze, Bonnie Schwartz, Dawn L. Sievers, Gabriella Solomon, Kelly Stack, B. Stefanow, Ean Taylor, Larry Trask, Rudolf Weiss, John C. White, Howard Williams, Walt Wolfram, and Mary Wu.

We are particularly grateful to Hanna and Antonio Damasio of the University of Iowa Medical School for information on their brain studies and the MRI and PET illustrations; to Colin Wilson for extensive assistance with chapter 7, phonology; and to Stephen Wilson for writing the excellent solutions manual available to instructors.

Finally, we wish to thank the editorial and production team at Wadsworth. They have been superb and supportive in every way: Michael Rosenberg, acquisitions editor; Lianne Ames, senior production editor; Amanda Robinson, developmental editor; Joan M. Flaherty, copy editor; Sandra Lord, permissions editor; Gail Farrar, project manager, and Mark Bergeron, design.

The responsibility for errors in fact or judgment is, of course, ours alone. We continue to be indebted to the instructors who have used the earlier editions and to their students, without whom there would be no seventh edition.

Robert Rodman
Nina Hyams

Contents

Part 1
The Nature of Human Language

Part 2
Grammatical Aspects of Language

Chapter 3
Morphology: The Word of Language   69

Chapter 4
The Sentence Patterns of Language   117

Part 3
The Psychology of Language

Chapter 8
Language Acquisition 341

Chapter 9
Language Processing: Human and Computer   397

Part 4
Language and Society

The Nature of Human Language

Reflecting on Noam Chomsky's ideas on the innateness of the fundamentals of grammar in the human mind, I saw that any innate features of the language capacity must be a set of biological structures, selected in the course of the evolution of the human brain.

—S. E. Luria, *A Slot Machine, A Broken Test Tube, An Autobiography*

The nervous systems of all animals have a number of basic functions in common, most notably the control of movement and the analysis of sensation. What distinguishes the human brain is the variety of more specialized activities it is capable of learning. The preeminent example is language.

—Norman Geschwind, 1979

Linguistics shares with other sciences a concern to be objective, systematic, consistent, and explicit in its account of language. Like other sciences, it aims to collect data, test hypotheses, devise models, and construct theories. Its subject matter, however, is unique: at one extreme it overlaps with such 'hard' sciences as physics and anatomy; at the other, it involves such traditional 'arts' subjects as philosophy and literary criticism. The field of linguistics includes both science and the humanities, and offers a breadth of coverage that, for many aspiring students of the subject, is the primary source of its appeal.

—David Crystal, 1987

CHAPTER 1

What Is Language?

When we study human language, we are approaching
what some might call the "human essence," the
distinctive qualities of mind that are, so far as we know,
unique to man.

Noam Chomsky, *Language and Mind*

Whatever else people do when they come together — whether they play, fight, make love, or make automobiles — they talk. We live in a world of language. We talk to our friends, our associates, our wives and husbands, our lovers, our teachers, our parents, our rivals, and even our enemies. We talk to bus drivers and total strangers. We talk face-to-face and over the telephone, and everyone responds with more talk. Television and radio further swell this torrent of words. Hardly a moment of our waking lives is free from words, and even in our dreams we talk and are talked to. We also talk when there is no one to answer. Some of us talk aloud in our sleep. We talk to our pets and sometimes to ourselves.

The possession of language, perhaps more than any other attribute, distinguishes humans from other animals. To understand our humanity, one must understand the nature of language that makes us human. According to the philosophy expressed in the myths and religions of many peoples, language is the source of human life and power. To some people of Africa, a newborn child is a *kintu,* a "thing," not yet a *muntu,* a "person." Only by the act of learning language does the child become a human being. According to this tradition, then, we all become "human" because we all know at least one language. But what does it mean to "know" a language?

Linguistic Knowledge

When you know a language, you can speak and be understood by others who know that language. This means you have the capacity to produce sounds that signify certain meanings and to understand or interpret the sounds produced by others. We are referring to normal-hearing individuals. Deaf persons produce and understand sign languages just as hearing persons produce and understand spoken languages. The languages of the deaf communities throughout the world are, except for their modality of expression, equivalent to spoken languages.

Most everyone knows a language. Five-year-old children are nearly as proficient at speaking and understanding as their parents. Yet the ability to carry out the simplest conversation requires profound knowledge that most speakers are unaware of. This is true for speakers of all languages, from Albanian to Zulu. A speaker of English can produce a sentence having two relative clauses without knowing what a relative clause is, such as

My goddaughter who was born in Sweden and who now lives in Iowa is named Disa, after a Viking queen.

In a parallel fashion, a child can walk without understanding or being able to explain the principles of balance and support, or the neurophysiological control mechanisms that permit one to do so. The fact that we may know something unconsciously is not unique to language.

What, then, do speakers of English or Quechua or French or Mohawk or Arabic know?

Knowledge of the Sound System

Part of knowing a language means knowing what sounds (or signs[1]) are in that language and what sounds are not. This unconscious knowledge is revealed by the way speakers

B.C. By Johnny Hart

"B.C." copyright © Creators Syndicate, Inc. Reprinted by permission of Johnny Hart and Creators Syndicate, Inc.

---

[1] The sign languages of the deaf will be discussed throughout the book. As stated, they are essentially the same as spoken languages, except that they use gestures instead of sound. A reference to "language" then, unless speech sounds or spoken languages are specifically mentioned, includes both spoken and signed languages.

of one language pronounce words from another language. If you speak only English, for example, you may substitute an English sound for a non-English sound when pronouncing "foreign" words like French *ménage à trois*. If you pronounce it as the French do, you are using sounds outside the English sound system.

French people speaking English often pronounce words like *this* and *that* as if they were spelled *zis* and *zat*. The English sound represented by the initial letters *th* in these words is not part of the French sound system, and the French mispronunciation reveals the speakers' unconscious knowledge of this fact.

Knowing the sound system of a language includes more than knowing the inventory of sounds. It includes knowing which sounds may start a word, end a word, and follow each other. The name of a former president of Ghana was *Nkrumah,* pronounced with an initial sound like the sound ending the English word *sink*. While this is an English sound, no word in English begins with the *nk* sound. Speakers of English who have occasion to pronounce this name, often mispronounce it (by Ghanaian standards) by inserting a short vowel sound, like *Nekrumah* or *Enkrumah*. Children who learn English recognize that *nk* does not begin a word, just as Ghanaian children learn that words in their language may begin with the *nk* sound.

We will learn more about sound systems in chapters 6 and 7.

Knowledge of Words

Knowing the sounds and sound patterns in our language constitutes only one part of our linguistic knowledge. Knowing a language is also to know that certain sound sequences signify certain concepts or **meanings.** Speakers of English know what *boy* means, and that it means something different from *toy* or *girl* or *pterodactyl*. When you know a language, you know words in that language, that is, the sound units that are related to specific meanings.

Arbitrary Relation of Form and Meaning

> The minute I set eyes on an animal I know what it is. I don't have to reflect a moment; the right name comes out instantly. I seem to know just by the shape of the creature and the way it acts what animal it is. When the dodo came along he [Adam] thought it was a wildcat. But I saved him. I just spoke up in a quite natural way and said, "Well, I do declare if there isn't the dodo!"
>
> Mark Twain, *Eve's Diary*

If you do not know a language, the words (and sentences) will be mainly incomprehensible, because the relationship between speech sounds and the meanings they represent in the languages of the world is, for the most part, an **arbitrary** one. You have to learn, when you are acquiring the language, that the sounds represented by the letters *house* signify the concept ; if you know French, this same meaning is represented by *maison;* if you know Twi, it is represented by *ɔdaŋ;* if you know Russian, by *dom;* if you know Spanish, by *casa*. Similarly, is represented by *hand* in English, *main* in French, *nsa* in Twi, and *ruka* in Russian.

The following are words in some different languages. How many of them can you understand?

a. kyinii
b. doakam
c. odun
d. asa
e. toowq
f. bolna
g. wartawan
h. inaminatu
i. yawwa

Speakers of the languages from which these words are taken know that they have the following meanings:

a. a large parasol (in a Ghanaian language, Twi)
b. living creature (in a Native American language, Papago)
c. wood (in Turkish)
d. morning (in Japanese)
e. is seeing (in a California Indian language, Luiseño)
f. to speak (in a Pakistani language, Urdu); aching (in Russian)
g. reporter (in Indonesian)
h. teacher (in a Venezuelan Indian language, Warao)
i. right on! (in a Nigerian language, Hausa)

These examples show that the sounds of words are given meaning only by the language in which they occur, despite what Eve says in Mark Twain's satire *Eve's Diary.* A pterodactyl could have been called *ron, blick,* or *kerplunkity.*

As Shakespeare, in his play *Romeo and Juliet,* has Juliet say:

> What's in a name? That which we call a rose
> By any other name would smell as sweet.

This arbitrary relationship between **form** (sounds) and **meaning** (concept) of a word in spoken languages is also true in sign languages used by deaf people. If you see someone using a sign language you do not know, it is doubtful that you will understand the message from the signs alone. A person who knows Chinese Sign Language (CSL) would find it difficult to understand American Sign Language (ASL), and vice versa, as seen in Figure 1.1.

Many signs were originally like miming, where the relationship between form and meaning was not arbitrary. Bringing the hand to the mouth to mean "eating," as in miming, would be nonarbitrary as a sign. Over time these signs may change, just as the pronunciation of words change, and the miming effect is lost. These signs become **conventional,** so knowing the shape or movement of the hands does not reveal the meaning of the gestures in sign languages.

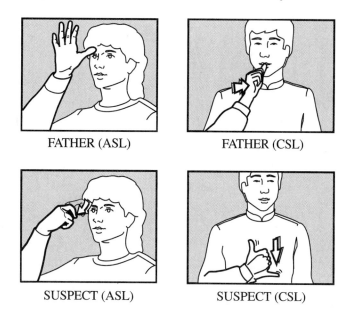

FATHER (ASL)　　　　FATHER (CSL)

SUSPECT (ASL)　　　　SUSPECT (CSL)

Figure 1.1　Arbitrary relation between gestures and meanings of the signs for *father* and *suspect* in ASL and CSL.[2] Copyright © 1987 by MIT Press. Reproduced by permission of MIT Press.

There is some **sound symbolism** in language — that is, words whose pronunciation suggests the meaning. Most languages contain **onomatopoeic** words like *buzz* or *murmur* that imitate the sounds associated with the objects or actions they refer to. Even here, the sounds differ among languages, reflecting the particular sound system of the language. In English *cock-a-doodle-doo* is an onomatopoeic word whose meaning is the crow of a rooster, whereas in Finnish the rooster's crow is *kukkokiekuu*. At the Internet address http://www.georgetown.edu/cball/animals/ you will find the onomatopoeic words in dozens of languages for the calls of dozens of animals. If you want to know the word for the sound that a turkey makes in Turkey, you can look it up. It's *glu-glu*.

Sometimes particular sound sequences seem to relate to a particular concept. In English many words beginning with *gl* relate to sight, such as *glare, glint, gleam, glitter, glossy, glaze, glance, glimmer, glimpse,* and *glisten*. However, such words are a very small part of any language, and *gl* may have nothing to do with "sight" in another language, or even in other words in English, such as *gladiator, glucose, glory, glutton, globe,* and so on.

English speakers know the *gl* words that relate to sight and those that do not; they know the onomatopoeic words and all the words in the basic vocabulary of the language. No speakers of English know all 450,000 words listed in *Webster's Third New International Dictionary*. Even if someone did, that person would not know English. Imagine

---

[2] From *What the Hands Reveal about the Brain* by H. Poizner, E. S. Klima, and U. Bellugi. 1987. Cambridge, MA: MIT Press.

trying to learn a foreign language by buying a dictionary and memorizing words. No matter how many words you learned, you would not be able to form the simplest phrases or sentences in the language, or understand a native speaker. No one speaks in isolated words. (Of course, you could search in your traveler's dictionary for individual words to find out how to say something like "car — gas — where?" After many tries, a native might understand this question and then point in the direction of a gas station. If you were answered with a sentence, however, you probably would not understand what was said or be able to look it up, because you would not know where one word ended and another began.) chapter 4 will explore how words are put together to form phrases and sentences, and chapter 5 will further explore word meanings.

The Creativity of Linguistic Knowledge

Knowledge of a language enables you to combine words to form phrases, and phrases to form sentences. You cannot buy a dictionary of any language with all its sentences, because no dictionary can list all the possible sentences. Knowing a language means being able to produce new sentences never spoken before and to understand sentences

never heard before. The linguist Noam Chomsky refers to this ability as part of the **creative aspect** of language use. Not every speaker of a language can create great literature, but you, and all persons who know a language, can and do create new sentences when you speak, and understand new sentences created by others.

To say that we are creative in our use of language means that language use is not limited to stimulus-response behavior. It's true that if someone steps on our toes we may automatically respond with a scream or a grunt, but these sounds are not part of language. They are involuntary reactions to stimuli. After we reflexively cry out, we can say: "Thank you very much for stepping on my toe, because I was afraid I had elephantiasis and now that I can feel it hurt I know I don't," or any one of an infinite number of sentences, because the particular sentence we produce is not controlled by any stimulus.

Even some involuntary cries like "ouch" are constrained by our own language system, as are the filled pauses that are sprinkled through conversational speech, such as *er, uh,* and *you know* in English. They contain only the sounds found in the language. French speakers, for example, often fill their pauses with the vowel sound that starts with their word for egg—*oeuf*—a sound that does not occur in English. Knowing a language includes knowing what sentences are appropriate in various situations. To say "Hamburger costs $4.00 a pound" after someone has just stepped on your toe would hardly be an appropriate response, although it would be possible.

Our creative ability not only is reflected in what we say but also includes our understanding of new or novel sentences. Consider the following sentence: "Daniel Boone decided to become a pioneer because he dreamed of pigeon-toed giraffes and cross-eyed elephants dancing in pink skirts and green berets on the wind-swept plains of the Midwest." You may not believe the sentence; you may question its logic; but you can understand it, although you probably never heard or read it before now.

Knowledge of a language, then, makes it possible to understand and produce new sentences. If you counted the number of sentences in this book that you have seen or heard before, the number would be small. Next time you write an essay or a letter, see how many of your sentences are new. Few sentences are stored in your brain, to be pulled out to fit some situation or matched with some sentence that you hear. Novel sentences never spoken or heard before cannot be stored in your memory.

Simple memorization of all the possible sentences in a language is impossible in principle. If for every sentence in the language a longer sentence can be formed, then there is no limit to the length of any sentence and therefore no limit to the number of sentences. In English you can say:

This is the house.

or

This is the house that Jack built.

or

This is the malt that lay in the house that Jack built.

or

This is the dog that worried the cat that killed the rat that ate the malt that lay in the house that Jack built.

And you need not stop there. How long, then, is the longest sentence? A speaker of English can say:

The old man came.

or

The old, old, old, old, old man came.

How many "olds" are too many? Seven? Twenty-three?

It is true that the longer these sentences become, the less likely we would be to hear or to say them. A sentence with 276 occurrences of "old" would be highly unlikely in either speech or writing, even to describe Methuselah. But such a sentence is theoretically possible. If you know English, you have the knowledge to add any number of adjectives as modifiers to a noun.

All human languages permit their speakers to form indefinitely long sentences; creativity is a universal property of human language.

Knowledge of Sentences and Nonsentences

To memorize and store an infinite set of sentences would require an infinite storage capacity. However, the brain is finite, and even if it were not, we could not store novel sentences. When you learn a language you must learn something finite — your vocabulary is finite (however large it may be) — and that can be stored. If putting one word after another in any order always formed sentences, then language could simply be a set of words. You can see that words are not enough by examining the following strings of words:

(1) a. John kissed the little old lady who owned the shaggy dog.
    b. Who owned the shaggy dog John kissed the little old lady.
    c. John is difficult to love.
    d. It is difficult to love John.
    e. John is anxious to go.
    f. It is anxious to go John.
    g. John, who was a student, flunked his exams.
    h. Exams his flunked student a was who John.

If you were asked to put an asterisk or star before the examples that seemed "funny" or "no good" to you, which ones would you mark? Our intuitive knowledge about what is or is not an allowable sentence in English convinces us to star *b, f,* and *h.* Which ones did you star?

Would you agree with the following judgments?

(2) a. What he did was climb a tree.
    b. *What he thought was want a sports car.[3]
    c. Drink your beer and go home!
    d. *What are drinking and go home?
    e. I expect them to arrive a week from next Thursday.
    f. *I expect a week from next Thursday to arrive them.
    g. Linus lost his security blanket.
    h. *Lost Linus security blanket his.

If you find the starred sentences unacceptable, as we do, you see that every string of words does not constitute a well-formed sentence in a language. Our knowledge of a language determines which strings of words are and which are not sentences. Therefore, in addition to knowing the words of the language, linguistic knowledge includes **rules** for forming sentences and making the kinds of judgments you made about the examples in (1) and (2). These rules must be finite in length and finite in number so that they can be stored in our finite brains. Yet, they must permit us to form and understand an infinite set of new sentences. They are not rules determined by a judge or a legislature, or even rules taught in a grammar class. They are unconscious constraints on sentence formation that are learned when language is acquired in childhood.

---

[3] The asterisk is used before examples that speakers, for any reason, find unacceptable. This notation will be used throughout the book.

A language, then, consists of all the sounds, words, and infinitely many possible sentences. When you know a language, you know the sounds, the words, and the rules for their combination.

Linguistic Knowledge and Performance

"What's one and one and one and one and one and one and one and one and one and one?" "I don't know," said Alice. "I lost count." "She can't do Addition," the Red Queen interrupted.

Lewis Carroll, *Through the Looking-Glass*

Speakers' linguistic knowledge permits them to form longer and longer sentences by joining sentences and phrases together or adding modifiers to a noun. Whether you stop at three, five, or eighteen adjectives, it is impossible to limit the number you could add if desired. Very long sentences are theoretically possible, but they are highly improbable. Evidently, there is a difference between having the knowledge necessary to produce sentences of a language, and applying this knowledge. It is a difference between what you know, which is your **linguistic competence,** and how you use this knowledge in actual speech production and comprehension, which is your **linguistic performance.**

"The Born Loser" copyright © 1993 by NEA, Inc. Reprinted by permission of NEA, Inc.

Speakers of all languages have the knowledge to understand or produce sentences of any length. When they attempt to use that knowledge, though — when they perform linguistically — there are physiological and psychological reasons that limit the number of adjectives, adverbs, clauses, and so on. They may run out of breath, their audience may leave, they may lose track of what they have said, and of course, no one lives forever.

When we speak, we usually wish to convey some message. At some stage in the act of producing speech, we must organize our thoughts into strings of words. Sometimes the message is garbled. We may stammer, or pause, or produce **slips of the tongue.** We may even sound like Tarzan in the cartoon, who illustrates the difference between linguistic knowledge and the way we use that knowledge in performance.

"The Far Side"® by Gary Larson copyright © 1991. All rights reserved. Used with permisson.

For the most part, linguistic knowledge is not conscious knowledge. The linguistic system — the sounds, structures, meanings, words, and rules for putting them all together — is learned subconsciously with no awareness that rules are being learned. Just as we may not be conscious of the principles that allow us to stand or walk, we are unaware of the rules of language. Our ability to speak and understand, and to make judgments about the grammaticality of sentences, reveals our knowledge of the rules of our language. This knowledge represents a complex cognitive system. The nature of this system is what this book is all about.

What Is Grammar?

> We use the term "grammar" with a systematic ambiguity. On the one hand, the term refers to the explicit theory constructed by the linguist and proposed as a description of the speaker's competence. On the other hand, it refers to this competence itself.
>
> N. Chomsky and M. Halle, *The Sound Pattern of English*

Descriptive Grammars

> There are no primitive languages. The great and abstract ideas of Christianity can be discussed even by the wretched Greenlanders.
>
> Johann Peter Suessmilch, 1756, in a paper delivered before the Prussian Academy

The **grammar** of a language consists of the sounds and sound patterns, the basic units of meaning such as words, and the rules to combine all of these to form sentences with the desired meaning. The grammar, then, is what we know. It represents our linguistic competence. To understand the nature of language we must understand the nature of grammar, and in particular, the internalized, unconscious set of rules that is part of every grammar of every language.

Every human being who speaks a language knows its grammar. When linguists wish to describe a language, they attempt to describe the grammar of the language that exists in the minds of its speakers. There will be some differences among speakers' knowledge, but there must be shared knowledge too. The shared knowledge — the common parts of the grammar — makes it possible to communicate through language. To the extent that the linguist's description is a true model of the speakers' linguistic capacity, it is a successful description of the grammar and of the language itself. Such a model is called a **descriptive grammar.** It does not tell you how you should speak; it describes your basic linguistic knowledge. It explains how it is possible for you to speak and understand, and it tells what you know about the sounds, words, phrases, and sentences of your language.

We have used the word *grammar* in two ways: the first in reference to the **mental grammar** speakers have in their brains; the second as the model or description of this internalized grammar. Almost two thousand years ago the Greek grammarian Dionysius Thrax defined grammar as that which permits us either to speak a language or to speak about a language. From now on we will not differentiate these two meanings, because the linguist's descriptive grammar is an attempt at a formal statement (or theory) of the speakers' grammar.

When we say in later chapters that there is a rule in the grammar such as "Every sentence has a noun phrase subject and a verb phrase predicate," we posit the rule in both the mental grammar and the descriptive model of it, the linguist's grammar. When we say that a sentence is **grammatical,** we mean that it conforms to the rules of both grammars; conversely, an **ungrammatical** sentence deviates in some way from these rules. If, however, we posit a rule for English that does not agree with your intuitions as a speaker, then the grammar we are describing differs in some way from the mental grammar that represents your linguistic competence; that is, your language is not the one described. No language or variety of a language (called a **dialect**) is superior to any other in a linguistic sense. Every grammar is equally complex, logical, and capable of producing an infinite set of sentences to express any thought. If something can be expressed in one language or one dialect, it can be expressed in any other language or dialect. It might involve different means and different words, but it can be expressed. We will have more to say about dialects in chapter 10.

No grammar, therefore no language, is either superior or inferior to any other. Languages of technologically undeveloped cultures are not primitive or ill-formed in any way.

Prescriptive Grammars

It is a rule up with which we should not put.

Winston Churchill

I don't want to talk grammar. I want to talk like a lady.

G. B. Shaw, *Pygmalion*

The views expressed in the preceding section are not those of all grammarians now or in the past. From ancient times until the present, "purists" have believed that language change is corruption, and that there are certain "correct" forms that all educated people should use in speaking and writing. The Greek Alexandrians in the first century, the Arabic scholars at Basra in the eighth century, and numerous English grammarians of the eighteenth and nineteenth centuries held this view. They wished to *prescribe* rather than *describe* the rules of grammar, which gave rise to the writing of **prescriptive grammars.**

In the Renaissance a new middle class emerged who wanted their children to speak the dialect of the "upper" classes. This desire led to the publication of many prescriptive grammars. In 1762 Bishop Robert Lowth wrote *A Short Introduction to English Grammar with Critical Notes.* Lowth prescribed a number of new rules for English, many of them influenced by his personal taste. Before the publication of his grammar, practically everyone — upper-class, middle-class, and lower-class — said *I don't have none, You was wrong about that,* and *Mathilda is fatter than me.* Lowth, however, decided that "two negatives make a positive" and therefore one should say *I don't have any;* that even when *you* is singular it should be followed by the plural *were;* and that *I* not *me, he* not *him, they* not *them,* and so forth should follow *than* in comparative constructions. Many of these prescriptive rules were based on Latin grammar, which had already given way to different rules in the languages that developed from Latin. Because Lowth was influential and because the rising new class wanted to speak "properly," many of these new rules were legislated into English grammar, at least for the **prestige dialect.**

The view that dialects that regularly use double negatives are inferior cannot be justified if one looks at the standard dialects of other languages in the world. Romance languages, for example, use double negatives, as the following examples from French and Italian show:

French: Je ne   veux parler avec personne.
I   not want speak with no-one.

Italian: Non voglio parlare con   nessuno.
not I-want speak   with no-one.

English translation: "I don't want to speak with anyone."

Grammars such as Lowth's are different from the descriptive grammars we have been discussing. Their goal is not to describe the rules people know, but to tell them what rules they should know.

In 1908 the grammarian Thomas R. Lounsbury wrote: "There seems to have been in every period in the past, as there is now, a distinct apprehension in the minds of very many worthy persons that the English tongue is always in the condition approaching collapse and that arduous efforts must be put forth persistently to save it from destruction."

Today our bookstores are filled with books by language "purists" attempting to do just that. Edwin Newman, for example, in his books *Strictly Speaking* and *A Civil Tongue,* rails against those who use the word *hopefully* to mean "I hope," as in "Hopefully, it will not rain tomorrow," instead of using it "properly" to mean "with hope." What Newman fails to recognize is that language changes in the course of time and words change meaning, and the meaning of *hopefully* has been broadened for most English speakers to include both usages. Other "saviors" of the English language blame television, the schools, and even the National Council of Teachers of English for failing to preserve the standard language, and they mount attacks against those college and university professors who suggest that African American English (AAE)[4] and other dialects are viable, living, complete languages.

Prescriptivists are bound to fail. Language is vigorous, dynamic, and constantly changing. All languages and dialects are expressive, complete, and logical, as much so as they were 200 or 2000 years ago. If sentences are muddled, it is not because of the language but because of the speakers. Prescriptivists should be more concerned about the thinking of the speakers than about the language they use. Hopefully, this book will convince you of this.

We as linguists wish you to know that all languages and dialects are rule governed and that what is grammatical in one language may be ungrammatical in another (equally prestigious) language. While we admit that the grammars and usages of particular groups in society may be dominant for social and political reasons, they are neither superior nor inferior, from a linguistic point of view, to the grammars and usages of less prestigious segments of society.

Having said all this, it is undeniable that the **standard** dialect (defined in chapter 10) may indeed be a better dialect for someone wishing to obtain a particular job or achieve a position of social prestige. In a society where "linguistic profiling" is used to

---

[4] AAE is also called African American Vernacular English (AAVE), Ebonics, and Black English (BE). It is spoken by some but by no means all African Americans. It is discussed in chapter 10.

discriminate against speakers of a minority dialect, it may behoove those speakers to learn the prestige dialect rather than wait for social change. But linguistically, prestige and standard dialects do not have superior grammars.

Finally, all of the preceding remarks apply to *spoken* language. Writing (see chapter 12), which is not acquired through exposure (see chapter 8), but must be taught, follows certain prescriptive rules of grammar, usage, and style that the spoken language does not, and is subject to little if any dialectal variation.

Teaching Grammars

The descriptive grammar of a language attempts to describe everything speakers know about their language. It is different from a **teaching grammar,** which is used to learn another language or dialect. Teaching grammars are used in school to fulfill language requirements. They can be helpful to persons who do not speak the standard or prestige dialect, but find it would be advantageous socially and economically to do so. Teaching grammars state explicitly the rules of the language, list the words and their pronunciations, and aid in learning a new language or dialect.

"B.C." Copyright © 1986 Creators Syndicate, Inc. Reprinted by permission of Johnny Hart and Creators Syndicate, Inc.

It is often difficult for adults to learn a second language without being instructed, even when living for an extended period in a country where the language is spoken. Teaching grammars assume that the student already knows one language and compares the grammar of the target language with the grammar of the native language. The meaning of a word is given by providing a **gloss** — the parallel word in the student's native language, such as *maison,* "house" in French. It is assumed that the student knows the meaning of the gloss "house," and so the meaning of the word *maison.*

Sounds of the target language that do not occur in the native language are often described by reference to known sounds. Thus the student might be aided in producing the French sound *u* in the word *tu* by instructions such as "Round your lips while producing the vowel sound in *tea.*"

The rules on how to put words together to form grammatical sentences also refer to the learners' knowledge of their native language. For example, the teaching grammar

Learn Zulu by Sibusiso Nyembezi states that "The difference between singular and plural is not at the end of the word but at the beginning of it," and warns that "Zulu does not have the indefinite and definite articles 'a' and 'the.'" Such statements assume students know the rules of their own grammar, in this case English. Although such grammars might be considered prescriptive in the sense that they attempt to teach the student what is or is not a grammatical construction in the new language, their aim is different from grammars that attempt to change the rules or usage of a language already learned.

This book is not primarily concerned with either prescriptive or teaching grammars, which, however, are considered in chapter 10 in the discussion of standard and nonstandard dialects.

Language Universals

> In a grammar there are parts that pertain to all languages; these components form what is called the general grammar. In addition to these general (universal) parts, there are those that belong only to one particular language; and these constitute the particular grammars of each language.
>
> Du Marsais, c. 1750

The way we are using the word *grammar* differs from most common usages. In our sense, the grammar includes everything speakers know about their language — the sound system, called **phonology;** the system of meanings, called **semantics;** the rules of word formation, called **morphology;** and the rules of sentence formation, called **syntax.** It also, of course, includes the vocabulary of words — the dictionary or **lexicon.** Many people think of the grammar of a language as referring largely to morphological rules like "add *–s* to third-person singular verbs," or syntactic rules such as "a sentence consists of a subject and a predicate." This is often what students mean when they talk about their class in "English grammar."

Our aim is more in keeping with that stated in 1784 by the grammarian John Fell in *Essay towards an English Grammar:* "It is certainly the business of a grammarian to find out, and not to make, the laws of a language." This business is just what the linguist attempts — to find out the "laws" of a language, and the laws that pertain to all languages. Those laws representing the universal properties of all languages constitute a **universal grammar.**

About 1630, the German philosopher Alsted first used the term *general grammar* as distinct from *special grammar.* He believed that the function of a general grammar was to reveal those features "which relate to the method and etiology of grammatical concepts. They are common to all languages." Pointing out that "general grammar is the pattern 'norma' of every particular grammar whatsoever," he implored "eminent linguists to employ their insight in this matter."[5]

Three and a half centuries before Alsted, the scholar Robert Kilwardby held that linguists should be concerned with discovering the nature of language in general. So con-

---

[5] V. Salmon. 1969. "Review of *Cartesian Linguistics* by N. Chomsky," *Journal of Linguistics* 5:165–87.

cerned was Kilwardby with universal grammar that he excluded considerations of the characteristics of particular languages, which he believed to be as "irrelevant to a science of grammar as the material of the measuring rod or the physical characteristics of objects were to geometry."[6] Kilwardby was perhaps too much of a universalist. The particular properties of individual languages are relevant to the discovery of language universals, and they are of interest for their own sake.

Someone attempting to study Latin, Greek, French, or Swahili as a second language may assert, in frustration, that those ancient scholars were so hidden in their ivory towers that they confused reality with idle speculation. Yet the more we investigate this question, the more evidence accumulates to support Chomsky's view that there is a universal grammar that is part of the human biologically endowed language faculty. It may be thought of "as a system of principles which characterizes the class of possible grammars by specifying how particular grammars are organized (what are the components and their relations), how the different rules of these components are constructed, how they interact, and so on."[7]

To discover the nature of this universal grammar whose principles characterize all human languages is a major aim of **linguistic theory.** The linguist's goal is to discover the "laws of human language" as the physicist's goal is to discover the "laws of the physical universe." The complexity of language, a product of the human brain, undoubtedly means this goal will never be fully achieved. All scientific theories are incomplete, and new hypotheses must be proposed to account for new data. Theories are continually changing as new discoveries are made. Just as physics was enlarged by Einstein's theories of relativity, so grows the linguistic theory of universal grammar as new discoveries shed new light on the nature of human language.

The Development of Grammar

Linguistic theory is concerned not only with describing the knowledge that an adult speaker has of his or her language, but also with explaining how that knowledge is acquired. All normal children acquire (at least one) language in a relatively short period with apparent ease. They do this despite the fact that parents and other caregivers do not provide them with any specific language instruction. Indeed, it is often remarked that children seem to "pick up" language just from hearing it spoken around them. Children are language learners par excellence — whether a child is male or female, from a rich family or a disadvantaged one, whether she grows up on a farm or in the city, attends day care or is home all day — none of these factors fundamentally affect the way language develops. A child can acquire any language he is exposed to with comparable ease — English, Dutch, French, Swahili, Japanese — and even though each of these languages has its own peculiar characteristics, children learn them all in very much the same way. For example, all children start out by using one word at a time. They then combine words into simple sentences. When they first begin to combine words into sentences,

---

[6] Ibid.

[7] N. Chomsky. 1979. *Language and Responsibility* (based on conversations with Misou Ronat), New York: Pantheon Press, p. 180.

certain parts of the sentence may be missing. For example, the English-speaking two-year-old might say *Cathy build house* instead of *Cathy is building the house*. On the other side of the world, a Swahili-speaking child will say *mbuzi kula majani,* which translates as "goat eat grass," and which also lacks many required elements. They pass through other linguistic stages on their way to adultlike competence, but by about age five children speak a language that is almost indistinguishable from the language of the adults around them.

In just a few short years, without the benefit of explicit guidance and regardless of personal circumstances, the young child — who may be unable to tie her shoes or do even the simplest arithmetic computation — masters the complex grammatical structures of her language and acquires a substantial lexicon. Just how children accomplish this remarkable cognitive achievement is a topic of intense interest to linguists. The child's success, as well as the uniformity of the acquisition process, point to a substantial innate component of language development. Chomsky, following the lead of the early rationalist philosophers, proposed that human beings are born with an innate "blueprint" for language, what we referred to earlier as Universal Grammar. Children are able to acquire language as quickly and effortlessly as they do because they do not have to figure out all the rules of their language, only those that are specific to their particular language. The universal properties — the laws of language — are part of their biological endowment. Linguistic theory aims to uncover those principles that characterize all human languages and to reveal the innate component of language that makes language acquisition possible. In chapter 8 we will discuss language acquisition in more detail.

Sign Languages: Evidence for Language Universals

It is not the want of organs that [prevents animals from making] . . . known their thoughts . . . for it is evident that magpies and parrots are able to utter words just like ourselves, and yet they cannot speak as we do, that is, so as to give evidence that they think of what they say. On the other hand, men who, being born deaf and mute . . . are destitute of the organs which serve the others for talking, are in the habit of themselves inventing certain signs by which they make themselves understood.

René Descartes, *Discourse on Method*

The sign languages of deaf communities provide some of the best evidence to support the notion that humans are born with the ability to acquire language, and that these languages are governed by the same universal properties.

Because deaf children are unable to hear speech, they do not acquire spoken languages as hearing children do. However, deaf children who are exposed to sign language learn it in stages parallel to those of hearing children learning oral languages. Sign languages are human languages that do not use sounds to express meanings. Instead, sign languages are visual-gestural systems that use hand, body, and facial gestures as the forms used to represent words. Sign languages are fully developed languages, and those who know sign language are capable of creating and comprehending unlimited numbers of new sentences, just like speakers of spoken languages.

Current research on sign languages has been crucial in the attempt to understand the biological underpinnings of human language acquisition and use. Some understanding of sign languages is therefore essential.

About one in a thousand babies is born deaf or with a severe hearing deficiency. One major effect is the difficulty that deaf children have in learning a spoken language. It is nearly impossible for those unable to hear language to learn to speak naturally. Normal speech depends largely on auditory feedback. A deaf child will not learn to speak without extensive training in special schools or programs designed especially for deaf people.

Although deaf persons can be taught to speak a language intelligibly, they can never understand speech as well as a hearing person. Seventy-five percent of spoken English words cannot be read on the lips accurately. The ability of many deaf individuals to comprehend spoken language is therefore remarkable; they combine lip reading with knowledge of the structure of language, the meaning redundancies that language has, and context.

If, however, human language is universal in the sense that all members of the human species have the ability to learn a language, it is not surprising that nonspoken languages have developed among nonhearing individuals. The more we learn about the human linguistic ability, the more it is clear that language acquisition and use are not dependent on the ability to produce and hear sounds, but on a much more abstract cognitive ability, biologically determined, that accounts for the similarities between spoken and sign languages.

AMERICAN SIGN LANGUAGE

The major language used by deaf people in the United States is **American Sign Language (ASL).** ASL is a fully developed language that historically is an outgrowth of the sign language used in France and brought to the United States in 1817 by the great educator Thomas Hopkins Gallaudet.

Like all human languages, ASL has its own grammar. That grammar encompasses knowledge of the system of gestures, equivalent to the phonology of spoken languages,[8] as well as the morphological, syntactic, and semantic systems, and a mental lexicon of signs.

In the United States there are several signing systems that educators have created in an attempt to represent spoken and/or written English. These artificial languages consist essentially in the replacement of each spoken English word (and grammatical elements such as the *s* ending for plurals and the *ed* ending for past tense) by a sign. The syntax and semantics of these manual codes for English are thus approximately the same as those of ordinary English. The result is unnatural in that it is similar to trying to speak French by translating every English word or ending into its French counterpart. Problems result because there are not always corresponding forms in the two languages.

---

[8] The term *phonology,* which was first used to describe the sound systems of language, has been extended to include the gestural systems of sign languages.

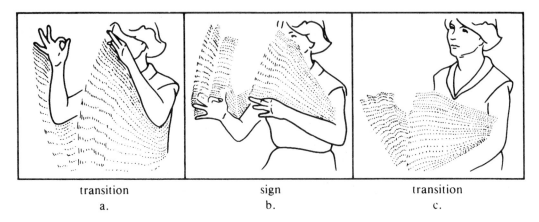

transition   sign   transition
a.   b.   c.

Figure 1.2   The ASL sign DECIDE: (a) and (c) show transitions from the sign; (b) illustrates the single downward movement of the sign. Reprinted from *The Signs of Language* by Edward Klima and Ursula Bellugi: Cambridge, Mass.: Harvard University Press. Copyright © 1979 by the President and Fellows of Harvard College.

In ASL the letters of the English alphabet are represented by a series of hand shapes and movements. This permits signers to represent new coinages, foreign words, acronyms, proper nouns for which there may not be a sign, technical vocabulary, or obsolete words as might be found in a signed interpretation of a play by Shakespeare.

Signs, however, are produced differently than are finger-spelled words. "The sign DECIDE cannot be analyzed as a sequence of distinct, separable configurations of the hand. Like all other lexical signs in ASL, but unlike the individual finger-spelled letters in D-E-C-I-D-E taken separately, the ASL sign DECIDE does have an essential movement but the hand shape occurs simultaneously with the movement. In appearance, the sign is a continuous whole."[9] This sign is shown in Figure 1.2.

Signers communicate ideas at a rate comparable to spoken communication. Moreover, language arts are not lost to the deaf community. Poetry is composed in sign language, and stage plays such as Sheridan's *The Critic* have been translated into sign language and acted by the National Theatre of the Deaf (NTD).

Deaf children acquire sign language much in the way that hearing children acquire a spoken language. Deaf children often sign themselves to sleep just as hearing children talk themselves to sleep. Deaf children report that they dream in sign language as French-speaking children dream in French and Hopi children dream in Hopi. Deaf children sign to their dolls and stuffed animals. Slips of the hand occur similar to slips of the tongue; finger fumblers amuse signers as tongue twisters amuse speakers. Sign languages resemble spoken languages in all major aspects, showing that there truly are universals of language despite differences in the modality in which the language is performed. This universality is predictable because regardless of the modality in which it is expressed, language is biologically based.

[9] Klima and Bellugi, *The Signs of Language,* pp. 38 and 62.

Animal "Languages"

No matter how eloquently a dog may bark, he cannot tell you that his parents were poor but honest.

Bertrand Russell

Is language the exclusive property of the human species? The idea of talking animals is as old and as widespread among human societies as language itself. All cultures have legends in which some animal plays a speaking role. All over West Africa, children listen to folktales in which a "spider-man" is the hero. "Coyote" is a favorite figure in many Native American tales, and many an animal takes the stage in Aesop's famous fables. The fictional Doctor Doolittle's forte was communicating with all manner of animals, from giant snails to tiny sparrows.

If language is viewed only as a system of communication, then many species communicate. Humans also use systems other than language to relate to each other and to send and receive "messages," like so-called "body language." The question is whether the communication systems used by other species are at all like human linguistic knowledge, which is acquired by children with no external instruction, and which is used creatively rather than in response to internal or external stimuli.

"Talking" Parrots

Most humans who acquire language use speech sounds to express meanings, but such sounds are not a necessary aspect of language, as evidenced by the sign languages. The use of speech sounds is therefore not a basic part of what we have been calling language. The chirping of birds, the squeaking of dolphins, and the dancing of bees may potentially represent systems similar to human languages. If animal communication systems are not like human language, it will not be due to a lack of speech.

Conversely, when animals vocally imitate human utterances, it does not mean they possess language. Language is a system that relates sounds or gestures to meanings. Talking birds such as parrots and mynah birds are capable of faithfully reproducing words and phrases of human language that they have heard, but their utterances carry no meaning. They are speaking neither English nor their own language when they sound like us.

Talking birds do not dissect the sounds of their imitations into discrete units. *Polly* and *Molly* do not rhyme for a parrot. They are as different as *hello* and *good-bye*. One property of all human languages (which will be discussed further in chapter 6) is the discreteness of the speech or gestural units, which are ordered and reordered, combined and split apart. Generally, a parrot says what it is taught, or what it hears, and no more. If Polly learns "Polly wants a cracker" and "Polly wants a doughnut" and also learns to imitate the single words *whiskey* and *bagel,* she will not spontaneously produce, as children do, "Polly wants whiskey" or "Polly wants a bagel" or "Polly wants whiskey and a bagel." If she learns *cat* and *cats,* and *dog* and *dogs,* and then learns the word *parrot,* she will be unable to form the plural *parrots* as children do by the age of three; nor can a parrot form an unlimited set of utterances from a finite set of units, nor understand

utterances never heard before. Recent reports of an African gray parrot named Alex studied by Dr. Irene M. Pepperberg suggest that new methods of training animals may result in more learning than was previously believed possible. When the trainer uses words in context, Alex seems to relate some sounds with their meanings. This is more than simple imitation, but it is not how children acquire the complexities of the grammar of any language. It is more like a dog learning to associate certain sounds with meanings, such as *heel, sit, fetch,* and so on. Alex's ability may go somewhat beyond that. However, the ability to produce sounds similar to those used in human language, even if meanings are related to these sounds, cannot be equated with the ability to acquire the complex grammar of a human language.

The Birds and the Bees

The birds and animals are all friendly to each other, and there are no disputes about anything. They all talk, and they all talk to me, but it must be a foreign language for I cannot make out a word they say.

Mark Twain, *Eve's Diary*

"Rose Is Rose" copyright © 2000 United Features Syndicate. Reprinted by permission.

Most animals possess some kind of "signaling" communication system. Among certain species of spiders there is a complex system for courtship. The male spider, before he approaches his ladylove, goes through an elaborate series of gestures to inform her that he is indeed a spider and a suitable mate, and not a crumb or a fly to be eaten. These gestures are invariant. One never finds a creative spider changing or adding to the courtship ritual of his species.

A similar kind of gestural language is found among the fiddler crabs. There are forty species, and each uses its own claw-waving movement to signal to another member of its "clan." The timing, movement, and posture of the body never change from one time to another or from one crab to another within the particular variety. Whatever the signal means, it is fixed. Only one meaning can be conveyed.

The imitative sounds of talking birds have little in common with human language, but the calls and songs of many species of birds do have a communicative function, and they resemble human languages in that there may be "dialects" within the same species. **Birdcalls** (consisting of one or more short notes) convey messages associated with the immediate environment, such as danger, feeding, nesting, flocking, and so on. **Bird songs** (more complex patterns of notes) are used to stake out territory and to attract mates. There is no evidence of any internal structure to these songs, nor can they be segmented into independently meaningful parts as words of human language can be. In a study of the territorial song of the European robin,[10] it was discovered that the rival robins paid attention only to the alternation between high-pitched and low-pitched notes, and which came first did not matter. The message varies only to the extent of how strongly the robin feels about his possession and to what extent he is prepared to defend it and start a family in that territory. The different alternations therefore express intensity and nothing more. The robin is creative in his ability to sing the same thing in many ways, but not creative in his ability to use the same units of the system to express many different messages with different meanings.

Despite certain superficial similarities to human language, birdcalls and songs are fundamentally different kinds of communicative systems. The kinds of messages that can be conveyed are limited, and messages are stimulus controlled.

---

[10] R. G. Busnel and J. Bertrand. 1962. "Recherche du Supporte de l'Information dans le Signal Acoustique de Défense Territoriale du Rougegorge," *C. R. Acad. Sci. Paris* 254:2236–38.

This distinction is also true of the system of communication used by honeybees. A forager bee is able to return to the hive and communicate to other bees where a source of food is located. It does so by performing a dance on a wall of the hive that reveals the location and quality of the food source. For one species of Italian honeybee, the dancing behavior may assume one of three possible patterns: round (which indicates locations near the hive, within 20 feet or so); sickle (which indicates locations at 20 to 60 feet from the hive); and tail-wagging (for distances that exceed 60 feet). The number of repetitions per minute of the basic pattern in the tail-wagging dance indicates the precise distance; the slower the repetition rate, the longer the distance.

The bees' dance is an effective system of communication for bees. It is capable, in principle, of infinitely many different messages, like human language; but unlike human language, the system is confined to a single subject — food source. An experimenter who forced a bee to walk to the food source showed the inflexibility. When the bee returned to the hive, it indicated a distance twenty-five times farther away than the food source actually was. The bee had no way of communicating the special circumstances in its message. This absence of creativity makes the bees' dance qualitatively different from human language.[11]

In the seventeenth century, the philosopher and mathematician René Descartes pointed out that the communication systems of animals are qualitatively different from the language used by humans:

> It is a very remarkable fact that there are none so depraved and stupid, without even excepting idiots, that they cannot arrange different words together, forming of them a statement by which they make known their thoughts; while, on the other hand, there is no other animal, however perfect and fortunately circumstanced it may be, which can do the same.[12]

Descartes goes on to state that one of the major differences between humans and animals is that human use of language is not just a response to external, or even internal, stimuli, as are the sounds and gestures of animals. He warns against confusing human use of language with "natural movements which betray passions and may be . . . manifested by animals."

To hold that animals communicate by systems qualitatively different from human language systems is not to claim human superiority. Humans are not inferior to the one-celled amoeba because they cannot reproduce by splitting in two; they are just different sexually. They are not inferior to hunting dogs, whose sense of smell is far better than that of human animals. All the studies of animal communication systems, including those of chimpanzees (discussed in chapter 8), provide evidence for Descartes' distinction between other animal communication systems and the linguistic creative ability possessed by the human animal.

---

[11] K. Von Frisch. *The Dance Language and Orientation of the Bees,* trans. L. E. Chadwick, Cambridge, MA: Harvard University Press, 1967.

[12] R. Descartes. 1967. "Discourse on Method," *The Philosophical Works of Descartes,* Vol. 1, trans. E. S. Haldane and G. R. Ross, Cambridge, England: Cambridge University Press, p. 116.

What We Know about Language

Much is unknown about the nature of human languages, their grammars and use. The science of linguistics is concerned with these questions. Investigations of linguists and the analyses of spoken languages date back at least to 1600 B.C.E. in Mesopotamia. We have learned a great deal since that time. A number of facts pertaining to all languages can be stated.

1. Wherever humans exist, language exists.
2. There are no "primitive" languages—all languages are equally complex and equally capable of expressing any idea in the universe. The vocabulary of any language can be expanded to include new words for new concepts.
3. All languages change through time.
4. The relationships between the sounds and meanings of spoken languages and between the gestures and meanings of sign languages are for the most part arbitrary.
5. All human languages use a finite set of discrete sounds or gestures that are combined to form meaningful elements or words, which themselves may be combined to form an infinite set of possible sentences.
6. All grammars contain rules of a similar kind for the formation of words and sentences.
7. Every spoken language includes discrete sound segments, like *p*, *n*, or *a*, that can all be defined by a finite set of sound properties or features. Every spoken language has a class of vowels and a class of consonants.
8. Similar grammatical categories (for example, noun, verb) are found in all languages.
9. There are universal semantic properties like "male" or "female," "animate" or "human," found in every language in the world.
10. Every language has a way of negating, forming questions, issuing commands, referring to past or future time, and so on.
11. Speakers of all languages are capable of producing and comprehending an infinite set of sentences. Syntactic universals reveal that every language has a way of forming sentences such as:

    Linguistics is an interesting subject.

    I know that linguistics is an interesting subject.

    You know that I know that linguistics is an interesting subject.

    Cecelia knows that you know that I know that linguistics is an interesting subject.

    Is it a fact that Cecelia knows that you know that I know that linguistics is an interesting subject?

12. Any normal child, born anywhere in the world, of any racial, geographical, social, or economic heritage, is capable of learning any language to which he or she is exposed. The differences we find among languages cannot be due to biological reasons.

It seems that Alsted and Du Marsais (and we could add many other universalists from all ages) were not spinning idle thoughts. We all possess human language.

≈≈≈ Summary

We are all intimately familiar with at least one language, our own. Yet few of us ever stop to consider what we know when we know a language. No book contains, or could possibly contain, the English or Russian or Zulu language. The words of a language can be listed in a dictionary, but not all the sentences can be; and a language consists of these sentences as well as words. Speakers use a finite set of rules to produce and understand an infinite set of possible sentences.

These rules are part of the **grammar** of a language, which develops when you acquire the language and includes the sound system (the **phonology**), the structure of words (the **morphology**), how words may be combined into phrases and sentences (the **syntax**), the ways in which sounds and meanings are related (the **semantics**), and the words or **lexicon.** The sounds and meanings of these words are related in an **arbitrary** fashion. If you had never heard the word *syntax* you would not, by its sounds, know what it meant. The gestures used by signers are also arbitrarily related to their meanings. Language, then, is a system that relates sounds (or hand and body gestures) with meanings. When you know a language you know this system.

This knowledge (**linguistic competence**) is different from behavior (**linguistic performance**). If you woke up one morning and decided to stop talking (as the Trappist monks did after they took a vow of silence), you would still have knowledge of your language. This ability or competence underlies linguistic behavior. If you do not know the language, you cannot speak it; but if you know the language, you may choose not to speak.

Grammars are of different kinds. The **descriptive grammar** of a language represents the unconscious linguistic knowledge or capacity of its speakers. Such a grammar is a model of the **mental grammar** every speaker of the language knows. It does not teach the rules of the language; it describes the rules that are already known. A grammar that attempts to legislate what your grammar should be is called a **prescriptive grammar.** It prescribes. It does not describe, except incidentally. **Teaching grammars** are written to help people learn a foreign language or a dialect of their own language.

The more that linguists investigate the thousands of languages of the world and describe the ways in which they differ from each other, the more they discover that these differences are limited. There are linguistic universals that pertain to each of the parts of grammars, the ways in which these parts are related, and the forms of rules. These principles comprise **universal grammar,** which defines the basis of the specific grammars of all possible human languages, and constitutes the innate component of the human language faculty that makes normal language development possible.

Strong evidence for Universal Grammar is found in the way children acquire language. Children learn language by exposure. They need not be deliberately taught, though parents may enjoy "teaching" their children to speak or sign. Children will learn any human language to which they are exposed, and they learn it in definable stages, beginning at a very early age. By four or five years of age, children have acquired nearly the entire adult grammar. This suggests that children are born with a genetically endowed faculty to learn and use human language, which is part of the Universal Grammar.

The fact that deaf children learn **sign language** shows that the ability to hear or produce sounds is not a prerequisite for language learning. All the sign languages in the world, which differ as spoken languages do, are visual-gestural systems that are as fully developed and as structurally complex as spoken languages. The major sign language used in the United States is **American Sign Language (ASL).**

If language is defined merely as a system of communication, then language is not unique to humans. There are, however, certain characteristics of human language not found in the communication systems of any other species. A basic property of human language is its **creative aspect** — a speaker's ability to combine the basic linguistic units to form an infinite set of "well-formed" grammatical sentences, most of which are novel, never before produced or heard.

Sign languages show us that the ability to hear or produce sounds is not a necessary condition for the acquisition of language; nor is the ability to imitate the sounds of human language a sufficient basis for learning language. "Talking" birds imitate sounds but can neither segment these sounds into smaller units, nor understand what they are imitating, nor produce new utterances to convey their thoughts.

Birds, bees, crabs, spiders, and most other creatures communicate in some way, but the information imparted is severely limited and stimulus-bound, confined to a small set of messages. The system of language represented by intricate mental grammars, which are not stimulus-bound and which generate infinite messages, is unique to the human species.

Because of linguistic research throughout history, we have learned much about Universal Grammar, the properties shared by all languages.

 # References for Further Reading

Bolinger, D. 1980. *Language — The Loaded Weapon: The Use and Abuse of Language Today.* London: Longman.

Chomsky, N. 1986. *Knowledge of Language: Its Nature, Origin, and Use.* New York and London: Praeger.

_____. 1975. *Reflections on Language.* New York: Pantheon Books.

_____. 1972. *Language and Mind.* Enlarged Edition. New York: Harcourt Brace Jovanovich.

Crystal, D. 1997. *Cambridge Encyclopedia of the English Language.* Cambridge, England: Cambridge University Press.

_____. 1984. *Who Cares about Usage?* New York: Penguin.

Gould, J. L., and C. G. Gould. 1983. "Can a Bee Behave Intelligently?" *New Scientist* 98:84–87.

Hall, R. A. 1950. *Leave Your Language Alone.* Ithaca, NY: Linguistica.

Jackendoff, R. 1997. *The Architecture of the Language Faculty.* Cambridge, MA: The MIT Press.

_____. 1994. *Patterns in the Mind: Language and Human Nature.* New York: Basic Books.

Klima, E. S., and U. Bellugi. 1979. *The Signs of Language.* Cambridge, MA: Harvard University Press.

Lane, H. 1984. *When the Mind Hears: A History of the Deaf.* New York: Random House.

Milroy, J., and L. Milroy. 1985. *Authority in Language: Investigating Language Prescription and Standardisation.* London: Routledge & Kegan Paul.

Newmeyer, F. J. 1983. *Grammatical Theory: Its Limits and Possibilities.* Chicago, IL: University of Chicago Press.

Nunberg, G. 1983. "The Decline of Grammar." *Atlantic Monthly,* December.

Pinker, S. 1999. *Words and Rules: The Ingredients of Language.* New York: HarperCollins.

_____. 1994. *The Language Instinct.* New York: William Morrow.

Safire, W. 1980. *On Age.* New York: Avon Books.

Sebeok, T. A., ed. 1977. *How Animals Communicate.* Bloomington, IN: Indiana University Press.

Shopen, T., and J. M. Williams, eds. 1980. *Standards and Dialects in English.* Rowley, MA: Newbury House.

Sternberg, M. L. A. 1987. *American Sign Language Dictionary.* New York: Harper & Row.

Stokoe, W. 1960. *Sign Language Structure: An Outline of the Visual Communication System of the American Deaf.* Silver Springs, MD: Linstok Press.

Von Frisch, K. 1967. *The Dance Language and Orientation of Bees,* L. E. Chadwick, trans. Cambridge, MA: Harvard University Press.

≋ Exercises

1. An English speaker's knowledge includes the sound sequences of the language. When new products are put on the market, the manufacturers have to think up new names for them that conform to the allowable sound patterns. Suppose you were hired by a manufacturer of soap products to name five new products. What names might you come up with? List them.

    We are interested in how the names are pronounced. Therefore, describe in any way you can how to say the words you list. Suppose, for example, you named one detergent *Blick*. You could describe the sounds in any of the following ways:

    bl as in *blood,*
    i as in *pit,*
    ck as in *stick*

    bli as in *bliss,*
    ck as in *tick*

    b as in *boy,*
    lick as in *lick*

2. Consider the following sentences. Put a star (*) after those that do not seem to conform to the rules of your grammar, that are ungrammatical for you. State, if you can, why you think the sentence is ungrammatical.

    a. Robin forced the sheriff go.

    b. Napoleon forced Josephine to go.

    c. The devil made Faust go.

    d. He passed by a large pile of money.

    e. He came by a large sum of money.

    f. He came a large sum of money by.

    g. Did in a corner little Jack Horner sit?

    h. Elizabeth is resembled by Charles.

    i. Nancy is eager to please.

    j. It is easy to frighten Emily.

    k. It is eager to love a kitten.

    l. That birds can fly amazes.

    m. The fact that you are late to class is surprising.

    n. Has the nurse slept the baby yet?

    o. I was surprised for you to get married.

    p. I wonder who and Mary went swimming.

    q. Myself bit John.

    r. What did Alice eat the toadstool with?

    s. What did Alice eat the toadstool and?

3. It was pointed out in this chapter that a small set of words in languages may be onomatopoeic; that is, their sounds "imitate" what they refer to. *Ding-dong, tick-tock, bang, zing, swish,* and *plop* are such words in English. Construct a list of ten new onomatopoeic words. Test them on at least five friends to see if they are truly nonarbitrary as to sound and meaning.

4. Although sounds and meanings of most words in all languages are arbitrarily related, there are some communication systems in which the "signs" unambiguously reveal their "meaning."

    a. Describe (or draw) five different signs that directly show what they mean. Example: a road sign indicating an S curve.

    b. Describe any other communication system that, like language, consists of arbitrary symbols. Example: traffic signals, where red means stop and green means go.

5. Consider these two statements: I learned a new word today. I learned a new sentence today. Do you think the two statements are equally probable, and if not, why not?

6. What do the barking of dogs, the meowing of cats, and the singing of birds have in common with human language? What are some of the basic differences?

7. A wolf is able to express subtle gradations of emotion by different positions of the ears, the lips, and the tail. There are eleven postures of the tail that express such emotions as self-confidence, confident threat, lack of tension, uncertain threat, depression, defensiveness, active submission, and complete submission. This system seems to be complex. Suppose that there were a thousand different emotions that the wolf could express in this way. Would you then say a wolf had a language similar to a human's? If not, why not?

8. Suppose you taught a dog to *heel, sit up, roll over, play dead, stay, jump,* and *bark* on command, using the italicized words as cues. Would you be teaching it language? Why or why not?

9. State some rule of grammar that you have learned is the correct way to say something, but that you do not generally use in speaking. For example, you may have heard that *It's me* is incorrect and that the correct form is *It's I*. Nevertheless you always use *me* in such sentences; your friends do also, and in fact, *It's I* sounds odd to you.

   Write a short essay presenting arguments against someone who tells you that you are wrong. Discuss how this disagreement demonstrates the difference between descriptive and prescriptive grammars.

10. Think of song titles that are "bad" grammar, but which, if corrected would lack effect. For example, the 1929 "Fats" Waller classic "Ain't Misbehavin'" is clearly superior to the bland "I am not misbehaving." Try to come up with five or ten such titles.

11. Linguists who attempt to write a descriptive grammar of linguistic competence are faced with a difficult task. They must understand a deep and complex system based on a set of sparse and often inaccurate data. (Children learning language face the same difficulty.) Albert Einstein and Leopold Infeld captured the essence of the difficulty in their book *The Evolution of Physics,* written in 1938:

   > In our endeavor to understand reality we are somewhat like a man trying to understand the mechanism of a closed watch. He sees the face and the moving hands, even hears its ticking, but he has no way of opening the case. If he is ingenious he may form some picture of a mechanism which could be responsible for all the things he observes, but he may never be quite sure his picture is the only one which could explain his observations. He will never be able to compare his picture with the real mechanism and he cannot even imagine the possibility of the meaning of such a comparison.

   Write a short essay that speculates on how a linguist might go about understanding the reality of a person's grammar (the closed watch) by observing what that person says, and doesn't say (the face and moving hands.) For example, a person might never say *the sixth sheik's sixth sheep is sick as a dog,* but the grammar should specify that it is a well-formed sentence, just as it should somehow indicate that *Came the messenger on time* is ill-formed.

CHAPTER

Brain and Language

The functional asymmetry of the human brain is unequivocal, and so is its anatomical asymmetry. The structural differences between the left and the right hemispheres are visible not only under the microscope but to the naked eye. The most striking asymmetries occur in language-related cortices. It is tempting to assume that such anatomical differences are an index of the neurobiological underpinnings of language.

Antonio and Hanna Damasio, University of Iowa, School of Medicine, Department of Neurology

[The brain is] the messenger of the understanding [and the organ whereby] in an especial manner we acquire wisdom and knowledge.

Hippocratic Treatise on the Sacred Disease, c. 377 B.C.E.

Attempts to understand the complexities of human cognitive abilities and especially the acquisition and use of language are as old and as continuous as history. Three long-standing problems of science include the nature of the brain, the nature of human language, and the relationship between the two. The view that the brain is the source of human language and cognition goes back over 2000 years. Assyrian and Babylonian cuneiform tablets mention disorders of language that may develop "when man's brain holds fire." Egyptian doctors in 1700 B.C.E. noted in their papyrus records that "the breath of an outside god" had entered their patients who became "silent in sadness." The philosophers of ancient Greece also speculated about the brain/mind relationship but neither Plato nor Aristotle recognized the brain's crucial function in cognition or language. Aristotle's wisdom failed him when he suggested that the brain is a cold sponge whose function is to cool the blood. Nevertheless, others writing in the same period showed greater insight, as shown by the Hippocratic treatises on the brain from which we quoted.

An important approach to understanding of the brain/mind relationship has been through the study of language. Conversely, research on the brain in humans and other primates is helping to answer questions concerning the neurological basis for language. The study of the biological and neural foundations of language is called **neurolinguistics.**

The Human Brain

"Rabbit's clever," said Pooh thoughtfully.

"Yes," said Piglet, "Rabbit's clever."

"And he has Brain."

"Yes," said Piglet, "Rabbit has Brain."

There was a long silence.

"I suppose," said Pooh, "that that's why he never understands anything."

A. A. Milne, *The House at Pooh Corner*[1]

The brain is the most complex organ of the body. It lies under the skull and consists of approximately 10 billion nerve cells (neurons) and billions of fibers that interconnect them. The surface of the brain is the **cortex,** often called "gray matter," consisting of billions of neurons. Beneath the cortex is the white matter, which consists primarily of connecting fibers. The cortex is the decision-making organ of the body. It receives messages from all the sensory organs, and it initiates all voluntary actions. It is "the seat of all which is exclusively human in the mind" and the storehouse of our memories. Somewhere in this gray matter resides the grammar that represents our knowledge of language.

The brain is composed of **cerebral hemispheres,** one on the right, and one on the left, joined by the **corpus callosum,** a network of 2 million fibers. (See Figure 2.1.)

In general, the left hemisphere supervises the right side of the body, and the right hemisphere supervises the left side. If you point with your right hand, it is the left hemisphere that controls your action, and conversely. This is referred to as **contralateral** brain function.

The Modularity of the Brain

Since the middle of the nineteenth century, scientists have assumed that it is possible to discover the particular brain areas where language capacities (competence and performance) are localized.

In the early part of that century Franz Joseph Gall put forth the theory of **localization,** that is, that different human abilities and behaviors were traceable to specific parts

---

[1] A. A. Milne. 1928. *House at Pooh Corner.* New York: E. P. Dutton.

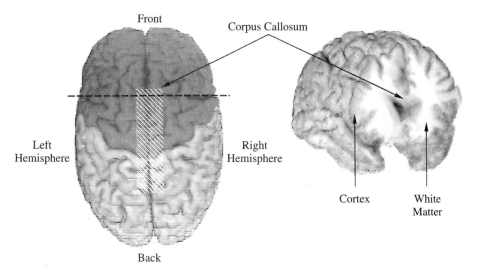

Front

Corpus Callosum

Left
Hemisphere

Right
Hemisphere

Cortex   White
Matter

Back

Figure 2.1   Three-dimensional reconstruction of the normal living human brain. The images were obtained from magnetic resonance data using the Brainvox technique. Left panel = view from top. Right panel = view from the front following virtual coronal section at the level of the dashed line. (Courtesy of Hanna Damasio)

of the brain. Some of Gall's views are amusing when looked at with our current knowledge. For example, he suggested that the frontal lobes of the brain were the location of language because when he was young he had noticed that the most articulate and intelligent of his fellow students had protruding eyes, which he believed reflected overdeveloped brain material. He also put forth a pseudoscientific theory called "organology" that later came to be known as **phrenology,** the practice of determining personality traits, intellectual capacities, and other matters by examination of the "bumps" on the skull. A disciple of Gall's, Johann Spurzheim, introduced phrenology to America,

"Peanuts" copyright © 1984 United Feature Syndicate, Inc. Reprinted by permission.

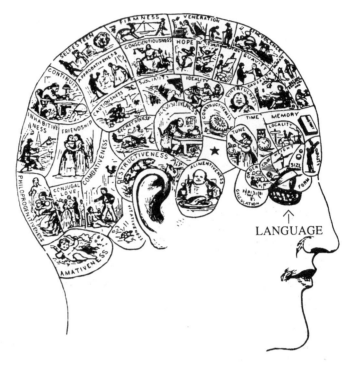

Figure 2.2   Phrenology skull model.

constructing elaborate maps and skull models such as the one shown in Figure 2.2, in which language is located directly under the eye.

Although phrenology has long been discarded as a scientific theory, Gall's view that the brain is not a uniform mass and that linguistic capacities are functions of localized brain areas has largely been upheld. Gall was in fact a pioneer and a courageous scientist in arguing against the prevailing view that the brain was an unstructured organ. He instead argued in favor of **modularity,** with the brain divided into distinct anatomical faculties (referred to as cortical organs) that were directly responsible for specific cognitive functions, including language.

Language was the first cognitive model to be localized in the brain via scientific evidence. In 1864 Paul Broca related language specifically to the left side of the brain. At a scientific meeting in Paris, he stated that we speak with the left hemisphere. He based his finding on the observation that damage to the front part of the left hemisphere (now called **Broca's area,** or **region**) resulted in loss of speech, whereas damage to the right side did not.[2] He determined this by autopsy investigations of eight patients who had lan-

---

[2] Broca, though a major figure in the history of neuroscience, held extremely racist and sexist views based on incorrect measurements of the brains of men and women and different races. His false view correlating brain size with intelligence is thoroughly demolished by Stephen Jay Gould in *The Mismeasure of Man.* 1981. New York: W.W. Norton.

guage deficits following brain injury. All of them had damage only to the frontal lobe of the left hemisphere. Language, then, is **lateralized,** the term used to refer to any cognitive function that is localized primarily on one side of the brain or the other.

Today, patients with injuries to Broca's area may have **Broca's aphasia. Aphasia** is the neurological term for any language disorder that results from brain damage caused by disease or trauma. Persons with Broca's aphasia may have labored speech, word-finding pauses, disturbed word orders, and difficulties with function words such as *to* and *if*. Language understanding may not appear abnormal, but controlled tests reveal a loss of comprehension of complex or ambiguous sentences.

Long before Broca, Greek Hippocratic physicians reported that loss of speech often occurred simultaneously with paralysis of the right side of the body. But it was Broca whose name is most closely associated with the left lateralization of language.

In 1874 thirteen years after Broca's Paris paper, Carl Wernicke presented a paper that described another variety of aphasia that occurred in patients with lesions in the back portion of the left hemisphere, now known as **Wernicke's area,** or **region.** Unlike Broca's patients, those with **Wernicke's aphasia** spoke fluently with good intonation and pronunciation, but with numerous instances of lexical errors (word substitutions), often producing **jargon** and **nonsense words.** They also had difficulty in comprehending speech.

Figure 2.3 is a view of the left side of the brain that shows Broca's and Wernicke's areas.

We no longer need to rely on surgery or autopsy to identify and locate brain lesions. Technologies such as magnetic resonance imaging (MRI) reveal lesions in the living

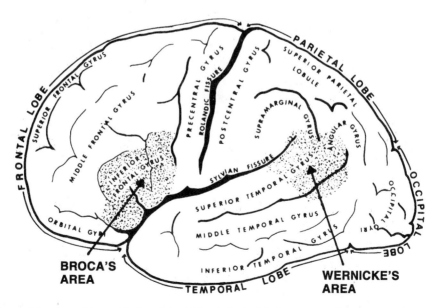

Figure 2.3   Lateral (external) view of the left hemisphere of the human brain, showing the position of Broca's and Wernicke's areas—two key areas of the cortex related to language processing.

brain. In addition, positron emission tomography (PET) scans have furthered the study of the brain, making it possible to detect changes in brain activities and relate these changes to localized brain damage and cognitive tasks. PET permits scientists to examine the brain and see what areas react to particular stimuli. It accomplishes this by computing a map of metabolic activity of the brain. Areas of greater activity are those most involved in the mental activity at the moment of the scan. MRI and PET studies reaffirm the lateralization of language.

For example, researchers at the State University of New York, Buffalo, conducted an experiment in which they used PET scans to locate and measure cortical activity when subjects were asked to produce the past tense forms of regular, irregular, and made-up verbs. They summed up their results by noting that "We find very different amounts and areas of cortical activation in the regular and irregular tasks . . ." All "cortical activation," though in different parts of the brain depending on the type of verb, was in the left hemisphere. These experiments support both the modular nature of the grammar and the left lateralization of language.[3]

Figures 2.4 and 2.5 show the MRI scans of the brains of a Broca's aphasic and a Wernicke's aphasic patient. The black areas show the sites of the lesions. Each diagram represents a slice of the left side of the brain.

There is now a consensus that the so-called higher mental functions are highly lateralized. Research shows that though the nervous system is generally left-right symmetrical, the two sides of the brain form an exception.

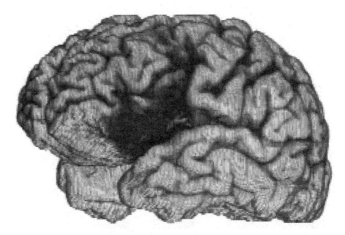

Figure 2.4   Three-dimensional reconstruction of the brain of a living patient with Broca's aphasia. Note area of damage in left frontal region (dark gray), which was caused by a stroke. (Courtesy of Hanna Damasio)[4]

[3] J. J. Jaeger, A. H. Lockwood, D. L. Kemmerer, R. D. Van Valin, B. W. Murphy, and H. G. Khalak. 1996. "A Positron Emission Tomographic Study of Regular and Irregular Verb Morphology in English," *Language,* 72(3).

[4] H. Damasio and A. R. Damasio. 1989. *Lesion Analysis in Neuropsychology.* New York: Oxford University Press, p. 53.

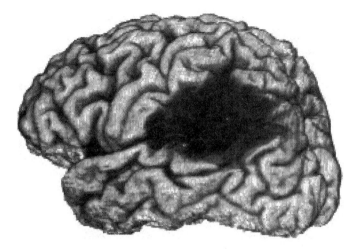

Figure 2.5   Three-dimensional reconstruction of the brain of a living patient with Wernicke's aphasia. Note area of damage in left posterior temporal and lower parietal region (dark gray), which was caused by a stroke. (Courtesy of Hanna Damasio)[5]

EVIDENCE FROM CHILDHOOD BRAIN LESIONS

It only takes one hemisphere to have a mind.

A. W. Wigan, 1844

The study of children with prenatal, perinatal, or childhood brain lesions suggests that although lateralization of language to the left hemisphere is a process that begins very early in life, language may be less lateralized initially, with the right hemisphere also playing some role. Studies of **hemiplegic** children — those with lesions in one side of the brain — show differential cognitive abilities. Those with damaged left hemispheres show greater deficiency in language acquisition and performance with the greatest impairments in their ability to form words and sentences.

In extreme cases of disease, it may be necessary to surgically remove one hemisphere of the brain. When this happens, the remaining hemisphere attempts to take over the functions of the missing one. Mature patients who have their right hemispheres excised retain their language abilities, though other cognitive losses may result. Surgical removal of the left hemisphere of adults is performed only to save the patient's life, because it inevitably results in severe loss of the language function.

It appears that even from birth the human brain is predisposed to specialize for language in the left hemisphere since language usually does not develop normally in children with early left-hemisphere brain lesions.

[5] Ibid., p. 107.

SPLIT BRAINS

Split-brain patients also provide evidence for language lateralization and for understanding brain functions. Persons suffering from intractable epilepsy may be treated by severing communication between their two hemispheres. Surgeons cut through the corpus callosum (Figure 2.1), the fibrous network that connects the two halves. When this pathway is broken, there is no communication between the "two brains."

The psychologist Michael Gazzaniga states:

> With [the corpus callosum] intact, the two halves of the body have no secrets from one another. With it sectioned, the two halves become two different conscious mental spheres, each with its own experience base and control system for behavioral operations. . . . Unbelievable as this may seem, this is the flavor of a long series of experimental studies first carried out in the cat and monkey.[6]

"ROGER DOESN'T USE THE LEFT SIDE OF THE BRAIN OR THE RIGHT SIDE. HE JUST USES THE MIDDLE."

Copyright © S. Harris.

When the brain is surgically split, certain information from the left side of the body is received only by the right side of the brain, and vice versa. For example, suppose a

---

[6] M. Gazzaniga. 1970. *The Bisected Brain.* New York: Appleton-Century-Crofts.

monkey is trained to respond with its hands to a certain visual stimulus, such as a flashing light. If the brain is split after the training period, and the stimulus is shown only to the left visual field (the right brain), the monkey will perform only with the left hand. Many such experiments show the independence of the two sides of the brain.

Studies of split-brain patients reveal that in the human brain, as in the monkey brain, the two hemispheres are distinct. Moreover, messages sent to the two sides of the brain result in different responses, depending on which side receives the message. Sensory information arrives in the opposite side of the brain from the side of the body that sends it. In a split-brain patient, information in the right hemisphere is inaccessible to the left hemisphere. If an apple is placed in the left hand of a split-brain human whose eyes are closed, the person can use it appropriately but cannot name it. The right brain senses the apple and distinguishes it from other objects, but the information cannot be relayed to the left brain for linguistic naming. By contrast, if an apple is placed in the right hand, the subject is immediately able to name it as well as to describe it.

Various experiments of this sort have provided information on the different capabilities of the two halves. The right brain does better than the left in pattern-matching tasks, in recognizing faces, and in spatial orientation. The left hemisphere is superior for language, for rhythmic perception, for temporal-order judgments, and for mathematical thinking. According to Gazzaniga, "the right hemisphere as well as the left hemisphere can emote and while the left can tell you why, the right cannot."[7]

Studies of human split-brain patients have shown that when the interhemispheric visual connections are severed, visual information from the right and left visual fields becomes confined to the left and right hemispheres, respectively. Because of the crucial endowment of the left hemisphere for language, written material delivered to the right hemisphere cannot be read if the brain is split, because the information cannot be transferred to the left hemisphere.

An image or picture that is flashed to the right visual field of a split-brain patient (and therefore processed by the left hemisphere) can be named. However, when the picture is flashed in the left visual field and lands in the right hemisphere, it cannot be named.

FURTHER EXPERIMENTS

Dichotic listening is an experimental technique that uses auditory signals to observe the behavior of the individual hemispheres of the human brain. Subjects hear two different sound signals simultaneously through earphones. They may hear *curl* in one ear and *girl* in the other, or a cough in one ear and a laugh in the other. When asked to state what they heard in each ear, subjects are more frequently correct in reporting linguistic stimuli (words, nonsense syllables, and so on) delivered directly to the right ear, but are more frequently correct in reporting nonverbal stimuli (musical chords, environmental sounds, and so on) delivered to the left ear. That is, if subjects hear *curl* in the right ear and *girl* in the left ear, they are more likely to report the word heard in the right ear correctly. If they hear a cough in the right ear and a laugh in the left, they are more apt to report the laughing stimulus correctly.

Both hemispheres receive signals from both ears, but the contralateral stimuli outweigh the **ipsilateral** (same side) stimuli because they are more intense and arrive more

---

[7] Ibid.

MOTHER GOOSE & GRIMM By Mike Peters

quickly. Their pathways are anatomically thicker (think of a four-lane highway versus a two-lane road), and are not delayed by the need to cross the corpus callosum. The accuracy with which subjects report what they heard is evidence that the left hemisphere is superior for linguistic processing, and the right hemisphere is superior for nonverbal information.

These experiments are important because they show not only that language is lateralized, but also that the left hemisphere is not superior for processing all sounds, only for those that are linguistic. That is, the left side of the brain is specialized for language, not sounds.

Other experimental techniques are also being used to map the brain and to investigate the independence of different aspects of language and the extent of the independence of language from other cognitive systems. Even before the advances in imaging technology of the 1970s, researchers were taping electrodes to different areas of the skull and investigating the electrical activity of the brain. In such experiments, scientists measure the electrical signals emitted from the brain in response to different stimuli (called **event-related brain potentials,** or **ERPs**). For example, ERP differences result when the subject hears speech sounds versus nonspeech sounds. Experiments also show ERP variation in timing and area of response when subjects heard sentences that were meaningless, such as

*The man admired Don's headache of the landscape[8]

as opposed to meaningful sentences such as

The man admired Don's sketch of the landscape.

These experiments show that neuronal activity in different locations varies with different stimuli and different tasks, and again show a left hemisphere specialization for grammar.

Additional evidence is provided by the patterns of neuronal activity in people reading different kinds of writing. Japanese has two writing systems. One system, *kana,* is based on the sound system of the language; each symbol corresponds to a syllable.

---

[8] As noted in Chapter 1, the asterisk indicates something unacceptable about the sentence.

The other system, *kanji,* is ideographic; each symbol corresponds to a word. Kanji is not based on the sounds of the language. Japanese people with left-hemisphere damage are impaired in their ability to read kana, while people with right hemisphere damage are impaired in their ability to read kanji. In addition, experiments with normal Japanese speakers that isolate the two hemispheres show that the right hemisphere is better than the left hemisphere at reading kanji.

The results of these studies, using different techniques and diverse subjects, both normal and brain damaged, are converging to provide the information we seek on the relationship between the brain and various language and nonlanguage cognitive systems.

More Evidence for Modularity

Although neurolinguistics is still in its infancy, our understanding has progressed a great deal since a day in September 1848, when a foreman of a road construction gang named Phineas Gage became a famous figure in medical history. He achieved medical immortality when an explosion drove a four-foot-long iron rod through his head. Despite the gaping tunnel in his brain, Gage maintained the ability to speak and understand, and retained whatever intellectual abilities he had before the injury. However, he suffered major changes in his personality, including his sexual behavior, and his ability to control his emotions or make plans. Both Gage and science benefited from this explosion. Phineas gained monetarily by becoming a one-man touring circus. He traveled the country charging money to those curious enough to see him and the iron rod. Nevertheless, he died penniless twelve years after the accident. Science benefited because scientists questioned why his intelligence remained intact.

No autopsy was performed when Gage died in 1861 (the year Broca delivered his seminal paper). Dr. John Harlowe, the doctor first called after Gage's accident, convinced Gage's sister that his body should be exhumed and his skull preserved for science. This was done and the skull and the iron bar have been kept in the Harvard Medical School since that time. Dr. Harlowe did indeed contribute to scientific knowledge in this way. Approximately 130 years after the exhumation, neurologists at the University of Iowa School of Medicine reconstructed Gage's brain. Using neuro-imaging techniques and a computer program called Brainvox, they showed that the damage to Gage's brain was neither to the motor area nor to the language areas, but to the prefrontal cortex.[9] They further observed that patients with damage to this area show the same kind of personality changes as did Gage.[10]

Despite the absurdity of Franz Joseph Gall's phrenology, the fact that damage to some parts of the brain results in language loss, whereas damage to other parts produces other kinds of deficits, supports his model of a structured brain with separate faculties.

APHASIA

In the preceding discussion, we saw that aphasia has been an important area of research in the attempts to understand the relation between brain and language. The interest in

[9] H. Damasio, T. Grabowski, R. Frank, A. M. Galaburda, and A. R. Damasio. 1994. "The Return of Phineas Gage: The Skull of a Famous Patient Yields Clues about the Brain," *Science* 264:1102–05.

[10] A. R. Damasio. 1994. *Descartes' Error: Emotion, Reason and the Human Brain.* New York: Avon Books.

aphasia did not start with Broca. In the New Testament, St. Luke reports that Zacharias could not speak but could write, showing the early recognition of the autonomy of different aspects of linguistic knowledge. In 30 B.C.E. the Roman writer Valerius Maximus describes an Athenian who was unable to remember his "letters" after being hit in the head with a stone. Pliny the Elder (C.E. 23–79) refers to this same Athenian, noting that "with the stroke of a stone, he fell presently to forget his letters only, and could read no more; otherwise his memory served him well enough."

Numerous clinical descriptions of patients with language deficits, but intact non-linguistic cognitive systems, were published between the fifteenth and eighteenth centuries. Johannes Gesner in 1770 did not attribute these language difficulties to either general intellectual deficits or loss of memory, but to a specific impairment to language memory. He wrote: "Just as some verbal powers can become weakened without injury to others, memory also can be specifically impaired to a greater or lesser degree with respect to only certain classes of ideas."

Other reports describe patients suffering from acquired dyslexia (loss of ability to read) who nevertheless preserved their ability to write, and patients who could write to dictation but could not read back what they had written.

Carl Linnaeus in 1745 published a case study of a man suffering from **jargon aphasia,** who spoke "as if it were a foreign language, having his own names for all words." An important observation regarding word substitution errors was made by Ryklof Michel von Goens in 1789 in his reference to a patient whom he described as follows: "After an illness, she was suddenly afflicted with a forgetting, or, rather, an incapacity or confusion of speech. . . . If she desired a *chair,* she would ask for a *table.* . . . Sometimes she herself perceived that she misnamed objects; at other times, she was annoyed when a *fan,* which she had asked for, was brought to her, instead of the *bonnet,* which she thought she had requested."

The description of these and similarly afflicted patients reveals that they substituted words that were semantically or phonologically similar to the intended ones, producing errors similar to the normal word substitution errors that unafflicted persons might produce.

Physicians of the day described other kinds of linguistic breakdown in detail. Gesner observed and wrote about bilingual asymmetry in which, for example, an abbot retained his ability following brain damage to read Latin but not German.

The historical descriptions of language loss following brain damage, together with the controlled scientific studies of aphasia that have been conducted in the last fifty years, provide substantial evidence that language is predominantly and most frequently a left-hemisphere function. In the great majority of cases, lesions to the left hemisphere result in aphasia but injuries to the right do not (although such lesions result in defects in facial recognition, pattern recognition, and other cognitive deficits). If both hemispheres were equally involved with language, this should not be the case.

The language difficulties suffered by aphasics are not due to any general cognitive or intellectual impairment. Nor are they due to loss of motor or sensory controls of the nerves and muscles of the speech organs or hearing apparatus. Aphasics can produce sounds and hear sounds. Whatever loss they suffer has to do only with the production or comprehension of language (or specific parts of the grammar).

Deaf signers with damage to the left hemisphere show aphasia for sign language similar to the language breakdown in hearing aphasics. Bellugi and her colleagues at the Salk Institute have found that deaf patients with lesions in Broca's area show language deficits similar to those found in hearing patients, namely severe dysfluent, agrammatic sign production.[11] While deaf aphasic patients show marked sign language deficits, they have no difficulty in processing nonlinguistic visual spatial relationships, just as hearing aphasics have no problem with processing nonlinguistic auditory stimuli. This is further evidence that the left hemisphere is not lateralized for hearing or speech, but for language.

Many aphasics do not show total language loss. Rather, different aspects of language are selectively impaired. Broca's aphasics may be **agrammatic** because of their particular problems with syntax, as the following sample of speech illustrates. Asked what brought him back to the hospital, the patient answered:

> Yes — ah — Monday ah — Dad — and Dad — ah — Hospital — and ah — Wednesday — Wednesday — nine o'clock and ah Thursday — ten o'clock ah doctors — two — two — ah doctors and — ah — teeth — yah. And a doctor — ah girl — and gums, and I.[12]

---

[11] H. Poizner, E. Klima, and U. Bellugi. 1987. *What the Hands Reveal about the Brain.* Cambridge, MA: MIT Press.

[12] H. Goodglass. 1973. "Studies on the Grammar of Aphasics," in *Psycholinguistics and Aphasia.* H. Goodglass and S. Blumstein, eds. Baltimore, MD: Johns Hopkins University Press.

Agrammatic aphasics often speak in ungrammatical utterances, frequently omitting articles, prepositions, and auxiliary verbs — let's call these "function words" for now. They might also drop parts of words like the past tense suffix -ed. On the hearing side of language use, they also have difficulty with sentences where comprehension depends on syntactic structure. For example, an agrammatic aphasic might be confused as to who is chasing whom in passive sentences such as:

The cat was chased by the dog

where it is plausible for either animal to chase the other. But they have less difficulty with

The car was chased by the dog

where the meaning of the sentence is provided by nonlinguistic context. They know that it is implausible for cars to chase dogs, and use that knowledge to interpret the sentence. In the first sentence, the interpretation depends on knowledge of the English passive construction, which tells normal speakers that the dog chased the cat, not the other way around.

Wernicke's aphasics, on the other hand, often produce fluent but unintelligible speech. They also have comprehension problems and difficulty in choosing words. One patient replied to a question about his health with:

I felt worse because I can no longer keep in mind from the mind of the minds
to keep me from mind and up to the ear which can be to find among ourselves.

Some aphasics have difficulty in naming objects that are presented to them, which shows a lexical defect. Others produce semantically meaningless jargon such as the patient who described a fork as "a need for a schedule," or another who, when asked about his poor vision, replied: "My wires don't hire right." While some of these aphasics substitute words that bear no semantic relationship to the correct word, others substitute words that are semantically related. Those errors resemble the speech errors that anyone might make, such as substituting *table* for *chair* or *boy* for *girl,* but they occur far more frequently when Wernicke's aphasia is the root cause.

Jargon aphasia results in the substitution of one sound for another. Patients with Wernicke's aphasia often produce such jargon. Thus *table* might be pronounced as *sable*. An extreme variety of phonetic jargon results in the production of nonsense words. One patient, a physician before his aphasia, when asked if he was a doctor, replied:

Me? Yes sir. I'm a male demaploze on my own. I still know my tubaboys what
for I have that's gone hell and some of them go.

The kind of selective impairment that we find in aphasics provides information on the organization of grammar. Patients that produce long strings of jargon that sound like sentences but make no sense show that knowledge of the sound sequences by which we represent words in our mental dictionaries can be disassociated from their meanings. If we find that damage to different parts of the brain results in different kinds of linguistic impairment, for example, syntactic vs. semantic, this supports the hypothesis that the mental grammar is not a homogeneous system, but rather consists of distinct modules, as is proposed in various linguistic models.

The substitution of semantically or phonetically related words provides evidence about the organization of our mental dictionaries. The substituted words are not random but are similar to the intended words either in their sounds or in their meanings.

Similar observations pertain to reading. Many such substitutions are made by aphasics who become dyslexic after brain damage. They are called **acquired dyslexics** because before the brain lesion they were normal readers (unlike developmental dyslexics who have difficulty learning to read). One group of these patients, when reading words printed on cards aloud, produced the kinds of substitutions shown in the following examples.[13]

Stimulus	Response 1	Response 2
act	*play*	*play*
applaud	*laugh*	*cheers*
example	*answer*	*sum*
heal	*pain*	*medicine*
south	*west*	*east*

Sometimes these patients would substitute the same related but wrong word on two testing occasions. Other times the words would be different, and yet other times they would read the correct word, showing that the problem was in performance (accessing the correct form in the lexicon) not in competence, since they could sometimes get to the right word and produce it.

The substitution of phonologically similar words, such as *pool* for *tool* or *crucial* for *crucible,* also provides information on the organization of the lexicon. Words in the lexicon are linked to other words through both sound and meaning. Words are not simply represented in a list, but rather in a network of connections.

Language tests of patients with aphasia give evidence for different word classes. The omission of function words[14] in the speech of agrammatic aphasics shows that that class of words is mentally distinct from content words like nouns. Patient G. R., who produced the semantically similar word substitutions cited above, was unable to read these function words at all. When presented with words like *which* or *would,* he just said, "No" or "I hate those little words." However he can read, though with many semantic mistakes, as shown in the following:

Stimulus	Response	Stimulus	Response
witch	*witch*	which	*no!*
bean	*soup*	been	*no!*
hour	*time*	our	*no!*
eye	*eyes*	I	*no!*
hymn	*bible*	him	*no!*
wood	*wood*	would	*no!*

---

[13] Patient G. R., as reported in F. Newcombe and J. Marshall. 1984. "Varieties of Acquired Dyslexia: A Linguistic Approach," *Seminars in Neurology* 4(2):181–95.

[14] Function words and word endings such as the *s* that forms plurals and the *ed* that forms past tense are called grammatical morphemes and will be discussed in Chapter 3.

These errors suggest that the mental dictionary in our brains is compartmentalized. Content words and function words are in different compartments. Furthermore, they give evidence that these two classes of words are processed in different areas or by different neural mechanisms, further supporting the view that the brain is structured in a complex, modular fashion. One can think of the grammar as a mental module in the brain with submodular parts.

Most of us have experienced word-finding difficulties in speaking if not in reading, as Alice did in "Wonderland" when she said:

> "And now, who am I? I will remember, if I can. I'm determined to do it!" But being determined didn't help her much, and all she could say, after a great deal of puzzling, was "L, I know it begins with L."

This **"tip-of-the-tongue" phenomenon** (often referred to as **TOT**) is not uncommon. But if you could *never* find the word you want, imagine how frustrated you would be. This is the fate of many aphasics when their impairment includes **anomia** — the inability to find the word you wish to speak.

DISTINCT CATEGORIES OF CONCEPTUAL KNOWLEDGE

Dramatic evidence for a differentiated and structured brain is provided by studies of both normal individuals and patients with lesions in other than Broca's and Wernicke's areas. Some patients have difficulty speaking a person's name; others have problems naming animals, and still others cannot name tools. The patients in each group have brain lesions in distinct regions of the left temporal lobe. MRI studies revealed the shape and location of the brain lesions of some of these patients. No overlap in the lesion sites in the three groups was found. In a follow-up study of normal subjects in a PET scan word-retrieval study, experimenters found differential activation of just those sites damaged in patients with lesions when they were asked to name persons, animals, or tools.[15]

Further evidence for the separation of cognitive systems is provided by the neurological and behavioral findings that follow brain damage. Some patients lose the ability to recognize sounds or colors or familiar faces while retaining all other functions. A patient may not be able to recognize his wife when she walks in the room until she starts to talk. This suggests the differentiation of visual and auditory processing, which is now highly substantiated.

The Autonomy of Language

In addition to brain-damaged individuals who lost their language ability, there are cases of children (without brain lesions) who have difficulties in acquiring language or are much slower than the average child. They show no other cognitive deficits, are not autistic or retarded, and have no perceptual problems. Such children are suffering from a **Specific Language Impairment (SLI).** Only their linguistic ability is affected, and often only specific aspects of the grammar are impaired.

---

[15] H. Damasio, T. J. Grabowski, D. Tranel, R. D. Hichwa, and A. R. Damasio. 1996. "A Neural Basis for Lexical Retrieval," *Nature* 380(11):499–505.

Children with SLI show that language may be impaired while general intelligence stays intact. But can language develop normally with general intelligence impaired? If such individuals can be found, it argues strongly for the view that language does not derive from some general cognitive ability.

The question as to whether the language faculty is already present from the time of birth or whether it is derivative of more general intelligence, is a controversial question receiving much attention and debate among linguists, psychologists, and neuropsychologists. A growing body of evidence supports the view that the human animal is biologically equipped from birth with an autonomous language faculty that itself is highly specific and that does not derive from general human intellectual ability.

Asymmetry of Abilities

> . . . the human mind is not an unstructured entity but consists of components which can be distinguished by their functional properties.
>
> Neil Smith and Ianthi-Maria Tsimpli.[16]

We know of numerous cases of intellectually handicapped individuals who, despite their disabilities in certain spheres, show remarkable talents in others. There are superb musicians and artists who lack the simple abilities required to take care of themselves. They were once called "idiot savants" but now, fortunately, are referred to as **savants.** Some of the most famous savants are human calculators who can perform arithmetic computations at phenomenal speed, or calendrical calculators who can tell you without pause on which day of the week falls any date in the last or next century.

Until recently, most of the savants have been reported to be linguistically handicapped. They may be good mimics who can repeat speech like parrots, but they show meager creative language ability.

While such cases argue for domain-specific abilities and suggest that certain talents do not require general intelligence, we cannot conclude from them that language is such a domain-specific ability. Nevertheless, the literature reports cases of language savants who have acquired the highly complex grammar of their language (as well as other languages in some cases) without parallel nonlinguistic abilities of equal complexity. Further investigation of these cases will contribute to the debate about the autonomy of the language faculty.

LAURA

Laura was a retarded young woman with a nonverbal IQ of 41–44.[17] She lacked almost all number concepts, including basic counting principles, could draw only at a preschool level, and had an auditory memory span limited to three units. Yet, when at the age of sixteen she was asked to name some fruits, she responded with *pears, apples,* and *pomegranates.* In this same period she produced syntactically complex sentences like *He was saying that I lost my battery-powered watch that I loved* and *Last year at school when I first went there, three tickets were gave out by a police last year.*

---

[16] N. Smith and I-M. Tsimpli. 1995. *The Mind of a Savant: Language Learning and Modularity.* Oxford: Blackwell.

[17] J. E. Yamada. 1990. *Laura: A Case for the Modularity of Language.* Cambridge, MA: MIT Press.

Laura could not add 2 + 2. She was not sure of when "last year" was or whether it was before or after "last week" or "an hour ago," nor did she know how many tickets were "gave out," nor whether three was larger or smaller than two. Nevertheless, Laura produced complex sentences with multiple phrases. She used and understood passive sentences, and she was able to inflect verbs for number and person to agree with the subject of the sentence. She formed past tenses in accord with adverbs that referred to past time. She could do all this and more, but she could neither read nor write nor tell time. She did not know who the president of the United States was or what country she lived in or even her own age. Her drawings of humans resembled potatoes with stick arms and legs. Yet, in a sentence imitation task, she both detected and corrected grammatical errors.

Laura is but one of many examples of children who display well-developed grammatical abilities, less-developed abilities to associate linguistic expressions with the objects they refer to, and severe deficits in nonlinguistic cognitive development.

In addition, any notion that linguistic competence results simply from communicative abilities, or develops to serve communication functions, is belied by studies of children with good linguistic skills, but nearly no communicative skills. The acquisition and use of language seem to depend on cognitive skills different from the ability to communicate in a social setting.

CHRISTOPHER

Christopher has a nonverbal IQ between 60 and 70 and must live in an institution because he is unable to take care of himself. The tasks of buttoning a shirt, cutting his fingernails, or vacuuming the carpet are too difficult for him. However, linguists find that his "linguistic competence in his first language is as rich and as sophisticated as that of any native speaker."[18] Furthermore, when given written texts in some fifteen to twenty languages, he translates them quickly, with few errors, into English. The languages include Germanic languages such as Danish, Dutch, and German; Romance languages such as French, Italian, Portuguese, and Spanish; as well as Polish, Finnish, Greek, Hindi, Turkish, and Welsh. He learned these languages from speakers who used them in his presence, or from grammar books. Christopher loves to study and learn languages. Little else is of interest to him. His situation strongly suggests that his linguistic ability is independent of his general intellectual ability.

The cases of Laura and Christopher argue against the view that linguistic ability derives from general intelligence, since for these two individuals language developed in spite of other intellectual deficits.

Genetic Evidence for Language Autonomy

Studies of genetic disorders also reveal that one cognitive domain can develop normally along with abnormal development in other domains. Children with Turner's syndrome (a chromosomal anomaly) have normal or advanced language skills along with serious nonlinguistic (visual and spatial) cognitive deficits. Similarly, the studies of the lan-

---

[18] N. Smith and I-M Tsimpli. 1995. *The Mind of a Savant: Language Learning and Modularity.* Oxford, England: Blackwell.

guage of adolescents with Williams syndrome reveal a unique behavioral profile in which there appears to be a selective preservation of linguistic functions in the face of many general cognitive deficits or moderate retardation. In addition, developmental dyslexia and at least some types of SLI also appear to have a genetic basis.

Epidemiological studies show that specific language impairment runs in families. A large multigenerational family, half of whom are language impaired, has been studied in detail.[19] All of the people in the study are adult native speakers of English. The impaired members of this family have a very specific grammatical problem. They do not reliably indicate the tense of the verb. They routinely produce sentences such as the following:

She remembered when she hurts herself the other day.
He did it then he fall.
The boy climb up the tree and frightened the bird away.

These results point to SLI as a heritable disorder.

Studies also show that monozygotic (identical) twins are more likely to both suffer from SLI than dizygotic (fraternal) twins.

Thus, evidence from aphasia, SLI, and other genetic disorders, along with the asymmetry of abilities in linguistic savants, strongly supports the view of the language faculty (and more specifically grammar,) as an autonomous, genetically determined, brain (mind) module.

Language and Brain Development

There is an intimate connection between language and the brain. Specific areas of the brain are devoted to language, and injury to these areas disrupts language. In the young child, injury to or removal of the left hemisphere has severe consequences for language development. Conversely, there is increasing evidence that normal brain development depends on early and regular exposure to language.

The Critical Period

Under normal circumstances, a child is introduced to language virtually at the moment of birth. Adults talk to him and to each other in his presence. Children do not require explicit language instruction, but they do need exposure to language in order to develop normally. Children who do not receive linguistic input during their formative years do not achieve nativelike grammatical competence. Behavioral tests and brain imaging studies show that late exposure to language alters the fundamental organization of the brain for language.

The *Critical Age Hypothesis* is part of the biological basis of language[20] and states that the ability to learn a native language develops within a fixed period, from birth to

---

[19] M. Gopnik. 1994. "Impairments of Tense in a Familial Language Disorder," *Journal of Neurolinguistics* 8(2):109–33.

[20] E. Lenneberg. 1967. *Biological Foundations of Language.* New York: Wiley.

"Jump Start" copyright © United Feature Syndicate. Reprinted with permission.

puberty. During this **critical period,** language acquisition proceeds easily, swiftly, and without external intervention. After this period, the acquisition of grammar is difficult and for some individuals never fully achieved. Children deprived of language during this critical period show atypical patterns of brain lateralization.

The notion of a critical period is true of many species and seems to pertain to species-specific, biologically triggered behavior. Ducklings, for example, during the period from nine to twenty-one hours after hatching, will follow the first moving object they see, whether or not it looks or waddles like a duck. Such behavior is not the result of conscious decision, external teaching, or intensive practice. It unfolds according to what appears to be a maturationally determined schedule that is universal across the species.

Instances of children reared in environments of extreme social isolation constitute "experiments in nature" for testing the critical age hypothesis. Such reported cases go back at least to the eighteenth century. In 1758 Carl Linnaeus first included *Homo ferus* (wild or feral man) as a subdivision of *Homo sapiens*. According to Linnaeus, a defining characteristic of *Homo ferus* was his lack of speech or observable language of any kind.

The most dramatic cases of children raised in isolation are those described as "wild" or "feral" children, who have reportedly been reared with wild animals or have lived alone in the wilderness. In 1920 two feral children, Amala and Kamala, were found in India, supposedly having been reared with wolves. A celebrated case, documented in François Truffaut's film *The Wild Child,* is that of Victor, "the wild boy of Aveyron," who was found in 1798. It was ascertained that he had been left in the woods when very young and had somehow survived.

Other children's isolation has resulted from deliberate efforts to keep them from normal social intercourse. In 1970 a child called Genie in the scientific reports[21] was discovered. She had been confined to a small room under conditions of physical restraint, and had received only minimal human contact from the age of eighteen months until almost fourteen years. None of these children, regardless of the cause of isolation, was able to speak or knew any language at the time of reintroduction to society.

---

[21] S. Curtiss. 1977. *Genie: A Linguistic Study of a Modern-Day "Wild Child."* New York: Academic Press.

This linguistic inability could simply be because they received no linguistic input, showing that exposure to language must trigger the innate neurological ability of the human brain to acquire language. In the documented cases of Victor and Genie, however, they were unable to acquire language after exposure, even with deliberate and painstaking linguistic teaching.

Genie did begin to acquire some language, but while she was able to learn a large vocabulary, including colors, shapes, objects, natural categories, and abstract as well as concrete terms, her syntax and morphology never fully developed. The UCLA linguist Susan Curtiss, who worked with Genie for a number of years, reports that Genie's utterances were, for the most part, "the stringing together of content words, often with rich and clear meaning, but with little grammatical structure." Many utterances produced by Genie at the age of fifteen and older, several years after her emergence from isolation, are like those of two-year old children, and not unlike utterances of Broca's aphasia patients.

Man motorcycle have.

Genie full stomach.

Genie bad cold live father house.

Want Curtiss play piano.

Open door key.

Genie's utterances lacked auxiliary verbs, the third-person singular agreement marker, the past-tense marker, and most pronouns. She did not invert subjects and verbs to form questions. Genie started learning language after the critical period, and was never able to fully acquire the grammatical rules of English, supporting the hypothesis.

Tests of lateralization (dichotic listening and ERP experiments) showed that Genie's language was lateralized to the *right* hemisphere, even though the left hemisphere is normally predisposed for language. Her test performance was similar to that found in split-brain and left hemispherectomy patients, yet Genie was not brain damaged. Curtiss speculates that after the critical period there is a functional atrophy of the usual language areas due to inadequate linguistic stimulation.

Chelsea is a woman whose situation also supports the critical-age hypothesis. She was born deaf in Northern California, isolated from any major urban center, and wrongly diagnosed as retarded. Her devoted and caring family never believed this to be so. They knew she was deaf, but in the small town where they lived there were no schools for the deaf, so she did not attend school. When she was thirty-one, a neurologist finally diagnosed her deafness, and she was fitted with hearing aids. She received extensive language therapy and was able to acquire a large vocabulary but, like Genie, has not been able to develop a grammar. A study of the localization of language in Chelsea's brain revealed an equal response to language in both hemispheres. In other words, Chelsea, like Genie, does not show the normal asymmetric organization for language.[22]

---

[22] H. Neville. 1987. Talk presented at the 38th annual conference of The Orton Dyslexia Society, San Francisco, CA.

More than 90 percent of children who are born deaf or become deaf before they have acquired language are born to hearing parents. These children have also provided information about the critical age for language acquisition. Because most of their parents do not know sign language at the time these children are born, many receive delayed language exposure. A number of studies have investigated the acquisition of ASL among deaf signers exposed to the language at different ages. Early learners who received ASL input from birth and up to six years of age did much better in the production and comprehension of complex signs than late learners who were not exposed to ASL until after the age of twelve. There was little difference, however, in the vocabularies or the word-order constraints (which are very regular in ASL).[23]

Another study compared patterns of lateralization in hearing children acquiring English, deaf children acquiring ASL, and deaf children who had not been exposed to sign language. The nonsigning deaf children did not show the same cerebral asymmetries as either the hearing children or the deaf signers.[24]

The cases of Genie and other isolated children, as well as deaf late learners of ASL, show that children cannot fully acquire language unless they are exposed to it within the critical period — a biologically determined window of opportunity during which time the brain is prepared to develop language. The critical period is linked to brain lateralization. The human brain is primed to develop language in specific areas of the left hemisphere, but the normal process of brain specialization depends on early and systematic experience with language.

Beyond the critical period, the human brain seems unable to acquire the grammatical aspects of language, even with substantial linguistic training. However, it is possible to acquire words and various conversational skills after this point. This evidence suggests that the critical period is for the acquisition of certain aspects of language, but not all aspects.

The "selective acquisition" of certain (but not all) components of language that occurs beyond the critical period is reminiscent of the selective impairment that occurs in aphasic syndromes and in SLI, in which specific linguistic abilities (but not all) are disrupted. This "selectivity" in both acquisition and impairment points to a strongly modularized language faculty. Language is separate from other cognitive systems and autonomous, and is itself a complex system with various components. In the chapters that follow, we will explore these different language components.

A Critical Period for Bird Songs

That's the wise thrush; he sings each song twice over,
Lest you should think he never could recapture
The first fine careless rapture!

Robert Browning, *Home-thoughts from Abroad*

---

[23] E. Newport. 1990. "Maturational Constraints on Language Learning," *Cognitive Science* 14:11–28.

[24] H. Neville. 1975. The Development of Cerebral Specialization in Normal and Congenitally Deaf Children: An Evoked Potential and Behavioral Study. Ph.D. dissertation: Cornell University.

Bird songs lack certain fundamental characteristics of human language such as discrete sounds and creativity. However, certain species show a critical period for acquiring their "language" similar to the critical period for human language acquisition. The bird species for which a critical period has been observed are those whose "language" acquisition is guided by something akin to the innate human language ability.

Calls and songs of the chaffinch vary depending on the geographical area that the bird inhabits. The message is the same but the form or "pronunciation" is different. Usually, a young bird sings a simplified version of the song shortly after hatching. Later, it undergoes further learning in acquiring the fully complex version. Since birds from the same brood acquire different chaffinch songs depending on the area in which they finally settle, part of the song must be learned. On the other hand, since the fledging chaffinch sings the song of its species in a simple degraded form, even if it has never heard it sung, some aspect of it is biologically determined, that is, innate.

The chaffinch acquires its fully developed song in several stages, just as human children acquire language. There is also a critical period in the song-learning of chaffinches (and white-crowned sparrows, zebra finches, and other species). If these birds are not exposed to the songs of their species during certain fixed periods after their birth (the period differs from species to species), song acquisition does not occur. The chaffinch is unable to learn new song elements after ten months of age. If it is isolated from other birds before attaining the full complexity of its song and is then exposed again after ten months, its song will not develop further. If white-crowned sparrows lose their hearing during a critical period after they have learned to sing, they produce a song that differs from other white crowns. They need to hear themselves sing to produce particular whistles and other song features. If, however, the deafness occurs after the critical period, the songs are normal.

In marked contrast to chaffinches and humans, some bird species show no critical period. The cuckoo sings a fully developed song even if it never hears another cuckoo sing. These communicative messages are entirely innate. For other species, songs appear to be completely learned; the bullfinch, for example, will learn any song it is exposed to, even that of another species. In a more recent example of unconstrained song learning, Danish ornithologists report that birds have begun to copy the ringing tones of cellular phones.[25]

From the point of view of human language research, the relationship between the innate and learned aspects of bird songs is significant. Apparently, the basic nature of the songs of some species is present from birth, which means that it is biologically determined. The same holds true for human language: its basic nature is innate. The details of bird songs, and of human language, are acquired through experience that must occur within a critical period.

---

[25] *The Progressive,* July 2001.

The Evolution of Language

As the voice was used more and more, the vocal organs would have been strengthened and perfected through the principle of the inherited effects of use; and this would have reacted on the power of speech. But the relation between the continued use of language and the development of the brain has no doubt been far more important. The mental powers in some early progenitor of man must have been more highly developed than in any existing ape, before even the most imperfect form of speech could have come into use.

Charles Darwin, *The Descent of Man*

If the human brain is structured and wired for the acquisition and use of language, how and when did this development occur? Two scholarly societies, the American Anthropological Association and the New York Academy of Sciences, held forums in 1974 and 1976 to review research on this question. It is not a new question, and seems to have arisen with the origin of the species.

In the Beginning: The Origin of Language

Nothing, no doubt, would be more interesting than to know from historical documents the exact process by which the first man began to lisp his first words, and thus to be rid for ever of all the theories on the origin of speech.

M. Muller, 1871

Drawing by Leo Cullum; copyright © 1995 The New Yorker Collection. All rights reserved.

All religions and mythologies contain stories of language origin. Philosophers through the ages have argued the question. Scholarly works have been written on the subject. Prizes have been awarded for the "best answer" to this eternally perplexing problem. Theories of divine origin, evolutionary development, and language as a human invention have all been suggested.

The difficulties inherent in answering this question are immense. Anthropologists believe that the species has existed for at least one million years, and perhaps for as long as five or six million years. Linguistic history (see chapter 11) suggests that spoken languages of the kind that exist today have been around for tens of thousands of years at the very least. But the earliest deciphered written records are barely six thousand years old. (The origin of writing is discussed in chapter 12). These records appear so late in the history of the development of language that they provide no clue to its origin.

For these reasons, scholars in the latter part of the nineteenth century, who were only interested in "hard science," ridiculed, ignored, and even banned discussions of language origin. In 1886 the Linguistic Society of Paris passed a resolution to ignore papers concerned with this subject.

Despite the difficulty of finding scientific evidence, speculations on language origin have provided valuable insights into the nature and development of language, which prompted the great Danish linguist Otto Jespersen to state that "linguistic science cannot refrain forever from asking about the whence (and about the whither) of linguistic evolution." A brief look at some of these speculative notions will reveal this.

God's Gift to Mankind?

> And out of the ground the Lord God formed every beast of the field, and every fowl of the air, and brought them unto Adam to see what he would call them; and whatsoever Adam called every living creature, that was the name thereof.
>
> Genesis 2:19

According to Judeo-Christian beliefs, God gave Adam the power to name all things. Similar beliefs are found throughout the world. According to the Egyptians, the creator of speech was the god Thoth. Babylonians believed that the language giver was the god Nabu, and the Hindus attributed our unique language ability to a female god: Brahma was the creator of the universe, but his wife Sarasvati gave language to us.

Belief in the divine origin of language is intertwined with the supernatural properties that have been associated with the spoken word. Children in all cultures utter "magic" words like *abracadabra* to ward off evil or bring good luck. Despite the childish jingle "Sticks and stones may break my bones, but names will never hurt me," name-calling is insulting, cause for legal punishment, and feared. In some cultures, when certain words are used, one is required to counter them by "knocking on wood," or some such ritualistic action.

In many religions only special languages may be used in prayers and rituals. The Hindu priests of the fifth century B.C.E. believed that the original pronunciations of Vedic Sanskrit was sacred and must be preserved. This led to important linguistic study, since their language had already changed greatly since the hymns of the Vedas had been written. The first linguist known to us is Panini, who, in the fourth century B.C.E., wrote a detailed grammar of Sanskrit in which the phonological rules revealed the earlier pronunciation for use in religious worship.

While myths, customs and superstitions do not tell us very much about language origin, they do tell us about the importance ascribed to language. There is no way to prove or disprove the divine origin of language, just as one cannot argue scientifically for or against the existence of God.

THE FIRST LANGUAGE

Imagine the Lord talking French! Aside from a few odd words in Hebrew, I took it completely for granted that God had never spoken anything but the most dignified English.

Clarence Day, *Life with Father*

Among the proponents of the divine origin theory, a great interest arose in the language used by God, Adam, and Eve. For millennia, "scientific" experiments have reportedly been devised to verify particular theories of the first language. The Greek historian Herodotus reported that the Egyptian pharaoh Psammetichus (664–610 B.C.E.) sought to determine the most primitive "natural" language by experimental methods. The monarch was said to have placed two infants in an isolated mountain hut, to be cared for by a mute servant. The pharaoh believed that without linguistic input the children would develop their own language and would thus reveal the original tongue of man. Patiently the Egyptian waited for the children to become old enough to talk. According to the story, the first word uttered was *bekos,* the word for "bread" in Phrygian, the language spoken in a province of Phrygia in the northwest corner of what is now Turkey. Based on this "experiment" this ancient language, which has long since died out, was thought to be the original language.

History is replete with other proposals. In the thirteenth century, the Holy Roman Emperor Frederick II of Hohenstaufen was said to have carried out a similar test, but the children died before they uttered a single word. James IV of Scotland (1473–1513), however, supposedly succeeded in replicating the experiment with the surprising results, according to legend, that the Scottish children "spak very guid Ebrew," providing "scientific evidence" that Hebrew was the language used in the Garden of Eden.

J. G. Becanus in the sixteenth century argued that German must have been the primeval language, since God would have used the "most perfect language." In 1830 the lexicographer Noah Webster asserted that the protolanguage must have been Chaldee (Aramaic), the language spoken in Jerusalem during the Roman occupation. In 1887 Joseph Elkins maintained that "there is no other language which can be more reasonably assumed to be the speech first used in the world's gray morning than can Chinese."

The belief that all languages originated from a single source — **the monogenetic theory of language origin** — is found not only in the Tower of Babel story in Genesis, but also in a similar legend of the Toltecs, early inhabitants of Mexico, and in the myths of other peoples as well.

We are no closer today to discovering the original language (or languages) than was Psammetichus, given the obscurities of prehistory. A more detailed discussion of the history of human languages is found in chapter 11.

HUMAN INVENTION OR THE CRIES OF NATURE?

Language was born in the courting days of mankind; the first utterances of speech I fancy to myself like something between the nightly love lyrics of puss upon the tiles and the melodious love songs of the nightingale.

Otto Jespersen[26]

The Greeks speculated about everything in the universe, including language. The earliest surviving linguistic treatise that deals with the origin and nature of language is Plato's *Cratylus*. A common view among the classical Greeks, expressed by Socrates in this dialogue, was that at some ancient time there was a "legislator" who gave the correct, natural name to everything, and that words echoed the essence of their meanings.

Despite all the contrary evidence, the idea that the earliest form of language was imitative, or echoic, was proposed up to the twentieth century. Called the bow-wow theory, it claimed that a dog would be designated by the word *bow-wow* because of the sounds of his bark.

A parallel view states that language at first consisted of emotional ejaculations of pain, fear, surprise, pleasure, anger, and so on. French philosopher Jean-Jacques Rousseau proposed that the earliest manifestations of language were "cries of nature."

Another hypothesis suggests that language arose out of the rhythmical grunts of men and women working together. Jespersen suggested a more charming view when he proposed that language derived from song as an expressive rather than a communicative need. To Jespersen, love was the great stimulus for language development.

Just as with the beliefs in a divine origin of language, these proposed origins are not verifiable by scientific means.

The Development of Language in the Species

There is much interest today among biologists as well as linguists in the relationship between the development of language and the evolutionary development of the human species. There are those who view language ability as a difference in degree between humans and other primates — a continuity view — and those who see the onset of language ability as a qualitative leap — the discontinuity view. There are those on both sides of the "discontinuity" view who believe that language is species specific.

In trying to understand the development of language, scholars past and present have debated the role played by the vocal tract and the ear. For example, it has been suggested that speech could not have developed in nonhuman primates because their vocal tracts were anatomically incapable of producing a large enough inventory of speech sounds. According to this hypothesis, the development of language is linked to the evolutionary development of the speech production and perception apparatus. This, of course, would be accompanied by changes in the brain and the nervous system toward greater complexity. Such a view implies that the languages of our human ancestors of millions of

---

[26] O. Jespersen. *Language, Its Nature, Development and Origin.*

years ago may have been syntactically and phonologically simpler than any language known to us today. The notion "simpler" is left undefined, though it has been suggested that this primeval language had a smaller inventory of sounds.

One evolutionary step must have resulted in the development of a vocal tract capable of producing the wide variety of sounds of human language, as well as the mechanism for perceiving and distinguishing them. However, the existence of mynah birds and parrots is evidence that this step is insufficient to explain the origin of language, since these creatures have the ability to imitate human speech, but not the ability to acquire language.

More important, we know from the study of humans who are born deaf and learn sign languages that are used around them that the ability to hear speech sounds is not a necessary condition for the acquisition and use of language. In addition, the lateralization evidence from brain-damaged deaf signers shows that the brain is neurologically equipped to learn language rather than speech.

The ability to produce and hear a wide variety of sounds therefore appears to be neither necessary nor sufficient for the development of language in the human species.

A major step in the development of language most probably relates to evolutionary changes in the brain. The linguist Noam Chomsky expresses this view:

> It could be that when the brain reached a certain level of complexity it simply automatically had certain properties because that's what happens when you pack 10^{10} neurons into something the size of a basketball.[27]

The biologist Stephen Jay Gould expresses a similar view:

> The Darwinist model would say that language, like other complex organic systems, evolved step by step, each step being an adaptive solution. Yet language is such an integrated "all or none" system, it is hard to imagine it evolving that way. Perhaps the brain grew in size and became capable of all kinds of things which were not part of the original properties.[28]

Other linguists, however, support a more Darwinian natural selection development of what is sometimes called "the language instinct":

> All the evidence suggests that it is the precise wiring of the brain's microcircuitry that makes language happen, not gross size, shape, or neuron packing.[29]

The attempt to resolve this controversy clearly requires more research. Another point that is not yet clear is what role, if any, hemispheric lateralization played in language evolution. Lateralization certainly makes greater specialization possible. Research conducted with birds and monkeys, however, shows that lateralization is not unique to the human brain. Thus, while it may constitute a necessary step in the evolution of language, it is not a sufficient one.

We do not yet have definitive answers to the origin of language in the brain of the human species. The search for these answers goes on and provides new insights into the nature of language and the nature of the human brain.

 Summary

The attempt to understand what makes language acquisition and use possible has led to research on the brain-mind-language relationship. **Neurolinguistics** studies the brain mechanisms and anatomical structures that underlie linguistic competence and performance, and how they developed over time.

The brain is the most complicated organ of the body, controlling motor and sensory activities and thought processes. Research conducted for over a century reveals that different parts of the brain control different body functions. The nerve cells that form the surface of the brain are called the **cortex,** which serves as the intellectual decision maker, receiving messages from the sensory organs and initiating all voluntary actions. The brain of all higher animals is divided into two parts called **the cerebral hemispheres,** which are connected by the **corpus callosum,** a pathway that permits the left and right hemispheres to communicate.

Although each hemisphere appears to be a mirror image of the other, they exhibit **contralateral** control of functions. The left hemisphere controls the right side of the body and the right hemisphere controls the left side. Despite the general symmetry of the human body, there is much evidence that the brain is asymmetric, with the left and right hemispheres specialized for different functions.

Evidence from studies of **aphasia** — language dysfunction as a result of brain injuries — and from surgical removal of parts of the brain, electrical stimulation studies, emission tomography results, dichotic listening, and experiments that measure brain electrical activity, show a lack of symmetry of function of the two hemispheres. These results are supported by studies of split-brain patients, who, for medical reasons, have had the corpus callosum severed. In the past, the studies of the brain and language depended on surgery or autopsy. Today, technologies such **as magnetic resonance imaging (MRI)** and **positron−emission tomography (PET)** make it possible to see the sites of lesions in the living brain, to detect changes in brain activities, and to relate these changes to localized brain damage and cognitive tasks.

For normal right-handers and many left-handers, the left side of the brain is specialized for language. This **lateralization** of functions is genetically and neurologically conditioned. Lateralization refers to any cognitive functions that are primarily localized to one side of the brain or the other.

In addition to aphasia, other evidence supports the lateralization of language. Children with early brain lesions in the left hemisphere resulting in the surgical removal of part or all of the left brain show specific linguistic deficits, while other cognitive abilities remain intact. If the right brain is damaged, however, language is unimpaired but other cognitive disorders may result.

Aphasia studies show impairment of different parts of the grammar. Patients with **Broca's aphasia** exhibit impaired syntax and speech problems. Patients with **Wernicke's**

[27] N. Chomsky. 1994. Video. *The Human Language Series*. Program Three. By G. Searchinger.

[28] S. J. Gould. 1994. Video. *The Human Language Series*. Program Three. By G. Searchinger.

[29] S. Pinker. 1995. *The Language Instinct,* New York: Morrow.

aphasia are fluent speakers who produce semantically empty utterances and have difficulty in comprehension. **Anomia** is a form of aphasia in which the patient has word-finding difficulties. Patients with **jargon aphasia** may substitute words unrelated semantically to their intended messages; others produce phonemic substitution errors, sometimes resulting in nonsense forms that make their utterances uninterpretable.

The language faculty is **modular.** It is independent from other cognitive systems with which it interacts. Evidence for modularity is found in studies of aphasia, of children with **Specific Language Impairment (SLI),** and of **savants.** Children with SLI suffer from language deficits, but are normal in other regards. Language savants are individuals with extraordinary language skills, but who are deficient in general intelligence. Their existence suggests that linguistic ability is not derived from some general cognitive ability, but exists independently.

The genetic basis for an independent language module is supported by studies of SLI in families and twins.

The **critical-age hypothesis** states that there is a window of opportunity between birth and puberty for learning a first language. The imperfect language learning of persons exposed to language after this period supports the hypothesis. Some songbirds also appear to have a critical period for the acquisition of their calls and songs.

The origin of language in the species has been a topic for much speculation throughout history. The idea that language was God's gift to humanity is present in religions throughout the world. The continuing belief in the miraculous powers of language is tied to this notion. The assumption of the divine origin of language stimulated interest in discovering the first primeval language. There are legendary experiments in which children were isolated in the belief that their first words would reveal the original language.

Other views suggest that language is a human invention, stemming from "cries of nature," early gestures, onomatopoeic words, or even from songs to express love. The ancient Greeks believed that a "legislator" gave the true names to all things.

Language most likely evolved with the human species, possibly in stages, possibly in one giant leap. Research by linguists, evolutionary biologists, and neurologists support this view, and the view that from the outset the human animal was genetically equipped to learn language. Studies of the evolutionary development of the brain provide some evidence for physiological and anatomic preconditions for language development.

≈≈≈ References for Further Reading

Caplan, D. 1987. *Neurolinguistics and Linguistic Aphasiology.* Cambridge, England: Cambridge University Press.

———. 1996. *Language: Structure, Processing, and Disorders.* Cambridge, MA: MIT Press.

Coltheart, M., K. Patterson, and J. C. Marshall, eds. 1980. *Deep Dyslexia.* London, England: Routledge & Kegan Paul.

Damasio, H. 1981. "Cerebral Localization of the Aphasias," in *Acquired Aphasia,* M. Taylor Sarno, ed., New York: Academic Press, pp. 27–65.

Gardner, H. 1978. "What We Know (and Don't Know) about the Two Halves of the Brain." *Harvard Magazine* 80: 24–27.

Gazzaniga, M. S. 1970. *The Bisected Brain.* New York: Appleton-Century-Crofts.

Geschwind, N. 1979. "Specializations of the Human Brain." *Scientific American* 206 (Sept): 180–199.

Grodzinsky, Y. 1990. *Theoretical Perspectives on Language Deficits.* Cambridge, MA: MIT Press.

Lenneberg, E. H. 1967. *Biological Foundations of Language.* New York: Wiley.

Lesser, R. 1978. *Linguistic Investigation of Aphasia.* New York: Elsevier.

Lieberman, P. 1984. *The Biology and Evolution of Language.* Cambridge, MA: Harvard University Press.

Newcombe, F., and J. C. Marshall. 1972. "World Retrieval in Aphasia," *International Journal of Mental Health* 1:38–45.

Patterson, K. E., J. C. Marshall, and M. Coltheart, eds. 1986. *Surface Dyslexia.* Hillsdale, NJ: Erlbaum.

Pinker, S. 1994. *The Language Instinct.* New York: William Morrow.

Poizner, H., E. S. Klima, and U. Bellugi. 1987. *What the Hands Reveal about the Brain.* Cambridge, MA: MIT Press.

Searchinger, G. 1994. *The Human Language Series: 1, 2, 3.* New York: Equinox Film/Ways of Knowing, Inc.

Segalowitz, S. 1983. *Two Sides of the Brain.* Englewood Cliffs, NJ: Prentice Hall.

Springer, S. P., and G. Deutsch. 1981. *Left Brain, Right Brain.* San Francisco, CA: W. H. Freeman.

Stam, J. 1976. *Inquiries into the Origin of Language: The Fate of a Question.* New York: Harper & Row.

Yamada, J. 1990. *Laura: A Case for the Modularity of Language.* Cambridge, MA: MIT Press.

≈ Exercises

1. The Nobel Prize laureate Roger Sperry has argued that split-brain patients have two minds:

> Everything we have seen so far indicates that the surgery has left these people with two separate minds, that is, two separate spheres of consciousness. What is experienced in the right hemisphere seems to lie entirely outside the realm of experience of the left hemisphere.

Another Nobel Prize winner in physiology, Sir John Eccles, disagrees. He does not think the right hemisphere can think; he distinguishes between "mere consciousness," which animals possess as well as humans, and language, thought, and other purely human cognitive abilities. In fact, according to him, human nature is all in the left hemisphere.

Write a short essay discussing these two opposing points of view, stating your opinion on how to define "the mind."

2. **A.** Some aphasic patients, when asked to read a list of words, substitute other words for those printed. In many cases there are similarities between the printed words and the

substituted words. The following data are from actual aphasic patients. In each case state what the two words have in common and how they differ:

Printed Word	Word Spoken by Aphasic
a. liberty	freedom
canary	parrot
abroad	overseas
large	long
short	small
tall	long
b. decide	decision
conceal	concealment
portray	portrait
bathe	bath
speak	discussion
remember	memory

B. What do the words in groups a and b reveal about how words are likely to be stored in the brain?

3. The following sentences spoken by aphasic patients, were collected and analyzed by Dr. Harry Whitaker. In each case state how the sentence deviates from normal nonaphasic language.

a. There is under a horse a new sidesaddle.

b. In girls we see many happy days.

c. I'll challenge a new bike.

d. I surprise no new glamour.

e. Is there three chairs in this room?

f. Mike and Peter is happy.

g. Bill and John likes hot dogs.

h. Proliferate is a complete time about a word that is correct.

i. Went came in better than it did before.

4. The investigation of individuals with brain damage has been a major source of information regarding the neural basis of language and other cognitive systems. One might suggest that this is like trying to understand how an automobile engine works by looking at a damaged engine. Is this a good analogy? If so, why? If not, why not? In your answer discuss how a damaged system can or cannot provide information about the normal system.

5. What are the arguments and evidence that have been put forth to support the notion that there are two separate parts of the brain?

6. Discuss the statement by A. W. Wigan that "It only takes one hemisphere to have a mind."

7. In this chapter, dichotic listening tests in which subjects hear different kinds of stimuli in each ear were discussed. These tests showed that there were fewer errors made in re-

porting linguistic stimuli such as the syllables *pa, ta, ka* when heard through an ear-phone on the right ear; other nonlinguistic sounds such as a police car siren were processed with fewer mistakes if heard by the left ear. This is due to the contralateral control of the brain. There is also a technique which permits visual stimuli to be received either by the right visual field, that is, the right eye alone (going directly to the left hemi-sphere) or the left visual field (going directly to the right hemisphere). What might some visual stimuli be that could be used in an experiment to further test the lateralization of language?

8. The following utterances were made either by Broca's aphasics or Wernicke's aphasics. Indicate which is which by writing a "B" or "W" next to the utterance.

   a. Goodnight and in the pansy I can't say but into a flipdoor you can see it

   b. Well . . . sunset . . .uh. . . horses nine, no, uh, two, tails want swish

   c. Oh, . . . if I could I would, and a sick old man disflined a sinter, minter.

   d. Words . . . words . . . words . . . two, four, six, eight, . . . blaze am he.

9. Shakespeare's Hamlet surely had problems. Some say he was obsessed with being overweight because the first lines he speaks in the play when alone on the stage in Act II, Scene 2 are:

   > O! that this too too solid flesh would melt,
   > Thaw, and resolve itself into a dew;

   Others argue that he may have had Wernicke's aphasia, as evidence by the following passage from Act II, Scene 2:

   > Slanders, sir: for the satirical rogue says here
   > that old men have grey beards, that their faces are
   > wrinkled, their eyes purging thick amber and
   > plum-tree gum and that they have a plentiful lack of
   > wit, together with most weak hams: all which, sir,
   > though I most powerfully and potently believe, yet
   > I hold it not honesty to have it thus set down, for you
   > yourself, sir, should be old as I am, if like a crab
   > you could go backward.

   Take up the argument. Is Hamlet aphasic? Argue either case.

Grammatical Aspects of Language

The theory of grammar is concerned with the question: What is the nature of a person's knowledge of his language, the knowledge that enables him to make use of language in the normal, creative fashion? A person who knows a language has mastered a system of rules that assigns sound and meaning in a definite way for an infinite class of possible sentences.

N. Chomsky, *Language and Mind*

CHAPTER

3

Morphology: The Words of Language

A word is dead
When it is said,
Some say.
I say it just
Begins to live
That day.

Emily Dickinson, "A Word"

Every speaker of every language knows tens of thousands of words. *Webster's Third International Dictionary of the English Language* has over 450,000 entries. Most speakers don't know all these words. It has been estimated that a child of six knows as many as 13,000 words and the average high school graduate about 60,000. A college graduate presumably knows many more than that, but whatever our level of education, we learn new words throughout our lives, such as words in this book that you will learn for the first time.

Words are an important part of linguistic knowledge and constitute a component of our mental grammars. But one can learn thousands of words in a language and still not know the language. Anyone who has tried to be understood in a foreign country by merely using a dictionary knows this is true. On the other hand, without words we would be unable to convey our thoughts through language.

What is a word? What do you know when you know a word? Suppose you hear someone say *morpheme* and haven't the slightest idea what it means, and you don't know what the "smallest unit of linguistic meaning" is called. Then you don't know the word *morpheme*. A particular string of sounds must be united with a meaning, and a meaning must be united with specific sounds in order for the sounds or the meaning to

69

be a word in our mental dictionaries. Once you learn both the sounds and their related meaning, you know the word. It becomes an entry in your mental **lexicon** (the Greek word for *dictionary*), part of your linguistic knowledge.

Someone who doesn't know English would not know where one word begins or ends in an utterance like *Thecatsatonthemat.* We separate written words by spaces but in the spoken language there are no pauses between most words. Without knowledge of the language, one can't tell how many words are in an utterance. A speaker of English has no difficulty in segmenting the stream of sounds into six individual words: *the, cat, sat, on, the,* and *mat.* Similarly, a speaker of the American Indian language Potawatomi knows that *kwapmuknanuk* (which means "they see us") is just one word.

The lack of pauses between words in speech has provided humorists and songwriters with much material. During World War II, the chorus of one of the Top Ten tunes sung by Bing Crosby and Bob Hope used this fact about speech to amuse us:

Mairzy doats and dozy doats	(Mares eat oats and does eat oats,
And liddle lamzy divey,	And little lambs eat ivy,
A kiddley-divey too,	A kid'll eat ivy too,
Wouldn't you?	Wouldn't you?)

Similarly, the comical hosts of the show *CarTalk,* aired on National Public Radio, close the show by reading a list of credits that includes the following cast of characters:

Copyeditor	Adeline Moore	(Add a line more)
Accounts payable	Ineeda Czech	(I need a check)
Pollution Control	Maury Missions	(More emissions)
Purchasing	Lois Bidder	(Lowest bidder)
Statistician	Marge Innovera	(Margin of error)
Russian chauffeur	Picov Andropov	(Pick up and drop off)
Legal firm	Dewey, Cheethum,	(Do we cheat them
	and Howe	and how)

The fact that the same sounds can be interpreted differently, even between languages, gave birth to an entertaining book. The title, *Mots D'Heures: Gousses, Rames,*[1] was derived from the fact that *Mother Goose Rhymes,* spoken in English, sounds to a French speaker like the French words meaning "Words of the Hours: Root and Branch." The first rhyme in French starts:

Un petit d'un petit
S'étonne aux Halles.

When interpreted as if it were English it would sound like:

Humpty Dumpty
Sat on a wall.

---

[1] Luis d'Antin Van Routen, ed. and annotator. 1993. *Mots d'Heures: Gousses Rames. The d'Antin Manuscript.* London: Grafton.

This shows that in a particular language, the form (sounds or pronunciation) and the meaning of a word are like two sides of a coin. *Un petit d'un petit* in French means "a little one of a little one" but in English the sounds represent the name *Humpty Dumpty.*

Similarly, in English, the sounds of the letters *bear* and *bare* represent four **homonyms** (also called **homophones**), different words with the same sounds, as shown in the sentences:

She can't bear (tolerate) children.

She can't bear (give birth to) children.

Bruin bear is the mascot of UCLA.

He stood there — bare and beautiful.

Couch and *sofa,* though they have the same meaning, are two words because they are represented by two different strings of sounds.

Sometimes we think we know a word even though we don't know what it means. In an introductory linguistics class, most of the 400 students had heard the word *antidisestablishmentarianism* and believed it to be the longest word in the English language. Yet, many of these students were unsure of its meaning. According to how we have defined what it means to "know a word"— pairing a string of sounds with a particular meaning — such individuals do not really know this word.

Information about the longest or shortest word in the language is not part of linguistic knowledge of a language, but general conceptual knowledge *about* a language. Children do not learn such facts the way they learn the sound/meaning correspondences of the words of their language. Both children and adults have to be told that *antidisestablishmentarianism* is the longest word in English or discover it through an analysis of entries in a dictionary. Actually, should they wish to research the question, they would find that the longest word in *Webster's Seventh International Dictionary* is *pneumonoultramicroscopicsilicovolcanoconiosis,* a disease of the lungs. As we shall see in chapter 8, children don't have to conduct such research. They learn words like *elephant, disappear, mother,* and all the other words they know without being taught them explicitly or looking them up in a dictionary.

Since each word is a sound-meaning unit, each word stored in our mental lexicon must be listed with its unique phonological representation, which determines its pronunciation, and with its meaning. For literate speakers, the spelling, or **orthography,** of most of the words we know is included.

Each word in your mental lexicon includes other information as well, such as whether it is a noun, a pronoun, a verb, an adjective, an adverb, a preposition, or a conjunction. That is, its **grammatical category,** or **syntactic class,** is specified. You may not consciously know that a form like *love* is listed as both a verb and a noun, but a speaker has such knowledge, as shown by the phrases *I love you* and *You are the love of my life.* If such information were not in the mental lexicon, we would not know how to form grammatical sentences, nor would we be able to distinguish grammatical from ungrammatical sentences. The classes of words, the syntactic categories — such as nouns, verbs, adjectives, and so on — and the semantic properties of words, which represent their meanings, will be discussed in later chapters.

Dictionaries

> Dictionary, n. A malevolent literary device for cramping the growth of a language and making it hard and inelastic.
>
> Ambrose Bierce, *The Devil's Dictionary*

The dictionaries that one buys in a bookstore contain some of the information found in our mental dictionaries. The first dictionary to be printed in England was the Latin-English *Promptuorium parvulorum* in 1499; another Latin-English dictionary by Sir Thomas Elyot was published in 1538. Noah Webster, who lived from 1758 until 1843, published *An American Dictionary of the English Language* in two volumes in 1828. It contained about seventy thousand entries.

"Rose Is Rose" copyright © 2001 United Feature Syndicate, Inc. Reprinted by permission.

One of the best efforts at lexicography (defined as "the editing or making of a dictionary" in *Webster's Third New Dictionary of the English Language: Unabridged*) was the *Dictionary of the English Language* by Dr. Samuel Johnson, published in 1755 in two volumes.

The aim of most early lexicographers, whom Dr. Johnson called "harmless drudges," was to *prescribe* rather than *describe* the words of a language. They strove to be, as stated in Webster's dictionaries, the "supreme authority" of the "correct" pronunciation and meaning of a word. To Johnson's credit, he stated in his preface that he could not construct the language but could only "register" it.

All dictionaries, from *The Oxford English Dictionary* (often referred to as the *OED* and called the greatest lexicographic work ever produced), to the more commonly used collegiate dictionaries, provide the following information about each word: (1) spelling, (2) the "standard" pronunciation, (3) definitions to represent the word's one or more meanings, and (4) parts of speech (e.g., noun, verb, preposition, etc.). Other information may include the etymology or history of the word, whether the word is nonstandard (such as *ain't*) or slang, vulgar, or obsolete. Many dictionaries provide quotations from published literature to illustrate the given definitions, as was first done by Johnson.

In recent years, perhaps due to the increasing specialization in science and the arts, or the growing fragmentation of the populace, we see the proliferation of hundreds of specialty and subspecialty dictionaries. A reference librarian at UCLA's Engineering and Mathematical Sciences Library estimates that her library has more than six hundred such books.

Dictionaries of slang and jargon (see chapter 10) have existed for many years; so have multilingual dictionaries. In addition to these, the shelves of bookstores and libraries are now filled with dictionaries written specifically for biologists, engineers, agriculturists, economists, artists, architects, printers, gays and lesbians, transvestites, athletes, tennis players, and almost any group that has its own set of words to describe what they think and what they do. Our own mental dictionaries probably include only a small set of the entries in all of these dictionaries, but each word is in someone's lexicon.

Content Words and Function Words

Languages make an important distinction between two kinds of words — content words and function words. Nouns, verbs, adjectives, and adverbs are the **content words.** These words denote concepts such as objects, actions, attributes, and ideas that we can think about like *children, anarchism, soar,* and *purple.* Content words are sometimes called the **open class** words because we can and regularly do add new words to these classes. A new word, *steganography,* which is the art of hiding information in electronic text, entered English with the Internet revolution. Verbs like *disrespect* and *download* entered the language quite recently, as have nouns like *byte* and *email.*

Different languages may express the same concept using words of different grammatical classes. For example, in Akan, the major language of Ghana, there are only a handful of adjectives. Most concepts that would be expressed with adjectives in English are expressed by verbs in Akan. Instead of saying "The sun is bright today," an Akan speaker will say "The sun brightens today."

There are other classes of words that do not have clear lexical meaning or obvious concepts associated with them, including conjunctions such as *and, or,* and *but;* prepositions such as *in* and *of;* the articles *the, a/an,* and pronouns such as *it* and *he.* These kinds of words are called **function words** because they have a grammatical function. For example, the articles indicate whether a noun is definite or indefinite —*the* boy or *a* boy. The preposition *of* indicates possession as in "the book of yours," but this word indicates many other kinds of relations too.

Function words are sometimes called **closed class** words. It is difficult to think of new conjunctions, prepositions, or pronouns that have recently entered the language. The small set of personal pronouns such as *I, me, mine, he, she,* and so on are part of this class. With the growth of the feminist movement, some proposals have been made for adding a neutral singular pronoun that would be neither masculine nor feminine and that could be used as the general, or **generic,** form. If such a pronoun existed, it might have prevented the department chairperson in a large university from making the incongruous statement: "We will hire the best person for the job regardless of his sex." The UCLA psychologist Donald MacKay has suggested that we use "e," pronounced like the letter name, for this pronoun with various alternative forms. Others point out that *they* and *their* are already being used as neutral third-person singular forms, as in "Anyone can do it if they try hard enough" or "Everyone can do their best." The use of the various forms of *they* is standard on the BBC (British Broadcasting System) as pronoun replacements for *anyone* and *everyone,* which may be regarded as singular or plural.

The difference between content and function words is illustrated by the following test that circulated recently over the Internet:

Please count the number of F's in the following text:

FINISHED FILES ARE THE
RESULT OF YEARS OF SCIENTIFIC
STUDY COMBINED WITH THE
EXPERIENCE OF YEARS.

If you are like most people, your answer will be 3. That answer is wrong. The correct answer is 6. Count again. This time pay attention to the function word OF.

What this little test illustrates is that the brain treats content and function words differently. Indeed, there is a great deal of psychological and neurological evidence to support this claim. For example, the effect that we just illustrated with the OF test is much more pronounced in brain-damaged people. As discussed in chapter 2, some brain-damaged patients have greater difficulty in using, understanding, or reading function words than they do with content words. Some are unable to read function words like *in* or *which* but can read the lexical content words *inn* and *witch*. Other patients do just the opposite. The two classes of words also seem to function differently in **slips of the tongue** produced by normal individuals. For example, a speaker may inadvertently switch words producing "the journal of the editor" instead of "the editor of the journal," but the switching or exchanging of function words has not been observed. There is also evidence for this distinction from language acquisition (discussed in chapter 8). In the early stages of development, children often omit function words from their speech, for example, "doggie barking." These two classes of words have different functions in language. Content words have semantic content (meaning). Function words play a grammatical role; they connect the content words to the larger grammatical context in ways that will be discussed in chapter 4.

Morphemes: The Minimal Units of Meaning

"They gave it me," Humpty Dumpty continued, "for an un-birthday present."
"I beg your pardon?" Alice said with a puzzled air.
"I'm not offended," said Humpty Dumpty.
"I mean, what is an un-birthday present?"
"A present given when it isn't your birthday, of course."

Lewis Carroll, *Through the Looking-Glass*

In the dialogue above, Humpty Dumpty is well aware that the prefix un- means "not," as further shown in the following pairs of words:

A	B
desirable	undesirable
likely	unlikely
inspired	uninspired
happy	unhappy
developed	undeveloped
sophisticated	unsophisticated

Webster's Third New International Dictionary lists about 2700 adjectives beginning with *un-*.

If we assume that the most basic unit of meaning is the word, what do we say about parts of words like *un-,* which has a fixed meaning? In all the words in the B column *un-* means the same thing — "not." *Undesirable* means "not desirable," *unlikely* means "not likely," and so on. All the words in column B consist of at least two meaningful units: *un + desirable, un + likely, un + inspired,* and so on.

Just as *un-* occurs with the same meaning in the words above, so does *phon* in the following words. (You may not know the meaning of some of them but you will when you finish this book.)

phone	phonology	phoneme
phonetic	phonologist	phonemic
phonetics	phonological	allophone
phonetician	telephone	euphonious
phonic	telephonic	symphony

Phon is a minimal form in that it can't be decomposed. *Ph* doesn't mean anything; *pho,* though it may be pronounced like *foe,* has no relation in meaning to it; and *on* is not the preposition spelled *o-n.* In all the words on the list, *phon* has the identical meaning, "pertaining to sound."

Words have internal structure, which is rule-governed. *Uneaten, unadmired,* and *ungrammatical* are words in English, but **eatenun, *admiredun,* and **grammaticalun* (to mean "not eaten," "not admired," "not grammatical") are not, because we do not form a negative meaning of a word by suffixing *un* but by prefixing it.

When Samuel Goldwyn, the pioneer moviemaker, announced: "In two words: impossible," he was reflecting the common view that words are the basic meaningful elements of a language. We have seen that this cannot be so, since some words contain several distinct units of meaning. The linguistic term for the most elemental unit of grammatical form is **morpheme.** The word is derived from the Greek word *morphe,* meaning "form." Linguistically speaking, then, Goldwyn should have said: "In two morphemes: im-possible."

The study of the internal structure of words, and of the rules by which words are formed, is **morphology.** This word itself consists of two morphemes, *morph + ology.* The suffix *-ology* means "science of" or "branch of knowledge concerning." Thus, the meaning of *morphology* is "the science of word forms."

Part of knowing a language is knowing its morphology. Like most linguistic knowledge, this is generally unconscious knowledge.

A single word may be composed of one or more morphemes:

one morpheme	boy
	desire
two morphemes	boy + ish
	desire + able
three morphemes	boy + ish + ness
	desire + able + ity
four morphemes	gentle + man + li + ness
	un + desire + able + ity
more than four	un + gentle + man + li + ness
	anti + dis + establish + ment + ari + an + ism[2]

A morpheme may be represented by a single sound, such as the morpheme *a* meaning "without" as in *amoral* or *asexual,* or by a single syllable, such as *child* and *ish* in *child + ish.* A morpheme may also consist of more than one syllable: by two syllables, as in *camel, lady,* and *water;* or by three syllables, as in *Hackensack* or *crocodile;* or by four or more syllables, as in *hallucinate.*

A morpheme — the minimal linguistic unit — is thus an arbitrary union of a sound and a meaning that cannot be further analyzed. This may be too simple a definition, but it will serve our purposes for now. Every word in every language is composed of one or more morphemes.

The decomposition of words into morphemes illustrates one of the fundamental properties of human language — **discreteness.** In all languages, discrete linguistic units combine in rule-governed ways to form larger units. Sound units combine to form morphemes, morphemes combine to form words, and words combine to form larger units — phrases and sentences.

Discreteness is one of the properties that distinguish human languages from the communication systems of other species. Our knowledge of these discrete units and the rules for combining them accounts for the creativity of human language. Linguistic creativity refers to a person's ability to produce and understand an infinite range of sentences and words never before heard.

---

[2] Some speakers have even more morphemes in this word than are shown.

With respect to words, linguistic creativity means that not only can we understand words that we have never heard before, but we can also create new words. In the first case, we can decompose a word into its component parts and if we know the meaning of those parts, we have a good guess at the meaning of the whole. In the second case, we can combine morphemes in novel ways to create new words whose meaning will be apparent to other speakers of the language. If you know that "to write" to a disk or a CD means to put information on it, you automatically understand that a *writable* CD is one that can take information; a *rewritable* CD is one where the original information can be written over; and an *unrewritable* CD is one that does not allow the user to write over the original information. You know the meanings of all these words by virtue of your knowledge of the individual morphemes *write, re-, -able,* and *un-* and the rules for their combination.

Bound and Free Morphemes

PREFIXES AND SUFFIXES

Our morphological knowledge has two components: knowledge of the individual morphemes and knowledge of the rules that combine them. One of the things we know about particular morphemes is whether they can stand alone or whether they must be attached to a host morpheme.

"LOOKS LIKE WE SPEND MOST OF OUR TIME INGING...
YOU KNOW, LIKE SLEEPING, EATING, RUNNING, CLIMBING..."

"Dennis the Menace" ® copyright © 1987 by North America
Syndicate. Used by permission of Hank Ketchum.

Some morphemes like *boy, desire, gentle,* and *man* may constitute words by themselves. These are **free morphemes.** Other morphemes like *-ish, -ness, -ly, dis-, trans-,* and *un-* are never words by themselves but are always parts of words. These affixes are **bound morphemes.** We know whether each affix precedes or follows other morphemes. Thus, *un-*, *pre-* (*premeditate, prejudge*), and *bi-* (*bipolar, bisexual*) are **prefixes.** They occur before other morphemes. Some morphemes occur only as **suffixes,** following other morphemes. English examples of suffix morphemes are *-ing* (e.g., *sleeping, eating, running, climbing*), *-er* (e.g., *singer, performer, reader,* and *beautifier*), *-ist* (e.g., *typist, copyist, pianist, novelist, collaborationist,* and *linguist*), and *-ly* (e.g., *manly, sickly, spectacularly,* and *friendly*), to mention only a few.

Morphemes are the minimal linguistic signs in all languages and many languages have prefixes and suffixes. But languages may differ in how they deploy their morphemes. A morpheme that is a prefix in one language may be a suffix in another and vice-versa. In English the plural morpheme *-s* is a suffix (e.g., *boys, machines, diskettes*). In Isthmus Zapotec, on the other hand, the plural morpheme *ka-* is a prefix:

zigi	"chin"	kazigi	"chins"
zike	"shoulder"	kazike	"shoulders"
diaga	"ear"	kadiaga	"ears"

Languages may also differ in what meanings they express through affixation. In English we do not add an affix to derive a noun from a verb. We have the verb *dance* as in "I like to dance" and we have the noun *dance* as in "The salsa is a Latin dance." The form is the same in both cases. In Turkish, you derive a noun from a verb with the suffix *-ak,* as in the following examples:

dur	"to stop"	dur + ak	"stopping place"
bat	"to sink"	bat + ak	"sinking place" or "marsh/swamp"

To express reciprocal action in English we use the phrase *each other,* as in *understand each other, love each other.* In Turkish a morpheme is added to the verb:

anla	"understand"	anla + sh	"understand each other"
sev	"love"	sev + ish	"love each other"

The reciprocal suffix in these examples is pronounced as *sh* after a vowel and as *ish* after a consonant. This is similar to the process in English in which we use *a* as the indefinite article morpheme before a noun beginning with a consonant, as in *a dog,* and *an* before a noun beginning with a vowel, as in *an apple.* We will discuss the various pronunciations of morphemes in chapter 7.

In Piro, an Arawakan language spoken in Peru, a single morpheme, *kaka,* can be added to a verb to express the meaning "cause to":

cokoruha	"to harpoon"	cokoruha + kaka	"cause to harpoon"
salwa	"to visit"	salwa + kaka	"cause to visit"

In Karuk, a Native American language spoken in the Pacific Northwest, adding *-ak* to a noun forms the locative adverbial meaning "in."

ikrivaam	"house"	ikrivaamak	"in a house"

It is accidental that both Turkish and Karuk have a suffix *-ak*. Despite the similarity in form, the two meanings are different. Similarly, the reciprocal suffix *-ish* in Turkish is similar in form to the English suffix *-ish* as in *greenish*. Also in Karuk, the suffix *-ara* has the same meaning as the English *-y*, that is, "characterized by" (*hairy* means "characterized by hair").

>   aptiik   "branch"   aptikara   "branchy"

These examples illustrate again the arbitrary nature of the sound-meaning relationship.

In Russian the suffix *-shchik* added to a noun is similar in meaning to the English suffix *-er* in words like *reader, teenager, Londoner, miler, first grader,* which may be affixed to words of different categories. The Russian suffix, however, is added to nouns only, as shown in the following examples:

Russian		**Russian**	
atom	"atom"	atomshchik	"atom-warmonger"
baraban	"drum"	barabanshchik	"drummer"
kalambur	"pun"	kalamburshchik	"punner"
beton	"concrete"	betonshchik	"concrete worker"
lom	"scrap"	lomshchik	"salvage collector"

These examples from different languages also illustrate free morphemes like *boy* in English, *dur* in Turkish, *salwa* in Piro, and *lom* in Russian.

INFIXES

Some languages also have **infixes,** morphemes that are inserted into other morphemes. Bontoc, spoken in the Philippines, is such a language, as illustrated by the following:

Nouns/Adjectives		**Verbs**	
fikas	"strong"	fumikas	"to be strong"
kilad	"red"	kumilad	"to be red"
fusul	"enemy"	fumusul	"to be an enemy"

In this language, the infix *-um-* is inserted after the first consonant of the noun or adjective. Thus, a speaker of Bontoc who learns that *pusi* means "poor," would understand the meaning of *pumusi*, "to be poor," on hearing the word for the first time, just as an English speaker who learns the verb *sneet* would know that *sneeter* is "one who sneets." A Bontoc speaker who knows that *ngumitad* means "to be dark" would know that the adjective "dark" must be *ngitad*.

English infixing has been the subject of the Linguist List, a discussion group on the Internet. The interest in infixes in English is because one can only infix full word obscenities into another word, usually into adjectives or adverbs. The most common infix in America is the word *fuckin'* and all the euphemisms for it, such as *friggin, freakin, flippin,* and *fuggin* as in *in-fuggin-credible, un-fuckin-believable,* or *Kalama-flippin-zoo,* based on the city in Michigan. In Britain, a common infix is *bloody,* an obscene term in British English, and its euphemisms, such as *bloomin*. In the movie and stage musical *My Fair Lady, abso + bloomin + lutely* occurs in one of the songs sung by Eliza Doolittle.

CIRCUMFIXES

Some languages have **circumfixes,** morphemes that are attached to another morpheme both initially and finally. These are sometimes called **discontinuous morphemes.** In Chickasaw, a Muskogean language spoken in Oklahoma, the negative is formed with both a prefix *ik-* and the suffix *-o*. The final vowel of the affirmative is deleted before the negative suffix is added. Examples of this circumfixing are:

Affirmative		**Negative**	
chokma	"he is good"	ik + chokm + o	"he isn't good"
lakna	"it is yellow"	ik + lakn + o	"it isn't yellow"
palli	"it is hot"	ik + pall + o	"it isn't hot"
tiwwi	"he opens (it)"	ik + tiww + o	"he doesn't open (it)"

An example of a more familiar circumfixing language is German. The past participle of regular verbs is formed by adding the prefix *ge-* and the suffix *-t* to the verb root. This circumfix added to the verb root *lieb* "love" produces *geliebt*, "loved" (or "beloved," when used as an adjective).

ROOTS AND STEMS

Morphologically complex words consist of a **root** and one or more affixes. A root is a lexical content morpheme that cannot be analyzed into smaller parts. Some examples of English roots are *paint* in *painter, read* in *reread,* and *ceive in conceive*. A root may or may not stand alone as a word (*paint* does; *ceive* doesn't). In languages that have circumfixes, the root is the form around which the circumfix attaches, for example, the Chickasaw root *chokm* in *ikchokmo* ("he isn't good"). In infixing languages the root is the form into which the infix is inserted, for example *fikas* in the Bontoc word *fumikas* ("to be strong").

Semitic languages like Hebrew and Arabic have a unique morphological system. Nouns and verbs are built on a foundation of three consonants, and one derives related words by varying the pattern of vowels and syllables. For example, the root for "write" in Egyptian Arabic is *ktb* from which the following words (among others) are formed:

katab	"he wrote"
kaatib	"writer"
kitáab	"book"
kútub	"books"

When a root morpheme is combined with an affix, it forms a **stem,** which may or may not be a word (*painter* is both a word and a stem; *-ceive + er* is only a stem). Other affixes can be added to a stem to form a more complex stem, as shown in the following:

root	Chomsky	(proper) noun
stem	Chomsky + ite	noun + suffix
word	Chomsky + ite + s	noun + suffix + suffix
root	believe	verb
stem	believe + able	verb + suffix
word	un + believe + able	prefix + verb + suffix
root	system	noun
stem	system + atic	noun + suffix
stem	un + system + atic	prefix + noun + suffix
stem	un + system + atic + al	prefix + noun + suffix + suffix
word	un + system + atic + al + ly	prefix + noun + suffix + suffix + suffix

As one adds each affix to a stem, a new stem and a new word are formed.

Huckles and Ceives

It had been a rough day, so when I walked into the party I was very chalant, despite my efforts to appear gruntled and consolate. I was furling my wieldy umbrella . . . when I saw her. . . . She was a descript person. . . . Her hair was kempt, her clothing shevelled, and she moved in a gainly way.

"How I Met my Wife," by Jack Winter. *The New Yorker*, July 25, 1994.

A morpheme was defined as the basic element of meaning, a phonological form that is arbitrarily united with a particular meaning and that cannot be analyzed into simpler elements. Although it holds for most of the morphemes in a language, this definition has presented problems for linguistic analysis for many years. Consider words like *cranberry, huckleberry,* and *boysenberry.* The *berry* part is no problem, but *huckle* and *boysen* occur only with *berry,* as did *cran* until *cranapple* juice came on the market, and other morphologically complex words using *cran-* followed. The *boysen-* part of *boysenberry* was named for a man named Boysen who developed it as a hybrid from the blackberry and raspberry. But few people are aware of this and it is a bound stem morpheme that occurs only in this word. *Lukewarm* is another word with two stem morphemes, with *luke* occurring only in this word, because it is not the same morpheme as the name *Luke.*

Bound forms like *huckle-, boysen-,* and *luke-* require a redefinition of the concept of morpheme. Some morphemes have no meaning in isolation but acquire meaning only in combination with other specific morphemes. Thus the morpheme *huckle,* when joined with *berry,* has the meaning of a special kind of berry that is small, round, and purplish blue; *luke* when combined with *warm* has the meaning "sort of" or "somewhat," and so on.

Some morphemes occur only in a single word (combined with another morpheme), while other morphemes occur in many words, but seem to lack a constant meaning from one word to another. Many words of Latin origin that entered the English language after the Norman Conquest of England in 1066 have this property. For example, the words *receive, conceive, perceive,* and *deceive* share a common root, *-ceive,* and the words *remit, permit, commit, submit, transmit,* and *admit* share the root *-mit.* For the original Latin speakers the morphemes corresponding to *ceive* and *mit* had clear meanings, the latter from the verb *mittere,*" to send," and the former from the verb *capere,* "to seize." But for modern English speakers, Latinate morphemes such as *-ceive* and *-mit* have no independent meaning. Their meaning depends on the entire word in which they occur.

There are other words that seem to be composed of prefix + root morphemes in which the roots, like *cran-* or *-ceive,* never occur alone, but always with a specific prefix. Thus we find *inept,* but *no *ept; ungainly,* but no **gainly; discern,* but no **cern; nonplussed,* but no **plussed.*

Similarly, the stems of *upholster, downhearted,* and *outlandish* do not occur by themselves: **holster* and **hearted* (with these meanings), and **landish* are not free morphemes. In addition, *downholster, uphearted,* and *inlandish,* their "opposites," are not words.

To complicate things a little further, there are words like *strawberry* in which the *straw* has no relationship to any other kind of *straw; gooseberry,* which is unrelated to *goose;* and *blackberry,* which may be blue or red. While some of these words may have historical origins, there is no present meaningful connection. *The Oxford English Dictionary* entry for the word *strawberry* states that

> The reason for the name has been variously conjectured. One explanation refers the first element to Straw . . . a particle of straw or chaff, a mote describing the appearance of the achenes scattered over the surface of the strawberry.

That may be true of the word's origin, but today, the *straw-* in *strawberry* is not the same morpheme as that found in *straw hat* or *straw-colored.*

The meaning of a morpheme must be constant. The agentive morpheme *-er* means "one who does" in words like *singer, painter, lover,* and *worker,* but the same sounds represent the comparative morpheme, meaning "more," in *nicer, prettier,* and *taller.* Thus, two different morphemes may be pronounced identically. The identical form represents two morphemes because of the different meanings. The same sounds may occur in another word and not represent a separate morpheme. The final syllable in *father, er,* is not a separate morpheme, since a father is not "one who faths." Similarly, in *water* the *-er* is not a distinct morpheme ending; *father* and *water* are single morphemes, or **monomorphemic** words. This follows from the concept of the morpheme as a sound-meaning unit.

Rules of Word Formation

"I never heard of 'Uglification,'" Alice ventured to say. "What is it?" The Gryphon lifted up both its paws in surprise. "Never heard of uglifying!" it exclaimed. "You know what to beautify is, I suppose?" "Yes," said Alice doubtfully: "it means — to make — anything — prettier." "Well, then," the Gryphon went on, "if you don't know what to uglify is, you are a simpleton."

Lewis Carroll, *Alice in Wonderland*

When the Mock Turtle listed the branches of Arithmetic for Alice as "Ambition, Distraction, Uglification, and Derision," Alice was very confused. She wasn't really a simpleton, since *uglification* was not a common word in English until Lewis Carroll used it. Still, most English speakers would immediately know the meaning of *uglification* even if we had never heard or used the word before because we know the meaning of its individual parts—the root *ugly* and the affixes—*-ify* and *-ation.*

We said earlier that knowledge of morphology includes knowledge of individual morphemes, their pronunciation, and their meaning, and knowledge of the rules for combining morphemes into complex words. The Mock Turtle added *-ify* to the adjective *ugly* and formed a verb. Many verbs in English have been formed in this way: *purify, amplify, simplify, falsify.* The suffix *-ify* conjoined with nouns also forms verbs: *objectify, glorify, personify.* Notice that the Mock Turtle went even further; he added the suffix *-cation* to *uglify* and formed a noun, *uglification,* as in *glorification, simplification, falsification, and purification.*

By using the **morphological rules** of English he created a new word. The rules that he used are as follows:

Adjective + ify   →   Verb   "to make Adjective"
Verb + cation   →   Noun   "the process of making Adjective"

Derivational Morphology

Bound morphemes like *-ify* and *-cation* are called **derivational morphemes.** When they are added to a root morpheme or stem, a new word with a new meaning is derived. The addition of *-ify* to *pure*—*purify*—means "to make pure" and the addition of *-ation*—*purification*—means "the process of making pure." If we invent an adjective, *pouzy,* to describe the effect of static electricity on hair, you will immediately understand the sentences "Walking on that carpet really pouzified my hair" and "The best method of pouzification is to rub a balloon on your head." This means that we must have a list of the derivational morphemes in our mental dictionaries as well as the rules that determine how they are added to a root or stem. The form that results from the addition of a derivational morpheme is called a **derived word.**

The Hierarchical Structure of Words

We saw above that morphemes are added in a fixed order. This order reflects the **hierarchical structure** of the word. A word is not a simple sequence of morphemes. It has an internal structure. For example, the word *unsystematic* is composed of three morphemes, *un-, system,* and *-atic.* The root is *system,* a noun, to which we add the suffix *-atic* resulting in an adjective, *systematic.* To this adjective, we add the prefix *un-* forming a new adjective, *unsystematic.*

In order to represent the hierarchical organization of words (and sentences) linguists use **tree diagrams.** The tree diagram for *unsystematic* is as follows:

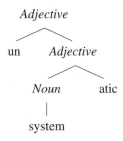

This tree represents the application of two morphological rules:

1. Noun + atic   →   Adjective
2. Un + Adjective   →   Adjective

Rule 1 attaches the derivational suffix *-atic* to the root noun, forming an adjective. Rule 2 takes the adjective formed by rule 1 and attaches the derivational prefix *un-.* The diagram shows that the entire word —*unsystematic*— is an adjective that is composed of an adjective —*systematic*— plus *un.* The adjective is itself composed of a noun —*system*— plus the suffix *atic.*

Like the property of discreteness discussed earlier, hierarchical structure is an essential property of human language. Words (and sentences) have component parts, which relate to each other in specific, rule-governed ways. Although at first glance it may seem that, aside from order, the morphemes *un-* and *-atic* each relate to the root *system* in the same way, this is not the case. The root *system* is "closer" to *-atic* than it is to *un-,* and *un-* is actually connected to the adjective *systematic,* and not directly to *system.* Indeed, *unsystem is not a word.

Further morphological rules can be applied to the structure given above. For example, English has a derivational suffix *-al,* as in *egotistical, fantastical,* and *astronomical.* In these cases, *-al* is added to an adjective —*egotistic, fantastic, astronomic*— to form a new adjective. The rule for *-al* is as follows:

3. Adjective + al   →   Adjective

Another affix is *-ly,* which is added to adjectives —*happy, lazy, hopeful*— to form adverbs *happily, lazily, hopefully.* Following is the rule for *-ly:*

4. Adjective + ly → Adverb

Applying these two rules to the derived form *unsystematic,* we get the following tree for *unsystematically:*

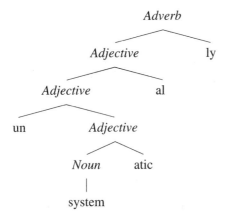

This is a rather complex word. Despite its complexity, it is well-formed because it follows the morphological rules of the language. On the other hand, a very simple word can be ungrammatical. Suppose in the above example, we first added *un-* to the root *system.* That would have resulted in a nonword, **unsystem.*

*Unsystem is not a possible word because there is no rule of English that allows *un-* to be added to nouns. The large soft-drink company whose ad campaign promoted the *Uncola* successfully flouted this linguistic rule to capture people's attention. Part of our linguistic competence includes the ability to recognize possible vs. impossible words, like **unsystem* and **Uncola.* Possible words are those that conform to the rules of morphology (as well as of phonology; see chapter 7); impossible words are those that do not.

Tree diagrams are the linguist's hypothesis of how speakers represent the internal structure of the morphologically complex words in their language. In speaking and writing, we string morphemes together sequentially as in *un + system + atic.* As shown by tree diagrams, however, our mental representation of words is much more complex.

The hierarchical organization of words is most clearly shown by structurally ambiguous words, words that have more than one meaning by virtue of having more than one structure. Consider the word *unlockable.* Imagine you are inside a room and you want some privacy. You would be unhappy to find the door is *unlockable* — "not able to be locked." Now imagine you are inside a locked room trying to get out. You would be very relieved to find that the door is *unlockable* —"able to be unlocked." These two meanings correspond to two different structures, as follows:

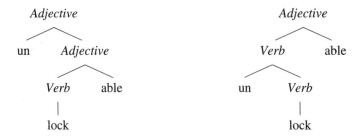

In the first structure the verb *lock* combines with the suffix *-able* to form an adjective *lockable* ("able to be locked"). Then the prefix *un-,* meaning "not," combines with the derived adjective to form a new adjective *unlockable* ("not able to be locked"). In the second case, the prefix *un-* combines with the verb *lock* to form a derived verb *unlock*.

Then the derived verb combines with the suffix *-able* to form *unlockable,* "able to be unlocked." An entire class of words in English follows this pattern: *unbuttonable, unzippable, and unlatchable,* among others. The ambiguity arises because the prefix *un-* can combine with an adjective, as illustrated in rule 2 above, or it can combine with a verb, as in *undo, unstaple, unearth,* and *unloosen.*

If words were only strings of morphemes without any internal organization, we could not explain the ambiguity of words like *unlockable*. These words also illustrate another important point, which is that structure is important to determining meaning. The same three morphemes occur in both versions of *unlockable,* yet there are two distinct meanings. The different meanings arise because of the two different structures.

More about Derivational Morphemes

Derivational morphemes have clear semantic content. In this sense they are like content words, except that they are not words. As we have seen, when a derivational morpheme is added to a root or stem, it adds meaning. The derived word may also be of a different grammatical class than the original word, as shown by suffixes such as *-able* and *-ly*. When a verb is suffixed with *-able,* the result is an adjective, as in *desire + able, adore + able*. When the suffix *-en* is added to an adjective, a verb is derived, as in *dark + en*. One may form a noun from an adjective, as in *sweet + ie*. Other examples are:

Noun to Adjective	Verb to Noun	Adjective to Adverb
boy + ish	acquitt + al	exact + ly
virtu + ous	clear + ance	quiet + ly
Elizabeth + an	accus + ation	
pictur + esque	confer + ence	
affection + ate	sing + er	
health + ful	conform + ist	
alcohol + ic	predict + ion	
life + like	free + dom	

Noun to Verb	Adjective to Noun	Verb to Adjective
moral + ize	tall + ness	read + able
vaccin + ate	specific + ity	creat + ive
brand + ish	feudal + ism	migrat + ory
haste + n	abstract + ion	run + (n)y

Not all derivational morphemes cause a change in grammatical class.

Noun to Noun	Verb to Verb	Adjective to Adjective
friend + ship	un + do	pink + ish
human + ity	re + cover	in + flammable

Many prefixes fall into this category:

a + moral	mono + theism
auto + biography	re + print
ex + wife	semi + annual
super + human	sub + minimal

There are also suffixes of this type:

vicar + age	New Jersey + ite
old + ish	fadd + ist
Paul + ine	music + ian
America + n	pun + ster

When a new word enters the lexicon by the application of morphological rules, other complex derivations may be blocked. For example, when *Commun + ist* entered the language, words such as *Commun + ite* (as in *Trotsky + ite*) or *Commun + ian* (as in *grammar + ian*) were not needed and were not formed. Sometimes, however, alternative forms coexist: for example, *Chomskyan* and *Chomskyist* and perhaps even *Chomskyite* (all meaning "follower of Chomsky's views of linguistics"). *Linguist* and *linguistician* are both used, but the possible word *linguite* is not.

Lexical Gaps

The redundancy of alternative forms such as those mentioned, all of which conform to the regular rules of word formation, may explain some of the **accidental,** or **lexical, gaps** in the lexicon. Accidental gaps are well-formed but nonexisting words. The actual words in the language constitute only a subset of the possible words. Speakers of a language may know tens of thousands of words. Dictionaries, as we noted, include hundreds of thousands of words, all of which are known by some speakers of the language. But no dictionary can list all **possible words** since it is possible to add to the vocabulary of a language in many ways. (Some of these will be discussed here and some in chapter 11 on language change.) There are always gaps in the lexicon — words that are not in the dictionary but that can be added. Some of the gaps are due to the fact that a permissible sound sequence has no meaning attached to it (like *blick,* or *slarm,* or *krobe*). Note that the sequence of sounds must be in keeping with the constraints of the language. **bnick*

"Peanuts" copyright © United Feature Syndicate. Reprinted by permission.

is not a "gap" because no word in English can begin with a *bn*. We will discuss such constraints in chapter 7.

Other gaps result when possible combinations of morphemes never come into use. Speakers can distinguish between impossible words such as *unsystem* and *speakly,* and possible, but nonexisting words such as *disobvious, linguisticism,* and *antiquify.* The ability to do this is further evidence that the morphological component of our mental grammar consists of not just a lexicon, a list of existing words, but also of rules that enable us to create and understand new words, and to recognize possible and impossible words.

Rule Productivity

Some morphological rules are **productive,** meaning that they can be used freely to form new words from the list of free and bound morphemes. The suffix *-able* appears to be a morpheme that can be conjoined with any verb to derive an adjective with the meaning of the verb and the meaning of *-able,* which is something like "able to be" as in *accept + able, blam(e) + able, pass + able, change + able, breath + able, adapt + able,* and so on. The meaning of *-able* has also been given as "fit for doing" or "fit for being done." The productivity of this rule is illustrated by the fact that we find *-able* affixed to new verbs such as *downloadable* and *faxable.*

We have already noted that there is a morpheme in English meaning "not" that has the form *un-* and that, when combined with adjectives like *afraid, fit, free, smooth, American,* and *British,* forms the **antonyms,** or **negatives,** of these adjectives. For example, *unafraid, unfit, un-American,* and so on. Note that unlike *-able, un-* does not change the grammatical category of the stem it attaches to.

We also saw that the prefix *un-* can be added to derived adjectives that have been formed by morphological rules:

un + believe + able
un + accept + able
un + speak + able
un + lock + able

We can also add *un-* to morphologically complex verbs that consist of a verb plus a particle plus *-able* such as:

pick + up +able
turn + around +able
chop + off + able
talk + about + able

Un- prefixation derives the following words:

un + pick + up + able,
un + chop + off + able,
un + talk + about + able,

Yet *un-* is not fully productive. We find *happy* and *unhappy, cowardly* and *uncowardly,* but not *sad* and **unsad, brave* and **unbrave,* or *obvious* and **unobvious.* The starred forms that follow may be merely accidental gaps in the lexicon. If someone refers to a person as being **unsad* we would know that the person referred to was "not sad," and an **unbrave* person would not be brave. But, as the linguist Sandra Thompson[3] points out, it may be the case that the "un-Rule" is most productive for adjectives that are themselves derived from verbs, such as *unenlightened, unsimplified, uncharacterized, unauthorized, undistinguished,* and so on.

Morphological rules may be more or less productive. The rule that adds an *-er* to verbs in English to produce a noun meaning "one who performs an action (once or habitually)" appears to be a very productive morphological rule. Most English verbs accept this suffix: *examiner, exam-taker, analyzer, lover, hunter, predictor,* and so forth (*-or* and *-er* have the same pronunciation and are the same morpheme even though they are spelled differently). Now consider the following:

sincerity	from	*sincere*
warmth	from	*warm*
moisten	from	*moist*

The suffix *-ity* is found in many other words in English, like *chastity, scarcity,* and *curiosity;* and *-th* occurs in *health, wealth, depth, width,* and *growth.* We find *-en* in *sadden, ripen, redden, weaken,* and *deepen.* Still, the phrase "**The fiercity of the lion*" sounds somewhat strange, as does the sentence "**I'm going to thinnen the sauce.*" Someone may use the word *coolth,* but, as Thompson points out, when words such as *fiercity, thinnen, fullen,* and *coolth* are used, usually it is either an error or an attempt at humor. It is possible that in such cases a morphological rule that was once productive (as shown by the existence of related pairs like *scarce/scarcity*) is no longer so. Our knowledge of the related pairs, however, may permit us to use these examples in forming new

---

[3] S. A. Thompson. 1975. "On the Issue of Productivity in the Lexikon," *Kritikon Litterarum* 4:332–49.

words, by analogy with the existing lexical items. Other derivational morphemes in English are not very productive, such as the suffixes meaning "diminutive," as in the words *pig + let* and *sap + ling*.

In the morphologically complex words that we have seen so far, we can easily predict the meaning based on the meaning of the morphemes that make up the word. *Unhappy* means "not happy" and *acceptable* means "fit to be accepted." However, one cannot always know the meaning of the words derived from free and derivational morphemes by knowing the morphemes themselves. The following *un-* forms have unpredictable meanings:

unloosen	"loosen, let loose"
unrip	"rip, undo by ripping"
undo	"reverse doing"
untread	"go back through in the same steps"
unearth	"dig up"
unfrock	"deprive (a cleric) of ecclesiastic rank"
unnerve	"fluster"

Morphologically complex words whose meanings are not predictable must be listed individually in our mental lexicons. However, the morphological rules must also be in the grammar, revealing the relation between words and providing the means for forming new words.

"Pullet Surprises"

That speakers of a language know the morphemes of that language, and the rules for word formation is shown as much by the errors made as by the nondeviant forms produced. Morphemes combine to form words. These words form a part our internal dictionaries. Given our knowledge of the morphemes of the language and the morphological rules, we may guess the meaning of a word we do not know. Sometimes we guess wrong.

Amsel Greene collected errors made by her students in vocabulary-building classes and published them in a book called *Pullet Surprises*.[4] The title is taken from a sentence written by one of her high school students: "In 1957 Eugene O' Neill won a Pullet Surprise." What is most interesting about these errors is how much they reveal about the stu-

"Drabble" copyright © 1986 United Feature Syndicate, Inc. Reprinted with permission.

---

[4] A. Greene. 1969. *Pullet Surprises.* Glenview, IL: Scott, Foresman.

dents' knowledge of English morphology. Consider the creativity of these students in the following examples:

Word	Student's Definition
deciduous	"able to make up one's mind"
longevity	"being very tall"
fortuitous	"well protected"
gubernatorial	"to do with peanuts"
bibliography	"holy geography"
adamant	"pertaining to original sin"
diatribe	"food for the whole clan"
polyglot	"more than one glot"
gullible	"to do with sea birds"
homogeneous	"devoted to home life"

The student who used the word *indefatigable* in the sentence

She tried many reducing diets, but remained indefatigable

clearly shows morphological knowledge: *in* meaning "not" as in *ineffective; de* meaning "off" as in *decapitate; fat* as in "fat"; *able* as in *able;* and combined meaning, "not able to take the fat off."

Sign Language Morphology

It appears that sign languages are rich in morphology. Like spoken languages, they have root and affix morphemes, free and bound morphemes, lexical content and grammatical morphemes, derivational and inflectional morphemes, and morphological rules for their combination to form signed words.

Figure 3.1 illustrates the derivational process in ASL that is equivalent to the formation of the nouns *comparison* and *measuring* from the verbs *compare* and *measure* in

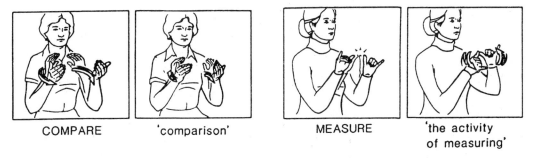

COMPARE   'comparison'   MEASURE   'the activity of measuring'

Figure 3.1   **Derivationally related sign in ASL.** (Copyright © 1987 MIT Press. Reprinted by permission of the MIT Press.)[5]

---

[5] H. Poizner, E. Klima, and U. Bellugi. 1987. *What the Hands Reveal about the Brain.* Cambridge, MA: MIT Press.

English. Everything about the root morpheme remains the same except for the movement of the hands.

Inflection of sign roots also occurs in ASL and all other sign languages, which characteristically modify the movement of the hands and the spatial contours of the area near the body in which the signs are articulated.

Word Coinage

We have seen that new words may be added to the vocabulary of a language by derivational processes. New words also enter a language in a variety of other ways. Some are created outright to fit some purpose. The advertising industry has added many words to English, such as *Kodak, nylon, Orlon,* and *Dacron.* Specific brand names such as *Xerox, Kleenex, Jell-O, Frigidaire, Brillo,* and *Vaseline* are now sometimes used as the generic name for different brands of these types of products. Notice that some of these words were created from existing words: *Kleenex* from the word *clean* and *Jell-O* from *gel,* for example.

In computer speech processing, the new words *cepstrum* and *cepstral* were purposely formed by reordering the letters of *spectrum* and *spectral.* Speakers do not agree on the pronunciation of these two words. Some say "sepstrum" with an *s*-sound, since the *c* precedes an *e.* Others say "kepstrum" since the *c* is pronounced as a *k* in the source word *spectrum.* Greek roots borrowed into English have also provided a means for coining new words. *Thermos* "hot" plus *metron* "measure" gives us *thermometer.* From *akros* "topmost" and *phobia* "fear," we get *acrophobia,* "dread of heights." To avoid going out Friday the thirteenth, you may say that you have *triskaidekaphobia,* a profound fear of the number 13. An ingenious cartoonist, Robert Osborn, has "invented" some phobias, to each of which he gives an appropriate name:[6]

logizomechanophobia	"fear of reckoning machines" from Greek *logizomai* "to reckon or compute" + *mekhane* "device" + *phobia*
ellipsosyllabophobia	"fear of words with a missing syllable" from Greek *elleipsis* "a falling short" + *syllabē* "syllable" + *phobia*
pornophobia	"fear of prostitutes" from Greek *porne* "harlot" + *phobia*

Latin, like Greek, has also provided prefixes and suffixes that are used productively with both native and nonnative roots. The prefix *ex-* comes from Latin:

ex-husband   ex-wife   ex-sister-in-law

---

[6] *An Osborn Festival of Phobias.* Copyright © 1971 Robert Osborn. Text copyright © 1971 Eve Wengler. Used by permission of Liveright Publishers, New York.

The suffix *-able/-ible* that was discussed earlier is also Latin, borrowed via French, and can be attached to almost any English verb, as we noted, and as further illustrated in:

writable   readable   answerable   movable

Compounds

... the Houynhnms have no Word in their Language to express any thing that is evil, except what they borrow from the Deformities or ill Qualities of the Yahoos. Thus they denote the Folly of a Servant, an Omission of a Child, a Stone that cuts their feet, a Continuance of foul or unseasonable Weather, and the like, by adding to each the Epithet of Yahoo. For instance, Hnhm Yahoo, Whnaholm Yahoo, Ynlhmnawihlma Yahoo, and an ill contrived House, Ynholmhnmrohlnw Yahoo.

Jonathan Swift, *Gulliver's Travels*

Two or more words may be joined to form new, **compound** words. The kinds of combinations that occur in English are nearly limitless, as the following table of compounds shows. Each entry in the table represents dozens of similar combinations.

	Adjective	**Noun**	**Verb**
Adjective	bittersweet	poorhouse	whitewash
Noun	headstrong	homework	spoonfeed
Verb	—	pickpocket	sleepwalk

Frigidaire is a compound formed by combining the adjective *frigid* with the noun *air*. Some compounds that have been introduced very recently into English are *carjack, mall rat, road rage, palm pilot,* and *slow-speed chase*. (Compounds are variously spelled with dashes, spaces, or nothing between the individual words.)

When the two words are in the same grammatical category, the compound will be in this category: noun + noun — *girlfriend, fighter-bomber, paper clip, elevator-operator, landlord, mailman;* adjective + adjective — *icy-cold, red-hot,* and *worldly-wise.* In English, the rightmost word in a compound is the **head** of the compound. The head is the part of a word or phrase that determines its broad meaning and grammatical category. Thus, when the two words fall into different categories, the class of the second or final word will be the grammatical category of the compound: noun + adjective = adjective — *headstrong, watertight, lifelong;* verb + noun = noun — *pickpocket, pinchpenny, daredevil, sawbones.* On the other hand, compounds formed with a preposition are in the category of the nonprepositional part of the compound; *overtake, hanger-on, undertake, sundown, afterbirth,* and *downfall, uplift.*

Though two-word compounds are the most common in English, it would be difficult to state an upper limit: Consider *three-time loser, four-dimensional space-time, sergeant-at-arms, mother-of-pearl, man about town, master of ceremonies,* and *daughter-in-law.* Dr. Seuss uses the rules of compounding when he explains "when tweetle beetles battle with paddles in a puddle, they call it a *tweetle beetle puddle paddle battle.*"[7]

---

[7] Dr. Seuss. 1965. *Fox in Sox*. New York: Random House, p. 51.

Spelling does not tell us what sequence of words constitutes a compound; whether a compound is spelled with a space between the two words, with a hyphen, or with no separation at all depends on the idiosyncrasies of the particular compound, as shown, for example, in *blackbird, gold-tail,* and *smoke screen.*

Like derived words, compounds have internal structure. This is clear from the ambiguity of a compound like *top + hat + rack,* which can mean "a rack for top hats" corresponding to the structure in tree diagram (1), or "the highest hat rack," corresponding to the structure in (2).

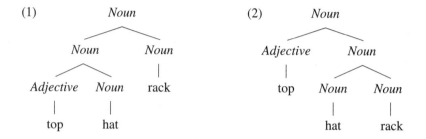

MEANING OF COMPOUNDS

The meaning of a compound is not always the sum of the meanings of its parts; a *blackboard* may be green or white. Everyone who wears a red coat is not a *Redcoat* (slang for British soldier during the American Revolutionary War.) The difference between the sentences "She has a red coat in her closet" and "She has a Redcoat in her closet" would have been highly significant in America in 1776.

"Hi & Lois" copyright © 1996 King Features Syndicate. Reprinted with special permission of King Features Syndicate.

Other compounds reveal other meaning relations between the parts, which are not entirely consistent because many compounds are idiomatic (idioms are discussed in chapter 5). A *boathouse* is a house for boats, but a *cathouse* is not a house for cats. (It is slang for a house of prostitution or whorehouse.) A *jumping bean* is a bean that jumps, a *falling star* is a star that falls, and a *magnifying glass* is a glass that magnifies; but a *looking glass* is not a glass that looks, nor is an *eating apple* an apple that eats, and *laughing gas* does not laugh. *Peanut oil* and *olive oil* are oils made from something, but what about *baby oil?* And is this a contradiction: horse meat is dog meat? Not at all, since the first is meat *from* horses and the other is meat *for* dogs.

In the example so far the meaning of each compound includes at least to some extent the meanings of the individual parts. However, many compounds do not seem to relate to the meanings of the individual parts at all. A *jack-in-a-box* is a tropical tree, and a *turncoat* is a traitor. A *highbrow* does not necessarily have a high brow, nor does a *bigwig* have a big wig, nor does an *egghead* have an egg-shaped head.

Like certain words with the prefix *un-*, the meaning of many compounds must be learned as if they were individual whole words. Some of the meanings may be figured out, but not all. If you had never heard the word *hunchback,* it might be possible to infer the meaning; but if you had never heard the word *flatfoot,* it is doubtful you would know it means "detective" or "policeman," even though the origin of the word, once you know the meaning, can be figured out.

The pronunciation of compounds differs from the way we pronounce the sequence of two words forming a noun phrase. In a compound, the first word is usually stressed (pronounced somewhat louder and higher in pitch) and in a noun phrase the second word is stressed. Thus we stress *Red* in *Redcoat* but *coat* in *red coat.* (Stress, pitch, and other "prosodic" features are discussed in chapters 6 and 7.)

UNIVERSALITY OF COMPOUNDING

Other languages have rules for conjoining words to form compounds, as seen by French *cure-dent,* "toothpick"; German *Panzerkraftwagen,* "armored car"; Russian *cetyrexetaznyi,* "four-storied"; Spanish *tocadiscos,* "record player." In the Native American language Papago the word meaning "thing" is *haʔichu,* and it combines with *doakam,* "living creatures," to form the compound *haʔichu doakam,* "animal life."

In Twi, by combining the word meaning "son" or "child," *ɔba,* with the word meaning "chief," *ɔhene,* one derives the compound *ɔheneba,* meaning "prince." By adding the word "house," *ofi,* to *ɔhene,* the word meaning "palace," *ahemfi,* is derived. The other changes that occur in the Twi compounds are due to phonological and morphological rules in the language.

In Thai, the word "cat" is *mɛɛw,* the word for "watch" (in the sense of "to watch over") is *fâw,* and the word for "house" is *bâan.* The word for "watch cat" (like a watchdog) is the compound *mɛɛwfâwbâan* — literally, "catwatchhouse."

Compounding is a common and frequent process for enlarging the vocabulary of all languages.

Acronyms

Acronyms are words derived from the initials of several words. Such words are pronounced as the spelling indicates: *NASA* from *N*ational *A*eronautics and *S*pace *A*gency, *UNESCO* from *U*nited *N*ations *E*ducational, *S*cientific, and *C*ultural *O*rganization, and

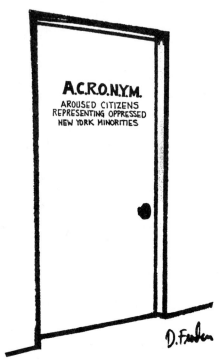

Drawing by D. Fradon. Copyright © 1974 The New Yorker Collection. All rights reserved.

UNICEF from *U*nited *N*ations *I*nternational *C*hildren's *E*mergency *F*und. *Radar* from "*ra*dio *de*tecting *and* *ra*nging," *laser* from "*l*ight *a*mplification by *s*timulated *e*mission of *r*adiation," *scuba* from "*s*elf-*c*ontained *u*nderwater *b*reathing *a*pparatus," and *RAM* from "*r*andom *a*ccess *m*emory," show the creative efforts of word coiners, as does *snafu,* which was coined by soldiers in World War II and is rendered in polite circles as "*s*ituation *n*ormal, *a*ll *f*ouled *u*p." Recently (1980s) coined additions are *AIDS*, from the initials of *a*cquired *i*mmune *d*eficiency *s*yndrome, and its partner *HIV* from *h*uman *i*mmunodeficiency *v*irus. Acronyms may be built on acronyms. *ROM* is a computer acronym for "*r*ead-*o*nly *m*emory"; *PROM* is "*p*rogrammable *r*ead-*o*nly *m*emory"; and *EPROM* "*e*rasable *p*rogrammable *r*ead-*o*nly *m*emory."[8] When the string of letters is not easily pronounced as a word, the acronym is produced by sounding out each letter, as in *NFL* for *N*ational *F*ootball *L*eague and *UCLA* for *U*niversity of *C*alifornia, *L*os *A*ngeles.

Acronyms are being added to the vocabulary daily with the proliferation of computers and widespread use of the Internet, including *MORF* (*m*ale *or f*emale?), *FAQ* (*f*requently *a*sked *q*uestions), *WYSIWYG* (*w*hat *y*ou *s*ee *i*s *w*hat *y*ou *g*et) and *POP* (*p*ost

---

[8] Contributed by Joan M. Flaherty.

*o*ffice *p*rotocol), among many more. Other common acronyms are *FYI* (*f*or *y*our *info*r-mation), *BTW* (*b*y *t*he *w*ay), and *TGIF* (*t*hank *G*od *i*t's *F*riday).

Back-Formations

Ignorance sometimes can be creative. A new word may enter the language because of an incorrect morphological analysis. For example, *peddle* was derived from *peddler* on the mistaken assumption that the *er* was the agentive suffix. Such words are called **back-formations.** The verbs *hawk, stoke, swindle,* and *edit* all came into the language as back-formations — of *hawker, stoker, swindler,* and *editor. Pea* was derived from a singular word, *pease,* by speakers who thought *pease* was a plural. Language purists sometimes rail against back-formations and cite *enthuse* and *liaise* (from *enthusiasm* and *liaison*) as examples of language corruption. However, language is not corrupt (although the speakers who use it may be), and many words have entered the language this way.

"Momma" by permission of Mell Lazarus and Creators Syndicate.

Some word coinage, similar to the kind of wrong morphemic analysis that produces back-formations, is deliberate. The word *bikini* is from the Bikini atoll of the Marshall Islands. Because the first syllable *bi-* in other words, like *bipolar,* means "two," some clever person called a topless bathing suit a *monokini.* Historically, a number of new words have entered the English lexicon in this way. Based on analogy with such pairs as *act/action, exempt/exemption, revise/revision,* new words *resurrect, preempt,* and *televise* were formed from the existing words *resurrection, preemption,* and *television.*

Abbreviations

Abbreviations of longer words or phrases also may become lexicalized, that is, words in their own right. *Fax* for *facsimile, telly,* the British word for *television, prof* for *professor, piano* for *pianoforte,* and *gym* for *gymnasium* are only a few examples of such "clipped" forms that are now used as whole words. Other examples are *ad, bike, math, gas, phone, bus,* and *van* (from *advertisement, bicycle, mathematics, gasoline, telephone, omnibus,* and *caravan*). More recently, *dis* and *rad* (from *disrespect* and *radical*) have entered the language, and *dis* has come to be used as a verb meaning "to show disrespect." This process is sometimes called **clipping.**

Words from Names

Eponyms are words derived from proper names and are another of the many creative ways that the vocabulary of a language expands.

Willard R. Espy has compiled a book of fifteen hundred such words.[9] They include common and widely used terminology:

sandwich	Named for the fourth Earl of Sandwich, who put his food between two slices of bread so that he could eat while he gambled.
robot	After the mechanical creatures in the Czech writer Karel Capek's play *R.U.R.,* the initials standing for "Rossum's Universal Robots."
gargantuan	Named for Gargantua, the creature with a huge appetite created by Rabelais.
jumbo	After an elephant brought to the United States by P. T. Barnum. ("Jumbo olives" need not be as big as an elephant, however.)

Espy admits to ignorance of the Susan, an unknown servant, from whom we derived the compound *lazy susan,* or the Betty or Charlotte or Chuck from whom we got *brown betty, charlotte russe,* or *chuck wagon.* He does point out that *denim* was named for the material used for overalls and carpeting, which originally was imported "de Nîmes" ("from Nîmes") in France, and *argyle* from the kind of socks worn by the chiefs of Argyll of the Campbell clan in Scotland.

The word *paparazzo,* "a freelance photographer who doggedly pursues celebrities," was a little known word until the death of Diana, Princess of Wales, in 1997, who was hounded by paparazzi (plural) before her automobile wreck. This eponym comes from the news photographer character Signor Paparazzo in the motion picture *La Dolce Vita.*

Blends

Two words may be combined to produce **blends.** Blends are similar to compounds but parts of the words that are combined are deleted, so they are "less than" compounds. *Smog,* from *smoke + fog; motel,* from *motor + hotel; infomercial* from *info + commercial;* and *urinalysis,* from *urine + analysis* are examples of blends that have attained full lexical status in English. The word *cranapple* may be a blend of *cranberry + apple.* *Broasted,* from *broiled + roasted,* is a blend that has limited acceptance in the language, as does Lewis Carroll's *chortle,* from *chuckle + snort.* Carroll is famous for both the coining and the blending of words. In *Through the Looking-Glass* he describes the "meanings" of the made-up words in "Jabberwocky" as follows:

> . . . "Brillig" means four o' clock in the afternoon — the time when you begin broiling things for dinner. . . . "Slithy" means "lithe and slimy.". . . You see

---

[9] W. R. Espy. 1978. *O Thou Improper, Thou Uncommon Noun: An Etymology of Words That Once Were Names.* New York: Clarkson N. Potter.

"The Wizard of Id" by permission of Johnny Hart and Creators Syndicate, Inc.

it's like a portmanteau — there are two meanings packed up into one word. . . . "Toves" are something like badgers — they're something like lizards — and they're something like corkscrews . . . also they make their nests under sun-dials — also they live on cheese. . . . To "gyre" is to go round and round like a gyroscope. To "gimble" is to make holes like a gimlet. And "the wabe" is the grass-plot round a sun-dial. . . . It's called "wabe" . . . because it goes a long way before it and a long way behind it. . . . "Mimsy" is "flimsy and miserable" (there's another portmanteau . . . for you).

Carroll's "portmanteaus" are what we have called blends, and such words can become part of the regular lexicon.

Blending is even done by children. The blend *crocogator* from *crocodile + alligator* is attributed to three-year old Elijah Peregrine. Grandmothers are not to be left out, and a Jewish one of African descent that we know came up with *shugeleh,* "darling," which we think is a blend of *sugar + bubeleh,* and which we confess we don't know how to spell. (*Bubeleh* is a Yiddish term of endearment.)

Grammatical Morphemes

"... and even ... the patriotic archbishop of Canterbury found it advisable —"

"Found what?" said the Duck.

"Found it," the Mouse replied rather crossly; "of course you know what 'it' means."

"I know what 'it' means well enough, when I find a thing," said the Duck; "it's generally a frog or a worm. The question is, what did the archbishop find?"

Lewis Carroll, *Alice's Adventures in Wonderland*

In the discussion of derivational morphology we saw that certain morphemes such as *-ceive* or *-mit* have meaning only when combined with other morphemes in a word, for example *transmit, remit, receive,* and *deceive.* Similarly, there are morphemes that have "meaning" only in combination with other words in a sentence. For example, what is the meaning of *it* in "It's hot in July" or "The Archbishop found it advisable"? What is the meaning of *to* in *He wanted her to go.* Function words such as *it* and *to* have a strictly grammatical meaning, or function, in the sentence. This means that they do not have any clear lexical meaning or concept associated with them. They are in the sentence because they are required by the rules of sentence formation — the syntax. For example, *to* in connection with a verb has the grammatical function of making the sentence an infinitive. Similarly, *have* in "The cows have walked here" marks the sentence as a present perfect, and the different forms of *be* in "The baby *is* crying" and "The baby's diaper *was* changed" function as a progressive and passive marker, respectively.

"Zits" reprinted with special permission of King Features Syndicate.

Inflectional Morphemes

Function words like *to, it,* and *be* are free morphemes. Many languages, including English, also have bound morphemes that have a strictly grammatical function. They mark properties such as tense, number, gender, case, and so forth. Such bound morphemes are called **inflectional morphemes.** They never change the syntactic category of the words or morphemes to which they are attached. Consider the forms of the verb in the following sentences:

(1) I sail the ocean blue.
(2) He sails the ocean blue.
(3) John sailed the ocean blue.
(4) John has sailed the ocean blue.
(5) John is sailing the ocean blue.

In sentence (2) the *-s* at the end of the verb is an agreement marker; it signifies that the subject of the verb is third person, is singular, and that the verb is in the present tense. It doesn't add lexical meaning. The suffix *-ed* indicates past tense, and is also required by the syntactic rules of the language when verbs are used with *have,* just as *-ing* is required when verbs are used with forms of *be.*

English is no longer a highly inflected language. But we do have other inflectional endings such as the plural suffix, which is attached to certain singular nouns, as in *boy/boys* and *cat/cats.* At the present stage of English history, there are a total of eight bound inflectional affixes:

English Inflectional Morphemes		Examples
-s	third-person singular present	She wait-**s** at home.
-ed	past tense	She wait-**ed** at home.
-ing	progressive	She is eat-**ing** the donut.
-en	past participle	Mary has eat-**en** the donuts.
-s	plural	She ate the donut-**s.**
-'s	possessive	Disa**'s** hair is short.
-er	comparative	Disa has short-**er** hair than Karin.
-est	superlative	Disa has the short-**est** hair.

Inflectional morphemes in English typically follow derivational morphemes. Thus, to the derivationally complex word *commit + ment* one can add a plural ending to form *commit + ment + s,* but the order of affixes may not be reversed to derive the impossible *commit + s + ment = *commitment.* However, with compounds the situation is complicated. Thus, for many speakers, the plural of *mother-in-law* is *mothers-in-law* whereas the possessive form is *mother-in-law's;* the plural of *court- martial* is *courts-martial* in a legal setting, but for most of the rest of us it's *court-martials.*

Compared to many languages of the world, English has relatively little inflectional morphology. Some languages are highly inflected. In Swahili, a Bantu language spoken in eastern and central Africa, a verb can be inflected with up to eight morphemes. For example, in *hatutawapikishia* the verb *pik* "to cook" has negative tense, subject agreement, object agreement, indicative mood, and prefixes as well as suffixes:

> Ha + tu + ta + wa + pik + i + sh + i + a   "We will not have made him cook for them"[10]

Even the more familiar European languages have many more inflectional endings than English. In the Romance languages (languages descended from Latin), the verb has different inflectional endings depending on the subject of the sentence. The verb is inflected to agree in person and number with the subject, as illustrated by the Italian verb *parlare* meaning "to speak":

Io parl**o**	"I speak"	Noi parl**iamo**	"We speak"
Tu parl**i**	"You (singular) speak"	Voi parl**ate**	"You (plural) speak"
Lui/Lei parl**a**	"He/she speaks"	Loro parl**ano**	"They speak"

Some languages can also add content morphemes to the verb. Many North American languages are of this type. For example, in Mohawk the word *wahonwatia'tawit-sherahetkenhten* means "she made the thing that one puts on one's body ugly for him." In such languages words are equivalent to sentences. As the linguist Mark Baker notes, languages like Mohawk "use a different division of labor from languages like English, with more burden on morphology and less on syntax to express complex relations."

Students often ask for definitions of derivational morphemes as opposed to inflectional morphemes. There is no easy answer. Perhaps the simplest answer is that derivational morphemes are affixes that are not inflectional. Inflectional morphemes signal grammatical relations and are required by the rule of sentence formation. Derivational

---

[10] Swahili examples provided by Kamil Deen.

morphemes, when affixed to roots and stems, change the grammatical word class and/or the basic meaning of the word, which may then be inflected as to number (singular or plural), tense (present, past, future), and so on.

Exceptions and Suppletions

The regular rule that forms plurals from singular nouns does not apply to words like *child, man, foot,* and *mouse.* These words are exceptions to the English inflectional rule of plural formation. Similarly, verbs like *go, sing, bring, run,* and *know* are exceptions to the regular past tense rule in English.

"Peanuts" copyright © United Feature Syndicate. Reprinted by permission.

When children are learning English, they first learn the regular rules, which they apply to all forms. Thus, we often hear them say *mans* and *goed.* Later in the acquisition process, they specifically learn irregular plurals like *men* and *mice,* and irregular past tense forms like *came* and *went.* These children's errors are actually evidence that the regular rules exist.

Irregular, or **suppletive,** forms are treated separately in the grammar. That is, one cannot use the regular rules of inflectional morphology to add affixes to words that are exceptions like *child/children,* but must replace the noninflected form with another word. It is possible that for regular words, only the singular form need be specifically stored in the lexicon since we can use the inflectional rules to form plurals. But this can't be so with suppletive exceptions.

When a new word enters the language it is generally the regular inflectional rules that apply. The plural of *geek,* when it was a new word in English, was *geeks,* not **geeken,* although we are advised that some geeks wanted the plural of *fax* to be **faxen,* like *oxen,* when *fax* entered the language as a clip of *facsimile.* Never fear: its plural is *faxes.* The exception to this may be a loan word, a word borrowed from a foreign language. For example, the plural of Latin *datum* has always been *data,* never *datums,* though nowadays *data,* the one-time plural, is treated by many as a singular word like *information.* The past tense of the verb *hit,* as in the sentence "Yesterday you hit the ball," and the plural of the noun *sheep,* as in "The sheep are in the meadow," show that some morphemes seem to have no phonological shape at all. We know that *hit* in the above sentence is *hit + past* because of the time adverb *yesterday,* and we know that *sheep* is the phonetic form of *sheep + plural* because of the plural verb form *are.* Thousands of years ago the Hindu grammarians suggested that some morphemes have a zero-form; that is, they have no phonological representation. Because we would like to hold to the definition of a morpheme as a constant sound-meaning form, however, we suggest that the morpheme *hit* is marked as both present and past in the lexicon, and the morpheme *sheep* is marked as both singular and plural, and that there are no "zero-forms."

When a verb is derived from a noun, even if it is homophonous with an irregular verb, the regular rules apply to it. Thus *ring,* when used in the sense of encircle, is derived from the noun *ring,* and as a verb it is regular. We say *the police ringed the bank with armed men,* not **rang the bank with armed men.*

Similarly, when a noun is used in a compound in which its meaning is lost, such as *flatfoot,* meaning "cop," its plural follows the regular rule, so one says *two flatfoots* to refer to a pair of cops slangily, not **two flatfeet.* It's as if the noun is saying: "If you don't get your meaning from me, you don't get my special plural form."

Morphology and Syntax

"Curiouser and curiouser!" cried Alice (she was so much surprised, that for the moment she quite forgot how to speak good English).

Lewis Carroll, *Alice's Adventures in Wonderland*

Some grammatical relations can be expressed either inflectionally (morphologically) or syntactically (as part of the sentence structure). We can see this in the following sentences:

England's queen is Elizabeth II.	The Queen of England is Elizabeth II.
He loves books.	He is a lover of books.
The planes which fly are red.	The flying planes are red.
He is hungrier than she.	He is more hungry than she.

Some of you may form the comparative of *beastly* only by adding *-er. Beastlier* is often used interchangeably with *more beastly.* There are speakers who say both. We know when either form of the comparative can be used, as with *beastly,* or when just one can be used, as with *curious,* as pointed out by Lewis Carroll in the quotation.

What one language signals with inflectional affixes, another does with word order, and another with function words. For example, in English, the sentence *Maxim defends Victor* means something different from *Victor defends Maxim.* The word order is critical. In Russian, all the following sentences mean "Maxim defends Victor": (The *č* is pronounced like the *ch* in *cheese;* the *š* like the *sh* in *shoe;* the *j* like the *y* in *yet.*)

Maksim zaščiščajet Viktora.
Maksim Viktora zaščiščajet.
Viktora Maksim zaščiščajet.
Viktora zaščiščajet Maksim.

The inflectional suffix *-a* added to the name *Viktor* to derive *Viktora* shows that Victor, not Maxim, is defended.

Like many languages, Russian has **case** markers, which are grammatical morphemes added to nouns to indicate whether the noun is a subject, object, possessor, or some other grammatical role. As shown in the preceding examples, *-a* is an accusative (object) case marker, and it can also mark genitive (possession) as in *mjech' Viktor + a* means

"Viktor's sword." *Viktor + u* is a dative form meaning "to Viktor," *Viktor + om* means "by Viktor," and *Viktor + je* means "about Viktor." Many of the grammatical relations that Russian expresses with case morphology, English expresses with prepositions.[11]

In English, to convey the future meaning of a verb we must use a function word *will,* as in "John will come Monday." In French, the verb is inflected with a future tense morpheme. Notice the difference between "John is coming Monday," *Jean **vient** lundi,* and "John will come Monday," *Jean **viendra** lundi.* Similarly, where English uses the grammatical markers *have* to form a perfect sentence and *be* to form a passive sentence, other languages use affixing to achieve the same meanings, as illustrated with Swahili. In Swahili the morpheme *-me* is a perfect marker and the morpheme *-w* is a passive marker:

*ni+**me**+pig+a m+pira*	*nimepiga mpira*	"I have hit a ball"
*m+pira i+li+pig+**w**+a*	*mpira ilipigwa*	"A ball was hit"

The meaning of the individual morphemes may not always indicate the meaning of a morphologically complex word. (For example, *lowlife* to mean "disreputable person.") This problem is not true of inflectional morphology. If we know the meaning of the word *linguist,* we also know the meaning of the plural form *linguists;* if we know the meaning of the verb *analyze,* we know the meaning of *analyzed, analyzes,* and *analyzing.* This reveals another difference between derivational and inflectional morphology.

Figure 3.2 shows the way one may classify English morphemes.

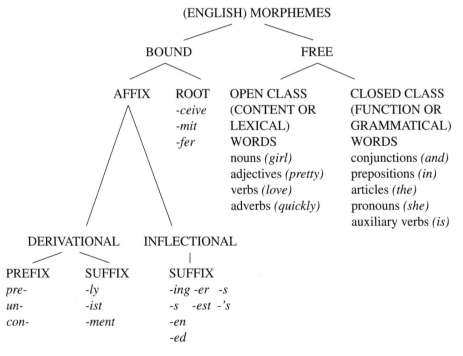

Figure 3.2   Classification of English Morphemes.

[11] These Russian examples were provided by Stella de Bode.

The mental grammar of the language internalized by the language learner includes a lexicon listing all the morphemes, as well as the derived words with unpredictable meanings. The morphological rules of the grammar permit speakers to use and understand the morphemes and words in forming and understanding sentences, and in forming and understanding new words.

Morphological Analysis: Identifying Morphemes

Speakers of a language have the knowledge to perceive the component morphemes of a word since their mental grammars include a mental lexicon of morphemes and the morphological rules for their combination. Of course, there are mistakes while learning, but these are quickly remedied. (See chapter 8 for details of how children learn their language.)

Suppose you didn't know English and were a linguist from the planet Mars wishing to analyze the language. How would you discover the morphemes of English? How would you determine whether a word in that language had one, two, or more morphemes?

The first thing to do would be to ask native speakers how they say various words. (It would help to have a Martian-English interpreter along; otherwise, copious gesturing is in order.) Assume you are talented in miming and manage to collect the following sets or *paradigms* of forms:

Adjective	Meaning
ugly	"very unattractive"
uglier	"more ugly"
ugliest	"most ugly"
pretty	"nice looking"
prettier	"more nice looking"
prettiest	"most nice looking"
tall	"large in height"
taller	"more tall"
tallest	"most tall"
etc.	

To determine what the morphemes are in such a list, the first thing a field linguist would do is to see if there are forms that mean the same thing in different words, that is, to look for **recurring** forms. We find them: *ugly* occurs in *ugly, uglier, ugliest,* all three of which words include the meaning "very unattractive." We also find that *er* occurs in *prettier* and *taller,* adding the meaning "more" to the adjectives to which it is attached. Similarly, *est* adds the meaning "most." Furthermore, by asking additional questions of our English speaker we find that *er* and *est* do not occur in isolation with the meanings of "more" and "most." We can therefore conclude that the following morphemes occur in English:

ugly	root morpheme
pretty	root morpheme

tall	root morpheme
er	bound morpheme "comparative"
est	bound morpheme "superlative"

As we proceed we find other words that end with *-er* (e.g., *singer, lover, bomber, writer, teacher*) in which the *-er* ending does not mean "comparative" but, when attached to a verb, changes it to a noun who "verbs," (e.g., *sings, loves, bombs, writes, teaches*). So we conclude that this is a different morpheme even though it is pronounced the same as the comparative. We go on and find words like *number, somber, umber, butter, member,* and many others in which the *er* has no separate meaning at all — a *somber* is not "one who sombs" and a *member* does not *memb* — and therefore these words must be monomorphemic.

Once you have practiced on the morphology of English, you might want to go on to describe another language. A "language" called Paku was invented by a linguist for an old 1970s TV series called *Land of the Lost.* This was the language used by the monkey people called Pakuni. Suppose you found yourself in this strange land and attempted to find out what the morphemes of Paku were. Again, you would collect your data from a native Paku speaker and proceed as the Martian did with English. Consider the following data from Paku:

me	"I"	meni	"we"
ye	"you (singular)"	yeni	"you (plural)"
we	"he"	weni	"they (masculine)"
wa	"she"	wani	"they (feminine)"
abuma	"girl"	abumani	"girls"
adusa	"boy"	adusani	"boys"
abu	"child"	abuni	"children"
Paku	"one Paku"	Pakuni	"more than one Paku"

By examining these words you find that all the plural forms end in *-ni* and the singular forms do not. You therefore conclude that *-ni* is a separate morpheme meaning "plural" that is attached as a suffix to a noun.

While these are rather simple examples of how one proceeds to conduct a morphological analysis, the principles remain the same, and by studying them you are on the road to becoming a morphologist.

≋ Summary

Knowing a language means knowing the words of that language. When you know a word you know both its **form** (sound) and its **meaning;** these are inseparable parts of the linguistic **sign.** The relationship between the form and meaning is **arbitrary.** That is, by hearing the sounds (form) you cannot know the meaning of those sounds without having learned it previously.

Each root, inflectional, and derivational morpheme is stored in your mental **lexicon** with information on its pronunciation (phonological representation), its meaning (semantic properties), and its syntactic category. Also contained in the lexicon are morphologically complex words whose meanings are unpredictable. For literate speakers, its spelling or **orthography** will also be present.

In spoken language, words are not separated by pauses (or spaces as in written language). One must know the language in order to segment the stream of speech into separate words.

Words are not the most elemental sound-meaning units; some words are structurally complex. The most elemental grammatical units in a language are **morphemes.** A morpheme is the minimal unit of linguistic meaning or grammatical function. Thus, *moralizers* is an English word composed of four morphemes: *moral + ize + er + s.*

The study of word formation and the internal structure of words is called **morphology.** Part of our linguistic competence includes knowledge of the morphology of the language. Morphemes combine according to the morphological rules of the language. A word consists of one or more morphemes. Lexical content morphemes that cannot be analyzed into smaller parts are called **root** morphemes. When a root morpheme is combined with affix morphemes it forms a **stem** or word. Other affixes can be added to a stem to form a more complex stem which may also be a word.

Some morphemes are **bound** in that they must be joined to other morphemes, are always parts of words, and are never words by themselves. Most morphemes are **free** in that they need not be attached to other morphemes; *free, king, serf,* and *bore* are free morphemes; *-dom,* as in *freedom, kingdom, serfdom,* and *boredom* is a bound morpheme. **Affixes,** that is, **prefixes, suffixes, infixes,** and **circumfixes,** are bound morphemes. Prefixes occur before, suffixes after, infixes in the middle of, and circumfixes around stems or roots.

Some morphemes, like *huckle* in *huckleberry* and *-ceive* in *perceive* and *receive,* have constant phonological form but meanings determined only by the words in which they occur. They are also bound morphemes.

Lexical content, or **root,** morphemes constitute the major word classes — nouns, verbs, adjectives, adverbs. These are **open class** items because their classes are easily added to.

Morphemes may be **derivational** or **inflectional. Morphological rules** are rules of word formation. Derivational morphemes, when added to a root or stem, may change the syntactic word class and/or the meaning of the word. For example, adding *-ish* to the noun *boy* derives an adjective, and prefixing *un-* to *pleasant* changes the meaning by adding a negative element. Inflectional morphemes are determined by the rules of syntax. They are added to complete words, whether simple **monomorphemic** words or complex **polymorphemic** words (i.e., words with more than one morpheme). Inflectional morphemes never change the syntactic category of the word.

Grammatical morphemes or **function words** constitute a **closed class;** that is, new function words do not enter the language. Function words and bound inflectional morphemes are inserted into sentences according to the syntactic structure. The past tense morpheme, often written as *-ed,* is added as a suffix to a verb, and the future tense morpheme *will,* is inserted in a sentence according to the syntactic rules of English.

There is a continuum of languages determined by how much they rely on morphology to express linguistic relations. English has relatively little reliance on morphology compared to Mohawk, in which a word equals a sentence. Between English and

Mohawk are languages like Swahili and Italian, which use affixation for some but not all grammatical information.

The grammars of sign languages also include a morphological component consisting of root, derivational and inflectional sign morphemes, and the rules for their combination.

Grammars also include ways of adding words and morphemes to the lexicon. Words can be **coined** outright, limited only by the coiner's imagination and the phonetic constraints of English word formation. **Compounds** are also a source of new words. Morphological rules combine two or more words to form complex combinations like *lamb chop, deep-sea diver,* and *laptop,* a word spawned by the computer industry. Frequently, the meaning of compounds cannot be predicted from the meanings of their individual morphemes.

Acronyms are words derived from the initials of several words — like *AWOL,* which came into the language as the initials for "*away without leave.*" **Blends** are similar to compounds but usually combine shortened forms of two or more morphemes or words. *Brunch,* a late morning meal, is a blend of *breakfast* and *lunch.* **Eponyms** (words taken from proper names such as *john* for "toilet" or "prostitute's customer"), **back-formations,** and **abbreviations** also add to the given stock of words.

While the particular morphemes and the particular morphological rules are language-dependent, the same general processes occur in all languages.

References for Further Reading

Anderson, S. R. 1992. *A-Morphous Morphology.* Cambridge, England: Cambridge University Press.

Aronoff, M. 1976. *Word Formation in Generative Grammar.* Cambridge, MA: MIT Press.

Bauer, L. 1983. *English Word-formation.* Cambridge, England: Cambridge University Press.

Hammond, M., and M. Noonan, eds. 1988. *Theoretical Morphology: Approaches in Modern Linguistics.* San Diego: Academic Press.

Jensen, J. T. 1990. *Morphology: Word Structure in Generative Grammar.* Amsterdam/Philadelphia: John Benjamins Publishing.

Marchand, H. 1969. *The Categories and Types of Present-Day English Word-Formation, 2nd ed.* Munich: C. H. Beck'sche Verlagsbuchhandlung.

Matthews, P. H. 1976. *Morphology: An Introduction to the Theory of Word Structure.* Cambridge, England: Cambridge University Press.

Scalise, S. 1984. *Generative Morphology.* Dordrecht, Holland/Cinnaminson, U.S.A: Foris Publications

Spencer, A. 1991. *Morphological Theory: An Introduction to Word Structure in Generative Grammar.* London: Basil Blackwell.

Winchester, S. 1999. *The Professor and the Madman.* HarperCollins.

Exercises

1. Here is how to estimate the number of words in your mental lexicon. Consult any standard dictionary.

   a. Count the number of entries on a typical page. They are usually bold-faced.

    b. Multiply the number of words per page by the number of pages in the dictionary.

    c. Pick four pages in the dictionary at random, say, pages 50, 75, 125, 303. Count the number of words on these pages.

    d. How many of these words do you know?

    e. What percentage of the words on the four pages do you know?

    f. Multiply the words in the dictionary by the percent you arrived at in (e). You know approximately that many English words.

2. Divide the following words by placing a + between their morphemes. (Some of the words may be monomorphemic and therefore indivisible.)

Example: replaces   re + place + s

    a. retroactive
    b. befriended
    c. televise
    d. margin
    e. endearment
    f. psychology
    g. unpalatable
    h. holiday
    i. grandmother
    j. morphemic
    k. mistreatment
    l. deactivation
    m. saltpeter
    n. airsickness

3. Match each expression under A with the one statement under B that characterizes it.

A	B
a. noisy crow	**1.** compound noun
b. scarecrow	**2.** root morpheme plus derivational prefix
c. the crow	**3.** phrase consisting of adjective plus noun
d. crowlike	**4.** root morpheme plus inflectional affix
e. crows	**5.** root morpheme plus derivational suffix
	6. grammatical morpheme followed by lexical morpheme

4. Write the one proper description from the list under B for the italicized part of each word in A.

A	B
a. terror*ized*	**1.** free root
b. un*civil*ized	**2.** bound root
c. terror*ize*	**3.** inflectional suffix
d. *luke*warm	**4.** derivational suffix
e. *im*possible	**5.** inflectional prefix
	6. derivational prefix
	7. inflectional infix
	8. derivational infix

5. **A.** Consider the following nouns in Zulu and proceed to look for the recurring forms. Note that the ordering of morphemes is not identical across languages. Thus, what is a prefix in one language may be a suffix or an infix in another.

umfazi	"married woman"	abafazi	"married women"
umfani	"boy"	abafani	"boys"
umzali	"parent"	abazali	"parents"
umfundisi	"teacher"	abafundisi	"teachers"
umbazi	"carver"	ababazi	"carvers"
umlimi	"farmer"	abalimi	"farmers"
umdlali	"player"	abadlali	"players"
umfundi	"reader"	abafundi	"readers"

   a. What is the morpheme meaning "singular" in Zulu?

   b. What is the morpheme meaning "plural" in Zulu?

   c. List the Zulu stems to which the singular and plural morphemes are attached, and give their meanings.

B. The following Zulu verbs are derived from noun stems by adding a verbal suffix.

fundisa	"to teach"	funda	"to read"
lima	"to cultivate"	baza	"to carve"

   d. Compare these words to the words in section A that are related in meaning, for example, umfundisi "teacher," abafundisi "teachers," fundisa "to teach." What is the derivational suffix that specifies the category verb?

   e. What is the nominal suffix (i.e., the suffix that forms nouns)?

   f. State the morphological noun formation rule in Zulu.

   g. What is the stem morpheme meaning "read"?

   h. What is the stem morpheme meaning "carve"?

6. Examine the following words from Michoacan Aztec.

nokali	"my house"	mopelo	"your dog"
nokalimes	"my houses"	mopelomes	"your dogs"
mokali	"your house"	ipelo	"his dog"
ikali	"his house"	nokwahmili	"my cornfield"
kalimes	"houses"	mokwahmili	"your cornfield"
		ikwahmili	"his cornfield"

   a. The morpheme meaning "house" is:

     (1) kal   (2) kali   (3) kalim   (4) ikal   (5) ka

   b. The word meaning "cornfields" is:

     (1) kwahmilimes   (2) nokwahmilimes   (3) nokwahmili   (4) kwahmili
     (5) ikwahmilimes

   c. The word meaning "his dogs" is:

     (1) pelos   (2) ipelomes   (3) ipelos   (4) mopelo   (5) pelomes

   d. If the word meaning "friend" is *mahkwa*, then the word meaning "my friends" is:

     (1) momahkwa   (2) imahkwas   (3) momahkwames
     (4) momahkwaes   (5) nomahkwames

   e. The word meaning "dog" is:

     (1) pelo   (2) perro   (3) peli   (4) pel   (5) mopel

7. The following infinitive and past participle verb forms are found in Dutch.

Root	Infinitive	Past Participle	
wandel	wandelen	gewandeld	"walk"
duw	duwen	geduwd	"push"
stofzuig	stofzuigen	gestofzuigd	"vacuum-clean"

With reference to the morphological processes of prefixing, suffixing, infixing, and circumfixing discussed in this chapter and the specific morphemes involved:

a. State the morphological rule for forming an infinitive in Dutch.

b. State the morphological rule for forming the Dutch past participle form.

8. Below are some sentences in Swahili:

mtoto	amefika	"The child has arrived."
mtoto	anafika	"The child is arriving."
mtoto	atafika	"The child will arrive."
watoto	wamefika	"The children have arrived."
watoto	wanafika	"The children are arriving."
watoto	watafika	"The children will arrive."
mtu	amelala	"The person has slept."
mtu	analala	"The person is sleeping."
mtu	atalala	"The person will sleep."
watu	wamelala	"The persons have slept."
watu	wanalala	"The persons are sleeping."
watu	watalala	"The persons will sleep."
kisu	kimeanguka	"The knife has fallen."
kisu	kinaanguka	"The knife is falling."
kisu	kitaanguka	"The knife will fall."
visu	vimeanguka	"The knives have fallen."
visu	vinaanguka	"The knives are falling."
visu	vitaanguka	"The knives will fall."
kikapu	kimeanguka	"The basket has fallen."
kikapu	kinaanguka	"The basket is falling."
kikapu	kitaanguka	"The basket will fall."
vikapu	vimeanguka	"The baskets have fallen."
vikapu	vinaanguka	"The baskets are falling."
vikapu	vitaanguka	"The baskets will fall."

One of the characteristic features of Swahili (and Bantu languages in general) is the existence of noun classes. Specific singular and plural prefixes occur with the nouns in each class. These prefixes are also used for purposes of agreement between the subject noun and the verb. In the sentences given, two of these classes are included (there are many more in the language).

a. Identify all the morphemes you can detect, and give their meanings.

Example: -toto "child"

m- noun prefix attached to singular nouns of Class I

a- prefix attached to verbs when the subject is a singular noun of Class I

Be sure to look for the other noun and verb markers, including tense markers.

b. How is the verb constructed? That is, what kinds of morphemes are strung together and in what order?

c. How would you say in Swahili:
   (1) The child is falling.
   (2) The baskets have arrived.
   (3) The person will fall.

9. One morphological process not discussed in this chapter is **reduplication** — the formation of new words through the repetition of part or all of a word — which occurs in many languages. The following examples from Samoan exemplify this kind of morphological rule.

manao	"he wishes"	mananao	"they wish"
matua	"he is old"	matutua	"they are old"
malosi	"he is strong"	malolosi	"they are strong"
punou	"he bends"	punonou	"they bend"
atamaki	"he is wise"	atamamaki	"they are wise"
savali	"he travels"	pepese	"they sing"
laga	"he weaves"		

a. What is the Samoan for:

   (1) they weave
   (2) they travel
   (3) he sings

b. Formulate a general statement (a morphological rule) that states how to form the plural verb form from the singular verb form.

10. Below are listed some words followed by incorrect definitions. (All these errors are taken from Amsel Greene's *Pullet Surprises*.)

Word	Student Definition
stalemate	"husband or wife no longer interested"
effusive	"able to be merged"
tenet	"a group of ten singers"
dermatology	"a study of derms"
ingenious	"not very smart"
finesse	"a female fish"

For each of these incorrect definitions, give some possible reasons why the students made the guesses they did. Where you can exemplify by reference to other words or morphemes, giving their meanings, do so.

11. Dal Yoo[12] expresses the belief that abbreviations and acronyms occur in the United States more than in any other country. He refers, for example, to the acronyms generated in the 1991 Gulf war, by both pro- and antiwar demonstrations such as SMASH for "*S*tudents *M*obilized *A*gainst *S*addam *H*ussein" and SCUD for "*S*adly *C*onfused *U*npatriotic *D*emonstrators." He also refers to a neon sign on a downtown high-rise building in Philadelphia reading PSFS for "*P*hiladelphia *S*avings *F*und *S*ociety," which was referred to by a local tour guide as meaning, instead, "*P*hiladelphia *S*mells *F*unny *S*ome-

---

[12] Dal Yoo. 1994. "The World of Abbreviations and Acronyms, *Verbatim: The Language Quarterly* (summer):4–5.

times." Dr. Yoo is a medical doctor who writes: "When I have no idea what the patient has, I apply my favorite of all the abbreviations, GOK syndrome 'God Only Knows.'" Such acronyms show how innovative our linguistic ability is.

   a. List ten acronyms currently in use in English. Do not use the ones given in the text.

   b. Invent ten acronyms (listing the words as well as the initials).

12. There are many asymmetries in English in which a root morpheme combined with a prefix constitutes a word but without the prefix is a nonword. A number of these are given in this chapter.

   A. Below are a list of such nonword roots. Add a prefix to each root to form an existing English word.

Words	Nonwords
_____	*descript
_____	*cognito
_____	*beknownst
_____	*peccable
_____	*promptu
_____	*plussed
_____	*domitable
_____	*nomer

   B. There are many more such multimorphemic words for which the root morphemes do not constitute words by themselves. See how many you can think of.

13. We have seen that the meaning of compounds is often not revealed by the meaning of its composite words. Crossword puzzles and riddles often make use of this by providing the meaning of two parts of a compound and asking for the resulting word. For example, infielder = diminutive/cease. Read this as asking for a word which means "infielder" by combining a word which means "diminutive" with a word which means "cease." The answer is *shortstop*. See if you can figure out the following:

   a. sci-fi TV series = headliner/journey

   b. campaign = farm building/tempest

   c. at-home wear = tub of water/court attire

   d. kind of pen = formal dance/sharp end

   e. conservative = correct/part of an airplane

14. Consider the cartoon:

"Drabble" copyright © 1997 United Feature Syndicate, Inc.

The humor is based on the ambiguity of the compound *ten-page book report*. Draw two trees similar to those in the text for *top hat rack* on page 94 to reveal the ambiguity.

15. One of the characteristics of Italian is that articles and adjectives have inflectional ending that mark agreement in gender (and number) with the noun they modify. Based on this information, answer the questions that follow the list of Italian phrases.

un uomo	"a man"
un uomo robusto	"a robust man"
un uomo robustissimo	"a very robust man"
una donna robusta	"a robust woman"
un vino rosso	"a red wine"
una faccia	"a face"
un vento secco	"a dry wind"

   a. What is the root morpheme meaning "robust"?
   b. What is the morpheme meaning "very"?
   c. What is the Italian for:
      (1) "a robust wine"
      (2) "a very red face"
      (3) "a very dry wine"

16. Below is a list of words from Turkish. In Turkish, articles and morphemes indicating location are affixed to the verb.

deniz	"an ocean"	evden	"from a house"
denize	"to an ocean"	evimden	"from my house"
denizin	"of an ocean"	denizimde	"in my ocean"
eve	"to a house"	elde	"in a hand"

   a. What is the Turkish morpheme meaning "to"?
   b. What kind of affixes in Turkish correspond to English prepositions (e.g., prefixes, suffixes, infixes, free morphemes)?
   c. What would the Turkish word for "from an ocean" be?
   d. How many morphemes are there in the Turkish word *denizimde*?

17. The following are some verb forms in Chickasaw, a member of the Muskogean family of languages spoken in south-central Oklahoma.[13] Chickasaw is an endangered language. Currently, there are only about 100 speakers of Chickasaw, most of whom are over 70 years old.

Sachaaha	"I am tall"
Chaaha	"He/she is tall"
Chichaaha	"you are tall"
Hoochaaha	"they are tall"
Satikahbi	"I am tired"
Chitikahbitok	"you were tired"
Chichchokwa	"you are cold"
Hopobatok	"he was hungry"
Hoohopobatok	"they were hungry"
Sahopoba	"I am hungry"

---

[13] The Chickasaw examples are provided by Pamela Munro.

a. What is the root morpheme for the following verbs?

(1) "to be tall"

(2) "to be hungry"

b. What is the morpheme meaning:

(1) past tense

(2) "I"

(3) "You"

(4) "He/she"

c. If the Chickasaw root for "to be old" is *sipokni,* how would you say:

(1) "You are old"

(2) "He was old"

(3) "They are old"

CHAPTER 4

Syntax: The Sentence Patterns of Language

To grammar even kings bow.

J. B. Molière, *Les femmes savantes*, II, 1672

ny speaker of a human language can produce and understand an infinite number of sentences. We can show this quite easily through examples such as the following:

The kind-hearted boy had many girlfriends.
The kindhearted, intelligent boy had many girlfriends.
The kindhearted, intelligent, handsome boy had many girlfriends.

.
.
.

John went to the movies.
John went to the movies and ate popcorn.
John went to the movies, ate popcorn, and drank a coke.

.
.
.

The cat chased the mouse.
The cat chased the mouse that ate the cheese.
The cat chased the mouse that ate the cheese that came from the cow.
The cat chased the mouse that ate the cheese that came from the cow that grazed in the field.

117

In each case the speaker could continue creating sentences by adding an adjective, or a noun connected by *and,* or a relative clause. In principle this could go on forever. All languages have mechanisms such as these — modification, coordination, and clause insertion — that make the number of sentences limitless. Obviously, the sentences of a language cannot be stored in a dictionary format in our heads. Sentences are composed of discrete units that are combined by rules. This system of rules explains how speakers can store infinite knowledge in a finite space — our brains.

The part of the grammar that represents a speaker's knowledge of sentences and their structures is called **syntax.** The aim of this chapter is to show you what syntactic structure is and what the rules that determine syntactic structure are like. Most of the examples will be from the syntax of English, but the principles that account for syntactic structures are universal.

Part of what we mean by *structure* is word order. As suggested by the "Shoe" cartoon, the meaning of a sentence depends largely on the order in which words occur in a sentence. Thus,

She has what a man wants

does not have the same meaning as

She wants what a man has.

Sometimes, however, a change of word order has no effect on meaning.

The Chief Justice swore in the new President.
The Chief Justice swore the new President in.

The grammars of all languages include **rules of syntax** that reflect speakers' knowledge of these facts.

Grammatical or Ungrammatical?

Although the following sequence consists of meaningful words, the entire expression is without meaning because it does not comply with the syntactic rules of the grammar.

Chief swore president the Justice the in new

In English and in every language, every sentence is a sequence of words, but not every sequence of words is a sentence. Sequences of words that conform to the rules of syntax are **well formed** or **grammatical,** and those that violate the syntactic rules are **ill formed** or **ungrammatical.**

What Grammaticality Is Based On

In chapter 1 you were asked to indicate strings of words as grammatical or ungrammatical according to your linguistic intuitions. Here is another list of word sequences. Disregarding the sentence meanings, use *your* knowledge of English and place an asterisk in front of the ones that strike you as peculiar or funny in some way.

1. (a) The boy found the ball
   (b) The boy found quickly
   (c) The boy found in the house
   (d) The boy found the ball in the house
2. (e) Disa slept the baby
   (f) Disa slept soundly
3. (g) Zack believes Robert to be a gentleman
   (h) Zack believes to be a gentleman
   (i) Zack tries Robert to be a gentleman
   (j) Zack tries to be a gentleman
   (k) Zack wants to be a gentleman
   (l) Zack wants Robert to be a gentleman
4. (m) Jack and Jill ran up the hill
   (n) Jack and Jill ran up the bill
   (o) Jack and Jill ran the hill up
   (p) Jack and Jill ran the bill up
   (q) Up the hill ran Jack and Jill
   (r) Up the bill ran Jack and Jill

We predict that speakers of English will "star" (b), (c), (e), (h), (i), (o), and (r). If we are right, this shows that grammaticality judgments are neither idiosyncratic nor capricious, but are determined by rules that are shared by the speakers of a language.

The syntactic rules that account for the ability to make these judgments include other constraints in addition to rules of word order. For example:

- The rules specify that *found* must be followed directly by an expression like *the ball* but not by *quickly* or *in the house* as illustrated in (a) through (d).
- The verb *sleep* patterns differently than *find* in that it may be followed solely by a word like *soundly* but not by other kinds of phrases such as *the baby* as shown in (e) and (f).
- Examples (g) through (l) show that *believe* and *try* function in opposite fashion while *want* exhibits yet a third pattern.
- Finally, the word order rules that constrain phrases such as *run up the hill* differ from those concerning *run up the bill* as seen in (m) through (r).

Sentences are not random strings of words. Some strings of words that we can interpret are not sentences. For example, we can understand example (o) even though we recognize it as ungrammatical. We can fix it up to make it grammatical. To be a sentence, words must conform to specific patterns determined by the syntactic rules of the language.

What Grammaticality Is Not Based On

Colorless green ideas sleep furiously. This is a very interesting sentence, because it shows that syntax can be separated from semantics — that form can be separated from meaning. The sentence doesn't seem to mean anything coherent, but it sounds like an English sentence.

Howard Lasnik, *The Human Language: Program One*

The ability to make grammaticality judgments does not depend on having heard the sentence before. You may never have heard or read the sentence

Enormous crickets in pink socks danced at the prom

but your syntactic knowledge tells you that it is grammatical.

Grammaticality judgments do not depend on whether the sentence is meaningful or not, as shown by the following sentences:

Colorless green ideas sleep furiously.
A verb crumpled the milk.

Although these sentences do not make much sense, they are syntactically well formed. They sound "funny," but they differ in their "funniness" from the following strings of words:

*Furiously sleep ideas green colorless.
*Milk the crumpled verb a.

You may understand ungrammatical sequences even though you know they are not well formed. Most English speakers could interpret

*The boy quickly in the house the ball found

although they know that the word order is irregular. On the other hand, grammatical sentences may be uninterpretable if they include nonsense strings, that is, words with no agreed-on meaning, as shown by the first two lines of "Jabberwocky" by Lewis Carroll:

'Twas brillig, and the slithy toves
Did gyre and gimble in the wabe;

Such nonsense poetry is amusing because the sentences comply with syntactic rules and sound like good English. Ungrammatical strings of nonsense words are not entertaining:

*Toves slithy the and brillig 'twas
wabe the in gimble and gyre did.

Grammaticality does not depend on the truth of sentences. If it did, lying would be impossible. Nor does it depend on whether real objects are being discussed, nor on whether something is possible. Untrue sentences can be grammatical, sentences discussing unicorns can be grammatical, and sentences referring to pregnant fathers can be grammatical.

Our unconscious knowledge of the syntactic rules of grammar permits us to make grammaticality judgments. These rules are not the prescriptive rules that are taught in school. Children develop the rules of grammar long before they attend school, as is discussed in chapter 8.

What Else Do You Know about Syntax?

Syntactic knowledge goes beyond being able to decide which strings are grammatical and which are not. It accounts for the multiple meanings, or **ambiguity,** of expressions like the one illustrated in the cartoon on page 122. The humor of the cartoon depends on the ambiguity of the phrase *synthetic buffalo hides,* which can mean "buffalo hides that are synthetic," or "hides of synthetic buffalo."

This example illustrates that within a phrase, certain words are grouped together. Sentences have **hierarchical structure** as well as word order. The words in the phrase *synthetic buffalo hides* can be grouped in two ways. When we group like this:

synthetic (buffalo hides)

we get the first meaning. When we group like this:

(synthetic buffalo) hides

we get the second meaning.

"Tumbleweeds" copyright © United Feature Syndicate, Inc. Reprinted with special permission of North America Syndicate.

The rules of syntax allow both these groupings, which is why the expression is ambiguous. The following diagrams illustrate the two structures:

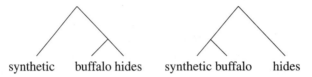

synthetic   buffalo hides   synthetic buffalo   hides

This is similar to the rules of morphology that allow multiple structures for words such as *unlockable,* as we saw in chapter 3.

Many sentences exhibit such ambiguities, often leading to humorous results. Consider the following two sentences, which appeared in classified ads:

For sale: an antique desk suitable for lady with thick legs and large drawers.

We will oil your sewing machine and adjust tension in your home for $10.00.

In the first ad, the humorous reading comes from the grouping . . . (*for lady with thick legs and large drawers*) as opposed to the intended . . . (*for lady*) (*with thick legs and large drawers*) where the legs and drawers belong to the desk. The second case is similar.

Because these ambiguities are a result of different structures, they are instances of **structural ambiguity.**

Contrast these sentences with

This will make you smart.

The two interpretations of this sentence are due to the two meanings of *smart* — "clever" or "burning sensation." Such lexical or word-meaning ambiguities, as opposed to structural ambiguities, will be discussed in chapter 5.

Syntactic knowledge also enables us to determine the **grammatical relations** in a sentence, such as **subject** and **direct object,** and how they are to be understood. Consider the following sentences:

   1. Mary hired Bill.
   2. Bill hired Mary.
   3. Bill was hired by Mary.

In (1) *Mary* is the subject and is understood to be the employer that did the hiring. *Bill* is the direct object and is understood to be the employee. In (2) *Bill* is the subject and *Mary* is the direct object, and as we would expect, the meaning changes so that we understand Bill to be Mary's employer. In (3) the grammatical relationships are the same as in (2), but we understand it to have the same meaning as (1), despite the structural differences between (1) and (3).

Syntactic rules reveal the grammatical relations among the words of a sentence and tell us when structural differences result in meaning differences and when they do not. Moreover, the syntactic rules permit speakers to produce and understand a limitless number of sentences never produced or heard before—the creative aspect of language use.

Thus, the syntactic rules in a grammar account for at least:

   1. The grammaticality of sentences
   2. Word order
   3. Hierarchical organization of sentences
   4. Grammatical relations such as subject and object
   5. Whether different structures have differing meanings or the same meaning
   6. The creative aspect of language

A major goal of linguistics is to show clearly and explicitly how syntactic rules account for this knowledge. A theory of grammar must provide a complete characterization of what speakers implicitly know about their language.

Sentence Structure

I really do not know that anything has ever been more exciting than diagramming sentences.

Gertrude Stein

Syntactic rules determine the order of words in a sentence, and how the words are grouped. The words in the sentence

The child found the puppy

may be grouped into (*the child*) and (*found the puppy*), corresponding to the subject and predicate of the sentence. A further division gives (*the child*) ((*found*)(*the puppy*)), and finally the individual words: ((*the*)(*child*)) ((*found*)((*the*) (*puppy*))). It is easier to see the parts and subparts of the sentence in a **tree diagram:**

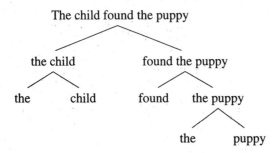

The "tree" is upside down with its "root" being the entire sentence, *The child found the puppy,* and its "leaves" being the individual words, *the, child, found, the, puppy.* The tree conveys the same information as the nested parentheses, but more clearly. The groupings and subgroupings reflect the hierarchical structure of the tree.

The tree diagram shows among other things that the phrase *found the puppy* divides naturally into two branches, one for the verb *found* and the other for the direct object *the puppy.* A different division, say *found the* and *puppy,* is unnatural.

The natural groupings of a sentence are called **constituents.** Various linguistic tests reveal the constituents of a sentence. For example, the set of words that can be used to answer a question is a constituent. So in answer to the question "what did you find?" a speaker might answer, *the puppy,* but not *found the.*

Pronouns can also substitute for natural groups. In answer to the question "where did you find the puppy?" a speaker can say, "I found *him* in the park." There are also words such as *do* that can take the place of the entire expression *found the puppy,* as in "John found the puppy and so *did* Bill," or "John found the puppy and Bill *did* too."

Constituents can also be "relocated" as in the following examples.

It was *the puppy* the child found
The puppy was found by the child

In the first example the constituent *the puppy* is relocated; in the second example both *the puppy* and *the child* are relocated. In all such rearrangements the constituents *the puppy* and *the child* remain intact. *Found the* does not remain intact, because it is not a constituent.

In the sentence *the child found the puppy,* the natural groupings or constituents are the subject *the child,* the predicate *found the puppy,* and the direct object *the puppy.*

Some verbs take a direct object and a prepositional phrase.

The child put the puppy in the garden.

We can use our tests to show that *in the garden* is also a constituent, as follows:

1. Where did the child put the puppy?   *In the garden.*
2. The child put the puppy *there.*
3. *In the garden* is where the child put the puppy.
4. It was *in the garden* that the child put the puppy.

In (1) *in the garden* is an answer to a question. In (2) the word *there* can substitute for the phrase *in the garden*. In (3) and (4) *in the garden* has been relocated.

Our knowledge of the **constituent structure** may be graphically represented as a tree structure. The tree structure for the sentence *The child put the puppy in the garden* is as follows:

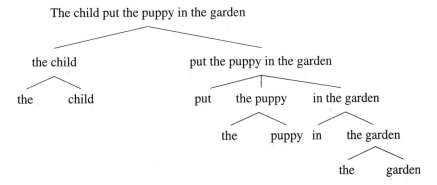

Every sentence in a language is associated with one or more constituent structures. If a sentence has more than one constituent structure, it is ambiguous, and each tree will correspond to one of the possible meanings. Multiple tree structures can account for structural ambiguity, as in the following examples:

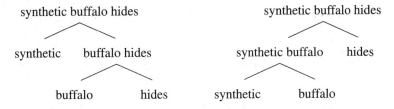

Syntactic Categories

Each grouping in the tree diagram of *The child put the puppy in the garden* is a member of a large family of similar expressions. For example, *the child* belongs to a family that includes *the police officer, your neighbor, this yellow cat, he,* and countless others. We can substitute any member of this family for *the child* without affecting the grammaticality of the sentence, although the meaning of course would change.

A police officer found the puppy in the garden.
Your neighbor found the puppy in the garden.
This yellow cat found the puppy in the garden.

A family of expressions that can substitute for one another without loss of grammaticality is called a **syntactic category.**

The child, a police officer, and so on belong to the syntactic category **Noun Phrase (NP),** one of several syntactic categories in English and every other language in the world. NPs may function as the subject or as an object in a sentence. They often

" I MISS THE GOOD OLD DAYS WHEN ALL
WE HAD TO WORRY ABOUT WAS NOUNS AND VERBS."

Copyright © S. Harris.

contain some form of a noun or proper noun, but may consist of a pronoun alone, or even contain a clause or a sentence.

Even though a proper noun like *John* and pronouns such as *he* and *him* are single words, they are technically NPs, because they pattern like NPs in being able to fill a subject or object or other NP slot.

John found the puppy.
He found the puppy.
The puppy loved him.
The puppy loved John.

NPs that are more complex are illustrated by:

Romeo who was a Montague loved *Juliet who was a Capulet.*

The NP subject of this sentence is *Romeo who was a Montague* and the NP object is *Juliet who was a Capulet.*

Part of the syntactic component of a grammar is the specification of the syntactic categories in the language, since this constitutes part of a speaker's knowledge. That is, speakers of English know that only items (a), (b), (e), (f), (g), and (i) in the following list are Noun Phrases even if they have never heard the term before.

1. (a) a bird
   (b) the red banjo
   (c) have a nice day
   (d) with a balloon

(e) the woman who was laughing

(f) it

(g) John

(h) went

(i) that the earth is round

As we discussed earlier, you can test this claim by inserting each expression into three contexts: "Who discovered _____ ?", "_____ was heard by everyone," and "What I heard was _____." Only those sentences into which NPs can be inserted are grammatical, because only NPs can function as subjects and objects.

There are other syntactic categories. The expression *found the puppy* is a **Verb Phrase (VP).** Verb Phrases always contain a **Verb (V)** and they may contain other categories, such as a Noun Phrase or **Prepositional Phrase (PP),** which is a preposition followed by a Noun Phrase. In (2) the VPs are those phrases that can complete the sentence "The child _____ ."

2. (a) saw a clown

   (b) a bird

   (c) slept

   (d) smart

   (e) is smart

   (f) found the cake

   (g) found the cake in the cupboard

   (h) realized that the earth was round

Inserting (a), (c), (e), (f), (g), and (h) will produce grammatical sentences, whereas the insertion of (b) or (d) would result in an ungrammatical string. Thus, in list 2 (a), (c), (e), (f), (g), and (h) are Verb Phrases.

Other syntactic categories are **Sentence (S), Adjective Phrase (AP), Determiner (Det), Adjective (Adj), Noun (N), Preposition (P), Adverb (Adv),** and **Auxiliary Verb (Aux),** but this is not a complete list. Some of these syntactic categories have traditionally been called "parts of speech." All languages have such syntactic categories. In fact, categories such as Noun, Verb, and Noun Phrase are present in the grammars of all human languages. Speakers know the syntactic categories of their language, even if they do not know the technical terms. Our knowledge of the syntactic classes is revealed when we substitute equivalent phrases, as we just did in examples (1) and (2), and when we use the various syntactic tests just discussed.

In addition to syntactic tests, there is experimental evidence for constituent structure. In these experiments subjects listen to sentences that have clicking noises inserted into them at random points. In some cases the click occurs at a constituent boundary, for example, between the subject NP and the VP. In other sentences, the click is inserted in the middle of a constituent, for example, between a determiner and an NP. The subjects are then asked to report where the click occurred. There were two important results: First, subjects noticed the click and recalled its location best when it occurred at a constituent boundary. Second, clicks that occurred inside the constituent were reported to have occurred between constituents. In other words, subjects displaced the clicks and put them at constituent boundaries. These results show that speakers perceive sentences in chunks corresponding to grammatical constituents. This argues for the psychological reality of constituent structure.[1]

Phrase Structure Trees

Who climbs the Grammar-Tree distinctly knows
Where Noun and Verb and Participle grows.

John Dryden, "The Sixth Satyr of Juvenal"

The following tree diagram provides labels for each of the constituents of the sentence *The child put the puppy in the garden.* These labels show that the entire sentence belongs to the syntactic category of Sentence, that *the child* and *the puppy* are Noun Phrases, that *put the puppy* is a Verb Phrase, that *in the garden* is a Prepositional Phrase, and so on.

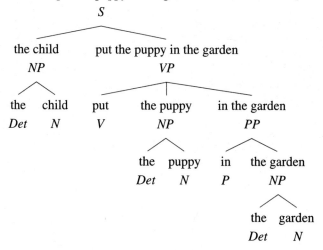

A tree diagram with syntactic category information is called **a phrase structure tree,** sometimes called a **constituent structure tree.** This tree shows that a sentence is both a linear string of words and a hierarchical structure with phrases nested in phrases. Phrase structure trees are graphic representations of a speaker's knowledge of the sentence structure in their language.

Three aspects of a speaker's syntactic knowledge are represented in phrase structure trees:

1. the linear order of the words in the sentence,
2. the groupings of words into syntactic categories,

---

[1] J. Fodor and T. Bever. 1965. "The Psychological Reality of Linguistic Segments," *Journal of Verbal Learning and Verbal Behavior* 4:414–20.

3. the hierarchical structure of the syntactic categories (e.g., a Sentence is composed of a Noun Phrase followed by a Verb Phrase, a Verb Phrase is composed of a Verb that may be followed by a Noun Phrase, and so on).

A phrase structure tree that explicitly reveals these properties can represent every sentence of English and of every human language. Notice, however, that the phrase structure tree above is correct, but redundant. The word *child* is repeated three times in the tree, *puppy* is repeated three times, and so on. We can streamline the tree by writing the words only once at the bottom of the diagram. Only the syntactic categories to which the words belong need to remain at the higher levels.

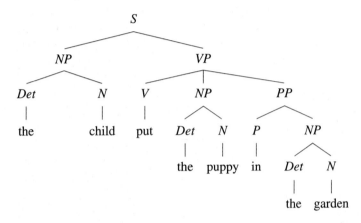

No information is lost in this simplified version. The syntactic category of each word appears immediately above it. In this way, *the* is shown to be a Determiner,[2] *child* a Noun, and so on. In chapter 3 we discussed the fact that the syntactic category of each word is listed in our mental dictionaries. We now see how this information is used by the syntax of the language. Words occur in trees under labels that correspond to their syntactic category. Nouns are under N, prepositions under P, and so on.

We have not given definitions of these syntactic categories. Traditional definitions usually refer to meaning and are either imprecise or wrong. For example, a noun is often defined as "a person, place, or thing." However, in the sentence *Seeing is believing, seeing* and *believing* are nouns but are neither persons, nor places, nor things. Syntactic categories are better defined in terms of the syntactic rules of the grammar. For example, defining a noun as "the head of an NP," or "a grammatical unit that occurs with a determiner," or "can be relocated in passive sentences" are more accurate characterizations.

The larger syntactic categories, such as Verb Phrase, are identified as consisting of all the syntactic categories and words below that point, or **node,** in the tree. The VP in the above phrase structure tree consists of syntactic category nodes V and NP, PP, and the words *put, the, puppy, in, the,* and *garden.* Since *the puppy* can be traced up the tree to the node NP, this constituent is a Noun Phrase. Since *in the garden* can be traced up

---

[2] The category Determiner includes the Articles *the* and *a* as well as a number of expressions such as *these, every, five, my, your cousin Mabel's,* and so forth.

the tree to a PP, this constituent is a Prepositional Phrase. The phrase structure tree reflects the speaker's intuitions about the natural groupings of words in sentence.

The phrase structure tree also states implicitly what combinations of words are not syntactic categories. For example, since there is no node above the words *put* and *the* to connect them, the two words do not constitute a syntactic category, reflecting our earlier judgments.

The phrase structure tree also shows that some syntactic categories are composed of other syntactic categories. The Sentence *The child put the puppy in the garden* consists of a Noun Phrase, *the child* and a Verb Phrase, *put the puppy in the garden.* The Verb Phrase consists of the Verb *put,* the Noun Phrase *the puppy,* and the Prepositional Phrase *in the garden.* Together, the Determiner *the* and the Noun *puppy* constitute a Noun Phrase, but individually neither is an NP. The Prepositional Phrase contains a Preposition *in* and the NP *the garden.* Every higher node is said to **dominate** all the categories beneath it. VP dominates V, NP, and PP, and also dominates Det, N, P, and PP. A node is said to **immediately dominate** the categories one level below it. VP immediately dominates V, NP, and PP. Categories that are immediately dominated by the same node are **sisters.** V, NP, and PP are sisters in the sentence *the child put the puppy in the garden.*

Heads and Complements

Phrase structure trees also show relationships among elements in a sentence. One kind of relationship is the relationship between the **head** of a phrase and the other members of the phrase. We said earlier that every VP contains a verb. The verb is the head of the VP. The VP may also contain other categories, such as a Noun Phrase or Prepositional Phrase. Loosely speaking, the entire phrase refers to whatever the head verb refers to. For example, the verb phrase *put the puppy in the garden* refers to event of "putting." The other constituents contained in the VP that complete its meaning are called **complements.** The direct object *the puppy* is a complement, as is the PP *in the garden.* A sentence can also be a complement to a verb, as in the sentence *I thought that the child found the puppy.*

Every phrasal category has a head of its same syntactic type. NPs are headed by nouns, PPs are headed by prepositions, Adjective Phrases (APs) are headed by adjectives, and so on; and every category can have complements. In the sentence *The man with the telescope smiled at me,* the PP *with the telescope* is the complement to the head noun *man.* Other examples of NP complements are shown in the following examples:

> The destruction of Rome
> A picture of Mary
> A person worthy of praise
> A boy who pitched a perfect game

Each of these examples is an NP containing a head noun followed by a PP (*of Rome, of Mary*), an AP (*worthy of praise*), or a sentence complement (*who pitched a perfect game*). The head-complement relation is universal. All languages have phrases that are headed and that contain complements.

However, the order of the two constituents may differ in different languages. In English, for example, we see that the head comes first, followed by the complement. English is an SVO (Subject-Verb-Object) language; the verb precedes its object in the VP. In the preceding examples, the noun *picture* precedes its PP complement *of Mary, destruction* comes before *of Rome, boy* before *who pitched a perfect game,* and the head noun *person* precedes its AP complement *worthy of praise.* In Japanese, on the other hand, complements precede the head, as shown in the following examples:

Taro-ga	inu-o	mituketa		
Taro	dog	found		(Taro found a dog)
Taro-ga	inu-o	isu-ni	oita	
Taro	dog	chair	put	(Taro put the dog on the chair)
Piza-o	tabeta	otoko		
Pizza	ate	man		(the man who ate pizza)

In the first sentence, the direct object *dog* precedes the verb *found.* In the second, both objects *dog* and *chair* precede the verb, while in the third the relative clause *piza-o tabeta,* "pizza eating," precedes the head noun *otoko,* "man," that it modifies.

SELECTION

Whether a verb takes one or more complements depends on the properties of the verb. For example, the verb *find* is a **transitive verb.** A transitive verb requires a Noun Phrase direct object complement. This additional specification, called **selection,** is included in the lexical entry of each word.

> The boy found the ball.
> *The boy found quickly.
> *The boy found in the house.

The examples where *found* does not have a direct object are not grammatical. Verbs select different kinds of complements, and the complements they select must be present. The verb *put* occurs with both an NP and a PP, and cannot occur with either alone:

Sam put the milk in the refrigerator.
*Sam put the milk.
*Disa put in the refrigerator.

Sleep is an **intransitive verb;** it cannot take an NP complement. Thus, if a verb fails to select a complement, it must not be present.

Michael slept.
*Michael slept a fish.

Some verbs such as *think* select a sentence as complement. Other verbs such as *tell* select an NP and an S, while *feel* selects an AP or an S:

I think that Sam won the race.
I told Sam that Michael was on his bicycle.
They felt strong as oxen.
They feel that they can win.
*They feel

Other categories besides verbs also select their complements. For example, the noun *belief* selects either a PP or an S, as shown by the following two examples:

the belief in freedom of speech
the belief that freedom of speech is a basic right

The noun *sympathy,* however, selects a PP, but not an S:

their sympathy for the victims
*their sympathy that the victims are so poor

The adjective *tired* selects a PP:

tired of stale sandwiches

Some selectional properties are optional. For example, the nouns *belief* and *sympathy* can also appear without complements, as can the adjective *tired:*

John has many beliefs.
The people showed their sympathy.
The students were tired.

In addition, many verbs such as *eat* are optionally transitive:

John ate a sandwich
John eats regularly.

The information about whether a complement is optional or obligatory is contained in the lexical entry of particular words.

The well-formedness of a phrase depends on at least two factors: whether the phrase conforms to the phrase structure requirements of the language, and whether the phrase conforms to the selectional requirements of the head.

WHAT HEADS THE SENTENCE?

We said earlier that all phrases have heads. One category that we have not yet discussed in this regard is Sentence (S). For uniformity's sake, we want all the categories to be headed, but what would the head of S be? To answer this question, let us consider sentences such as the following:

Sam will kick the ball.
Sam has kicked the ball.
Sam is kicking the ball.
Sam may kick the ball.

Words like *will, have, is,* and *may* are in a class of Auxiliary Verbs (Aux), which includes *might, would, could, can,* and several others. The auxiliaries other than *be* and *have* are also referred to as **modals.** Auxiliaries are function words, as discussed in chapter 3. They occur in structures such as the following:

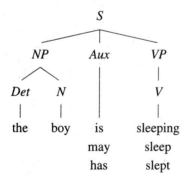

Auxiliary verbs specify a time frame for the sentence, whether the situation described by the sentence will take place, already took place, or is taking place now. A modal such as *may* contains "possibility" as part of its meaning, and says it is possible that the situation will occur at some future time. The category Aux is a natural category to head S. Just as the VP is about the event described by the verb — *eat ice cream* is about "eating" — so a sentence is about a situation or state of affairs that occurs at some point in time.

To better express the idea that Aux is the head of S, the symbols **INFL (=Inflection)** and **IP (=Inflection Phrase)** are often used instead of Aux and S, as in the following phrase structure tree:

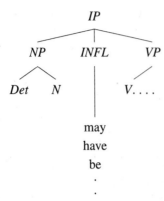

We will continue to use the symbols S and Aux, but you should think of Aux and S as having the same relationship to each other as V and VP, N and NP, and so on.

Not all sentences have auxiliaries. For example, the sentence *Sam kicked the ball* has no modal, *have* or *be*. There is, however, a time reference for this sentence, namely, the past tense on the verb *kicked*. In sentences without auxiliaries, the tense of the sentence is its head. Instead of having a function word under the category Aux (or INFL), we have a tense specification, *present* or *past,* as in the following tree. The verb in the VP must agree with the tense in Aux. For example, if the tense of the sentence is *past* then the verb must have an *-ed* affix (or must be an irregular past tense verb such as *ate*).

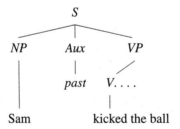

A property of English and many languages is that the head of S may contain only an abstract tense specification and no actual word as is the case for English past tense. But for English future tense, the word *will* occurs as the Aux. The word *do* is a tense-bearing word that is found in negative sentences such as *John did not go* and questions such as *Where did John go?* In these sentences *did* means "past tense."

In addition to specifying the time reference of the sentence, Aux specifies the agreement features of the subject. For example, if the subject is "we," Aux contains the features first-person plural; if the subject is "he" or "she," Aux contains the features third-person singular. Thus, another function of the syntactic rules is to use Aux as a "matchmaker" between the subject and the verb. When the subject and the verb bear the same features, Aux makes a match; when they have incompatible features, Aux cannot make a match and the sentence is ungrammatical. This matchmaker function of syntactic rules is more obvious in languages such as Italian, which have many different agreement morphemes, as discussed in chapter 3. Consider the Italian sentence for "I go to school."

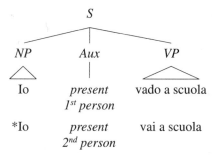

The verb *vado,* "go," in the first sentence bears the first-person singular morpheme, *-o,* which matches the agreement feature in Aux, which in turn matches the subject *Io,* "I." Hence, the sentence is grammatical. In the second sentence, there is a mismatch between the first-person subject and the second-person features in Aux (and on the verb), and so the sentence is ungrammatical.

The Infinity of Language

So, naturalists observe, a flea
Hath smaller fleas that on him prey;
And these have smaller fleas still to bite 'em,
And so proceed ad infinitum.

Jonathan Swift, "On Poetry, A Rhapsody"

As we noted earlier, the number of sentences in a language is infinite, because speakers can lengthen any sentence by various means, such as adding an adjective or, as in the

"Cathy" cartoon, including sentences within sentences. Even children know how to produce and understand very long sentences, and know how to make them even longer, as illustrated by the children's rhyme about the house that Jack built.

> This is the farmer sowing the corn,
> that kept the cock that crowed in the morn,
> that waked the priest all shaven and shorn,
> that married the man all tattered and torn,
> that kissed the maiden all forlorn,
> that milked the cow with the crumpled horn,
> that tossed the dog,
> that worried the cat,
> that killed the rat,
> that ate the malt,
> that lay in the house that Jack built.

The child begins the rhyme with *This is the house that Jack built,* continues by lengthening it to *This is the malt that lay in the house that Jack built,* and so on.

You can add any of the following to the beginning of the rhyme and still have a grammatical sentence:

> I think that . . .
> What is the name of the unicorn that noticed that . . .
> Ask someone if . . .
> Do you know whether . . .

Phrase structure trees also capture this limitless aspect of language. An NP may appear immediately under a PP, which may occur immediately under a higher NP, as in *the man with the telescope:*

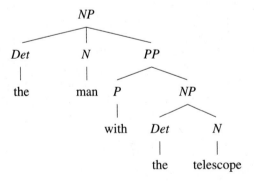

The complex (but comprehensible) Noun Phrase *the girl with the feather on the ribbon on the brim,* as shown in the following phrase structure tree, illustrates that one can repeat the number of NPs under PPs under NPs without a limit.

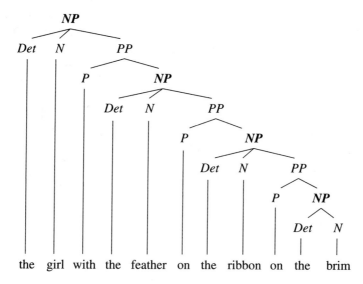

the girl with the feather on the ribbon on the brim

The NP diagrammed above, though cumbersome, violates no rules of syntax and is a grammatical Noun Phrase. Moreover, it can be made even longer by expanding the final NP — *the brim* — by adding a PP — *of her hat* — to derive the longer phrase — *the girl with the feather on the ribbon on the brim of her hat.*

The repetition of categories within categories is common in all languages. It allows speakers to use the same syntactic categories several times, with different functions, in the same sentence. Our brain capacity is finite, able to store only a finite number of categories and rules for their combination. Yet, these finite means place an infinite set of sentences at our disposal.

This linguistic property also illustrates the difference between competence and performance discussed in chapter 1. All speakers of English have as part of their linguistic competence — their mental grammars — the ability to put NPs in PPs in NPs ad infinitum. However, as the structures grow longer they become increasingly more difficult to produce and understand. This could be due to short-term memory limitations, muscular fatigue, breathlessness, or any number of performance factors. (We will discuss performance factors more fully in chapter 9.)

Thus, while such rules give a speaker access to infinitely many sentences, no speaker utters or hears an infinite number in a lifetime; nor is any sentence of infinite length, although in principle there is no upper limit on sentence length. This property of grammars also accounts for the creative aspect of language use, since it permits speakers to produce and understand sentences never spoken before.

Phrase Structure Rules

Everyone who is master of the language he speaks . . . may form new . . . phrases, provided they coincide with the genius of the language.

Michaelis, *Dissertation* (1769)

A phrase structure tree is a formal device for representing the knowledge that a speaker has of the structure of sentences in his language. When we speak, we are not aware that we are producing sentences with such structures, but controlled experiments show that we use them in speech production and comprehension, as we will see in chapter 9.

When we look at phrase structure trees that represent the sentences of English, certain patterns emerge. In ordinary sentences, the S always subdivides into NP Aux VP. As we said earlier, NPs always contain Nouns; VPs always contain Verbs; PPs consist of a Preposition followed by a Noun Phrase; and APs consist of an Adjective possibly followed by a complement.

Of all logically possible tree structures, few actually occur, just as not all word combinations constitute grammatical phrases or sentences. For example, a non-occurring tree structure in English is:

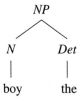

The speaker of a language knows whether any sentence or phrase is a possible or impossible structure in her language. The structure given in the preceding tree is not possible in English.

Just as a speaker cannot have an infinite list of sentences in her head, so she cannot have an infinite set of phrase structure trees in her head. Rather, a speaker's knowledge of the permissible and impermissible structures must exist as a finite set of rules that "generate," or provide a tree for, any sentence in the language. These are **phrase structure rules.** Phrase structure rules specify the structures of a language precisely and concisely. They express the regularities of the language, such as the head complement order, and other relationships.

For example, in English a Noun Phrase may simply contain a Determiner followed by a Noun. One of the several allowable NP subtrees looks like this:

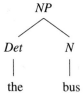

The phrase structure rule that makes this explicit is:

NP → Det N

This rule conveys two facts:

A Noun Phrase can contain a Determiner followed by a Noun.
A Determiner followed by a Noun is a Noun Phrase.

To the left of the arrow is the category whose components appear on the right side. The right side of the arrow also shows the linear order of these components. Phrase structure rules make explicit speakers' knowledge of the order of words and the grouping of words into syntactic categories.

An NP may also contain a complement, as in the example *a picture of Mary* or *the destruction of Rome*. We can accommodate this fact by revising the rule to include an optional Prepositional Phrase. The parentheses around the PP indicate that it is optional. Not all NPs in the language have PPs inside them.

NP → Det N (PP)

This revised rule says that an NP can contain a Det followed by a Noun followed by an optional PP.

The phrase structure trees of the previous section show that the following phrase structure rules are also part of the grammar of English.

1. VP → V NP
2. VP → V NP PP

Rule 1 states that a Verb Phrase can consist of a Verb followed by a Noun Phrase. Rule 2 states that a Verb Phrase can also consist of a Verb followed by a Noun Phrase followed by a Prepositional Phrase. These rules are general statements, which do not refer to any specific Verb Phrase, Verb, Noun Phrase, or Prepositional Phrase.

Rules 1 and 2 can be summed up in one statement: A Verb Phrase may be a Verb followed by a Noun Phrase, which may or may not be followed by a Prepositional Phrase. By putting parentheses around the optional element, we can abbreviate rules 1 and 2 to a single rule:

VP → V NP (PP)

In fact, the NP is also optional, as shown in the following trees:

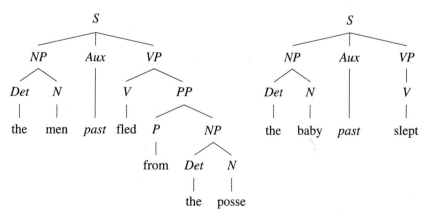

In the first case we have a Verb Phrase consisting of a Verb plus a Prepositional Phrase, corresponding to the rule VP → V PP. In the second case, the Verb Phrase consists of a Verb alone, corresponding to the rule VP → V. All the facts about the Verb Phrase we have seen so far are explicit in the single rule:

VP → V (NP) (PP)

This rule states that a Verb Phrase may consist of a Verb followed optionally by a Noun Phrase and/or a Prepositional Phrase.

Other rules of English are:

S → NP Aux VP
PP → P NP
AP → Adj (PP)

Growing Trees: The Relationship between Phrase Structure Rules and Phrase Structure Trees

I think that I shall never see
A poem lovely as a tree

Joyce Kilmer, "Trees"

Phrase structure trees may not be as lovely to look at as the trees Kilmer was thinking of, but if a poem is written in grammatical English, its phrases and sentences can be represented by trees, and those trees can be specified by phrase structure rules.

The rules that we have discussed, repeated here, define some of the phrase structure trees of English.

S → NP Aux VP
NP → Det N (PP)
VP → V (NP) (PP)
PP → P NP
AP → Adj (PP)

There are several possible ways to view phrase structure rules. We can regard them as tests that trees must pass to be grammatical. Each syntactic category mentioned in the tree is examined to see if the syntactic categories immediately beneath it agree with the phrase structure rules. If we were examining an NP in a tree, it would pass the test if the categories beneath it were Det N, or Det N PP, in that order, and fail the test otherwise, insofar as our (incomplete) set of phrase structure rules is concerned. (In a more comprehensive grammar of English, the NP rule would include many more structures, as would other rules.)

We may also view the rules as a way to construct phrase structure trees that conform to the syntactic structures of the language. This is by no means suggestive of how speakers actually produce sentences. It is just another way of representing their knowledge, and it applies equally to speakers and listeners.

In generating or specifying trees, certain conventions are followed. The S occurs at the top of the tree despite being called "the root." Another convention specifies how the rules are applied: First, find a rule with an S on the left side of the arrow, and put the categories on the right side below the S, as shown here:

Once started, continue by matching any syntactic category at the bottom of the partially constructed tree to a category on the left side of a rule, then expand the tree with the categories on the right side. For example we may expand the tree by applying the NP rule to produce:

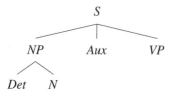

The categories at the bottom are Det, N, and VP, but only VP occurs to the left of an arrow in the set of rules and so needs to be expanded. The VP rule is actually four rules abbreviated by parentheses. They are:

VP → V
VP → V NP
VP → V PP
VP → V NP PP

Any of them may apply next; the order in which the rules appear in the grammar is irrelevant. (Indeed, we might equally have begun by expanding the VP rather than the NP.) Suppose VP → V PP is next. Then the tree has grown to look like this:

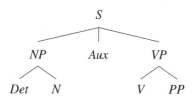

Convention dictates that we continue in this way until none of the categories at the bottom of the tree appears on the left side of any rule. The PP must expand into a P and an NP, and the NP into a Det and an N. We can use a rule as many times as it can apply. In this tree, we used the NP rule twice. After we have applied all the rules that can apply, the tree looks like this:

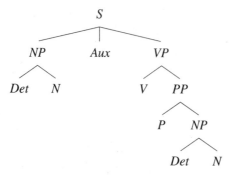

By following these conventions, we can generate only trees specified by the phrase structure rules. By implication, any tree not so specified will be ungrammatical. Whether we choose to use the rules to generate only well-formed trees or use the rules to test the grammaticality of all possible trees is immaterial. Both methods achieve the goal of revealing syntactic knowledge. Most books on language use the rules to generate trees.

Categories such as NP, VP, AP, IP (= S) are **phrasal categories.** The categories N, V, P, Adj, and Adv are **lexical categories.** The categories such as Det and Aux that house function words are **functional categories.** Phrase structure trees always have lexical and functional categories at the bottom since the rules must apply until no phrasal categories remain. The lexical and functional categories are "the parts of speech" in a traditional "grammar" book. You may know some of them by other names. Members of Aux are sometimes called "helping verbs." Members of Det may be called "articles," "demonstrative pronouns," and so on.

The previous tree structure corresponds to a very large number of sentences because there are numerous combinations of nouns, verbs, prepositions, and so on that conform to this structure. Here are just a few:

The boat sailed up the river.
A girl laughed at the monkey.
The sheepdog rolled in the mud.
The lions roared in the jungle.

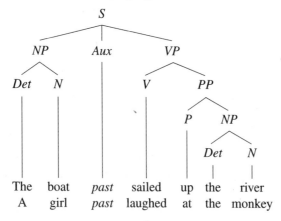

At any point during the construction of a tree, any rule may be used as long as its left-side category occurs somewhere at the bottom of the tree. At the point where we chose the rule VP → V PP, we could equally well have chosen VP → V or VP → V NP PP. This would have resulted in different structures corresponding to sentences such as:

The boys left. (VP → V)
The wind swept the kite into the sky. (VP → V NP PP)

Since there is an infinite number of possible sentences in every language, there are limitless numbers of trees, but only a finite set of phrase structure rules that specify the trees allowed by a grammar of the language.

Structural Ambiguities

The structure of every sentence is a lesson in logic.

John Stuart Mill, *Inaugural address at St. Andres*

As mentioned earlier, certain ambiguous sentences have more than one phrase structure tree, each corresponding to a different meaning. The sentence *The boy saw the man with the telescope* is ambiguous. Its two meanings correspond to the following two phrase structure trees.

(1)

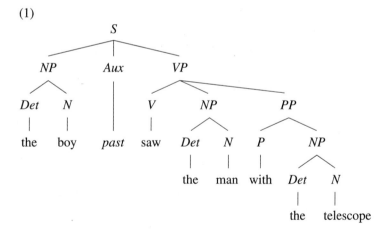

(2)

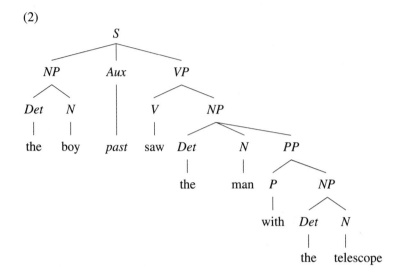

One meaning of this sentence is "the boy used a telescope to see the man." The first phrase structure tree represents this meaning. The key element is the position of the PP directly under the VP. Although the PP is under VP, it is not a complement because it is not selected by the verb. The verb *see* selects an NP only. In this sentence, the PP has an adverbial function and modifies the verb.

In its other meaning, "the boy saw a man who had a telescope," the PP *with the telescope* occurs under the direct object NP, where it modifies the noun *man*. In this second meaning, the complement of the verb *see* is the entire NP—*the man with the telescope*.

The PP in the first structure is generated by the rule:

VP → V NP PP

In the second structure the PP is generated by the rule:

NP → Det N PP

Two interpretations are possible because the rules of syntax permit different structures for the same linear order of words.

Trees That Won't Grow

Just as speakers know which structures and strings of words are permitted by the syntax of their language, they know which are not. The phrase structure rules specify this knowledge implicitly.

Since the rule S → NP Aux VP is the only S rule in our (simplified) grammar of English, the following word sequences and their corresponding structures do not constitute English sentences.

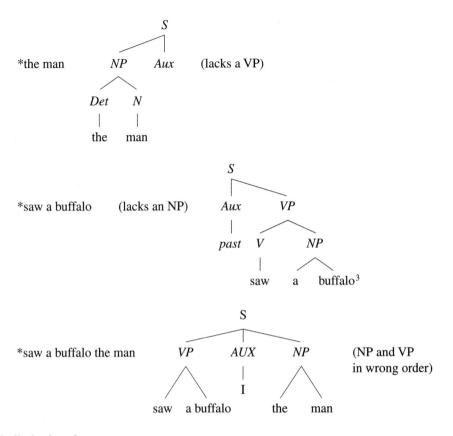

*the man   (lacks a VP)

*saw a buffalo   (lacks an NP)

*saw a buffalo the man   (NP and VP in wrong order)

Similarly, *boy the*

cannot be an NP in English because none of the NP rules of English syntax allows a Determiner to follow a Noun.

---

[3] Nonpertinent parts of the tree are sometimes omitted, in this case the Det and N of the NP, *a buffalo*.

"The Far Side"® copyright © 1983 Farworks, Inc. All rights reserved. Used with permission.

More Phrase Structure Rules

Normal human minds are such that . . . without the help of anybody, they will produce 1000 (sentences) they never heard spoke of . . . inventing and saying such things as they never heard from their masters, nor any mouth.

Huarte De San Juan, c. 1530–1592

Many English sentences have structures that are not accounted for by the phrase structure rules given so far, including:

1. Pretty girls whispered softly.
2. The cat and the dog were friends.
3. The teacher believes that the student knows the answer.

Sentence 1 may be represented by this phrase structure tree:

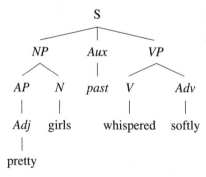

From this example we see that a Determiner is optional in the NP. Moreover, a new phrasal category, and two new lexical categories appear in the tree: Adjective Phrase

"B.C." copyright ©. Reprinted by permission of Johnny Hart and Creators Syndicate, Inc.

(AP), Adjective (Adj), and Adverb (Adv). All this suggests modifications to both the NP and the VP rules:

NP → (Det) (AP) N (PP)
VP → V (NP) (PP) (Adv)
AP → Adj (PP) [4]

The addition of an optional Adverb to the VP rule allows for four more sentence types:

The wind blew softly.
The wind swept through the trees noisily.
The wind rattled the windows violently.
The wind forced the boat into the water suddenly.

The NP in sentence 2, *The cat and the dog,* is a **coordinate structure.** A coordinate structure results when two constituents of the same category (in this case, two NPs) are joined with a conjunction such as *and* or *or*. The NP has the following structure:

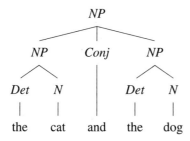

_____

[4] As pointed out earlier, any number of adjectives may be strung together. For simplicity our rules will allow only one adjective and would need to be changed to fully account for the English speaker's knowledge.

The phrase structure rule that generates this coordinate structure is:

NP → NP conj NP

Sentence 3 is particularly interesting. It includes another sentence within itself. The inside sentence, *the student knows the answer,* is **embedded** in the larger sentence *The teacher believes that the student knows the answer.* What is the structure of such sentences?

Recall that verbs (like other heads) take complements. These complements can be of different categories, for example, a PP or an AP. In sentence 3 the complement to the verb *believe* is a sentence — S. The embedded sentence *that the students know the answer* bears the same local relationship to the verb that a simple direct object does in a sentence such as *The teacher believes the student.* We know therefore that the embedded sentence is inside the VP with the verb:

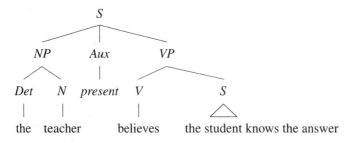

However, the structure is incomplete. It is missing a piece of the sentence, the word *that.* The word *that* belongs to the class of **complementizers,** which also includes words such as *if* and *whether* in sentences like:

I don't know whether I should talk about this.
The teacher asked if the students understood the syntax lesson.

A complementizer is an element that turns a sentence into a complement. In English, the word *that* is not always required in embedded sentences. The sentence *I know John is happy* is as grammatical as *I know that John is happy.* In many languages, a sentence can be a complement (that is, it can be embedded in another sentence) only if it is accompanied by a word like *that.* In English the other complementizers *if* and *whether* cannot be omitted, as illustrated by the ungrammaticality of the B sentences:

A	**B**
Sam asked if he could play soccer.	*Sam asked he could play soccer.
I wonder whether Michael walked the dog.	*I wonder Michael walked the dog.

So the structure of the embedded sentence must contain an S, and it must contain a position for a complementizer. But how are these two elements situated with respect to each other? If we do some constituency tests, as we did earlier for NP and VP, we see that the complementizer and the S form a constituent. For example, the question test, the relocation test, and the pronoun test all show that the embedded S and the complementizer act together as a constituent.

Sam asked if he could play soccer.
What did Sam ask? If he could play soccer.
I wonder whether Michael walked the dog.
Whether Michael walked the dog is always a question
The teacher believes that the students know the answer.
The teacher believes it.
That the students know the answer is believed by the teacher.
It is a problem that Sam lost his watch.
That Sam lost his watch is a problem.

It is not possible to leave the complementizer behind or omit it.

*What did Sam ask if.
*Michael walked the dog is always a question.
*The students know the answer is believed by the teacher (that).
*Sam lost his watch is a problem.

We now have all the information we need to determine the structure of the embedded sentence. The embedded sentence is a complement to the verb, therefore inside the VP. The complementizer *that* forms a constituent with S, which means there must be a category dominating both *that* and S that is inside the VP. The relevant structure is:

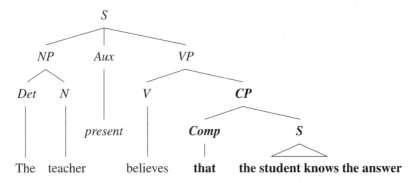

The complementizer (*that, if, whether*) appears under a node Comp, which, like Det and Aux, is a functional category. Comp is the head of a category CP (Complementizer Phrase). CP is the complement to the verb. The structure is parallel to a simple structure with an NP complement, such as *The teacher believes the student,* except that there is a CP instead of an NP.

We have omitted the internal structure of the embedded S in the preceding tree because it is the same as the internal structure of a root sentence, as described by the phrase structure rule for S. This suggests a rule for the category CP:

CP → Comp S

In addition, we need another VP rule:

VP → V CP

If we combine this with the previous VP rules, we get:

VP → V (NP) (PP) (CP)

We now see how the grammar reflects the knowledge that all speakers have to embed sentences in sentences, as illustrated by the cartoon at the beginning of this section. Here is an illustrative phrase structure tree:

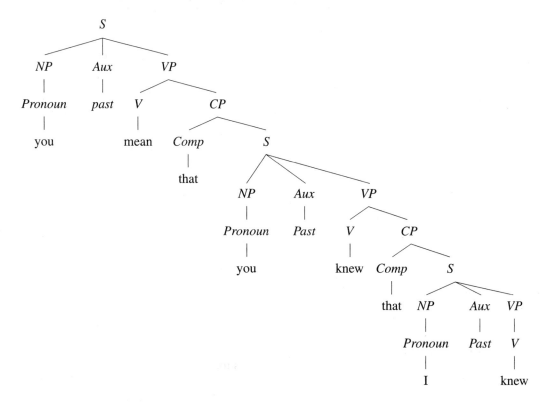

Here are the phrase structure rules we have discussed so far. These are all the phrase structure rules we will present in this chapter.

1. S → NP Aux VP
2. NP → (Det) (AP) N (PP)
3. VP → V (NP) (PP) (Adv) (CP)
4. PP → P NP
5. AP → Adj (PP)
6. CP → Comp S

A complete grammar of English would have more rules. However, even this mini-grammar can specify an infinite number of possible sentences because several categories (S, NP, VP) appear on both the left and right sides of several rules. Thus, the rules explain our observations that language is creative and that speakers with their finite brains can still produce and understand an infinite set of sentences.

Many structures of English remain unaccounted for by our mini-grammar. For example, many types of Determiners besides the articles *the* and *a* may precede the noun in a Noun Phrase, such as *each, several, these, many of The Grateful Dead's,* and so on.

> *Each* boy found several eggs.
> They sang *many of The Grateful Dead's* songs.

Also, rules 3 and 5 show that a whole sentence (preceded by a complementizer) may be embedded in a VP. There are other forms of embedded sentences such as the following:

> Hilary is waiting *for you to sing* (Cf. You sing.)
>
> The host regrets *the president's having left early*. (Cf. The president has left early.)
>
> The host wants *the president to leave early*. (Cf. The president leaves early.)
>
> The host believes *the president to be punctual*. (Cf. The president is punctual.)

Although, the detailed structure of these different embedded sentences is beyond the scope of this introduction, you should note that an embedded sentence may be an **infinitive.** An infinitive sentence does not have a tense. The embedded sentences *for you to sing, the president to leave early, and the president to be punctual* are infinitives. Such verbs as *want* and *believe* among many others can take an infinitive complement. This information, like other selectional properties, belongs to the lexical entry of the selecting verb (the higher verb in the tree).

We noted earlier that Aux is the head of S, and that the tense features of the sentence are in Aux. In sentences without tense, Aux is specified as "infinitive." Whether the sentence is tensed or infinitive has consequences for other aspects of the sentence. For example, reflexive pronouns can be subjects of infinitives but not of embedded tensed sentences:

> Frank believes himself to be a superstar.
> *Frank thinks himself is a superstar.

Also, the subject of an infinitive can be questioned while the subject of a tensed clause cannot:

> Paul believed Melissa to be his wife.
> Who did Paul believe to be his wife?
> Sam thinks that Michael is his cousin.
> *Who does Sam think that is his cousin?

These sentences provide further evidence of the central role that Aux plays in the structure of the sentence, and of its "headlike" properties.

Sentence Relatedness

> Most wonderful of all are . . . [sentences], and how they make friends one with another.
>
> O. Henry, as modified by a syntactician

Sentences may be related in various ways. For example, they may have the same phrase structure, but differ in meaning because they contain different words. We saw this earlier in sets of sentences such as *The boat sailed up the river* and *A girl laughed at the monkey*.

Two sentences with different meanings may contain the same words in the same order, and differ only in structure, like *the boy saw the man with the telescope*. These are cases of structural ambiguity.

Two sentences may differ in structure, possibly with small differences in grammatical morphemes, but with no difference in meaning:

The father wept silently.	The father silently wept.
The astronomer saw a quasar with a telescope.	With a telescope the astronomer saw a quasar.
Mary hired Bill.	Bill was hired by Mary.
I know that you know.	I know you know.

Two sentences may have structural differences that correspond systematically to meaning differences.

The boy is sleeping.	Is the boy sleeping?
The boy can sleep.	Can the boy sleep?
The boy will sleep.	Will the boy sleep?

Earlier we discussed auxiliaries. Auxiliaries are very important in forming certain types of sentences in English, including questions. In questions, the auxiliary appears at the beginning of the sentence. This difference in position is not accounted for by the phrase structure rules we have presented, which specify that in a sentence the NP comes first, followed by Aux, followed by VP.

We could easily add a phrase structure rule to our mini-grammar that would generate the questions above. It would look like the following:

S → Aux NP VP

Although such a rule might do the job of producing the right word order, it would fail to capture the generalization that interrogatives are systematically related (in both form and meaning) to their declarative counterparts. For example, the declarative sentence *John is sleeping* is well formed, as is the question *Is John sleeping?* The declarative sentence *The rock is sleeping* is semantically odd, as is the question *Is the rock sleeping?* A speaker of English will be able to immediately provide the interrogative counterpart to any declarative sentence that we present.

Phrase structure rules account for much syntactic knowledge, but they do not account for the fact that certain sentence types in the language relate systematically to other sentence types.

Since the grammar must account for all of a speaker's syntactic knowledge, we must look beyond phrase structure rules.

Transformational Rules

Method consists entirely in properly ordering and arranging the things to which we should pay attention.

René Descartes, *Oeuvres*, Vol. X

A way to capture the relationship between a declarative and a question is to allow the phrase structure rules to generate the structure corresponding to the declarative sentence, and have another formal device, called a **transformational rule,** move the auxiliary in front of the subject.

The rule "Move Aux" is formulated as follows:

Take the first auxiliary verb following the subject NP and move it to the left of the subject.

For example:

The boy is sleeping → Is the boy ___ sleeping

The rule takes a basic structure generated by the phrase structure rules and derives a second tree (the dash represents the position from which a constituent has been moved):

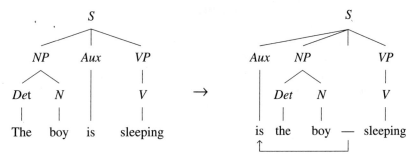

Questions are generated in two steps.

1. The phrase structure rules generate a basic structure.
2. Aux movement applies to produce the derived structure.

The basic structures of sentences, also called **deep structures,** are specified by the phrase structure rules. Variants on those basic sentence structures are derived via transformations. By generating questions in two steps, we are claiming that for speakers there is a relationship between a question and its corresponding statement. Intuitively, we know that such sentences are related. The transformational rule is a formal way of representing this relationship.

The structures that result from the application of transformational rules are called **surface structures.** The phonological rules of the language (pronunciation rules) apply to surface structures. If no transformations apply, then deep structure and surface structure are the same. If transformations apply, then surface structure is the result after all transformations have had their effect. Much syntactic knowledge that is not expressed by phrase structure rules is accounted for by transformations, which can alter phrase structure trees by moving, adding, or deleting elements.

Other sentence types that are transformationally related are:

active- passive

The cat chased the mouse → The mouse was chased by the cat

***there* sentences**

There was a man on the roof → A man was on the roof

PP preposing

The astronomer saw the quasar with the telescope → With the telescope, the astronomer saw the quasar.

Structure Dependent Rules

Transformations act on structures without regard to the words that they contain. They are **structure dependent.** The transformational rule of PP preposing moves any PP as long as it is immediately under the VP, as in *In the house, the puppy found the ball,* or *With the telescope, the boy saw the man,* and so on.

Evidence that transformations are structure dependent is the fact that the sentence *With a telescope, the boy saw the man* is not ambiguous. It has only the meaning "the boy used a telescope to see the man," the meaning corresponding to the phrase structure in which the PP is immediately dominated by the VP shown on page 143. In the structure corresponding to the other meaning "the boy saw a man who had a telescope" the PP is in the NP as in the tree on page 144. The PP preposing transformation does not move a PP that is part of a complement. (Recall that *the man with a telescope* is a complement to the verb *saw*).

Another rule allows *that* to be omitted when it precedes a sentence complement but not in subject position, as illustrated by these pairs:

I know that you know.	I know you know.
That you know bothers me.	*You know bothers me.

This is a further demonstration that rules are structure dependent.

Agreement rules are also structure dependent. In many languages, including English, the verb must agree with the subject. The verb has an "s" added whenever the subject is third-person singular.

The guy seems kind of cute.
The guys seem kind of cute.

Now consider these sentences:

The guy we met at the party next door *seems* kind of cute.
The guys we met at the party next door *seem* kind of cute.

The verb *seem* must agree with the subject, *guy* or *guys*. Even though there are various words between the head noun and the verb, the verb always agrees with the head noun. Moreover, there is no limit to how many words may intervene, as the following sentence illustrates:

The guys (guy) we met at the party next door that lasted until three A.M. and was finally broken up by the cops who were called by the neighbors seem (seems) kind of cute.

The phrase structure tree of such a sentence explains this aspect of linguistic competence:

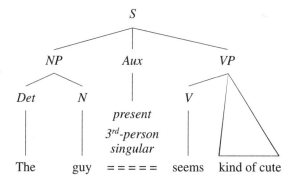

In the tree, "= = = = = =" represents the intervening structure, which may, in principle, be indefinitely long and complex. But speakers of English know that agreement depends on sentence structure, not the linear order of words. Agreement is between the subject and the main verb, where the subject is structurally defined as the NP immediately below the S, and the main verb is structurally defined as the Verb in the VP. The agreement relation is mediated by Aux, which contains the tense and agreement features that match up the subject and verb. Other material can be ignored as far as the rule of agreement is concerned, although in actual performance, if the distance is too great, the speaker may forget what the head noun was.

A final illustration of structure dependency is found in the declarative-question pairs discussed above. Consider the following sets of sentences:

The boy who is sleeping was dreaming.
Was the boy who is sleeping dreaming?
*Is the boy who sleeping was dreaming?
The boy who can sleep will dream.
Will the boy who can sleep dream?
*Can the boy who sleep will dream?

The ungrammatical sentences show that to form a question, it is the Auxiliary of the top-most S, that is, the one following the entire first NP, that moves to the position before the subject, not simply the *first* Auxiliary in the sentence. We can see this in the following simplified phrase structure trees.

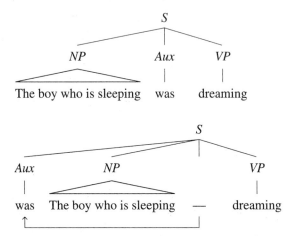

To produce the correct results, transformations such as Move Aux must refer to phrase structure, not to the linear order of elements.

Structure dependency is a principle of Universal Grammar, and is found in all languages. For example, in languages that have subject-verb agreement, the dependency is between the verb and the head noun, and never some other noun such as the closest one, as shown in the following examples from Italian, German, Swahili, and English, respectively (the third-person singular agreement morpheme is in boldface):

La madre con tanti figli lavor**a** molto.
Die Mutter mit den vielen Kindern arbeite**t** viel.
Mama **a**nao watoto wengi.
The mother with many children work**s** a lot.

Syntactic Dependencies

Sentences are organized according to two basic principles: constituent structure and syntactic dependencies. As we discussed earlier, constituent structure refers to the hierarchical organization of the subparts of a sentence. The second important property is that there are dependencies among elements in the sentence. In other words, the presence of a particular word or morpheme can depend on the presence of some other word or morpheme in a sentence. We have already seen at least two examples of syntactic dependencies. Selection is one kind of dependency. Whether there is a direct object in a sentence depends on whether the verb is transitive or intransitive. More generally, complements depend on the properties of the head of the phrase. Agreement is another kind of dependency. The features in Aux (and on the verb) must match the features of the subject.

WH QUESTIONS

Whom are you? said he, for he had been to night school.

George Ade, Bang! Bang!: The Steel Box

The following sentences illustrate another kind of dependency:

1. (a) What will Max chase?
   (b) Where has Pete put his ball?
   (c) Which dog do you think loves bones?

There are some points of interest in these sentences. First, the verb *chase* in sentence (a) is transitive, yet there is no direct object following it. There is a "gap" where the direct object should be. The verb *put* in sentence (b) selects a direct object and a prepositional phrase, yet there is no PP following *his ball*. Finally, we note that the embedded verb *loves* in sentence (c) bears the third-person *–s* morpheme, yet there is no obvious subject to trigger this agreement. Normally these omissions would result in ungrammaticality, as in the examples in (2):

2. (a) *Max will chase _____.
   (b) *Pete has put his ball _____.
   (c) *Do you think _____ loves bones.

The possibility of a gap in the sentence depends on there being a *wh* phrase at the beginning of the sentence. The sentences in (1) are grammatical because the *wh phrase* is acting like the object in (a), the prepositional phrase object in (b), and the embedded subject in (c).

We can capture the relationship between the *wh* phrase and the missing constituent if we assume that in each case the *wh* phrase originated in the position of the gap:

3. (a) Max will chase what?
   (b) Pete has put his ball where?
   (c) You think which dog loves bones?

The *wh* phrase is then moved to the beginning of the sentence by a transformational rule: Move *wh*.

If we allow the phrase structure rules to apply so that *wh* questions are CPs, then the *wh* phrase can move to the empty Comp position at the beginning of the sentence.

Wh questions are generated by the grammar in three steps:

1. The phrase structure rules generate the basic (deep) structure with the *wh* phrase occupying an NP position: direct object in 3(a); prepositional object in 3(b); and subject in 3(c).
2. Move Aux moves the auxiliary to beginning of the sentence.
3. Move *wh* moves the *wh* phrase to Comp.

The following tree shows the deep structure in the sentence *What will Max chase?*

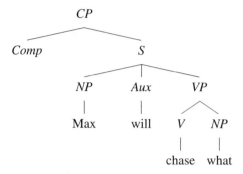

The surface structure representation of this sentence is:[5]

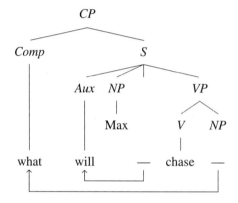

In question 1(c), there is an auxiliary "do." Unlike the other auxiliaries (e.g., *can, have, be,* etc.), *do* is not part of the deep structure of the question. The deep structure of the question *Which dog do you think likes bones* is "you think which dog likes bones." Like all transformations, the rule of Move Aux is structure dependent and ignores the content of the category. It will move Aux even when Aux contains only a tense feature such as *past.* In this case another transformational rule, called "*do* support," inserts *do* into the structure to carry the tense:

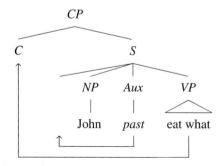

---

[5] For ease of exposition we have presented Comp with only a single slot to accommodate moved constituents. In fact, Comp may have two positions, one for *wh* and one for the Aux.

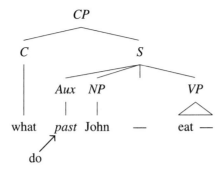

The first tree represents the deep structure to which Move Aux and wh movement apply. The second tree shows the output of those transformations and the insertion of "do." "Do" combines with past to yield "did."

Unlike the other rules we have seen, which operate inside a phrase or clause, *wh* movement can move the *wh* phrase outside of its own clause. In fact there is no limit to the distance that a *wh* phrase can move, as illustrated by the following sentences. The dashes indicate the position from which the *wh* phrase has been moved.

> Who did Helen say the senator wanted to hire ____?
>
> Who did Helen say the senator wanted the congressional representative to try to hire ____?
>
> Who did Helen say the senator wanted the congressional representative to try to convince the Speaker of the House to get the Vice President to hire ____?
>
> .
> .
> .

"Long-distance" dependencies created by *wh* movement are a fundamental part of human language. They provide further evidence that sentences are not simply strings of words but are supported by a rich scaffolding of phrase structure trees. These trees express the underlying structure of the sentence as well as their relation to other sentences in the language.

UG Principles and Parameters

> Whenever the literary German dives into a sentence, that is the last you are going to see of him till he emerges on the other side of the Atlantic with his Verb in his mouth.
>
> Mark Twain, *A Connecticut Yankee in King Arthur's Court*

As we emphasize throughout this book, Universal Grammar provides the basic design for human language. Individual languages are variations on this basic design. Imagine a development of new houses. All of the houses have the same floor plan but the occupants have some choices to make. They can have carpet or hardwood floors, curtains or blinds, they can choose their kitchen cabinets and the countertops, the bathroom tiles, and so on. This is more or less how the syntax operates. Languages conform to a basic structure and then there are points of variation.

All languages have phrase structure rules. In all languages, phrases consist of heads and complements, and sentences are headed by Aux (or INFL), which houses notions such as tense, agreement and modality. However, languages may have different word orders within the phrases and sentences. The word order differences between English and Japanese, discussed earlier, illustrate the interaction of general and language-specific properties. UG specifies the structure of a phrase. It must have a head and may take one or more complements. However, each language gets to decide for itself the relative order of these constituents: English is head initial, Japanese is head final. We call the points of variation **parameters.**

All languages seem to have movement rules. The transformational rule Move Aux is a version of a more general rule that exists in languages such as Dutch, in which the auxiliary moves, if there is one:

Aux Raising

Zal Femke fiesten?	(Will Femke ride her bicycle?)
will Femke bicycle ride	
Kan Elmer baskenballen?	(Can Elmer play basketball?)
can Elmer play basketball	

And otherwise, the main verb moves:

Verb Raising

Hoeveel studenten onderwijst Els?	(How many students does Els teach?)
how many students teaches Els	
Leest Meindert veel boeken?	(Does Meindert read many books?)
reads Meindert many books	

In English main verbs other than *be* do not move. Instead, English has "do" support to carry the tense, as noted earlier.

All languages have expressions for requesting information about *who, when, where, what,* and *how.* Even if the question words do not always begin with "wh," we will refer to such questions as *wh* questions.

In some languages, such as Japanese and Swahili, the *wh* phrase does not move. It remains in its original deep structure position. In Japanese the sentence is marked with a question morpheme, *no:*

Taro-ga	nani-o	mituketa-no?
Taro	what	found ?

Recall that Japanese word order is SOV, so the *wh* phrase *nani* ("what") is an object and occurs before the verb.

In Swahili the *wh* phrase—*nani* by pure coincidence—also does not move to Comp:

Ulipatia	nani	kitabu
you gave	who	a book

However, in all languages with *wh* movement (that is, movement of the question phrase), the moved element goes to Comp. The "landing site" of the moved phrase is determined by UG. Among the *wh* movement languages, there is some variation. In the Romance languages such as Italian, the *wh* phrase moves as in English, but when the *wh* phrase questions the object of a preposition, the preposition must move together with the *wh* phrase, whereas in English the preposition can be "stranded" behind:

A chi ha dato il libro?
To whom (did) you give the book?

*Chi hai dato il libro a?
Who did you give the book to?

In some dialects of German, "long-distance" *wh* movement leaves a trail of *wh* phrases in the Comp position of the embedded sentence: [6]

Mit   wem   glaubst du   mit   wem   Hans spricht?
With whom think   you with whom Hans talks
(Whom do you think Hans talks to?)

Wen   willst du   wen   Hans anruft?
Whom want you whom Hans call
(Whom do you want Hans to call?)

In Czech the question phrase "how much" can be moved, leaving behind the NP it modifies:

Jak   velké Václav koupil auto?
how big   Václav bought car
(How big a car did Václav buy?)

Despite these variations, *wh* movement adheres to certain constraints. Although a *wh* phrase such as *what, who, which boy* can be inserted into any NP position, and it is then free in principle to move to Comp, there are specific instances in which *wh* movement is blocked. For example, the rule cannot move a *wh* phrase out of a relative clause such as ". . . the senator that wanted to hire who" as in 1(b), or a clause beginning with *whether* or *if* as in 2(c) and (d). (Remember that the position from which the *wh* phrases have been moved is indicated with ____.)

1. (a) Emily paid a visit to the senator that wants to hire who?
   (b) *Who did Emily pay a visit to the senator that wants to hire ____?
2. (a) Miss Marple asked Sherlock whether Poirot had solved the crime.
   (b) Who did Miss Marple ask ____ whether Poirot had solved the crime?
   (c) *Who did Miss Marple ask Sherlock whether ____ had solved the crime?
   (d) *What did Miss Marple ask Sherlock whether Poirot had solved ____?

---

[6] Other languages such as Romani, the language of Roma, once called gypsies, exhibits similar properties.

The only difference between the grammatical 2(b) and the ungrammatical 2(c) and (d) is that in the former case the *wh* phrase originates in the higher clause, whereas in the latter cases the *wh* phrase comes from inside the *whether* clause. This illustrates that the constraint against movement depends on structure and not on the length of the sentence.

In fact some sentences can be very short and still not allow *wh* movement:

3. (a) Sam Spade insulted the fat man's henchman.
   (b) Who did Sam Spade insult?
   (c) Whose henchman did Sam Spade insult?
   (d) *Whose did Sam Spade insult henchman?
4. (a) John ate bologna and cheese.
   (b) John ate bologna with cheese.
   (c) *What did John eat bologna and?
   (d) What did John eat bologna with?

The sentences in 3 show that a *wh* phrase cannot be extracted from inside a possessive NP. In 3(b) it is of course okay to question the whole direct object, and prepose the *wh* word. In 3(c) it is even okay to question a piece of the possessive NP, providing the entire *wh* phrase is moved. But 3(d) shows that it is not permitted to move the *wh* word alone out of the possessive NP.

Sentence 4(a) is a coordinate structure and has approximately the same meaning as 4(b), which is not a coordinate structure. In 4(c) moving a *wh* word out of the coordinate structure results in ungrammaticality, whereas in 4(d), it's okay to move the *wh* word out of the PP. The ungrammaticality of 4(c), then, is related to its structure and not to its meaning.

The constraints on *wh* movement are not specific to English. Such constraints operate in all languages that have *wh* movement. Like the principle of structure dependency and the principles governing the organization of phrases, the constraints on *wh* movement are part of Universal Grammar. These aspects of grammar need not be learned. They are part of what the child brings to the task of acquiring a language.

What children must learn are the language specific aspects of grammar. Where there are parameters of variation, children must determine what is correct for their language. The Japanese child must determine that the verb comes after the object in the VP, and the English-speaking child acquires the VO order. The Dutch-speaking child acquires a rule that moves the verb, while the English-speaking child must restrict his rule to auxiliaries. Italian, English, and Czech children learn that to form a question the *wh* phrase moves, while Japanese and Swahili children determine that there is no movement. We will have more to say about how children "fix" the parameters of UG in chapter 8.

Sign Language Syntax

All languages have rules of syntax similar in kind, if not in detail, to those of English, and sign languages are no exception. Signed languages have phrase structure rules that provide hierarchical structure and order constituents. A signer is as capable as an oral speaker of distinguishing *dog bites man* from *man bites dog* through the order of signing. The basic order of ASL is SVO. Unlike English, however, adjectives follow the head noun in ASL.

ASL has a category Aux, which expresses notions such as tense, agreement, modality, and so on. In Thai, to show that an action is continuous, the auxiliary verb *kamlang* is inserted before the verb. Thus *kin* means "eat" and *kamlang kin* means "is eating." In English a form of *be* is inserted and the main verb is changed to an -ing form. In ASL the sign for a verb such as *eat* may be articulated with a sweeping, repetitive movement to achieve the same effect. The sweeping repetitive motion is a kind of the auxiliary.

Many languages, including English, have a transformation that moves a direct object to the beginning of the sentence to draw particular attention to it, as in:

Many greyhounds, my wife has rescued.

The transformation is called **topicalization** because an object to which attention is drawn generally becomes the topic of the sentence or conversation. (The deep structure underlying this sentence is *my wife has rescued many greyhounds*.)

In ASL a similar reordering of signs accompanied by raising the eyebrows and tilting the head upwards accomplishes the same effect. The head motion and facial expressions of a signer function as markers of the special word order, much as intonation does in English, or the attachment of prefixes or suffixes might in other languages.

There are constraints on topicalization similar to those on *wh* movement illustrated in a previous section. In English the following strings are ungrammatical:

*Henchman, Sam Spade insulted the fat man's.
*This film, John asked Mary whether she liked.
*Cheese, John ate bologna and for lunch.

Compare this with the grammatical:

The fat man's henchman, Sam Spade insulted.
This film, John asked Mary to see with her.
Bologna and cheese, John ate for lunch.

Sign languages exhibit similar constraints. An attempt to express in ASL sequences like **Henchman, Sam Spade insulted the fat man's* or the other starred examples would result in an ungrammatical sequence of signs.

ASL has *wh* phrases. The *wh* phrase in ASL may move or it may remain in its deep structure position as in Japanese and Swahili. The ASL equivalents of *who did Bill see yesterday* and *Bill saw who yesterday* are both grammatical. As in topicalization, *wh* questions are accompanied by a non-manual marker. For questions, this marker is a facial expression with furrowed brows and the head tilted back. Non-manual markers are an integral part of the grammar of ASL, much like intonation in spoken languages.

ASL and other sign languages show an interaction of universal and language-specific properties, just as spoken languages do. The grammatical rules of sign languages are structure dependent, and movement rules are constrained in various ways, as illustrated above. Other aspects are particular to sign languages, such as the facial gestures, which are part of the grammar of sign languages but not of spoken languages. The fact that the principles and parameters of UG hold in both the spoken and manual modalities shows that the human brain is designed to acquire and use language, not simply speech.

Summary

Speakers of a language recognize the grammatical sentences of their language and know how the words in a sentence must be ordered and grouped to convey a certain meaning. All speakers are capable of producing and understanding an unlimited number of new sentences never before spoken or heard. They also recognize ambiguities, know when different sentences mean the same thing, and correctly perceive the grammatical relations in a sentence such as **subject** and **direct object.** This kind of knowledge comes from their knowledge of the **rules of syntax.**

Sentences have structure that can be represented by **phrase structure trees** containing **syntactic categories.** Phrase structure trees reflect the speaker's mental representation of sentences. Ambiguous sentences may have more than one phrase structure tree.

Phrase structure trees reveal the linear order of words, and the constituency of each syntactic category. There are different kinds of syntactic categories: **phrasal categories,** such as NP and VP, are decomposed into other syntactic categories; **lexical categories,** such as Noun and Verb, and **functional categories,** such as Det, Aux, and Comp. The internal structure of the phrasal categories is universal. It consists of a **head** and its **complements.** The particular order of elements within the phrase is accounted for by the **phrase structure rules** of each language. The sentence is headed by Aux, which carries such information as tense, agreement, and modality.

A grammar is a formally stated, explicit description of the mental grammar or speaker's linguistic competence. Phrase structure rules characterize the basic phrase structure trees of the language, the **deep structures.**

Some categories that appear on the left side of a phrase structure rule may also occur on the right side. Such rules allow the same syntactic category to appear repeatedly in a phrase structure tree, such as a sentence embedded in another sentence. These rules reflect a speaker's ability to produce an infinite number of sentences.

The **lexicon** represents the knowledge that speakers have about the vocabulary of their language. This knowledge includes the syntactic category of words and what elements may occur together, expressed as **selectional restrictions.**

Transformational rules account for relationships between sentences such as declarative and interrogative pairs including *wh* questions. Transformations can move constituents or insert function words such as *do* into a sentence. Much of the meaning of a sentence is interpreted from its deep structure. The output of the transformational rules is the **surface structure** of a sentence, the structure to which the phonological rules of the language apply.

The basic design of language is universal. Universal Grammar specifies that syntactic rules are **structure dependent** and that movement rules may not move phrases out of certain structures such as coordinate structures. These constraints exist in all languages — spoken and signed — and need not be learned. UG also contains parameters of variation such as the order of heads and complements, and the variations on movement rules. A child acquiring a language must "fix" the parameters of UG for any particular language.

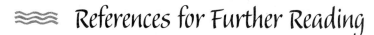

References for Further Reading

Akmajian, A., R. A. Demers, and R. M. Harnish. 1995. *Linguistics: An Introduction to Language and Communication,* 4th ed. Cambridge, MA: MIT Press.

Baker, M.C. 2001. *The Atoms of Language: The Mind's Hidden Rules of Grammar.* NY: Basic Books.

Chomsky, N. 1982. *Some Concepts and Consequences of the Theory of Government and Binding.* Cambridge, MA: MIT Press.

_____. 1972. *Language and Mind,* rev. ed. New York: Harcourt Brace Jovanovich.

_____. 1965. *Aspects of the Theory of Syntax.* Cambridge, MA: MIT Press.

_____. 1957. *Syntactic Structures.* The Hague: Mouton.

Gazdar, G., E. Klein, G. Pullum, and I. Sag. 1985. *Generalized Phrase Structure Grammar.* Cambridge, MA: Harvard University Press.

Haegeman, L. 1991. *Introduction to Government and Binding Theory.* Oxford, England: Basil Blackwell.

Horrocks, G. 1987. *Generative Grammar.* New York: Longman.

Jackendoff, R. S. 1994. *Patterns in the Mind: Language and Human Nature.* New York: Basic Books.

McCawley, J. D. 1988. *The Syntactic Phenomena of English, Vols. I, II.* Chicago: University of Chicago Press.

Napoli, D. J. 1993. *Syntax: Theory and Problems.* New York: Oxford University Press.

Newmeyer, F. J. 1981. *Linguistic Theory in America: The First Quarter Century of Transformational-Generative Grammar.* New York: Academic Press.

Pinker, S. 1999. *Words and Rules: The Ingredients of Language.* New York: HarperCollins.

Radford, A. 1997. *Syntax: A Minimalist Introduction.* New York: Cambridge University Press.

_____. 1988. *Transformational Grammar.* New York: Cambridge University Press.

Exercises

1. Besides distinguishing grammatical from ungrammatical strings, the rules of syntax account for other kinds of linguistic knowledge, such as

   a. when a sentence is structurally ambiguous. (Cf. The boy saw the man with a telescope.)

   b. when two sentences of different structure mean the same thing. (Cf. The father wept silently and The father silently wept.)

   c. when two sentences of different structure and meaning are nonetheless structurally related, like declarative sentences and their corresponding interrogative form. (Cf. The boy can sleep and Can the boy sleep?)

   In each case, draw on your linguistic knowledge of English to provide an example different from the ones in the chapter, and explain why your example illustrates the point. If you know a language other than English, provide examples in that language, if possible.

2. Consider the following sentences:

    a. I hate war.

    b. You know that I hate war.

    c. He knows that you know that I hate war.

        A. Write another sentence that includes sentence (c).

        B. What does this set of sentences reveal about the nature of language?

        C. How is this characteristic of human language related to the difference between linguistic competence and performance? (*Hint:* Review these concepts in chapter 1.)

3. Paraphrase each of the following sentences in two ways to show that you understand the ambiguity involved:

    Example: Smoking grass can be nauseating.
    i. Putting grass in a pipe and smoking it can make you sick.
    ii. Fumes from smoldering grass can make you sick.

    a. Dick finally decided on the boat.

    b. The professor's appointment was shocking.

    c. The design has big squares and circles.

    d. That sheepdog is too hairy to eat.

    e. Could this be the invisible man's hair tonic?

    f. The governor is a dirty street fighter.

    g. I cannot recommend him too highly.

    h. Terry loves his wife and so do I.

    i. They said she would go yesterday.

    j. No smoking section available.

4. Draw two phrase structure trees representing the two meanings of the sentence *The magician touched the child with the wand*. Be sure you indicate which meaning goes with which tree.

5. Write out the phrase structure rules that each of the following rules abbreviate. Give an example sentence illustrating each expansion.

    (*Hint:* Do not mix the rules. That is, VP → V Det N is not one of the rule expansions of the VP rule. There are 16 rules altogether.)

    VP → V (NP) (PP) (Adv)

    NP → (Det) (AP) N (PP)

6. In all languages, sentences can occur within sentences. For example, in exercise 2, sentence (b) contains sentence (a), and sentence (c) contains sentence (b). Put another way, sentence (a) is embedded in sentence (b), and sentence (b) is embedded in sentence (c). Sometimes embedded sentences appear slightly changed from their "normal" form, but you should be able to recognize and underline the embedded sentences in the examples below. Underline in the non-English sentences, when given, not in the translations. (The first one is done as an example):

    a. Yesterday I noticed <u>my accountant repairing the toilet</u>.

    b. Becky said that Jake would play the piano.

    c. I deplore the fact that bats have wings.

  d. That Guinevere loves Lorian is known to all my friends.

  e. Who promised the teacher that Maxine wouldn't be absent?

  f. It's ridiculous that he washes his own Rolls-Royce.

  g. The woman likes for the waiter to bring water when she sits down.

  h. The person who answers this question will win $100.

  i. The idea of Romeo marrying a 13-year-old is upsetting.

  j. I gave my hat to the nurse who helped me cut my hair.

  k. For your children to spend all your royalty payments on recreational drugs is a shame.

  l. Give this fork to the person I'm getting the pie for.

  m. khăw chyâ wăa khruu maa. (Thai)

    He believe that teacher come

    He believes that the teacher is coming.

  n. Je me demande quand il partira. (French)

    I me ask   when he will leave

    I wonder when he'll leave.

  o. Jan zei dat Piet dit boek niet heeft gelezen. (Dutch)

    Jan said that Piet this book not has read

    Jan said that Piet has not read this book.

7. Following the patterns of the various tree examples in the text, draw phrase structure trees for the following sentences:

  a. The puppy found the child.

  b. A frightened passenger landed the crippled airliner.

  c. The house on the hill collapsed in the wind.

  d. The ice melted.

  e. The hot sun melted the ice.

  f. A fast car with twin cams sped by the children on the grassy lane.

  g. The old tree swayed in the wind.

  h. The children put the toy in the box.

  i. The reporter realized that the senator lied.

  j. Broken ice melts in the sun.

  k. The guitar gently weeps.

  l. A stranger whispered to the Soviet agent on the corner quietly that a dangerous spy from the CIA lurks in the alley by the old tenement.

8. Use the rules on page 150 to create five phrase structure trees of sentences not given in the chapter of 6, 7, 8, 9, and 10 words. Use your mental lexicon to fill in the bottom of the tree.

9. We stated that the rules of syntax specify all and only the grammatical sentences of the language. Why is it important to say "only"? What would be wrong with a grammar that specified as grammatical sentences all of the truly grammatical ones plus a few that were not grammatical?

10. Here is a set of made-up phrase structure rules. The "initial" symbol is still S, and the "terminal symbols" (the ones that do not appear to the left of an arrow) are actual words:

   i.   S → A B C

   ii.   A → *the*

   iii. B → *children*

   iv.   C → *ran*

   v.   C → C *and* D

   vi.   D → *ran and* D

   vii. D → *ran*

   A. Give three phrase structure trees that these rules characterize.

   B. How many phrase structure trees could these rules characterize? Explain your answer.

11. Using one or more of the constituency tests (question word substitution, pronoun substitution, and relocation) discussed in the chapter, determine which boldfaced portions in the sentences are constituents. Provide the grammatical category of the constituents.

   a. Martha found **a lovely pillow** for the couch.

   b. The **light in this room** is terrible.

   c. I wonder **if Bonnie has finished packing her books.**

   d. Melissa hated the students **in her class.**

   e. **Pete and Max** are fighting over **the bone.**

12. The two sentences below contain a **verbal particle.**

   i. He ran *up* the bill.

   ii. He ran the bill *up*.

   The verbal particle *up* and the verb *run* depend on each other for the unique meaning of the phrasal verb *run up*. We know this because *run up* has a meaning different from *run in* or *look up*.

   Sentences (i) and (ii) have the same deep structure:

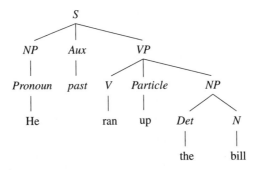

   The surface structure of (ii), however, illustrates a **discontinuous dependency.** The verb is separated from its particle by the direct object NP.

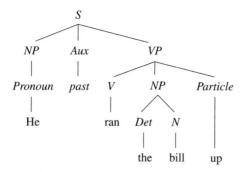

A particle movement transformation derives this surface structure from the deep structure.

A. Explain why the particle movement transformation would not derive *he ran the hill up* from the deep structure of *he ran up the hill.*

B. Many of the transformations encountered in this chapter are **optional.** Whether they apply or not, the ultimate surface structure is grammatical. This is true of the particle movement transformation in most cases, but there is one condition under which the particle movement transformation is obligatory. That is, failure to apply the rule will lead to ungrammatical results. What is that condition? (This exercise may require native English competency.)

13. In terms of selectional restrictions, explain why the following are ungrammatical.

    a. *The man located.

    b. *Jesus wept the apostles.

    c. *Robert is hopeful of his children.

    d. *Robert is fond that his children love animals.

    e. *The children laughed the man.

14. In the chapter, we considered only transitive verbs, ones that select an NP direct object like *chase*. English also has **ditransitive verbs,** ones that may be followed by two NPs, such as *give:*

The emperor gave the vassal a castle.

Think of three other ditransitive verbs in English and give example sentences.

15. For each verb, list the different types of complements it selects and provide an example of each type:

    a. want

    b. force

    c. try

    d. believe

    e. say

16. All of the *wh* words exhibit the "long-distance" behavior illustrated with *who* in the chapter. Invent three sentences beginning with *what, which,* and *where,* in which the *wh* word is not in its deep structure position in the sentence. Give both versions of your sentence. Here is an example with the *wh* word *when: When could Marcy catch a flight out of here?* from *Marcy could catch a flight out of here when?*

17. There are many systematic, structure-dependent relationships among sentences similar to the one discussed in the chapter between declarative and interrogative sentences. Here is another example, based on ditransitive verbs (see exercise 14):

The boy wrote the senator a letter.

The boy wrote a letter to the senator.

A philanthropist gave the Animal Rights movement $1,000,000.

A philanthropist gave $1,000,000 to the Animal Rights movement.

A. Describe the relationship between the first and second members of the pairs of sentences.

B. State why a transformation deriving one of these structures from the other is plausible.

18. State at least three differences between English and the following languages, using just the sentence(s) given. Ignore lexical differences — that is, the different vocabulary. Here is an example:

Thai:	dèg	khon	níi	kamlang	kin.
	boy	*classifier*	this	*progressive*	eat

"This boy is eating."

	măa	tua	nán	kin	khâaw.
	dog	*classifier*	that	eat	rice

"That dog ate rice."

Three differences are (1) Thai has "classifiers." They have no English equivalent. (2) The words (Determiners, actually) "this" and "that" follow the noun in Thai, but precede the noun in English. (3) The "progressive" is expressed by a separate word in Thai. The verb does not change form. In English, the progressive is indicated by the presence of the verb *to be* and the adding of *-ing* to the verb.

a. French

cet	homme	intelligent	comprendra	la question.
this	man	intelligent	will understand	the question

"This intelligent man will understand the question."

ces	hommes	intelligents	comprendront	les questions.
these	men	intelligent	will understand	the questions

"These intelligent men will understand the questions."

b. Japanese

watashi	ga	sakana	o	tabete	iru.
I	*subject marker*	fish	*object marker*	eat (*ing*)	am

"I am eating fish."

c. Swahili

mtoto	alivunja	kikombe.				
m-	toto	a-	li-	vunja	ki-	kombe
class marker	child	he	*past*	break	*class marker*	cup

"The child broke the cup."

watoto	wanavunja	vikombe.				
wa-	toto	wa-	na-	vunja	vi-	kombe
class marker	child	they	*present*	break	*class marker*	cup

"The children break the cups."

d. Korean

kɨ	sonyɔn-iee	wɨyu-lɨl	masi-ass-ta.			
kɨ	sonyɔn-	iee	wɨyu-	lɨl	masi-	ass-	ta
the	boy	*subject marker*	milk	*object marker*	drink	*past*	*assertion*

"The boy drank milk."

kɨ-nɨn	muɔs-il	mɔk-ass-ninya.			
kɨ-	nɨn	muɔs-	il	mɔk-	ass-	ninya
he	*subject marker*	what	*object marker*	eat	*past*	*question*

"What did he eat?"

e. Tagalog

nakita	ni	Pedro-ng	puno	na	ang	bus.		
nakita	ni	Pedro -ng	puno	na	ang	bus.
saw	*article*	Pedro that	full	already	*topic marker*	bus

"Pedro saw that the bus was already full."

19. Transformations may delete elements. For example, the surface structure of the ambiguous sentence *George wants the presidency more than Martha* may be derived from two possible deep structures:

a. George wants the presidency more than he wants Martha.

b. George wants the presidency more than Martha wants the presidency.

A deletion transformation either deletes *he wants* from the structure of example (a), or *wants the presidency* from the structure of example (b). This is a case of **transformationally induced ambiguity:** two different deep structures with different semantic interpretations are transformed into a single surface structure.

Explain the role of a deletion transformation similar to the ones just discussed in the following cartoon:

"Hagar the Horrible" copyright © King Features Syndicate, Inc. Reprinted with special permission.

20. (advanced) Compare the following French and English sentences:

French	English
Jean boit toujours du vin.	John always drinks some wine.
Jean drinks always some wine	*John drinks always some wine
Marie lit jamais le journal.	Mary never reads the newspaper.
Marie reads never the newspaper	*Mary reads never the newspaper.
Pierre lave souvent ses chiens.	Peter often washes his dogs.
Pierre washes often his dogs	*Peter washes often his dogs.

A. Based on the above data, what would you hypothesize concerning the position of adverbs in French and English?

B. Now suppose that UG specifies that *in all languages* adverbs of frequency (e.g., *always, never, often, sometimes*) are between the Aux and VP constituents, as in the tree below. What rule would you need to hypothesize to derive the correct surface structure word order for French? (*Hint:* adverbs are not allowed to move.)

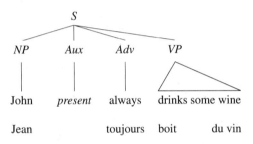

C. Are there any verbs in English that follow the same pattern as the French verbs?

21. In this chapter we proposed that there is a category Aux that is a separate constituent from the subject NP and the VP. One source of evidence that Aux is a separate constituent is that it undergoes movement in questions:

Have you seen John?

Will John come to the party?

Think of at least two other sentence types in English that demonstrate the constituency of Aux.

The Meanings of Language

Language without meaning is meaningless.

Roman Jakobson

For thousands of years philosophers have pondered the **meaning** of *meaning,* yet speakers of a language can understand what is said to them and can produce strings of words that are meaningful to other speakers.

To understand language we need to know the meaning of words and of the morphemes that compose them. We also must know how the meanings of words combine into phrase and sentence meanings. Finally, we must consider context when determining meaning.

The study of the linguistic meaning of morphemes, words, phrases, and sentences is called **semantics.** Subfields of semantics are **lexical semantics,** which is concerned with the meanings of words, and the meaning relationships among words; and **phrasal,** or **sentential, semantics,** which is concerned with the meaning of syntactic units larger than the word. The study of how context affects meaning — for example, how the sentence *It's cold in here* comes to be interpreted as "close the windows" in certain situations — is called **pragmatics.**

Lexical Semantics (Word Meanings)

"There's glory for you!"
"I don't know what you mean by 'glory,'" Alice said.
Humpty Dumpty smiled contemptuously.
"Of course you don't—till I tell you. I meant 'there's a nice knock-down argument for you!'"

"But 'glory' doesn't mean 'a nice knock-down argument,'" Alice objected.

"When I use a word," Humpty Dumpty said, in rather a scornful tone, "it means just what I choose it to mean—neither more nor less."

"The question is," said Alice, "whether you can make words mean so many different things."

Lewis Carroll, *Through the Looking-Glass*

Learning a language includes learning the agreed-upon meanings of certain strings of sounds and learning how to combine these meaningful units into larger units that also convey meaning. We are not free to change the meanings of these words at will; if we did we would be unable to communicate with anyone.

As we see from the quotation, Humpty Dumpty was unwilling to accept this convention. Alice, on the other hand, is right. You cannot make words mean whatever you want them to mean. Of course, if you wish to redefine the meaning of each word as you use it, you are free to do so, but this would be an artificial and clumsy use of language, and most people would not wait around very long to talk to you.

Fortunately, there are few Humpty Dumptys. All the speakers of a language share a basic vocabulary—the sounds and meanings of morphemes and words.

Dictionaries are filled with words and their meanings. So is the head of every human being who speaks a language. You are a walking dictionary. You know the meanings of thousands of words. Your knowledge of their meanings permits you to use them to express your thoughts and to understand them when heard, even though you probably seldom stop and ask yourself: "What does *boy* mean?" or "What does *walk* mean?" The meaning of words is part of linguistic knowledge and is therefore a part of the grammar. Your mental storehouse of information about words and morphemes is what we have been calling the **lexicon.**

Semantic Properties

Words and morphemes have meanings. We shall talk about the meaning of words, even though words may be composed of several morphemes, as noted in chapter 3.

Suppose someone said:

The assassin killed Thwacklehurst.

"B.C." reprinted by permission of Johnny Hart and Creators Syndicate, Inc.

If the word *assassin* is in your mental dictionary, you know that it was some *person* who murdered some *important person* named Thwacklehurst. Your knowledge of the meaning of *assassin* tells you that an animal did not do the killing, and that Thwacklehurst was not a little old man who owned a tobacco shop. Knowledge of *assassin* includes knowing that the individual to whom that word refers is human, is a murderer, and is a killer of important people. These pieces of information, then, are some of the **semantic properties** of the word on which speakers of the language agree. The meaning of all nouns, verbs, adjectives, and adverbs—the **content words**—and even some of the function words such as *with* and *over* can at least partially be specified by such properties.

The same semantic property may be part of the meaning of many words. "Female" is a semantic property that helps to define

tigress	hen	aunt	maiden
doe	mare	debutante	widow
ewe	vixen	girl	woman

The words in the last two columns are also distinguished by the semantic property "human," which is also found in

doctor	dean	professor	
bachelor	parent	baby	child

The meanings of the last two of these words are also specified as "young." That is, part of the meaning of the words *baby* and *child* is that they are "human" and "young." (We will continue to indicate words by using *italics* and semantic properties by using double quotation marks.)

The meanings of words have other properties. The word *father* has the properties "male" and "adult," as do *uncle* and *bachelor;* but *father* also has the property "parent," which distinguishes it from the other two words.

Mare, in addition to "female" and "animal," must also have a property "equine." Words have general semantic properties such as "human" or "parent," as well as specific properties that give the word its particular meaning.

The same semantic property may occur in words of different categories. "Female" is part of the meaning of the noun *mother,* of the verb *breast-feed,* and of the adjective *pregnant.* "Cause" is a verbal property of *darken, kill, uglify,* and so on.

darken	cause to become dark
kill	cause to die
uglify	cause to become ugly

Other semantic properties of verbs are shown in the following table:

Semantic Property	Verbs Having It
motion	bring, fall, plod, walk, run . . .
contact	hit, kiss, touch . . .
creation	build, imagine, make . . .
sense	see, hear, feel . . .

For the most part no two words have exactly the same meaning (but see the discussion of synonyms below). Additional semantic properties make for increasingly finer distinctions in meaning. *Plod* is distinguished from *walk* by the property "slow," and *stalk* from *plod* by properties like "purposeful" and "menace."

The humor of the cartoon at the head of this section (p. 174) is that the verb *roll over* has a specific semantic property, something like "activity about the longest axis." The snake's attempt to roll about its shortest axis indicates trouble with semantic *properties*.

EVIDENCE FOR SEMANTIC PROPERTIES

Semantic properties are not directly observable. Their existence must be inferred from linguistic evidence. One source of such evidence is the speech errors, or "slips of the tongue," that we all produce. Consider the following unintentional word substitutions that some speakers have actually spoken.

Intended Utterance	Actual Utterance (Error)
bridge of the nose	bridge of the neck
when my gums bled	when my tongues bled
he came too late	he came too early
Mary was young	Mary was early
the lady with the dachshund	the lady with the Volkswagen
that's a horse of another color	that's a horse of another race
he has to pay her alimony	he has to pay her rent

These errors and thousands of others that have been collected and catalogued reveal that the incorrectly substituted words are not random substitutions but share some semantic property with the intended words. *Nose, neck, gums,* and *tongues* are all "body parts" or "parts of the head." *Young, early,* and *late* are related to "time." *Dachshund* and *Volkswagen* are both "German" and "small." The common semantic properties of *color* and *race* and of *alimony* and *rent* are rather obvious.

The semantic properties that describe the linguistic meaning of a word should not be confused with other nonlinguistic properties, such as physical properties. Scientists know that water is composed of hydrogen and oxygen, but such knowledge is not part of a word's meaning. We know that water is an essential ingredient of lemonade or a bath. We need not know any of these things, though, to know what the word *water* means, and to be able to use and understand this word in a sentence.

SEMANTIC PROPERTIES AND THE LEXICON

The lexicon is the part of the grammar that contains the knowledge that speakers have about individual words and morphemes, including semantic properties. Words that share a semantic property are said to be in a semantic class, for example, the semantic class of "female" words. Semantic classes may intersect, such as the class of words with the properties "female" and "young." The words *girl* and *filly* are members of this class.

In some cases, the presence of one semantic property can be inferred from the presence or absence of another. For example, words with the property "human" also have the property "animate," and lack the property "equine."

"Tumbleweeds" copyright © Tom K. Ryan. Reprinted with special permission of North American Syndicate, Inc.

One way of representing semantic properties is by use of **semantic features.** Semantic features are a formal or notational device that indicates the presence or absence of semantic properties by pluses and minuses. For example, the lexical entries for words such as *father, girl,* and *mare* would appear as follows (with other information omitted):

woman	father	girl	mare	stalk
+female	+male	+female	+female	+motion
+human	+human	+human	- human	+slow
- young	+parent	+young	- young	+purposeful
. . .	. . .	. . .	+equine	. . .
			. . .	

Intersecting classes share some features; members of the class of words referring to human females are marked "plus" for the features *human* and *female.*

Another difference between nouns may be captured by the use of the feature [+/-Count]. Consider these data:

I have two dogs.	*I have two rice(s)
He has many dogs.	*He has many rice(s)
*He has much dogs	He has much rice.

Nouns that can be enumerated—*one potato, two potatoes*—are called **count nouns.** They may also be preceded by the quantifier *many* but not by *much.* Nouns such as *rice, water,* and *milk,* which cannot be enumerated or preceded by *many,* are called **mass nouns.** They may be distinguished in the lexicon with one feature:

dog	potato	rice	water	milk
+count	+count	-count	-count	-count

MORE SEMANTIC RELATIONSHIPS

Our linguistic knowledge about words, their semantic properties, and the relationships among them are illustrated by the "Garfield" cartoon, which shows that "small" is a semantic property of *morsel,* but not of *glob.*

"Garfield" copyright © 1990 United Feature Syndicate, Inc. Reprinted with permission.

Consider the following knowledge about words that speakers of English have:

If something *swims,* it is in a liquid.
If something is *splashed,* it is a liquid.

If you say you saw a bug swimming in a container of "goop," anyone who under-stands English would agree that goop is surely a liquid, that is, has the semantic feature [+liquid]. Even without knowing what goop refers to, you know you can talk about pour-ing goop, drinking goop, or plugging a hole where goop is leaking out and forming droplets. The words *pour, drink, leak,* and *droplet* are all used with items relating to the property "liquid."

Similarly, we would know that "sawing goop in half," "melting goop," or "bending goop" are semantically ill-formed expressions because none of these activities apply sensibly to objects that are [+liquid].

In some languages, the fact that certain verbs can occur appropriately with certain nouns is reflected in the verb morphology. For example in the Native American lan-guage Navajo, there are different verb forms for objects with different semantic proper-ties. The verbal suffix *–leh* is used with words with semantic features [+long], [+flexible], such as *rope;* whereas the verbal suffix *tuh* is used for words like *spear,* which is [+long], [-flexible].

In other languages, nouns occur with **classifiers,** grammatical morphemes that mark their semantic class. In Swahili, for example, nouns that refer to human beings are marked with a prefix *m-* if singular and *wa-* if plural, as in *mtoto* "child" and *watoto* "chil-dren." Nouns that refer to human artifacts such as beds, chairs, and cutlery are marked with the classifiers *ki* if singular and *vi* if plural, for example, *kiti* "chair" and *viti* "chairs."

–nyms

Most wonderful of all are words, and how they . . . [relate] one with another.

O. Henry, as modified by a semantician

Words are related to one another in a variety of ways. These relationships have words to describe them that often end in the bound morpheme *-nym.*

HOMONYMS AND POLYSEMY

"Mine is a long and sad tale!" said the Mouse, turning to Alice and sighing.

"It is a long tail, certainly," said Alice, looking with wonder at the Mouse's tail, "but why do you call it sad?"

Lewis Carroll, *Alice's Adventures in Wonderland*

"Bizarro" copyright © 1996 Dan Piraro. Reprinted with permission of Universal Press Syndicate. All rights reserved.

Knowing a word means knowing both its sounds (pronunciation) and its meaning. Both are crucial in determining whether words are the same or different. If words differ in pronunciation but have the same meaning, such as *sofa* and *couch,* they are different words. Likewise, words with identical pronunciation but significantly different meanings, such as *tale* and *tail,* are also different words. Spelling is not relevant, only pronunciation. Thus, *bat* the animal and *bat* for hitting baseballs are different words because they have different meanings although they are pronounced identically.

Words like *tale* and *tail* are **homonyms.**[1] Homonyms are different words that are pronounced the same, but may or may not be spelled the same. *To, too,* and *two* are homonyms despite their spelling differences.

---

[1] The term *homophone* is sometimes used instead of *homonym.*

Homonyms can create ambiguity. A word or a sentence is **ambiguous** if it can be understood or interpreted in more than one way. The sentence

I'll meet you by the bank

may mean "I'll meet you by the financial institution" or "I'll meet you by the riverside." The ambiguity is due to the two words *bank* with two different meanings. Sometimes additional context can help to disambiguate the sentence:

I'll meet you by the bank, in front of the automated teller machine.
I'll meet you by the bank. We can go skinny-dipping.

Homonyms are good candidates for humor as well as for confusion.

"How is bread made?"
"I know *that!*" Alice cried eagerly.
"You take some flour —"
"Where do you pick the flower?" the White Queen asked. "In a garden, or in the hedges?"
"Well, it isn't *picked* at all," Alice explained; "it's ground —"
"How many acres of ground?" said the White Queen.

The humor of this passage is based on the two sets of homonyms: *flower* and *flour* and the two meanings of *ground*. Alice means *ground* as the past tense of *grind,* whereas the White Queen is interpreting *ground* to mean "earth."

When a word has multiple meanings that are related conceptually or historically, it is said to be **polysemous** (polly-seamus). Open a dictionary of English to any page and you will find words with more than one definition, for example, *guard, music,* and *rot.* Each of these words is polysemous because each has several meanings.

Bear is polysemous, with meanings "to tolerate," "to carry," "to support" among others found in the dictionary. *Bear* is also a homonym. Homonyms generally have separate dictionary entries, often marked with superscripts "1," "2," and so forth. One "bear" is the polysemous verb just mentioned. The other "bear" refers to the animal. It, too, is polysemous, with other meanings such as "a falling stock market." *Bare,* which is pronounced the same as *bear,* is a third homonym.

A related concept is **heteronym.** Two words are heteronyms if they are spelled the same, but pronounced differently, and have different meanings. *Dove* the bird and *dove* the past tense of *dive* are heteronyms, as are *bass, bow, lead, wind,* and hundreds of others.

Homographs are words that are spelled the same, but have different meanings, such as *dove* the bird, and *dove,* the past tense of *dive.* When homonyms are spelled the same, they are also homographs, for example *bear* and *bear,* but not all homonyms are homographs (*bear* and *bare*). On the other hand, by definition, all heteronyms are also homographs. The following table should help sort out these confusing, overlapping terms.

	Homonyms	**Heteronyms**	**Homographs**
Pronounced identically	Yes	No	Yes/No
Spelled identically	Yes/No	Yes	Yes

SYNONYMS

Does he wear a turban, a fez or a hat?
Does he sleep on a mattress, a bed or a mat, or a Cot,
The Akond of Swat?
Can he write a letter concisely clear,
Without a speck or a smudge or smear or Blot,
The Akond of Swat?

Edward Lear, *The Akond of Swat*

Not only are there words that sound the same but have different meanings, but there are words that sound different but have the same or nearly the same meaning. Such words are called **synonyms.** There are dictionaries of synonyms that contain many hundreds of entries, such as:

apathetic/phlegmatic/passive/sluggish/indifferent
pedigree/ancestry/genealogy/descent/lineage

A sign in the San Diego Zoo Wild Animal Park states:

Please do not *annoy, torment, pester, plague, molest, worry, badger, harry, harass, heckle, persecute, irk, bullyrag, vex, disquiet, grate, beset, bother, tease, nettle, tantalize,* or *ruffle* the animals.

It has been said that there are no perfect synonyms—that is, no two words ever have *exactly* the same meaning. Still, the following two sentences have very similar meanings.

He's sitting on the sofa. / He's sitting on the couch.

Some individuals may prefer to use *sofa* instead of *couch,* but if they know the two words, they will understand both sentences and interpret them to mean essentially the same thing. The degree of semantic similarity between words depends largely on the number of semantic properties they share. *Sofa* and *couch* refer to the same type of object and share most of their semantic properties.

There are words that are neither synonyms nor near synonyms, yet have many semantic properties in common. *Man* and *boy* both refer to male humans; the meaning of *boy* includes the additional semantic property of "youth," whereby it differs from the meaning of *man.*

A polysemous word may share one of its meanings with another word, a kind of partial synonymy. For example, *mature* and *ripe* are polysemous words that are synonyms when applied to fruit, but not when applied to (smelly) animals. *Deep* and *profound* mean the same when applied to thought, but only *deep* can modify *water.*

Sometimes words that are ordinarily opposites can mean the same thing in certain contexts; thus a *good* scare is the same as a *bad* scare and a *fat* chance is about as likely as a *slim* chance. Similarly, a word with a positive meaning in one form, such as the adjective *perfect,* when used adverbially, undergoes a "weakening" effect, so that a "perfectly good bicycle" is neither perfect nor always good. "Perfectly good" means something more like "adequate."

When synonyms occur in otherwise identical sentences, the sentences are **paraphrases;** that is, they have the same meaning (except possibly for minor differences in emphasis). For example:

She forgot her handbag.
She forgot her purse.

This use of synonyms creates **lexical paraphrase,** just as the use of homonyms creates lexical ambiguity.

ANTONYMS

As a rule, man is a fool;
When it's hot, he wants it cool;
When it's cool, he wants it hot;
Always wanting what is not.

Anonymous

The meaning of a word may be partially defined by saying what it is *not. Male* means *not* female. *Dead* means *not* alive. Words that are opposite in meaning are often called **antonyms.** Ironically, the basic property of words that are antonyms is that they share all but one semantic property. *Beautiful* and *tall* are not antonyms; *beautiful* and *ugly,* or *tall* and *short,* are. The property they do not share is present in one and absent in the other.

There are several kinds of antonymy. There are complementary pairs:

alive/dead   present/absent   awake/asleep

They are complementary in that not *alive* = *dead* and not *dead* = *alive,* and so on.

There are **gradable** pairs of antonyms:

big/small   hot/cold   fast/slow   happy/sad

The meaning of adjectives in gradable pairs is related to the object they modify. The words themselves do not provide an absolute scale. Thus we know that "a small elephant" is much bigger than "a large mouse." *Fast* is faster when applied to an airplane than to a car.

With gradable pairs, the negative of one word is not synonymous with the other. For example, someone who is *not happy* is not necessarily *sad.* It is also true of gradable antonyms that more of one is less of another. More bigness is less smallness; wider is less narrow; taller is less short.

Gradable antonyms are often found among sets of words that partition a continuum:

tiny - small - medium - large - huge - gargantuan
euphoric - elated - happy - so-so - sad - gloomy - despondent

Another characteristic of certain pairs of gradable antonyms is that one is **marked** and the other **unmarked.** The unmarked member is the one used in questions of degree.

We ask, ordinarily, "How *high* is the mountain?" (not "How low is it?")[2] We answer "Ten thousand feet high" but never "Ten thousand feet low," except humorously or ironically. Thus *high* is the unmarked member of *high/low*. Similarly *tall* is the unmarked member of *tall/short, fast* the unmarked member of *fast/slow,* and so on.

Another kind of "opposite" involves pairs like

give/receive buy/sell teacher/pupil

They are called **relational opposites,** and they display symmetry in their meaning. If X *gives* Y to Z, then Z *receives* Y from X. If X is Y's *teacher,* then Y is X's *pupil.* Pairs of words ending in *-er* and *-ee* are usually relational opposites. If Mary is Bill's *employer,* then Bill is Mary's *employee.*

Comparative forms of gradable pairs of adjectives often form relational pairs. Thus, if Sally is *taller* than Alfred, then Alfred is *shorter* than Sally. If a Cadillac is *more expensive* than a Ford, then a Ford is *cheaper* than a Cadillac.

If meanings of words were indissoluble wholes, there would be no way to make the interpretations we do. We know that *big* and *red* are not opposites because they have too few semantic properties in common. They are both adjectives, but *big* has a semantic property "about size," whereas *red* has a semantic property "about color." On the other hand, *buy/sell* are relational opposites because both contain the semantic property "transfer of goods or services," and they differ only in one property, "direction of transfer."

Relationships between certain semantic features can reveal knowledge about antonyms. Consider:

A word that is [+married] is [-single].
A word that is [+single] is [-married].

These show that any word that bears the semantic property "married," such as *wife,* is understood to lack the semantic property "single"; and conversely, any word that bears the semantic property "single," such as *bachelor,* will not have the property "married."

Some words are their own antonyms. These "autoantonyms" are words such as *cleave* "to split apart" or "to cling together" and *dust* "to remove something" or "to spread something," as in dusting furniture or dusting crops. Antonymic pairs that are pronounced the same but spelled differently are similar to autoantonyms: *raise* and *raze* are one such pair.

Formation of Antonyms   In English there are a number of ways to form antonyms. You can add the prefix *un-:*

likely/unlikely able/unable fortunate/unfortunate

or you can add *non-:*

entity/nonentity conformist/nonconformist

---

[2] If the topic of conversation were "low mountains," say for the purpose of novice mountain climbing, then it might be appropriate to ask "How low is Mount Airy?" The marked/unmarked distinction is in effect if there are no contextual factors.

or you can add *in-:*

> tolerant/intolerant   discreet/indiscreet   decent/indecent

Other prefixes may also be used to form negative words morphologically: *mis-,* as in *misbehave, dis-,* as in *displease.*

These strategies occasionally backfire, however. *Loosen* and *unloosen; flammable* and *inflammable; valuable* and *invaluable,* and a few other "antiautonyms" actually have the same or nearly the same meaning.

Hyponyms

Speakers of English know that the words *red, white,* and *blue* are "color" words, that is, their lexical representations have the feature [+color] indicating a class to which they all belong. Similarly *lion, tiger, leopard,* and *lynx* have the feature [+feline]. Such sets of words are called **hyponyms.** The relationship of *hyponymy* is between the more general term such as *color* and the more specific instances of it such as *red.* Thus *red* is a hyponym of *color,* and *lion* is a hyponym of *feline;* or equivalently, *color* has the hyponym *red* and *feline* has the hyponym *lion.*

Sometimes no single word in the language encompasses a set of hyponyms. Thus *clarinet, guitar, horn, marimba, piano, trumpet,* and *violin* are hyponyms because they are "musical instruments" but there isn't a single word meaning "musical instrument" that has these words as its hyponyms.

Metonyms

A **metonym** substitutes for the object that is meant, the name of an attribute or concept associated with that object. The use of *crown* for *king,* or for the government ruled by a king, is an example of metonymy. So is the use of *brass* to refer to military leaders. Metonyms are often employed by the news services. Sportswriters are especially adept, using *gridiron* for football; *diamond* for baseball; *ice* for hockey; *turf* for horseracing; and so on. Metonyms for governments such as *Kremlin, Whitehall, Washington,* and *Baghdad* are commonplace. Metonyms need not be a single word. *Madison Avenue* is a metonym referring to the advertising industry; *Scotland Yard* refers to the Criminal Investigation Department in the United Kingdom. The association is that the Metropolitan Police were once housed in an area of London called Great Scotland Yard.

RETRONYMS

Day baseball, silent movie, surface mail, and *whole milk* are all expressions that once were redundant. In the past, all baseball games were played in daylight, all movies were silent, electronic mail didn't exist, and low-fat and skim milk were not yet conceived.

Retronym is the term reserved for these expressions. Strictly speaking, it does not apply to the individual words themselves, but the combination. Still, it's an interesting member of the *-nym* family of words.

Proper Names

"My name is Alice . . . "

"It's a stupid name enough!" Humpty Dumpty interrupted impatiently. "What does it mean?"

"Must a name mean something?" Alice asked doubtfully.

"Of course it must," Humpty Dumpty said with a short laugh. "My name means the shape I am—and a good handsome shape it is, too. With a name like yours, you might be any shape, almost."

Lewis Carroll, *Through the Looking-Glass*

"Tumbleweeds" copyright ©1987 Field Enterprises, Inc. Reprinted with special permission of North America Syndicate.

Proper names are a language's shortcuts. Imagine if we couldn't name people, places, institutions, or gods. How would you describe yourself uniquely without use of proper names? You can't say: "Eldest daughter of John and Mary Smith," obviously. How about: "The young woman who lives at 5 Oak Street?" No way! "Valedictorian of the senior class at Central High School." Sorry.

Proper names are different from most words in the language in that they refer to a specific object or entity, but usually have little meaning, or sense, beyond the power of referral.[3] That's part of the humor in Humpty Dumpty's remark about names meaning shapes.

The meaning of words like *dog* and *sincerity* impart a sense that permits you to recognize specific instances of that class of entities, or even have an abstract vision of what is meant, but you cannot pet *dog* or doubt *sincerity*. You can only pet a specific dog, Fido, or doubt a specific instance of sincerity, such as a political promise. Nothing in the world corresponds to *dog* the way *Paris* refers to the city of Paris.

Thus, proper names refer to unique (within context) objects or entities. The objects may be extant, such as those designated by

Disa Karin Viktoria Lubker
Lake Michigan
The Empire State Building

or extinct, such as

Socrates
Troy

or even fictional

Sherlock Holmes
Luke Skywalker
Oz

Proper names are **definite,** which means they refer to a unique object insofar as the speaker and listener are concerned. If I say

Mary Smith is coming to dinner

my spouse understands Mary Smith to refer to our friend Mary Smith, and not to one of the dozens of Mary Smiths in the phone book.

Proper names in English are not in general preceded by *the:*

*the John Smith
*the California

There are some exceptions, such as the names of rivers, ships, and erected structures:

the Mississippi
the *Queen Mary*
the Empire State Building
the Eiffel Tower
the Golden Gate Bridge

---

[3] Of course, if a word with sense, such as *lake,* is incorporated into a proper name, as in *Lake Louise,* then the proper noun has the semantic properties of *lake.* Care is needed though, since a restaurant named *Lake Louise* would not have any lakelike meaning.

and there are special cases such as *the John Smiths* to refer to the family of John Smith. Also, for the sake of clarity or literary effect, it is possible to precede a proper name by an article if the resulting noun phrase is followed by a modifying expression such as a prepositional phrase or a sentence:

The Paris of the 1920s . . .
The New York that everyone knows and loves . . .

In some languages, such as Greek and Hungarian, articles normally occur before proper names. Thus we find in Greek: *O Spiros agapai tin Sophia,* which is literally "The Spiro loves the Sophie," where *O* is the masculine nominative form of the definite article and *tin* the feminine accusative form. This indicates that some of the restrictions we observed are particular to English, and may be due to syntactic rather than semantic rules of language.

Proper names cannot usually be pluralized, though they can be plural, like *the Great Lakes* or *the Pleiades.* There are exceptions, such as the John Smiths already mentioned or expressions like *the Linguistics Department has three Bobs,* meaning three people named Bob, but they are special locutions used in particular circumstances. Because proper names generally refer to unique objects, it is not surprising that they occur mainly in the singular. For the same reason, proper names cannot in general be preceded by adjectives. Many adjectives have the semantic effect of narrowing the field of reference, so that the noun phrase *a red house* is a more specific description than simply a *house;* but what proper names refer to is already completely narrowed down, so modification by adjectives seems peculiar. Again, as in all these cases, extenuating circumstances give rise to exceptions. Language is nothing if not flexible, and we find expressions such as *young John* used to discriminate between two people named John. We also find adjectives applied to emphasize some quality of the object referred to, such as *the wicked Borgias* or *the brilliant Professor Einstein.*

Proper names are found in all languages and are therefore a linguistic universal.

Names may be coined or drawn from the stock of names that the language provides. However, once a proper name is coined, it cannot be pluralized or preceded by *the* or any adjective (except for cases like those just cited), and it will be used to refer uniquely. These rules are among the many rules already in the grammar, and speakers know they apply to all proper names, even new ones.

Phrase and Sentence Meaning

"Then you should say what you mean," the March Hare went on.

"I do," Alice hastily replied, "at least—I mean what I say—that's the same thing, you know."

"Not the same thing a bit!" said the Hatter. "You might just as well say that 'I see what I eat' is the same thing as 'I eat what I see'!"

"You might just as well say," added the March Hare, "that 'I like what I get' is the same thing as 'I get what I like'!"

> "You might just as well say," added the Dormouse . . . "that 'I breathe when I sleep' is the same thing as 'I sleep when I breathe'!"
> "It is the same thing with you," said the Hatter.
>
> Lewis Carroll, *Alice's Adventures in Wonderland*

Words and morphemes are the smallest meaningful units in language. We have been studying their meaning relationships and semantic properties as lexical semantics. For the most part, however, we communicate in phrases and sentences. The **Principle of Compositionality** states that the meaning of a phrase or sentence depends both on the meaning of its words and how those words are combined structurally. The sentences *John loves Mary* and *Mary loves John* mean different things even though they contain the same words. The sentence *Visiting relatives can be boring* can have two meanings because it has two structures.

Some of the semantic relationships we observed between words are also found between sentences. For example, two words may be synonyms; two sentences may be paraphrases. They may be paraphrases because they contain synonymous words, but they may also be paraphrases because of structural differences that do not affect meaning, such as

They ran the bill up.
They ran up the bill.

Similarly, words may be homonyms, hence ambiguous when spoken. Sentences may be ambiguous because they contain homonymous words, as in *I need to buy a pen for Shelby*, or due to their structure, as in the sentence *the boy saw the man with the telescope,* discussed in chapter 4.

Words have antonyms; sentences can be negated. Thus the opposite of *he is alive* is both *he is dead,* using an antonym, and *he is not alive,* using syntactic negation.

Words are used for naming purposes; sentences can also be used that way. Both words and sentences may refer to, or point out, objects; and both may have some meaning beyond this referring capability, as we shall see in a later section.

The study of how word meanings combine into phrase and sentence meanings, and the meaning relationships among these larger units, is called **phrasal,** or **sentential, semantics** to distinguish it from lexical semantics.

Phrasal Meaning

> . . . I placed all my words with their interpretations in alphabetical order. And thus in a few days, by the help of a very faithful memory, I got some insight into their language.
>
> Jonathan Swift, *Gulliver's Travels*

Although it is sometimes thought that learning a language is merely learning the words of that language and what they mean—a myth apparently accepted by Gulliver—there is more to it than that, as you know from reading this book. You might have known it already if you ever tried to learn a foreign language. We comprehend phrases and sentences because we know the meaning of individual words, and we know rules for combining their meanings.

NOUN–CENTERED MEANING

We know the meanings of *red* and *balloon*. The semantic rule to interpret the combination *red balloon* adds the property "redness" to the properties of *balloon*. Since *balloon* is the head of the phrase, it is modified by *red*. The properties of *balloon* are not added to the properties of *red*. If we add the word *the* to form *the red balloon,* the expression means "a particular instance of a balloon that is red." Semantic rules of interpretation that are sensitive to syntactic structure determine how the meanings of *the, red,* and *balloon* are combined to give a meaning to *the red balloon.*

The phrase *large balloon* would be interpreted differently because part of the meaning of *large* is that it is a relative concept. *Large balloon* means "*large for a balloon.*" What is large for a balloon may be small for a house and gargantuan for a cockroach. Nonetheless, the semantic rules of our mental grammar allow us to comprehend the meanings of *large balloon, large house,* and *large cockroach.*

The semantic rules for adjective-noun combinations are complex. A *good friend* is a kind of friend, just as a *red balloon* is a kind of a balloon. The semantic properties of the modifier are added to the head noun. But some adjectives belie the heads of phrases. Thus a *false friend* is not any kind of a friend at all. The semantic properties of "friendness" are "canceled out" by the adjective "false." The semantic rules for noun phrases containing *good* and *false* are different. A third kind of rule governs adjectives like *alleged;* the meaning of *alleged murderer* is someone accused of murder, but the semantic rules in this case do not tell us whether an alleged murderer is or is not a murderer.

The examples in the previous three paragraphs, and many examples below, all illustrate the Principle of Compositionality, and how it is manifested differently depending on the semantic properties of the individual words, and the syntactic structures in which they occur, in particular, which word is the head of the phrase.

Exemplars of Class of Adjective (Adj)	Truth of "An Adj X is an X" (e.g., *A red ball is a ball*)
good, red, large, . . .	True
false, counterfeit, phony, . . .	False
alleged, purported, putative, . . .	Undetermined

There are many more rules involved in the semantics of noun phrases. Because noun phrases may contain prepositional phrases, semantic rules are needed for such expressions as *the house with the white fence.* We have seen how the rules account for *the house* and *the white fence.* The semantic rules for prepositions indicate that two objects stand in a certain relationship determined by the meaning of the particular preposition. For *with,* that relationship is "accompanies" or "is part of." A preposition like *in* means a certain spatial relationship, and so on for other prepositions. As nearly always, the meanings center on the head of the phrase, so *the house with the white fence* is a kind of house because *house* is the head of the noun phrase. Similarly, *red brick* is a brick that is red: *brick* is the head. But *brick red* is a shade of red because *red* is the head of the Adjective Phrase.

In noun compounds, the final noun is generally the head; it provides the core meaning and specifies the syntactic class of the compound. So a *doghouse* is a kind of a house, namely one suitable for dogs, whereas a *housedog* is a kind of dog. Similar analyses apply to compounds consisting of mixed categories. The Noun-Adjective compound *headstrong* is an adjective; the Noun-Verb compound *spoonfeed* is a verb; the Verb-Noun compound *pickpocket* is a Noun, and so on. Exceptions are compounds like *redneck,* which is a type of person not a type of neck. These items must be individually stored along with their meaning in the mental lexicon. Their meaning cannot be predicted by rule.

Meanings build on meanings. Noun-phrase meanings are combinations of meanings of nouns, adjectives, articles, and even sentences. (The noun phrase *the man who knew too much* is a combination of *the, man,* and the sentence *he knew too much.*)[4] All these combinations make sense because the semantic rules of grammar, like rules of phonology or syntax, operate systematically and predictably to incorporate the meanings of the phrasal components into the meaning of the phrase.

Sense and Reference

It is natural . . . to think of there being connected with a sign . . . besides . . . the reference of the sign, also what I should like to call the sense of the sign. . . .

Gottlob Frege, *On Sense and Reference*

"There's nothing here under 'Superman'—is it possible you made the reservation under another name?"

Drawing by Michael Maslin; copyright © 1992 The New Yorker Collection. All rights reserved.

Knowing the meaning of certain noun phrases means knowing how to discover what objects the noun phrases refer to. For example in the sentence

The mason put the red brick on the wall

knowing the meaning of the Noun Phrase *the red brick* enables us to identify the object being referred to. We need only know in principle how to identify the object: A blind-

---

[4] Another semantic rule determines that *who* means the same as *the man.*

folded person would also comprehend the meaning. The object "pointed to" in such a noun phrase is called its **referent,** and the noun phrase is said to have **reference.**

For many noun phrases there is more to meaning than just reference. For example, the noun phrases *the red brick* and *the first brick from the right* may refer to the same object, that is, may be **coreferential.** Nevertheless, we would be reluctant to say that the two expressions have the same meaning because they have the same reference. Some additional meaning is present; it is often termed **sense.** Thus a noun phrase may have *sense* and *reference,* which together comprise its meaning. Knowing the sense of a noun phrase allows you to identify its referent. Sometimes the term **extension** is used for reference, and **intension** for sense.

Certain proper names appear to have only reference. A name like Chris Jones may point out a certain person, its referent, but seems to have little linguistic meaning beyond that. Nonetheless, some proper names do seem to have meaning over and above their ability to refer. Humpty Dumpty suggested that his name means "a good round shape." Certainly, the name Sue has the semantic property "female," as evinced by the humor in "A Boy Named Sue," a song sung by Johnny Cash. *The Pacific Ocean* has the semantic properties of *ocean,* and even such names as *Fido, Dobbins,* and *Bossie* are associated with dogs, horses, and cows, respectively.

Sometimes two different proper names have the same referent, such as Superman and Clark Kent or Dr. Jekyll and Mr. Hyde. It is a hotly debated question in the philosophy of language as to whether two such expressions have the same meaning, or differ in sense.

Other descriptions make a clear distinction between reference and sense. Consider the noun phrase, *the president of the United States.* Its reference at the time of this writing is George W. Bush; this will change in time. Its sense is "head of state of the United States of America." The sense is more enduring.

While some proper nouns appear to have reference but no sense, other noun phrases lack a reference, but have sense. If they didn't we would be unable to understand sentences like these:

The present king of France is bald.
By the year 3000, our descendants will have left Earth.

We can understand sentences that refer to nonexistent objects like present kings of France, unicorns, and so on.

In a later section on "deictic expressions," we will see examples of expressions that have sense, but rely on context for reference.

VERB-CENTERED MEANING

In all languages, the verb plays a central role in the meaning and structure of sentences. The verb determines the number of objects and limits the semantic properties of both its subject and its objects. For example, *find* requires an animate subject and selects a direct object; *put* selects for both a direct object and a prepositional object that has a locative meaning. Languages of the world, as we'll see in chapter 11, may be classified according to whether the verb occurs initially, medially, or finally in their basic sentences. All this is evidence for the centrality of the verb.

Thematic Roles   The noun phrase subject of a sentence and the constituents of the verb phrase are semantically related in various ways to the verb. The relations depend on the meaning of the particular verb. For example, the NP *the boy* in *the boy found a red brick* is called the **agent**, or "doer," of the action of finding. The NP *a red brick* is the **theme** and undergoes the action. (The boldfaced words are technical terms of semantic theory.) Part of the meaning of *find* is that its subject is an agent and its direct object is a theme.

"B.C." copyright © 1986 News America Syndicate. Reprinted by permission of Johnny Hart and Creators Syndicate, Inc.

The noun phrases within a verb phrase whose head is the verb *put* have the relation of theme and **goal.** In the verb phrase *put the red brick on the wall, the red brick* is the theme and *on the wall* is the goal. The entire verb phrase is interpreted to mean that the theme of *put* changes its position to the goal. *Put*'s subject is also an agent, so that in *The boy put the red brick on the wall,* "the boy" performs the action. The knowledge speakers have about *find* and *put* may be revealed in their lexical entries:

> find, V, ____ NP, (Agent, Theme)
> put, V, ____ NP PP, (Agent, Theme, Goal)

This formal representation is one way of stating the selectional restrictions of the verb, and the semantic relationships between the subject and the selected objects.

The semantic relationships that we have called *theme, agent,* and *goal* are among the **thematic roles** of the verb. Other thematic roles are **location,** where the action occurs; **source,** where the action originates; **instrument,** an object used to accomplish the action; **experiencer,** one receiving sensory input; **causative,** a natural force that brings about a change; and **possessor,** one who owns or has something. (The list is not complete.) These may be summed up:

Thematic Role	Description	Example
Agent	the one who performs an action	*Joyce* ran
Theme	the one or thing that undergoes an action	Mary found ***the puppy***
Location	the place where an action happens	It rains ***in Spain***

Thematic Role	Description	Example
Goal	the place to which an action is directed	Put the cat **on the porch**
Source	the place from which an action originates	He flew **from Iowa** to Idaho
Instrument	the means by which an action is performed	Jo cuts hair **with a razor**
Experiencer	one who perceives something	**Helen** heard Robert playing the piano
Causative	a natural force that causes a change	**The wind** damaged the roof
Possessor	one who has something	The tail of **the dog** wagged furiously

Our knowledge of verbs includes their syntactic category, which objects if any they select, and the thematic roles that their NP subject and object(s) have; and this knowledge is explicitly represented in the lexicon.

Thematic roles are the same in sentences that are paraphrases. In both these sentences

The dog bit the stick
The stick was bitten by the dog

the dog is the agent and *the stick* is the theme.

Thematic roles may remain the same in sentences that are *not* paraphrases, as in the following instances:

The boy opened the door with the key.
The key opened the door.
The door opened.

In all three of these sentences, *the door* is the theme, the object that is opened. In the first two sentences, *the key,* despite its different structural positions, retains the thematic role of instrument. The semantics of the three sentences, which speakers of English know, is determined by the meaning of *open,* including how it selects objects, and the thematic roles of the subjects and object(s) under the various selectional options.

The three examples illustrate the fact that English allows many thematic roles to be the subject of the sentence (that is, the first NP under the S). These sentences had as subjects an agent (*the boy*), an instrument (*the key*), and a theme (*the door*). The sentences below illustrate other kinds of subjects.

This hotel forbids dogs.
It seems that Samson has lost his strength.

In the first example, *this hotel* has the thematic role of location. In the second, the subject *it* is semantically empty and lacks a thematic role entirely.

Thematic Roles in Other Languages

> The immense value of becoming acquainted with a foreign language is that we are thereby led into a new world of tradition and thought and feeling.
>
> Havelock Ellis, *The Task of Social Hygiene*, chapter 10

Contrast English with German. German is much stingier about which thematic roles can be subjects. For example, in order to express the idea "this hotel forbids dogs," a German speaker would have to say:

In diesem Hotel sind Hunde verboten

literally, "in this hotel are dogs forbidden." German does not permit the thematic role of location to occur as a subject; it must be expressed as a prepositional phrase. If we translated the English sentence word for word into German, the results would be ungrammatical in German:

*Dieses Hotel verbietet Hunde.

Differences such as these between English and German show that learning a foreign language is not a matter of simple word-for-word translation. You must learn the grammar, and that includes learning the syntax and semantics and how the two interact.

In many languages, thematic roles are reflected in the **case,** or **grammatical case,** of the noun. The case of a noun refers to its morphological shape, often manifested as suffixes on the noun stem. English does not have an extensive case system, but the possessive form of a noun, as in *the boy's red brick,* is called the genitive, or possessive, case.

In languages such as Finnish, the noun assumes a morphological shape according to its thematic role in the sentence. In Finnish, *koulu* is the root meaning "school," and *-sta* is a case ending that means "directional source." Thus *koulusta* means "from the school." Similarly, *kouluun* (*koulu* + *-un*) means "to the school."

Some of the information carried by grammatical case in languages like Finnish is borne by prepositions in English. Thus *from* and *to* often indicate the thematic roles of source and goal. Instrument is marked by *with,* location by prepositions such as *on* and *in,* possessor by *of* and agent, experiencer, and causative by *by* in passive sentences. The role of theme is generally unaccompanied by a preposition, as its most common syntactic function is direct object. What we are calling thematic roles in this section has sometimes been studied as case theory.

In German, case distinctions appear on articles as well as on nouns and adjectives. Thus in

Sie liebt den Mann

"She loves the man," the article *den* is in the accusative case. In the nominative case it would be *der*. Languages with a rich system of case are often more constraining as to which thematic roles can occur in subject position. German, as we saw above, is one such language.

The Theta-Criterion The process of assigning thematic roles is sometimes called **theta assignment.** This term refers to the grammatical activity of spreading information from the verb to its noun phrase and prepositional phrase satellites. In a sentence like *the boy opened the door with the key, open* is represented in the lexicon as follows:

open, V, _____ NP, PP (Agent, Theme, Instrument)

Theta assignment assigns Agent to the subject noun phrase, Theme to the direct object, and Instrument to the prepositional phrase.

In chapter 4, we noted that the meaning of a sentence corresponds most closely to its deep structure. This is because theta assignment happens at deep structure. We find the evidence in sentences such as *Who will Bill kiss? Who* is the theme of *kiss,* and *Bill* is the agent, despite their relative positions in the sentence. If we examine the deep structure, *Bill will kiss who,* we see that theta assignment assigns the role of subject to *Bill* and theme to *who,* in accordance with the lexical entry of *kiss:*

kiss, V, _____ NP (Agent, Theme)

The transformational rules of *wh* movement and Move Aux produce the surface structure *Who will kiss Bill?* leaving the thematic role relationships intact. In fact, an important constraint on transformations is that they do not affect thematic roles, which are determined in deep structure.

A universal principle has been proposed called the **theta-criterion,** which states in part that a particular thematic role may occur only once in a sentence. Thus sentences like

*The boy opened the door with the key with a lock-pick

are semantically anomalous because two noun phrases bear the thematic role of instrument. The theta-criterion is a constraint on theta assignment. It permits one assignment per thematic role. If all objects do not receive a thematic role after theta assignment is completed, the result is anomalous.

In English the thematic role of possessor is indicated two ways syntactically: either as *the boy's red hat* or as *the red hat of the boy.* However, *the boy's red hat of Bill* is semantically anomalous according to the theta-criterion because both *the boy* and *Bill* have the thematic role of possessor.

The semantic relations that exist between verbs and noun phrases are part of every speaker's linguistic competence, and account for much of the meaning in language.

Sentential Meaning

The meaning of sentences is built, in part, from the meaning of noun phrases and verb phrases — the Principle of Compositionality again. Adverbs may add to or qualify the meaning. *The boy found the ball yesterday* specifies a time component to the meaning of the boy's finding the ball. Adverbs such as *quickly, fortunately,* and *often* would affect the meaning in other ways.

Like noun phrases, sentences have sense, or intension, which is usually what we are referring to when we talk about the meaning of a sentence. Some linguists would also say that certain sentences have reference, or extension, namely ones that can be true or false. Their extension is *true* if the sentence is true, and *false* if the sentence is false.

The "Truth" of Sentences

. . . Having Occasion to talk of Lying and false Representation, it was with much Difficulty that he comprehended what I meant. . . . For he argued thus: That the Use of Speech was to make us understand one another and to receive Information of Facts; now if any one said the Thing which was not, these Ends were defeated; because I cannot properly be said to understand him. . . . And these were all the Notions he had concerning that Faculty of Lying, so perfectly well understood, and so universally practiced among human Creatures.

Jonathan Swift, *Gulliver's Travels*

The sense of a declarative sentence permits you to know under what circumstances that sentence is true. Those "circumstances" are called the **truth conditions** of the sentence. The truth conditions of a declarative sentence are the same as the *sense* of the sentence.

In the world as we know it, the sentence

The Declaration of Independence was signed in 1776

is true, and the sentence

The Declaration of Independence was signed in 1976

is false. We know the meaning of both sentences equally well, and knowing their meaning means knowing their sense, or intension, or truth conditions. We compare their truth conditions with "the real world" or historical fact, and can thus say which sentence is true and which false. The truth or falsehood of these sentences is their *reference,* their *extension.*

You can, however, understand well-formed sentences of your language without knowing their truth value, just as you can understand the expression *the fifteenth Pope of the Catholic Church* without knowing the reference. Knowing the truth conditions is not the same as knowing the facts. Rather, the truth conditions permit you to examine the world and learn the facts. If you did not know the linguistic meaning — if the sentence were in an unknown language — you could never determine its truth, even if you had memorized an encyclopedia. You may not know the truth of

The Mecklenburg Charter was signed in 1770

but if you know its meaning you know in principle how to discover its truth, even if you do not have the means to do so. For example, consider the sentence

The moon is made of green cheese.

We knew before space travel that going to the moon would test the truth of the sentence. Now consider this sentence:

Rufus believes that the Declaration of Independence was signed in 1976.

This sentence is true if some individual named Rufus does indeed believe the statement, and it is false if he does not. Those are its truth conditions. It does not matter that a sub-part of the sentence is false. An entire sentence may be true even if one or more of its parts are false, and vice versa. The sense of a sentence is determined by the semantic rules that permit you to combine its subparts and still know under what conditions it is true or false.

PARAPHRASE

We can now give a formal definition of *paraphrase:*

> Two sentences are paraphrases if they have the same truth conditions.

This means whenever one is true, the other is true; and when one is false, the other is false, without exception. The following sets of sentences are paraphrases. Despite subtle differences in emphasis, they have the same truth conditions:

> The horse threw the rider.
> The rider was thrown by the horse.

Active-passive pairs like this example are often paraphrases, but not always. When quantifiers are involved—words like *every, each, many, few,* and *several* — an active and its corresponding passive may have different truth conditions; that is, they may not be paraphrases. Consider

> Every person in this room speaks two languages.
> Two languages are spoken by every person in this room.

These two sentences do *not* have the same truth conditions; they are not paraphrases. Suppose there are three people in the room, Tom, Dick, and Harry. Tom speaks English and Russian; Dick speaks French and Italian; and Harry speaks Chinese and Thai. Then the first sentence is true. The second, however, is false because there are no two languages that everyone speaks.

Here are other sets of paraphrases involving more or less the same vocabulary in different syntactic structures:

> It is easy to play sonatas on this piano.
> This piano is easy to play sonatas on.
> On this piano it is easy to play sonatas.
> Sonatas are easy to play on this piano.

> Booth assassinated Lincoln.
> It was Booth who assassinated Lincoln.
> It was Lincoln who was assassinated by Booth.
> The person who assassinated Lincoln was Booth.

> The students gave money to the beggar.
> The students gave the beggar money.

In these three sets, the sentences in each set are related via transformations. Since transformations do not change thematic roles, they tend in many cases to preserve the truth conditions, that is, to preserve meaning.

Paraphrase may also arise with certain semantic concepts such as "ability," "permission," and "obligation." These may be expressed through auxiliary verbs:

He *can* go.
He *may* go.
He *must* go.

They may also be expressed phrasally, without the auxiliaries:

He is *able* to go. / He has *the ability* to go.
He is *permitted* to go. / He has *permission* to go.
He is *obliged* to go. / He has an *obligation* to go.

Finally, it is often possible to substitute a phrase for a word without affecting the sense of the sentence.

John saw Mary.
John perceived Mary using his eyes.

The professor lectured the class.
The professor delivered a lecture to the class.

ENTAILMENT

Sometimes knowing the truth of one sentence **entails,** or necessarily implies, the truth of another sentence. For example, if you know that it is true that

Corday assassinated Marat

then you know that it is true that

Marat is dead.

It is logically inconsistent for the former to be true and the latter false. Thus the *sentence Corday assassinated Marat* entails the sentence *Marat is dead.*

The sentence *The brick is red* entails *The brick is not white; Mortimer is a bachelor* entails *Mortimer is male,* and so on. These entailments are part of the semantic rules we have been discussing. Much of what we know about the world comes from knowing the entailments of true sentences.

CONTRADICTION

Contradiction is negative entailment; that is, the truth of one sentence necessarily implies the falseness of another sentence, for example:

Elizabeth II is Queen of England.
Elizabeth II is a man.

Scott is a baby.
Scott is an adult.

If the first sentence of each pair is true, the second is necessarily false. This relationship is called *contradiction* because the truth of one sentence contradicts the truth of the other. For a somewhat different use of the word *contradictory,* see exercise 12.

Events Versus States

Some sentences describe **events,** such as *John kissed Mary,* or *John ate oysters.* Other sentences describe **states** such as *John knows Mary,* or *John likes oysters.* These differences appear to have syntactic consequences. Eventive sentences sound natural when passivized, when expressed progressively, when used imperatively, and with certain adverbs:

Eventives

Mary was kissed by John.	Oysters were eaten by John.
John is kissing Mary.	John is eating oysters.
Kiss Mary!	Eat oysters!
John deliberately kissed Mary.	John deliberately ate oysters.

The stative sentences seem peculiar, if not ungrammatical or anomalous, when cast in the same form. (The preceding "?" indicates the strangeness.)

Statives

?Mary is known by John	?Oysters are liked by John.
?John is knowing Mary	?John is liking oysters
?Know Mary!	?Like oysters!
?John deliberately knows Mary	?John deliberately likes oysters

These examples show yet another way in which syntax and semantics interact.

Pronouns and Coreferentiality

Another example of how syntax and semantics interact has to do with **reflexive pronouns,** such as *herself* and *themselves.* The meaning of a reflexive pronoun always refers back to some antecedent. In *Jane bit herself, herself* refers to Jane. Syntactically,

"Hi and Lois" copyright © 1999 King Features Syndicate, Inc. Reprinted with special permission of King Features Syndicate.

reflexive pronouns and their antecedents must occur within the same S in the phrase structure tree. Compare the phrase structure tree of *Jane bit herself* with that of **Jane said that herself slept:*

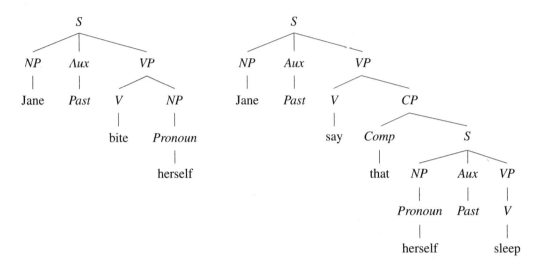

In the first tree *Jane* and *herself* are in the same S, and are understood to be coreferential, that is, to refer to the same person. In the second tree, *Jane* and *herself* are in different S-rooted trees and cannot be coreferential. Moreover, syntactic and semantic rules do not allow reflexive pronouns to be subjects — that's the humor of the cartoon — so the second tree is ungrammatical. It would even be ungrammatical if the sentence were **Jane said that Bill bit herself*, with *herself* as the direct object, because the only possible referent for *herself* is not in the same S-rooted tree.

Sentence structure also plays a role in determining when a pronoun and a noun phrase in different clauses can be coreferential. For example in

John believes that he is a genius

the pronoun *he* can be interpreted as John or as some person other than John. However in

He believes that John is a genius

the coreferential interpretation is impossible. *John* and *he* cannot refer to the same person. It may appear that a pronoun antecedent cannot occur to the left of its noun phrase if the two are to be coreferential, but this is deceiving. It is really a matter of structure. In the sentence

The fact that he is considered a genius bothers John

he and *John* can be interpreted as coreferential. The critical factor is that the pronoun is in a "lower" S, as this abbreviated phrase structure tree shows:

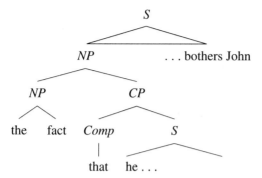

A precise statement of the rule that is at work here goes beyond the scope of this introductory text. The point is that syntax and semantics interrelate in complex ways, and that sentence structure is crucial. This is further proof that knowing a language is knowing the syntactic structures and the semantic rules, and how they interact.

To Mean or Not to Mean

> For all a rhetorician's rules
> Teach nothing but to name his tools.
>
> Samuel Butler, Hudibras

The meaning of an expression is not always obvious, even to a native speaker of the language. There are many ways in which meanings may be obscured, or at least require some imagination or special knowledge to be apprehended. Poets, pundits, and yes, even professors, can be difficult to understand.

We would like to examine three ways in which meaning may be veiled or even absent. They are **anomaly**—expressions that appear to follow the rules of syntax, but go awry semantically; **metaphor,** or nonliteral, indirect, but often creative meaning; and **idioms,** wherein the meaning of an expression is unrelated to the meaning of its parts, though it is conventionally understood.

Anomaly: No Sense and Nonsense

> Don't tell me of a man's being able to talk sense; everyone can talk sense. Can he talk nonsense?
>
> William Pitt

> There is no greater mistake in the world than the looking upon every sort of nonsense as want of sense.
>
> Leigh Hunt

If in a conversation someone said to you

My brother is an only child

you might think that he was making a joke or that he did not know the meaning of the words he was using. You would know that the sentence was strange, or *anomalous;* yet it is certainly an English sentence. It conforms to all the syntactic rules of the language. It is strange because it represents a contradiction; the meaning of *brother* includes the fact that the individual referred to is a male human who has at least one sibling, and cannot sensibly be "an only child."

The sentence

That bachelor is pregnant

is anomalous for similar reasons; the word bachelor contains the semantic property "male," whereas the word "pregnant" has the semantic property "female." This clash of semantic properties makes the sentence anomalous. The anomaly arises from trying to equate something that is [+male] with something that is [-male].

The semantic properties of words determine what other words they can be combined with. A sentence widely used by linguists that we encountered in chapter 4 illustrates this fact:

Colorless green ideas sleep furiously.

The sentence obeys all the syntactic rules of English. The subject is *colorless green ideas* and the predicate is *sleep furiously*. It has the same syntactic structure as the sentence

Dark green leaves rustle furiously

but there is obviously something wrong semantically with the sentence. The meaning of *colorless* includes the semantic property "without color," but it is combined with the adjective *green,* which has the property "green in color." How can something be both "without color" and "green in color"? Other such semantic violations also occur in the sentence.

Other English "sentences" make no sense at all because they include "words" that have no meaning; they are **uninterpretable.** They can be interpreted only if some meaning for each nonsense word can be dreamt up. Lewis Carroll's "Jabberwocky" is probably the most famous poem in which most of the content words have no meaning — they do not exist in the lexicon of the grammar. Still, all the sentences "sound" as if they should be or could be English sentences:

'Twas brillig, and the slithy toves
Did gyre and gimble in the wabe;
All mimsy were the borogoves,
And the mome raths outgrabe.

. . .

He took his vorpal sword in hand:
Long time the manxome foe he sought —

> So rested he by the Tumtum tree,
> And stood awhile in thought.

Without knowing what *vorpal* means, you nevertheless know that

> He took his vorpal sword in hand

means the same thing as

> He took his sword, which was vorpal, in hand.
> It was in his hand that he took his vorpal sword.

Knowing the language, and assuming that *vorpal* means the same thing in the three sentences (because the same sounds are used), you can decide that the sense — the truth conditions — of the three sentences are identical. In other words, you are able to decide that two things mean the same thing even though you do not know what either one means. You decide by assuming that the semantic properties of *vorpal* are the same whenever it is used.

We now see why Alice commented, when she had read "Jabberwocky":

> "It seems very pretty, but it's *rather* hard to understand!" (You see she didn't like to confess, even to herself, that she couldn't make it out at all.) "Somehow it seems to fill my head with ideas — only I don't exactly know what they are! However, *somebody* killed *something:* that's clear, at any rate —"

The semantic properties of words show up in other ways in sentence construction. For example, if the meaning of a word includes the semantic property "human" in English, we can replace it by one sort of pronoun but not another. This semantic feature determines that we call a boy *he* and a table *it,* and not vice versa.

According to Mark Twain, Eve had such knowledge in her grammar, for she writes in her diary:

> If this reptile is a man, it ain't an *it,* is it? That wouldn't be grammatical, would it? I think it would be *he*. In that case one would parse it thus: nominative *he;* dative, *him;* possessive, *his'n*.

Semantic violations in poetry may form strange but interesting aesthetic images, as in Dylan Thomas's phrase *a grief ago. Ago* is ordinarily used with words specified by some temporal semantic feature:

a week ago		*a table ago
an hour ago	but not	*a dream ago
a month ago		*a mother ago
a century ago		

When Thomas used the word *grief* with *ago* he was adding a durational feature to grief for poetic effect.

In the poetry of e. e. cummings there are phrases like

the six subjunctive crumbs twitch.
a man . . . wearing a round jeer for a hat.
children building this rainman out of snow.

Though all of these phrases violate some semantic rules, we can understand them; it is the breaking of the rules that creates the imagery desired.

Anomaly occurs in many ways in language. It may involve contradictory semantic properties, nonsense words, violation of semantic rules, and so on. The fact that we are able to understand, or at least interpret, anomalous expressions, and at the same time recognize their anomalous nature, demonstrates our knowledge of the semantic system and semantic properties of the language.

Metaphor

Our doubts are traitors.

Shakespeare

Walls have ears.

Cervantes

The night has a thousand eyes and the day but one.

Frances William Bourdillon

Anyone who ever sat down to write a term paper on some "fascinating" but abstract subject such as "the fall of the rupee in nineteenth-century British-ruled India" knows how hard it is to find the right words. Often, you find yourself using concrete language to describe the abstract events. The use of *fall* to describe the decline in the value of a monetary unit illustrates this.

Language concepts, combined with our experience in the world, may be stretched to encompass a variety of (possibly remotely) related concepts. For example, a metaphor is an expression that ordinarily designates one concept — its literal meaning — but is used to designate another concept, thus creating an implicit comparison. Metaphor is an important part of semantics. Without metaphor, our ability to communicate efficiently and effectively would be crippled. Metaphor is an important component of language creativity.

Interpreted literally, metaphors may appear anomalous. *Walls have ears* is certainly anomalous, but it can be interpreted as meaning "you can be overheard even when you think nobody is listening." In some sense the sentence is ambiguous, but the literal meaning is so unlikely that listeners use their imagination for another interpretation. The Principle of Compositionality is very "rubbery," and when it fails to produce an acceptable literal meaning, listeners stretch it. That "stretching" is based on semantic properties that are inferred, or that provide some kind of resemblance.

The literal meaning of a sentence such as

My new car is a lemon

is anomalous. You could, if driven to the wall (another metaphor), provide some literal interpretation that is plausible if given sufficient context. For example, *the new car* may be a miniature toy carved out of a piece of citrus fruit. The more common meaning, however, would be metaphorical and interpreted as referring to a newly purchased automobile that breaks down and requires constant repairs. The imagination stretching in this case may relate to the semantic property "tastes sour" that *lemon* possesses.

Metaphors are not necessarily anomalous when taken literally. The literal meaning of the sentence

Dr. Jekyll is a butcher

is that a physician named Jekyll also works as a retailer of meats or a slaughterer of animals used for food. The metaphorical meaning is that the doctor named Jekyll is harmful, possibly murderous, and apt to operate unnecessarily.

Similarly, the sentence

John is a snake in the grass

can be interpreted literally to refer to a pet snake on the lawn named John. Metaphorically, the sentence has nothing to do with a scaly, limbless reptile.

To interpret metaphors we need to understand both the literal meaning and facts about the world. To understand the metaphor

Time is money

it is necessary to know that in our society we are often paid according to the number of hours or days worked. In fact, "time," which is an abstract concept, is the subject of multiple metaphors. We "save time," "waste time," "manage time," push things "back in time," live on "borrowed time," and suffer the "ravages of time" as the "sands of time" drift away.

Metaphor has a strong cultural component. *My car is a lemon* may not be understood in a culture that lacks both cars and lemons, like that of the native peoples of northern Greenland. Shakespeare uses metaphors that are lost on many of today's playgoers. "I am a man whom Fortune hath cruelly scratched," is most effective as a metaphor in a society like Shakespeare's that commonly depicts "Fortune" as a woman.

Many expressions now taken literally may have originated as metaphors. Indeed, the once highly metaphorical "My car is a lemon" is becoming more literal as legislatures pass "lemon laws," and the usage becomes more common. Metaphor is one of the driving forces behind language change (see chapter 11).

Metaphorical use of language is language creativity at its highest. Nevertheless, the basis of metaphorical use is the ordinary linguistic knowledge about words, their semantic properties, and their combining powers that all speakers possess.

Idioms

Knowing a language includes knowing the morphemes, simple words, compound words, and their meanings. In addition, it means knowing fixed phrases, consisting of more than one word, with meanings that cannot be inferred from the meanings of the individual words. Here is where the Principle of Compositionality is superseded by expressions that act very much like individual morphemes in that they are not decomposable, but

have a fixed meaning that must be learned. The usual semantic rules for combining meanings do not apply. All languages contain many such expressions, called **idioms,** or **idiomatic phrases,** as in these English examples:

sell down the river
haul over the coals
eat my hat
let their hair down
put his foot in his mouth
throw her weight around
snap out of it
cut it out
hit it off
get it off
bite your tongue
give a piece of your mind

Idioms are similar in structure to ordinary phrases except that they tend to be frozen in form and do not readily enter into other combinations or allow the word order to change. Thus,

1. She put her foot in her mouth

has the same structure as

2. She put her bracelet in her drawer

but

The drawer in which she put her bracelet was hers
Her bracelet was put in her drawer

are sentences related to sentence (2).

The mouth in which she put her foot was hers
Her foot was put in her mouth

do not have the idiomatic sense of sentence (1), except, perhaps, humorously.

On the other hand, the words of some idioms can be moved without affecting the idiomatic sense:

The FBI kept tabs on radicals.
Tabs were kept on radicals by the FBI.
Radicals were kept tabs on by the FBI.

Idioms can break the rules on combining semantic properties. The object of *eat* must usually be something with the semantic property "edible," but in

He ate his hat
Eat your heart out

this restriction is violated.

Idioms often lead to humor:

What did the doctor tell the vegetarian about his surgically implanted heart valve from a pig?
That it was okay as long as he didn't "eat his heart out."

Idioms, grammatically as well as semantically, have special characteristics. They must be entered into the lexicon or mental dictionary as single items with their meanings specified, and speakers must learn the special restrictions on their use in sentences.

Most idioms originate as metaphorical expressions that establish themselves in the language and become frozen in their form and meaning.

Pragmatics

Pragmatics is concerned with the interpretation of linguistic meaning in context. Two kinds of contexts are relevant. The first is *linguistic* context — the discourse that precedes the phrase or sentence to be interpreted. Taken by itself, the sentence

> Amazingly, he already loves her

is essentially uninterpretable. Its linguistic meaning is clear: "Something male and animate has arrived at a state of adoration of something female and animate, and the speaker finds it astonishing." However, without context, that's as far as it goes. There are no referents for *he* and *her,* and the reason for *amazingly* is vague. If the sentence preceding it were *John met Mary yesterday,* its interpretation would be clearer.

> John met Mary yesterday
> Amazingly, he already loves her

The discourse suggests the second kind of context — *situational,* or knowledge of the world. To fully interpret the sentences the listener must know the real-world referents of John and Mary. Moreover the interpretation of *amazingly* is made clear by the general belief or knowledge that a person ordinarily needs more than a day to complete the act — the completion indicated by *already* — of falling in love.

Situational context, then, includes the speaker, hearer, and any third parties present, along with their beliefs and their beliefs about what the others believe. It includes the physical environment, the subject of conversation, the time of day, and so on, ad infinitum. Almost any imaginable extralinguistic factor may, under appropriate circumstances, influence the way language is interpreted.

Pragmatics is also about language use. It tells that calling someone a *son of a bitch* is not a zoological opinion, it's an insult. It tells us that when a beggar on the street asks *do you have any spare change?* it is not a fiduciary inquiry, it's a request for money. It tells us that when a justice of the peace says, in the appropriate setting, *I now pronounce you husband and wife,* an act of marrying was performed.

Linguistic Context: Discourse

Put your discourse into some frame, and start not so wildly from my affair.

William Shakespeare, *Hamlet*

Linguistic knowledge accounts for speakers' ability to combine phonemes into morphemes, morphemes into words, and words into sentences. Knowing a language also permits combining sentences to express complex thoughts and ideas. These larger linguistic units are called **discourse.**

The study of discourse, or **discourse analysis,** is concerned with how speakers combine sentences into broader speech units. Discourse analysis involves questions of style, appropriateness, cohesiveness, rhetorical force, topic/subtopic structure, differences between written and spoken discourse, as well as grammatical properties.

Our immediate concern is to point out a few aspects of discourse that may influence the interpretation of linguistic meaning.

PRONOUNS

The 911 operator, trying to get a description of the gunman, asked, "What kind of clothes does he have on?"

Mr. Morawski, thinking the question pertained to Mr. McClure, [the victim, who lay dying of a gunshot wound], answered, "He has a bloody shirt with blue jeans, purple striped shirt."

The 911 operator then gave police that description [the victim's] of a gunman.

The News and Observer, Raleigh, North Carolina, 1/21/89

Pronouns may be used in place of noun phrases or may be used to refer to an entity presumably known to the discourse participants. When that presumption fails, miscommunication such as the one at the head of this section may result.

Pronominalization occurs both in sentences and across the sentences of a discourse. Within a sentence, the sentence structure limits the choice of pronoun. We saw previously that the occurrence of reflexive pronouns depends on syntactic structure, which also determines whether a pronoun and noun phrase can be interpreted as coreferential.

In a discourse, prior linguistic context plays a primary role in pronoun interpretation. In the following discourse:

It seems that the man loves the woman.
Many people think he loves her.

the most natural interpretation of *her* is "the woman" referred to in the first sentence, whoever she happens to be. But it is also possible for *her* to refer to a different person, perhaps one indicated with a gesture. In such a case *her* would be spoken with added emphasis:

Many people think he loves *her!*

Similar remarks apply to the reference of *he,* which is ordinarily coreferential with *the man,* but not necessarily so. Again, intonation and emphasis would provide clues.

As far as syntactic rules are concerned, pronouns are noun phrases, and may occur almost anywhere that a noun phrase may occur.[5] Semantic rules of varying complexity establish whether a pronoun and some other noun phrase in the discourse can be interpreted as coreferential. A minimum condition of coreferentiality is that the pronoun and its antecedent have the same feature values for the semantic properties of number and gender.[6]

---

[5] There are a few exceptions. For example, *He ran up it* sounds strange. Compare *He ran up a large bill.*

[6] An exception to this, discussed in chapter 3, is the use of *they* in *anyone is eligible when they sign up.*

When semantic rules and contextual interpretation determine that a pronoun is coreferential with a noun phrase, we say that the pronoun is **bound** to that noun phrase antecedent. If *her* in the previous example refers to "the woman," it would be a bound pronoun. When a pronoun refers to some object not explicitly mentioned in the discourse, it is said to be **free** or **unbound.** The reference of a free pronoun must ultimately be determined by the situational context.

First- and second-person nonreflexive (*I, we, you*) pronouns are bound to the speaker and hearer, respectively. Reflexive pronouns are always bound; they require an antecedent in the sentence.

In the preceding example, semantic rules permit *her* either to be bound to *the woman,* or to be a free pronoun, referring to some person not explicitly mentioned. The ultimate interpretation is context-dependent.

Referring to the discourse above, strictly speaking, it would not be ungrammatical if the discourse went this way:

It seems that the man loves the woman.
Many people think the man loves the woman.

However, most people would find that the discourse sounds stilted. Often in discourse, the use of pronouns is a stylistic decision, which is part of pragmatics. Here are several examples of pronouns used in place of phrases:

Jan saw **the boy with the telescope**.
Dan also saw **him**.   (Pronoun)

Him has replaced *the boy with the telescope*. Technically, what we call pro*nouns* are "Pro-*noun phrases*" in that they replace entire noun phrases. As mentioned in chapter 4, pro-forms may substitute for other categorical expressions than noun phrases, for example:

Emily **hugged Cassidy** and Zachary **did** too. (Pro-verb phrase)
I am sick, **which** depresses me.   (Pro-sentence)

In the first sentence *did* replaces the Verb Phrase *hugged Cassidy.* In the second, *which* replaces the entire sentence *I am sick.*

Sometimes in discourse, or even within sentences, entire phrases may be omitted and not replaced by a pro-form but still understood because of context. Such utterances taken in isolation appear to violate the rules of syntax, as in the sentence **My uncle dried,* but in the following discourse it is perfectly acceptable:

First speaker: My aunt washed the dishes.
Second speaker: My uncle dried.

The second speaker is understood to mean "My uncle dried the dishes." In the following example, Bill is understood to have washed the cherries. This illustrates a process that linguists call **gapping.**

Jill washed the grapes and Bill the cherries.

In a similar process, called **sluicing,** what follows a *wh* word in an embedded sentence is omitted, but understood.

Your ex-husband is dancing with someone, but I don't know who.
My cat ate something, and I wish I knew what.
She said she was coming over, but she didn't say when.

Missing from the end of the first sentence is *he is dancing with;* missing from the second sentence is *she ate;* and from the third sentence, *she was coming over.*

THE ARTICLES *THE* AND *A*

"Peanuts" copyright © 1991 United Feature Syndicate, Inc. Reprinted with permission.

There are discourse rules that apply regularly, such as those that determine the occurrence of the articles *the* and *a*. The article *the* is used to indicate that the referent of a noun phrase is agreed upon by speaker and listener. If someone says

I saw the boy

it is assumed that a certain boy is being discussed. No such assumption accompanies

I saw a boy

which is more of a description of what was seen than a reference to a particular individual.

Often a discourse will begin with the use of indefinite articles, and once everyone agrees on the referents, definite articles start to appear. A short example illustrates this transition:

I saw *a* boy and *a* girl holding hands and kissing.
Oh, it sounds lovely.
Yes, *the* boy was quite tall and handsome, and he seemed to like *the* girl a lot.

These examples show that some rules of discourse are similar to grammatical rules in that a violation produces unacceptable results. If the final sentence of this discourse were

> Yes, a boy was quite tall and handsome, and he seemed to like a girl a lot

most speakers would find it unacceptable.

The presence or absence of *the* may make a large difference in the meaning of a sentence. Compare these two sentences:

> The terrorists are in control of the government.
> The terrorists are in *the* control of the government.

In the first, the terrorists are in charge; in the second, the government is in charge of the terrorists.

The article *a* may be interpreted, or used, specifically or nonspecifically. When used specifically, there is one reference; when used nonspecifically, multiple references are possible. Consider the sentence, *Helen wants to marry a college professor.* It has two possible meanings. In the first, Helen wants to marry Robert, and Robert is a college professor. This is the specific use of the article *a.* In the second meaning, Helen doesn't have a particular person in mind to marry, but she is confining her search for a mate to college professors. This is the nonspecific use of the article.

The census bureau is very good at producing ambiguities of specificity. It often proclaims such facts as: "A woman gives birth in the United States every 15 seconds." Of course context — pragmatics — prevent communication from going awry in most of these cases.

Situational Context

> Depending on inflection, *ah bon* [in French] can express shock, disbelief, indifference, irritation, or joy.
>
> Peter Mayle, *Toujours Provence*

Much discourse is telegraphic. Verb phrases are not specifically mentioned, entire clauses are left out, direct objects disappear, pronouns abound. Yet, people still understand people, and part of the reason is that rules of grammar and rules of discourse combine with contextual knowledge to fill in what's missing and make the discourse cohere. Much of the contextual knowledge is knowledge of who is speaking, who is listening, what objects are being discussed, and general facts about the world we live in, called **situational context.**

Often what we say is not literally what we mean. When we ask at the dinner table if someone "can pass the salt" we are not querying their ability to do so, we are requesting that they do so. If I say "you're standing on my foot," I am not making idle conversation; I am asking you to stand somewhere else. We say "it's cold in here" to mean "shut the window," or "turn up the heat," or "let's leave," or a dozen other things that depend on the real-world situation at the time of speaking.

In the following sections, we will look at several ways that real-world context influences and interacts with meaning.

MAXIMS OF CONVERSATION

Though this be madness, yet there is method in't.

William Shakespeare, *Hamlet*

Speakers recognize when a series of sentences "hangs together" or when it is disjointed. The following discourse, which gave rise to Polonius' above remark, does not seem quite right — it is not coherent.

POLONIUS: What do you read, my lord?
HAMLET: Words, words, words.
POLONIUS: What is the matter, my lord?
HAMLET: Between who?
POLONIUS: I mean, the matter that you read, my lord.
HAMLET: Slanders, sir: for the satirical rogue says here that old men have gray beards, that their faces are wrinkled, their eyes purging thick amber and plum-tree gum, and that they have a plentiful lack of wit, together with most weak hams: all which, sir, though I most powerfully and potently believe, yet I hold it not honesty to have it thus set down; for yourself, sir, should grow old as I am, if like a crab you could go backward.[7]

Hamlet, who is feigning insanity, refuses to answer Polonius' questions "in good faith." He has violated certain conversational conventions, or **maxims of conversation.**[8] One such maxim, **the maxim of quantity,** states that a speaker's contribution to the discourse should be as informative as is required — neither more nor less. Hamlet has violated this maxim in both directions. In answering "Words, words, words" to the question of what he is reading, he is providing too little information. His final remark goes to the other extreme in providing too much information.

He also violates the **maxim of relevance** when he "misinterprets" the question about the reading matter as a matter between two individuals.

The "run-on" nature of Hamlet's final remark, a violation of the **maxim of manner,** is another source of incoherence. This effect is increased in the final sentence by the somewhat bizarre metaphor that compares growing younger with walking backward, a violation of the **maxim of quality,** which requires sincerity and truthfulness.

Here is a summary of the four conversational maxims, parts of the broad **Cooperative Principle.**

Name of Maxim	Description of Maxim
Quantity	Say neither more nor less than the discourse requires.
Relevance	Be relevant.

---

[7] *Hamlet,* Act II, Scene ii.
[8] These maxims were first discussed by H. Paul Grice.

Name of Maxim	Description of Maxim
Manner	Be brief and orderly; avoid ambiguity and obscurity.
Quality	Do not lie; do not make unsupported claims.

Unless speakers (like Hamlet) are being deliberately uncooperative, they adhere to these maxims, and to other conversational principles,[9] and assume others do too.

Bereft of context, if one man says (truthfully) to another *I have never slept with your wife* that would be grounds for provocation because that very topic of conversation should be unnecessary, a violation of the maxim of quantity.

Asking an able-bodied person at the dinner table, *can you pass the salt?* if answered literally, would force the responder into stating the obvious, a violation of the maxim of quantity. To avoid this, the person asked seeks a reason for the question, and deduces that the asker would like to have the saltshaker.

The maxim of relevance explains how saying *it's cold in here* to a person standing by an open, drafty window might be interpreted as a request to close it, else why make the remark to that particular person in the first place.[10]

Conversational conventions such as these allow the various sentence meanings to be sensibly combined into discourse meaning and integrated with context, much as rules of sentence grammar allow word meanings to be sensibly (and grammatically) combined into sentence meaning.

SPEECH ACTS

You can use language to do things. You can use language to make promises, lay bets, issue warnings, christen boats, place names in nomination, offer congratulations, or swear testimony. The theory of **speech acts** describes how this is done.

By saying *I warn you that there is a sheepdog in the closet,* you not only say something, you *warn* someone. Verbs like *bet, promise, warn,* and so on are **performative verbs.** Using them in a sentence does something extra over and above the statement.

"Zits" copyright © 1998 Zits Partnership. Reprinted with special permission of King Features Syndicate.

---

[9] *Turn-taking,* knowing when it's your turn to speak, is governed by conversational principles not discussed here.

[10] Because these maxims are not precisely stated, other analyses for these situations are possible. The point is that much communication relies on these maxims and similar principles.

There are hundreds of performative verbs in every language. The following sentences illustrate their usage:

I *bet* you five dollars the Yankees win.
I *challenge* you to a match.
I *dare* you to step over this line.
I *fine* you $100 for possession of oregano.
I *move* that we adjourn.
I *nominate* Batman for mayor of Gotham City.
I *promise* to improve.
I *resign!*
I *pronounce* you husband and wife.

In all these sentences, the speaker is the subject (that is, the sentences are in first person) who by uttering the sentence is accomplishing some additional action, such as daring, nominating, or resigning. In addition, all these sentences are affirmative, declarative, and in the present tense. They are typical **performative sentences.**

An informal test to see whether a sentence contains a performative verb is to begin it with the words *I hereby. . . .* Only performative sentences sound right when begun this way. Compare *I hereby apologize to you* with the somewhat strange *I hereby know you.* The first is generally taken as an act of apologizing. In all the examples given, insertion of *hereby* would be acceptable. Snoopy in the following cartoon knows that *hereby* is used in performative sentences. The humor comes when he uses it for the nonperformative verb *despise.*

"PEANUTS" © United Feature Syndicate. Reprinted by permission.

Actually, every utterance is some kind of speech act. Even when there is no explicit performative verb, as in *It is raining,* we recognize an implicit performance of *stating.* On the other hand, *Is it raining?* is a performance of questioning, just as *Leave!* is a performance of *ordering.* In all these instances we could use, if we chose, an actual performative verb: *I state that it is raining; I ask if it is raining; I order you to leave.*

In studying speech acts, the importance of context is evident. In some situations *Band practice, my house, 6 to 8* is a reminder; but the same sentence may be a warning in a different context. We call this underlying purpose — a reminder, a warning, a promise, a threat, or whatever — the **illocutionary force** of a speech act.

Because the illocutionary force of a speech act depends on the context of the utterance, speech act theory is a part of pragmatics.

PRESUPPOSITIONS

What does 'yet' mean, after all? 'I haven't seen *Reservoir Dogs yet.*' What does that mean? It means you're going to go, doesn't it?

Nick Hornby, *High Fidelity*

Speakers often make implicit assumptions about the real world, and the sense of an utterance may depend on those assumptions. The **presupposition(s)** of an utterance are facts whose truth is required for the utterance to be appropriate. Consider the following sentences:

1. Have you stopped hugging your sheepdog?
2. Who bought the badminton set?
3. John doesn't write poems anymore.
4. The present King of France is bald.
5. Would you like another beer?

Sentence (1) is inappropriate if the person addressed has never hugged their sheepdog. Thus, in sentence (1) the speaker is said to *presuppose*, or assume, the truth of the fact that the listener has at some past time hugged their sheepdog. In (2) there is the presupposition that someone has already bought a badminton set, and in (3) it is assumed that John once wrote poetry.

We have already run across the somewhat odd (4), which we decided we could understand even though France does not currently have a king. The use of the definite article *the* usually presupposes an existing referent. When presuppositions are inconsistent with the actual state of the world, the utterance is felt to be strange unless the participants agree upon a fictional setting, as in a play, for example. The French cry: "The king is dead, long live the king," was made when the old king died and the new king was crowned. By force of that context, the two uses of *the king,* even in the same sentence, were interpreted to refer to two different individuals.

Sentence (5) presupposes or implies that you have already had at least one beer. Part of the meaning of the word *another* includes this presupposition. The Mad Hatter in *Alice's Adventures in Wonderland* appears not to understand presuppositions.

"Take some more tea," the March Hare said to Alice, very earnestly.

"I've had nothing yet," Alice replied in an offended tone, "so I can't take more."

"You mean you can't take *less*," said the Hatter: "It's very easy to take *more* than nothing."

The humor in this passage comes from the meaning of the word *more,* which presupposes some earlier amount.

These phenomena may also be described as **implication.** Part of the meaning of *more* implies that there has already been something. The definite article *the,* in these terms, implies the existence of the referent within the current context.

Presuppositions can be used to communicate information indirectly. If someone says *my brother is rich,* we assume that person has a brother, even though that fact is not explicitly stated. Much of the information exchanged in a conversation or discourse is of this kind. Often, after a conversation has ended, we realize that we learned something that was not specifically mentioned. That something is often a presupposition. Presuppositions are indispensable to making discourse efficient. If we had to spell out every presupposition specifically, conversation would be very tedious indeed. Instead of *John doesn't write poems anymore* we might have to say: *A person that we both know and agree that his name is John, and who knows how to write, and who is able to write poetry, wrote poetry in some past time, and now he does not write poetry.*

The use of language in a courtroom is restricted so that presuppositions cannot influence the court or jury. The famous type of question, *Have you stopped beating your wife?* is disallowed in court, because accepting the validity of the question means accepting its presuppositions. The question itself imparts information in a way that is difficult to cross-examine or even be consciously aware of.

Presuppositions are so much a part of natural discourse that they become second nature and we do not think of them, any more than we are directly aware of the many other rules and maxims that govern language and its use in context.

DEIXIS

When language is spoken, it occurs in a specific location, at a specific time, is produced by a specific person and is (usually) addressed to some specific other person or persons. Only written language can ever be free of this kind of anchoring in the extralinguistic situation. A sentence on a slip of paper can move through space and time, 'speaker'-less, and addressee-less. All natural, spoken languages have devices that link the utterance with its spatio-temporal and personal context. This linkage is called 'deixis.'

Christine Tanz, *Studies in the Acquisition of Deictic Terms*

"Dennis the Menace" used by permission of Hank Ketcham and copyright © by North America Syndicate.

In all languages, the reference of many words and expressions relies entirely on the situational context of the utterance, and can only be understood in light of these circumstances. This aspect of pragmatics is called **deixis** (pronounced "dike-sis"). First- and second-person pronouns such as

> my   mine   you   your   yours   we   ours   us

are always deictic because their reference is entirely dependent on context. You must know who the speaker and listener are to interpret them.

Third-person pronouns are deictic if they are *free*. If they are *bound,* their reference is known from linguistic context. One peculiar exception is the "pronoun" *it* when used in sentences such as

> *It* appears as though sheepdogs are the missing link.
> The patriotic archbishop of Canterbury found *it* advisable . . .

In these cases, *it* does not function as a true pronoun by referring to some entity. Rather, it is a grammatical morpheme, a placeholder as it were, required to satisfy the English rules of syntax.

Expressions such as

> this person
> that man
> these women
> those children

are deictic, for they require situational information in order for the listener to make a referential connection and understand what is meant. These examples illustrate **person deixis.** They also show that the use of **demonstrative articles** like *this* and *that* is deictic.

There is also **time deixis** and **place deixis.** The following examples are all deictic expressions of time:

now	then	tomorrow
this time	that time	seven days ago
two weeks from now	last week	next April

To understand what specific times such expressions refer to, we need to know when the utterance was said. Clearly, *next week* has a different reference when uttered today than a month from today. If you found an undated notice announcing a "BIG SALE NEXT WEEK," you would not know whether the sale had already taken place.

Expressions of place deixis require contextual information about the place of the utterance, as shown by the following examples:

here	there	this place
that place	this ranch	those towers over there
this city	these parks	yonder mountains

The "Dennis the Menace" cartoon at the beginning of this section indicates the confusion that may result if deictic expressions are misinterpreted.

Directional terms such as

before/behind   left/right   front/back

are deictic insofar as you need to know the orientation in space of the conversational participants to know their reference. In Japanese the verb *kuru* "come" can only be used for motion toward the place of utterance. A Japanese speaker cannot call up a friend and ask

May I *kuru* to your house?

as you might, in English, ask "May I come to your house?" The correct verb is *iku*, "go," which indicates motion away from the place of utterance. In Japanese these verbs thus have a deictic aspect to their meaning.

Deixis abounds in language use and marks one of the boundaries of semantics and pragmatics. Deictic expressions such as *I, an hour from now, behind me,* have meaning to the extent that they have *sense.* To complete their meaning, to determine their *reference,* it is necessary to know the context.

 ## Summary

Knowing a language means to know how to produce and understand sentences with particular meanings. The study of linguistic meaning is called **semantics. Lexical semantics** is concerned with the meanings of morphemes and words; **phrasal semantics** with phrases and sentences. The study of how context affects meaning is called **pragmatics.**

The meanings of morphemes and words are defined in part by their **semantic properties,** whose presence or absence is indicated by **semantic features.** Evidence for semantic properties is found in "slips of the tongue" that people make, which indicates their knowledge of these properties.

When two words are pronounced the same but have different meanings, they are **homonyms** (e.g., *bear* and *bare*). **Heteronyms** are words spelled the same but pronounced differently and having different meanings, such as *sow* "female pig," and *sow* "to plant seeds." **Homographs** are words that are spelled the same and have different meanings, such as *trunk* of an elephant and *trunk* for storing clothes. The use of homonyms and heteronyms may result in **ambiguity,** which occurs when an utterance has more than one meaning.

When two words have the same meaning but different sounds, they are **synonyms** (e.g., *sofa* and *couch*). The use of synonyms may result in **lexical paraphrases,** two sentences with the same meaning.

When a word has differing meanings that are conceptually and historically related, it is said to be **polysemous.** For example, *good* means "well behaved" in *good child,* and "sound" in *good investment.* Polysemous words may be partially synonymous in that they share one or more of their meanings with other words, such as *ripe* and *mature.*

Two words that are opposite in meaning are **antonyms.** Antonyms have the same semantic properties except for the one that accounts for their oppositeness. There are antonymous pairs that are **complementary** (*alive/dead*), **gradable** (*hot/cold*), and **relational opposites** (*buy/sell, employer/employee*).

Other meaning relations are also described by "-nym" words. **Hyponyms** are words like *red, white,* and *blue,* which share a feature indicating they all belong to the class of color words. **Metonyms** are "substitute" words, such as *Rome* meaning "The Catholic Church"; and **retronyms** are expressions like *broadcast television* that once were redundant, but that now make necessary distinctions as a result of changes in the world — in this case, the advent of cable television.

Proper names are "shortcut" words used to designate particular objects uniquely, that is, they are **definite.** Proper names cannot ordinarily be preceded by an article or an adjective, or be pluralized, in English.

The **Principle of Compositionality** states that the meaning of sentences and phrases is determined by the meaning of the individual morphemes and words they contain, together with the syntactic structure of the larger expression. All languages have rules for combining the meanings of parts into the meaning of the whole. For example, *red balloon* has the semantic properties of *balloon* to which the semantic properties of *red* are added, because *balloon* is the head of the phrase. *Brick red* has the semantic properties of *red* modified by those of *brick,* because *red* is the head of that adjective phrase. Such combinations are not always additive. The phrase *counterfeit dollar* does not simply have the semantic properties of *dollar* plus something else.

Words, phrases, and sentences generally have **sense,** which is a part of their meaning. By knowing the sense of an expression, you can determine its **reference,** if any, namely, what it points to in the world. Some meaningful expressions (e.g., *the present King of France*) have sense but no reference; others, such as proper nouns, often have reference but no sense. Deictic terms have sense, but require context to determine their reference. The sense of a declarative sentence is its **truth conditions,** that aspect of meaning that allows you to determine whether the sentence is true or false. The reference of a declarative sentence, when it has one, is its truth value, either true or false. Two sentences are **paraphrases** if they have the same truth conditions. Words like *you, yesterday,* and *behind* have sense, but their reference is context dependent.

The meaning of a sentence is determined in part by the **thematic roles** of the noun phrases in relation to the verb. These semantic relationships indicate who, to whom, toward what, from which, with what, and so on.

In building larger meanings from smaller meanings, the semantic rules interact with the syntactic rules of the language. For example, if a noun phrase and a nonreflexive pronoun occur within the same S, semantic rules cannot interpret them to be **coreferential,** that is, having the same referent. Thus in *Mary bit her, her* refers to someone other than Mary. Pronoun reference is structure dependent. In *he annoys John, he* and *John* may not be coreferential, but in *The fact that he can't swim annoys John, he* and *John* can be coreferential because the pronoun is in a "lower" S.

Often, the truth of one sentence **entails** the truth or falseness another. If the sentence *I managed to kiss my sheepdog* is true, then the sentence *I kissed my sheepdog* is necessarily true by the semantic rules for entailment.

Sentences are **anomalous** when they deviate from certain semantic rules. *The six subjunctive crumbs twitched* and *The stone ran* are anomalous. Other sentences are **uninterpretable** because they contain **nonsense words,** such as *An orkish sluck blecked nokishly.*

Many sentences have both a literal and a nonliteral or **metaphorical** interpretation. *He's out in left field* may be a literal description of a baseball player or a metaphorical description of someone mentally deranged. The use of metaphor is fundamental to the creativity and flexibility of language.

Idioms are phrases that do not adhere to the Principle of Compositionality, that is, whose meaning is *not* the combination of the meanings of the individual words, (e.g., *put her foot in her mouth*). Idioms often violate co-occurrence restrictions of semantic properties.

The general study of how context affects linguistic interpretation is **pragmatics.** Context may be *linguistic* — what was previously spoken or written — or *knowledge of the world,* what we've called **situational context.**

Discourse consists of several sentences, including exchanges between speakers. Pragmatics is important when interpreting discourse, for example, in determining whether a pronoun in one sentence has the same referent as a noun phrase in another sentence. Pro-forms can replace various constituents such as NPs, VPs, and sentences. In addition, parts of sentences can be omitted, but speakers can interpret what is missing. Linguistic context often reveals the reference of the pro-form or the missing parts. For example, it supplies the "will wash" in *Jan will wash grapes and Jon _____ cherries.*

Well-structured discourse follows certain rules and **maxims,** such as "be relevant," that make the discourse coherent. There are also grammatical rules that affect discourse, such as those that determine when to use the definite article *the.*

Pragmatics includes **speech acts, presuppositions,** and **deixis.** Speech act theory is the study of what an utterance does beyond just saying something. The effect of what is done is called the **illocutionary force** of the utterance. For example, use of a **performative verb** like *bequeath* may be an act of bequeathing, which may even have legal status.

Presuppositions are implicit assumptions that accompany certain utterances. *Have you stopped hugging Sue?* carries with it the presupposition that at one time you hugged Sue. Presuppositions are necessary in language for efficiency; otherwise, we would always longwindedly have to state "the obvious."

Deictic terms such as *you, there,* and *now* require knowledge of the circumstances (the person, place, or time) of the utterance to be interpreted referentially.

 # References for Further Reading

Austin, J. L. 1962. *How to Do Things with Words.* Cambridge, MA: Harvard University Press.
Brown, G., and G. Yule. 1983. *Discourse Analysis.* Cambridge, England: Cambridge University Press.

Chierchia, G., and A. McConnell-Ginet. 1990. *Meaning and Grammar.* Cambridge, MA: MIT Press.

Davidson, D., and G. Harman, eds. 1972. *Semantics of Natural Languages.* Dordrecht, The Netherlands: Reidel.

Fraser, B. 1995. *An Introduction to Pragmatics.* Oxford: Blackwell Publishers.

Green, G. M. 1989. *Pragmatics and Natural Language Understanding.* Hillsdale, NJ: Lawrence Erlbaum Associates.

Grice, H. P. 1989. "Logic and Conversation." Reprinted in *Studies in the Way of Words.* Cambridge, MA: Harvard University Press.

Hawkins, J. A. 1985. *A Comparative Typology of English and German.* Austin: University of Texas Press.

Hurford, J. R., and B. Heasley. 1983. *Semantics: A Coursebook.* Cambridge, England: Cambridge University Press.

Jackendoff, R. 1993. *Patterns in the Mind.* New York: HarperCollins.

_____. 1983. *Semantics and Cognition.* Cambridge, MA: MIT Press.

Katz, J. 1972. *Semantic Theory.* New York: Harper & Row.

Lakoff, G. 1987. *Women, Fire, and Dangerous Things: What Categories Reveal about the Mind.* Chicago: University of Chicago Press.

Lakoff, G., and M. Johnson. 1980. *Metaphors We Live By.* Chicago: University of Chicago Press.

Larson, R., and G. Segal. 1995. *Knowledge of Meaning.* Cambridge, MA: MIT Press.

Levinson, S. C. 1983. *Pragmatics.* Cambridge, England: Cambridge University Press.

Lyons, J. 1977. *Semantics.* Cambridge, England: Cambridge University Press.

Mey, J. L. 1993. *Pragmatics: An Introduction.* Oxford, England: Blackwell Publishers.

Saeed, J. 1997. *Semantics.* Oxford, England: Blackwell Publishers.

Searle, J. R. 1969. *Speech Acts: An Essay in the Philosophy of Language.* Cambridge, England: Cambridge University Press.

Sperber, D., and D. Wilson. 1986. *Relevance: Communication and Cognition.* Oxford, England: Basil Blackwell.

Tanz, C. 1980. *Studies in the Acquisition of Deictic Terms.* Cambridge, England: Cambridge University Press.

Exercises

1. For each group of words given below, state what semantic property or properties distinguish between the classes of (a) words and (b) words. If asked, also indicate a semantic property the (a) words and the (b) words share.

   Example: (a) widow, mother, sister, aunt, maid

           (b) widower, father, brother, uncle, valet

              The (a) and (b) words are "human."

              The (a) words are "female" and the (b) words are "male."

   A. (a) bachelor, man, son, paperboy, pope, chief

        (b) bull, rooster, drake, ram

        The (a) and (b) words are _____

        The (a) words are _____

        The (b) words are _____

B. (a) table, stone, pencil, cup, house, ship, car

    (b) milk, alcohol, rice, soup, mud

    The (a) words are _____

    The (b) words are _____

C. (a) book, temple, mountain, road, tractor

    (b) idea, love, charity, sincerity, bravery, fear

    The (a) words are _____

    The (b) words are _____

D. (a) pine, elm, ash, weeping willow, sycamore

    (b) rose, dandelion, aster, tulip, daisy

    The (a) and (b) words are _____

    The (a) words are _____

    The (b) words are _____

E. (a) book, letter, encyclopedia, novel, notebook, dictionary

    (b) typewriter, pencil, pen, crayon, quill, charcoal, chalk

    The (a) words are _____

    The (b) words are _____

F. (a) walk, run, skip, jump, hop, swim

    (b) fly, skate, ski, ride, cycle, canoe, hang-glide

    The (a) and (b) words are _____

    The (a) words are _____

    The (b) words are _____

G. (a) ask, tell, say, talk, converse

    (b) shout, whisper, mutter, drawl, holler

    The (a) and (b) words are _____

    The (a) words are _____

    The (b) words are _____

H. (a) absent – present, alive – dead, asleep – awake, married – single

    (b) big – small, cold – hot, sad – happy, slow – fast

    The (a) and (b) words are _____

    The (a) words are _____

    The (b) words are _____

I. (a) alleged, counterfeit, false, putative, accused

    (b) red, large, cheerful, pretty, stupid

    (*Hint:* Is an alleged murderer always a murderer? Is a pretty girl always a girl?)

    The (a) words are _____

    The (b) words are _____

2. Explain the semantic ambiguity of the following sentences by providing two or more sentences that paraphrase the multiple meanings. *Example:* "She can't bear children" can mean either "She can't give birth to children" or "She can't tolerate children."

a. He waited by the bank.

b. Is he really that kind?

c. The proprietor of the fish store was the sole owner.

d. The long drill was boring.

e. When he got the clear title to the land, it was a good deed.

f. It takes a good ruler to make a straight line.

g. He saw that gasoline can explode.

h. You should see her shop.

i. Every man loves a woman.

j. Bill wants to marry a Norwegian woman. (NB: This is difficult.)

3. The following sentences may be lexically or structurally ambiguous, or both. Provide paraphrases showing you comprehend all the meanings.

   Example: I saw him walking by the bank.

   Meaning 1:   I saw him and he was walking by the bank of the river.

   Meaning 2:   I saw him and he was walking by the financial institution.

   Meaning 3:   I was walking by the bank of the river when I saw him.

   Meaning 4:   I was walking by the financial institution when I saw him.

   a. We laughed at the colorful ball.

   b. He was knocked over by the punch.

   c. The police were urged to stop drinking by the fifth.

   d. I said I would file it on Thursday.

   e. I cannot recommend visiting professors too highly.

   f. The license fee for pets owned by senior citizens who have not been altered is $1.50. (Actual notice)

   g. What looks better on a handsome man than a tux? Nothing! (Attributed to Mae West)

   h. Wanted: Man to take care of cow that does not smoke or drink. (Actual notice)

   i. For Sale: Several old dresses from grandmother in beautiful condition. (Actual notice)

   j. Time flies like an arrow. (*Hint:* There are at least four paraphrases, but some of them require imagination.)

4. Here are a few more *retronyms:*

   straight razor, one-speed bike, conventional warfare, acoustic guitar, bar soap

   A. Explain why the five examples given are retronyms.

   B. Think of five retronyms not in the above list or previously mentioned.

   C. Think of one that is perhaps not yet widely used in the language, but which you think soon will be needed. For example, *low-definition television.*

5. **A.** There are more than 300 heteronyms in English. How many can you think of? Ten would be okay, 25 would be terrific, and 100 would once have gotten your name en-

shrined. In our Sixth Edition, we promised to publish the names of readers who sent us 100 or more. They are hereby enshrined.[11]

B. The Internet has made exercises such as this a matter of look up. As a challenge, how many autoantonyms—words like *dust* that are their own antonyms—can you think of? Try for 5 or 10, and when you give up, put *autoantonym* in an Internet search engine and you'll quickly find a couple of dozen.

C. Oh, and what the heck. While you're at it you might as well try to come up with some antiautonyms—pairs like *loosen/unloosen* that you might think are antonyms, but turn out to be synonyms. Go for three. Then hit the Internet.

6. There are other *-nym* words that describe semantic relations and facts about words and word classes. We mentioned *acronyms* in chapter 3, though not in this chapter. How many more *-nym* words and their meaning can you come up with? Try for three. Five would be great. Ten is possible. (*Hint:* One such *-nym* word was the winning word in the 1997 National Spelling Bee.)

7. There are several kinds of antonymy. By writing a *c, g,* or *r* in column *C,* indicate whether the pairs in columns *A* and *B* are complementary, gradable, or relational opposites.

A	B	C
good	bad	
expensive	cheap	
parent	offspring	
beautiful	ugly	
false	true	
lessor	lessee	
pass	fail	
hot	cold	
legal	illegal	
larger	smaller	
poor	rich	
fast	slow	
asleep	awake	
husband	wife	
rude	polite	

---

[11] From Baylor University: Elizabeth Arosemana, Elvin Barao, Nancy Barr, Leslie Hardy, Marlo Kaufman, Professor M. Lynne Murphy, Maria Park, and Heidy Shields; from Hunter College in New York: Marcia Schonzeit; and from Florida International University: Corinna Scholz. Special thanks to Bruce C. Johnson, University of North Colorado, who pointed out a number of difficulties in determining whether two words are heteronyms, including whether proper nouns count (*male, Male*), whether foreign words commonly used in English count (*corps (sg.), corps (pl.)*), and whether words spelled with diacritics count (*pate, pâté*).

8. For each definition write in the first blank the word that has that meaning and in the second (and third if present) a differently spelled homonym that has a different meaning.

Example: "A pair:" t(*wo*)   t(*oo*)   t(*o*)

a. "Naked":	b _____	b _____	
b. "Base metal":	l _____	l _____	
c. "Worships":	p _____	p _____	p _____
d. "Eight bits":	b _____	b _____	b _____
e. "One of five senses":	s _____	s _____	c _____
f. "Several couples":	p _____	p _____	p _____
g. "Not pretty":	p _____	p _____	
h. "Purity of gold unit":	k _____	c _____	
i. "A horse's coiffure":	m_____	m_____	M_____
j. "Sets loose":	f _____	f _____	f _____

9. Here are some proper names of U.S. restaurants. Can you figure out the basis for the name? (This is for fun—don't let yourself be graded.)

a. Mustard's Last Stand   *Custer's last stand*

b. Aunt Chilada's   *Enchilada*

c. Lion on the Beach   *Lying on the beach*

d. Pizza Paul and Mary   *Peter Paul + Mary*

e. Franks for the Memories   *Thanks...*

f. Weiner Take All   *Winner...*

g. Dressed to Grill   *... to kill*

h. Deli Beloved   *dearly beloved*

i. Gone with the Wings   *Gone ... wind*

j. Aunt Chovy's Pizza   *anchovy*

k. Polly Esther's   *polyester*

l. Dewey, Cheatam & Howe

(*Hint:* This is also the name of a mythical law firm.)

m. Thai Me Up Café (truly—it's in L.A.)   *tie*

n. Romancing the Cone   *... Stone*

10. The following sentences consist of a verb, its noun phrase subject, and various complements and prepositional phrases. Identify the thematic role of each NP by writing the letter *a, t, l, i, s, g, e, c,* or *p* above the noun, standing for *agent, theme, location, instrument, source, goal, experiencer, causative,* or *possessor.*

       a   *t*   *s*   *i*

Example: The boy took the books from the cupboard with a handcart.

a. Mary found a ball in the house.

b. The children ran from the playground to the wading pool.

c. One of the men unlocked all the doors with a paper clip.

A   +   i
d. John melted the ice with a blowtorch.

e. The sun melted the ice.

f. The ice melted.

g. With a telescope, the boy saw the man.

h. The farmer loaded hay onto the truck.

i. The farmer loaded the hay with a pitchfork.

j. The hay was loaded on the truck by the farmer.

11. Some linguists and philosophers distinguish between two kinds of truthful statements: one follows from the definition or meaning of a word; the other simply happens to be true in the world as we know it. Thus, *kings are monarchs* is true because the word *king* has the semantic property "monarch" as part of its meaning; but *kings are rich* is circumstantially true. We can imagine a poor king, but a king who is not a monarch is not truly a king. Sentences like *kings are monarchs* are said to be **analytic,** true by virtue of meaning alone. Write *A* by any of the following sentences that are analytic, and *S* for "situational" by the ones that are not analytic.

a. Queens are monarchs. A

b. Queens are female. A

c. Queens are mothers. S

d. Dogs are four-legged. S

e. Dogs are animals. A

f. Cats are felines. A

g. Cats are stupid. S

h. George Washington is George Washington. A

i. George Washington was the first president. A

j. Uncles are male. A

12. The opposite of *analytic* (see previous exercise) is **contradictory.** A sentence that is false due to the meaning of its words alone is contradictory. *Kings are female* is an example. Write a *C* by the contradictory sentences and *S* for situational by sentences that are not contradictory.

a. My aunt is a man. C

b. Witches are wicked. S

c. My brother is an only child. C

d. The evening star isn't the morning star. S

e. The evening star isn't the evening star. C

f. Babies are adults. C

g. Babies can lift one ton. S

h. Puppies are human. C

i. My bachelor friends are all married. C

j. My bachelor friends are all lonely. S

13. Go on an idiom hunt. In the course of some hours in which you converse or overhear conversations, write down all the idioms that are used. If you prefer, watch the "Soaps" for an hour or two and write down the idioms. Show your parents (or whomever) this book when they find you watching TV and you claim you're doing your homework.

14. Find a complete version of "The Jabberwocky" from *Through the Looking-Glass* by Lewis Carroll. Look up all the nonsense words in a good dictionary and see how many of them are lexical items in English. Note their meaning.

15. In sports and games many expressions are "performative." By shouting *You're out*, the first base umpire performs an act. Think up a half-dozen or so similar examples and explain their use.

read up to p.207

16. A criterion of a performative utterance is whether you can begin it with "I hereby." Notice that if you say sentence (a) aloud it sounds like a genuine apology, but to say sentence (b) aloud sounds funny because you cannot perform an act of knowing:

a. I hereby apologize to you.

b. I hereby know you.

Determine which of the following sentences are performative sentences by inserting "hereby" and seeing whether they sound right.

c. I testify that she met the agent.

d. I know that she met the agent.

e. I suppose the Yankees will win.

f. He bet her $2500 that Clinton would win.

g. I dismiss the class.

h. I teach the class.

i. We promise to leave early.

j. I owe the IRS $1,000,000.

k. I bequeath $1,000,000 to the IRS.

l. I swore I didn't do it.

m. I swear I didn't do it.

17. The following sentences make certain presuppositions. What are they?

Example: The police ordered the minors to stop drinking.
            Presupposition: The minors were drinking.

a. Please take me out to the ball game again.
Presupposition:

b. Valerie regretted not receiving a new T-bird for Labor Day.
Presupposition:

c. That her pet turtle ran away made Emily very sad.
Presupposition:

d. The administration forgot that the professors support the students. (Compare: *The administration believes that the professors support the students,* in which there is no such presupposition.)
Presupposition:

e. It is an atrocity that the World Trade Center was attacked on September 11, 2001.
Presupposition:

f. Isn't it an atrocity that the World Trade Center was attacked on September 11, 2001?

Presupposition:

g. Disa wants more popcorn.

Presupposition:

h. Why don't pigs have wings?

Presupposition:

i. Who discovered Pluto in 1930?

Presupposition:

18. **A.** Consider the following "facts" and then answer the questions:

Roses are red and bralkions are too.
Booth shot Lincoln and Czolgosz, McKinley.
Casca stabbed Caesar and so did Cinna.
Frodo was exhausted as was Sam.

(a) What color are bralkions?

(b) What did Czolgosz do to McKinley?

(c) What did Cinna do to Caesar?

(d) What state was Sam in?

B. Now consider these facts and answer the questions:

Black Beauty was a stallion.
Mary is a widow.
John remembered to send Mary a birthday card.
John didn't remember to send Jane a birthday card.
Flipper is walking.

(T = true; F = false)

(e) Black Beauty was male?	T _____	F _____
(f) Mary was never married?	T _____	F _____
(g) John sent Mary a card?	T _____	F _____
(h) John sent Jane a card?	T _____	F _____
(i) Flipper has legs?	T _____	F _____

Part A illustrates your ability to interpret meanings when syntactic rules have deleted parts of the sentence; Part B illustrates your knowledge of semantic features and presupposition.

19. Circle any deictic expression in the following sentences. (*Hint:* Proper names and noun phrases that contain the definite article *the* are not considered deictic expressions.)

a. I saw her standing there.

b. Dogs are animals.

c. Yesterday, all my troubles seemed so far away.

d. The name of this rock band is "The Beatles."

e. The Declaration of Independence was signed in 1776.

f. The Declaration of Independence was signed last year.

g. Copper conducts electricity.

h. The treasure chest is to your right.

i. These are the times that try men's souls.

j. There is a tide in the affairs of men which taken at the flood leads on to fortune.

20. State for each pronoun in the following sentences whether it is free, bound, or either bound or free. Consider each sentence independently.

Example: John finds himself in love with her.

himself — bound; her — free

Example: John said that he loved her.

he — bound or free; her — free

a. Louise said to herself in the mirror: "I'm so ugly."

b. The fact that he considers her pretty pleases Maria.

c. Whenever I see you, I think of her.

d. John discovered that a picture of himself was hanging in the post office, and that fact bugged him, but it pleased her.

e. It seems that she and he will never stop arguing with them.

f. Persons are prohibited from picking flowers from any but their own graves. (On a sign in a cemetery.)

Phonetics:
The Sounds of Language

I gradually came to see that Phonetics had an important
bearing on human relations — that when people of
different nations pronounce each other's languages
really well (even if vocabulary & grammar not perfect), it
has an astonishing effect of bringing them together, it
puts people on terms of equality, a good understanding
between them immediately springs up.

Daniel Jones

Phonetics is concerned with describing the speech
sounds that occur in the languages of the world. We
want to know what these sounds are, how they fall into
patterns, and how they change in different
circumstances. . . . The first job of a phonetician is . . . to
try to find out what people are doing when they are
talking and when they are listening to speech.

Peter Ladefoged, *A Course in Phonetics*, 1982, 2nd Edition

Knowledge of a language includes knowledge of the morphemes, words, phrases, and sentences. It also includes the sounds of the language and how they may be "strung" together to form meaningful units. Although there may be some sounds in one language that are not in another, the sounds of all the languages of the world together constitute a limited set of the sounds that the human vocal tract can produce. This chapter will discuss these speech sounds, how they are produced, and how they may be characterized.

Sound Segments

"Keep out! Keep out! K-E-E-P O-U-T."

The study of speech sounds is called **phonetics.** To describe speech sounds it is necessary to know what an individual sound is, and how each sound differs from all others. This is not as easy as it may seem, and the fact that we generally avoid the confusion of the sign painter in the cartoon is actually remarkable.

A speaker of English knows that there are three sounds in the word *cat,* the initial sound represented by the letter *c,* the second by *a,* and the final sound by *t.* Yet, physically the word is just one continuous sound. You can **segment** the one sound into parts because you know English. The ability to analyze a word into its individual sounds does not depend on knowledge of spelling. *Not* and *knot* have three sounds even though the first sound in *knot* is represented by the two letters *kn.* The printed word *psycho* has six letters that represent only four sounds — *ps, y, ch, o.*

It is difficult if not impossible to segment the sounds of someone clearing their throat into a sequence of discrete units. This is because these sounds are not the sounds of any morphemes in any human language; it is not because they form a single continuous sound. You do not produce one sound, then another, then another when you say the word *cat.* You move your organs of speech continuously and produce a continuous signal.

Although the sounds we produce and hear are continuous, everyone throughout history who has attempted to analyze language has recognized that speech is divisible into units. According to an ancient Hindu myth, the god Indra was the first to segment speech into its separate elements. After he succeeded, the sounds could be perceived as language. Indra may thus be the first phonetician.

Speakers of English can separate *keepout* into the two words *keep* and *out* because they know the language. However, we do not pause between words even though we sometimes have that illusion. Children learning a language reveal this problem. A two-year-old child going down stairs heard his mother say, "hold on." He replied, "I'm holing don, I'm holing don," not knowing where the break between words occurred. In fact, the errors in deciding where a boundary falls between two words has changed the form of words. At an earlier stage of English, the word *apron* was *napron*. However, the phrase *a napron* was so often misperceived as *an apron* that the word lost its initial *n*.

Some phrases and sentences that are clearly distinct when printed may be ambiguous when read aloud as in the children's jingle: *I scream, you scream, we all scream for ice cream.* Read the following pairs aloud and see why we often misinterpret what we hear:

grade A	gray day
It's hard to recognize speech.	It's hard to wreck a nice beach.
The sun's rays meet.	The sons raise meat.

The lack of breaks between spoken words and individual sounds often makes us think that speakers of foreign languages run their words together, not realizing that we also do so. X-ray motion pictures of someone speaking make this lack of breaks in speech very clear. One can see the tongue, jaw, and lips in continuous motion as the individual sounds are produced.

Yet, if you know a language you have no difficulty segmenting the continuous sounds. It doesn't matter if the language is written or not, or if the person perceiving the individual sounds can read or not. People who cannot read or write are nevertheless aware of the individual sounds, and some writing systems do not use spaces between words on a page, yet everyone who knows the language knows how to segment sentences into words, and words into sounds.

Identity of Speech Sounds

It is quite amazing, given the continuity of the speech signal, that we are able to understand the individual words in an utterance. This ability is more surprising because no two speakers ever say the "same thing" identically. The speech signal produced when one speaker says *cat* is not the same as that of another speaker's *cat*. Even two utterances of *cat* by the same speaker will differ to some degree. George Bernard Shaw pointed to the impossibility of constructing any set of symbols that will specify all the minute differences between sounds in his statement:

> By infinitesimal movements of the tongue countless different vowels can be produced, all of them in use among speakers of English who utter the same vowels no oftener than they make the same fingerprints.

Nevertheless, speakers understand each other because they know the same language.

Our knowledge of a language determines when we judge physically different sounds to be the same; we know which aspects or properties of the signal are linguistically important and which are not. For example, if someone coughs in the middle of saying "How (cough) are you?" a listener will ignore the cough and interpret this simply as "How are you?" Men's voices are usually lower in overall pitch than women's; some

"Boy, he must think we're pretty
stupid to fall for that again."

"Rubes" by Leigh Rubin. By permission of Leigh Rubin and Creators
Syndicate.

speakers speak slowly, some quickly; others have a "nasal twang." Such pitch or tempo differences, or personal styles of speaking, are not linguistically significant.

Our linguistic knowledge, our mental grammar, makes it possible to ignore nonlinguistic differences in speech. Furthermore, we are capable of making many sounds that we know intuitively are not speech sounds in our language. Many English speakers can make a clicking sound that writers sometimes represent as *tsk tsk tsk*. These sounds are not part of the English sound system. They never occur as part of the words of the utterances we produce. It is even difficult for many English speakers to combine this clicking sound with other sounds. Yet clicks are speech sounds in Xhosa, Zulu, Sosotho, and Khoikhoi — languages spoken in southern Africa — just like the *k* or *t* in English. Speakers of those languages have no difficulty producing them as parts of words. *Xhosa,* the name of a language spoken in South Africa, begins with one of these clicks. Thus, *tsk* is a speech sound in Xhosa but not in English. The sound represented by the letters *th* in the word *think* is a speech sound in English but not in French. The sound produced with a closed mouth when we are trying to clear a tickle in our throats is not a speech sound in any language, nor is the sound produced when we sneeze.

The science of phonetics attempts to describe all the sounds used in human language — sounds that constitute a subset of the totality of sounds that humans can produce.

The way we use our linguistic knowledge to produce a meaningful utterance is complicated. It is a chain of events that starts with an idea or message in the speaker's brain or mind and ends with a similar message in the hearer's brain. The language faculty forms the message in words and transmits it by nerve signals to the organs of speech, which produce the physical sounds.

We can describe the speech sounds at any stage in this chain of events. The study of the physical properties of the sounds themselves is **acoustic phonetics.** The study of the way listeners perceive these sounds is **auditory phonetics.** Our primary concern in this chapter is **articulatory phonetics,** the study of how the vocal tract produces the sounds of language.

Spelling and Speech

The one-l lama,
He's a priest.
The two-l llama,
He's a beast.

And I will bet
A silk pajama
There isn't any
Three-l lllama.

Ogden Nash[1]

Drawing by Leo Cullum, copyright © 1988 The New Yorker Collection. All rights reserved.

Alphabetic spelling represents the pronunciations of words. However, **orthography** does not represent the sounds of the words in a language systematically. It is confusing to discuss the production of the different sounds as they are spelled in English words.

Suppose some horrible catastrophe destroyed all Earthlings, and years later extraterrestrials exploring Earth discover some fragments of English writing that include the following sentence:

Did h**e** bel**ie**ve that C**ae**sar could s**ee** the p**eo**ple s**ei**ze the s**ea**s?

How would an ET phonetician decide that **e, ie, ae, ee, eo, ei,** and **ea** all represented the same sound? To add to the confusion, this sentence might crop up later:

The sill**y** am**oe**ba stole the k**ey** to the mach**i**ne.

English speakers learn how to pronounce these words when learning to read and write, and therefore they know that **y, oe, ey,** and **i** represent the same sound as the boldface letters in the first sentence.

On the other hand, consider:

My f**a**ther w**a**nted m**a**ny **a** village d**a**me badly

Here the letter **a** represents the several sounds in *father, wanted, many,* and so on.

In any science, the objects of study, when different, must be given different names or symbols, and the science of phonetics is no exception. Each distinct sound must have a distinct symbol to represent it; and each symbol must represent one and only one distinct sound.

The Phonetic Alphabet

> The English have no respect for their language, and will not teach their children to speak it. They cannot spell it because they have nothing to spell it with but an old foreign alphabet of which only the consonants — and not all of them — have any agreed speech value.
>
> G. B. Shaw, Preface to *Pygmalion*

The discrepancy between spelling and sounds gave rise to a movement of "spelling reformers" called orthoepists. They wanted to revise the alphabet so that one letter would correspond to one sound and one sound to one letter, thus creating a **phonetic alphabet** to simplify spelling.

George Bernard Shaw followed in the footsteps of three centuries of spelling reformers in England. In typical Shavian manner he pointed out that we could use the English spelling system to spell *fish* as *ghoti* — the *gh* like the sound in *enough,* the *o* like the sound in *women,* and the *ti* like the sound in *nation.* Shaw was so concerned about English spelling that he included a provision in his will for a new "Proposed English Alphabet" to be administered by a "Public Trustee" who would have the duty of seeking and publishing a more efficient alphabet. This alphabet was to have at least forty letters to enable "the said language to be written without indicating single sounds by groups of letters or by diacritical marks." After Shaw's death in 1950, 450 designs for such an al-

"B.C." reprinted by permission of Johnny Hart and Creators Syndicate, Inc.

phabet were submitted from all parts of the globe. Four alphabets were judged equally good, and the prize money was shared among their designers, who collaborated to produce the alphabet designated in Shaw's will. Shaw also stipulated in his will that his play *Androcles and the Lion* be published in the new alphabet, with "the original Doctor Johnson's lettering opposite the transliteration page by page and a glossary of the two alphabets." This version of the play came out in 1962.

It is easy to understand why spelling reformers believe there is a need for a phonetic alphabet. Several letters may represent a single sound:

to   too   two   through   threw   clue   shoe

A single letter may represent different sounds:

d*a*me   d*a*d   f*a*ther   c*a*ll   vill*a*ge   m*a*ny

A combination of letters may represent a single sound:

*sh*oot	*ch*aracter	*Th*omas	*ph*ysics
ei*th*er	de*a*l	rou*gh*	na*ti*on
c*oa*t	gla*ci*al	*th*eater	pl*ai*n

Some letters have no sound at all in certain words:

*m*nemonic	autum*n*	resi*g*n	*gh*ost
*p*terodactyl	*w*rite	hol*e*	corp*s*
*p*sychology	s*w*ord	de*b*t	*g*naw
bou*gh*	lam*b*	is*l*and	*k*not

The spelling may fail to represent sounds that occur. In many words, the letter *u* represents a *y* sound followed by a *u* sound:

c*u*te	(compare: c*oo*t)
f*u*tile	(compare: r*u*le)
*u*tility	(compare: *U*zbekistan)

One letter may represent two sounds; the final *x* in *Xerox* represents a *k* followed by an *s*.

Whether we support or oppose spelling reform, it is clear that we cannot depend on the spelling of words to describe the sounds of English. The alphabets designed to fulfill Shaw's will were not the first phonetic alphabets. In Shaw's lifetime, the phonetician Henry Sweet, the prototype for Shaw's character Henry Higgins in the play *Pygmalion* or the musical play or movie *My Fair Lady,* produced a phonetic alphabet.

In 1888 the interest in the scientific description of speech sounds led the **International Phonetic Association (IPA)** to develop a phonetic alphabet to symbolize the sounds of all languages. Since many languages use a Roman alphabet like that used in the English writing system, the IPA utilized many Roman letters as well as invented symbols. These alphabetic characters have a consistent value, unlike ordinary letters that may or may not represent the same sounds in the same or different languages.

A phonetic alphabet should include enough symbols to represent the "crucial" linguistic differences. At the same time it should not, and cannot, include noncrucial differences, since such differences are infinitely varied.

Table 6.1 is a list of the phonetic symbols that we will use to represent English speech sounds. The symbols do not tell us everything about the sounds, which may vary from person to person, and which may depend on their position in a word. These symbols are intended for use by persons knowing English. They are not all the phonetic symbols needed for English sounds. When we discuss the sounds in more detail later in the chapter, we will add appropriate symbols.

The symbol [ə] is called a *schwa*. We use it only to represent vowels in unstressed syllables (we will discuss stress below). In the word *phoNEtic,* for example, the first syllable (*pho*) and last syllable (*tic*) are unstressed, while the middle syllable (*NE*) is stressed. So we spell it phonetically as [fənɛtək]. (There is great variation in the way

Table 6.1   A Phonetic Alphabet for English Pronunciation

	Consonants						Vowels			
p	pill	**t**	till	**k**	kill	**i**	beet	ɪ	bit
b	bill	**d**	dill	**g**	gill	**e**	bait	ɛ	bet
m	mill	**n**	nil	**ŋ**	ring	**u**	boot	ʊ	foot
f	feel	**s**	seal	**h**	heal	**o**	boat	ɔ	bore
v	veal	**z**	zeal	**l**	leaf	**æ**	bat	**a**	pot/bar
θ	thigh	**č**	chill	**r**	reef	**ʌ**	butt	**ə**	sofa
ð	thy	**ǰ**	Jill	**j**	you	**aj**	bite	**aw**	bout
ʃ/š	shill	**ʍ**	which	**w**	witch	**ɔj**	boy		
ʒ/ž	azure								

speakers of English produce this unstressed vowel, but it is often phonetically similar to the sound [ʌ] of *cut* [kʌt].) All other vowel symbols are used in syllables that are not unstressed.

Speakers of different English dialects pronounce some words differently from those of other speakers. For example, some of you may pronounce the words *which* and *witch* identically. If you do, the initial sound of both words is symbolized by **w** in the chart. Some speakers of English pronounce *bought* and *pot* with the same vowel; others pronounce them with the vowel sounds in *bore* and *bar,* respectively. We have thus listed both words in the chart of symbols. It is difficult to include all the phonetic symbols needed to represent all English dialect differences. We are sorry if a vowel sound in your dialect is not included in the table.

Some of the symbols in Table 6.1 are those traditionally used by linguists in the United States in place of IPA symbols. Here are some equivalences:

U.S.	IPA
š	ʃ
ž	ʒ
č	tʃ
ǰ	dʒ
ʊ	ʊ

We will use [š], [ʃ] and [ž], [ʒ] interchangeably to familiarize readers with both notations, since both are common in books on language and linguistics. We will however, use [č] and [ǰ] instead of the IPA symbols for the first and last sounds in *church* and *judge,* respectively.

Using these symbols, we can now unambiguously represent the pronunciation of words. For example, in the six words below, *ou* represents six distinct vowel sounds; the *gh* is silent in all but *rough,* where it is pronounced [f]; the *th* represents two sounds, and the *l* in *would* is also silent.

Spelling	Pronunciation
though	[ðo]
thought	[θɔt]
rough	[rʌf]
bough	[baw]
through	[θru]
would	[wʊd]

We will always use square brackets around the phonetic transcription to distinguish it from ordinary spelling.

Articulatory Phonetics

The voice is articulated by the lips and the tongue . . . Man speaks by means of the air which he inhales into his entire body and particularly into the body cavities. When the air is expelled through the empty space it produces a sound, because of the resonances in the skull. The tongue articulates by its strokes; it gathers the air in the throat and pushes it against the palate and the teeth, thereby giving the sound a definite shape. If the tongue would not articulate each time, by means of its strokes, man would not speak clearly and would only be able to produce a few simple sounds.

Hippocrates (460–377 B.C.E)

The production of any sound involves the movement of air. Most speech sounds are produced by pushing lung air through the opening between the vocal cords, up the throat, and into the mouth or nose, and finally out of the body. Some technical jargon — see chapter 10 for a discussion of "jargon" in general — is required. The opening between the vocal cords is the **glottis** and is located in the **larynx** (often referred to as the "voice box," and pronounced "lair rinks."). The tubular part of the throat above the larynx is the **pharynx** (rhymes with *larynx,* and produces a very high score at Scrabble). What sensible people call "the mouth," we linguists call the **oral cavity** to distinguish it from the **nasal cavity,** which is the nose and the plumbing that connects it to the throat, plus your sinuses. All of it together is the **vocal tract.** Figure 6-1 should make these descriptions more clear.

What distinguishes one sound from the other? If you bang a large round drum you will get one sound; if you bang a small round drum you will get a different sound; if you bang a small oblong drum you will get still another sound. The size and shape of the vessel containing the air that is moving makes a difference. This is also true in the production of speech sounds. The vocal tract acts as the vessel of air. When it changes shape, different sounds are produced.

Airstream Mechanisms

Most of the sounds of the world's languages are produced by pushing air out of the lungs through the vocal tract. Since the air comes from the lungs, it is **pulmonic;** and since it

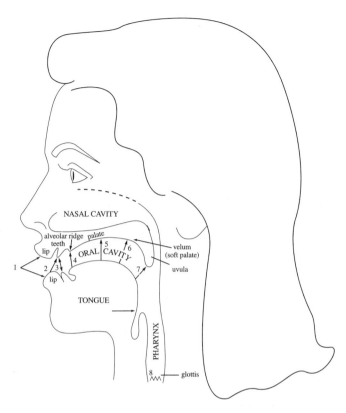

Places of articulation: 1. bilabial; 2. labiodental; 3. interdental; 4. alveolar; 5. (alveo)palatal; 6. velar; 7. uvular; 8. glottal.

Figure 6.1   The vocal tract.

is pushed out, it is **egressive.** All of the speech sounds of English have a **pulmonic egressive airstream mechanism.**

Other airstream mechanisms are rare in the world's languages, but are still part of phonetics. Another kind of egressive sound is made when air in the mouth is pressurized by an upward movement of the closed glottis, and then released suddenly, producing a sharp sound called an **ejective.** An ejective "p" sound makes a distinctive pop.

Sounds may also be **ingressive.** In one kind of ingressive sound, the air is sucked into the mouth to make **clicks** (such as *tsk*). In a different kind, air is drawn from the mouth into the throat to make **implosives.** There are four airstream mechanisms in all, then. Pulmonic egressive is the most common. The other three are the mechanisms that produce ejectives, clicks, and implosives.

Ejectives are found in many American Indian and African languages, as well as languages spoken in the Caucasus, a region between the Black and Caspian Seas. Implosives also occur in the languages of the American Indians and throughout Africa, India, and Pakistan. Clicks occur in the Southern Bantu languages such as Xhosa and Zulu, and in the languages spoken by the Bushmen and Khoikhoi. A detailed description of these different airstream mechanisms goes beyond the requirements of an introductory text. We mention them to show that sounds can be classified according to the airstream mechanism used to produce them. In the rest of this chapter, we will discuss only sounds produced by a pulmonic egressive airstream mechanism.

Consonants

The sounds of all languages fall into two classes: consonants and vowels. Consonants are produced with some restriction or closure in the vocal tract that impedes the flow of air from the lungs. In phonetics, the terms *consonant* and *vowel* refer to types of <u>sounds,</u> not to the letters that represent them. In speaking of the alphabet, we may call "a" a vowel and "b" a consonant, but that means only that we use the letter "a" to represent vowel sounds, and the letter "b" to represent consonant sounds.

PLACES OF ARTICULATION

Different consonantal sounds result according to the **place of articulation,** which is where in the vocal tract the airflow restriction occurs. Movement of the tongue and lips, called the **articulators,** cause the restriction, reshaping the oral cavity in various ways to produce the various consonants. In this section, we discuss the major consonantal place features. As you read the description of each class of sounds, pronounce them and try to feel which articulators are moving and to where. Refer to Figure 6.1 to remind yourself of the terminology.

Bilabials [p] [b] [m]   When we produce a [p], [b], or [m] we articulate by bringing both lips together. These sounds are therefore called **bilabials.**

Labiodentals [f] [v]   We also use our lips to form [f] and [v] as in *fine* [fajn] and *vine* [vajn]. We articulate these sounds by touching the bottom lip to the upper teeth, which is why these sounds are called **labiodental,** *labio-* referring to lips and *dental* to teeth.

Interdentals [θ] [ð]   In ordinary spelling, the sounds [θ] and [ð] are both represented by *th,* for example, *thin* [θɪn] and *then* [ðɛn]. To articulate these **interdental** ("between the teeth") sounds, one inserts the tip of the tongue between the upper and lower teeth. However, for some speakers the tongue merely touches the teeth, making a sound more correctly called **dental.** We will nevertheless continue to use *interdental* since it describes the most common articulation.

Alveolars [t] [d] [n] [s] [z] [l] [r]   Alveolar sounds are articulated by raising the front part of the tongue to the **alveolar ridge** (see Figure 6.1). Pronounce the words *do* [du], *new* [nu], *two* [tu], *sue* [su], *zoo* [zu]. You should feel your tongue touch or almost touch the bony tooth ridge as you produce the first sounds in these words.

For the **lateral [l],** the tip of the tongue rises to the alveolar ridge leaving the rest of the tongue down, permitting the air to escape laterally over its sides. You can feel it in the "la" of "tra la la."

The sound [r] is produced in a variety of ways. Many English speakers produce [r] by curling the tip of the tongue back behind the alveolar ridge. In that case the [r] is a **retroflex** sound. In some languages, the [r] may be an alveolar **trill,** produced by the tip of the tongue vibrating against the roof of the mouth. Other symbols can be used for these different *r* sounds, and in a very detailed phonetic description, we would include some of them. For the purposes of this book, however, we will use the symbol [r] for all the varieties produced by speakers of English.

Palatals [ʃ]/[š] [ʒ]/[ž] [č] [ǰ]   To produce the sounds in the middle of the words *mission* [mɪšən] and *measure* [mɛžər], the front part of the tongue is raised to a point on the hard palate just behind the alveolar ridge. These are **palatal** sounds. (The term **alveopalatal** is also used.)

The palatal region is also the place of articulation of [č] and [ǰ], the sounds that begin and end the words *church* and *judge*.

Velars [k] [g] [ŋ]   Another class of sounds is produced by raising the back of the tongue to the soft palate or **velum.** The initial and final sounds of the words *kick* [kɪk], *gig* [gɪg], and the final sounds of the words *back* [bæk], *bag* [bæg], and *bang* [bæŋ] —[k], [g], and [ŋ] —are all velar sounds.

Uvulars [R] [q] [ɢ]   Uvular sounds are produced by raising the back of the tongue to the uvula, the fleshy appendage that hangs down in the back of the throat. The *r* in French is sometimes a uvular trill and is symbolized by [R]. Uvular sounds occur in other languages. Arabic, for example, has two uvular sounds symbolized as [q] and [ɢ].

Glottal [ʔ] [h]   The [h] sound that starts words such as *house* [haws], *who* [hu], and *hair* [hɛr] is a glottal sound. Although classified as a consonant, there is no airflow restriction in pronouncing [h]. Its sound is from the flow of air through the open glottis. The tongue and lips are usually in the position for the production of the following vowel.

If the air is stopped completely at the glottis by tightly closed vocal cords, the sound produced is a **glottal stop.** This is the sound sometimes used instead of [t] in *button* and *Latin*. It also may occur in colloquial speech at the end of words like *don't, won't,* and *can't*. In some American dialects (we'll discuss dialects in chapter 10), it regularly replaces the *tt* sound in words like *bottle* or *glottal*. If you say "ah-ah-ah-ah-" with one "ah" right after another and do not sustain the vowel sound, you will be producing glottal stops between the vowels. In some languages, the glottal stop functions like the stops [p], [t], [k] in English. The IPA symbol for a glottal stop looks something like a question mark without the dot on the bottom [ʔ].

Table 6.2 summarizes the classification of English consonants by their place of articulation. The glottal stop is not included in this table since only some speakers use it in some words. The uvular sounds do not occur regularly in English.

Table 6.2   Place of Articulation of English Consonants

Bilabial	p	b	m			
Labiodental	f	v				
Interdental	θ	ð				
Alveolar	t	d	n	s	z	l	r
Palatal	ʃ	ʒ	č	ǰ		
Velar	k	g	ŋ			
Glottal	h					

MANNERS OF ARTICULATION

We have described a number of classes of consonants according to their place of articulation, yet we are still unable to distinguish the sounds in each class from each other. What distinguishes [p] from [b], or [b] from [m]? All are bilabial sounds. What is the difference between [t], [d], and [n], which are all alveolar sounds?

Speech sounds also vary in the way the airstream is affected as it flows from the lungs up and out of the mouth and nose. It may be blocked or partially blocked; the vocal cords may vibrate or not vibrate. We refer to this as the **manner of articulation.**

Voiced and Voiceless Sounds   If the vocal cords are apart during airflow, the air flows freely through the glottis and supraglottal cavities (the parts of the vocal tract above the glottis; see Figure 6.1). The sounds produced in this way are **voiceless** sounds: [p], [t], [k], and [s] in the English words *seep* [sip], *seat* [sit], and *seek* [sik] are voiceless sounds.

If the vocal cords are together, the airstream forces its way through and causes them to vibrate. Such sounds are **voiced** and are illustrated by the sounds [b], [d], [g], and [z] in the words *bate* [bet], *date* [det], *gate* [get], *cob* [kab], *cod* [kad], *cog* [kag], and *daze* [dez]. If you put a finger in each ear and say the voiced "z-z-z-z-z," you can feel the vibrations of the vocal cords. If you now say the voiceless "s-s-s-s-s," you will not feel these vibrations (although you might hear a hissing sound in your mouth). When you whisper, you are making all the speech sounds voiceless.

The voiced/voiceless distinction is very important in English. This phonetic feature, or property, distinguishes the words in word pairs like the following:

rope/robe	fate/fade	rack/rag	wreath/wreathe
[rop]/[rob]	[fet]/[fed]	[ræk]/[ræg]	[riθ]/[rið]

The first word of each pair ends with a voiceless sound and the second word with a voiced sound. All other aspects of the sounds in each word pair are identical; the position of the lips and tongue is the same.

The voiced/voiceless distinction also occurs in the following pairs, where the first word begins with a voiceless sound and the second with a voiced sound:

fine/vine	seal/zeal	choke/joke
[fajn]/[vajn]	[sil/zil]	[čok]/[ǰok]

peat/beat	tote/dote	kale/gale
[pit]/[bit]	[tot]/[dot]	[kel]/[gel]

In our discussion of [p], we did not distinguish the initial sound in the word *pit* from the second sound in the word *spit*. There is, however, a phonetic difference in these two voiceless stops. During the production of voiceless sounds, the glottis is open and the air passes freely through the opening between the vocal cords. When a voiceless sound is followed by a voiced sound such as a vowel, the vocal cords must close so that they can vibrate.

Voiceless sounds fall into two classes depending on the timing of the vocal cord closure. In English, when we pronounce the word *pit,* there is a brief period of voicelessness immediately after the *p* sound is released. That is, after the lips come apart, the vocal cords remain open for a very short time. Such sounds are called **aspirated** because an extra puff of air escapes through the open glottis.

When we pronounce the *p* in *spit,* however, the vocal cords start vibrating as soon as the lips open. Such sounds are **unaspirated.** The *t* in *tick* and the *k* in *kin* are also aspirated voiceless stops, while the *t* in *stick* and the *k* in *skin* are unaspirated. Hold your palm about 2 inches in front of your lips and say *pit.* You will feel a puff of air, which you will not feel when you say *spit.*

Figure 6.2 shows in diagrammatic form the timing of the articulators (in this case the lips) in relation to the state of the vocal cords.

In the production of the voiced [b], the vocal cords are vibrating throughout the closure of the lips, and continue to vibrate for the vowel production after the lips part. Most English speakers do not voice initial [b] fully. That is, the vocal cords remain open for a fraction of a second after the lips seal. Voiced consonants in other languages such as French are typically fully voiced throughout. These are idiosyncratic differences between languages, or even dialects of languages and individual speakers.

We indicate aspirated sounds by writing the phonetic symbol with a raised *h,* as in the following examples:

pate	[p^{h}et]	spate	[spet]
tale	[t^{h}el]	stale	[stel]
kale	[k^{h}el]	scale	[skel]

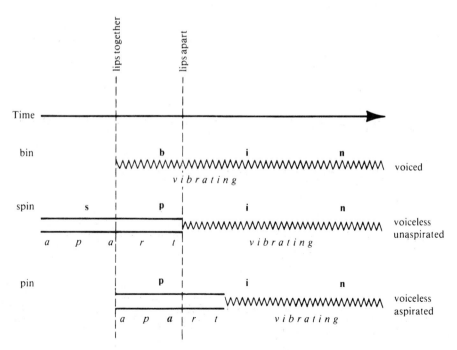

Figure 6.2   Timing of articulation and vocal-cord vibrations for voiced, voiceless, unaspirated, and voiceless aspirated stops.

Nasal and Oral Sounds   The voiced/voiceless distinction differentiates the bilabials [b] and [p]. The sound [m] is also a bilabial, and it is voiced. What distinguishes it from [b]?

Figure 6.1 shows the roof of the mouth divided into the (hard) palate and the soft palate (or velum). The palate is a hard bony structure at the front of the mouth. You can feel it with your thumb. As you slide your thumb along the hard palate back toward the throat, you will feel the velum, which is where the flesh becomes soft and pliable. The velum terminates in the uvula, which you can see in a mirror if you open your mouth wide and say "aaah." The velum is movable, and when it is raised all the way to touch the back of the throat, the passage through the nose is cut off and air can escape only through the mouth.

Sounds produced with the velum up, blocking the air from escaping through the nose, are **oral sounds,** since the air can escape only through the oral cavity. Most sounds in all languages are oral sounds.

When the velum is not in its raised position, air escapes through both the nose and the mouth. Sounds produced this way are **nasal sounds.** The sound [m] is a nasal consonant. Thus [m] is distinguished from [b] because it is a nasal sound, while [b] is an oral sound.

The diagrams in Figure 6.3 show the position of the lips and the velum when [m], [b], and [p] are articulated. The sounds [p], [b], and [m] are produced by stopping the airflow at the lips; [m] and [b] differ from [p] by being voiced; [m] differs from [b] by being nasal.

The same oral/nasal difference occurs in *dear* [dir] and *near* [nir], *rug* [rʌg] and *rung* [rʌŋ]. The velum is raised in the production of [d] and [g], preventing the air from flowing through the nose, whereas in [n] and [ŋ] the velum is down, letting the air go through both the nose and the mouth when the closure is released. The sounds [m], [n], and [ŋ] are therefore nasal sounds, and [b], [d], and [g] are oral sounds.

These **phonetic features** permit the classification of all speech sounds into four classes: voiced, voiceless, nasal, and oral. One sound may belong to more than one class, as shown in Table 6.3.

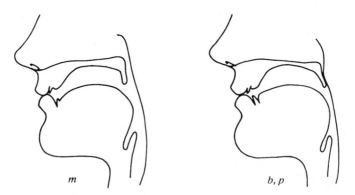

Figure 6.3   Position of lips and velum for *m* (lips together, velum down), and *b, p* (lips together, velum up).

Table 6.3   Four Classes of Speech Sounds

	Oral	Nasal
Voiced	b d g	m n ŋ
Voiceless	p t k	*

*Nasal consonants in English are usually voiced. Both voiced and voiceless nasal sounds occur in other languages.

We now have three ways of classifying consonants: by voicing, by place of articulation, and oral vs. nasal. For example, [p] is a voiceless, bilabial, oral sound; [n] is a voiced, alveolar, nasal sound, and so on.

Stops [p] [b] [m] [t] [d] [n] [k] [g] [ŋ] [č] [ǰ] [ʔ]   We are seeing finer and finer distinctions of speech sounds. However, both [t] and [s] are voiceless, alveolar, oral sounds. What distinguishes them? After all, *sack* and *tack* are different words.

In producing consonants, the airstream may be completely stopped or just partially obstructed. Sounds that are stopped completely in the oral cavity for a brief period are, not surprisingly, called **stops.** The sound [t] is a stop, but the sound [s] is not, and that is what makes them different speech sounds.

The final sounds in the words *top* [tap], *bomb* [bam], *dude* [dud], *dune* [dun], *root* [rut], *rack* [ræk], *rag* [ræg], and *rang* [ræŋ] are stops that occur in English.

In the production of the nasal stops [m], [n], [ŋ], although the air flows freely through the nose, the airflow is blocked completely in the mouth; therefore, nasal consonants are stops.

Sounds in which there is no stoppage in the oral tract are **continuants.** All the sounds of a language are either stops or continuants (nonstop).

Nonnasal, or oral, stops are also called **plosives** because the air that is blocked in the mouth "explodes" when the closure is released. This explosion does not occur during the production of nasal stops because the air escapes continuously through the nose.

[p], [b], and [m] are *bilabial stops,* with the airstream stopped at the mouth by the complete closure of the lips.

[t], [d], and [n] are *alveolar stops;* the airstream is stopped by the tongue making a complete closure at the alveolar ridge.

[k], [g], and [ŋ] are *velar stops* with the complete closure at the velum.

[ʔ] is a *glottal stop.* Although there is no stoppage of air in the oral cavity, the air is completely stopped at the glottis.

[č] and [ǰ] are *palatal affricates* with complete stop closures. We will describe them below.

We have been discussing the sounds that occur in English. Some sounds, including stops, occur in other languages but not in English. For example, in Quechua, spoken in Bolivia and Peru, uvular stops occur, where the back of the tongue is raised and moved rearward to form a complete closure with the uvula. The phonetic symbol [q] denotes the voiceless version of this stop, which is the initial sound in the name of the language "Quechua." The voiced uvular stop [G] also occurs in Quechua. We find glottal stops in a number of languages such as Arabic.

Fricatives [f] [v] [θ] [ð] [s] [z] [š] [ž]   In the production of some continuants, the airflow is so severely obstructed that it causes friction, and the sounds are therefore called fricatives. The sounds [f], [v], [θ], [ð], [s], [z], [š], and [ž] are pronounced in this manner.

[f] and [v] are *labiodental fricatives;* the friction is created at the lips and teeth, where a narrow passage permits the air to escape. The [f] is voiceless and the [v] is voiced. The following pairs follow this pattern.

[θ] and [ð] are the *interdental fricatives,* represented by *th* in *thin* and *then.* The friction occurs at the opening between the tongue and teeth.

[s] and [z] are *alveolar fricatives,* with the friction created at the alveolar ridge.

[š] and [ž] are the *palatal fricatives,* and contrast in such pairs as *mission* [mɪšən] and *measure* [mɛžər]. They are produced with friction created as the air passes between the tongue and the palate behind the alveolar ridge. In English, the voiced palatal fricative never begins words (except in words borrowed from French like *genre,* which some English speakers produce with a French pronunciation). The voiceless palatal sound begins the words *shoe* [šu] and *sure* [šur] and ends the words *rush* [rʌš] and *push* [pʊš].

Most modern English dialects do not include velar fricatives, although they occurred in an earlier stage of English in such words as *right, knight, enough,* and *through,* where the *gh* occurs in the spelling. If you raise the back of the tongue as if you were about to produce a [k] or [g], but stop just short of touching the velum, you will produce a velar fricative. The *ch* ending in the German pronunciation of the composer's name *Bach* is a velar fricative. Some speakers of modern English substitute a voiceless velar fricative in words like *bucket* and a voiced velar fricative in such words as *wagon* for the velar stops, especially in rapid, informal speech. The IPA symbol for the voiceless velar fricative is [x], and for the voiced velar fricative, it is [ɣ].

In languages like French, the uvular trill [R] occurs as the sound represented by *r* in French words such as *rouge,* "red." Voiced glottal fricatives, which do not occur in English, do occur in other languages, such as Czech. Speakers of Arabic produce pharyngeal fricatives by pulling the tongue root toward the back wall of the pharynx. It is difficult to pull the tongue back far enough to make a complete pharyngeal stop closure, but both voiced and voiceless pharyngeal fricatives can be produced, and can be distinguished from velar fricatives.

All fricatives are continuants: Although the airstream is obstructed as it passes through the oral cavity, it is not completely stopped.

Affricates [č], [ǰ]   Some sounds are produced by a stop closure followed immediately by a gradual release of the closure that produces an effect characteristic of a fricative. These sounds are affricates. The palatal sounds that begin the words *church* and *judge* are voiceless and voiced affricates, respectively. Phonetically, an affricate is a sequence of a stop plus a fricative. Thus, the *ch* in *church* is the same as the sound combination [t] + [š], as you can see by pronouncing *white shoes* and *why choose* rapidly. The two expressions are indistinguishable. The voiceless and voiced affricates are symbolized as [tš] (IPA [tʃ]) and [dž] (IPA [dʒ]), respectively. In the American tradition, [č], [ǰ] are the more common symbols for these sounds, and are used in this book.

Because the air is stopped completely during the initial articulation of an affricate, these sounds are also classified as stops.

Liquids [l] [r]   In the production of the sounds [l] and [r], there is some obstruction of the airstream in the mouth, but not enough to cause any real constriction or friction. These sounds are *liquids*. The lateral liquid [l] and the retroflex liquid [r] are described in the earlier alveolar section. They are both voiced sounds. In some contexts the liquids sound similar, as they do to Dennis in the cartoon.

"WHO'S MAKING ALL THOSE MISTAKES? THEY'RE *ALWAYS* PASSING THE CORRECTION PLATE."

"Dennis the Menace"® used by permission of Hank Ketcham and © by North America Syndicate.

As mentioned earlier, the *r* sounds that occur in various dialects of English, and in various languages, differ somewhat from each other. We are using the symbol [r] for this whole class of sounds. An alveolar trilled *r* occurs in many languages, such as Spanish. In addition, uvular trills occur, produced by vibrating the uvula. Some French speakers use uvular trills in the pronunciation of *r;* others use uvular fricatives. In yet other languages, the *r* is produced by a single **tap** or **flap** of the tongue against the alveolar ridge, and we sometimes call that sound "a flap." In Spanish both the trilled *r* and the flap occur, the former in *perro,* "dog," and the latter in *pero,* "but."

Some speakers of British English pronounce the *r* in the word *very* as a flap. It sounds like a "very fast *d*." Most American speakers produce a flap instead of a [t] or [d] in words like *writer, rider, latter,* and *ladder.* The IPA symbol for the alveolar tap or flap is [ɾ]. American linguists often use the upper case [D] to represent this sound.

In English, [l] and [r] are regularly voiced. When they follow voiceless sounds, as in *please* and *price,* they may be partially devoiced, that is, the voicing doesn't begin until part way through the consonant. Many languages have a voiceless *l* as an independent sound, in which case it is actually a fricative. Welsh is such a language; the name *Lloyd* in Welsh starts with the voiceless fricative *l*.

Some languages may lack liquids entirely, or may have only a single one. The Cantonese dialect of Chinese has the single liquid [l]. Some English words are difficult for Cantonese speakers to pronounce, and they may substitute an [l] for an [r] when speaking English.

The reason that speakers of languages with only one liquid tend to substitute that sound for the nonoccurring liquid is the acoustic similarity of these sounds. This auditory similarity is the reason that linguists group them in one class, and why they function as a single class of sounds in certain circumstances. For example, in English, the only two consonants that occur after an initial [k], [g], [p], or [b] are the liquids [l] and [r]. Thus we have *crate* [kret], *clock* [klak], *plate,* [plet], *pray* [pre], *bleak* [blik], *break* [brek], but no word starting with [ps], [bt], [pk], and so on. (Notice that in words like *psychology* or *pterodactyl* the *p* is not pronounced. Similarly, in *knight* or *knot* the *k* is not pronounced, although at an earlier stage of English it was.)

Glides [j] [w]   The sounds [j] and [w], the initial sounds of *you* [ju] and *woo* [wu], are produced with little or no obstruction of the airstream in the mouth. They are always preceded or followed directly by a vowel. In articulating [j] or [w], the tongue moves rapidly in gliding fashion either toward or away from a neighboring vowel, hence the term *glide*. Glides are transitional sounds that are sometimes called *semivowels*.

The glide [j] is a palatal sound; the blade of the tongue (the front part minus the tip) is raised toward the hard palate in a position almost identical to that in producing the vowel sound [i] in the word *beat* [bit]. In pronouncing *you* [ju], the tongue moves rapidly from the [j] to the [u] vowel.

The glide [w] is produced by both raising the back of the tongue toward the velum and simultaneously rounding the lips. It is thus a **labio-velar** glide, or a rounded velar glide. In the dialect of English where speakers have different pronunciations for the words *which* and *witch,* the velar glide in the first word is voiceless, symbolized as [ʍ] (an "upside-down" *w*), and in the second word it is voiced, symbolized as [w]. When the pronunciation of the two words is the same, it is the voiced [w]. The position of the tongue and the lips for [w] is similar to that for producing the vowel sound in *suit* [sut]. In pronouncing *we* [wi], the tongue moves rapidly from the [w] to the [i] vowel.

PHONETIC SYMBOLS FOR AMERICAN ENGLISH CONSONANTS

We are now capable of distinguishing all of the consonant sounds of English via the properties of voicing, nasality, and place and manner of articulation. For example, [f] is a voiceless, (oral), labiodental fricative; [n] is a (voiced), nasal, alveolar stop. The parenthesized features are usually not mentioned since they are redundant; all sounds are oral unless nasal is specifically mentioned, and all nasals are voiced in English.

Table 6.4 lists the consonants by their phonetic features. The rows stand for manner of articulation and the columns for place of articulation. Symbols for aspirated stops and the glottal stop are not included. The entries are the minimal number of basic sounds needed to distinguish all morphemes and words in English. For example, the one symbol [p] for all voiceless bilabial stops, together with the symbol [b] for the voiced

Table 6.4   Minimal Set of Phonetic Symbols for American English Consonants

	Bilabial	Labiodental	Interdental	Alveolar	Palatal	Velar	Glottal
Stop (oral)							
voiceless	p			t		k	
voiced	b			d		g	
Nasal (stop)	m			n		ŋ	
Fricative							
voiceless		f	θ	s	š		h[1]
voiced		v	ð	z	ž		
Affricate							
voiceless					č		
voiced					ǰ		
Glide							
voiceless	ʍ					ʍ	h[1]
voiced	w[2]				j	w[2]	
Liquid				l r			

1. [h] is sometimes classified as a fricative because of the hissing sound produced by air or noise at the glottis. It is also sometimes classified with the glides because in many languages it combines with other sounds the way that glides do.

2. [w] is classified as both a bilabial because it is produced with both lips rounded and as a velar because the back of the tongue is raised toward the velum.

bilabial stop, are sufficient to differentiate the word *peat* [pit] from *beat*. If a more detailed, or narrow, phonetic transcription of these words is desired, the symbol [p^h] can be used as in [p^hit].

Examples of words in which these sounds occur are given in Table 6.5.

Table 6.5   Examples of Consonants in English Words

	Bilabial	Labiodental	Interdental	Alveolar	Palatal	Velar	Glottal
Stop (oral)							
voiceless	*p*ie			*t*ie		*k*ite	
voiced	*b*uy			*d*ie		*g*uy	
Nasal (stop)	*m*y			*n*ight		si*ng*	
Fricative							
voiceless		*f*ie	*th*igh	*s*ue	mi*ss*ion		*h*igh
voiced		*v*ie	*th*y	*z*oo	mea*s*ure		
Affricate							
voiceless					*ch*ime		
voiced					*j*ive		
Glide							
voiceless	*wh*ich[1]					*wh*ich[1]	
voiced	*w*ipe				*y*ank	*w*ipe	
Liquid				*l*ie, *r*ye			

1. For speakers with a voiceless *w*.

Vowels

F W WNT T TLK RLLY GD, W'LL HV T NVNT VWLS.

THAVES 10-16

"Frank and Ernest" copyright © 1980 Newspaper Enterprise Association, Inc.

The quality of a vowel depends on the configuration of the vocal tract during its production. Different parts of the tongue may be high or low in the mouth; the lips may be spread or pursed; the velum may be raised or lowered. The passage through which the air travels, however, is never so narrow as to obstruct the free flow of the airstream.

Vowel sounds carry pitch and loudness; you can sing vowels. They may be long or short. Vowels can "stand alone" — they can be produced without consonants before or after them. You can say the vowels of *beat,* [bit], *bit* [bɪt], or *boot* [but], for example, without the initial [b] or the final [t], but you cannot say a [b] or a [t] alone without at least a "little bit" of vowel sound.

Linguists and speech scientists can describe vowels acoustically, or electronically. We will discuss that in chapter 9. In this chapter, we describe vowels by their articulatory features, just as we described consonants. Many beginning students of phonetics find this method more difficult to apply to vowel articulations than to consonant articulations. When you articulate a [t], you can feel your tongue touch the alveolar ridge. When you make a [p], you can feel your two lips come together, or you can watch your lips move in a mirror. Because we produce vowels without articulators touching or even coming close, it is often difficult to feel what is happening. You may not understand at first what we mean by "front," "back," "high," and "low" vowels, but we encourage you to persist. It will come.

These terms do have meaning, though. If you watch an X-ray movie of someone talking, you can see why vowels have traditionally been classified according to three questions:

1. How high is the tongue?
2. What part of the tongue is involved, and is that part up, down, or neutral in the mouth?
3. What is the position of the lips?

TONGUE POSITION

HIGGINS: Tired of listening to sounds?

PICKERING: Yes. It's a fearful strain. I rather fancied myself because I can pronounce twenty-four distinct vowel sounds, but your hundred and thirty beat me. I can't hear a bit of difference between most of them.

HIGGINS: Oh, that comes with practice. You hear no difference at first, but you keep on listening and presently you find they're all as different as A from B.

G. B. Shaw, *Pygmalion*

The upper two diagrams in Figure 6.4 show that the tongue is high in the mouth in the production of the vowels [i] and [u] in the words *he* [hi] and *who* [hu]. In *he* the front part (but not the tip) of the tongue is raised; in *who* it is the back of the tongue. (Prolong the vowels of these words and try to feel the raised part of your tongue.)

To produce the vowel sound [a] of *hah* [ha], the back of the tongue is low in the mouth, as the lower diagram in Figure 6.4 shows. (The reason a doctor examining your throat may ask you to say "ah" is that the tongue is low and easy to see over.) This vowel is therefore a low, back vowel.

The vowels [ɪ] and [ʊ] in the words *hit* [hɪt] and *put* [pʊt] are similar to those in *he* [hi] and *who* [hu] with slightly lowered tongue positions.

The vowel [æ] in *hack* [hæk] is produced with the front part of the tongue low in the mouth, similar to the low vowel [a], but with the front rather than the back part of the tongue lowered. Say "hack, hah, hack, hah, hack, hah, . . ." and you should feel your tongue moving forward and back in the low part of your mouth.

The vowels [e] and [o] in *bait* [bet] and *boat* [bot] are *mid vowels*, produced by raising the tongue to a position midway between the high and low vowels just discussed.

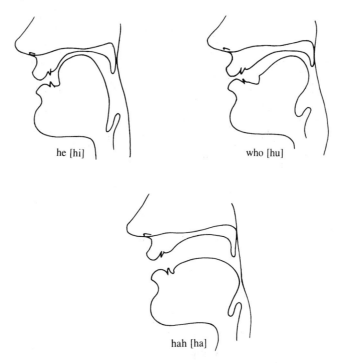

he [hi]   who [hu]

hah [ha]

Figure 6.4   Position of the tongue in producing the vowels in he, who, and hah.

[ɛ] and [ɔ] in the words *bet* [bɛt] and *bore* [bɔr] are also mid vowels, produced with a slightly lower tongue position than [e] and [o].

To produce the vowel [ʌ] in the word *butt* [bʌt], the tongue is not strictly high nor low, front nor back. It is a lower mid, central vowel. The schwa vowel [ə], which occurs as the first sound in *about* [əbawt], or the final sound of *sofa* [sofə], is also articulated with the tongue in a more or less neutral position between the extremes of high/low, front/back. The schwa is used only to represent unstressed vowels. (We will discuss stress below.)

LIP ROUNDING

Vowels also differ as to whether the lips are rounded or spread. The vowels [u], [ʊ], [o], and [ɔ], in *boot, put, boat,* and *bore* are **rounded vowels.** They are produced with the lips pursed, or rounded, and the back of the tongue at decreasing heights, as shown in Figure 6.5. You can get a feel for the rounding by prolonging the word *who,* as if you were an owl: *whooooooooooo.* Now pose for the camera and say *cheese,* only say it with a prolonged vowel: *cheeeeeeeeeeese.* The high front [i] in *cheese* is unrounded, with the lips in the shape of a smile, and you can feel it. The low vowel [a] in the words *bar, bah,* and *aha* is the only English back vowel that occurs without lip rounding. All nonback vowels in English are also unrounded.

This is not true of all languages. French and Swedish, for example, have both front and back rounded vowels. In English, a high back unrounded vowel does not occur, but in Mandarin Chinese, Japanese, the Cameroonian language FeʔFeʔ, and many other languages, this vowel is part of the phonetic inventory of sounds. There is a Chinese word meaning "four" with an initial [s] followed by a vowel similar to the one in *boot* but with unrounded, spread lips. This Chinese word is distinguished from the word meaning "speed," pronounced like the English word *sue,* with a high back rounded vowel.

Figure 6.5 shows the vowels based on tongue "geography." The position of the vowel relative to the horizontal axis is a measure of the vowel's front/back dimension.

Part of the Tongue Involved

Tongue Height	FRONT ⟵——— CENTRAL ———⟶ BACK					
HIGH	i beet				boot	u
↑	ɪ bit				put	ʊ
						↵ **ROUNDED**
MID	e bait				boat	o
	ɛ bet	ə Rosa				
↓		ʌ butt			bore	ɔ
LOW	æ bat				bomb	a

Figure 6.5   Classification of American English vowels.

Its position relative to the vertical axis is a measure of tongue height. For example, we see that [i] is a high front vowel, [o] is a mid back (rounded) vowel, and [ʌ] is a lower mid, central vowel, tending toward backness.

Diphthongs

A **diphthong** is a sequence of two sounds, vowel + glide. Diphthongs are present in the phonetic inventory of many languages, including English. The vowels we have studied so far are simple vowels, called **monophthongs.** The vowel sound in the word *bite* [bajt], however, is the [a] vowel sound of *father* followed by the [j] glide, resulting in the diphthong [aj]. Similarly, the vowel in *bout* [bawt] is [a] followed by the glide [w], resulting in [aw]. (Some speakers of English pronounce this diphthong as [æw], with the front low unrounded vowel instead of the back vowel.) The third diphthong that occurs in English is the vowel sound in *boy* [bɔj], which is the vowel [ɔ] of *bore* (without the [r]) followed by the palatal glide [j], resulting in [ɔj].

Nasalization of Vowels

Vowels, like consonants, can be produced with a raised velum that prevents the air from escaping through the nose, or with a lowered velum that permits air to pass through the nasal passage. When the nasal passage is blocked, *oral* vowels result; when the nasal passage is open, *nasal* (or *nasalized*) vowels result. In English, nasal vowels occur for the most part before nasal consonants in the same syllable, and oral vowels occur in all other places.

The words *bean, bin, bane, been, ban, boon, bun, bone, beam, bam, boom, bing, bang,* and *bong* are examples of words that contain nasalized vowels. To show the nasalization of a vowel in a phonetic transcription, a **diacritic** mark [~] (tilde) is placed over the vowel, as in *bean* [bĩn] and *bone* [bõn].

In languages like French, Polish, and Portuguese, nasalized vowels occur without nasal consonants. The French word meaning "sound" is *son* [sõ]. The *n* in the spelling is not pronounced but indicates that the vowel is nasal.

Tense and Lax Vowels

Figure 6.5 shows that the vowel [i] has a slightly higher tongue position than [ɪ]. This is also true for [e] and [ɛ], [u] and [ʊ], and [o] and [ɔ]. The first vowel in each pair is generally produced with greater tension of the tongue muscles than its counterpart, and they are often a little longer in duration. These vowels can be distinguished from the shorter and less tense vowels by the phonetic features **tense** and **lax** as shown in the following:

Tense (Longer)[2]		Lax (Shorter)	
i	beat	ɪ	bit
e	bait	ɛ	bet
u	boot	ʊ	put
o	boat	ɔ	bore

---

[2] The term *long* refers to duration, not to the "long vowels" of traditional grammar and dictionaries, where a "long *i*" is [aj], and the "short *i*" is [ɪ], and so on.

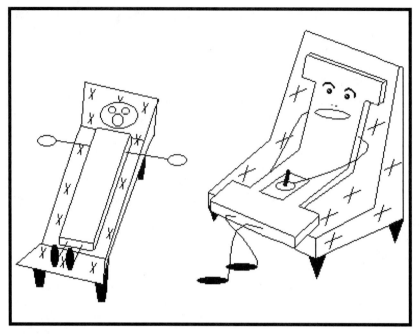

"You know, your problem is that you're just too tense."

Some speakers of English may diphthongize the tense vowels somewhat. For these speakers, the tense front vowels are followed by a short [j] glide, so [ij] and [ej] replace [i] and [e]. The tense back vowels are followed by a short [w] glide, so [uw] and [ow] replace [u] and [o]. These are sometimes written as [iʲ], [eʲ], [uʷ], and [oʷ]. We will continue to denote these sounds as [i], [e], [u], and [o].

DIALECT DIFFERENCES

As already mentioned, but perhaps worth repeating because of the many dialects of English, the vowels in Figure 6.5 do not represent all the vowels of all dialects of English. One dialect spoken in the United Kingdom, called British RP or "Received Pronunciation" (as the dialect spoken by the upper classes and "received" in court), has a low rounded back vowel in the word *hot* that does not occur in American English dialects, and that contrasts with the unrounded low back vowel [a] in *bah*. The long tense vowels in British RP are all diphthongs. Thus the vowel in *bay* is [ej] and the vowel in *bow* is [ow], as is true for some dialects of American English. On the other hand, in some dialects of English spoken in Ireland, these vowels are pure monophthongs. These are just a few examples of dialect differences that occur primarily in the pronunciation of vowels.

Major Classes

Biologists describe classes of life in broader or narrower terms. They may distinguish between animals and plants, or within animals, between vertebrates and invertebrates, and within vertebrates, between mammals and reptiles, and so on.

Linguists describe speech sounds in a similar manner. All sounds are consonants or vowels. Within consonants, all are voiced or unvoiced, and so on. All the classes of sounds described so far in this chapter combine to form larger, more general classes that are important in the patterning of sounds in the world's languages.

NONCONTINUANTS AND CONTINUANTS

As we mentioned, stop sounds are **noncontinuants.** There is a total obstruction of the airstream in the *oral cavity*. They include the nasal stops (despite the fact that air flows continuously out the nose). All other consonants, and all vowels, are continuants, in which the stream of air flows continuously out the mouth.

OBSTRUENTS AND SONORANTS

The nonnasal stops, the fricatives, and the affricates form a major class of sounds called **obstruents.** The airstream may be fully obstructed, as in nonnasal stops and affricates, or partially obstructed, as in the production of fricatives.

Fricatives are continuant obstruents. The air flows continuously out the mouth, though it is obstructed enough to cause the frictional sound that characterizes this class of consonants.

Nonnasal stops and affricates are noncontinuant obstruents; there is a complete blockage of the air during the production of these sounds. The closure of a stop is released abruptly as opposed to the closure of an affricate, which is released gradually, causing friction.

Sounds that are not obstruents are **sonorants.** Sonorants are produced with relatively free airflow through either the mouth or nose. They have greater acoustic energy than obstruents. Nasal stops are sonorants because although the air is blocked in the mouth, it continues to resonate and move through the nose. Vowels, the liquids [l] and [r], and the glides [w] and [j] are also sonorants because the air resonates as it flows relatively undisturbed through the vocal tract.

CONSONANTS AND VOWELS

As stated, the sounds of all the languages of the world fall into two major natural classes —consonants and vowels. Consonants include a number of subclasses: stops (including affricates and nasals), fricatives, liquids, and glides. The class of vowels include oral, nasal, front, central, back, high, mid, and low vowels.

Nasals and liquids are sonorants because they resonate; yet, they resemble the obstruents in that the oral cavity is constricted or even closed during their articulation. Linguists group nasals, liquids, and obstruents into a larger class of sounds that they (confusingly) call **consonantal.** This is done not out of perversity, but because these sounds form a natural class, as we will see in the next chapter.

While all consonantal sounds are consonants, not all consonants are consonantal. Glides, in particular, are nonconsonantal consonants. They pattern with the vowels to make up the class of nonconsonantal sounds that are sometimes referred to as **vocalic** sounds.

Here are some other terms used to form classes of consonants. These are not exhaustive (though they may exhaust you while learning them). A full course in phonetics would note further classes that we omit.

Labials [p] [b] [m] [f] [v]   The class of labial consonants includes the class of bilabial sounds — [p] [b] [m] — as well as the labiodentals, [f] and [v]. Labial sounds are those articulated with the involvement of the lips.

Coronals [t] [d] [n] [s] [z] [š] [ž] [č] [ǰ] [l]   Coronals include the alveolars, [t] [d] [n] [s] [z]; the palatals, [š] [ž]; the affricates, [č] [ǰ]; and the liquid [l]. (Some articulations of [r] are also coronal.) These are sounds articulated by raising the tongue blade.

Anterior [p] [b] [m] [f] [v] [θ] [ð] [t] [d] [n] [s] [z]   Anterior sounds are consonants produced in the front part of the mouth, that is, from the alveolar area forward. They include the labials, the interdentals, and the alveolars.

Sibilants [s] [z] [š] [ž] [č] [ǰ]   Another class of consonantal sounds is characterized by an acoustic rather than an articulatory property of its members. The friction created in the production of fricatives and affricates causes a hissing sound, which is a mixture of high-frequency sounds. These sounds form the class of sibilants.

Syllabic Sounds

In the following chapter, we will give a precise definition of *syllable*. Traditionally it has been difficult to provide such a definition, although speakers seem to be able to determine the syllabic structure of a word. From an auditory point of view, syllables have peaks of sonorance (which are also difficult to define). Every vowel is at the center of a single syllable.

Liquids and nasals can also be syllabic — function as a syllable — as shown by the words *Rachel* [rečl̩], *faker* [fekr̩], *rhythm* [rɪðm̩], and *button* [bʌtn̩]. (The diacritic mark under the [l̩] [r̩] [m̩] and [n̩] show that these sounds are **syllabic**.) Placing a schwa [ə] before the syllabic liquid or nasal also shows that these are separate syllables. The four words could be written as [rečəl], [fekər], [rɪðəm], and [bʌtən]. We will use this transcription. Similarly, the vowel sound in words like *bird* and *verb* are sometimes written as a syllabic r, [br̩d] and [vr̩b]. For consistency we shall transcribe these words using the schwa — [bərd] and [vərb] — the only instances where a schwa represents a stressed vowel.

Prosodic Suprasegmental Features

Speech sounds that are identical in their place or manner features may differ in length (duration), pitch, or loudness. Tense vowels are generally longer than lax vowels, but only by a small amount, perhaps a few milliseconds. (A millisecond is 1/1000 of a second.) However, when a vowel is prolonged to around twice its normal length, it is considered in some languages a different vowel, and it can make a difference between words. In Japanese the word *biru* with a short *i* means "building," but with the *i* prolonged, spelled *bi:ru* or *biiru,* the meaning is "beer." We have just illustrated the two ways of denoting a long, or **geminate,** vowel: add a colon or simply write it twice.

Japanese, and many other languages such as Finnish and Italian, also have long (geminate) consonants that make a difference in words. When a consonant is long, either the closure or obstruction is prolonged. Pronounced with a short k, the word *saki,* means "ahead" in Japanese; pronounced with a long k — prolonging the velar closure — the word *sakki* means "before."

English is not a language in which vowel or consonant length can change a word. You might say "stooooooop!" to emphasize your desire to make someone stop, but the word is not changed. You may also say in English "Whatttttt a dump!" to express your dismay at a hotel room, prolonging the *t*-closure, but the word *what* is not changed.

When we speak, we also change the **pitch** of our voice. The pitch depends on how fast the vocal cords vibrate; the faster they vibrate, the higher the pitch. If the larynx is small, as in women and children, the shorter vocal cords vibrate faster and the pitch is higher, all other things being equal. That is why women and children have higher pitched voices than men, in general.

In many languages, certain syllables in a word are louder, slightly higher in pitch, and somewhat longer in duration (but not geminate) than other syllables in the word. They are **stressed** syllables. For example, the first syllable of *digest,* the noun meaning "summation of articles" is stressed, while in *digest,* the verb meaning "to absorb food," the second syllable receives greater stress. Stress can be marked in a number of ways: for example, by putting an accent mark over the stressed vowel in the syllable, as in *dígest* versus *digést*.

English is a "stress" language. In general, at least one syllable is stressed in an English word. French is not a stress language. The syllables have approximately the same loudness, length, and pitch. When native English speakers attempt to speak French, they often stress syllables, so that native French speakers hear French with "an English accent." When French speakers speak English, they fail to put stress where a native English speaker would, and that contributes to what English speakers would call a "French accent."

Length, pitch, and the complex feature stress are **prosodic,** or **suprasegmental,** features. They are features over and above the segmental values such as voicing or place of articulation, thus the "supra" in *suprasegmental.* The term *prosodic* comes from poetry, where it refers to the metrical structure of verse. One of the essential characteristics of poetry is the placement of stress on particular syllables, which defines the versification of the poem.

TONE AND INTONATION

We have already seen how length and stress can make sounds with the same segmental properties different. In some languages, these differences make different words, such as the two *digests.* Pitch, too, can make a difference in certain languages.

Speakers of all languages vary the pitch of their voices when they talk. The effect of pitch on a syllable differs from language to language. In English, it doesn't matter whether you say *cat* with a high pitch or a low pitch. It will still mean "cat." But if you say [ba] with a high pitch in Nupe (a language spoken in Nigeria), it will mean "to be sour," whereas if you say [ba] with a low pitch, it will mean "to count." Languages that use the pitch of individual vowels or syllables to contrast meanings of words are called **tone** languages.

The majority of the languages in the world are tone languages. There are more than one thousand tone languages in Africa alone. Many languages of Asia, such as Chinese, Thai, and Burmese, are tone languages, as are many Native American languages.

Thai is a language that has contrasting pitches or tones. The same string of segmental sounds represented by [naa] will mean different things if one says the sounds with a low pitch, a mid pitch, a high pitch, a falling pitch from high to low, or a rising pitch from low to high. Thai therefore has five linguistic tones.

[naa]	[__]	low tone	"a nickname"
[naa]	[—]	mid tone	"rice paddy"
[naa]	[⁻]	high tone	"young maternal uncle or aunt"
[naa]	[⌐]	falling tone	"face"
[naa]	[◡]	rising tone	"thick"

Diacritics are used to represent distinctive tones in the phonetic transcriptions.

[`]	L	low tone	
[⁻]	M	mid tone	
[´]	H	high tone	
[^]	HL	falling tone	(High to Low)
[ˇ]	LH	rising tone	(Low to High)

We can use these diacritics placed above the vowels to represent the tonal contrasts in any language where the pitch of the vowel is important in conveying meaning as illustrated by the three contrastive tones in Nupe:

| [bá] | "be sour" | [bā] | "cut" | [bà] | "count" |
| H | | M | | L | |

Akan, sometimes called Twi, the major language of Ghana, has two tones, which are shown in these contrasting two-syllables words.

dù	à	[_ _]	"tail"	dù	á	[_ ⁻]	"tree"
|	|			|	|		
L	L			L	H		

kɔ̀	tó	[_ ⁻]	"go buy"	kɔ́	tɔ̀	[⁻ _]	"crab"
|	|			|	|		
L	H			H	L		

In some tone languages the pitch of each tone is level; in others, the direction of the pitch (whether it glides from high to low or from low to high) is important. Tones that glide are called **contour tones;** tones that do not are called **level,** or **register,** tones. The contour tones of Thai are represented by using a high tone followed by a low tone for a falling glide, and a low followed by a high for a rising tone.

In a tone language, it is not the absolute pitch of the syllables that is important but the relations among the pitches of different syllables. After all, some individual speakers have high-pitched voices, others low-pitched, and others medium-pitched. In many tone languages we find a falling-off of the pitch, a continual downdrifting of the tones.

In the following sentence in Twi, the relative pitch rather than the absolute pitch is important.

"Kofi searches for a little food for his friend's child."

```
Kòfí    hwèhwé   áduàŋ   kàkrá mà   ǹ' ádàmfò   bá
| |     |  |     |  |     |  |  |    |  | |  |    |
L H     L  H     H  L     L  H  L    L  H L  L    H
```

The actual pitches of these syllables would be rather different from each other, as shown in the following musical staff-like figure (the higher the number, the higher the pitch):

7	fí
6	hwé á
5	Kò	krá
4	hwè	á
3	duàŋ kà	bá
2	mà ǹ'
1	dàmfò

The lowering of the pitch is called **downdrift.** In languages with downdrift — and many tone languages in Africa are downdrift languages — a high tone that occurs after a low tone, or a low tone after a high tone, is lower in pitch than the preceding similarly marked tone. Notice that the first high tone in the sentence is given the pitch value 7. The next high tone (which occurs after an intervening low tone) is 6; that is, it is lower in pitch than the first high tone.

This example shows that in analyzing tones, just as in analyzing segments, all the physical properties need not be considered; only essential features are important in language — in this case, whether the tone is "high" or "low" in relation to the other pitches, but not the specific pitch of that tone.

Languages that are not tone languages, such as English, are called **intonation** languages. The **pitch contour** of the utterance varies, but in an intonation language as opposed to a tone language, pitch is not used to distinguish words from each other.

Diacritics

In the discussions of vowel nasalization, prosodic features, and tone, we presented a number of diacritic marks that modify the basic phonetic symbols. A tilde [~] over the vowel symbol means nasalization; a colon [:] after the vowel symbol marks length or gemination; an acute accent shows stress; and various other marks indicate the various tones.

Other diacritics provide additional ways of showing phonetic differences of speech sounds. For example, to differentiate the voiceless lateral liquid that occurs in some pronunciations of words like *place* [pl̥es], or the voiceless alveolar nasal that may occur in a word like *snow* [sn̥o], a little round "o" is written under the symbol, as you can see.

Linguists often use **cover symbols** to refer to classes of sounds. A capital C represents the class of consonants, V the class of vowels, G the glides, and L the liquids. (It's true. Linguists are just as lazy as the government bureaucrats who make up all those acronyms.)

We can summarize these diacritics and additional symbols as follows:

C = Consonant	C: = long C	
V = Vowel	V: = long V	V́ = stressed V
	Ṽ = nasalized V	V̥ = voiceless vowel
L = Liquid	L̥ = voiceless L	
G = Glide	G̥ = voiceless glide	

Tones

V́ = High	V̀ = Low	V̄ = Mid
V̌ = Rising	V̂ = Falling	

Phonetic Symbols and Spelling Correspondences

Table 6.6 shows the sound/spelling correspondences for American English consonants and vowels. (We have not given all possible spellings for every sound, however these examples should help you relate English orthography to the English sound system.) We have included the symbols for the voiceless aspirated stops to illustrate that what speakers usually consider one sound — for example [p] — may phonetically be two (or more) sounds, [p], [pʰ].

Some of these pronunciations may differ from yours, making some of the examples confusing. For example, as we mentioned, some speakers of American English pronounce the words *cot* and *caught* identically. In the dialect described here, *cot* and *caught* are pronounced differently, so *cot* is one of the examples of the vowel sound [a]. Many speakers who pronounce *cot* and *caught* the same pronounce *car* and *core* with

"Why do I have to keep writin' in
these K's when they don't make
any noise anyway?"

"The Family Circus" copyright © 1987 Cowles Syndicate, Inc. Reprinted with special
permission of King Features Syndicate.

different vowels. If you use the vowel of *car* to say *cot* and the vowel of *core* to say *caught,* you will be approximating the dialect that distinguishes the two words. In addition, some speakers of English pronounce an *r* sound only when it occurs before a vowel, and would therefore pronounce the words *car* and *fear* without the [r], although we mention *fear* as one example of [r].

The English used for examples in this book is rather arbitrary. It is in fact a mixture of several dialects. Our aim is to teach phonetics in general, and to show you how phonetics might describe the speech sounds of any of the world's languages with the proper symbols and diacritics. We illustrate how to do this using American English, and providing the major phonetic symbols for describing most varieties of American English. We are aware that this may present problems for speakers of different dialects. We apologize for this, but we have not figured out a way to solve this problem satisfactorily without introducing complexities unsuitable for this introduction to language.

The symbols listed in Table 6.6 are not sufficient to represent the pronunciation of words in all languages, or even all dialects of English around the world. The symbol [x], for example, is needed for the voiceless velar fricative in the German word *Bach,* or the Scottish English word for "lake," *loch.* The symbol [ʁ] is needed for the French uvular

Table 6.6   Phonetic Symbol/English Spelling Correspondences

Consonants

Symbol	Examples
p	spit tip apple ample
pʰ	pit prick plaque appear
b	bit tab brat bubble
m	mitt tam smack Emmy camp comb
t	stick pit kissed write
tʰ	tick intend pterodactyl attack
d	Dick cad drip loved ride
n	nick kin snow mnemonic gnostic pneumatic know
k	skin stick scat critique elk
kʰ	curl kin charisma critic mechanic close
g	girl burg longer Pittsburgh
ŋ	sing think finger
f	fat philosophy flat phlogiston coffee reef cough
v	vat dove gravel
s	sip skip psychology pass pats democracy scissors fasten deceive descent
z	zip jazz razor pads kisses Xerox design lazy scissors maize
θ	thigh through wrath ether Matthew
ð	thy their weather lathe either
š	shoe mush mission nation fish glacial sure
ž	measure vision azure casual decision rouge (for those who do not pronounce this word with the final sound of *judge*)
č	choke match feature rich righteous
ǰ	judge midget George magistrate residual
l	leaf feel call single
r	reef fear Paris singer
j	you yes feud use
w	witch swim queen
ʍ	which where whale (for speakers who pronounce *which* differently than *witch*)
h	hat who whole rehash
ʔ	bottle button glottal (for some speakers)
ɾ	writer rider latter ladder

Table 6.6   (Continued)

Vowels	
Symbol	**Examples**
i	beet beat be receive key believe amoeba people Caesar Vaseline serene
ɪ	bit consist injury bin
e	bate bait ray great eight gauge reign they
ɛ	bet serenity says guest dead said
æ	pan act laugh comrade
u	boot lute who sewer through to too two move Lou
U	put foot butcher could
ʌ	cut tough among oven does cover flood
o	coat go beau grow though toe own over
ɔ	caught stalk core saw ball awe
a	cot father palm sergeant honor hospital melodic
ə	sofa alone symphony suppose melody tedious the America
aj	bite sight by die dye Stein aisle choir liar island height sign
aw, æw	about brown doubt coward
ɔj	boy doily

fricative. English does not have rounded front vowels, but languages such as French and Swedish do. Front rounded vowels are symbolized as follows:

[y] as in French *tu* [ty] "you" The tongue position for [i] but with the lips rounded

[ø] as in French *bleu* [blø] "blue" The tongue position for [e] but with the lips rounded

[œ] as in French *heure* "hour" The tongue position for [ɛ] but with the lips rounded

Sign-Language Primes

Just as sign languages have their own morphological, syntactic, and semantic systems, they also have their equivalent of phonetics and phonology. The formal units corresponding to phonetic elements of spoken language are referred to as **primes.** The signs of the language that correspond to morphemes or words can be specified by primes of three classes: hand configuration; the motion of the hand(s) toward or away from the body; and the place of articulation, or the locus, of the sign's movement relative to the body. For example, the sign meaning "arm" is a flat hand, moving to touch the upper arm. It has three prime features: flat hand, motion upward, upper arm.

Figure 6.6 illustrates the hand-configuration primes.

/B/	/A/	/G/	/C/	/5/	/V/
[B]	[A]	[G]	[C]	[5]	[V]
flat hand	fist hand	index hand	cupped hand	spread hand	V hand

/0/	/F/	/X/	/H/	/L/	/Y/
[0]	[F]	[X]	[H]	[L]	[Y]
0 hand	pinching hand	hook hand	index-mid hand	L hand	Y hand

/8/	/K/	/I/	/R/	/W/	/3/	/E/
[8]	[K]	[I]	[R]	[W]	[3]	[E]
mid-finger hand	chopstick hand	pinkie hand	crossed-finger hand	American-3 hand	European-3 hand	nail-buff hand

Figure 6.6   ASL hand configuration (with descriptive phrases that are used to refer to them). The letters and numbers refer to the signs used for these symbols when words are finger-spelled. Reprinted from *The Signs of Language* by Edward Klima and Ursula Bellugi: Cambridge, Mass.: Harvard University Press, Copyright © 1979 by the President and Fellows of Harvard College.

Summary

The science of speech sounds is called **phonetics.** It aims to provide the set of features or properties to describe and distinguish all the sounds in human languages throughout the world.

When we speak, the physical sounds we produce are continuous stretches of sound, which are the physical representations of strings of discrete linguistic **segments.** Knowledge of a language permits one to separate the continuous sound into linguistic units — words, morphemes, and sounds.

The discrepancy between spelling and sounds in English and other languages motivated the development of phonetic alphabets in which one letter corresponds to one sound. The major **phonetic alphabet** in use is that of the **International Phonetic Association (IPA),** which includes modified Roman letters and **diacritics** by means of which the sounds of all human languages can be represented. To distinguish between the **orthography,** or spelling, of words, and their pronunciations, we write **phonetic transcriptions** between square brackets, as in [fənɛtɪk] for *phonetic.*

All English speech sounds come from the movement of lung air through the vocal tract. The air moves through the **glottis,** or between vocal cords, up the pharynx, through the oral (and possibly the nasal) cavity, and out the mouth or nose. Other languages may use different **airstream mechanisms.**

Human speech sounds fall into classes according to their phonetic properties. All speech sounds are either **consonants** or **vowels,** and all consonants are either **obstruents** or **sonorants.** Consonants have some obstruction of the airstream in the vocal tract, and the location of the obstruction defines their **place of articulation,** some of which are **bilabial, labiodental, alveolar, palatal, velar, uvular,** and **glottal.**

Consonants are further classified according to their **manner of articulation.** They may be **voiced** or **voiceless, oral** or **nasal;** long or short. They may be **stops, fricatives, affricates, liquids,** or **glides.** During the production of **voiced** sounds, the vocal cords are together and vibrating, whereas in voiceless sounds they are apart and not vibrating. Voiceless sounds may also be **aspirated** or **unaspirated.** In the production of aspirated sounds, the vocal cords remain apart for a brief time after the stop closure is released, resulting in a puff of air at the time of the release. Consonants may be grouped according to certain features to form larger classes such as **labials, coronals, anteriors,** and **sibilants.**

Vowels form the nucleus of syllables. They differ according to the position of the tongue and lips: **high, mid,** or **low** tongue; **front, central,** or **back** of the tongue; **rounded** or **unrounded** lips. The vowels in English may be **tense** or **lax.** Tense vowels are slightly longer in duration than lax vowels. Vowels may also be **stressed** (longer, higher in pitch, and louder) or unstressed. Vowels, like consonants, may be nasal or oral, though most vowels in all languages are oral.

Length, pitch, loudness, and **stress** are **prosodic,** or **suprasegmental,** features. They are imposed over and above the segmental values of the sounds in a syllable.

In many languages, the pitch of the vowel or syllable is linguistically significant. For example, two words may contrast in meaning if one has a high pitch and another a low pitch. Such languages are **tone** languages. There are also **intonation** languages in which the rise and fall of pitch may contrast meanings of sentences. In English the statement *Mary is a teacher* will end with a fall in pitch, but as a question, *Mary is a teacher?* the pitch will rise.

English and other languages use **stress** to distinguish different words, such as *cóntent* and *contént,* In some languages, long vowels and long consonants contrast with their shorter counterparts. Thus *biru* and *biiru (bi:ru), saki* and *sakki* are different words in Japanese. Long sounds are sometimes referred to as **geminates.**

Diacritics to specify such properties as **nasalization, length, stress,** and **tone** may be combined with the phonetic symbols for more detailed phonetic transcriptions. A phonetic transcription of *main* would use a tilde diacritic to indicate the nasalization of the vowel: [mẽn]

In sign languages, instead of phonetic features there are three classes of **primes** — hand configuration, the motion of the hand(s) toward or away from the body, and the place of articulation, or the locus, of the sign's movements.

References for Further Reading

Abercrombie, D. 1967. *Elements of General Phonetics.* Chicago: Aldine.

Catford, J. C. 1977. *Fundamental Problems in Phonetics.* Bloomington, IN: Indiana University Press.

Clark, J., and C. Yallop. 1990. *An Introduction to Phonetics and Phonology.* Oxford, England: Blackwell Publishers.

Crystal, D. 1985. *A Dictionary of Linguistics and Phonetics.* Oxford, England: Blackwell Publishers.

Fromkin, V. A. (ed). 1978. *Tone: A Linguistic Survey.* New York: Academic Press.

International Phonetic Association. 1989. *Principles of the International Phonetics Association, rev. ed.* London: IPA.

Ladefoged, P. 1993. *A Course in Phonetics, 3rd ed.* Fort Worth: Harcourt Brace Jovanovich.

Ladefoged, P., and I. Maddieson. 1996. *The Sounds of the World's Languages.* Oxford, England: Blackwell Publishers.

MacKay, I. R. A. 1987. *Phonetics: The Science of Speech Production, 2nd ed.* Boston: Little Brown.

Pullum, G. K., and W. A. Ladusaw. 1986. *Phonetic Symbol Guide.* Chicago: University of Chicago Press.

Exercises

1. Write the phonetic symbol for the first sound in each of the following words according to the way you pronounce it.

   Examples: ooze [u]   psycho   [s]

a. judge	[ ]		**f.** thought	[ ]
b. Thomas	[ ]		**g.** contact	[ ]
c. though	[ ]		**h.** phone	[ ]
d. easy	[ ]		**i.** civic	[ ]
e. pneumonia	[ ]		**j.** usual	[ ]

2. Write the phonetic symbol for the *last* sound in each of the following words.

Example: boy [ɔj] (Dipththongs should be treated as one sound.)

a. fleece   [   ]   **f.** cow   [   ]

b. neigh   [   ]   **g.** rough   [   ]

c. long   [   ]   **h.** cheese   [   ]

d. health   [   ]   **i.** bleached   [   ]

e. watch   [   ]   **j.** rags   [   ]

3. Write the following words in phonetic transcription, according to your pronunciation.

Examples: knot [nat], delightful [dilajtfəl] or [dəlajtfəl]. Some students may pronounce a number of words identically.

a. physics   **h.** Fromkin

b. merry   **i.** tease

c. marry   **j.** weather

d. Mary   **k.** coat

e. yellow   **l.** Rodman

f. sticky   **m.** heath

g. transcription   **n.** "your name"

4. Below is a phonetic transcription of a verse in the poem "The Walrus and the Carpenter" by Lewis Carroll. The speaker who transcribed it may not have exactly the same pronunciation as you; there are many correct versions. However, there is *one* major error in each line that is an impossible pronunciation for any American English speaker. The error may consist of an extra symbol, a missing symbol, or a wrong symbol in the word. Note that the phonetic transcription that is given is a **narrow** transcription; aspiration is marked, as is the nasalization of vowels. This is to illustrate a detailed transcription. However, none of the errors involve aspiration or nasalization of vowels.

Write the word in which the error occurs in the correct phonetic transcription.

                                          Corrected Word

a. ðə tʰãjm hæz cʌ̃m   [kʰʌ̃m]

b. ðə wɔlrəs sed

c. tʰu tʰɔlk əv mẽni θĩŋz

d. əv šuz ãnd šɪps

e. ænd silĩŋ wæx

f. əv kʰæbəgəz ænd kʰĩŋz

g. ænd waj ðə si ɪs bɔjlĩŋ hat

h. ænd wɛθər pʰɪgz hæv wĩŋz

5. The following are all English words written in phonemic transcription. Write the words using normal English orthography.

a. /hit/

b. /strok/

c. /fez/

    d. /ton/

    e. /boni/

    f. /skrim/

    g. /frut/

    h. /pričər/

    i. /krak/

6. Write the symbol that corresponds to each of the following phonetic descriptions, then give an English word that contains this sound.

    Example: voiced alveolar stop   [d] *dough*

    a. voiceless bilabial unaspirated stop   [   ]

    b. low front vowel   [   ]

    c. lateral liquid   [   ]

    d. velar nasal   [   ]

    e. voiced interdental fricative   [   ]

    f. voiceless affricate   [   ]

    g. palatal glide   [   ]

    h. mid lax front vowel   [   ]

    i. high back tense vowel   [   ]

    j. voiceless aspirated alveolar stop   [   ]

7. In each of the following pairs of words, the bold italicized sounds differ by one or more phonetic properties (features). Give the symbol for each italicized sound, state their differences and, in addition, state what properties they have in common.

    Example: phone — phonic   The *o* in *phone* is mid, tense, round.
                          The *o* in *phonic* is low, unround.
                          Both are back vowels.

    a. ba*th* — ba*the*

    b. redu*c*e — redu*c*tion

    c. c*oo*l — c*o*ld

    d. wi*f*e — wi*v*es

    e. cat*s* — dog*s*

    f. i*m*polite — i*n*decent

8. Write a phonetic transcription of the italicized words in the following poem entitled "English" published long ago in a British newspaper.

    I take it you already ***know***

    Of ***tough*** and ***bough*** and ***cough*** and ***dough?***

    Some may stumble, but not ***you,***

    On ***hiccough, thorough, slough*** and ***through?***

    So now you are ready, perhaps,

    To learn of less familiar traps?

    Beware of ***heard,*** a dreadful ***word***

That looks like *beard* and sounds like *bird.*

And *dead,* it's *said* like *bed,* not *bead;*

For goodness' sake, don't call it *deed!*

Watch out for *meat* and *great* and *threat.*

(They rhyme with *suite* and *straight* and *debt.*)

A *moth* is not a moth in *mother,*

Nor *both* in *bother, broth* in *brother.*

9. For each group of sounds listed, state the phonetic feature(s) they all share.

    Example: [p] [b] [m]   Features: bilabial, stop, consonant

    a. [g] [p] [t] [d] [k] [b]

    b. [u] [ʊ] [o] [ɔ]

    c. [i] [ɪ] [e] [ɛ] [æ]

    d. [t] [s] [š] [p] [k] [č] [f] [h]

    e. [v] [z] [ž] [ǰ] [n] [g] [d] [b] [l] [r] [w] [j]

    f. [t] [d] [s] [š] [n] [č] [ǰ]

10. Write the following sentences in regular English spelling.

    a. nom čamski ɪz e lɪŋgwɪst hu tičəz æt ɛm aj ti

    b. fonɛtɪks ɪz ðə stʌdi əv spič sawndz

    c. ɔl spokən læŋgwɪǰəz juz sawndz prədust baj ðə ʌpər rɛspərətɔri sɪstəm

    d. ɪn wʌn dajəlɛkt əv ɪŋglɪš kat ðə nawn ænd kɔt ðə vərb ar pronawnst ðə sem

    e. sʌm pipəl θɪŋk fonɛtɪks ɪz vɛri ɪntərɛstɪŋ

    f. vɪktɔrijə framkɪn rabərt radmən ænd ninə hajəmz ar ðə ɔθərz əv ðɪs bʊk.

11. What phonetic property or feature distinguishes the sets of sounds in column A from those in Column B?

A	B
a. [i] [ɪ]	[u] [ʊ]
b. [p] [t] [k] [s] [f]	[b] [d] [g] [z] [v]
c. [p] [b] [m]	[t] [d] [n] [k] [g] [ŋ]
d. [i] [ɪ] [u] [ʊ]	[e] [ɛ] [o] [ɔ] [æ] [a]
e. [f] [v] [s] [z] [š] [ž]	[č] [ǰ]
f. [i] [ɪ] [e] [ə] [ɛ] [æ]	[u] [ʊ] [o] [ɔ] [a]

12. **A.** Which of the following sound pairs have the same manner of articulation?

i.	[h] [ʔ]	**vi.**	[f] [š]
ii.	[r] [w]	**vii.**	[k] [θ]
iii.	[m] [ŋ]	**viii.**	[s] [g]
iv.	[ð] [v]	**ix.**	[j] [w]
v.	[r] [t]	**x.**	[j] [ǰ]

    B. For each sound in part A, identify the manner of articulation.

Phonology: The Sound Patterns of Language

Speech is human, silence is divine, yet also brutish and dead; therefore we must learn both arts.

Thomas Carlyle (1795–1881)

Phonology is the study of telephone etiquette.

A high school student[1]

From the Arctic Circle to the Cape of Good Hope, people speak to each other. The totality of the sounds they produce constitutes the universal set of human speech sounds. The same relatively small set of phonetic properties or features characterizes all these sounds. The same classes of these sounds are used in all spoken languages, and the same kinds of patterns of speech occur all over the world. Some of these sounds occur in the languages you speak and some do not. When you learn a language, you learn which sounds occur in your language and how they pattern. The study of the ways in which speech sounds form systems and patterns is **phonology.**

The term *phonology,* like *grammar,* is used in two ways: as the mental representation of linguistic knowledge, and as the description of this knowledge. Thus, *phonology* refers either to the representation of the sounds and sound patterns in a speaker's mental grammar, or to the study of the sound patterns in a language or in human language in general.

---

[1] As reported in Amsel Greene. 1969. *Pullet Suprises.* Glenview, IL: Scott, Foresman & Co.

Phonological knowledge permits a speaker to produce sounds that form meaningful utterances, to recognize a foreign "accent," to make up words, to add the appropriate phonetic segments to form plurals and past tenses, to produce aspirated and unaspirated voiceless stops in the appropriate context, to know what is or is not a sound in one's language, and to know that different phonetic strings may represent the same morpheme.

A speaker's phonological knowledge includes information about what sounds can occur at the beginning of a word, what sounds can occur at the end of a word, and what sounds can appear next to each other within a syllable. For example, native English speakers know that the final sound of the word *ring,* which we represent as [ŋ], cannot occur at the beginning of a word. To see this, say the words *ring out* [riŋawt] then say it again but try to omit the initial *ri.* Phonetically, you are trying to say [ŋawt] to rhyme with *bout,* but you are likely to find this weird or difficult unless you happen to speak a language that permits [ŋ] to begin a word. In English [ŋawt] is not a possible word.

Similarly, native English speakers know that certain sound combinations are not possible at the beginning of a word: *blick* [blɪk] is a possible but not actual word of English, whereas *bnick* [bnɪk] is not a possible word at all. You also know that an English word cannot end in a sequence [tp] so that *ritp* is an impossible word; but a word may end in [pt] so that *ripped* [rɪpt] is an actual word and *mipped* [mɪpt] is possible but nonoccurring.

At this point we should address two questions about phonology that often arise. First, you might be wondering whether it could be the case that *ngawt* [ŋawt] is not a possible word of English simply because [ŋ] is difficult to pronounce at the beginning of a word. The answer is both yes and no. It is true that [ŋ] is difficult to articulate at the beginning of a word *for native English speakers,* because the phonology of English does not allow [ŋ] in that position. But there are other languages, such as Lardil (spoken on Mornington Island in Australia), that *do* allow [ŋ] to occur at the beginning of a word, and we do not know of any evidence that suggests that speakers of those languages find words with initial [ŋ] particularly difficult to pronounce. The same point holds for the other examples just given; for example, [tp] may end a word in the American Indian language Papago. Though English speakers generally find words that do not conform to the sound pattern of English difficult to pronounce, speakers of languages in which those same words *do* conform to the sound pattern have no difficulty producing them. The differences among the sound patterns of the world's languages are so great that no general notion of "difficulty of articulation" can fully explain all of the phonological facts about a particular language.

The second question that arises is, what role does phonological knowledge play in determining the phonetic detail of how words or sentences are pronounced? Up to this point, we have discussed the use of this knowledge only to determine whether a certain string of sounds is a possible word. But phonological knowledge tells us much more than that. It tells us where we can delete sounds, add sounds, and even change one sound into another — all in keeping with the pronunciation patterns that are part of the grammar of the language. Because this activity usually takes place at an unconscious level, it takes a little work to become attuned to it, just as you (may have) struggled in chapter 6 to become aware of the difference in aspiration between the [pʰ] of *pit* and the [p] of *spit.* However, you will soon see that interesting phonological activity underlies even the seemingly effortless process of forming the plurals of English nouns.

The Pronunciation of Morphemes

Copyright © Don Addis.

Knowledge of phonology determines how we pronounce morphemes (see chapter 3) in different contexts. Often, certain morphemes are pronounced differently depending on their context, and we will introduce a way of describing this variation with phonological *rules*. Along the way, we will encounter many types of phonological rules. We begin with some examples from English, and then move on to examples from other languages.

The Pronunciation of Plurals

You know that almost all English nouns have both singular and plural forms: *cat* (sg.) and *cats* (pl.); *dog* (sg.) and *dogs* (pl.); and so on. But have you ever paid close attention to how plural forms are pronounced? Listen to a native speaker of English saying the plural forms of all the following nouns, and try to focus on variation in the pronunciation of the plural morpheme.

A	B	C	D
cab	cap	bus	child
cad	cat	bush	ox
bag	back	buzz	mouse
love	cuff	garage	criterion
lathe	faith	match	sheep
cam		badge	
can			
bang			
call			
bar			
spa			
boy			

Some of the variation in the pronunciation of the plural morpheme is easy to hear, and is reflected in how the plural forms are spelled. The nouns in columns A, B, and C — and the vast majority of English nouns — form their written plurals by adding "s" or "es." But the plurals of the words in column D are not formed in the usual way. The plural of *child* is not *childs;* the plural of *mouse* is *mice* ([majs]); the plural of *criterion* is *criteria* ([kʰrajtiriə]); and the plural of *sheep* is identical to the singular form [šip]. Largely, learners of English must simply memorize these and other irregular plural forms on a word-by-word basis, because there is no way to predict what shape they will take.

Looking now at the nouns in columns A through C, however, we observe a more interesting phonological pattern — not all of which is apparent from English orthography. If you listen closely, you should hear the following variation in the pronunciation of the English plural morpheme. The plurals of all the nouns in column A are formed by adding the *voiced* alveolar fricative [z] to the end of the singular form. The plurals of the nouns in column B are formed by adding the *voiceless* alveolar fricative [s] to the end of the singular form. And the plurals in column C are created by adding *schwa* [ə] followed by [z]. We thus have our first example of a morpheme with different pronunciations: the regular plural morpheme can be pronounced as [z], [s], or [əz]

How do we know how to pronounce this plural morpheme? The spelling is misleading, yet if you know English, you pronounce it as we indicated without a thought. When faced with this type of question, it is useful to make a chart that records the phonological contexts in which each variant of the morpheme is known to occur. The more technical term for the variants is allomorphs, and phonological contexts are often referred to as environments. Writing the words from the four columns in phonetic transcription, we have our first chart for the plural morpheme. (Recall from chapter 6 that in English voiceless stops are aspirated at the beginning of a stressed syllable, and that aspiration is indicated with a superscript [ʰ]).

Allomorph	Environment
[z]	After [kʰæb], [kʰæd], [bæg], [lʌv], [leð], [kʰæm], [kʰæn], [bæŋ], [kʰɔl], [bar], [spa], [bɔj]
[s]	After [kʰæp], [kʰæt], [bæk], [kʰʌf], [feθ]
[əz]	After [bʌs], [buš], [bʌz], [gəraž], [mæč], [bæǰ]

Our goal now is to simplify the chart so that the pattern behind the distribution of the allomorphs is revealed. We are searching for one or more properties of the environments that are responsible for selecting, or **conditioning,** the allomorphs. For example, we want to know what properties of [kʰæb] determine that the plural morpheme will take the form [z] rather than [s] or [əz].

To guide our search, we look for **minimal pairs** in our list of words. A minimal pair is two words with different meanings that are identical except for one sound segment that occurs in the same place in the string. For example, *cab* [kʰæb] and *cad* [kʰæd] are a minimal pair that differ only in their final segments. Other minimal pairs in our data include *cap/cab, bag/back,* and *bag/badge.*

Minimal pairs whose members take different allomorphs are particularly useful for our search. For example, consider *cab* [kʰæb] and *cap* [kʰæp], which take the allomorphs [z] and [s] to form the plural. If we assume that exactly one segment of the singular form conditions the choice of the plural allomorph, then this pair shows that the conditioning segment must be the final one — because that is the only segment in which [kʰæb] and [kʰæp] differ. The minimal pair *bag* [bæg] and *badge* [bæǰ] similarly points to the final segment as the conditioning factor. These two words are identical except for their final segments, which provide the conditions for different plural allomorphs ([z] and [əz], respectively).

We now see that English regular plural allomorphy (i.e., distribution of allomorphs) is conditioned by the final segment of the singular form — the segment that immediately precedes the plural morpheme. This fact allows us to simplify our chart by removing all information about the environments except the final segment. (We treat diphthongs such as [ɔj] as single segments.)

Allomorph	Environment
[z]	After [b], [d], [g], [v], [ð], [m], [n], [ŋ], [l], [r], [a], [ɔj]
[s]	After [p], [t], [k], [f], [θ]
[əz]	After [s], [š], [z], [ž], [č], [ǰ]

Having isolated the segments that condition the regular plural allomorphy, we now want to understand *why* each particular segment conditions the allomorph that it does. For example, is there a reason that [b] conditions the voiced allomorph [z] whereas [p] conditions the voiceless allomorph [s]? We answer questions of this type by inspecting the *phonetic properties* of the conditioning segments. If we can find properties shared by all segments that condition a particular allomorph, then we will be able to simplify the chart further by replacing the list of segments with those properties.

It turns out that the conditioning of the English regular plural allomorphs relies on just two phonetic properties of the preceding segment, both of which were discussed in chapter 6. All of the segments that condition the [z] allomorph are voiced sounds that are not sibilants. All of the segments that condition the [s] allomorph are voiceless sounds that are not sibilants. And all of the segments that condition the [əz] are sibilants. These observations allow us to simplify the chart as follows.

Allomorph	Environment
[z]	After voiced nonsibilant segments
[s]	After voiceless nonsibilant segments
[əz]	After sibilant segments

This chart is an impressive achievement. We have taken what at first looked like a random list of words paired with allomorphs and extracted a simple generalization, or pattern, from it. The alternant selected to form the regular plural of a given noun is determined by the last segment of the singular form of the noun, and in particular by two phonetic properties of that segment: whether or not the segment is voiced, and whether or not the segment is a sibilant. From the perspective of language acquisition, children acquiring English do not have to memorize the individual sounds that condition the [z], [s], and [əz] allomorphs, because the sounds that condition a particular allomorph have certain properties in common.

A more concise way of stating the same information that appears in the chart is in terms of **phonological rules,** which are similar to rules of syntax and morphology. These are not rules that someone teaches you in school or that you must obey because someone insists on it. They are rules that you know unconsciously and that express phonological patterns such as the one shown in the chart.

To write the rules that are relevant for this example, we assumed that the regular, productive plural morpheme has the phonological form /z/, with the meaning "plural." The slashes around this segment indicate that this is the basic form of the morpheme — the form in which the morpheme is pronounced if no phonological rules apply to it. Given this basic form, the variation in pronunciation of the regular plural morpheme follows two rules:

1. Insert a [ə] before the plural morpheme when a regular noun ends in a sibilant —/s, z, š, ž, č, ǰ/ — giving [əz].
2. Change the plural morpheme to voiceless [s] when a voiceless sound precedes it.

Later in this chapter we will introduce an even more concise way of stating phonological rules, but these two rules are perfectly explicit and sufficient for our discussion at this point.

These two plural-formation rules will derive the phonetic forms of plurals for all regular nouns. Since the basic form of the plural is /z/, if neither (1) nor (2) applies, then the plural morpheme will be realized as [z]; no segments will be added and no features will be changed. The following chart is an abbreviated scheme showing how the plurals of *bus, butt,* and *bug* are formed. At the top are the basic forms. The two rules apply or not as appropriate as one moves downward. At the bottom are the phonetic realizations — the way the words are pronounced.

	bus + pl.	*butt* + pl.	*bug* + pl.
Basic representation	/bʌs + z/	/bʌt + z/	/bʌg + z/
Apply rule (1)	ə	NA*	NA
Apply rule (2)	NA	s	NA
Phonetic representation	[bʌsəz]	[bʌts]	[bʌgz]

*NA means "not applicable."

As we have formulated these rules, (1) must apply before (2). If we applied the rules in reverse order, we would derive an incorrect phonetic form for the plural of *bus,* as a diagram similar to the previous one illustrates:

Basic representation	/bʌs + z/
Apply rule (2)	s
Apply rule (1)	ə
Phonetic representation	*[bʌsəs]

The rules that determine the phonetic form of the plural morpheme and other morphemes of the language are **morphophonemic rules.** Their application concerns the phonology of specific morphemes. Thus the plural morphophonemic rules apply to the plural morpheme specifically, not to all morphemes in English. If you find this new term a bit daunting, you're not alone, as the cartoon below shows.

EXCEPTIONS TO THE PLURAL RULE

No rule is so general which admits not some exception.

Robert Burton, *The Anatomy of Melancholy*

As we noted at the beginning of this section, some words are exceptions to the general pattern. The regular plural rule does not work for words like *child, ox, woman, foot, mouse,* and *sheep.* Children often learn these exceptional plurals after they have discovered the regular rules, which they acquire at a very early age (discussed in detail in chapter 8). The late Harry Hoijer, a well-known anthropological linguist, used to play a game with his two-year-old daughter. He would say a noun and she would give him the plural form if he said the singular and the singular if she heard the plural. One day he said *ox* [aks] and she responded [ak], apparently not knowing the word and thinking that the [-s] at the end must be the plural suffix. As we will see in chapter 8, children also sometimes "regularize" exceptional forms, saying *mouses* and *sheeps*. This is evidence that the rule exists as part of the mental grammar.

If the grammar represented each unexceptional or regular word in both its singular and plural forms — for example, *cat* [kʰæt], *cats* [kʰæts]; *cap* [kʰæp], *caps* [kʰæps]; and so on — it would imply that the plurals of *cat* and *cap* were mentally the same as the irregular plurals of *child* and *ox*. Of course, they are not. If a new toy appeared on the market called a *glick* [glɪk], a young child who wanted two of them would ask for two *glicks* [glɪks] even if the child had never heard the word *glicks*. The child knows the regular rule to form plurals and need not learn the plural of each noun; children learn the exceptions, and that knowledge remains for a lifetime. Experiments conducted by linguists show that very young children can apply this rule to words they have never heard. A grammar that describes such knowledge (the internalized mental grammar) must then include the general rule.

Allomorphy in English: Further Examples

In this section, we will discuss two more examples of rule-governed allomorphy in English. We will not make a chart of all the environments in which each allomorph occurs and then simplify the chart by looking for properties that are shared by all environments that select a particular allomorph. Instead, we will focus on the end products of that type of analysis: the rules that determine the context in which each allomorph occurs.

The formation of the regular past tense of English verbs has some interesting parallels with the formation of regular plurals. Recall that past-tense spellings, like plurals, may be misleading as to the actual pronunciation.

A	B	C	D
grab	reap	state	is
hug	peak	raid	run
seethe	unearth		sing
love	huff		have
buzz	kiss		go
rouge	wish		hit
judge	pitch		
fan			
ram			
long			
kill			
care			
tie			
bow			
hoe			
add [d]	**add [t]**	**add [əd]**	

The productive regular past-tense morpheme in English is pronounced [d] (column A), [t] (column B), or [əd] (column C), depending on the final segment of the verb to which it is attached. (Try to hear these differences by pronouncing the past tense forms yourself.) The column D verbs are exceptions. The following rules describe these variations in the pronunciation of the regular past-tense morpheme.

1. Insert a [ə] before the past-tense morpheme when a regular verb ends in an alveolar stop — /t d/ – giving [əd].

2. Change the past-tense morpheme to a voiceless [t] when a voiceless sound precedes it.

The past-tense morpheme has the basic form /d/, pronounced [d], if no rules apply.

Like the rules for the regular English plural, the rules for the regular past tense are morphophonological, because they apply to the past-tense morpheme specifically, not to all morphemes in English.

The English negative prefix *in-* which, like *un-*, means "not," has three allomorphs:

Allomorph	Environment	Examples
[ɪn]	before vowels	inexcusable, inattentive
	before alveolars	intolerable, indefinable, innovation, insurmountable
[ɪm]	before labials	impossible, imbalance, immaterial
[ɪŋ]	before velars	incomplete, inglorious

The pronunciation of this morpheme is often revealed by the spelling as *im-* when it is prefixed to morphemes beginning with *p*, *b*, or *m*. Because we have no letter "ŋ" in our alphabet, the velar [ŋ] is written as *n* in words like *incomplete*. You may not realize that you pronounce the *n* in *inconceivable, inglorious, incongruous,* and other such words as [ŋ] because this rule is as unconscious as other rules in your grammar. It is the job of linguists and phoneticians to bring such rules to consciousness or to reveal them as part of the grammar. If you say these words in normal tempo without pausing after the *in-*, you should feel the back of your tongue rise to touch the velum.

The rule that accounts for the pronunciation of the *in-* prefix is called the **homorganic nasal rule** — *homorganic* meaning "same place" — because the nasal consonant is produced at the same place of articulation as the following consonant:

> Change the place of articulation of a nasal consonant so that it agrees with (i.e., is the same as) the place feature of articulation of a following consonant.

With this rule we can give the *in-* negative prefix morpheme the basic representation /ɪn/. Before vowels and before morphemes beginning with *t* or *d*, the homorganic nasal rule has no effect on the basic form. (Another rule, to be discussed later, nasalizes the vowel so that its pronunciation is [ĩ].) The rule changes the alveolar feature of *n* to labial before a morpheme beginning with a labial consonant *p, b,* or *m* to agree with the place of articulation, as in *impossible* and *immodest.* Similarly, this feature-changing rule changes alveolar to velar, so the *n* in /ɪn/ is pronounced as the velar nasal [ŋ] before morphemes that begin with the velar consonants *k* or *g* in words like *incoherent.*

Allomorphy in Other Languages

English is not the only language that has morphemes that are pronounced differently in different phonological environments. Allomorphy exists in most languages, and can be described by rules similar to the ones we have written for English. For example, the negative morpheme in the West African language Akan also has three nasal allomorphs: [m] before *p,* [n] before *t,* and [ŋ] before *k,* as the following examples show:

mɪ pɛ	"I like"	mɪ mpɛ	"I don't like"
mɪ tɪ	"I speak"	mɪ ntɪ	"I don't speak"
mɪ kɔ	"I go"	mɪ ŋkɔ	"I don't go"

The rule that describes this case of allomorphy is the same as the one for the English *in-* prefix:

Change the place of articulation of a nasal consonant to agree with the place of articulation of a following consonant.

The Native American language Ojibwa offers a different example of allomorphy. The following data come from a discussion of Ojibwa by Jonathan Kaye.[2] Examine the words and see if you can discover the allomorphy pattern before reading further.[3]

anokkiː	"she works"	nitanokkiː	"I work"
aːkkosi	"she is sick"	nitaːkkos	"I am sick"
ayeːkkosi	"she is tired"	kitayeːkkos	"you are tired"
ineːntam	"she thinks"	kitineːntam	"you think"
maːcaː	"she leaves"	nimaːcaː	"I leave"
takoššin	"she arrives"	nitakoššin	"I arrive"
pakiso	"she swims"	kipakis	"you swim"
wiːsini	"she eats"	kiwiːsin	"you eat"

Both the prefix that means "I" and the prefix than means "you" have two allomorphs. These prefixes end in the consonant [t] when they are added to stems that begin in vowels, as in [nit+anokkiː], where the stem is [anokkiː], and [kit+ayeːkkos], where the stem is [ayeːkkosi]. But the [t] does not appear when the prefixes are added to stems that begin in consonants, as in [ni+maːcaː], where the stem is [maːcaː], and [ki+pakis], where the stem is [pakis]. If we assume that the two prefixes are basically /nit/ and /kit/, then we can write a rule that deletes the final consonant of the prefixes in this environment:

Delete a consonant before another consonant.

Descriptions of Ojibwa report that this rule is morphophonemic (i.e., only applies to particular morphemes). Can you see several examples in the data that suggest that this is the case?

---

[2] Jonathan Kaye. 1981. Chapter 8 in C. Baker and John McCarthy, eds. *The Logical Problem of Language Acquisition.* Cambridge, MA: MIT Press. Reprinted by permission of MIT Press.

[3] The diacritic symbol ː that appears after *i, a,* and *e* indicates a longer version of the vowel. It has no bearing on the point of this particular example. Also, ignore the deletion of the final, short vowel in the second column of the Ojibwa words.

Phonemes: The Phonological Units of Language

> In the physical world the naive speaker and hearer actualize and are sensitive to sounds, but what they feel themselves to be pronouncing and hearing are "phonemes."
>
> Edward Sapir, 1933

The phonological rules that we discussed in the preceding section apply only to particular morphemes. However, there are other purely phonological rules that can apply in principle to any morpheme in the language. These rules reveal the activity of phonology in an even more striking fashion than those we saw previously.

To discuss these rules, we first need to introduce some additional phonological concepts. This section introduces the notions of **phoneme** and **allophone**: phonological rules apply to phonemes to produce variants, or allophones, in different environments. Phonemes are the individual sounds that appear in what we have been calling the "basic" form of morphemes (e.g., the basic form /z/ for the English regular plural morpheme). Phonemes are abstract mental units. Allophones are the actual pronunciations of those abstract units in different environments.

Vowel Nasalization in English

Our first example of a purely phonological rule — one that is not sensitive to morphology — determines the contexts in which vowels are nasalized in English. In chapter 6 it was noted that both oral and nasal vowels occur *phonetically* in English. The following examples show this.

bean	[bĩn]	bead	[bid]
roam	[rõm]	robe	[rob]

There is a general rule of English that tells us when nasalized vowels occur — always before nasal consonants, never before oral consonants. We do not have to learn that the nasalized versions of /i/, /u/ and /a/ occur in *bean, boom,* and *bomb* ([bĩn], [būm], [bãm]). Rather, we generalize from the occurrences of oral and nasal vowels in English, and form a mental rule that automatically nasalizes [i], [u], and all other vowels before nasal consonants.

The general principle that predicts when a vowel will be oral and when it will be nasal is exemplified in Table 7.1.

Table 7.1   Nasal and Oral Vowels: Words and Nonwords

Words						**Nonwords***		
be	[bi]	bead	[bid]	bean	[bĩn]	*[bĩ]	*[bĩd]	*[bin]
lay	[le]	lace	[les]	lame	[lẽm]	*[lẽ]	*[lẽs]	*[lem]
baa	[bæ]	bad	[bæd]	bang	[bæ̃ŋ]	*[bæ̃]	*[bæ̃d]	*[bæŋ]

As the examples in Table 7.1 illustrate, oral vowels in English occur in final position and before nonnasal consonants; nasalized vowels occur only before nasal consonants within the same syllable. The "nonwords" show us that nasalized vowels do not occur finally or before nonnasal consonants, nor do oral vowels occur before nasal consonants. We can state these generalizations in a more concise way with the following phonological rule. (The syllables referred to in this rule are similar, but not identical, to those found in dictionary entries. We will discuss how linguists define syllables later in the chapter.)

> A vowel or diphthong becomes nasalized before a nasal segment (within the same syllable).

This rule makes explicit the fact that nasalized vowels occur in English syllables only before nasal consonants. If one substituted oral vowels for the nasal vowels in *bean* and *roam,* the meanings of the two words would remain the same. Try to say these words keeping your velum up until your tongue makes the stop closure of the [n] or your lips come together for the [m]. It will not be easy because in English we automatically lower the velum when producing vowels before nasals in the same syllable. Now try to produce *bead* and *robe* with a nasal vowel. The pronunciation [bĩd] would still be understood as *bead* although your pronunciation would be heard as being very nasal, and people might say you had a "nasal twang." In short, the oral and nasal variants of a given vowel can be substituted for one another without changing the meaning of a word.

But notice that *different* vowels cannot generally be substituted for one another without a change in meaning. For example, if you tried to produce the word *beat* with the vowel [æ] instead of [i], you would not be understood as saying *beat* in a strange way. Rather, you would be understood as saying a completely different word: namely, *bat*. To put it another way, we can find minimal pairs of words, such as *beat* and *bat,* that have different meanings and whose pronunciations differ only in that one has [i] in the position where the other has [æ]. The sounds [i] and [æ] can therefore distinguish or contrast words. They are distinctive sounds in English. Such distinctive sounds are called phonemes.

The following list of words illustrates some of the other vowel phonemes of English. The words in the list differ only in their vowels; each vowel thus represents a distinct phoneme.

beat	[bit]	[i]	boot	[but]	[u]
bit	[bɪt]	[ɪ]	but	[bʌt]	[ʌ]
bait	[bet]	[e]	boat	[bot]	[o]
bet	[bɛt]	[ɛ]	bought	[bɔt]	[ɔ]
bat	[bæt]	[æ]	bout	[bawt]	[aw]
bite	[bajt]	[aj]	bot	[bat]	[a]

The vowels [ʊ] and [ɔj], which do not appear in the list above, are also phonemes of English. They contrast meanings in other minimal pairs:

[ʊ]	[i]	book	[bʊk]	beak	[bik]
[ɔj]	[aj]	boy	[bɔj]	buy	[baj]

The diphthongs [ɔj], [aj], and [aw] are considered single vowel sounds although each includes a glide because they function like the monophthongal vowels, as further illustrated by the following list that includes all three diphthongs:

bile [bajl]   bowel [bawl]   boil [bɔjl]

Phonemes are not physical sounds. They are abstract mental representations of the phonological units of a language, the units used to represent the forms of words in our mental lexicons. The phonological rules apply to the phonemic representation to determine the pronunciations of the words.

Now that we have introduced the concept of a phoneme, we return to the topic that began this section: oral and nasalized vowels in English. Do the oral and nasalized versions of the same vowel qualify as different phonemes?

The answer is no, the oral and nasalized variants of a vowel are not distinct phonemes. We saw that changing an oral vowel to a nasalized vowel, or vice versa, does not change the meaning of a word (although it may make your pronunciation sound odd). Another way of saying the same thing is that oral and nasal vowels *do not contrast* in English. Yet another way of putting it is that there are no minimal pairs in English that differ only in that one member of the pair has the oral version of a vowel, while the other member of the pair has the nasalized version of the same vowel. However we say it, the conclusion is the same: there is just *one* set of vowel phonemes in English. Each member of that set has an oral version (or allophone) and a nasalized version (or allophone).

A particular version, or "realization," of a phoneme is referred to as a phone. The different phones that are the realizations of the same phoneme are called the *allophones* of that phoneme. An allophone is therefore a *predictable phonetic variant* of a phoneme. In English, each vowel phoneme has both an oral and a nasalized allophone. The choice of the allophone is not random or haphazard. It is *rule-governed.*

To distinguish between a phoneme and its allophones (the ways in which the phoneme is pronounced in different contexts), we use slashes / / to enclose phonemes and continue to use square brackets [ ] for allophones or phones. For example, [i] and [ĩ] are allophones of the phoneme /i/; [ɪ] and [ɪ̃] are allophones of the phoneme /ɪ/ etc. Thus we will represent *bead* and *bean* phonemically as /bid/ and /bin/. We refer to these as phonemic transcriptions of the two words. The rule for the distribution of oral and nasal vowels in English shows that phonetically these words will be pronounced as [bid] and [bĩn]. The pronunciations are indicated by phonetic transcriptions, and written between square brackets.

In chapter 6 we mentioned another example of allophones of a single phoneme. We noted that some speakers of English substitute a glottal stop for the [t] at the end of words such as *don't* or *can't,* or in the middle of words like *bottle* or *button.* The substitution of the glottal stop does not change the meanings of any words; [dõnt] and [dõnʔ] do not contrast in meaning, nor do [batəl] and [baʔəl]. On the other hand, [ræbəl] and [ræʔəl] do contrast, as the pronunciations of *rabble* and *rattle,* but [rætəl] with a [t] or [ræɾəl] with the flap [ɾ] or [ræʔəl] with a glottal stop are all possible pronunciations of the word *rattle.* The phones [t], [ɾ], and [ʔ] do not contrast; they are all allophones of the phoneme /t/.

In the preceding discussion, we used minimal pairs to determine which vowel phones are and are not phonemes of English. We can do the same for the consonant phones that occur in the language. For example, *fine* and *vine,* and *chunk* and *junk* are minimal pairs in English; [f], [v], [č], and [ǰ] are therefore allophones of different phonemes in English, which we may write /f/, /v/, /č/, and /ǰ/.

Seed [sid] and *soup* [sup] are not a minimal pair because they differ in two sounds, the vowels and the final consonants. It is therefore not evident as to which differences in sound cause the differences in meaning. *Bar* [bar] and *rod* [rad] do not constitute a minimal pair because although only one sound differs in the two words, the [b] occurs initially and the [d] occurs finally. However, [d] and [p] do contrast in the minimal pair *deed* [did] and *deep* [dip], and [b] and [d] contrast in the following minimal pairs:

bead	[bid]	deed	[did]
bowl	[bol]	dole	[dol]
rube	[rub]	rude	[rud]
lobe	[lob]	load	[lod]

Substituting a [d] for a [b] changes both the phonetic form and its meaning. [b] and [d] also contrast with [g] as in:

bill   dill   gill   rib   rid   rig

Therefore [b], [d], and [g] are all phonemes in English and *bill, dill,* and *gill* constitute a minimal set.

A minimal set of vowels is illustrated in the "B. C." cartoon below, namely [ɪ], [i], [ʊ], [o] in *crick, creek, crook, croak:*

"B.C." reprinted by permission of Johnny Hart and Creators Syndicate, Inc.

One could easily extend this set to include [e], [æ], [a] as in *crake, crack,* and *crock.*

We have many minimal sets in English, which makes it relatively easy to determine what the English phonemes are. In some languages, particularly those with relatively long words of many syllables, it is not as easy to find minimal sets or even minimal pairs to illustrate the contrasting sounds, and thereby identify the phoneme set. Even in English, which has many monosyllabic words, and hundreds of minimal pairs, there are very few minimal pairs in which the phones [θ] and [ð] contrast, though we know English has the phonemes /θ/ and /ð/. In a computer search, only one pair was found in which they contrast at the beginning of words, one in which they contrast in the middle of words, and four in which they contrast at the ends of words. All four pairs in which they contrast finally are noun-verb pairs, the result of historical sound change, which we will discuss in chapter 11.

[θ]	[ð]
thigh	**thy**
e**th**er	ei**th**er
mou**th** (noun)	mou**the** (verb)
tee**th**	tee**the**
loa**th**	loa**the**
wrea**th**	wrea**the**
shea**th**	shea**the**

Even if these pairs did not occur, we would analyze [θ] and [ð] as distinct phonemes. Each contrasts with other sounds in the language, as for example *thick* [θɪk] and *sick* [sɪk], *though* [ðo] and *dough* [do]. Note also that we cannot substitute the voiced and voiceless interdental fricatives in the words in which they do occur without producing nonsense forms; for example, if we substitute the voiced [ð] for the voiceless [θ] in *thick,* we get [ðɪk], which has no meaning.

Minimal Pairs in ASL

There are minimal pairs in sign languages, just as there are in spoken languages. Figure 7.1 shows minimal contrasts involving hand configurations, place of articulation, and movement.

The signs meaning "candy," "apple," and "jealous" are articulated at the same place of articulation on the face, involve the same movement, but contrast minimally only in hand configuration. "Summer," "ugly," and "dry" are a minimal set contrasting only place of articulation, and "tape," "chair," and "train" only in movement.

Complementary Distribution

Minimal pairs illustrate that some speech sounds are contrastive in a language, and these sounds represent the set of phonemes. We also saw that some sounds are not distinct; they do not contrast meanings. The sounds [t] and [ʔ] were cited as examples that do not contrast. The substitution of one for the other does not create a minimal pair.

Oral and nasal vowels in English are also nondistinct sounds. Unlike the [t], [ʔ], and [ɾ] — the allophones of /t/ — the oral and nasal allophones of each vowel phoneme never occur in the same phonological context, as we saw in Table 7.1. They complement each other and are therefore in complementary distribution, as Table 7.2 further illustrates.

Where oral vowels occur, nasal vowels do not occur, and vice versa. In this sense the phones are said to complement each other or to be in **complementary distribution.** We offer two of analogies to help you understand this concept. Both analogies draw upon your everyday experience of reading and writing English.

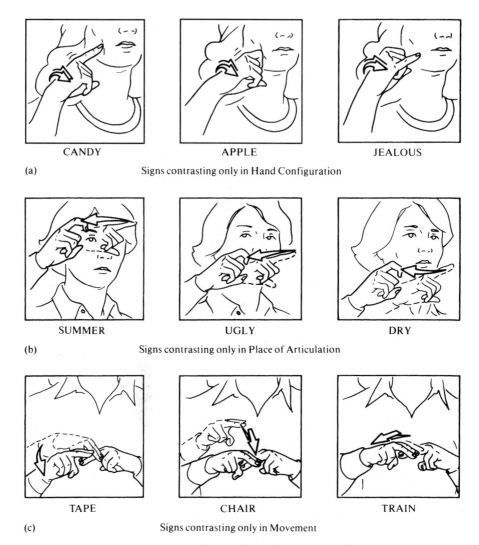

Figure 7.1   Minimal contrasts illustrating major formational parameters Reprinted from *The Signs of Language* by Edward Klima and Ursula Bellugi:, pp. 42, 46, Cambridge, Mass.: Harvard University Press, Copyright © 1979 by the President and Fellows of Harvard College.

Table 7.2   Distribution of Oral and Nasal Vowels in English Syllables

	In Final Position	Before Nasal Consonants	Before Oral Consonants
Oral vowels	Yes	No	Yes
Nasal vowels	No	Yes	No

The first analogy focuses on *printed* letters such as those that appear on the pages of this book. Each printed letter of English has two main variants: lowercase and uppercase (or capital). If we restrict our attention to words that are not names or acronyms (such as UNICEF or NAACP), we can formulate a simple rule that does a fair job of determining how letters will be printed:

> A letter is printed in uppercase if it is the first letter of a sentence; otherwise, it is printed in lowercase.

Even ignoring names and acronyms, this rule does not perfectly predict whether a given letter will be lowercase or uppercase. (For example, the initial letter of a quotation is uppercase even when the quotation does not appear at the beginning of a written sentence. And writers sometimes place words or syllables in all capitals to signal emphasis or stress.) But the rule is approximately right, and it helps to explain why written sentences such as the following appear so strange:

> phonology is the study of the sound patterns of human languageS. pHO-NOLOGY iS tHE sTUDY oF tHE sOUND pATTERNS oF hUMAN lANGUAGES.

To the extent that the rule is correct, the lowercase and uppercase variants of an English letter *are in complementary distribution*. The uppercase variant occurs in one particular environment (namely, at the beginning of the sentence). And the lower case variant occurs in every other environment (or elsewhere). Therefore, just as every English vowel phoneme has an oral and a nasalized allophone that occurs in different phonological environments, we can say that every letter of the English alphabet has two variants, or "allographs," that occur in different written environments. In both cases, the two variants of a single mental representation (phoneme or letter) are in *complementary distribution* because they never appear in the same environment.

We end the discussion of this analogy with two brief remarks. First, as we have noted all along, the lowercase and uppercase variants of a letter are in complementary distribution only if we ignore names, acronyms, quotations, and so on. This limitation is actually instructive, because it shows that we can be confident in statements of complementary distribution only if we have carefully checked all possible environments. Try to keep this in mind as you work through the problems at the end of this chapter. Second, we should make it clear that complementary distribution in English writing does not reflect complementary distribution in English phonology. For example, the initial sound of the word *atlas* is pronounced as an oral [æ] regardless of whether the word is spelled with a lowercase *a* or an uppercase *A*.

Our second analogy turns to *cursive* handwriting, which you are likely to have learned in elementary school. Writing in cursive is in one sense more similar to the act of speaking than printing is, because in cursive writing each letter of a word (usually) connects to the following letter — just as nearby sounds influence one another during speech. The figure below illustrates that the connections between the letters of a word in cursive writing create different variants of a letter in different environments:

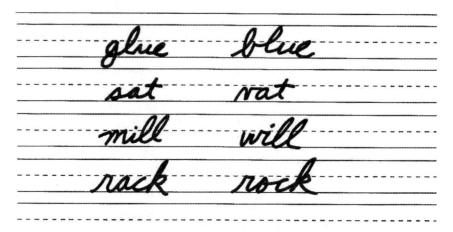

Compare how the letter *l* appears after a *g* (as in *glue*) and after a *b* (as in *blue*). In the first case, the *l* begins near the bottom of the line. But in the second case, the *l* begins near the middle of the line (which is indicated by the dotted line). In other words, the same letter *l* has two variants. It doesn't matter where the *l* begins, it's still an *l*. Likewise, it doesn't matter whether a vowel in English is nasalized or not, it's still that vowel. Which variant occurs in a particular word is determined by the immediately preceding letter. The variant that begins near the bottom of the line appears after letters like *g* that end near the bottom of the line. The variant that begins near the middle of the line appears after letters like *b* that end near the middle of the line. The two variants of *l* are therefore in complementary distribution.

This pattern of complementary distribution is not specific to *l* but occurs for other cursive letters in English. By examining the pairs *sat* and *vat, mill* and *will*, and *rack* and *rock*, you can see the complementary distribution of the variants of *a, i*, and *c*, respectively. In each case, the immediately preceding letter determines which variant occurs, with the consequence that the variants of a given letter are in complementary distribution.

We turn now to a general discussion of phonemes and allophones. When sounds are in complementary distribution they do not contrast with each other. The replacement of one sound for the other will not change the meaning of the word although it might not sound like typical English pronunciation. Given these facts about the patterning of sounds in a language, a phoneme can be defined as a set of phonetically similar sounds that are in complementary distribution. A set can, of course, consist of only one member. Some phonemes are represented by only one sound — they have one allophone. When there is more than one allophone in the set, the phones must be *phonetically similar,* that is, share most phonetic features. In English, the velar nasal [ŋ] and the glottal fricative [h] are in complementary distribution; [ŋ] does not occur word initially and [h] does not occur word finally. But they share very few phonetic features; [ŋ] is a voiced velar nasal stop; [h] is a voiceless glottal fricative. Therefore, they are not allophones of the same phoneme; [ŋ] and [h] are allophones of different phonemes.

Speakers of a language generally perceive the different allophones of a single phoneme as the same sound or phone. For example, most speakers of English are unaware that the vowels in *bead* and *bean* are different phones. This is because mentally, speakers produce and hear phonemes, not phones.

Distinctive Features

We generally are not aware of the phonetic properties or features that distinguish the phonemes of our language. Phonetics provides the means to describe these sounds, showing how they vary; phonology tells us which variations of sounds function as phonemes to contrast the meanings of words.

For two phones to contrast meanings, there must be some phonetic difference between them. The minimal pairs *seal* [sil] and *zeal* [zil] show that [s] and [z] represent two contrasting phonemes in English. They cannot be allophones of one phoneme since one cannot replace the [s] with the [z] without changing the meaning of the word. Furthermore, they are not in complementary distribution; both occur word initially before the vowel [i]. They are therefore allophones of the two different phonemes /s/ and /z/. From the discussion of phonetics in chapter 6, we know that [s] and [z] differ in voicing: [s] is voiceless and [z] is voiced. The phonetic feature of voicing therefore distinguishes the two words. Voicing thus plays a special role in English (and in many other languages). It also distinguishes *feel* and *veal* [f]/[v] and *cap* and *cab* [p]/[b]. When a feature distinguishes one phoneme from another, it is a **distinctive feature** (or a phonemic feature).

When two words are alike phonetically except for one feature, the phonetic feature is distinctive since this difference alone accounts for the contrast or difference in meaning.

Feature Values

One can think of voicing and voicelessness as the presence or absence of a single feature, *voiced.* This single feature may have two values: plus (+), which signifies its presence, and minus (−), which signifies its absence. For example, [b] is [+ voiced] and [p] is [− voiced].

The presence or absence of nasality can similarly be designated as [+ nasal] or [− nasal] with [m] being [+ nasal] and [b] and [p] being [− nasal]. A [− nasal] sound is an oral sound.

The phonetic and phonemic symbols are *cover symbols* for a set, or bundle, of distinctive features, a shorthand method of specifying the phonetic properties of the segment. Phones and phonemes are not indissoluble units; they are composed of phonetic features, similar to the way molecules are composed of atoms. A more explicit description of the phonemes /p/, /b/, and /m/ may thus be given in a **feature matrix.**

	p	b	m
Stop	+	+	+
Labial	+	+	+
Voiced	−	+	+
Nasal	−	−	+

Aspiration is not listed as a feature in this phonemic specification of these units because it is a **nondistinctive feature** and it is not necessary to include both [p] and [pʰ] as phonemes. In a phonetic transcription, however, the aspiration would be specified where it occurs.

A phonetic feature is distinctive when the + value of that feature in certain words contrasts with the – value of that feature in other words. At least one feature value difference must distinguish each phoneme from all the other phonemes in a language.

Since the phonemes /b/, /d/, and /g/ contrast by virtue of their place of articulation features — *labial, alveolar,* and *velar* — these place features are also distinctive in English. Since uvular sounds do not occur in English, the place feature *uvular* is nondistinctive. The distinctive features of the voiced stops in English are shown in the following:

	b	m	d	n	g	ŋ
Stop	+	+	+	+	+	+
Voiced	+	+	+	+	+	+
Labial	+	+	–	–	–	–
Alveolar	–	–	+	+	–	–
Velar	–	–	–	–	+	+
Nasal	–	+	–	+	–	+

Each phoneme in this chart differs from all the other phonemes by at least one distinctive feature.

The following minimal pairs further describe some of the distinctive features in the phonological system of English.

bat	[bæt]	mat	[mæt]	The difference between *bat* and *mat* is due only to the difference in nasality between [b] and [m]. [b] and [m] are identical in all features except for the fact that [b] is oral or [– nasal] and [m] is nasal or [+ nasal]. Therefore, nasality (or [± nasal][4]) is a distinctive feature of English consonants.
rack	[ræk]	rock	[rak]	The two words are distinguished only because [æ] is a front vowel and [a] is a back vowel. They are both low, unrounded vowels. Therefore, backness (or [± back]) is a distinctive feature of English vowels.
see	[si]	zee	[zi]	The difference is due to the voicelessness of the [s] contrasted with the voicing of the [z]. Therefore, voicing (or [± voiced]) is a distinctive feature of English consonants.

PREDICTABILITY OF REDUNDANT (NONDISTINCTIVE) FEATURES

We have seen that nasality is a distinctive feature of English consonants. Given the arbitrary relationship between form and meaning, there is no way to predict that the word *meat* begins with a nasal bilabial stop [m] and that the word *beat* begins with an oral bilabial stop [b]. You learn this when you learn the words. We also saw that nasality is not a distinctive feature for English vowels. The nasality feature value of the vowels in *bean,*

---

[4] The symbol ± before a feature is read "plus or minus" that feature, showing that it is a binary-valued feature (i.e., a feature that has exactly two possible values).

mean, comb, and *sing* is predictable since they occur before nasal consonants in the same syllable. When a feature value is predictable by rule, it is a **redundant** or **predictable feature.** Thus nasality is a redundant feature in English vowels, but a **nonredundant** (distinctive or phonemic) feature for English consonants.

This is not the case in all languages. In French, nasality is a distinctive feature for both vowels and consonants: *gars* pronounced [ga], "lad," contrasts with *gant* [gã], which means "glove," and *bal* [bal] "dance" contrasts with *mal* [mal] "bad." Thus, French has both oral and nasal consonant phonemes and vowel phonemes; English has oral and nasal consonant phonemes, but only oral vowel phonemes.

Like French, the Ghanaian language Akan has both oral and nasal vowel phonemes. In other words, nasalization is a distinctive feature for vowels in Akan, as the following examples illustrate:

[ka]	"bite"	[kã]	"speak"
[fi]	"come from"	[fĩ]	"dirty"
[tu]	"pull"	[tũ]	"den"
[nsa]	"hand"	[nsã]	"liquor"
[či]	"hate"	[čĩ]	"squeeze"
[pam]	"sew"	[pãm]	"confederate"

These examples show that vowel nasalization is not predictable in Akan. As shown by the last minimal pair — [pam]/[pãm] — there is no rule that nasalizes vowels before nasal consonants. If there were, there could be no word, like [pam], which has an oral consonant before a nasal vowel. Unlike English, oral and nasal vowels contrast in Akan. If you substitute an oral vowel for a nasal vowel, or vice versa, you will change the meaning of the word. Both oral and nasal vowel phonemes must therefore exist in Akan.

Two languages may have the same phonetic segments (phones) but have two different phonemic systems. Phonetically, both oral and nasalized vowels exist in English and Akan. However, English does not have nasalized vowel phonemes, but Akan does. The same phonetic segments function differently in the two languages. Nasalization of vowels in English is redundant and nondistinctive; nasalization of vowels in Akan is nonredundant and distinctive.

Another nondistinctive feature in English is aspiration. In the previous chapter we pointed out that in English both aspirated and unaspirated voiceless stops occur. The voiceless aspirated stops [pʰ], [tʰ], and [kʰ] and the voiceless unaspirated stops [p], [t], and [k] are in complementary distribution in English as shown in the following:

Syllable Initial before a Stressed Vowel			After a Syllable Initial /s/			Nonword*		
[pʰ]	**[tʰ]**	**[kʰ]**	**[p]**	**[t]**	**[k]**			
pill	*till*	*kill*	*spill*	*still*	*skill*	[pɪl]*	[tɪl]*	[kɪl]*
[pʰɪl]	[tʰɪl]	[kʰɪl]	[spɪl]	[stɪl]	[skɪl]	[spʰɪl]*	[tʰɪl]*	[skʰɪl]*
par	*tar*	*car*	*spar*	*star*	*scar*	[par]*	[tar]*	[car]*
[pʰar]	[tʰar]	[kʰar]	[spar]	[star]	[skar]	[spʰar]*	[tʰar]*	[skʰar]*]

Where the unaspirated stops occur, the aspirated ones do not, and vice versa. You could say *spit* if you pleased with an aspirated [pʰ], as [spʰɪt], and it would be understood as *spit,* but listeners would probably think you were spitting out your words. Given this distribution, we see that aspiration is a redundant, nondistinctive feature in English; aspiration is predictable, occurring as a feature of voiceless stops when they occur initially in a stressed syllable.

This is the reason speakers of English (if they are not analyzing the sounds as linguists or phoneticians) perceive the [pʰ] in *pill* and the [p] in *spill* to be the "same" sound. They do so because the difference between them, in this case the feature aspiration, is *predictable, redundant, nondistinctive,* and *nonphonemic* (all equivalent terms).

This example illustrates why we referred to the phoneme as an abstract unit, similar to a deep structure in syntax. We do not utter phonemes; we produce phones, the allophones of the phonemes of the language. In English /p/ is a phoneme that is realized phonetically (pronounced) as both [p] or [pʰ], depending on context. The phones or sounds [p] and [pʰ] are allophones of the phoneme /p/.

MORE ON REDUNDANCIES

The value of some features of a single phoneme is predictable or redundant due to the specification of the other features of that segment. That is, given the presence of certain feature values, one can predict the value of other features in that segment.

In English all front vowels are predictably, or redundantly, nonround. The nonlow back vowels (/u ʊ o ɔ/) are redundantly round. Redundant features in phonemic representations need not be specified. If a vowel in English is [– back] it is also automatically [– round], and the feature value for round is absent from its representation. A blank would occupy its place, indicating that the value of that feature is predictable by a phonological rule of the language. The case is similar for vowels specified as [– back, – low], which are predictably [– round].

Similarly, in English all nasal consonant phonemes are predictably voiced. Voicing is nondistinctive for nasal consonants and need not be specified in marking the value of the voicing feature for this set of phonemes.

This can be accounted for at the phonemic level by the following:

Redundancy Rule: If a phoneme is [+ nasal] it is also [+ voiced].

Nevertheless, phonetically in English, the nasal phonemes may be voiceless (indicated by the small ring under the symbol) when they occur after a syllable initial *s* as in *snoop,* which phonemically is /snup/ and phonetically may be [sn̥up]. The voicelessness is predictable from the context.

In Burmese, however, we find the following minimal pairs.

/ma/	[ma]	"health"	/m̥a/	[m̥a]	"order"
/na/	[na]	"pain"	/n̥a/	[n̥a]	"nostril"

The fact that some nasal phonemes are [+ voiced] and others [– voiced] must be specified in Burmese; the English redundancy rule does not occur in Burmese grammar. We can illustrate this phonological difference between English and Burmese in the following phonemic distinctive feature matrices:

Burmese:	/m/	/m̥/	**English: /m/**
Nasal	+	+	+
Labial	+	+	+
Voicing	+	–	

Note that the value for the voicing feature is left blank for the English phoneme /m/ since the [+] value for this feature is specified by the redundancy rule just given.

As noted earlier, the value of some features in a segment is predictable because of the segments that precede or follow. The phonological context determines the value of the feature rather than the presence of other feature values in that segment. Aspiration cannot be predicted in isolation but only when a voiceless stop occurs in a word, since the presence or absence of the feature depends on where the voiceless stop occurs and what precedes or follows it. It is determined by its phonological environment. Similarly, the oral or nasal quality of a vowel depends on its environment. If it is followed by a nasal consonant, it is predictably [+ nasal].

Unpredictability of Phonemic Features

We saw above that the same phones (phonetic segments) can occur in two languages but pattern differently because the phonemic system, the phonology of the languages, is different. English, French, and Akan have oral and nasal vowel phones; in English, oral and nasal vowels are allophones of one phoneme, whereas in French and Akan they represent distinct phonemes.

Aspiration of voiceless stops further illustrates the asymmetry of the phonological systems of different languages. Both aspirated and unaspirated voiceless stops occur in English and Thai, but they function differently in the two languages. Aspiration in English is not a distinctive feature — one that can create a phonemic difference — because its presence or absence is predictable. In Thai it is not predictable, as the following examples show:

Voiceless Unaspirated		**Voiceless Aspirated**	
[paa]	*forest*	[pʰaa]	*to split*
[tam]	*to pound*	[tʰam]	*to do*
[kat]	*to bite*	[kʰat]	*to interrupt*

The voiceless unaspirated and the voiceless aspirated stops in Thai are not in complementary distribution. They occur in the same positions in the minimal pairs; they contrast and are therefore phonemes in Thai. In both English and Thai, the phones [p], [t], [k], [pʰ], [tʰ], and [kʰ] occur. In English they represent the phonemes /p/, /t/, and /k/; in Thai they represent the phonemes /p/, /t/, /k/, /pʰ/, /tʰ/, and /kʰ/. Aspiration is a distinctive feature in Thai; it is a nondistinctive redundant feature in English.

The phonetic facts alone do not reveal what is distinctive or phonemic.

> The *phonetic representation* of utterances shows what speakers know about the pronunciation of utterances.

The *phonemic representation* of utterances shows what speakers know about the abstract phonological system, the patterning of sounds.

That *pot/pat* and *spot/spat* are phonemically transcribed with an identical /p/ reveals the fact that English speakers consider the [pʰ] in *pot* [pʰat] and the [p] in *spot* [spat] to be phonetic manifestations of the same phoneme /p/.

In chapter 6, we pointed out that in English, the tense vowels /i/, /e/, /u/, and /o/ are also higher (articulated with a higher tongue position) and longer in duration than their lax vowel counterparts ɪ, ɛ, ʊ, and ɔ. The distinction between the tense and lax vowels can be shown simply by using the feature tense/lax, or [± tense]. Using this specification, the small difference in tongue height between the tense and lax vowels is nondistinctive, as is the length difference. The distinctive feature of tense serves to distinguish between pairs of phonemes like /u/ and /ʊ/.

In other languages, long and short vowels that are identical except for length are contrastive. Thus, length can be a nonpredictable distinctive feature. Vowel length is phonemic in Danish, Finnish, Arabic, and Korean. Consider the following minimal pairs in Korean:

il	"day"	i:l	"work"
seda	"to count"	se:da	"strong"
kul	"oyster"	ku:l	"tunnel"

Vowel length is also phonemic in Japanese, as shown by the following:

biru	"building"	bi:ru	"beer"
tsuji	"a proper name"	tsu:ji	"moving one's bowels"

When teaching at a university in Japan, one of the authors of this book inadvertently pronounced Ms. Tsuji's name (with a short /u/) as Tsu:ji-san (with a long /u:/). (The -*san* is a suffix used to show respect.) The effect of this error on the class quickly taught him to respect the phonemic nature of vowel length in Japanese.

Consonant length is also contrastive in Japanese. A consonant may be lengthened by prolonging the closure: a long *t* [t:] or [tt] can be produced by holding the tongue against the alveolar ridge twice as long as for a short *t* [t]. The following minimal pairs illustrate that length is a phonemic feature for Japanese consonants:

šite	"doing"	šitte	"knowing"
saki	"ahead"	sakki	"before"

Luganda, an African language, also contrasts long and short consonants; *kkula* means "treasure" and *kula* means "grow up." (In both these words the first vowel is produced with a high pitch and the second with a low pitch.)

The Italian word for "grandfather" is *nonno* /nonno/, contrasting with the word for "ninth" which is *nono* /nono/.

The phonemic contrast between long and short consonants and vowels can be symbolized by the colon, /t:/ or /a:/, or by doubling the segment, /tt/ or /aa/. As discussed in chapter 6, such long segments are sometimes referred to as geminates. Since phonemic symbols are simply cover symbols for a number of distinctive feature values, it does not matter how we choose to represent geminates, with a colon or with doubled letters. Feature specification is what truly distinguishes between long and short. Thus in /non:o/ or /nonno/ the second consonant is marked as [+ long]; in /nono/ it is [– long], and that's the long and the short of it.

Natural Classes

It's as large as life, and twice as natural!

Lewis Carroll, *Through the Looking-Glass*

Suppose you were writing a grammar of English and wished to include all the generalities that children acquire about the set of phonemes and their allophones. The way that we have chosen to show what speakers of the language know about the predictable aspects of speech is to include these generalities as phonological rules in the phonological component of the grammar. As we have seen, phonological rules in English determine the conditions under which vowels are nasalized or voiceless stops are aspirated. They also apply to all the words in the vocabulary of the language, and they even apply to nonsense words that are not in the language but could enter the language (like *sint, peeg,* or *sparg,* which would be /sɪnt/, /pig/, and /sparg/ phonemically and [sɪ̃nt], [pʰig], and [sparg] phonetically).

All languages also have general rules, such as the morphophonemic rules discussed at the beginning of the chapter. And sometimes there are exceptions even to quite general, purely phonological rules. But what is of greater interest at the moment is that the more linguists examine the phonologies of the many thousands of languages of the world, the more they find that similar phonological rules apply to the same broad general classes of sounds like the ones we have mentioned — nasals, voiceless stops, alveolars, labials, and so on.

For example, many languages of the world include the rule that nasalizes vowels before nasal consonants. This rule, which we discussed earlier in the chapter, can be stated as:

Nasalize a vowel when it precedes a nasal consonant in the same syllable.

It will apply to all vowel phonemes when they occur in a context before any segment marked [+ nasal] in the same syllable, and will add the feature [+ nasal] to the feature matrix of the vowels. Our description of vowel nasalization in English needs only this rule. It need not include a list of the individual vowels to which the rule applies, or a list of the sounds that result from its application.

Another rule that we discussed earlier in the chapter, and that occurs frequently in the world's languages, changes the place of articulation of nasal consonants to match the place of articulation of a following consonant. Thus, an /n/ will become an [m] before a /p/, /b/, or /m/; and will become a velar [ŋ] before a /k/ or /g/. In other words, the rule creates homorganic consonants, ones that agree in their place of articulation. This homorganic nasal rule occurs in Akan as well as English and many other languages.

Many languages have rules that refer to [+ voiced] and [– voiced] sounds. For example, the aspiration rule in English applies to the class of [– voiced] stops. As in the vowel nasality rule, we do not need to list the individual segments in the rule since it applies to all the voiceless stops /p/, /t/, and /k/, as well as /č/, which may be analyzed as the voiceless stop /t/ plus the palatal fricative /š/

That similar rules apply to the same classes of sounds across languages is not surprising since, as we will see shortly, such rules often have phonetic explanations and these classes of sounds are defined by phonetic features. For this reason such classes are called **natural classes** of speech sounds. A natural class is a group of sounds that share one or more distinctive features.

Although one does find complex rules in languages — including rules that apply to an individual member of a natural class — rules pertaining to natural classes occur more frequently, and an explanation is provided for this fact by reference to phonetic properties.

The relationships among phonological rules and natural classes illustrates why individual phonemic segments are better regarded as combinations or complexes of features than as indissoluble whole segments. If such segments are not specified as feature matrices, the similarities among /p/, /t/, and /k/ or /m/, /n/, and /ŋ/ would not be revealed. It would appear that it should be just as likely for a language to have a rule such as

1. Nasalize vowels before *p, i,* or *z.*

as to have a rule such as

2. Nasalize vowels before *m, n,* or *ŋ.*

Rule 1 has no phonetic explanation whereas rule 2 does. It is easier to lower the velum to produce a nasalized vowel in anticipation of a following nasal consonant than to prevent the velum from lowering before the consonant closure.

A natural class may always be specified by fewer features than any of its individual members. The class that includes the phonemes /p, t, k, b, d, g, m, n, ŋ, č, ǰ/ can be defined by specifying one feature, [– continuant]. The phoneme /p/ requires three feature specifications (bilabial, voiceless, stop) to distinguish it uniquely, as do the other phonemes in this set.

A class of sounds that can be defined by fewer features than another class of sounds is clearly more general. Thus, the class of [– continuant] sounds is in some sense more natural than the class that includes all the noncontinuants except /p/. The only way to refer to such a class is to list all the segments in that class. It cannot be done with feature notation alone.

A phonological segment may be a member of a number of classes. For example, /s/ is a member of the class that can be designated as [+ consonantal], or of the class [+ alveolar], or of the class [+ coronal], or of the class [+ continuant, – voice], and so on.

The various classes of sounds discussed in chapter 6 also define natural classes to which the phonological rules of all languages may refer. They also can be specified by

+ and – feature values. Table 7.3 illustrates how these feature values combine to define some major classes of phonemes. The presence of +/– indicates that the sound may or may not possess a feature depending on its context. For example, word-initial nasals are [– syllabic] but some word-final nasals can be [+ syllabic], as in *button* [bʌtn̩].

Table 7.3   Feature Specification of Major Natural Classes of Sounds

	Obstruents O	Nasals N	Liquids L	Glides G	Vowels V
Features					
Consonantal	+	+	+	–	–
Sonorant	–	+	+	+	+
Syllabic	–	+/–	+/–	–	+
Nasal	–	+	–	–	+/–

Feature Specifications for American English Consonants and Vowels

Using the phonetic properties or features provided in chapter 6, and the additional features in this chapter, we can provide feature matrices for all the phonemes in English using the + or – value. One then can easily identify the members of each class of phonemes by selecting all the segments marked + or – for a single feature. Thus, the class of high vowels /i, ɪ, u, ʊ/ are marked [+ high] in the vowel feature chart of Table 7.4; the class of stops, /p, b, m, t, d, n, k, g, ŋ, c, ǰ/ are the phonemes marked [– continuant] in the consonant chart in Table 7.5.

Table 7.4   Specification of Phonemic Features of American English Stressed Vowels

Features	i	ɪ	e	ɛ	æ	u	ʊ	o	ɔ	a	ʌ
High	+	+	–	–	–	+	+	–	–	–	–
Mid	–	–	+	+	–	–	–	+	+	–	+
Low	–	–	–	–	+	–	–	–	–	+	–
Back	–	–	–	–	–	+	+	+	+	+	–
Central	–	–	–	–	–	–	–	–	–	–	+
Rounded	–	–	–	–	–	+	+	+	+	–	–
Tense	+	–	+	–	–	+	–	+	–	–	–

Note: The feature [± mid] is not required to distinguish each vowel from every other one. The vowels marked [+ mid] are already distinguished from high and low vowels by being specified as [– high, – low]. The one stressed central vowel [ʌ] is sometimes specified as a back vowel. We have included the features [mid] and [central] to show more clearly the phonetic quality of the vowel phonemes.

Table 7.5 Phonemic Features of American English Consonants

Features	p	b	m	t	d	n	k	g	ŋ	f	v	θ	ð	s	z	š	ž	č	ǰ	l	r	j	w	h
Consonantal	+	+	+	+	+	+	+	+	+	+	+	+	+	+	+	+	+	+	+	+	+	−	−	−
Sonorant	−	−	+	−	−	+	−	−	+	−	−	−	−	−	−	−	−	−	−	+	+	+	+	+
Syllabic	−	−	−/+	−	−	−/+	−	−	−/+	−	−	−	−	−	−	−	−	−	−	−/+	−/+	−	−	−
Nasal	−	−	+	−	−	+	−	−	+	−	−	−	−	−	−	−	−	−	−	−	−	−	−	−
Voiced	−	+	+	−	+	+	−	+	+	−	+	−	+	−	+	−	+	−	+	+	+	+	+	−
Continuant	−	−	−	−	−	−	−	−	−	+	+	+	+	+	+	+	+	−	−	+	+	+	+	+
Labial	+	+	+	−	−	−	−	−	−	+	+	−	−	−	−	−	−	−	−	−	−	−	+	−
Alveolar	−	−	−	+	+	+	−	−	−	−	−	−	−	+	+	−	−	−	−	+	+	−	−	−
Palatal	−	−	−	−	−	−	−	−	−	−	−	−	−	−	−	+	+	+	+	−	−	+	−	−
Anterior	+	+	+	+	+	+	−	−	−	+	+	+	+	+	+	−	−	−	−	+	+	−	−	−
Velar	−	−	−	−	−	−	+	+	+	−	−	−	−	−	−	−	−	−	−	−	−	−	+	−
Coronal	−	−	−	+	+	+	−	−	−	−	−	+	+	+	+	+	+	+	+	+	+	+	−	−
Sibilant	−	−	−	−	−	−	−	−	−	−	−	−	−	+	+	+	+	+	+	−	−	−	−	−

Note: The [+ voicing] feature value is redundant for English nasals, liquids, and glides (except for /h/) and could have been left blank for this reason. The feature specifications for [± coronal], [± anterior], and [± sibilant] are also redundant. These redundant predictable feature specifications are provided simply to illustrate the segments in these natural classes. Note that we have not included the allophones [pʰ, tʰ, kʰ], since the aspiration is predictable at the beginning of syllables and these phones are not distinct phonemes in English. The phonemes /r/ and /l/ are distinguished by the feature [lateral], not shown here. /l/ is the only phoneme that would be [+ lateral].

The Rules of Phonology

> But that to come
> Shall all be done by the rule.
>
> William Shakespeare, *Antony and Cleopatra*

Throughout this chapter we have emphasized that the relationship between the phonemic representations of words and the phonetic representations that reflect the pronunciation of these words is *rule-governed*. The phonological rules relate the phonemic representations to the phonetic representations and are part of a speaker's knowledge of the language.

The phonemic representations are minimally specified because some features or feature values are predictable. The underspecification reflects the redundancy in the phonology, which is also part of a speaker's knowledge of the sound system. The grammars we write aim at revealing this knowledge so it is necessary to exclude predictable features; if we included these features we would fail in our goal of accurately representing what speakers know.

The phonemic representation, then, should include only the nonpredictable, distinctive features of the phonemes in a word. The phonetic representation, derived by applying the phonological rules, includes all the linguistically relevant phonetic aspects of the sounds. It does not include all the physical properties of the sounds of an utterance, however, because the physical signal may vary in many ways that have little to do with the phonological system. The absolute pitch of the sound, the rate of speech or its loudness is not linguistically significant. The phonetic transcription is therefore also an abstraction from the physical signal; it includes the nonvariant phonetic aspects of the utterances, those features that remain relatively the same from speaker to speaker and from one time to another.

Although the specific rules of phonology differ from language to language, the kinds of rules, what they do, and the natural classes they refer to are the same cross-linguistically.

Assimilation Rules

We have seen that nasalization of vowels in English is nonphonemic because it is predictable by rule. The vowel nasalization rule is an **assimilation** rule, or a rule that makes neighboring segments more similar by copying or spreading a phonetic property from one segment to the other. For the most part, assimilation rules stem from articulatory or physiological processes. There is a tendency when we speak to increase the **ease of articulation,** that is, to articulate efficiently. We have noted that it is easier to lower the velum while a vowel is being pronounced before a nasal stop closure than to wait for the actual moment of closure and force the velum to move suddenly.

We now wish to look more closely at the phonological rules we have been discussing. Previously, we stated the vowel nasalization rule as:

Nasalize vowels when they occur before nasal consonants (within the same syllable).

This rule specifies the class of sounds affected by the rule:

Vowels

It states what phonetic change will occur by applying the rule:

Change phonemic oral vowels to phonetic nasal vowels.

And it specifies the context or phonological environment.

Before nasal consonants within the same syllable.

All three kinds of information — class of phonemes affected, phonetic change, phono-logical environment — must be included in the statement of a phonological rule or it will not explicitly state the regularities that constitute speakers' unconscious phonological knowledge.

Phonologists often use a shorthand notation to write rules, similar to the way scientists and mathematicians use symbols. Every physicist knows that $E = mc^2$ means "Energy equals mass times the square of the velocity of light." Children know that $2 + 6 = 8$ can be stated in words as "two plus six equals eight." We can also use such notations to state the nasalization rule as:

V → [+ nasal] / __ [+ nasal] (C) $

The arrow abbreviates "becomes." The segment on the left of the arrow becomes, or takes on, any feature on the right of the arrow in the specified environment. It means that a vowel becomes nasalized or takes on the feature [+ nasal]. The environment follows the "slash" and in this case indicates that the vowel to be nasalized must be followed by a nasal consonant (the [+ nasal] part); and optionally by any consonant (the (C) part); and then the syllable must end, indicated by the $. (We'll discuss syllables in more detail below.) For example, the condition is met in the word *dam* because the vowel precedes a nasal consonant at the end of the syllable (and word); the condition is also met in the word *damp* because the vowel precedes a nasal consonant and another consonant, whose presence or absence doesn't affect nasalization. The condition is *not* met in a word like *dab,* because *b* is not [+ nasal]; nor is it met by *dozen* (insofar as the *o* is concerned) because the nasal is in a different syllable. The parentheses surrounding the (C) denote optionality, that is, a "don't care" condition. If the optional (C) were not there, however, the rule could not apply in words like *damp* or *dent* because the nasal consonant is not followed by $ but by another segment. (Technically, our rule is not quite complete. It doesn't take words like *dumps* [dãmps] into account where two consonants come between the nasal and the syllable boundary $.)

What occurs on the left side of the arrow fulfills the first requirement for a rule: It specifies the class of sounds affected by the rule. What occurs on the immediate right side of the arrow specifies the change that occurs, thus fulfilling the second requirement of a phonological rule.

To fulfill the third requirement of a rule — the phonological environment where the rule applies — we use the underscore _____ to denote the position of the segment to be changed relative to the conditioning environment. Then the conditioning environment is symbolized. In this case the segment to be changed precedes a nasal consonant, and possibly another consonant, and is in the same syllable. That's what ____ [+ nasal] (C) $ means.

In summary:

→ means "becomes" or "is changed to"

/ means "in the environment of"

____ is placed before or after the segments that condition the change.

( ) enclose optional segments, whose presence or absence are irrelevant to the rule

$ indicates a syllable boundary

The nasalization rule stated formally using symbols can be read in words:

A vowel becomes nasalized in the environment before a nasal segment, possibly followed by a consonant, in the same syllable.

Any rule written in formal notation can be stated in words. The use of the formal notation is, as stated above, a shorthand way of presenting the information. Notation also reveals *the function* of the rule more explicitly than words. It is easy to see in the formal statement of the rule that this is an assimilation rule since the change to [+ nasal] occurs before [+ nasal] segments.

Assimilation rules in languages reflect **coarticulation** — the spreading of phonetic features either in the anticipation or in the perseveration (the "hanging on") of articulatory processes. This tendency may become regularized as rules of the language.

The following example illustrates how the English vowel nasalization rule applies to the phonemic representation of words and shows the assimilatory nature of the rule; that is, the change from the [− nasal] feature value of the vowel in the phonemic representation to a [+ nasal] in the phonetic representation:

	"Bob"			**"bomb"**		
Phonemic representation	/b	a	b/	/b	a	m/
Nasality: phonemic feature value	−	−	−	−	−	+
Apply nasal rule		NA*			↓	
Nasality: phonetic feature value	−	−	−	−	+	+
Phonetic representation	[b	a	b]	[b	ã	m]

* NA means "not applicable."

There are many other examples of assimilation rules in English and other languages. Recall that the voiced /z/ of the English regular plural suffix is changed to [s] after a voiceless sound, and that similarly the voiced /d/ of the English regular past tense suffix is changed to [t] after a voiceless sound. We can describe both of these changes with the following morphophonemic rule:

Notation: [+ voice] → [− voice] / [− voice] ____

Words: A voiced segment becomes voiceless when the preceding segment is voiceless. (Application of this rule is restricted to the plural and past tense morphemes.)

Another morphophonemic rule that we discussed earlier in this chapter changes the place of articulation of the English negative prefix *in-* to be the same as the place of articulation of a following consonant. Recall that this rule also applies to the negative morpheme in the West African language Akan. Although the formal statement of this rule is too complicated to give here, its function is essentially the same as the rule immediately above: both rules make two consonants that appear next to one another more similar.

There is an optional (**"free variation"**) assimilation rule in English that applies particularly in fast or casual speech. The rule devoices the nasals and liquids in words like *snow* /sno/ [sn̥o], *slow* /slo/ [sl̥o], *smart* /smart/ [sm̥art], *probe* /prob/ [pʰr̥ob], and so on.

The feature [− voiced] of the /s/ or /p/ perseveres or hangs on through at least part of the following segment. Because voiceless nasals and liquids do not occur phonemically — do not contrast with their voiced counterparts — the vocal cords need not react quickly. The devoicing will not change the meaning of the words; [slat] and [sl̥at] both mean "slot."

Vowels may also be devoiced, or become voiceless, in a voiceless environment. When you whisper, you make all the sounds voiceless including the vowels, so try whispering if you're wondering what a voiceless vowel might sound like. In Japanese, high vowels are devoiced when preceded and followed by voiceless obstruents; in words like *sukiyaki* the /u/ becomes [u̥] — a voiceless or whispered *u*. This Japanese assimilation rule can be stated as follows:

$$\begin{bmatrix} - \text{ consonantal} \\ + \text{ syllabic} \end{bmatrix} \rightarrow [- \text{ voiced}] / \begin{bmatrix} - \text{ sonorant} \\ - \text{ voiced} \end{bmatrix} \_\_ \begin{bmatrix} - \text{ sonorant} \\ - \text{ voiced} \end{bmatrix}$$

This rule states that any Japanese vowel (a segment that is nonconsonantal and syllabic) becomes devoiced ([− voiced]) in the environment of, or when it occurs (/) between, voiceless obstruents.[5] Notice that the underscore does not occur immediately after the slash or at the end of the rule, but between the segment matrices represented as [− sonorant, − voiced].

This rule requires three kinds of information:

   (a) the class of sounds affected: vowels
   (b) the phonetic change: devoicing
   (c) the phonological environment: between two voiceless obstruents

---

[5] The rule applies most often to high vowels but may apply to other vowels as well.

The rule does not specify the class of segments to the left of the arrow as [+ voiced] because phonemically all vowels in Japanese are voiced. It therefore simply has to include the change on the right side of the arrow.

We can illustrate the application of this Japanese assimilation rule as we did the English vowel nasalization rule:

"sukiyaki"								
Phonemic representation	/s	u	k	i	j	a	k	i/
Voicing: phonemic feature value	−	+	−	+	+	+	−	+
Apply devoicing rule		↓						
Voicing: phonetic feature value	−	−	−	+	+	+	−	+
Phonetic representation	[s	ṵ	k	i	j	a	k	i]

Feature-Changing Rules

The English vowel nasalization and devoicing rules, and the Japanese devoicing rule, change feature specifications. That is, in English the [− nasal] value of phonemic vowels is changed to [+ nasal] phonetically through an assimilation process when the vowels occur before nasals. Vowels in Japanese are phonemically voiced, and the rule changes vowels that occur in the specified environment into phonetically voiceless segments.

The rules we have discussed are phonetically plausible, as are other assimilation rules, and can be explained by natural phonetic processes. This fact does not mean that all these rules occur in all languages. In fact, if they always occurred they would not have to be learned; they would apply automatically and universally, and therefore would not have to be included in the grammar of any language. They are not, however, universal.

There is a nasal assimilation rule in Akan that nasalizes voiced stops when they follow nasal consonants, as shown in the following example:

/ɔ bá/   [ɔbá]   "he comes"   /ɔ m̀ bá/   [ɔmmá]   "he doesn't come"
he come   *he not come*

The /b/ of the verb "come" becomes an [m] when it follows the negative morpheme /m/. (The diacritics are tone marks.)

This assimilation rule also has a phonetic explanation; the velum is lowered to produce the nasal consonant and remains down during the following stop. Although it is a phonetically "natural" assimilation rule, it does not occur in the grammar of English; the word *amber,* for example, shows an [m] followed by a [b]. It is not pronounced "ammer."

Assimilation rules such as the ones we have discussed in English, Japanese, and Akan often have the function of changing the value of phonemic features. They are **feature-changing** or **feature-spreading** rules.

Because of this feature-changing rule in Akan, the phone [m] is an allophone of /b/ as well as an allophone of /m/ in that language. The more general point that this example illustrates is the following:

There is no one-to-one relationship between phonemes and their allophones.

This fact can be illustrated in another way:

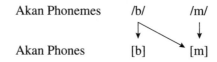

We will provide more examples of the one-to-many or many-to-one mapping between phonemes and allophones as this section progresses.

Dissimilation Rules

It is understandable that so many languages have assimilation rules; they permit greater ease of articulation. It might seem strange, then, to learn that languages also have **dissimilation** rules, rules in which a segment becomes less similar to another segment. Such rules also have a natural explanation, often from the hearer's, rather than the speaker's, perspective. That is, in listening to speech, if sounds are too similar, we may miss the contrast. Also, it may be easier to articulate dissimilar sounds. The difficulty of tongue twisters like "the sixth sheik's sixth sheep is sick" is based on the repeated similarity of sounds. If one were to make some sounds less similar, as in "the fifth sheik's fourth sheep is sick," it would be easier to say.

An example of easing pronunciation through dissimilation is found in some varieties of English, where there is a fricative dissimilation rule. This rule applies to sequences /fθ/ and /sθ/, changing them to [ft] and [st]. Here the fricative /θ/ becomes dissimilar to the preceding fricative by becoming a stop. For example, the words *fifth* and *sixth* come to be pronounced as if they were spelled *fift* and *sikst*.

The liquids /l/ and /r/ are sometimes interchanged to create dissimilarity. For example, English adopted the French word *marbre* meaning "marble" and in doing so dissimilated the second /r/ to an /l/.

A classic example of the same kind of dissimilation occurred in Latin, and the results of this process show up in the derivational morpheme /-ar/ in English. In Latin a derivational suffix *-alis* was added to nouns to form adjectives. When the suffix was added to a noun that contained the liquid /l/, the suffix was changed to *-aris,* that is, the liquid /l/ was changed to the liquid /r/. These words came into English as adjectives ending in *-al* or in its dissimilated form *-ar,* as shown in the following examples:

-al	**-ar**
anecdot-al	angul-ar
annu-al	annul-ar
ment-al	column-ar
pen-al	perpendicul-ar
spiritu-al	simil-ar
ven-al	vel-ar

All the *-ar* adjectives contain an /l/, and as *columnar* illustrates, the /l/ need not be the consonant directly preceding the dissimilated segment.

Though dissimilation rules are somewhat rare, they are found throughout the world's languages. The African language Kikuyu has a dissimilation rule in which a prefix added to a verb begins with a velar fricative if the verb begins with a stop but with a velar stop if the verb begins with a continuant.

Feature Addition Rules

Some phonological rules are neither assimilation nor dissimilation rules. The aspiration rule in English, which aspirates voiceless stops at the beginning of a syllable, simply adds a nondistinctive feature. Generally, aspiration occurs only if the following vowel is stressed. The /p/ in *pit* and *repeat* is an aspirated [pʰ], but the /p/ in *inspect* or *compass* is usually an unaspirated [p]. Using the feature [+ stress] to indicate a stressed syllable, (C) to represent an optional consonant, V́ to symbolize stressed vowels, and $ to represent the syllable boundary, the aspiration rule may be stated:

$$\begin{bmatrix} - \text{continuant} \\ - \text{voiced} \end{bmatrix} \rightarrow [+ \text{aspirated}] \,/\, \$ \underline{\qquad} (C) \begin{bmatrix} - \text{consonantal} \\ + \text{stress} \end{bmatrix}^{6}$$

Stated in words, the same rule is:

Voiceless stops ([– continuant, – voiced]) become aspirated when they occur syllable initially before stressed vowels ($ ____(C)V́)

Aspiration is neither present nor absent in any phonemic feature matrices in English. The aspiration rule adds a feature, unlike assimilation or dissimilation rules, which change phonetic feature values already present.

Remember that /p/ and /b/ (and all such symbols) are simply cover symbols that do not reveal the phonemic distinctions. In phonemic and phonetic feature matrices, these differences are made explicit, as shown in the following phonemic matrices:

	p	b	
Consonantal	+	+	
Continuant	–	–	
Labial	+	+	
Voiced	–	+	← distinctive difference

The nondistinctive feature "aspiration" is not included in these phonemic representations because aspiration is predictable.

Segment Deletion and Insertion Rules

Phonological rules may delete or add entire phonemic segments. These are different from the feature-changing and feature-adding rules we have seen so far. In French, for example, as demonstrated by Sanford Schane,[7] word-final consonants are deleted

---

[6] The presence of the optional consonant (C) in the environment covers cases like *place*, *twin*, and *krait* in which the voiceless stops are also aspirated.

[7] Sanford Schane. 1968. *French Phonology and Morphology*, Cambridge, MA: MIT Press.

when the following word begins with an obstruent, a liquid, or a nasal consonant, but are retained when the following word begins with a vowel or a glide, as illustrated in Table 7.6.

Table 7.6   Distribution of Word-Final Consonants in French

Before an obstruent:	/pətit tablo/	[pəti tablo]	"small picture"
	/noz tablo/	[no tablo]	"our pictures"
Before a liquid:	/pətit livr/	[pəti livr]	"small book"
	/noz livr/	[no livr]	"our books"
Before a nasal:	/pətit navet/	[pəti navɛ]	"small turnip"
	/noz navets/	[no navɛ]	"our turnips"
Before a vowel:	/pətit ami/	[pətit ami]	"small friend"
	/noz amis/	[noz ami]	"our friends"
Before a glide:	/pətit wazo/	[pətit wazo]	"small bird"
	/noz wazo/	[noz wazo]	"our birds"

Table 7.6 represents a general rule in French that applies to all word-final consonants. We distinguished the five classes of conditioning sounds by the features *consonantal, sonorant, syllabic,* and *nasal* in Table 7.3. We noted that obstruents, liquids, and nasal consonants are [+ consonantal], and vowels and glides are [– consonantal]. We can now see why such natural classes are significant. Using the symbol ∅ to represent deletion, and # to signify a word boundary, we can state the French rule simply as:

[+ consonantal] → ∅ / ___ # # [+ consonantal]

This rule can be stated in words as:

A [+ consonantal] segment (obstruent, liquid, or nasal) is deleted (→ ∅) in the environment (/) at the end of a word (____#) which is followed by a word beginning with an obstruent, liquid, or nasal (# [+ consonantal]).

or simply as

Delete a consonant before a word beginning with any consonant that is not a glide.

Given this rule in the grammar of French, *petit* would be phonemically /pətit/. It need not be additionally represented as /pəti/, because the rule determines the phonetic shape of the word.

Earlier in the chapter we saw a deletion rule in Ojibwa that deletes the final consonant of the /nit-/ and /kit-/ prefixes when these are added to stems that begin in consonants. This rule is like the preceding French rule, except that the Ojibwa rule applies between two morphemes in the same word rather than between words. The Ojibwa rule can be written as follows, where "+" stands for the boundary between two morphemes, and should not be confused with the other use of "+" to indicate the presence of a feature:

$$[+ \text{consonantal}] \rightarrow \varnothing / \underline{\quad} + [+ \text{consonantal}]$$

In some cases different phonetic forms of the same morpheme in English are derived by segment deletion rules, as the following examples illustrate:

A		**B**	
sign	[sãjn]	signature	[sɪgnəčər]
design	[dəzãjn]	designation	[dɛzɪgnešə̃n]
paradigm	[pʰærədãjm]	paradigmatic	[pʰærədɪgmærək]

In none of the words in column A is there a phonetic [g], but in each corresponding word in column B a [g] occurs. Our knowledge of English phonology accounts for these phonetic differences. The "[g]-no [g]" alternation is regular, and we apply it to words that we never have heard. Suppose someone says:

"He was a salignant [səlɪgnə̃nt] man."

Not knowing what the word means (which, of course, you couldn't since we made it up) you might ask:

"Why, did he salign [səlãjn] somebody?"

It is highly doubtful that a speaker of English would pronounce the verb form without the *-ant* as [səlɪgn], because the phonological rules of English would delete the /g/ when it occurred in this context. This rule might be stated as:

Delete a /g/ when it occurs before a final nasal consonant.[8]

The rule is even more general, as evidenced by the pair *gnostic* [nastɪk] and *agnostic* [ægnastɪk], and by the cartoon:

"Tumbleweeds" copyright © 1994 T. K. Ryan. Reprinted with permission of North American Syndicate, Inc.

---

[8] The /g/ may be deleted under other circumstances as well, as indicated by its absence in *signing* and *signer*.

This more general rule may be stated as:

Delete a /g/ when it occurs word initially before a nasal consonant or before a word-final nasal.

Given this rule, the phonemic representation of the stems in *sign/signature, design/designation, resign/resignation, repugn/repugnant, phlegm/phlegmatic, paradigm/paradigmatic, diaphragm/diaphragmatic,* and *gnosis/agnostic* will include a phonemic /g/ that will be deleted by the regular rule if a prefix or suffix is not added. By stating the class of sounds that follow the /g/ (nasal consonants) rather than any specific nasal consonant, the rule deletes the /g/ before both /m/ and /n/.

The phonological rules that delete whole segments, add segments and features, and change features account for the various phonetic forms of some morphemes. The following words further illustrate this point:

A			**B**		
bomb	/bamb/	[bãm]	bombardier	/bambədir/	[bãmbədir]
iamb	/ajæmb/	[ajæ̃m]	iambic	/ajæmbɪk/	[ajæ̃mbək]
crumb	/krʌmb/	[kʰrʌ̃m]	crumble	/krʌmbl/	[kʰrʌ̃mbəl]

A speaker of English knows when to pronounce a /b/ and when not to. The relationship between the pronunciation of the A words and their B counterparts is regular and can be accounted for by the following rule:

Delete a word-final /b/ when it occurs after an /m/.

Notice that the underlying phonemic representation of the A and B stems is the same and contains the /b/.

The rules that delete the segments are general phonological rules, but their application to phonemic representations results in different phonetic forms of the same morpheme.

Deletion rules also show up as optional rules in fast speech or casual speech in English. They result, for example, in the common contractions changing *he is* [hi ɪz] to *he's* [hiz] and *I will* [aj wɪl] to *I'll* [ajl]. Often we delete the unstressed vowels that are shown in bold type in words like the following:

mys**t**ery gen**e**ral mem**o**ry fun**e**ral vig**o**rous Barb**a**ra

These words in casual speech sound as if they were written:

mystry genral memry funral vigrous Barbra

Phonological rules may also insert consonants or vowels, which is called **epenthesis.** In some cases, epenthesis occurs to "fix up" nonpermitted sequences. In English morphemes, nasal/nonnasal consonant clusters must be homorganic: both labial, both alveolar, or both velar. We find /m/ before /p/ and /b/ as in *ample* and *amble;* /n/ before /t/ and /d/, as in *gentle* and *gender;* and /ŋ/ before /k/ and /g/, as in *ankle* and *angle.*

(You may not have realized that the nasal in the last two words has a velar articulation because the spelling obscures this fact. If you pronounce these words carefully, you will feel that the back of your tongue touches the velum in the articulation of both the *n* and the *k*.) The phoneme /m/ does not occur syllable internally before /t, d, k, g/; nor /n/ before /p, b, k, g/ nor /ŋ/ before /p, b, t, d/. Because of this sequential constraint, many speakers pronounce the name *Fromkin* with an epenthetic [p] as if it were written *Frompkin,* and the Fromkin family occasionally receives letters addressed with this spelling.

Epenthesis has occurred throughout the history of English. For example, the earlier form of the word *empty* had no *p*. Similarly a *d* was inserted in the word *ganra* giving us the modern *gander*. (We'll discuss historical language change in chapter 11.)

Two epenthesis rules that were discussed earlier in the chapter insert schwa before the English regular plural and regular past-tense endings when they occur in certain environments. The rule for the plural suffix is stated below, where null becomes schwa (∅ → ə) is the part of the rule that actually performs the insertion.

$$\varnothing \rightarrow \text{ə} \, / \, [+ \text{sibilant}] \, \underline{\quad} \, [+ \text{sibilant}]$$

The rule for the past-tense suffix differs only in the phonological environment:

$$\varnothing \rightarrow \text{ə} \, / \, [+ \text{alveolar}, + \text{stop}] \, \underline{\quad} [+ \text{alveolar}, + \text{stop}]$$

There is a plausible explanation for insertion of a [ə] in the plural forms of nouns ending with sibilants and in the past-tense forms of verbs ending with alveolar stops. If we added a [z] to *squeeze* we would get [skwizz], which would be hard for English speakers to distinguish from [skwiz]; similarly, if we added [d] to *load,* it would be [lodd] phonetically in the past and [lod] in the present, which would also be difficult to perceive, because in English we do not contrast long and short consonants. This and other examples suggest that the allomorphy patterns in a language are closely related to other generalizations about the phonology of that language.

Movement (Metathesis) Rules

Phonological rules may also reorder sequences of phonemes, in which case they are called **metathesis** rules. In some dialects of English, for example, the word *ask* is pronounced [æks], but the word *asking* is pronounced [æskɪn] or [æskĭŋ]. In these dialects, a metathesis rule reorders the /s/ and /k/ in certain contexts. In Old English the verb was *aksian,* with the /k/ preceding the /s/. A historical metathesis rule switched these two consonants, producing *ask* in most dialects of English. Children's speech shows many cases of metathesis (which are corrected as the child approaches the adult grammar): *aminal* [ǽmənəl] for *animal* and *pusketti* [pʰəskɛti] for *spaghetti* are common children's pronunciations.

In Hebrew there is a metathesis rule that reverses a pronoun-final consonant with the first consonant of the following verb if the verb starts with a sibilant. These reversals are in "reflexive" verb forms, as shown in the following examples:

Nonsibilant-Initial Verbs		Sibilant-Initial Verbs	
kabel	"to accept"	*tsadek*	"to justify"
lehit-kabel	"to be accepted"	*lehits-tadek* (not **lehit-tsadek*)	"to apologize"
pater	"to fire"	*šameš*	"to use for"
lehit-pater	"to resign"	*lehiš-tameš* (not **lehit-šameš*)	"to use"
bayeš	"to shame"	*sader*	"to arrange"
lehit-bayeš	"to be ashamed"	*lehis-tader* (not **lehit-sader*)	"to arrange "oneself"

We see, then, that phonological rules have a number of functions, among which are the following:

1. Change feature values (vowel nasalization rule in English).
2. Add new features (aspiration in English).
3. Delete segments (final consonant deletion in French).
4. Add segments (schwa insertion in English plural and past tense).
5. Reorder segments (metathesis rule in Hebrew).

These rules, when applied to the phonemic representations of words and phrases, result in phonetic forms that differ from the phonemic forms. If such differences were unpredictable, it would be difficult to explain how we can understand what we hear or how we produce utterances that represent the meanings we wish to convey. The more we look at languages, however, the more we see that many aspects of the phonetic forms of utterances that appear at first to be irregular and unpredictable are actually rule-governed. We learn, or construct, these rules when we are learning the language as children (see chapter 8). The rules form an important part of the sound pattern that we acquire.

From One to Many and from Many to One

The discussion on how phonemic representations of utterances are realized phonetically included an example from the language Akan to show that the relationship between a phoneme and its allophonic realization may be complex. The same phone may be an allophone of two or more phonemes, as [m] was shown to be an allophone of both /b/ and /m/ in Akan.

We can also illustrate this complex mapping relationship in English. Consider the vowels in the following pairs of words:

	A		**B**	
i	compete	[i]	competition	[ə]
ɪ	medicinal	[ɪ]	medicine	[ə]
e	maintain	[e]	maintenance	[ə]
ɛ	telegraph	[ɛ]	telegraphy	[ə]

	A		**B**	
æ	analysis	[æ]	analytic	[ə]
a	solid	[a]	solidity	[ə]
o	phone	[o]	phonetic	[ə]
u	Talmu**d**ic	[ʊ]	Talmu**d**	[ə]

In column A all the boldfaced vowels are stressed vowels with a variety of vowel phones; in column B all the boldfaced unstressed vowels are pronounced [ə]. How can one explain the fact that the root morphemes that occur in both words of the pairs have different pronunciations?

In the chapter on morphology we defined a morpheme as a sound/meaning unit. Changing either would make a different morpheme. It doesn't seem plausible (nor is it necessary) for speakers of English to represent these root morphemes with distinct phonemic forms if there is some general rule that relates the stressed vowels in column A to the unstressed schwa vowel [ə] in column B.

Speakers of English know (unconsciously of course) that one can derive one word from another by the addition of derivational morphemes. This is illustrated by adding *-ition* or *-ance* to verb roots to form nouns, or *-al* and *-ic* to nouns to form adjectives. In English the syllable that is stressed depends to a great extent on the phonemic structure of the word, the number of syllables, and other factors. In a number of cases, the addition of derivational suffixes changes the stress pattern of the word, and the vowel that was stressed in the root morpheme becomes unstressed in the derived form. (The stress rules are too complex for an introductory text. The curious reader may consult the references at the end of the chapter.) When a vowel is unstressed in English it is pronounced as [ə], which is a reduced vowel.

The phonemic representation of all of the root morphemes in column A contains an unreduced vowel that becomes [ə] when it is not stressed. We can conclude, then, that [ə] is an allophone of all English vowel phonemes. The rule to derive the schwa is simple to state:

Change a vowel to a [ə] when it is unstressed.

There are exceptions, however. When an unstressed vowel occurs as the final segment of some words, it retains its full vowel quality, as shown in words like *confetti, motto,* or *democracy.* A comprehensive rule would be more complex to state.

The rule that reduces unstressed vowels to schwas is another example of a rule that changes feature values.

In a phonological description of a language that we do not know, it is not always possible to determine phonemic representation from the phonetic transcription. However, given the phonemic representation and the phonological rules, we can always derive the correct phonetic transcription. Of course, in our internal mental grammars this derivation is no problem, because the words occur in their phonemic forms in our lexicons and we know the rules of the language.

Another example will illustrate this aspect of phonology. In English, /t/ and /d/ are both phonemes, as is illustrated by the minimal pairs *tie/die* and *bat/bad.* When /t/ or /d/

occurs between a stressed and an unstressed vowel they both become a flap [ɾ]. For many speakers of English, *writer* and *rider* are pronounced identically as [rajɾər]; yet these speakers know that *writer* has a phonemic /t/ because of *write* /rajt/, whereas *rider* has a phonemic /d/ because of *ride* /rajd/. The flap rule may be stated as:

> An alveolar stop becomes a voiced flap when preceded by a stressed vowel and followed by an unstressed vowel.

The application of this rule is illustrated as follows:

Phonemic *representation*	write /rajt/	writer /rajt + ər/ ↓	ride /rajd/	rider /rajd + ər/ ↓
Apply rule	NA	ɾ	NA	ɾ
Phonetic *representation*	[rajt]	[rajɾər]	[rajd]	[rajɾər]

We are omitting other phonetic details that are also determined by phonological rules, such as the fact that in *ride* the vowel is slightly longer than in *write* because it is followed by a voiced [d], which is a phonetic rule in many languages. We are using the example only to illustrate the fact that two distinct phonemes may be realized phonetically by the same phone.

Such cases show that we cannot arrive at a phonological analysis by simply inspecting the phonetic representation of utterances. If we just looked for minimal pairs as the only evidence for phonology, we would have to conclude that [ɾ] is a phoneme in English because it contrasts phonetically with other phonetic units: *riper* [rajpər], *rhymer* [rãjmər], *riser* [rajzər], and so forth. The fact that *write* and *ride* change their phonetic forms when suffixes are added shows that there is an intricate mapping between phonemic representations of words and phonetic pronunciations.

Notice that in the case of the schwa rule and the flap rule the allophones derived from the different phonemes by rule are different in features from all other phonemes in the language. That is, there is no /ɾ/ phoneme, but there is a [ɾ] phone. This was also true of aspirated voiceless stops and nasalized vowels. The set of phones is larger than the set of phonemes.

The English flap rule also illustrates an important phonological process called **neutralization;** the voicing contrast between /t/ and /d/ is neutralized in the specified environment. That is, /t/ never contrasts with /d/ in the environment between a stressed and an unstressed vowel.

Similar rules showing there is no one-to-one relation between phonemes and phones exist in other languages. In both Russian and German, when voiced obstruents occur at the end of a word or syllable, they become voiceless. Both voiced and voiceless obstruents do occur in German as phonemes, as is shown by the following minimal pair:

> *Tier* [tiːr] "animal"   *dir* [diːr] "to you"

At the end of a German word, however, only [t] occurs; the words meaning "bundle" *Bund*[9] /bʊnd/ and "colorful" *bunt* /bʊnt/ are phonetically identical and pronounced [bũnt] with a final [t].

The German devoicing rule, like the vowel reduction rule in English and the homorganic nasal rule, changes the specifications of features. In German, the phonemic representation of the final stop in *Bund* is /d/, specified as [+ voiced]; it is changed by rule to [– voiced] to derive the phonetic [t] in word-final position.

This rule in German further illustrates that we cannot discern the phonemic representation of a word given only the phonetic form; [bũnt] can be derived from either /bʊnd/ or /bʊnt/. The phonemic representations and the rules of the language together determine the phonetic forms.

The Function of Phonological Rules

The function of the phonological rules in a grammar is to provide the phonetic information necessary for the pronunciation of utterances. We may illustrate this point in the following way:

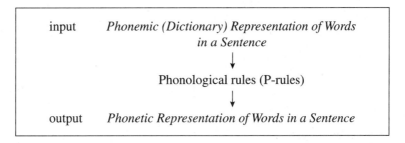

input   *Phonemic (Dictionary) Representation of Words in a Sentence*

Phonological rules (P-rules)

output   *Phonetic Representation of Words in a Sentence*

The input to the P-rules is the phonemic representation; the P-rules apply to the phonemic strings and produce as output the phonetic representation.

The application of rules in this way is called a **derivation.** We have given examples of derivations that show how phonemically oral vowels become nasalized, how phonemically unaspirated voiceless stops become aspirated, how contrastive voiced and voiceless alveolar stops in English merge to become flaps, and how German voiced obstruents are devoiced. A derivation is thus an explicit way of showing both the effects and the function of phonological rules in a grammar.

All the examples of derivations we have so far considered show the applications of just one phonological rule, except the plural and past-tense rules, which are actually one rule with two parts. In any event, it is common for more than one rule to apply to a word. For example, the word *tempest* is phonemically /tɛmpɛst/ (as shown by the pronunciation of *tempestuous* [tʰɛ̃mpʰɛsčuəs]) but phonetically [tʰɛ̃mpəst]. Three rules apply to it: the aspiration rule, the vowel nasalization rule, and the schwa rule. We can derive the phonetic form from the phonemic representation as follows:

---

[9] In German, nouns are capitalized in written form.

Underlying phonemic representation	/ t	ε	m	p	ε	s	t /
Aspiration rule	tʰ						
Nasalization rule		ɛ̃					
Schwa rule					ə		
Surface phonetic representation	[tʰ	ɛ̃	m	p	ə	s	t]

We are using phonetic symbols instead of matrices in which the feature values are changed. These notations are equivalent, however, as long as we understand that a phonetic symbol is a cover term representing a matrix with all distinctive features marked either + or − (unless, of course, the feature is nondistinctive, such as the nasality value for phonemic vowels in English).

Slips of the Tongue: Evidence for Phonological Rules

"The Wizard of Id " reprinted by permission of Johnny Hart and Creators Syndicate, Inc.

Slips of the tongue, or **speech errors,** in which we deviate in some way from the intended utterance, show phonological rules in action. Some of these tongue slips are called **spoonerisms,** after William Archibald Spooner, a distinguished head of an Oxford College in the early 1900s who is reported to have referred to Queen Victoria as "That queer old dean" instead of "That dear old queen," and berated his class of students by saying, "You have hissed my mystery lecture. You have tasted the whole worm" instead of the intended "You have missed my history lecture. You have wasted the whole term." We all make speech errors, and they tell us interesting things about language and its use. Consider the following speech errors:

	Intended Utterance	**Actual Utterance**
1.	gone to seed	god to seen
	[gãn tə sid]	[gad tə sĩn]

Intended Utterance	Actual Utterance
2. stick in the mud	smuck in the tid
[stɪk ĩn ðə mʌd]	[smʌk ĩn ðə tʰɪd]
3. speech production	preach seduction
[spič prədʌkšə̃n]	[pʰrič sədʌkšə̃n]

In the first example, the final consonants of the first and third words were reversed. Notice that the reversal of the consonants also changed the nasality of the vowels. The vowel [ã] in the intended utterance is replaced by [a]; in the actual utterance, the nasalization was lost because it no longer occurred before a nasal consonant. The vowel in the third word, which was the nonnasal [i] in the intended utterance, became [ĩ] in the error, because it was followed by /n/. The nasalization rule applied.

In the other two errors, we see the application of the aspiration rule. In the intended *stick,* the /t/ would have been realized as an unaspirated [t] because it follows the syllable initial /s/; when it was switched with the /m/ in *mud,* it was pronounced as the aspirated [tʰ], because it occurred initially. The third example also illustrates the aspiration rule in action.

Prosodic Phonology

Syllable Structure

Words are composed of one or more syllables. A **syllable** is a phonological unit composed of one or more phonemes. Every syllable has a **nucleus,** which is usually a vowel (but which may be a syllabic liquid or nasal). The nucleus may be preceded by one or more phonemes called the syllable **onset** and followed by one or more segments called the **coda.** From a very early age, children learn that certain words rhyme. In rhyming words, the nucleus and the coda of the final syllable of both words are identical, as in the following jingle:

> Jack and **Jill**
> Went up the **hill**
> To fetch a pail of water.
> Jack fell d**own**
> And broke his cr**own**
> And Jill came tumbling after.

For this reason, the nucleus + coda constitute the subsyllabic unit called a **rime** (note the spelling).

A syllable thus has a hierarchical structure. Using the Greek letter *sigma*, σ, as the symbol for the phonological unit syllable, the hierarchical structure of the monosyllabic word *splints* can be shown.

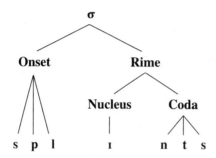

Word Stress

In many languages, including English, one or more of the syllables in every content word (i.e., every word except for functions words like *to, the, a, of,* etc.) are stressed. A stressed syllable, which can be marked by an acute accent (´) is perceived as more prominent than unstressed syllables in the following examples:

pérvert (noun) as in "My neighbor is a pervert."
pervért (verb) as in "Don't pervert the idea."

súbject (noun) as in "Let's change the subject."
subjéct (verb) as in "He'll subject us to criticism."[10]

In some words, more than one vowel is stressed, but if so, one of these stressed vowels receives greater stress than the others. We have indicated the most highly stressed vowel by an acute accent over the vowel (we say this vowel receives the **accent,** or **primary stress,** or **main stress**); the other stressed vowels are indicated by a grave accent (`) over the vowels (these vowels receive secondary stress).

| rèsignátion | lìnguístics | sỳstemátic |
| fùndaméntal | ìntrodúctory | rèvolútion |

Generally, speakers of a language know which syllable receives primary stress, which receives secondary stress, and which are not stressed at all; it is part of their knowledge of the language. Sometimes it is hard to distinguish between primary and secondary stress; it is easier to distinguish between stressed and unstressed syllables. If you are unsure of where the primary stress is in a word (and you are a good speaker of English), try shouting the word as if talking to a person across a busy street. Often, the difference in stress becomes more apparent. (This should not be attempted in a public place such as a library.)

The stress pattern of a word may differ among English-speaking people. For example, in most varieties of American English the word *láboratòry* [lǽbərətɔ̀ri] has two stressed syllables, but in most varieties of British English it receives only one stress [ləbɔ́rətri]. Because vowel qualities in English are closely related to stress — recall that vowels generally reduce to schwa or delete when they are not stressed — the British and American vowels differ in this word. In fact, in the British version the fourth vowel is deleted because it is not stressed.

There are a number of ways to represent stress. We have used acúte accent marks for primary stress and gràve accent marks for secondary stress. We can also specify which syllable in the word is stressed by marking the syllable *s* if strongly stressed, *w* if weakly stressed, and unmarked if unstressed.

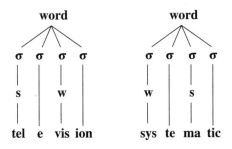

---

[10] These pairs show that stress can be contrastive in English. In these cases it distinguishes between nouns and verbs.

Stress is also sometimes shown by placing a 1 over the primary stressed syllable, a 2 over the syllable with secondary stress, and leaving unstressed vowels unmarked.

2	1		2	1		1	2
fundamental			introductory			secondary	

Stress is a property of the syllable rather than a segment; it is a prosodic or suprasegmental feature. To produce a stressed syllable, one may change the pitch (usually by raising it), make the syllable louder, or make it longer. We often use all three of these phonetic means to stress a syllable.

Sentence and Phrase Stress

By Howie Schneider. Copyright © 1975 by NEA, Inc.

When words are combined into phrases and sentences, one syllable receives greater stress than all others. That is, just as there is only one primary stress in a word spoken in isolation, only one of the vowels in a phrase (or sentence) receives primary stress or accent. All the other stressed vowels are reduced to secondary stress. This is illustrated by these examples:

	1	1	1 2		
	tight + rope → tightrope			("a rope for acrobatics")	
	1	1	2 1		
	tight + rope → tight rope			("a rope drawn taut")	
	1	1	1 2		
	hot + dog → hotdog			("frankfurter")	
	1	1	2 1		
	hot + dog → hot dog			("an overheated dog")	
	1	1	1 2		
	red + coat → Redcoat			("a British soldier")	
	1	1	2 1		
	red + coat → red coat			("a coat that is red")	

$$1 \qquad 1 \qquad 1 \qquad 2$$
white + house → White House　　("the President's house")
$$1 \qquad 1 \qquad 2 \qquad 1$$
white + house → white house　　("a house painted white")

Speaking naturally, say these examples aloud, and at the same time listen or feel the stress pattern. This may not work if English is not your native language, for which we apologize, but suggest you listen to a native speaker say them.

In English we place primary stress on an adjective followed by a noun when the two words are combined in a compound noun (which may be written as one word, two words separated by a hyphen, or two separate words), but we place the stress on the noun when the words are part of a noun phrase. The differences between the following pairs are therefore predictable:

Compound Noun	Adjective + Noun
tightrope	tight rope
Redcoat	red coat
hotdog	hot dog
White House	white house

These pairs show that stress may be predictable from the morphology and syntax. The phonology interacts with the other components of the grammar. The stress differences between the noun and verb pairs discussed in the previous section (*subject* as noun or verb) are also predictable from the syntactic word category.

Intonation

"B. C." reprinted by permission of Johnny Hart and Creators Syndicate, Inc.

In chapter 6, we discussed pitch as a phonetic feature in reference to tone languages and intonation languages. In this chapter we have discussed the use of phonetic features to distinguish meaning. We can now see that pitch is a *phonemic* feature in tone languages such as Chinese, Thai, and Akan. We refer to these relative pitches as **contrasting tones**. In intonation languages such as English, pitch still plays an important role, but in the form of the *pitch contour,* or *intonation* of the phrase or sentence.

In English, intonation contours may reflect syntactic or semantic differences. If we say *John is going* with a falling pitch at the end, it is a statement; but if the pitch rises at the end, it may be interpreted as a question.

Similarly, *What's in the tea, honey?* may, depending on intonation, be a query to someone called "honey" regarding the contents of the tea (falling intonation on *honey*), or may be a query regarding whether the tea contains honey (rising intonation on *honey*).

A sentence that is ambiguous in writing may be unambiguous when spoken due to differences in the pitch contour, as we saw in the previous paragraph. Here is a somewhat more subtle example. Written, sentence 1 is unclear as to whether Tristram intended for Isolde to read and follow directions, or merely to follow him:

1. Tristram left directions for Isolde to follow.

Spoken, if Tristram wanted Isolde to follow him, the sentence would be pronounced with a rise in pitch on the first syllable of *follow,* followed by a fall in pitch, as indicated (oversimplistically) in sentence 2.

2. Tristram left directions for Isolde to follow.

In this pronunciation of the sentence, the primary stress is on the word *follow.*

If the meaning is to read and follow a set of directions, the highest pitch comes on the second syllable of *directions,* as illustrated, again oversimplistically, in sentence 3.

3. Tristram left directions for Isolde to follow.

The primary stress in this pronunciation is on the word *directions.*

The way we have indicated pitch ignores much detail. Before the big rise in pitch the voice does not remain on the same monotone low pitch. These pitch diagrams merely indicate when there is a special change in pitch.

Pitch plays an important role in both tone languages and intonation languages, but in different ways, depending on the phonological system of the respective languages.

Sequential Constraints

Suppose you were given the following four phonemes of English and asked to arrange them to form all *possible* words:

/b/   /ɪ/   /k/   /l/

You would most likely produce the following:

/b   l   ɪ   k /
/k   l   ɪ   b /
/b   ɪ   l   k /
/k   ɪ   l   b /

These are the only permissible arrangements of these phonemes in English. */lbkɪ/, */ɪlbk/, */bkɪl/, and */ɪlkb/ are not possible English words. Although /blɪk/ and /klɪb/ are not now existing words, if you heard someone say:

"I just bought a beautiful new blick"

you might ask: "What's a blick?"

If, on the other hand, you heard someone say:

"I just bought a beautiful new bkli"

you might reply, "You just bought a new *what?*"

Your knowledge of English phonology includes information about what sequences of phonemes are permissible, and what sequences are not. After a consonant like /b/, /g/, /k/, or /p/, another stop consonant in the same syllable is not permitted by the phonology. If a word begins with an /l/ or an /r/, the next segment must be a vowel. That is why */lbɪk/ does not sound like an English word. It violates the restrictions on the sequencing of phonemes. People who like to work crossword puzzles are often more aware of these constraints than the ordinary speaker, whose knowledge, as we have emphasized, may not be conscious.

Other such constraints exist in English. If the initial sounds of *chill* or *Jill* begin a word, the next sound must be a vowel. The words /čat/ or /čon/ or /čæk/ are possible in English, as are /ǰæl/ or /ǰil/ or /ǰalɪk/, but */člɔt/ and */ǰpurz/ are not. No more than three sequential consonants can occur at the beginning of a word, and these three are restricted to /s/ + /p, t, k/ + /l, r, w, y/. There are even restrictions if this condition is met. For example, /stl/ is not a permitted sequence, so *stlick* is not a possible word in English, but *strick* is, along with *spew* /spyu/, *sclaff* /sklæf/ ("to strike the ground with a golf club"), and *squat* /skwat/.

Other languages have different sequential restrictions. In Polish *zl* is a permissible combination, as in *zlev,* a sink. Croatian permits words like the name *Mladen.* Japanese has severe constraints on what may begin a syllable; most combinations of consonants (e.g., /br/, /sp/) are impermissible.

The limitations on sequences of segments are called **phonotactic constraints.** Phonotactic constraints have as their basis the syllable, rather than the word. That is, only the clusters that can begin a syllable can begin a word, and only a cluster that can end a syllable can end a word.

In multisyllabic words, clusters that seem illegal may occur, for example the /kspl/ in *explicit* /ɛksplɪsɪt/. However, there is a syllable boundary between the /ks/ and /pl/ which we can make explicit using $: /ɛk $ splɪs $ ɪt/. Thus we have a permitted syllable coda /k/ that ends a syllable adjoined to a permitted onset /spl/ that begins a syllable.

On the other hand, English speakers know that "condstluct" is not a possible word because the second syllable would have to start with an impermissible onset, either /stl/ or /tl/.

In the language Asante Twi, a word may end only in a vowel or a nasal consonant. The sequence /pik/ is not a possible Twi word because it breaks the phonotactic rules of the language, whereas /mba/is not a possible word in English though it is a word in Twi.

All languages have constraints on the permitted sequences of phonemes, though different languages have different constraints. Just as spoken language has sequences of sounds that are not permitted in the language, so sign languages have forbidden combinations of features. They differ from one sign language to another, just as the constraints on sounds and sound sequences differ from one spoken language to another. A permissible sign in a Chinese sign language may not be a permissible sign in ASL, and vice versa. Children learn these constraints when they learn the spoken or signed language, just as they learn what the phonemes are and how they are related to phonetic segments.

LEXICAL GAPS

The words *bot* [bat] and *crake* [krek] are not known to all speakers of English, and [bʊt] (to rhyme with *put*), *creck* [krɛk], *cruke* [kruk], *cruk* [krʌk], and *crike* [krajk] are not now words in English, though they are possible words.

Advertising professionals often use possible but nonoccurring words for the names of new products. Although we would hardly expect a new product or company to come on the market with the name *Zhleet* [žlit] — an impossible word in English — we do not bat an eye at *Bic, Xerox* /zıraks/, *Kodak, Glaxo*, or *Spam* because those once nonoccurring words obey the phonotactic constraints of English.

A *possible word* is one that contains phonemes in sequences that obey the phonotactic constraints of the language. An actual, occurring word is the union of a possible word with a meaning. Possible words without meaning are sometimes called *nonsense words* and are also referred to as *accidental gaps* in the lexicon, or *lexical gaps*. Thus " words " such as *creck* and *cruck* are nonsense words and represent accidental gaps in the lexicon of English.

Phonological Analysis: Discovering Phonemes

Children recognize phonemes at an early age without being taught, as we shall see in chapter 8. Before reading this book, or learning anything about phonology, you knew a *p* sound was a phoneme in English because it contrasts words like *pat* and *cat, pat* and *sat, pat* and *mat*. But you probably did not know that the *p* in *pat* and the *p* in *spit* are different sounds. There is only one /p/ phoneme in English, but that phoneme has more than one allophone, including an aspirated one and an unaspirated one.

The linguist from Mars from chapter 3, who is trying to write a grammar of English, would have to decide whether the different *p* sounds in English represent separate phonemes or are allophones of a single phoneme. How can this be done? How would any phonologist discover the phonological system of a language?

To do a phonemic analysis, the words to be analyzed must be transcribed in great phonetic detail, because we do not know in advance which phonetic features are distinctive and which are not.

Consider the following Finnish words:

1.	[kudot]	"failures"	**3.**	[katot]	"roofs"
2.	[kate]	"cover"	**4.**	[kade]	"envious"

5. [madon] "of a worm"   **7.** [ratas]   "wheel"
6. [maton] "of a rug"   **8.** [radon]   "of a track"

Given these words, do the voiceless/voiced alveolar stops [t] and [d] represent different phonemes or are they allophones of the same phone?

Here are a few hints as to how a phonologist might proceed:

1. Check to see if there are any minimal pairs.
2. Items (2) and (4) are minimal pairs: [kate] "cover" and [kade] "envious."
    Items (5) and (6) are minimal pairs: [madon] "of a worm" and [maton] "of a rug."
3. [t] and [d] in Finnish thus represent the distinct phonemes /t/ and /d/.

That was an easy problem.

Now consider these data from Greek, focusing on the following sounds:[11]

[x] voiceless velar fricative
[k] voiceless velar stop
[c] voiceless palatal stop
[ç] voiceless palatal fricative

1. [kano]	"do"		**9.** [çeri]	"hand"
2. [xano]	"lose"		**10.** [kori]	"daughter"
3. [çino]	"pour"		**11.** [xori]	"dances"
4. [cino]	"move"		**12.** [xrima]	"money"
5. [kali]	"charms"		**13.** [krima]	"shame"
6. [xali]	"plight"		**14.** [xufta]	"handful"
7. [çeli]	"eel"		**15.** [kufeta]	"bonbons"
8. [ceri]	"candle"		**16.** [oçi]	"no"

To determine the status of [x], [k], [c], and [ç], you should answer the following questions.

1. Are there are any minimal pairs in which these sounds contrast?
2. Are any noncontrastive sounds in complementary distribution?
3. If noncontrasting phones are found, what are the phonemes and their allophones?
4. What are the phonological rules by which the allophones can be derived?

1. By analyzing the data we find that [k] and [x] contrast in a number of minimal pairs, for example, in [kano] and [xano]. [k] and [x] are therefore distinctive. [c] and [ç] also contrast in [çino] and [cino] and are therefore distinctive. But what about the velar fricative [x] and the palatal fricative [ç]? And the velar stop [k] and the palatal stop [c]? We can find no minimal pairs that would conclusively show that these represent separate phonemes.

---

[11] Those phones that we haven't discussed are allophones of /k/ in some varieties of English, e.g., [x] and [c] may occur as allophones of /k/ in words like *sicken* [sɪxən] and ski [sci]; [ç] is often the initial phone in the word *hue* /hyu/.

2. We now proceed to answer the second question: Are these noncontrasting phones in complementary distribution? One way to see if sounds are in complementary distribution is to list each phone with the environment in which it is found, as follows:

Phone	Environment
[k]	before [a], [o], [u], [r]
[x]	before [a], [o], [u], [r]
[c]	before [i], [e]
[ç]	before [i], [e]

We see that [k] and [x] are not in complementary distribution; they both occur before back vowels. Nor are [c] and [ç] in complementary distribution. They both occur before front vowels. But the stops [k] and [c] are in complementary distribution; [k] occurs before back vowels and [r], and never occurs before front vowels. [c] occurs only before front vowels and never before back vowels or [r]. Similarly, [x] and [ç] are in complementary distribution for the same reason. We therefore conclude that [k] and [c] are allophones of one phoneme and the fricatives [x] and [ç] are also allophones of one phoneme. The pairs of allophones also fulfill the criterion of phonetic similarity. The first two are [− anterior] stops; the second are [− anterior] fricatives. (This similarity discourages us from pairing [k] with [ç], and [c] with [x], which are less similar to each other.)

3. Which of the phone pairs are more basic, and hence the ones whose features would define the phoneme? When two allophones can be derived from one phoneme, one selects as the underlying segment the allophone that makes the rules and the phonemic feature matrix as simple as possible, as we illustrated with the English unaspirated and aspirated voiceless stops.

In the case of the velar and palatal stops and fricatives in Greek, the rules appear equally simple. However, in addition to the simplicity criterion, we wish to state rules that have natural phonetic explanations. Often these turn out to be the simplest solution. In many languages, velar sounds become palatal before front vowels. This is an assimilation rule; palatal sounds are produced toward the front of the mouth as are front vowels. Thus we select /k/ as a phoneme with the allophones [k] and [c], and /x/ as a phoneme with the allophones [x] and [ç].

4. We can now state the rule by which the palatals can be derived from the velars.

Palatalize velar consonants before front vowels.

Using feature notation we can state the rule as:

[+ velar] → [+ palatal] / _____ [− back]

Because only consonants are marked for the feature [velar], and only vowels for the feature [back], it is not necessary to include the features [consonantal] or [syllabic] in the rule. Nor need we include any other features that are redundant in defining the segments to which the rule applies, or the environment in which the rule applies. Thus [+ palatal] in the change part of the rule is sufficient, and the feature [− back] also suffices to specify the front vowels. The simplicity criterion constrains us to state the rule as simply as we can.

Summary

Part of one's knowledge of a language is knowledge of the **phonology** or sound system of that language — the inventory of **phones,** the phonetic segments that occur in the language, and the ways in which they pattern. This patterning determines the inventory of **phonemes** — the segments that differentiate words.

Phonetic segments are enclosed in square brackets, [ ], and phonemes between slashes, / /. When similar phones occur in **complementary distribution,** they are **allophones** — predictable phonetic variants — of phonemes. For example, in English, aspirated voiceless stops such as the initial sound in *pill* are in complementary distribution (never occur in the same phonological environment) as the unaspirated voiceless stops in words such as *spill.* Thus the aspirated [pʰ] and the unaspirated [p] are allophones of the phoneme /p/. This generalizes also to the voiceless stops /t/ and /k/. On the other hand, phones in the same environment that differentiate words, like the [b] and [m] in *boat* [bot] and *moat* [mot], represent two distinct phonemes, /b/ and /m/.

Some phones may be allophones of more than one phoneme. There is no one-to-one correspondence between the phonemes of a language and their allophones. In English, for example, stressed vowels become unstressed according to regular rules and ultimately reduce to schwa [ə], which is an allophone of each English vowel.

Phonological segments — phonemes and phones — are composed of **phonetic features** such as **voiced, nasal, labial,** and **continuant,** whose presence or absence is indicated by + or – signs. They distinguish one segment from another. When a phonetic feature causes a word contrast, as **nasal** does in *boat* and *moat,* it is a distinctive feature. Thus, in English, the binary valued feature [± nasal] is a distinctive feature whereas [± aspiration] is not.

When two words (different forms with different meanings) are distinguished by a single phone occurring in the same position, they constitute a **minimal pair.** Some pairs, such as *boat* and *moat,* contrast by means of a single distinctive feature, in this case, [± nasal], where /b/ is [– nasal] and /m/ is [+ nasal]. Other minimal pairs may show sounds contrasting in more than one feature, for example, *dip* versus *sip,* where /d/, a voiced alveolar stop, is [+ voiced, – continuant] and /s/, a voiceless alveolar fricative, is [– voiced, + continuant]. Minimal pairs and sets also occur in sign languages. Signs may contrast by hand configuration, place of articulation, or movement.

Some sounds differ phonetically but are nonphonemic because they are in **free variation,** which means that either sound may occur in the identical environment without changing the word's meaning. The glottal stop [ʔ] in English is in free variation with the [t] in words like *don't* or *bottle* and is therefore not a phoneme in English.

Phonetic features that are **predictable** are nondistinctive and **redundant.** The nasality of vowels in English is a redundant feature since all vowels are nasalized before nasal consonants. One can thus predict the + or – value of this feature in vowels. A feature may therefore be distinctive in one class of sounds and **nondistinctive** in another. Nasality is distinctive for English consonants, and nondistinctive predictable for English vowels.

Phonetic features that are nondistinctive in one language may be distinctive in another. Aspiration is distinctive in Thai and nondistinctive in English; both aspirated and unaspirated voiceless stops are phonemes in Thai.

The phonology of a language also includes constraints on the sequences of phonemes in the language, as exemplified by the fact that in English two stop consonants may not occur together at the beginning of a word. Similarly, the final sound of the word *sing,* the velar nasal, never occurs word initially. These sequential constraints determine what are *possible* but nonoccurring words in a language, and what phonetic strings are impermissible. For example, *blick* [blɪk] is not now an English word but it could become one, whereas *kbli* [kbli] or *ngos* [ŋos] could not. Possible but nonoccurring words constitute **accidental gaps** and are **nonsense words.**

Words in some languages may also be phonemically distinguished by **prosodic** or **suprasegmental** features, such as **pitch, stress,** and segment duration or **length.** Languages in which syllables or words are contrasted by pitch are called **tone** languages. **Intonation** languages may use pitch variations to distinguish meanings of phrases and sentences.

In English, words and phrases may be differentiated by **stress,** as in the contrast between the noun *pérvert* in which the first syllable is stressed, and the verb *pervért* in which the final syllable is stressed. In the compound noun *hótdog* versus the adjective + noun phrase *hot dóg,* the former is stressed on *hot,* the latter on *dog.*

Vowel **length** and consonant **length** may be phonemic features. Both are contrastive in Japanese, Finnish, Italian, and many other languages.

The relationship between the phonemic representation of words and sentences and the phonetic representation (the pronunciation of these words and sentences) is determined by phonological rules. Phonological rules in a grammar apply to phonemic strings and alter them in various ways to derive their phonetic pronunciation:

1. They may be **assimilation rules,** which change feature values of segments, thus spreading phonetic properties. The rule that nasalizes vowels in English before nasal consonants is such a rule.
2. They may be **dissimilation rules,** which change feature values to make two phonemes in a string more dissimilar, like the Latin liquid rule.
3. They may *add* **nondistinctive features,** which are predictable from the context. The rule that aspirates voiceless stops at the beginning of words and syllables in English is such a rule.
4. They may *insert* segments that are not present in the phonemic string. Insertion is also called **epenthesis.** The schwa insertion part of the rule of English plural formation is an example of epenthesis, e.g., *kisses* [kɪsəz].
5. They may *delete* phonemic segments in certain contexts. Contraction rules in English are **deletion** rules.
6. They may *transpose* or move segments in a string. These **metathesis** rules occur in many languages, such as Hebrew. The rule in certain varieties of American English that changes an *sk* to [ks] in final position is also a metathesis rule.

Phonological rules often refer to entire classes of sound rather than to individual sounds. These are **natural classes,** characterized by the phonetic features that pertain to all the members of a class such as voiced sounds which are represented in feature notation as [+ voiced]. A natural class can be defined by fewer features than required to distinguish a member of that class. Natural classes reflect the ways in which we articulate sounds, or, in some cases, the acoustic characteristics of sounds. The occurrence of such classes, therefore, does not have to be learned in the same way as groups of sounds that are not phonetically similar. Natural classes provide explanations for the occurrence of many phonological rules.

In the writing of rules, one can use formal notations, which often reveal linguistic generalizations of phonological processes.

A morpheme may have different phonetic representations; these are determined by the **morphophonemic** and phonological rules of the language. Thus the regular plural morpheme is phonetically [z], [s], or [əz], depending on the final phoneme of the noun to which it is attached.

To discover the phonemes of a language, linguists (or students of linguistics) can use a methodology such as looking for minimal pairs of words, or for sounds that are in complementary distribution. The feature matrix of the allophone of a phoneme that results in the simplest statement of the phonological rules is selected as the underlying phoneme from which all the phonetic allophones are derived.

The phonological and morphophonemic rules in a language show that the phonemic shape of words or phrases is not identical with their phonetic form. The phonemes are not the actual phonetic sounds, but are abstract mental constructs that are realized as sounds by the operation of rules such as those described in this chapter. No one is taught these rules, yet everyone knows them subconsciously.

≋ References for Further Reading

Anderson, S. R. 1974. *The Organization of Phonology.* New York: Academic Press.

_____. 1985. *Phonology in the Twentieth Century: Theories of Rules and Theories of Representations.* Chicago: University of Chicago Press.

Chomsky, N., and M. Halle. 1968. *The Sound Pattern of English.* New York: Harper & Row.

Clark, J., and C. Yallop. 1990. *An Introduction to Phonetics and Phonology.* Oxford, England: Basil Blackwell.

Clements, G. N., and S. J. Keyser. 1983. *CV Phonology: A Generative Theory of the Syllable.* Cambridge, MA: MIT Press.

Dell, F. 1980. *Generative Phonology.* London, England: Cambridge University Press.

Goldsmith, J. A. 1990. *Autosegmental and Metrical Phonology.* Oxford, England: Basil Blackwell.

Hogg, R., and C. B. McCully. 1987. *Metrical Phonology: A Coursebook.* Cambridge, England: Cambridge University Press.

Hyman, L. M. 1975. *Phonology: Theory and Analysis.* New York: Holt, Rinehart & Winston.

Kenstowicz, M. J. 1995. *Phonology in Generative Grammar.* Oxford, England: Blackwell Publishers.

Kenstowicz, M., and C. Kisseberth. 1979. *Generative Phonology: Description and Theory.* New York: Academic Press.

≋ Exercises

All the data in languages other than English are given in phonetic transcription without square brackets unless otherwise stated. The phonetic transcriptions of English words are given within square brackets.

1. The following sets of minimal pairs show that English /p/ and /b/ contrast in initial, medial, and final positions.

Initial	*Medial*	*Final*
pit/bit	rapid/rabid	cap/cab

   Find similar sets of minimal pairs for each pair of consonants given:

   a. /k/–/g/   **d.** /b/–/v/   **g.** /s/–/š/

   b. /m/–/n/   **e.** /b/–/m/   **h.** /č/–/ǰ/

   c. /l/–/r/   **f.** /p/–/f/   **i.** /s/–/z/

2. A young patient at the Radcliffe Infirmary in Oxford, England, following a head injury, appears to have lost the spelling-to-pronunciation and pronunciation-to-spelling rules that most of us can use to read and write new words or nonsense strings. He also is unable to get to the phonemic representation of words in his lexicon. Consider the following examples of his reading pronunciation and his writing from dictation.

Stimulus	**Reading Pronunciation**	**Writing from Dictation**
fame	/fæmi/	FAM
café	/sæfi/	KAFA
time	/tajmi/	TIM
note	/noti/ or /nɔti/	NOT
praise	/pra-aj-si/	PRAZ
treat	/tri-æt/	TRET
goes	/go-ɛs/	GOZ
float	/flɔ-æt/	FLOT

   What rules or patterns relate his reading pronunciation to the written stimulus? What rules or patterns relate his spelling to the dictated stimulus? For example: in reading, *a* corresponds to /a/ or /æ/; in writing from dictation /e/ and /æ/ correspond to written A.

3. Consider the distribution of [r] and [l] in Korean in the following words:

   [ɯ] is a high back unrounded vowel. It does not affect your analysis in this problem.

rubi	"ruby"	mul	"water"
kiri	"road"	pal	"leg"
saram	"person"	sɔul	"Seoul"
irɯm	"name"	ilgop	"seven"
ratio	"radio"	ibalsa	"barber"

   Are [r] and [l] allophones of one or two phonemes?

   a. Do they occur in any minimal pairs?

   b. Are they in complementary distribution?

   c. In what environments does each occur?

d. If you conclude that they are allophones of one phoneme, state the rule that can derive the phonetic allophonic forms.

4. Here are some additional data from Korean:

son	"hand"	šihap	"game"
som	"cotton"	šilsu	"mistake"
sosəl	"novel"	šipsam	"thirteen"
sɛk	"color"	šinho	"signal"
isa	"moving"	mašita	"is delicious"

Are [s] and [š] allophones of the same phoneme or is each an allophone of a separate phoneme?

There are no minimal pairs that will help to answer this question. Determine, instead, whether they are in complementary distribution. If they are, state their distribution. If they are not in complementary distribution, state the contrasting environment.

5. In Southern Kongo, a Bantu language spoken in Angola, the nonpalatal segments [t, s, z] are in complementary distribution with their palatal counterparts [č, š, ž], as shown in the following words:

tobola	"to bore a hole"	čina	"to cut"
tanu	"five"	čiba	"banana"
kesoka	"to be cut"	ŋkoši	"lion"
kasu	"emaciation"	nselele	"termite"
kunezulu	"heaven"	ažimola	"alms"
nzwetu	"our"	lolonži	"to wash house"
zevo	"then"	zeŋga	"to cut"
žima	"to stretch"		

a. State the distribution of each pair of segments. (Assume that the nonoccurrence of [t] before [e] is an accidental gap.)

Example: [t]—[č]: [t] occurs before the back vowels [o, a, u];
　　　　　　[č] occurs before [i].

　　　[s]—[š]
　　　[z]—[ž]

b. Using considerations of simplicity, which phone should be used as the basic phoneme for each pair of nonpalatal and palatal segments in Southern Kongo?

c. State in your own words the **one** phonological rule that will derive all the phonetic segments from the phonemes. Do not state a separate rule for each phoneme; a general rule can be stated that will apply to all three phonemes you listed in b. Try to give a formal statement of your rule.

6. In some dialects of English the following words have different vowels, as is shown by the phonetic transcriptions.

A		B		C	
bite	[bʌjt]	bide	[bajd]	die	[daj]
rice	[rʌjs]	rise	[rajz]	by	[baj]
ripe	[rʌjp]	bribe	[brajb]	sigh	[saj]
wife	[wʌjf]	wives	[wajvz]	rye	[raj]
dike	[dʌjk]	dime	[dãjm]	guy	[gaj]
		nine	[nãjn]		
		rile	[rajl]		
		dire	[dajr]		
		writhe	[rajð]		

a. How may the classes of sounds that end the words in columns A and B be characterized? That is, what feature specifies all the final segments in A and all the final segments in B?

b. How do the words in column C differ from those in columns A and B?

c. Are [ʌj] and [aj] in complementary distribution? Give your reasons.

d. If [ʌj] and [aj] are allophones of one phoneme, should they be derived from /ʌj/ or /aj/? Why?

e. Give the phonetic representations of the following words as they would be spoken in the dialect described here:

life _____ lives _____ lie _____

file _____ bike _____ lice _____

f. Formulate a rule that will relate the phonemic representations to the phonetic representations of the words given above.

7. Pairs like *top* and *chop, dunk* and *junk, so* and *show* reveal that /t/ and /č/, /d/ and /ǰ/, and /s/ and /š/ are distinct phonemes in English. Although it is difficult to find a minimal pair to distinguish /z/ and /ž/, they occur in similar if not identical environments, such as *razor* and *azure*. Consider these same pairs of nonpalatalized and palatalized consonants in the following data. (The palatal forms are optional forms that often occur in casual speech.)

Nonpalatalized		Palatalized	
[hɪt mi]	"hit me"	[hɪč ju]	"hit you"
[lid hĩm]	"lead him"	[liǰ ju]	"lead you"
[pʰæs ʌs]	"pass us"	[pʰæš ju]	"pass you"
[luz ðẽm]	"lose them"	[luž ju]	"lose you"

Formulate the rule that specifies when /t/, /d/, /s/, and /z/ become palatalized as [č], [ǰ], [š], and [ž]. Restate the rule using feature notations. Does the formal statement reveal the generalizations?

8. Here are some Japanese words in phonetic transcription. [č] is the voiceless palatal affricate that occurs in the English word *church*. [ts] is an alveolar affricate and should be taken as a *single* symbol. It is pronounced as the final sound(s) in *cats*. Japanese words (except certain loan words) never contain the phonetic sequences *[ti] or *[tu].

tatami	"mat"	tomodači	"friend"	uči	"house"
tegami	"letter"	totemo	"very"	otoko	"male"
čiči	"father"	tsukue	"desk"	tetsudau	"help"
šita	"under"	ato	"later"	matsu	"wait"
natsu	"summer"	tsutsumu	"wrap"	čizu	"map"
kata	"person"	tatemono	"building"	te	"hand"

  a. Based on these data, are [t], [č], and [ts] in complementary distribution?

  b. State the distribution — first in words, then using features — of these phones.

  c. Give a phonemic analysis of these data insofar as [t], [č], and [ts] are concerned. That is, identify the phonemes, and the allophones.

  d. Give the phonemic representation of the phonetically transcribed Japanese words given below. Assume phonemic and phonetic representations are the same except for [t], [č], and [ts].

tatami_____   tsukue_____   tsutsumu_____

tomodači _____   tetsudau _____   čizu _____

uči _____   šita _____   kata_____

tegami _____   ato _____   koto _____

totemo _____   matsu _____   tatemono _____

otoko _____   deguči _____   te _____

hiči _____   natsu_____   tsuri _____

9. The following words are Paku, a language spoken by the Pakuni in the NBC television series *Land of the Lost* (a language created by V. Fromkin). V́ = a stressed vowel ([+ stress])

a. ótu	"evil" (N)		**h.** mpósa	"hairless"	
b. túsa	"evil" (Adj)		**i.** ã́mpo	"hairless one"	
c. etógo	"cactus" (sg)		**j.** ãmpṍni	"hairless ones"	
d. etogṍni	"cactus" (pl)		**k.** ã́mi	"mother"	
e. Páku	"Paku" (sg)		**l.** ãmĩ́ni	"mothers"	
f. Pakṹni	"Paku" (pl)		**m.** áda	"father"	
g. épo	"hair"		**n.** adã́ni	"fathers"	

  (1) Is stress predictable? If so, what is the rule?

  (2) Is nasalization a distinctive feature for vowels? Give the reasons for your answer.

10. Consider the following English verbs. Those in column A have stress on the next-to-last syllable (called the penultimate), whereas the verbs in column B and C have their last syllable stressed.

A	B	C
astónish	collápse	amáze
éxit	exíst	impróve
imágine	resént	surpríse
cáncel	revólt	combíne
elícit	adópt	recáll
práctice	insíst	atóne

a. Transcribe the words under A, B, and C phonemically. (Use a schwa for the unstressed vowels even if they can be derived from different phonemic vowels. This should make it easier for you.)

e.g., *astonish* /əstanɪš/, *collapse* /kəlæps/, *amaze* /əmez/

b. Consider the phonemic structure of the stressed syllables in these verbs. What is the difference between the final syllables of the verbs in columns A and B? Formulate a rule that predicts where stress occurs in the verbs in columns A and B.

c. In the verbs in column C, stress also occurs on the final syllable. What must you add to the rule to account for this fact? (*Hint:* For the forms in columns A and B, the final consonants had to be considered; for the forms in column C, consider the vowels.)

11. Below are listed the phonetic transcriptions of ten "words." Some are English words, some are not words now but are possible words or nonsense words, and others are definitely "foreign" (they violate English sequential constraints).

   Write the English words in regular spelling. Mark the other words "foreign" or "possible." For each word you mark as "foreign," state your reason.

	Word	Possible	"Foreign"	Reason
Example:				
[θrot]	throat			
[slig]		X		
[lsig]			X	No English word can begin with a liquid followed by an obstruent.

	Word	Possible	"Foreign"	Reason
a. [pʰril]				
b. [skrič]				
c. [know]				
d. [maj]				
e. [gnostɪk]				
f. [jūnəkɔrn]				
g. [fruit]				
h. [blaft]				
i. [ŋar]				
j. [æpəpʰlɛksi]				

12. Consider these phonetic forms of Hebrew words:

[v]–[b]		**[f]–[p]**	
bika	"lamented"	litef	"stroked"
mugbal	"limited"	sefer	"book"
šavar	"broke" (masc.)	sataf	"washed"
šavra	"broke" (fem.)	para	"cow"
ʔikev	"delayed"	mitpaxat	"handkerchief"
bara	"created"	haʔalpim	"the Alps"

Assume that these words and their phonetic sequences are representative of what may occur in Hebrew. In your answers, consider classes of sounds rather than individual sounds.

a. Are [b] and [v] allophones of one phoneme? Are they in complementary distribution? In what phonetic environments do they occur? Can you formulate a phonological rule stating their distribution?

b. Does the same rule, or lack of a rule, that describes the distribution of [b] and [v] apply to [p] and [f]? If not, why not?

c. Here is a word with one phone missing. A blank appears in place of the missing sound: hid___ik.

Check the one correct statement.

(1) [b] but not [v] could occur in the empty slot.

(2) [v] but not [b] could occur in the empty slot.

(3) Either [b] or [v] could occur in the empty slot.

(4) Neither [b] nor [v] could occur in the empty slot.

d. Which of the following statements is correct about the incomplete word ___ana?

(1) [f] but not [p] could occur in the empty slot.

(2) [p] but not [f] could occur in the empty slot.

(3) Either [p] or [f] could fill the blank.

(4) Neither [p] nor [f] could fill the blank.

e. Now consider the following possible words (in phonetic transcription):

laval   surva   labal   palar   falu   razif

If these words actually occurred in Hebrew, would they:

(1) Force you to revise the conclusions about the distribution of labial stops and fricatives you reached on the basis of the first group of words given above?

(2) Support your original conclusions?

(3) Neither support nor disprove your original conclusions?

13. In the African language Maninka, the suffix *-li* has more than one pronunciation (like the *-ed* past-tense ending on English verbs, as in *reaped* [t], *robbed* [d], and *raided* [əd]). This suffix is similar to the derivational suffix *-ing*, which, when added to the verb *cook*, makes it a noun as in "Her cooking was great," or the suffix *-ion*, which also derives a noun from a verb as in *create + ion*.

Consider these data from Maninka:

bugo	"hit"	bugoli	"hitting"
dila	"repair"	dilali	"repairing"
don	"come in"	donni	"coming in"
dumu	"eat"	dumuni	"eating"
gwen	"chase"	gwenni	"chasing"

   a. What are the two forms of the "ing" morpheme?

   (1) _____   (2) _____

   b. Can you predict which phonetic form will occur? If so, state the rule.

   c. What are the "-ing" forms for the following verbs?

   da   "lie down" _____   famu   "understand" _____

   men   "hear"_____   sunogo   "sleep" _____

14. Consider the following phonetic data from the Bantu language Luganda. (The data have been somewhat altered to make the problem easier.) In each line except the last, the same root occurs in both columns A and B, but it has one prefix in column A, meaning "a" or "an," and another prefix in column B, meaning "little."

A		B	
ẽnato	"a canoe"	akaato	"little canoe"
ẽnapo	"a house"	akaapo	"little house"
ẽnobi	"an animal"	akaobi	"little animal"
ẽmpipi	"a kidney"	akapipi	"little kidney"
ẽŋkoosa	"a feather"	akakoosa	"little feather"
ẽmmããmmo	"a peg"	akabãammo	"little peg"
ẽŋŋõõmme	"a horn"	akagõõmme	"little horn"
ẽnnĩmiro	"a garden"	akadĩmiro	"little garden"
ẽnugẽni	"a stranger"	akatabi	"little branch"

Base your answers to the following questions on only these forms. Assume that all the words in the language follow the regularities shown here.

   a. Are nasal vowels in Luganda phonemic?

   Are they predictable?

   b. Is the phonemic representation of the morpheme meaning "garden" /dimiro/?

   c. What is the phonemic representation of the morpheme meaning "canoe"?

   d. Are [p] and [b] allophones of one phoneme?

   e. If /am/ represents a bound prefix morpheme in Luganda, can you conclude that [ãmdãno] is a possible phonetic form for a word in this language starting with this prefix?

f. Is there a phonological homorganic nasal rule in Luganda?

g. If the phonetic representation of the word meaning "little boy" is [akapoobe], give the phonemic and phonetic representations for "a boy."

Phonemic_____ Phonetic _____

h. Which of the following forms is the phonemic representation for the prefix meaning "a" or "an"?

(1) /en/   (2) /ẽn/   (3) /ẽm/   (4) /em/   (5) /eŋ/

i. What is the *phonetic* representation of the word meaning "a branch"?

j. What is the *phonemic* representation of the word meaning "little stranger"?

k. State the three phonological rules revealed by the Luganda data.

15. Here are some Japanese verb forms given in phonetic symbols rather than in the Japanese orthography. They represent two styles (informal and formal) of present-tense verbs. Morphemes are separated by +.

Gloss	Informal	Formal
"call"	yob + u	yob + imasu
"write"	kak + u	kak + imasu
"eat"	tabe + ru	tabe + masu
"see"	mi + ru	mi + masu
"leave"	de + ru	de + masu
"go out"	dekake + ru	dekake + masu
"die"	šin + u	šin + imasu
"close"	šime + ru	šime + masu
"swindle"	kata + ru	kata + masu
"wear"	ki + ru	ki + masu
"read"	yom + u	yom + imasu
"lend"	kas + u	kaš + imasu
"wait"	mats + u	mač + imasu
"press"	os + u	oš + imasu
"apply"	ate + ru	ate + masu
"drop"	otos + u	otoš + imasu
"have"	mots + u	moč + imasu
"win"	kats + u	kač + imasu
"steal a lover"	neto + ru	neto + masu

a. List each of the Japanese verb roots in their phonemic representations.

b. Formulate the rule that accounts for the different phonetic forms of these verb roots.

c. There is more than one allomorph for the suffix designating formality and more than one for the suffix designating informality. List the allomorphs of each. Formulate the rule or rules for their distribution.

The Psychology of Language

The field of psycholinguistics, or the psychology of language, is concerned with discovering the psychological processes that make it possible for humans to acquire and use language.

Jean Berko Gleason and Nan Bernstein Ratner *Psycholinguistics* (1993)

CHAPTER

Language Acquisition

The acquisition of language "is doubtless the greatest intellectual feat any one of us is ever required to perform."

Leonard Bloomfield, *Language* (1933)

The capacity to learn language is deeply ingrained in us as a species, just as the capacity to walk, to grasp objects, to recognize faces. We don't find any serious differences in children growing up in congested urban slums, in isolated mountain villages, or in privileged suburban villas.

Dan Slobin, *The Human Language Series 2* (1994)

341

*E*very aspect of language is extremely complex. Yet very young children — before the age of five — already know most of the intricate system we have been calling the grammar of a language. Before they can add 2 + 2, children are conjoining sentences, asking questions, using appropriate pronouns, negating sentences, forming relative clauses, and using the syntactic, phonological, morphological, and semantic rules of the grammar.

A normal human being can go through life without learning to read or write. Millions of people in the world today do. These same people speak and understand a language, and they can discuss ideas as complex and abstract as literate speakers can. Learning to speak and understand a language, and learning to read and write, are different. Similarly, millions of humans never learn algebra or chemistry or how to use a computer. They must be taught these skills or systems, but they do not have to be taught to walk or to talk. In fact, "We are designed to walk. . . . That we are taught to walk is impossible. And pretty much the same is true of language. Nobody is taught language. In fact you can't prevent the child from learning it."[1]

The study of the grammars of human languages has revealed a great deal about language acquisition, about what a child does and does not do when learning a language. First, it is obvious that children do not learn a language by storing all the words and all the sentences in some giant mental dictionary. The list of words is finite, but no dictionary can hold all the sentences, which are infinite in number. Rather, they learn to construct and understand sentences, most of which they have never produced or heard before.

Children must therefore construct the rules that permit them to use their language creatively. No one teaches them these rules. Their parents are no more aware of the phonological, morphological, syntactic, and semantic rules than are the children. Even if you remember your early years, do you remember anyone telling you to form a sentence by adding a verb phrase to a noun phrase, or to add [s] or [z] to form plurals? Children seem to act like efficient linguists equipped with a perfect theory of language, and they use this theory to construct the grammar of the language they hear.

In the preceding chapters you saw something of the richness and complexity of human language (but only a bit). How do children acquire such an intricate system so quickly and effortlessly? Even more difficult, the child must figure out the rules of language from very "noisy" data. She hears sentence fragments, false starts, speech errors, and interruptions. No one tells the child "this is a grammatical utterance and this is not." Yet, somehow she is able to "recreate" the grammar of the language of her speech community based on the language she hears around her. How does the child accomplish this phenomenal task?

Mechanisms of Language Acquisition

There have been various proposals concerning the psychological mechanisms involved in acquiring a language. Early theories of language acquisition were heavily influenced by behaviorism, a school of psychology prevalent in the 1950s. As the name implies,

---

[1] N. Chomsky. 1994. *The Human Language Series 2.* G. Searchinger. New York: Equinox Films/Ways of Knowing, Inc.

behaviorism focused on people's behaviors, which are directly observable, rather than on the mental systems underlying these behaviors. Language was viewed as a kind of verbal behavior and it was proposed that children learn language through imitation, reinforcement, analogy, and similar processes.[2]

Do Children Learn through Imitation?

CHILD: My teacher holded the baby rabbits and we patted them.
ADULT: Did you say your teacher held the baby rabbits?
CHILD: Yes.
ADULT: What did you say she did?
CHILD: She holded the baby rabbits and we patted them.
ADULT: Did you say she held them tightly?
CHILD: No, she holded them loosely.

Courtney Cazden[3]

"Flintstones " reprinted by permission of Hanna-Barbera.

At first glance the question of how children acquire language doesn't seem to be such a difficult one to answer. Don't children just listen to what is said around them and imitate the speech they hear? **Imitation** is involved to some extent, of course, but the early words and sentences that children produce show that they are not simply imitating adult speech. Children do not hear words like *holded* or *tooths* or sentences such as *Cat*

---

[2] B. F. Skinner, one of the founders of behaviorist psychology, proposed a model of language acquisition in his book *Verbal Behavior* (1957). Two years later, in a devastating reply to Skinner, *Review of Verbal Behavior* (1959), Chomsky showed that language is a complex cognitive system that could not be acquired by behaviorist principles.

[3] C. Cazden. 1972. *Child Language and Education.* New York: Holt, Rinehart and Winston, p. 92.

stand up table or many of the other utterances they produce between the ages of two and three, such as the following:[4]

> a my pencil
> two foot
> what the boy hit?
> other one pants
> Mommy get it my ladder
> cowboy did fighting me

Even when children are trying to imitate what they hear, they are unable to produce sentences that they would not spontaneously produce.

ADULT:	He's going out.	CHILD:	He go out
ADULT:	That's an old-time train.	CHILD:	Old-time train.
ADULT:	Adam, say what I say		
	Where can I put them?	CHILD:	Where I can put them?

Imitation cannot account for another important phenomenon: children who are unable to speak for neurological or physiological reasons learn the language spoken to them and understand it. When they overcome their speech impairment, they immediately use the language for speaking.

Do Children Learn through Reinforcement?

CHILD:	Nobody don't like me.
MOTHER:	No, say "Nobody likes me."
CHILD:	Nobody don't like me.
	(dialogue repeated eight times)
MOTHER:	Now, listen carefully, say *"Nobody likes me."*
CHILD:	Oh, nobody don't likes me.

Another proposal is that children learn to produce correct (grammatical) sentences because they are positively reinforced when they say something right, and negatively reinforced when they say something wrong. One kind of reinforcement is correction of "bad grammar" and reward for "good grammar." Roger Brown and his colleagues at Harvard University studied parent-child interactions. They report that reinforcement seldom occurs, and when it does, it is usually incorrect pronunciation or incorrect reporting of facts that is corrected. They note, for example, that the ungrammatical sentence "Her curl my hair" was not corrected because Eve's mother was in fact curling her hair. However, when Eve uttered the syntactically correct sentence "Walt Disney comes on Tuesday" she was corrected because the television program was shown on Wednesday. They conclude that it is "truth value rather than syntactic well-formedness that

---

[4] Unless otherwise noted, the examples of child language in this chapter were taken from CHILDES (Child Language Data Exchange System), a computerized database of the spontaneous speech of children as they acquire many different languages. B. MacWhinney and C. Snow. 1985. "The Child Language Data Exchange System," *Journal of Child Language* 12:271–96.

chiefly governs explicit verbal reinforcement by parents — which renders mildly paradoxical the fact that the usual product of such a training schedule is an adult whose speech is highly grammatical but not notably truthful."[5]

Even if syntactic correction occurred more often than it actually does, it would not explain how or what children learn from such adult responses, or how children discover and construct the correct rules. In fact, attempts to correct a child's language are doomed to failure. Children do not know what they are doing wrong and are unable to make corrections even when they are pointed out, as shown by the preceding example and the following one:

CHILD: Want other one spoon, Daddy.
FATHER: You mean, you want *the other spoon*.
CHILD: Yes, I want other one spoon, please, Daddy.
FATHER: Can you say "the other spoon"?
CHILD: Other . . . one . . . spoon.
FATHER: Say . . . "other."
CHILD: Other.
FATHER: Spoon.
CHILD: Spoon.
FATHER: Other . . . spoon.
CHILD: Other . . . spoon. Now give me other one spoon?

Such conversations between parents and children do not occur often. This conversation was between a linguist studying child language and his child. Mothers and fathers are usually delighted that their young children are talking and consider every utterance a gem. The "mistakes" children make are cute and repeated endlessly to anyone who will listen.

Do Children Learn Language through Analogy?

It has also been suggested that children put words together to form phrases and sentences by **analogy**, by hearing a sentence and using it as a sample to form other sentences. But this doesn't work, as Lila Gleitman points out:

> So suppose the child has heard the sentence "I painted a red barn." So now, by analogy, the child can say "I painted a blue barn." That's exactly the kind of theory that we want. You hear a sample and you extend it to all of the new cases by similarity. . . . In addition to "I painted a red barn" you might also hear the sentence "I painted a barn red." So it looks as if you take those last two words and switch their order. . . . So now you want to extend this to the case of seeing, because you want to look at barns instead of paint them. So you have heard, "I saw a red barn." Now you try (by analogy) a . . . new sentence — "I saw a barn red." Something's gone wrong. This is an analogy, but the analogy didn't work. It's not a sentence of English.[6]

---

[5] Brown, R.O. 1973. *Early Syntactic Development.* Cambridge, MA: MIT Press, p. 330.

[6] *The Human Language Series 2.* 1994. By G. Searchinger. New York: Equinox Films/Ways of Knowing, Inc.

This problem arises constantly. Consider another example. The child hears the following pair of sentences:

The boy was sleeping.   Was the boy sleeping?

Based on pairs of sentences like this, he formulates a rule for forming questions, "move the auxiliary to the position preceding the subject." He then acquires the more complex relative clause construction:

The boy who is sleeping is dreaming about a new car.

He now wants to form a question. What does he do? If he forms a question on analogy to the simple yes-no question, he will move the first auxiliary *is* as follows.

*Is the boy who sleeping is dreaming about a new car?

Studies of spontaneous speech, as well as experiments, show that children never make mistakes of this sort. As discussed in chapter 4, sentences have structure, and the rules of grammar, such as the rule that moves the auxiliary, are sensitive to structure and not to linear order. Children seem to know about the structure dependency of rules at a very early age.

Recently, a computer model of language representation and acquisition called **connectionism** has been proposed that relies in part on behaviorist learning principles such as analogy and reinforcement. In the connectionist model no grammatical rules are stored anywhere. Linguistic knowledge, such as knowledge of the past tense, is represented by a set of neuronlike connections between different phonological forms, for example, between *play* and *played, dance* and *danced, drink* and *drank,* and so on. Repeated exposure to particular verb pairs in the input reinforces the connection between them, mimicking rule-like behavior. Based on similarities between words, the model can produce a past-tense form that it was not previously exposed to. On analogy to *dance-danced,* it will convert *prance* to *pranced;* on analogy to *drink-drank* it will convert *sink* to *sank.*

As a model of language acquisition, connectionism faces some serious challenges. The model relies on specific properties of the input data. However, investigation of the input that actual children receive shows that it is not consistent with the assumptions of this model. Past-tense learning cannot be based on phonological form alone but must also be sensitive to information in the lexicon. For example, the past tense of a verb derived from a noun is always regular even if an irregular form exists. When a fly ball is caught in a baseball game, we say the batter *flied out* not *flew out.* Similarly, when an irregular plural is part of a larger noun, it may be regularized. When we see several images of Walt Disney's famous rodent we describe them as Mickey Mouses, not Mickey Mice.

Do Children Learn through Structured Input?

Yet another suggestion is that children are able to learn language because adults speak to them in a special "simplified" language sometimes called **motherese**, or **child directed speech** (CDS) (more informally, **baby talk.**) This theory of acquisition places a lot of emphasis on the role of the environment in facilitating language acquisition.

In our culture adults do typically talk to young children in a special way. We tend to speak more slowly and more clearly, we exaggerate our intonation, and sentences are generally grammatical. However, motherese is not syntactically simpler. It contains a range of sentence types, including syntactically complex sentences such as questions: *Do you want your juice now?* Embedded sentences: *Mommy thinks you should sleep now.* Imperatives: *Pat the dog gently!* Negatives with tag questions: *We don't want to hurt him, do we?* Indeed, it is fortunate that motherese is not syntactically restricted. If it were, children might not have sufficient information to extract the rules of their language.

Although infants prefer to listen to motherese than normal adult speech, controlled studies show that motherese does not significantly affect the child's language development. In many cultures adults do not use a special register with children, and there are even communities in which adults hardly talk to babies at all. Children acquire language in much the same way, irrespective of these varying circumstances. Finally, adults seem to be the followers rather than the leaders in this enterprise. The child does not develop because he is exposed to ever more adultlike language. Rather, the adult adjusts his language to the child's increasing linguistic sophistication.

The exaggerated intonation and other properties of motherese may be useful for getting a child's attention and holding it, but it is not a driving force behind language development.

Analogy, imitation, and reinforcement cannot account for language development because they are based on the (implicit or explicit) assumption that what the child acquires is a set of sentences or forms rather than a set of grammatical rules. Theories that assume that acquisition depends on a specially structured input also place too much emphasis on the environment rather than on the grammar-making abilities of the child. These proposals do not explain the creativity that children show in acquiring language, why they go through stages, or why they make some kinds of "errors" but not others.

Children Construct Grammars

> Language learning is not really something that the child does; it is something that happens to the child placed in an appropriate environment, much as the child's body grows and matures in a predetermined way when provided with appropriate nutrition and environmental stimulation.
>
> Noam Chomsky[7]

Language acquisition is a creative process. Children are not given explicit information about the rules, by either instruction or correction. They must somehow extract the rules of the grammar from the language they hear around them, and their linguistic environment does not need to be special in any way for them to do this. Observations of children acquiring different languages under different cultural and social circumstances

---

[7] N. Chomsky. 1988. *Language and the Problem of Knowledge: The Managua Lectures.* Cambridge, MA: MIT Press.

reveal that the developmental stages are similar, possibly universal. Even deaf children of deaf signing parents go through stages in their signing development that parallel those of children acquiring spoken languages. These factors lead many linguists to believe that children are equipped with an innate template or blueprint for language — **Universal Grammar** (UG) — and this blueprint aids the child in the task of constructing a grammar for her language. This is referred to as the **innateness hypothesis.**

The Innateness Hypothesis

How comes it that human beings, whose contacts with the world are brief and personal and limited, are able to know as much as they do know?

Bertrand Russell[8]

"WHAT'S THE BIG SURPRISE? ALL THE LATEST THEORIES OF LINGUISTICS SAY WE'RE BORN WITH THE INNATE CAPACITY FOR GENERATING SENTENCES."

Copyright © S. Harris.

The innateness hypothesis receives its strongest support from the observation that the grammar a person ends up with is vastly underdetermined by linguistic experience. In other words, we end up knowing far more about language than is exemplified in the language we hear around us. This argument for the innateness of UG is called the **poverty of the stimulus.**

Although children hear many utterances, the language they hear is incomplete, noisy, and unstructured. We said earlier that child directed speech is largely well formed, but children are also exposed to adult-adult interactions. These utterances include slips of the tongue, false starts, ungrammatical and incomplete sentences, and no information as to which utterances are well formed. Most important, children come to know aspects

---

[8] B. Russell. 1948. *Human Knowledge: Its Scope and Limits.* New York: Simon and Schuster.

of the grammar about which they receive *no* information. In this sense, the data they are exposed to is **impoverished.** It is less than what is necessary to account for the richness and complexity of the grammar they attain.

For example, we noted that the rules children construct are **structure dependent.** Children do not produce questions by moving the "first" auxiliary as in (1). Instead, they correctly invert the auxiliary of the main clause, as in (2). [We use _____ to mark the position from which a constituent moves.]

1. *Is the boy who _____ sleeping is dreaming of a new car.
2. Is the boy who is sleeping _____ dreaming of a new car.

To come up with a rule that moves the auxiliary of the main clause rather than the first auxiliary, the child must know something about the structure of the sentence.

Children are not told about structure dependency. They are not told about constituent structure. The input they get is a sequence of sounds, not a set of phrase structure trees. No amount of imitation, reinforcement, analogy, or structured input will lead the child to formulate a phrase structure tree or a principle of structure dependency. Yet, children do create phrase structures, and the rules they acquire are sensitive to this structure.

The knowledge that children and adults have of abstract principles (principles not identified in the input) can be shown in countless ways. The rules for formation of *wh* questions provide another illustration.

Statement	**Question**
<u>Jack</u> went up the hill.	<u>Who</u> went up the hill?
<u>Jack and Jill</u> went up the hill.	<u>Who</u> went up the hill?
Jack and <u>Jill</u> went home.	Jack and <u>who</u> went home?
Jill ate <u>bagels and lox</u>.	Jill ate <u>what</u>?
Jill ate cookies and <u>ice cream</u>.	Jill ate cookies and <u>what</u>?

To ask a question the child learns to replace the noun phrase (NP) *Jack, Jill, ice cream,* or *school,* or the coordinate NPs *Jack and Jill* or *bagels and lox* with the appropriate *wh* question word, *who* or *what* or *where.*

The *wh* phrase can replace any subject or object NP. But in coordinate structures, the *wh* phrase must stay in the original NP position. It can't be moved, as the following sentences show.

*Who did Jack and _____ go up the hill?
*What did Jill eat bagels and _____?

These sentences are ungrammatical, yet the following are acceptable:

Statement	**Question**
Jill ate bagels with lox.	What did Jill eat bagels with _____?
Jack went up the hill with Jill.	Who did Jack go up the hill with _____?

What accounts for the difference between the "and" questions and the "with" questions? *Bagels and lox* is a coordinate NP, that is, two NPs conjoined with *and* (NP and

NP). But *bagels with lox* is an NP composed of an NP followed by a prepositional phrase (NP + PP), as shown by the following diagrams.

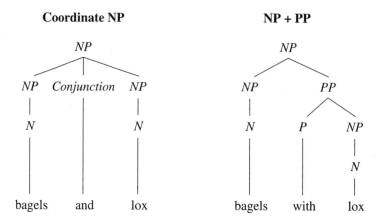

Coordinate NP

NP + PP

In all languages that linguists have investigated, a coordinate structure constraint is part of the grammar. It prohibits the movement of a *wh* phrase out of a coordinate structure. Children do make errors in their early *wh* questions, but they never produce sentences that violate the coordinate structure constraint like the starred ones above . No one has told them that these sentences are impossible. No one corrects them because children never utter them to begin with. How do children know that *wh* phrases are frozen inside a coordinate structure? According to the innateness hypothesis, children come "prewired" with knowledge of Universal Grammar, including structure dependency and the coordinate structure constraint, among many other principles.

Of course the child must also learn many aspects of grammar from the specific linguistic environment. For example, English-speaking children learn that the subject comes first and that the verb precedes the object inside the VP. More technically, English is an SVO language. Japanese children acquire an SOV language. They learn that the object precedes the verb. Japanese children also learn that to form a yes-no question, the morpheme *-ka* is suffixed to a verb stem. In Japanese, sentence constituents are not rearranged. English-speaking children must learn that yes-no questions are formed by moving constituents. In yes-no questions the auxiliary moves from its original position to the beginning of the sentence, as follows:

You will come home → Will you ____ come home?

English-speaking children must also learn that in *wh* questions the *wh* phrase moves as follows (with the additional complexity of inserting *do*):

You like who → Who do you like ____?

In Mandarin Chinese, as in many other Asian languages, speakers form questions by leaving the question word in its original position, as in the example below; Chinese children obviously learn the Chinese way of forming questions:

Ni xihuan shei
'You like who'

According to the innateness hypothesis, the child extracts from the linguistic environment those rules of grammar that are language specific, such as word order and movement rules. However, he does not need to learn universal principles like structure dependency and the coordinate structure constraint, or general rules of sentence formation such as the fact that heads of categories can take complements. They are part of the innate blueprint for language that children use to construct the grammar of their language. For example, the English-speaking child must learn that forming a question involves movement of an auxiliary. This rule takes time to acquire and children may initially form questions with uninverted auxiliaries as follows.

Where Mommy is going?
What you can do?

Nevertheless, children never make the mistake of moving the wrong auxiliary in a complex sentence or a *wh* phrase out of a coordinate structure.

The innateness hypothesis provides an answer to *the logical problem of language acquisition* posed by Chomsky: What accounts for the ease, rapidity, and uniformity of language acquisition in the face of impoverished data? The answer is that children acquire a complex grammar quickly and easily without any particular help beyond exposure to the language because they do not start from scratch. UG helps them to extract the rules of their language and to avoid many grammatical errors. Because the child constructs his grammar according to an innate blueprint, all children proceed through similar developmental stages as we will discuss in the next section.

The innateness hypothesis also predicts that all languages will conform to the principles of UG. We are still far from understanding the full nature of the principles of UG. Research on more and more languages provides a way to test principles like the coordinate structure constraint, that linguists propose are part of our genetic makeup for language. If we investigate a language in which posited UG principles are absent, we will have to correct our theory and substitute other principles, as scientists must do in any field. But there is little doubt that human languages conform to abstract universal principles, and that the human brain is specially equipped for acquisition of human language grammars.

Stages in Language Acquisition

... for I was no longer a speechless infant; but a speaking boy. This I remember; and have since observed how I learned to speak. It was not that my elders taught me words ... in any set method; but I ... did myself ... practice the sounds in my memory. ... And thus by constantly hearing words, as they occurred in various sentences ... I thereby gave utterance to my will.

St. Augustine *Confessions* (transl. F. J. Sheed, 1944), (circa 400 C.E.)

Children do not wake up one fine morning with a fully formed grammar in their heads. Relative to the complexity of the adult grammar that they eventually attain, the process of language acquisition is fast, but it is not instantaneous. From first words to virtual adult competence takes three to four years, during which time children pass through linguistic stages. They begin by babbling, they then acquire their first words, and in just a few months they begin to put words together into sentences.

Observations of children in different language areas of the world reveal that the stages are similar, possibly universal. Some of the stages last for a short time; others remain longer. Some stages may overlap for a short period, though the transition between stages is often sudden.

The earliest studies of child language acquisition come from diaries kept by parents. More recent studies include the use of tape recordings, videotapes, and controlled experiments. Linguists record the spontaneous utterances of children and purposefully elicit other utterances to study the child's production and comprehension. Researchers have also invented ingenious techniques for investigating the linguistic abilities of infants, who are not yet speaking.

What the studies show is that child language is not just a degenerate form of adult language. At each stage of development the child's language conforms to a set of rules, a grammar. Although child grammars and adult grammars differ in certain respects, they also share many formal properties. Like adults, children have grammatical categories such as NP and VP, rules for building phrase structures and for moving constituents, as well as phonological rules, morphological rules, and semantic rules, and they adhere to universal principles such as structure dependency.

As we will illustrate, children's early utterances may not completely resemble comparable adult sentences. This is because the words and sentences the child produces conform to the phonology, morphology, and syntax that he has developed to that point. This may be why children do not respond to correction. *Nobody don't like me* and *want 'nother one spoon, daddy* may contain errors from the perspective of the adult grammar, but they are not errors from the child's point of view. They reflect his current grammar. Indeed, the so-called errors that children make provide us with a window into their grammar.

The Perception and Production of Speech Sounds

> An infant crying in the night:
> An infant crying for the light:
> And with no language but a cry.
>
> Alfred Lord Tennyson, "In Memoriam H.H.S."

The old idea that the neonate is born with a mind that is like a blank slate is belied by a wealth of evidence that infants are highly sensitive to some subtle distinctions in their environment and not to others. That is, the mind appears to be attuned at birth to receive certain kinds of information.

Experiments have shown that infants will increase their sucking rate when stimuli (visual or auditory) presented to them are varied, but will decrease the sucking rate when the same stimuli are presented repeatedly. Infants will respond to visual depth and distance distinctions, to differences between rigid and flexible physical properties of objects, and to human faces rather than to other visual stimuli.

Similarly, newborns respond to phonetic contrasts found in human languages even when these differences are not phonemic in the language spoken in the baby's home. A baby hearing a human voice over a loudspeaker saying [pa] [pa] [pa] will slowly decrease her rate of sucking. If the sound changes to [ba] or even [pʰa], the sucking rate increases dramatically. Controlled experiments show that adults find it difficult to differentiate between the allophones of one phoneme, but for infants it comes naturally. Japanese infants can distinguish between [r] and [l] while their parents cannot; babies can hear the difference between aspirated and unaspirated stops even if students in an introductory linguistics course cannot. Babies can discriminate between sounds that are phonemic in other languages and nonexistent in the language of their parents. For example, in Hindi, there is a phonemic contrast between a retroflex [ʈ] and the alveolar [t]. To English-speaking adults, these sound the same; to their infants, they do not.

Babies will not react, however, to distinctions that never correspond to phonemic contrasts in any human language, such as sounds spoken more or less loudly or sounds that lie between two phonemes. Furthermore, a vowel that we perceive as [i] or [u] or [a] is a different physical sound when produced by a male, female, or child, but babies ignore the nonlinguistic aspects of the speech signal just as we do. An [i] is an [i] is an [i] to an infant even if the physical sound is different. They do not increase their sucking rate when, after hearing many [i]s spoken by a male, they then hear an [i] spoken by a female. Yet, computational linguists still have difficulty programming computers to recognize these different signals as the "same."

An infant could not have learned to perceive linguistically relevant distinctions and ignore others, such as sex of the speaker. Infants appear to be born with the ability to perceive just those sounds that are phonemic in some language. They can perceive voicing contrasts such as [pa] versus [ba], contrasts in place of articulation such as [da] versus [ga], and contrasts in manner of articulation such as [ra] versus [la], or [ra] versus [wa], among many others. This partially accounts for the fact that children can learn any human language to which they are exposed. Infants have the sensory and motor abilities to produce and perceive speech sounds. During the first years of life the infant's job is to uncover the sounds of this language. From around six months, they begin to lose the ability to discriminate between sounds that are not phonemic in their own language. Their linguistic environment molds their initial perceptions. Japanese infants can no longer hear the difference between [r] and [l], which do not contrast in Japanese, whereas babies in English-speaking homes retain this perception. They have begun to learn the sounds of the language of their parents. Before that, they appear to know the sounds of human language in general.

The shaping by the linguistic environment that we see in perception also occurs in the speech the infant is producing. At around six months, the infant begins to babble. The sounds produced in this period include many which do not occur in the language of the household. However, **babbling** is not linguistic chaos. The twelve most frequent consonants in the world's languages make up 95 percent of the consonants infants use in their babbling. There are linguistic constraints even during this very early stage. The early babbles consist mainly of repeated consonant-vowel sequences, like *mama, gaga,* and *dada.* Later babbles are more varied.

Gradually, the child's babbles come to include only those sounds and sound combinations that occur in the target language. Babbles begin to sound like words though they may not have any specific meaning attached to them. At this point adults can distinguish the babbles of an English-babbling infant from those of an infant babbling in Cantonese or Arabic. During the first year of life the infant's perceptions and productions are being fine-tuned to the language(s) of the surroundings.

Deaf infants produce babbling sounds that are different from those of hearing children. Babbling is related to auditory input and is linguistic in nature. Studies of vocal babbling of hearing children, and manual babbling of deaf children, support the view that babbling is a linguistic ability related to the kind of language input the child receives. These studies show that four to seven month old hearing infants exposed to spoken language produce a restricted set of phonetic forms. At the same age, deaf children exposed to sign language produce a restricted set of signs. In each case the forms are drawn from the set of possible sounds or possible gestures found in spoken and signed languages.

Babbling illustrates the readiness of the human mind to respond to linguistic cues from a very early stage. During the babbling stage, the intonation contours produced by hearing infants begin to resemble the intonation contours of sentences spoken by adults. The semantically different intonation contours are among the first linguistic contrasts that children perceive and produce. During this same period, the vocalizations produced by deaf babies are random and nonrepetitive. Similarly, the manual gestures produced by hearing babies differ greatly from those produced by deaf infants exposed to sign language. The hearing babies move their fingers and clench their fists randomly with little or no repetition of gestures. The deaf infants, however, use more than a dozen different hand motions repetitively, all of which are elements of American Sign Language, or the other sign languages used in deaf communities of other countries.

The generally accepted view is that humans are born with a predisposition to discover the units that serve to express linguistic meanings, and that at a genetically specified stage in neural development, the infant will begin to produce these units — sounds or gestures — depending on the language input the baby receives. This suggests that babbling is the earliest stage in language acquisition, in opposition to the earlier view that babbling was prelinguistic and merely neuromuscular in origin.

First Words

From this golden egg a man, Prajapati, was born. . . . A year having passed, he wanted to speak. He said bhur and the earth was created. He said bhuvar and the space of the air was created. He said suvar and the sky was created. That is why a child wants to speak after a year. . . . When Prajapati spoke for the first time, he uttered one or two syllables. That is why a child utters one or two syllables when he speaks for the first time.

Hindu Myth

Sometime after the age of one, children begin to use repeatedly the same string of sounds to mean the same thing. At this stage children realize that sounds are related to meanings. They have produced their first true words. This is an amazing feat. How do they discover where one word begins and another leaves off? Speech is a continuous stream broken only by breath pauses. Children are in the same fix that you might be in if you

tuned in a foreign language radio station. You wouldn't have the foggiest idea of what was being said, or what the words were. Remarkably, infants solve the problem in a relatively short time. The age of the child when this occurs varies, and has nothing to do with the child's intelligence (It is reported that Einstein did not start to speak until three or four.)

The child's first utterances differ from adult language. The following words of one child, J. P. at the age of 16 months,[9] illustrate the point:

[ʔaw]	"not," "no," "don't"	[s:]	"aerosol spray"
[bʌʔ]/[mʌʔ]	"up"	[sʲuː]	"shoe"
[da]	"dog"	[haj]	"hi"
[iʔo]/[siʔo]	"Cheerios"	[sr]	"shirt" "sweater"
[sa]	"sock"	[sæː]/[əsæː]	"what's that?" "hey, look!"
[aj]/[ʌj]	"light"	[ma]	"mommy"
[baw]/[daw]	"down"	[dæ]	"daddy"

J. P.'s mother reports that earlier he had used the words [bu] for "book," [ki] for "kitty," and [tsi] for "tree," but seemed to have lost them.

Most children go through a stage in which their utterances consist of only one word. This stage is the **holophrastic** stage (from *holo,* "complete" or "undivided," and *phrase,* "phrase" or "sentence") because these one-word utterances seem to convey a more complex message. For example, when J. P. says "down," he may be making a request to be put down, or he may be commenting on a toy that has fallen down from the shelf. When he says "cheerios" he may simply be naming the box of cereal in front of him, or he may be asking for some Cheerios. This suggests that children have a more complex mental representation than their language at this point allows them to express. The comprehension experiments we will discuss next confirm the hypothesis that children's grammatical competence is ahead of their productive abilities.

---

[9] We give special thanks to John Peregrine Munro for providing us with such rich data, and to Drs. Pamela and Allen Munro, J. P.'s parents, for their painstaking efforts in recording these data.

The Development of Grammar

Children are neurologically prepared to acquire all aspects of grammar, from phonetics to pragmatics. This section presents evidence and illustrations of the breadth of Universal Grammar, and the innateness of the several components of grammar discussed in preceding chapters.

Acquisition of Phonology

In terms of his phonology, J. P. is like most children at this stage. His first words are generally monosyllabic with a CV (consonant-vowel) form. The vowel part may be a diphthong, depending on the language being acquired. His phonemic or phonetic inventory — at this stage they are equivalent — is much smaller than is found in the adult language. The linguist Roman Jakobson suggested that children first acquire the small set of sounds common to all languages of the world, no matter what language they hear, and in later stages a child acquires the less common sounds of his own language. For example, most languages have the sounds [p] and [s], but [θ] is a rare sound. J. P.'s sound system was as Jakobson's theory predicted. His phonological inventory at an early stage included the consonants [b, m, d, k], which are frequently occurring sounds in the world's languages.

"Baby Blues" copyright © 1997 Baby Blues Partnership. Reprinted with special permission of King Features Syndicate, Inc.

In general the order of acquisition of classes of sounds goes by manner of articulation: nasals are acquired first, then glides, stops, liquids, fricatives, and affricates. Natural classes characterized by place of articulation features also appear in children's utterances according to an ordered series: labials, velars, alveolars, and palatals. It is not surprising that *mama* is an early word for many children.

In early language, children may not make a linguistic distinction between voiced and voiceless consonants, although they can perceive the difference. If the first year is devoted to figuring out the phonetic inventory of the target language, the second year involves learning how these sounds are used in the phonology of the language, especially which contrasts are phonemic. When they first begin to contrast one set — that is, when they learn that /p/ and /b/ are distinct phonemes — they also begin to distinguish between

/t/ and /d/, /s/ and /z/, and all the other voiceless-voiced phonemic pairs. As we would expect, the generalizations refer to natural classes of speech sounds.

Controlled experiments show that children at this stage can perceive or comprehend many more phonological contrasts than they can produce. The same child who says [waebɪt] instead of "rabbit," and who does not seem to distinguish [w] and [r], will not make mistakes on a picture identification task in which she must point to either a ring or a wing. In addition, children sometimes produce a sound in a way that makes it indiscernible to adult observers. Acoustic analyses of children's utterances show that the child's pronunciation of *wing* and *ring* are physically different sounds, though they may seem the same to the adult ear. As a further example, a spectrographic analysis of *ephant,* "elephant," produced by a three-year-old child clearly showed an [l] in the representation of the word even though the adult experimenter could not hear it.[10]

Many anecdotal reports also show the disparity between the child's production and perception at this stage. An example is the exchange between the linguist Neil Smith and his two-year-old son Amahl. (At this age Amahl's pronunciation of "mouth" is [maws].)

NS: What does [maws] mean?
A: Like a cat.
NS: Yes, what else?
A: Nothing else.
NS: It's part of your head.
A: [fascinated]
NS: [touching A's mouth] What's this?
A: [maws]

According to Smith, it took Amahl a few seconds to realize his word for "mouse" and for "mouth" were the same. It is not that Amahl and other children do not hear the correct adult pronunciation. They do, but they are unable in these early years to produce it themselves. Another linguist's child (yes, linguists love to experiment on their own children) pronounced the word *light* as *yight* [jajt] but would become very angry if someone said to him, "Oh, you want me to turn on the yight." "No no," he would reply, "not yight — yight!"

Therefore, even at this stage, it is not possible to determine the extent of the grammar of the child — in this case, the phonology — simply by observing speech production. It is sometimes necessary to use various experimental and instrumental techniques to tap the child's competence.

A child's first words show many substitutions of one feature for another or one phoneme for another. In the preceding examples, *mouth* [mawθ] is pronounced *mouse* [maws], with the alveolar fricative [s] replacing the less common interdental fricative [θ]; *light* [lajt] is pronounced *yight* [jajt], with the glide [j] replacing the liquid [l]; and *rabbit* is pronounced *wabbit,* with the glide [w] replacing the liquid [r]. Glides are acquired earlier than liquids, and hence substituted for them. These substitutions are

---

[10] K. Zuraw and T. Masilon. 1996. *Weak Syllable Deletion:: An Articulatory Phonological Account.* Unpublished UCLA manuscript.

simplifications of the adult pronunciation. They make articulation easier until the child achieves greater articulatory control.

Children's early pronunciations are not haphazard, however. The phonological substitutions are rule governed. The following is an abridged lexicon for another child, Michael, between the ages of 18 and 21 months:[11]

[pun]	"spoon"	[majtl]	"Michael"
[peyn]	"plane"	[dajtər]	"diaper"
[tɪs]	"kiss"	[pati]	"Papi"
[taw]	"cow"	[mani]	"Mommy"
[tin]	"clean"	[bərt]	"Bert"
[polər]	"stroller"	[bərt]	"(big) Bird"

Michael systematically substituted the alveolar stop [t] for the velar stop [k] as in his words for "cow," "clean," "kiss," and his own name. He also replaced labial [p] with [t] when it occurred in the middle of a word, as in his words for "Papi" and "diaper." He reduced consonant clusters in "spoon," "plane," and "stroller," and he devoiced final stops as in "Big Bird." In devoicing the final [d] in "bird," he created an ambiguous form [bərt] referring both to Bert and Big Bird. No wonder only parents understand their children's first words!

Michael's substitutions are typical of the phonological rules that operate in the very early stages of acquisition. Other common rules are reduplication — "bottle" becomes [baba], "water" becomes [wawa]; and the dropping of a final consonants — "bed" becomes [be], "cake" becomes [ke]. These two rules show that the child prefers a simple CV syllable.

Of the many phonological rules that children create, no one child will necessarily use all rules. Early phonological rules generally reflect natural phonological processes that also occur in adult languages. For example, various adult languages have a rule of syllable-final consonant devoicing (German does, English does not). Children do not create bizarre or whimsical rules. Their rules conform to the possibilities made available by UG.

THE ACQUISITION OF WORD MEANING

Suddenly I felt a misty consciousness as of something forgotten — a thrill of returning thought; and somehow the mystery of language was revealed to me. . . . Everything had a name, and each name gave birth to a new thought.

Helen Keller[12]

In addition to phonological regularities, the child's early vocabulary provides insight into how children use words and construct word meaning. For J. P. the word *up* was

---

[11] Data from Michael Jaeggli.

[12] H. Keller quoted in J. P. Lash. 1980. *Helen and Teacher: The Story of Helen Keller and Anne Sullivan Macy.* New York: Delacorte press.

originally used only to mean "Get me up!" when he was either on the floor or in his high chair, but later he used it to mean "Get up!" to his mother as well. J. P. used his word for *sock* not only for socks but also for other undergarments that are put on over the feet, such as undershorts. This illustrates how a child may extend the meaning of a word from a particular referent to encompass a larger class.

When J. P. began to use words, the stimulus had to be visible, but that requirement did not last very long. He first used "dog" only when pointing to a real dog, but later he used the word for pictures of dogs in various books. A new word that entered J. P.'s vocabulary at seventeen months was "uh-oh," which he would say after he had an accident like spilling juice, or when he deliberately poured his yogurt over the side of his high chair. His use of this word shows his developing use of language for social purposes. At this time he added two new words meaning "no," [do:] and [no], which he used when anyone attempted to take something from him that he wanted, or tried to make him do something he did not want to do. He used them either with the imperative meaning of "Don't do that!" or with the assertive meaning of "I don't want to do that." Even at this early stage, J. P. was using words to convey a variety of ideas and feelings, as well as his social awareness.

But how do children learn the meanings of words? Most people do not see this aspect of acquisition as posing a great problem. The intuitive view is that children look at an object, the mother says a word, and the child connects the sounds with the object. However, this is not as easy as it seems, as the following quote demonstrates:

> A child who observes a cat sitting on a mat also observes . . . a mat supporting a cat, a mat under a cat, a floor supporting a mat and a cat, and so on. If the adult now says "The cat is on the mat" even while pointing to the cat on the mat, how is the child to choose among these interpretations of the situation?[13]

Even if the mother simply says "cat," and the child by accident associates the word with the animal on the mat, the child may interpret cat as "Cat," the name of a particular animal, or of an entire species. In other words, to learn a word for a class of objects such as "cat" or "dog," children have to figure out exactly what the word refers to. Upon hearing the word *dog* in the presence of a dog, how does the child know that "dog" can refer to any four-legged, hairy, barking creature. Should it include poodles, tiny Yorkshire terriers, bulldogs, and great Danes, all of which look rather different from one another? What about cows, lambs, and other four-legged mammals? Why are they not "dogs"? The important and very difficult question is: What are the relevant features that define the class of objects we call *dog* and how does a child acquire knowledge of them? Even if a child succeeds in associating a word with an object, nobody provides explicit information about how to extend the use of that word to other objects to which that word refers.

It is not surprising, therefore, that children often overextend a word's meaning, as J. P. did with the word *sock*. A child may learn a word such as *papa* or *daddy,* which she

---

[13] L. R. Gleitman and E. Wanner. 1982. *Language Acquisition. The State of the State of the Art.* Cambridge, England: Cambridge University Press, p. 10.

first uses only for her own father and then extend its meaning to apply to all men, just as she may use the word *dog* to mean any four-legged creature. After the child has acquired her first seventy-five to one hundred words, the overextended meanings start to narrow until they correspond to those of the other speakers of the language. How this occurs is still not entirely understood.

The mystery surrounding the acquisition of word meanings has intrigued philosophers and psychologists as well as linguists. We know that all children view the world in a similar fashion and apply the same general principles to help them determine a word's meaning. For example, overextensions are usually based on physical attributes such as size, shape, and texture. *Ball* may refer to all round things, *bunny* to all furry things, and so on. However, children will not make overextensions based on color. In experiments, children will group objects by shape and give them a name, but they will not assign a name to a group of red objects.

If an experimenter points to an object and uses a nonsense word like *blick* to a child, saying *that's a blick,* the child will interpret the word to refer to the whole object, not one of its parts or attributes. Given the poverty of stimulus for word learning, principles like the "form over color principle" and the "whole object principle" help the child organize experience in ways that facilitate word learning. Without such principles, it is doubtful that children could learn words as quickly as they do. Children learn approximately 14 words a day for the first six years of their lives. That averages to about 5,000 words per year. How many students know 10,000 words of a foreign language after two years of study?

Furthermore, as children are learning the meaning of words, they are also developing the syntax of the language and the syntactic categories. Syntax can help the child acquire meaning. A child will interpret a word like *blicking* to be a verb if the word is used while the investigator points to a picture of a person or thing performing an action, and will interpret the word *blick* to be a noun if used in the expression *a blick* or *the blick* while looking at the same picture. For example, suppose a child is shown a picture of some funny animal jumping up and down and hears either *See the blicking* or *See the blick.* Later, when asked to show "blicking," the child will jump up and down, but if asked to show a blick, will point to the funny animal. This process is called **syntactic bootstrapping.** Children use their knowledge of syntax to learn the syntactic category of the word: If the word is a verb it has a meaning referring to an action, if the word is a noun it refers to an object of some kind.

THE ACQUISITION OF MORPHOLOGY

The child's acquisition of morphology provides the clearest evidence of rule learning. Children's errors in morphology reveal that the child acquires the regular rules of the grammar and overgeneralizes them. This **overgeneralization** manifests itself when children treat irregular verbs and nouns as if they were regular. We have probably all heard children say *bringed, goed, drawed,* and *runned,* or *foots, mouses, sheeps,* and *childs.*

These mistakes tell us more about how children learn language than the correct forms they use. The child cannot be imitating; children use such forms in families where the parents never utter such "bad English." In fact, children can go through three phases in the acquisition of an irregular form:

"Baby Blues" copyright © 1997 Baby Blues Partnership. Reprinted with special permission of King Features Syndicate, Inc.

Phase 1	**Phase 2**	**Phase 3**
broke	breaked	broke
brought	bringed	brought

In phase 1 the child uses the correct term such as *brought* or *broke*. At this point the child's grammar does not relate the form *brought* to *bring*, or *broke* to *break*. The words are treated as separate lexical entries. Phase 2 is crucial. This is when the child constructs a rule for forming the past tense and attaches the regular past-tense morpheme to all verbs — *play, hug, help,* as well as *break* and *bring*. Children look for general patterns, for systematic occurrences. What they do not know at phase 2 is that there are exceptions to the rule. Now their language is more regular than the adult language. During phase 3 the child learns that there are exceptions to the rule, and then once again uses *brought* and *broke,* with the difference being that these irregular forms will be related to the root forms.

The child's morphological rules emerge quite early. In a classic study,[14] preschool children and children in the first, second, and third grades were shown a drawing of a nonsense animal like the funny creature below. Each "animal" was given a nonsense name. The experimenter would then say to the child, pointing to the picture, "This is a wug."

Then the experimenter would show the child a picture of two of the animals and say, "Now here is another one. There are two of them. There are two _____?"

The child's task was to give the plural form, "wugs" [wʌgz]. Another little make-believe animal was called a "bik," and when the child was shown two biks, he or she again was to say the plural form [bɪks]. The children applied the regular plural formation rule

---

[14] J. Berko. 1958. "The Child's Learning of English Morphology," *Word* 14:150–77.

to words they had never heard. Their ability to add [z] when the animal's name ended with a voiced sound, and [s] when there was a final voiceless consonant, showed that the children were using rules based on an understanding of natural classes of phonological segments, and not simply imitating words they had previously heard.

More recently, studies of children acquiring languages with more inflectional morphology than English reveal that they learn agreement and case morphology at a very early age. For example, Italian verbs must be inflected for number and person to agree with the subject. This is similar to the English agreement rule "add *s* to the verb" for third-person, singular subjects — *He giggles a lot* but *We giggle a lot* — except that in Italian there are more verb forms that must be acquired. Italian-speaking children between the ages of 1;10 (one year, ten months) and 2;4 correctly inflect the verb, as the following utterances of Italian children show:[15]

Tu legg**i** il libro	"You (2nd-person singular) read the book."
Io vad**o** fuori	"I go (1st-p. sg.) outside."
Dorme miao dorme	"Sleeps (3rd-p. sg.) cat sleeps."
Legg**iamo** il libro	"(We) read (1st-p. plural) the book."

Children acquiring other richly inflected languages such as Spanish, German, Catalan, and Swahili quickly acquire agreement morphology. It is rare for them to make agreement errors just as it is rare for an English-speaking child to say "I goes."

In these languages there is also gender and number agreement between the head noun and the article and adjectives inside the noun phrase. Children as young as two years old respect these agreement requirements, as shown by the following Italian examples.

E mia gonn**a**.	"(It) is my (feminine singular) skirt."
Questo mi**o** bimbo.	"This my (masculine singular) baby."
Guarda **la** mela piccolin**a**.	"Look at the little (fem. sg.) apple."
Guarda **il** topo piccolin**o**.	"Look at the little (masc. sg.) mouse."

Many languages have case morphology where nouns have different forms depending on their grammatical function: subject, object, possessor, and so on. Studies show that children acquiring Russian and German, two languages with extensive case systems, acquire case morphology at a very early age.

Children also show knowledge of the derivational rules of their language and use these rules to create novel words. In English, for example, we can derive verbs from nouns. From the noun *microwave* we now have a verb *to microwave;* from the noun *e(lectronic) mail* we derived the verb *to e-mail*. Children acquire this derivational rule early and use it often since there are lots of gaps in their verb vocabulary.

Child Utterance	**Adult Translation**
You have to scale it.	"You have to weigh it."
I broomed it up.	"I swept it up."
He's keying the door.	"He's opening the door (with a key).

---

[15] The data in examples were collected by M. Moneglia and E. Cresti and reported in N. Hyams. 1986. *Language Acquisition and the Theory of Parameters.* Dordrecht, the Netherlands: Reidel Publishers.

These novel forms provide further evidence that language acquisition is a creative process and that children's utterances reflect their internal grammars, which include both derivational and inflectional rules.

THE ACQUISITION OF SYNTAX

When children are still in the holophrastic stage, adults listening to the one-word utterances often feel that the child is trying to convey a more complex message. Indeed, new experimental techniques show that at that stage (and even earlier) children have knowledge of some syntactic rules. In these experiments the infant sits on his mother's lap and hears a sentence over a speaker while seeing two video displays depicting different actions, one of which corresponds to the sentence. Infants tend to look longer at the video that matches the sentence they hear. This methodology allows researchers to tap the linguistic knowledge of children who are only using single words or who are not talking at all. Results show that children as young as seventeen months can understand the difference between sentences such as "Ernie is tickling Bert" and "Bert is tickling Ernie." Because these sentences have all the same words, the child cannot be relying on the words alone to understand the meanings. He must also understand the word order rules and how they determine the grammatical relations of subject and object. Results such as these strongly suggest that children's syntactic competence is ahead of their productive abilities, which is also how their phonology develops.

"Doonesbury" copyright © 1982 and 1984 G. B. Trudeau.

Around the time of their second birthday, children begin to put words together. At first these utterances appear to be strings of two of the child's earlier holophrastic utterances, each word with its own single-pitch contour. Soon, they begin to form actual two-word sentences with clear syntactic and semantic relations. The intonation contour of the two words extends over the whole utterance rather than being separated by a pause between the two words. The following utterances illustrate the kinds of patterns that are found in children's utterances at this stage.

allgone sock	hi Mommy
byebye boat	allgone sticky
more wet	it ball
Katherine sock	dirty sock

These early utterances can express a variety of semantic and syntactic relations. For example, noun + noun sentences such as *Mommy sock* can express a subject + object relation in the situation when the mother is putting the sock on the child, or a possessive relation when the child is pointing to Mommy's sock. Two nouns can also be used to show a subject-locative relation, as in *sweater chair* to mean "The sweater is on the chair," or to show attribution as in *dirty sock.* Often children have a variety of modifiers such as *allgone, more,* and *bye bye.*

Since children mature at different rates and the age at which children start to produce words and put words together varies, chronological age is not a good measure of a child's language development. Instead, researchers use the child's **mean length of utterances** (MLU) to compare children's progress. MLU is the average length of the utterances the child is producing at a particular point. MLU is usually measured in terms of morphemes rather than words, so the words *boys, danced,* and *crying* are each two morphemes long. Children with the same MLU are likely to have similar grammars even though they are different ages.

In their earliest multiword utterances, children are inconsistent in their use of function words (grammatical morphemes) such as *to* and *the,* auxiliary verbs such as *can* and *is,* and verbal inflection. Many (though not all) utterances consist only of open-class or content words, while some or all of the function words, auxiliaries, and verbal inflection may be missing. During this stage children often sound as if they are reading a Western Union message, which is why such utterances are sometimes called **telegraphic speech:**[16]

Cat stand up table
What that?
He play little tune
Andrew want that
Cathy build house
No sit there

J. P.'s early sentences were similar. (The words in parentheses are missing from J. P.'s sentences):

---

[16] Before the days of e-mail and faxes, people would send telegrams to get a message to someone faster than by postal mail. They would be charged by the word, so to save money they would omit words that were not required to express the meaning. The words left out of sentences would be mainly grammatical morphemes like *the, is, are, of,* and *for.* A notable instance of this occurred when a New York reporter wired a colleague in Hollywood inquiring about the age of the movie star Cary Grant. "How old Cary Grant?" said the four-word message. The reply came back instantly: "Old Cary Grant fine, how you?"

Age in Months

25	[danʔ ɪ ʔ tˢɪʔ]	"don't eat (the) chip"
	[bʷaʔ tat]	"block (is on) top"
26	[mamis tu hæs]	"Mommy's two hands"
	[mo bʌs go]	"where bus go?"
	[dædi go]	"where Daddy go?"
27	[ʔaj gat tu dʲus]	"I got two (glasses of) juice"
	[do bajʔ mi]	"don't bite (kiss) me"
	[kʌdər sʌni ber]	"Sonny color(ed a) bear"
28	[ʔaj gat pwe dɪs]	"I('m) play(ing with) this"
	[mamis tak mɛns]	"Mommy talk(ed to the) men"

It takes many months before children use grammatical morphemes and auxiliary verbs consistently, which is defined to mean "in 90 percent of the contexts in which they are required." For example, the auxiliary *is* is required when the subject of the sentence is third-person singular and the verb has the progressive affix *-ing,* as in *Daddy ____ building a house.*

In an early study of children's morphological development, researchers examined the spontaneous utterances of three English-speaking children — Adam, Eve, and Sarah — over a period of years, noting their use of grammatical morphemes. They found that different morphemes reach the 90 percent criterion level at different times, and that the sequence was the same for all three children. The progressive morpheme *-ing,* as in *Me going,* was found to be among the earliest inflectional morphemes to be used consistently. The prepositions *in* and *on* were next, and then the regular plural ending, as in *two doggies* /tu dɔgiz/. The third-person singular marker (as in *Johnny comes*) and the possessive morpheme (as in *Daddy's hat*), which have the same phonological shape as the plural /s/, reached the 90 percent criterion six months to one year after the plural was acquired. This showed that the acquisition of these morphemes depends on the syntax, not the phonology. Eventually all the other inflections became stable features and the children's utterances sounded like those spoken by adults.

Though the children's utterances are described as telegraphic, the child does not deliberately leave out function words as would an adult sending a telegram. The sentences reflect the child's grammar at that particular stage of language development. Although these sentences may lack certain morphemes, they nevertheless appear to have hierarchical constituent structures and syntactic rules similar to those in the adult grammar. For example, children almost never violate the word order rules of their language. In languages with relatively fixed word order such as English, children use SVO order from the earliest stage. In languages with freer word order such as Russian, children typically use several (though not all) of the permissible orders.

In languages with freer word order, like Turkish and Russian, grammatical relations such as subject and object are generally marked by inflectional morphology, such as case markers. Children acquiring these languages quickly learn the morphological case markers. For example, two-year old Russian-speaking children mark subjects with nominative case, objects with accusative case, and indirect objects with dative case, with very few errors. Most errors arise with words that have an idiosyncratic or irregular case ending. This is reminiscent of the overgeneralization errors that children make with irregular verb morphology in English. Children take longer to acquire aspects of grammar that are not predictable by rule.

As we noted earlier, children acquiring Italian and other languages that mark subject agreement on the verb use correct agreement as soon as they produce multiword utterances. We repeat two of the examples here.

Tu leggi il libro.	"You read (2nd-p. sg.) the book."
Gira il pallone.	"Turns (3rd-p. sg.) the balloon."
	(The balloon turns.)

Various languages have been investigated and they all reveal that children rarely make subject-verb agreement errors.

Children have other agreement rules as well, such as the article-noun-adjective agreement found in Italian. There is nothing intrinsically masculine or feminine about the nouns that are marked for such grammatical gender. Children produce the correct forms based on the syntactic classification of these nouns and the agreement rules of the language.

The correct use of word order, case marking, and agreement rules shows that even though children may often omit function morphemes, they are aware of constituent structure and syntactic rules. Their utterances are not simply words randomly strung together. From a very early stage onwards, children have a grasp of the principles of phrase and sentence formation, and of the kinds of structure dependencies mentioned in chapter 4, as revealed by these constituent structure trees:

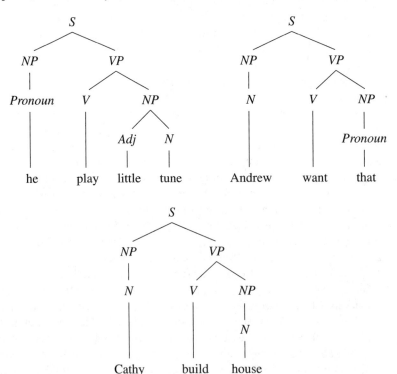

Sometime between the ages of 2;6 and 3;6 there is a virtual language explosion. At this point it is difficult to identify distinct stages because the child is undergoing so much development so rapidly. By the age of 3;0 most children are consistent in their use of function morphemes. Moreover, they have begun to produce and understand complex structures including coordinated sentences and embedded sentences of various kinds.

> He was stuck and I got him out.
> I want this doll because she's big.
> I know what to do.
> I like to play with something else.
> I think she's sick.
> Look at the train Ursula bought.
> I gon' make it like a rocket to blast off with.
> It's too early for us to eat.

THE ACQUISITION OF PRAGMATICS

In addition to acquiring the rules of grammar, children must learn the appropriate use of language in context, or pragmatics. The cartoon below is funny because of the inappropriateness of the interaction, showing that Zoe hasn't completely acquired the pragmatic "maxims of conversation" discussed in chapter 5.

"Baby Blues" copyright © 1997 Baby Blues Partnership. Distributed by King Features Syndicate, Inc. Reprinted with permission.

Context is needed to determine the reference of pronouns. As also discussed in chapter 5, a sentence like "Amazingly, he loves her" is uninterpretable unless both speaker and hearer understand who the pronouns *he* and *her* refer to. If the sentence were preceded by "I saw John and Mary kissing in the park," then it would be clear to the listener who the pronouns refer to. Children are not always sensitive to the needs of their interlocutors and they may fail to establish the referents for pronouns. It is not unusual for a three- or four-year-old (or even older children) to use pronouns "out of the blue," like the child who cries to his mother "He hit me" when mom has no idea who did the deed.

The speaker and listener form part of the context of an utterance. The meaning of *I* and *you* depends on who's talking and who's listening, and this changes from situation to situation. Younger children (around age two) have difficulty with the "shifting reference" of these pronouns. A typical error that children make at this age is to refer to themselves as "you," for example, saying "You want to take a walk" when he means "I want to take a walk."

Children also show a lack of pragmatic awareness by the way they sometimes use articles. Like pronouns, the interpretation of articles depends on context. The definite article (*the*) as in "the boy" can be used felicitously only when it is clear to speaker and hearer what boy is being discussed. In a discourse the indefinite article (*a/an*) must be used for the first mention of a new referent, the definite article (or pronoun) may be used in subsequent mentions, as illustrated below:

A boy walked into the class.
He was in the wrong room.
The teacher directed the boy to the right classroom.

Children do not always respect the pragmatic rules for articles. In experimental studies, three-year-olds are just as likely to use the definite article as the indefinite article for introducing a new referent. In other words, the child tends to assume that his listener knows who he is talking about without having established this in a linguistically appropriate way.

It may take a child several months or years to master those aspects of pragmatics that involve establishing the reference for function morphemes such as determiners and pronouns. Other aspects of pragmatics are acquired very early. Children in the holophrastic stage use their one-word utterances with different illocutionary force. The utterance "up" spoken by J. P. at sixteen months might be a simple statement such as "The teddy is up on the shelf," or a request "Pick me up."

The Development of Auxiliaries: A Case Study

We have seen in this chapter that language acquisition involves development in various components — the lexicon, phonology, morphology and syntax, as well as pragmatics. These different modules interact in complex ways to chart an overall course of language development.

As an example, let us take the case of the English auxiliaries. As noted earlier, children in the telegraphic stage do not typically use auxiliaries such as *can, will,* and or *do,* and they often omit *be* and *have* from their utterances. Several syntactic constructions in English depend on the presence of an auxiliary, the most central of which are questions and negative sentences. To negate a main verb requires the auxiliary *do* or a modal as in the following examples:

I don't like this movie
I won't see this movie.

An adult does not say "I not read this book."

Similarly, as discussed in chapter 4, English yes-no and *wh* questions are formed by moving an auxiliary to precede the subject, as in the following examples:

Can I leave now?
Where should John put the book?

Although the two-year-old does not have productive control of auxiliaries, she is able to form negative sentences and questions. During the telegraphic stage the child produces questions of the following sort:

Yes-No Questions	*Wh* **Questions**
I ride train?	What cowboy doing?
Mommy eggnog?	Where milk go?
Have some?	Where kitty?

These utterances have a rising intonation pattern typical of yes-no questions in English, but since there are no auxiliaries, there can be no auxiliary movement. In *wh* questions there is also no auxiliary but there is generally a *wh* phrase that has moved to the beginning of the sentence. English-speaking children do not produce sentences such as "Cowboy doing what?" in which the *wh* phrase remains in its deep structure position.

The two-year-old has an insufficient lexicon. The lack of auxiliaries means that she cannot use a particular syntactic device associated with question formation in English — auxiliary movement. However, she has the pragmatic knowledge of how to make a request or ask for information, and she has the appropriate prosody, which depends on knowledge of phonology and the syntactic structure of the question. She also knows the grammatical rule that requires a *wh* phrase to be in the Comp position. Many components of language must be in place to form an adultlike question.

In languages that do not require auxiliaries to form a question, children appear more adultlike. For example, in Dutch and Italian, it is the main verb that moves. Since many main verbs are acquired before auxiliaries, Dutch and Italian children in the telegraphic stage produce questions that follow the adult rule:[17]

Dutch

En wat doen ze daar?	And what do they there	(And what are they doing there?)
Wordt mama boos?	Becomes mama angry	(Is mommy angry?)
Weet je n kerk?	Know you a church	(Do you know a church?)
Valt ie hier om?	Falls in here	(Does it fall here?)

Italian

Cosa fanno questi bambini?[18]	What do these children	(What are these babies doing?)
Chando vene a mama?	When comes the mommy	(When is Mommy coming?)
Vola cici?	Flies birdie	(Is the birdie flying?)
Veni teno?	Comes train	(Is the train coming?)

---

[17] In the child language examples from languages other than English, we have included a word-by-word translation and in parentheses the intended meaning of the utterance.

[18] Italian data from J. Schaeffer. 1990. *The Syntax of the Subject in Child Language: Italian Compared to Dutch.* Unpublished master's thesis, State University of Utrecht.

The Dutch and Italian children show us there is nothing intrinsically difficult about syntactic movement rules. The delay that English-speaking children show in producing adultlike questions is mainly because auxiliaries are acquired later than main verbs and English is idiosyncratic in forming questions by moving only auxiliaries.

The lack of auxiliaries during the telegraphic stage also affects the formation of negative sentences. An English-speaking child's negative sentences look like the following:

He no bite you.
Wayne not eating it.
Kathryn not go over there.
You no bring choo-choo train.
That no fish school.

Because of the absence of auxiliaries, these utterances do not look very adultlike. However, children at this stage understand the pragmatic force of negation. The child who says "no!" when asked to take a nap knows exactly what he means.

As children acquire the auxiliaries, they generally use them correctly, that is, the auxiliary usually appears before the subject, but not always.

Yes-No Questions

Does the kitty stand up?
Can I have a piece of paper?
Will you help me?
We can go now?

Wh Questions

Which way they should go?
What can we ride in?
What will we eat?

The introduction of auxiliaries into the child's grammar also affects negative sentences. We now find correctly negated auxiliaries, though *be* is still missing in many cases.[19]

Paul can't have one.
Donna won't let go.
I don't want cover on it.
I am not a doctor.
It's not cold.
Paul not tired.
I not crying.

The child always places the negation in the correct position in relation to the auxiliary or *be*. Main verbs follow negation and *be* precedes negation. Children virtually never produce errors such as "Mommy dances not" or "I not am going."

---

[19] The fact that *be* seems to be omitted for a longer period than the other auxiliaries may be simply because it is easier for the researcher to note when there is a missing *be*.

In languages such as French and German, which are like Italian and Dutch in having a rule that moves inflected verbs, the verb shows up before the negative marker. French and German children respect this rule.

French

Veux pas lolo	"want not water"	(I don't want water)
Marche pas	"walks not"	(She doesn't walk)
Ça tourne pas	"that turns not"	(that doesn't turn)

German

Macht nich aua	"makes not ouch"	(It doesn't hurt.)
Brauche nich lala	"need not pacifier"	(I don't need a pacifier.)
Schmeckt auch nich	"tastes also not"	(It doesn't taste good either.)
Ich mach das nich	"I do that not"	(I don't/won't do that.)

Whether they are acquiring Dutch, German, Italian, French, or any other language, all children pass through a "telegraphic" stage, which is but one of many stages that a child goes through on the way to adult linguistic competence. Each of these stages corresponds to a system of rules that the child has internalized — a grammar — and includes a lexicon and pragmatic rules. Although the child's language may not look exactly like the adult language, it is rule-governed and not a haphazard approximation to the adult language.

Though the stages of language development are universal, they are shaped by the grammar of the particular adult language the child is acquiring. German, French, Italian, and English-speaking children all go through a telegraphic stage in which they do not use auxiliaries, but they form negative sentences and questions in different ways because the rules of question and negative formation are different in the respective adult languages. This tells us something essential about language acquisition: Children are sensitive to the rules of the adult language at the earliest stages of development. Just as their phonology is quickly fine-tuned to the adult language, so is their syntactic system.

The ability of children to form complex rules and construct grammars of the languages used around them in a relatively short time is indeed phenomenal. The similarity of the language acquisition stages across diverse peoples and languages shows that children are equipped with special abilities to know what generalizations to look for and what to ignore, and how to discover the regularities of language.

Children develop language the way they develop the ability to sit up, stand, crawl, or walk. They are not taught to do these things, but all normal children begin to do them at around the same age. Learning to walk or learning language is different from learning to read or to ride a bicycle. Many people never learn to read because they are not taught to do so, and there are large groups of people in many parts of the world that have no *written* language. However, they all have language.

Setting Parameters

There are aspects of syntax that children acquire very quickly, even while they are still in the telegraphic stage. Most of these early developments correspond to what we earlier referred to as the **parameters** of UG. One such parameter that we discussed in chapter 4, the Head Parameter, determines whether the head of a phrase comes before or after its complements, for example, whether the order of the VP is VO as in English or OV as in Japanese. Children produce the correct word order of their language in their earliest multiword utterances, and they understand word order even when they are in the one-word stage of production. According to the parameter model of UG, the child does not actually have to formulate a word order rule. Rather, he must choose between two already specified values: head first or head last? He determines the correct value based on the language he hears around him. The English-speaking child can quickly figure out that the head comes before its complements; a Japanese-speaking child can equally well determine that his language is head final.

Other parameters of UG involve the verb movement rules. In some languages the verb can move out of the VP to higher positions in the phrase structure tree. We saw this in the Dutch and Italian questions discussed in the last section. In other languages, such as English, verbs do not move (only auxiliaries do). The verb movement parameters provide the child with an option: my language does/does not allow verb movement. As we saw, Dutch- and Italian-speaking children quickly set the verb movement parameters to the "does allow" value, and so they form questions by moving the verb. English-speaking children never make the mistake of moving the verb — even when they don't yet have auxiliaries. In both cases, the children have set the parameter at the correct value for their language. Even after English-speaking children acquire the auxiliaries and the Aux movement rule, they never overgeneralize this movement to include verbs. This supports the hypothesis that the parameter is set early in development and cannot be undone. In this case as well, the child does not have to formulate a rule of verb movement; he does not have to learn when the verb moves and where it moves to. This is all given by UG. He simply has to decide whether verb movement is possible in his language.

The parameters of UG limit the grammatical options to a small well-defined set — is my language head first or head last, does my language have verb movement, and so on. Parameters greatly reduce the acquisition burden on the child and contribute to explaining the ease and rapidity of language acquisition.

The Acquisition of Signed Languages

Deaf children who are born to deaf signing parents are naturally exposed to sign language just as hearing children are naturally exposed to spoken language. Given the universal aspects of sign and spoken languages, it is not surprising that language development in these deaf children parallels the stages of spoken language acquisition. Deaf children babble, they then progress to single signs similar to the single words in the holophrastic stage, and finally they begin to combine signs. There is also a telegraphic stage in which the function signs may be omitted. Use of function signs becomes consistent at around the same age for deaf children as function words in spoken languages. The ages at which signing children go through each of these stages are comparable to the ages of children acquiring a spoken language.

Like the acquisition of spoken languages, the acquisition of signed languages involves the interaction of universal and language-particular components. In our discussion of the acquisition of questions in English, we saw that children easily acquire *wh* movement, which is governed by universal principles, but they show some delay in their use of Aux movement. This is because they first must learn the auxiliaries, which are specific to English.

In *wh* questions in ASL, the *wh* word can move or it can be left in its original position. Both of the following sentences are grammatical:

＿＿＿＿＿＿＿＿＿＿＿＿＿＿＿＿＿whq

WHO BILL SEE YESTERDAY?

＿＿＿＿＿＿＿＿＿＿＿＿＿＿＿＿＿whq

BILL SAW WHO YESTERDAY?

(NB: We follow the convention of writing the glosses for signs in uppercase letters.)

There is no Aux movement in ASL, but a question is accompanied by a facial expression with furrowed brows and the head tilted back. This is represented by the "whq" above the ASL glosses. This non-manual marker is part of the grammar of ASL. It is like the rising intonation we use when we ask questions in English and other spoken languages.

In one study of the acquisition of *wh* questions in ASL, researchers found that children easily learned the rules associated with the *wh* phrase. The children would sometimes move the *wh* phrase and sometimes leave it in place, as adult signers do. But the children often omitted the non-manual marker, which is not possible in the adult language. Like the English auxiliaries, the non-manual markers are specific to ASL and so they take longer to learn.

Sometimes the parallels between the acquisition of signed and spoken languages are surprising. Some of the grammatical morphemes in ASL are semantically transparent or **iconic,** that is, they look like what they mean. For example, the sign for the pronoun "I" involves the speaker pointing to his chest. The sign for the pronoun "you" is a point to the chest of the addressee. As we discussed earlier, at around age two children acquiring spoken languages often reverse the pronouns "I" and "you." Interestingly, at this same age signing children make this same error. They will point to themselves when they mean "you" and point to the addressee when they mean "I." Children acquiring ASL make this error despite the transparency or iconicity of these particular signs. This is because signing children (like signing adults) treat these pronouns as linguistic symbols and not simply as pointing gestures. As part of the language, the shifting reference of these pronouns presents the same problem for signing children that it does for speaking children.

Hearing children of deaf parents acquire both sign language and spoken language when exposed to both. Studies show that Canadian bilingual children who acquire Langues des Signes Quebecoise (LSQ), or Quebec Sign Language, develop the two languages exactly as bilingual children acquiring two spoken languages.[20] The LSQ–French bilinguals reached linguistic milestones in each of their languages in parallel

---

[20] L. Petitto, M. Katerelos, B. Levy, K. Guana, K. Tetreault, and V. Ferraro. 2001. "Bilingual Signed and Spoken Language Acquisition from Birth: Implications for the Mechanisms Underlying Early Bilingual Language Acquisition," *Journal of Child Language* 28:453–96.

with Canadian children acquiring French and English. They produced their first words, as well as their first word combinations, at the same time in each language. In reaching these milestones neither group showed any delay as compared to monolingual children.

Deaf children of hearing parents who are not exposed to sign language from birth suffer a great handicap in acquiring language. It may be many years before these children are able to make use of a spoken language or before they encounter a conventional sign language. Yet the instinct to acquire language is so strong in humans that these deaf children begin to develop their own manual gestures to express their thoughts and desires. A study of six such children revealed that they not only developed individual signs but joined pairs and formed sentences with definite syntactic order and systematic constraints. Although these "home signs," as they are called, are not fully developed languages like ASL or LSQ, they have a linguistic complexity and systematicity that could not have come from the input, since there was no input. Cases such as these demonstrate not only the strong drive that humans have to communicate through language, but also the innate basis of language structure.

Knowing More Than One Language

> He that understands grammar in one language, understands it in another as far as the essential properties of Grammar are concerned. The fact that he can't speak, nor comprehend, another language is due to the diversity of words and their various forms, but these are the accidental properties of grammar.
>
> Roger Bacon (1214–1294)

People can acquire a second language under many different circumstances. You may have learned a second language when you began middle school, or high school, or college. Moving to a new country often means acquiring a new language. Other people live in communities or homes in which more than one language is spoken and may acquire two (or more) languages simultaneously. The term **second language acquisition,** or **L2 acquisition,** generally refers to the acquisition of a second language by someone (adult or child) who has already acquired a first language. **Bilingual language acquisition** refers to the (more or less) simultaneous acquisition of two languages beginning in infancy (or before the age of three years).

Childhood Bilingualism

| Bilingual Hebrew-English- speaking child: | "I speak Hebrew and English." |
| Monolingual English-speaking child: | "What's English?" |

Approximately half of the people in the world are native speakers of more than one language. This means that as children they had regular and continued exposure to more than one language. In many parts of the world, especially in Africa and Asia, bilingualism (even multilingualism) is the norm. In contrast, many Western countries (though by no means all of them) view themselves as monolingual, even though they may be home to

"Gina is by lingal . . . that means she can say the same thing twice, but you can only understand it once."

"Dennis the Menace"® used by permission of Hank Ketcham and by North American Syndicate.

speakers of many languages. In the United States and many European countries, bilingualism is often viewed as a transitory phenomenon associated with immigration.

Bilingualism is always an intriguing topic. People wonder how it's possible for a child to acquire two (or more) languages at the same time. There are many questions, such as: doesn't the child confuse the two languages; does bilingual language development take longer than monolingual development; are bilingual children brighter or does acquiring two languages negatively affect the child's cognitive development in some way; how much exposure to each language is necessary for a child to become bilingual?

Much of the early research into bilingualism focused on the fact that bilingual children sometimes "mix" the two languages in the same sentences, as the following examples from French-English bilingual children illustrate. In the first example, a French word appears in an otherwise English sentence. In the other two examples, all of the words are English but the syntax is French.

His nose is perdu.	(His nose is lost.)
A house pink	(A pink house)
That's to me	(That's mine)

In early studies of bilingualism, this kind of language mixing was viewed in a negative light. It was taken as an indication that the child was confused or having difficulty with the two languages. In fact, many parents, sometimes on the advice educators or psychologists, would stop raising their children bilingually when faced with this issue. However, it now seems clear that some amount of language mixing is a normal part of the early bilingual acquisition process, and not necessarily an indication of any language problem.

THEORIES OF BILINGUAL DEVELOPMENT

These mixed utterances raise an interesting question about the grammars of bilingual children. Does the bilingual child start out with only one grammar that is eventually differentiated, or does she construct a separate grammar for each language right from the start? The **unitary system hypothesis** says that the child initially constructs only one lexicon and one grammar. The presence of "mixed" utterances such as the ones just given is often taken as support for this hypothesis. In addition, at the early stages, bilingual children often have words for particular objects in only one language. For example, a Spanish-English bilingual child may know the Spanish word for milk, *leche,* but not the English word, or she may have the word *water* but not *agua.* This kind of complementarity has also been taken as support for the idea that the child has only one lexicon.

However, careful examination of the vocabularies of bilingual children reveals that although they may not have exactly the same words in both languages, there is enough overlap to make the single lexicon idea implausible. The reason children may not have the same set of words in both languages is that they use their two languages in different circumstances and acquire the vocabulary appropriate to each situation. For example, the bilingual English-Spanish child may hear only Spanish during mealtime and so he will first learn the Spanish words for foods. Also, bilingual children initially have smaller vocabularies in each of their languages than the monolingual child has in her one language. This makes sense since a child can only learn so many words a day, and the bilingual child has two lexicons to build. For these reasons the bilingual child may have more lexical gaps than the monolingual child at a comparable stage of development, and those gaps may be different for each language.

The **separate systems hypothesis** says that the bilingual child builds a distinct lexicon and grammar for each language. To test the separate systems hypothesis it is necessary to look at how the child acquires those pieces of grammar that are different in his two languages. For example, if both languages have SVO word order, this would not be a good place to test this hypothesis. A number of studies have shown that where the two languages diverge, children acquire the different rules of each language. Spanish-English and French-German bilingual children have been shown to use the word orders appropriate to each language, as well as the correct agreement morphemes for each language. Other studies have shown that children set up two distinct sets of phonemes and phonological rules for their languages.

The separate systems hypothesis also receives support from the study of the LSQ-French bilinguals discussed earlier. These children have semantically equivalent words in the two languages, just as spoken-spoken bilinguals do. In addition, these children, like all bilingual children, were able to adjust their language choice to the language of their addressees, showing that they differentiated the two languages. Like most bilingual children, the LSQ-French bilinguals produced "mixed" utterances — utterances that had words from both languages. What is especially interesting is that these children showed "simultaneous" language mixing. They would produce a LSQ sign and a French word at the same time, something that is only possible if one language is spoken and the other signed. However, this finding has implications for bilingual language acquisition in general. It shows that the language mixing of bilingual children is not due to confusion, but is rather the result of two grammars operating simultaneously.

If bilingual children have two grammars and two lexicons, what explains the mixed utterances? Various explanations have been offered. One suggestion is that children mix because they have lexical gaps; if the French-English bilingual child does not know the English word *lost,* she will use the word she does know, *perdu* — the "any port in a storm strategy." Another possibility is that the mixing in child language is like the special language usage of many adult bilinguals referred to as **code-switching** (discussed in chapter 10). In specific social situations, bilingual adults may switch back and forth between their two languages in the same sentence, for example, "I put the forks en las mesas" (I put the forks on the tables). Code-switching reflects the grammars of both languages working simultaneously; it is not "bad grammar" or "broken English." Adult bilinguals code-switch only when speaking to other bilingual speakers. It has been suggested that the mixed utterances of bilingual children are a form of code-switching. In support of this proposal, various studies have shown that bilingual children as young as two make contextually appropriate language choices: In speaking to monolinguals the children use one language, in speaking to bilinguals they mix the two languages.

Two Monolinguals in One Head

Although we must study many bilingual children to reach any firm conclusions, the evidence accumulated so far seems to support the idea that children construct multiple grammars at the outset. Moreover, it seems that bilingual children develop their grammars along the same lines as monolingual children. They go through a babbling stage, a holophrastic stage, a telegraphic stage, and so on. During the telegraphic stage they show the same characteristics in each of their languages as the monolingual children. For example, monolingual English-speaking children omit verb endings in sentences such as "Eve play there," "Andrew want that," and German-speaking children use infinitives as in "Thorstn das haben" (Thorstn that to have). Spanish- and Italian-speaking monolinguals never omit verbal inflection or use infinitives in this way. Remarkably, two-year-old German-Italian bilinguals use infinitives when speaking German but not when they speak Italian. Young Spanish-English bilingual children drop the English verb endings but not the Spanish ones, and German-English bilinguals omit verbal inflection in English and use the infinitive in German.[21] Results such as these have led some researchers to suggest that the bilingual child is like "two monolinguals in one head."

The Role of Input

One issue that concerns researchers studying bilingualism, as well as parents of bilingual children, is the relation between language input and "proficiency." What role does input play in helping the child to separate the two languages? One input condition that is thought to promote bilingual development is *une personne-une langue* (one person, one language). In this condition, each person, say Mom and Dad, speaks only one language

---

[21] M. Salustri, J. Berger-Morales, and J. Gilkerson. *An Analysis of the Spontaneous Utterances of Two Bilingual Children: Evidence for the Separate Systems Hypothesis.* Unpublished UCLA manuscript; S. Unsworth. 2000. *The Referential Properties of Root Infinitives in Bilingual (German/English) First Language Acquisition.* Unpublished master's thesis, University of Durham.

to the child. The idea is that keeping the two languages separate in the input will make it easier for the child to keep them separate. Whether this affects bilingual development in some important way has not been established. In practice this "ideal" input situation may be difficult to attain. It may also be unnecessary. We saw earlier that babies are attuned to various phonological properties of the input language such as prosody and phonotactics. This may provide a sufficient basis for the bilingual child to keep the two languages separate.

Another question is, how much input does a child need in each language to become "native" in both? The answer is not straightforward. It seems intuitively clear that if a child hears 12 hours of English a day and only 2 hours of Spanish, he will probably develop English much more quickly and completely than Spanish. In fact, under these conditions he may never achieve the kind of grammatical competence in Spanish that we associate with the normal monolingual Spanish speaker. In reality, bilingual children are raised in varying circumstances. Some may have more or less equal exposure to the two languages; some may hear one language more than the other but still have sufficient input in the two languages to become "native" in both; some may ultimately have one language that is "dominant" to a lesser or greater degree. Researchers simply do not know how much language exposure is necessary in the two languages to produce a "balanced bilingual." For practical purposes, the rule of thumb is that the child should receive roughly equal amounts of input in the two languages to achieve native proficiency in both.

Cognitive Effects of Bilingualism

Another issue is the effect of bilingualism on intellectual or cognitive development. Does being bilingual make you more or less intelligent, more or less creative, and so on? Historically, research into this question has been fraught with methodological problems and has often been heavily influenced by the prevailing political and social climate. Many early studies (before the 1960s) showed that bilingual children did worse than monolingual children on IQ and other cognitive and educational tests. The results of more recent research indicate that bilingual children outperform monolinguals in certain kinds of problem solving. Also, bilingual children seem to have better **metalinguistic awareness.** Metalinguistic awareness refers to a speaker's conscious awareness *about* language and the use of language. This is in contrast to linguistic knowledge, which, as we have seen, is knowledge *of* language and is unconscious. Bilingual children have an earlier understanding of the arbitrary relation between an object and its name, for instance. And they have sufficient metalinguistic awareness to speak the contextually appropriate language, as we mentioned.

Whether children enjoy some cognitive or educational benefit from being bilingual seems to depend a great deal on extralinguistic factors such as the social and economic position of the child's group or community, the educational situation, and the relative "prestige" of the two languages. Studies that show the most positive effects (for example, better school performance) generally involve children reared in societies where both languages are valued, and whose parents were interested and supportive of their bilingual development.

Second Language Acquisition

In contrast to the bilinguals just discussed, many people are introduced to a second language (L2) after they have achieved native competence in a first language (L1). If you have had the experience of trying to master a second language as an adult, no doubt you found it to be a challenge quite unlike your first language experience.

"Rhymes with Orange" copyright © 2001 Hilary B. Price. Reprinted with special permission of King Features Syndicate, Inc.

IS L2 ACQUISITION THE SAME AS L1 ACQUISITION?

With some exceptions, adults do not simply "pick up" a second language. It usually requires conscious attention, if not intense study and memorization, to become proficient in a second language. Again, with the exception of some remarkable individuals, adult second-language learners (L2ers) do not often achieve nativelike grammatical competence in the L2, especially with respect to pronunciation. They generally have an accent and they may make syntactic or morphological errors that are unlike the errors of children acquiring their first language (L1ers). For example, L2ers often make word order errors, especially early in their development, as well as morphological errors in grammatical gender and case. L2 errors may **fossilize** so that no amount of teaching or correction can undo them

Unlike L1 acquisition, which is uniformly successful across children and languages, adults vary considerably in their ability to acquire an L2 completely. Some people are very talented language learners. Others are hopeless. Most people fall somewhere in the middle. Success may depend on a range of factors, including age, talent, motivation, and whether you are in the country where the language is spoken or sitting in a classroom five mornings a week with no further contact with native speakers. For all these reasons, many people, including many linguists who study L2 acquisition, believe that second language acquisition is something different from first language acquisition. This hypothesis is referred to as the **fundamental difference hypothesis** of L2 acquisition.

In certain important respects, however, L2 acquisition is like L1 acquisition. Like L1ers, L2ers do not acquire their second language overnight; they go through stages.

Like L1ers, L2ers construct grammars. These grammars reflect their competence in the L2 at each stage and so their language at any particular point, though not nativelike, is rule-governed and not haphazard. The intermediate grammars that L2ers create on their way to the target have been called **interlanguage grammars.**

Consider word order in the interlanguage grammars of Romance (Italian, Spanish, and Portuguese) speakers acquiring German as a second language. The word order of the Romance languages is Subject-(Auxiliary)-Verb-Object (like English). German has two basic word orders depending on the presence of an auxiliary. Sentences with auxiliaries have Subject-Auxiliary-Object-Verb, as in (1). Sentences without auxiliaries have Subject-Verb-Object, as in (2).

1. Hans hat ein Buch gekaufen.   "Hans has a book bought."
2. Hans kauft ein Buch.   "Hans bought a book."

Studies show that Romance speakers acquire German word order in pieces. During the first stage they use German words but the S-Aux-V-O word order of their native language, as follows:[22]

Stage 1: Mein vater hat gekaufen ein buch.
          "My father has bought a book."

At the second stage, they acquired the VP word order Object-Verb.

Stage 2: Vor personalrat auch meine helfen.
          in the personnel office [a colleague] me helped
          "A colleague in the personnel office helped me. "

At the third stage they acquired the rule that places the verb or (auxiliary) in second position

Stage 3: Jetzt kann sie mir eine frage machen.
          now can she me a question ask
          "Now she can ask me a question."

          I kenne nich die welt.
          I know not the world.
          "I don't know the world."

These stages differ from those of children acquiring German as a first language. For example, German children know from the start that the language has SOV word order. However, like L1ers, L2ers attempt to uncover the grammar of the target language.

Unlike children acquiring their first language, second-language learners often do not reach the target. Proponents of the fundamental difference hypothesis believe that L2ers construct grammars according to different principles than those used in L1 acquisition, principles that are not specifically designed for language acquisition, but for the problem-solving skills used for tasks like playing chess or learning math. According to

---

[22] Data from P. Jordens. 1988. "The Acquisition of Word Order in L2 Dutch and German," in P. Jordens and J. Lalleman, eds. *Language Development*. Dordrecht: Foris. (These stages are simplified for expository purposes.)

this view, L1ers have specifically linguistic principles of UG to help them, but adult L2ers do not. In response to this position, others have noted that adults are superior to children in solving all sorts of nonlinguistic problems. If they were using these problem-solving skills to learn their L2, shouldn't they be uniformly more successful than they are? Also, linguistic savants such as Christopher, discussed in chapter 2, argue against the view that L2 acquisition involves only nonlinguistic cognitive abilities. Christopher's IQ and problem-solving skills are minimal at best. Yet, he has become proficient in several languages.

Many L2 acquisition researchers reject the idea that L2 acquisition is fundamentally different from L1 acquisition. They point to various studies that show that interlanguage grammars do not generally violate principles of UG, which makes the process seem more similar to L1 acquisition. In the German L2 examples above, the interlanguage rules may be wrong for German, or wrong for Romance, but they are not impossible rules. These researchers also note that although L2ers may fall short of L1ers in terms of their final grammar, they may acquire rules in the same way as L1ers.

NATIVE LANGUAGE INFLUENCE IN L2 ACQUISITION

One respect in which L1 acquisition and L2 acquisition are clearly different is that adult L2ers already have a fully developed grammar of their first language. As discussed in chapter 1, linguistic competence is unconscious knowledge. We cannot suppress our ability to use the rules of our language. We cannot decide not to understand English. Similarly, L2ers — especially at the beginning stages of acquiring their L2 — seem to rely on their L1 grammar to some extent. This is shown by the kinds of errors L2ers make, which often involve the **transfer of grammatical rules** from their L1. This is most obvious in phonology. L2ers generally speak with an accent because they may transfer the phonemes, phonological rules, or syllable structures of their first language to their second language. We see this in the Japanese speaker, who does not distinguish between *write* [rajt] and *light* [lajt] because the r/l distinction is not phonemic in Japanese; in the French speaker, who says "ze cat in ze hat" because French does not have [ð]; in the German speaker, who devoices final consonants, saying [hæf] for *have;* and in the Spanish speaker, who inserts a schwa before initial consonant clusters, as in [əskul] for *school* and [əsnab] for *snob.*

Similarly, English speakers may have difficulty with unfamiliar sounds in other languages. For example, in Italian long (or double) consonants are phonemic. Italian has minimal pairs such as the following:

ano	"anus"	anno	"year"
pala	"shovel"	palla	"ball"
dita	"fingers"	ditta	"company"

English-speaking L2 learners of Italian have difficulty in hearing and producing the contrast between long and short consonants. This can lead to very embarrassing situations, for example on New Year's Eve, when instead of wishing people *buon anno* (good year), you wish them *buon ano.*

Native language influence is also found in the syntax and morphology. Sometimes this influence shows up as a wholesale transfer of a particular piece of grammar. For example, a Spanish speaker acquiring English might drop subjects in non-imperative sentences because this is possible in Spanish, as illustrated by the following examples.[23]

> Hey, is not funny.
> In here have the mouth.
> Live in Columbia.

Or speakers may begin with the word order of their native language, as we saw in the Romance-German interlanguage examples.

Native language influence may show up in more subtle ways. For example, people whose L1 is German acquire English yes/no questions faster than Japanese speakers do. This is because German has a verb movement rule for forming yes-no questions that is very close to the English Aux movement rule, while in Japanese there is no syntactic movement in question formation.

The Creative Component of L2 Acquisition

It would be an oversimplification to think that L2 acquisition involves only the transfer of L1 properties to the L2 interlanguage. There is a strong creative component to L2 acquisition. Many language-particular parts of the L1 grammar do not transfer. Items that a speaker considers irregular, infrequent, or semantically difficult are not likely to transfer to the L2. For example, speakers will not typically transfer L1 idioms such as *He hit the roof* meaning "He got angry." They are more likely to transfer structures in which the semantic relations are transparent. For example, a structure such as (1) will transfer more readily than (2).

1. It is awkward to carry this suitcase.
2. This suitcase is awkward to carry.

In (1) the NP "this suitcase" is in its logical direct object position, while in (2) it has been moved to the subject position away from the verb that selects it.

Many of the "errors" that L2ers do make are not derived from their L1. For example, in one study Turkish speakers at a particular stage in their development of German used SVAdv (Subject-Verb-Adverb) word order in embedded clauses (the *wenn* clause in the following example) in their German interlanguage, even though both their native language and the target language have SAdvV order:

Wenn	ich	geh	zuruck	ich	arbeit	elektriker	in turkei
if	I	go	back,	I	work (as an)	electrician	in Turkey

The embedded SVAdv order is most likely an overgeneralization of the verb second requirement in main clauses that we discussed above. As we noted earlier, overgeneralization is a clear indication that a rule has been acquired.

Why certain L1 rules transfer to the interlanguage grammar and others don't is not well understood. It is clear, however, that although construction of the L2 grammar is influenced by the L1 grammar, there are also developmental principles — possibly uni-

---

[23] Examples from S. Hillis. 1989. *Access to Universal Grammar and Second Language Acquisition.* UCLA Ph.D. dissertation.

versal — that operate in L2 acquisition. This is best illustrated by the fact that speakers with different L1s go through similar L2 stages. For example, Turkish, Serbo-Croatian, Italian, Greek, and Spanish speakers acquiring German as an L2 all drop articles to some extent. Since some of these L1s have articles, this cannot be due to transfer but must involve some more general property of language acquisition

A CRITICAL PERIOD FOR L2 ACQUISITION?

Age is a significant factor in L2 acquisition. The younger a person is when exposed to a second language, the more likely she is to achieve nativelike competence.

In an important study of the effects of age on ultimate attainment in L2 acquisition, Jacqueline Johnson and Elissa Newport tested several groups of Chinese and Korean speakers who had acquired English as a second language.[24] The subjects, all of whom had been in the United States for at least five years, were tested on their knowledge of specific aspects of English morphology and syntax. They were asked to judge the grammaticality of sentences such as:

The little boy is speak to a policeman.
The farmer bought two pig.
A bat flewed into our attic last night.

Johnson and Newport found that the test results depended heavily on the age at which the person had arrived in the United States. The people who arrived as children (between the age of three and eight) did as well on the test as American native speakers. Those who arrived between the ages of eight and fifteen did not perform like native speakers. Moreover, every year seemed to make a difference for this group. The person who arrived at age nine did better than the one who arrived at age ten; those who arrived at age eleven did better than those who arrived at age twelve and so on. The group that arrived between the ages of seventeen and thirty-one had the lowest scores.

Does this mean that there is a critical period for L2 acquisition, an age beyond which it is *impossible* to acquire the grammar of a new language? Most researchers would hesitate to make such a strong claim. Although age is an important factor in achieving nativelike L2 competence, it is certainly possible to acquire a second language as an adult. Indeed, many teenage and adult L2 learners become quite proficient, and a few highly talented ones even manage to pass for native speakers.

It is more appropriate to say that there is a gradual decline in L2 acquisition abilities with age and that there are "sensitive periods" for the nativelike mastery of certain aspects of the L2. The sensitive period for phonology is the shortest. To achieve nativelike pronunciation of an L2 generally requires exposure during childhood. Other aspects of language, such as syntax, may have a larger window.

Recent research with "heritage language" learners provides additional support for the notion of sensitive periods in L2 acquisition. UCLA psychologist Terry Au and her colleagues investigated the acquisition of Spanish by college students who had overheard the language as children (and sometimes knew a few words), but who did not oth-

---

[24] J. Johnson and E. Newport. 1989. "Critical Period Effects in Second Language Learning: The Influence of Maturational State on the Acquisition of English as a Second Language," *Cognitive Psychology* 21:60–99.

erwise speak or understand Spanish. The "overhearers" were compared to people who had no exposure to Spanish before the age of fourteen. All of the students were native speakers of English studying their "heritage language" as a second language. Au's results showed that the "overhearers" acquired a nativelike accent while the other students did not. However, the overhearers did not show any advantage in acquiring the grammatical morphemes of Spanish. Early exposure may leave an "imprint" that facilitates the late acquisition of certain aspects of language.[25]

Second-Language Teaching Methods

Many approaches to foreign-language instruction have developed over the years. In one method, **grammar-translation,** the student memorizes words, inflected words, and syntactic rules and uses them to translate from English to L2 and vice versa. The **direct method** abandons memorization and translation; the native language is never used in the classroom, and the structure of the L2 language or how it differs from the native language is not discussed. The direct method attempts to stimulate learning a language as if the students found themselves in a foreign country with only natives to speak to. The direct method seems to assume that adults can learn a foreign language in a way they learned their native language as children. Practically, it is difficult to duplicate the social, psychological, or physical environment of the child, or even the number of hours that the learner is exposed to the language to be acquired, even if there is no critical-age factor.

An audio-lingual language-teaching method is based on the assumption that language is acquired mainly through imitation, repetition, and reinforcement, an assumption which is very likely to be as wrong for L2 acquisition as it is for L1 acquisition. All language acquisition involves creativity on the part of the learner.

Most individual methods have serious limitations: Probably a combination of many methods is required as well as motivation on the part of the student, intensive and extensive exposure, native or near-native speaking teachers who can serve as models, and instruction and instructional material that is based on linguistic analysis of all aspects of the language.

Can Chimps Learn Human Language?

> . . . It is a great baboon, but so much like man in most things . . . I do believe it already understands much English; and I am of the mind it might be taught to speak or make signs.
>
> Entry in Samuel Pepys' *Diary*, August 1661

In this chapter, the discussion has centered on human language acquisition. Recently, much effort has been expended to determine whether nonhuman primates (chimpanzees, monkeys, gorillas, and so on) can learn human language.

---

[25] T. Au, L. Knightly, S. Jun, and J. Oh. In press. "Overhearing a Language During Childhood," *Psychological Science*.

In their natural habitat, primates communicate with each other in systems that include visual, auditory, olfactory, and tactile signals. Many of these signals seem to have meaning associated with the animals' immediate environment or emotional state. They can signal danger and can communicate aggressiveness and subordination. Females of some species emit a specific call to indicate that they are anestrus (sexually quiescent), which inhibits attempts by males to copulate. However, the natural sounds and gestures produced by all nonhuman primates show their signals to be highly stereotyped and limited in the type and number of messages they convey. Their basic vocabularies occur primarily as emotional responses to particular situations. They have no way of expressing the anger they felt yesterday or the anticipation of tomorrow.

Despite their limited natural systems of communication, these animals have provoked an interest in whether they have the capacity to acquire complex linguistic systems that are similar to human language.

Gua

In the 1930s, Winthrop and Luella Kellogg raised their infant son with an infant chimpanzee named Gua to determine whether a chimpanzee raised in a human environment and given language instruction could learn a human language. Gua understood about one hundred words at sixteen months, more words than their son at that age, but she never went beyond that. Moreover, comprehension of language involves more than understanding the meanings of isolated words. When their son could understand the difference between *I say what I mean* and *I mean what I say,* Gua could not understand either sentence.

Viki

A chimpanzee named Viki was raised by Keith and Cathy Hayes, and she too learned a number of individual words, even learning to articulate, with great difficulty, the words *mama, papa, cup,* and *up.* That was the extent of her language production.

Washoe

Psychologists Allen and Beatrice Gardner recognized that one disadvantage suffered by the primates was their physical inability to pronounce many different sounds. Without a sufficient number of phonemic contrasts, spoken human language is impossible. Many species of primates are manually dexterous, and this fact inspired the Gardners to attempt to teach American Sign Language to a chimpanzee that they named Washoe, after the Nevada county in which they lived. Washoe was brought up in much the same way as a human child in a deaf community, constantly in the presence of people who used ASL. She was deliberately taught to sign, whereas children raised by deaf signers acquire sign language without explicit teaching, as hearing children learn spoken language.

By the time Washoe was four years old (June 1969), she had acquired eighty-five signs with such meanings as "more," "eat," "listen," "gimme," "key," "dog," "you," "me," "Washoe," and "hurry." According to the Gardners, Washoe was also able to produce sign combinations such as "baby mine," "you drink," "hug hurry," "gimme flower," and "more fruit."

Sarah

At about the same time that Washoe was growing up, psychologist David Premack and his wife Ann Premack raised a chimp named Sarah in their home and attempted to teach her an artificial language designed to resemble human languages in some aspects. The "words" of Sarah's "language" were plastic chips of different shapes and colors that had metal backs. Sarah and her trainers "talked" to each other by arranging these symbols on a magnetic board. Sarah was taught to associate particular symbols with particular meanings. The form-meaning relationship of these "morphemes" or "words" was arbitrary; a small red square meant "banana," and a small blue rectangle meant "apricot," while the color red was represented by a gray chip and the color yellow by a black chip. Sarah learned a number of "nouns," "adjectives," and "verbs," symbols for abstract concepts like "same as" and "different from," "negation," and "question."

There were drawbacks to the Sarah experiment. She was not allowed to "talk" spontaneously, but only in response to her trainers. There was the possibility that her trainers unwittingly provided cues that Sarah responded to.

Learning Yerkish

To avoid these and other problems, Duane and Sue Rumbaugh and their associates at the Yerkes Regional Primate Research Center began in 1973 to teach a different kind of artificial language, called Yerkish, to three chimpanzees: Lana, Sherman, and Austin. The words of Yerkish, called lexigrams, are geometric symbols displayed on a computer keyboard. Certain fixed orders of these lexigrams constitute grammatical sentences in Yerkish. The computer records every button pressed so that a complete 24/7 record of the chimps' "speech" was obtained. The researchers are particularly interested in the ability of primates to communicate using abstract, functional symbols.

Koko

Another experiment aimed at teaching sign language to primates involved a gorilla named Koko, who was taught by her trainer, Francine "Penny" Patterson. Patterson claims that Koko has learned several hundred signs, is able to put signs together to make sentences, and is capable of making linguistic jokes and puns, composing rhymes such as BEAR HAIR (which is a rhyme in spoken language but not ASL), and inventing metaphors such as FINGER BRACELET for ring.

Nim Chimpsky

The psychologist H. S. Terrace and his associates studied a chimpanzee named Nim Chimpsky in a project specifically designed to test the linguistic claims that had emerged from prior primate experiments.[26] An experienced teacher of ASL taught Nim to sign. Under carefully controlled experimental conditions that included thorough record-

---

[26] Collaborating with Terrace were Laura Petitto, Richard Sanders, and Thomas Bever. The results of Project Nim are reported in H. S. Terrace (1979), *Nim: A Chimpanzee Who Learned Sign Language,* New York: Knopf.

"Bizzaro" copyright © 1994 Dan Piraro. Reprinted with permission of Universal Press Syndicate. All rights reserved.

keeping and many hours of videotaping, Nim's teachers hoped to show beyond a reasonable doubt that chimpanzees had a humanlike linguistic capacity, in contradiction to the view put forth by Noam Chomsky (after whom Nim was ironically named) that human language is species-specific. In the nearly four years of study, Nim learned about 125 signs, and during the last two years Nim's teachers recorded more than 20,000 utterances including two or more signs. Nim produced his first ASL sign (DRINK) after just four months, which greatly encouraged the research team at the start of the study. Their enthusiasm soon diminished when he never seemed to go much beyond the two-word stage. Terrace concluded that "his three-sign combinations do not . . . provide new information. . . . Nim's most frequent two- and three-sign combinations [were] PLAY ME and PLAY ME NIM. Adding NIM to PLAY ME is simply redundant," writes Terrace. This kind of redundancy is illustrated by a sixteen-sign utterance of Nim's: GIVE ORANGE ME GIVE EAT ORANGE ME EAT ORANGE GIVE ME EAT ORANGE GIVE ME YOU. Other typical sentences do not sound much like the early sentences of children we cited earlier.

> Nim eat Nim eat.
> Drink eat me Nim.
> Me Eat Me eat.
> You me banana me banana you.

Nim rarely signed spontaneously as children do when they begin to use language (spoken or sign). Only 12 percent of his utterances were spontaneous. Most of Nim's signing occurred only in response to prompting by his trainers and was related to eating, drinking, and playing; that is, it was stimulus-controlled. As much as 40 percent of his output was simply repetitions of signs made by the trainer. Children initiate conversations more and more frequently as they grow older, and their utterances repeat less and less of the adult's prior utterance. Some children rarely imitate in conversation. Children become increasingly more creative in their language use, but Nim showed almost no tendency toward such creativity. Furthermore, children's utterances increase in length and complexity as time progresses, finally mirroring the adult grammar, whereas Nim's language did not.

The lack of spontaneity and the excessive noncreative imitative nature of Nim's signing led to the conclusion that Nim's acquisition and use of language is qualitatively different from a child's. After examining the films of Washoe, Koko, and others, Terrace drew similar conclusions regarding the signing of the other primates.

Signing chimpanzees are also unlike humans in that when several of them are together they do not sign to each other as freely as humans would under similar circumstances. There is also no evidence to date that a signing chimp (or one communicating with plastic chips or computer symbols) will teach another chimp language, or that offspring will acquire language from their parent.

Clever Hans

Like Terrace, the Premacks and the Rumbaughs suggest that the sign-language studies lacked sufficient control and that the reported results were too anecdotal to support the view that primates are capable of acquiring a human language. They also question whether each of the others' studies, and all those attempting to teach sign language to primates, suffer from what has come to be called the Clever Hans phenomenon.

Clever Hans was a performing horse that became famous at the end of the nineteenth century because of his apparent ability to do arithmetic, read, spell, and even solve problems of musical harmony. He answered the questions posed by his interrogators by stamping out numbers with his hoof. It turned out, not surprisingly, that Hans did not know that $2 + 2 = 4$, but he was clever enough to pick up subtle cues conveyed unconsciously by his trainer as to when he should stop tapping his foot.

Sarah, like Clever Hans, took prompts from her trainers and her environment to produce the plastic-chip sentences. In responding to the string of chips standing for

SARAH INSERT APPLE PAIL BANANA DISH

all Sarah had to figure out was to place certain fruits in certain containers, and she could decide which by merely seeing that the apple symbol was next to the pail symbol, and the banana symbol was next to the dish symbol. There is no evidence that Sarah actually grouped strings of words into constituents. There is also no indication that Sarah would understand a new compound sentence of this type. The creative ability so much a part of human language is not demonstrated by this act.

Problems also exist in Lana's acquisition of Yerkish. Thompson and Church[27] studied the Lana project and were able to simulate Lana's behavior with a computer model. They concluded that the chimp's "linguistic" behavior can all be accounted for by her learning to associate lexigrams with objects, persons, or events, and to produce one of several "stock sentences" depending on situational cues (like Clever Hans).

How Sarah and Lana learned to manipulate symbols differs in several significant respects from how children learn language. In the case of the chimpanzees, each new rule or sentence form was introduced in a deliberate, highly constrained way. When parents speak to children, however, they do not confine themselves to a few words in a particular order for months, rewarding the child with a chocolate bar or a banana each time the child correctly responds to a command. Nor do they wait until the child has mastered one rule of grammar before going on to a different structure. Unless they were linguists, parents wouldn't know how to do such a thing. Young children require no special language training.

Kanzi

Research on the linguistic ability of nonhuman primates continues. Two investigators studied a different species of chimp, a male bonobo (or pygmy chimpanzee) named Kanzi. They used the same plastic lexigrams and computer keyboard as used with Lana. They concluded that Kanzi "has not only learned, but also invented grammatical rules that may well be as complex as those used by human two-year-old children."[28] The grammatical rule referred to was the combination of a lexigram (such as that meaning "dog") followed by a gesture meaning "go." After combining these, Kanzi would then go to an area where dogs were located to play with them. Greenfield and Savage-Rumbaugh claim that this "ordering" rule was not an imitation of his caretakers' utterances, whom they say use an opposite ordering, in which "go" was followed by "dogs."

The investigators report that Kanzi's acquisition of "grammatical skills" was slower than that of human children, taking about three years (starting when he was five and a half years old).

Most of Kanzi's so-called sentences are fixed formulas with little if any internal structure. Kanzi has not yet exhibited the linguistic knowledge of a human three-year-old, whose complexity level includes knowledge of structure dependencies and hierarchical structure. Moreover, unlike Kanzi who used a different word order from her caretakers, children rapidly set the word order parameters of UG to correspond to the input.

As often happens in science, the search for the answers to one kind of question leads to answers to other questions. The linguistic experiments with primates have led to many advances in our understanding of primate cognitive ability. Premack has gone on to investigate other capacities of the chimp mind, such as causality; the Rumbaughs and Greenfield are continuing to study the ability of chimpanzees to use symbols. These

---

[27] C. R. Thompson and R. M. Church. 1980. "An Explanation of the Language of a Chimpanzee," *Science* 208:313–14.

[28] The study, conducted by UCLA psychologist P. Marks Greenfield and Georgia State University biologist E. S. Savage-Rumbaugh, was reported in an article in *The Chronicle of Higher Education,* 26 September 1990.

studies also point out how remarkable it is that human children, by the age of three and four, without explicit teaching, and without overt reinforcement, create new and complex sentences never spoken and never heard before.

≋ Summary

When children acquire a language, they acquire the grammar of that language — the phonological, morphological, syntactic, and semantic rules. They also acquire the pragmatic rules of the language as well as a lexicon. Children are not taught language. Rather, they extract the rules (and much of the lexicon) from the language around them.

A number of learning mechanisms have been suggested to explain the acquisition process. Imitations of adult speech, reinforcement, and analogy have all been proposed. None of these possible learning mechanisms account for the fact that children creatively form new sentences according to the rules of their language, or for the fact that children make certain kinds of errors but not others. Empirical studies of the **motherese** show that grammar development does not depend on structured input. **Connectionist models** of acquisition also depend on the child having specially structured input.

The ease and rapidity of children's language acquisition and the uniformity of the stages of development for all children and all languages, despite the **poverty of the stimulus** they receive, suggest that the language faculty is innate and that the infant comes to the complex task already endowed with a Universal Grammar. UG is not a grammar like the grammar of English or Arabic, but represents the principles to which all human languages conform. Language acquisition is a creative process. Children create grammars based on the linguistic input and are guided by UG.

Language development proceeds in stages. These stages are universal. During the first year of life, children develop the sounds of their language. They begin by producing and perceiving many sounds that do not exist in their language input. Gradually, their productions and perceptions are fine-tuned to the environment. Children's late **babbling** has all the phonological characteristics of the input language. Deaf children exposed at birth to sign languages also produce manual babbling, showing that babbling is a universal first-stage in language acquisition that is dependent on the linguistic input received.

At the end of the first year, children utter their first words. During the second year, they learn many more words and they develop much of the phonological system of the language. Children's first utterances are one-word "sentences" (the **holophrastic** stage). After a few months, the child puts two or more words together. These early sentences are not random combinations of words: The words have definite patterns and express both syntactic and semantic relationships.

During the **telegraphic stage,** the child produces longer sentences that often lack function or grammatical morphemes. The child's early grammar still lacks many of the rules of the adult grammar, but is not qualitatively different from it. Children at this stage have correct word order and rules for agreement and case, which show their knowledge of structure.

Children make various kinds of errors. For example, they will **overgeneralize** morphology. This shows that they are acquiring rules. They also need to learn rules that are particular to their specific language, and there may be errors related to this learning. There are other kinds of errors that children never make, errors that would involve violating principles of Universal Grammar.

Deaf children exposed to **sign language** show the same stages of language acquisition as do hearing children exposed to spoken languages.

Children may acquire more than one language at a time. **Bilingual** children seem to go through the same stages as monolingual children except that they develop two grammars and two lexicons simultaneously. This is true for children acquiring two spoken languages as well as for children acquiring a spoken language and a signed language. Whether the child will be equally proficient in the two languages depends on the input she receives and the social conditions under which the languages are acquired.

Like first language learners, **L2 learners** construct grammars of the target language and they also go through stages — called **interlanguage grammars.** In **second language acquisition,** influence from the speaker's first language makes L2 acquisition appear different from L1 acquisition. Adults often do not achieve nativelike competence in their L2, especially in pronunciation. The difficulties encountered in attempting to learn languages after puberty may be due to the fact that there are sensitive periods for L2 acquisition. Some theories of second language acquisition suggest that the same principles operate that account for first language acquisition. A second view suggests that the acquisition of a second language in adulthood involves general learning mechanisms rather than the specifically linguistic principles used by the child.

There are a number of second-language teaching methods that have been proposed, some of them reflecting different theories of the nature of language and language acquisition.

Questions as to whether language is unique to the human species have led researchers to attempt to teach nonhuman primates systems of communication that purportedly resemble human language. Chimpanzees like Sarah and Lana have been taught to manipulate symbols to gain rewards, and other chimpanzees, like Washoe and Nim Chimpsky, have been taught a number of ASL signs. A careful examination of the utterances in ASL by these chimps shows that unlike children, their language exhibits little spontaneity, is highly imitative (echoic), and reveals little syntactic structure. It has been suggested that the pygmy chimp Kanzi shows grammatical ability greater than the other chimps studied, but he still does not have the ability of even a three-year-old child.

The universality of the language acquisition process, of the stages of development, of the relatively short period in which the child constructs a complex grammatical system without overt teaching, and the limited results of the chimpanzee experiments, suggest that the human species is innately endowed with special language acquisition abilities, and that language is biologically and genetically part of the human neurological system.

All normal children everywhere learn language. This ability is not dependent on race, social class, geography, or even intelligence (within a normal range). This ability is uniquely human.

References for Further Reading

Atkinson, M. 1992. *Children's Syntax: An Introduction to Principles and Parameters Theory*. Oxford: Blackwell Publishers.

Brown, R. 1973. *A First Language: The Early Stages*. Cambridge, MA: Harvard University Press.

Cairns, H. 1996. *The Acquisition of Language*. Austin, TX: PRO-ED.

Crain, S., and D. Lillo-Martin. 1999. *An Introduction to Linguistic Theory and Language Acquisition*. Oxford: Blackwell Publishers.

Gass, S., and L. Selinker. 1994. *Second Language Acquisition*. Hillsdale, NJ: Lawrence Erlbaum Associates.

Feldman, H., S. Goldin-Meadow, and L. Gleitman. 1978. "Beyond Herodotus: The Creation of Language by Linguistically Deprived Deaf Children." In A. Lock, ed., *Action, Symbol, and Gesture: The Emergence of Language*. New York: Academic.

Fischer, S. D., and P. Siple. 1990. *Theoretical Issues in Sign Language Research. Vol. 1. Linguistics*. Chicago, IL: University of Chicago Press.

Fletcher, P., and B. MacWhinney, eds. 1995. *The Handbook of Child Language Acquisition*. Cambridge, MA: Blackwell Publishers.

Goldin-Meadow, S., and C. Mylander. 1990. "Beyond the Input Given: The Child's Role in the Acquisition of Language," *Language* 66(2):323–55.

Golinkoff, R., and K. Hirsh-Pasek. 1996. *The Origins of Grammar*. Cambridge, MA: MIT Press

Hakuta, K. 1986. *Mirror of Language: The Debate on Bilingualism*. New York: Basic Books.

Hyams, N. 1986. *Language Acquisition and the Theory of Parameters*. Dordrecht, The Netherlands: Reidel.

Hyltenstam, K., and L. Obler. 1989. *Bilingualism Across the Lifespan. Aspects of Acquisition, Maturity and Loss*. Cambridge, England: Cambridge University Press.

Ingram, D. 1989. *First Language Acquisition: Method, Description and Explanation*. New York: Cambridge University Press.

Jusczyk, P. W. 1997. *The Discovery of Spoken Language*. Cambridge, MA: MIT Press.

Jakobson, R. 1971. *Studies on Child Language and Aphasia*. The Hague: Mouton.

Klima, E. S., and U. Bellugi. 1979. *The Signs of Language*. Cambridge, MA: Harvard University Press.

Landau, B., and L. R. Gleitman. 1985. *Language and Experience: Evidence from the Blind Child*. Cambridge, MA: Harvard University Press.

Petitto, L. 1987. On the Autonomy of Language and Gesture: Evidence from the Acquisition of Personal Pronouns in American Sign Language, *Cognition* 27(1):1–52.

Premack, A. J., and D. Premack. 1972. "Teaching Language to an Ape." *Scientific American* (October):92–99.

Ritchie, W., and T. Bhatia eds. 1996. *The Handbook of Second Language Acquisition*. San Diego, CA: Academic Press.

Rumbaugh, D. M. 1977. *Acquisition of Linguistic Skills by a Chimpanzee*. New York: Academic Press.

Sebeok, T. A., and J. Umiker-Sebeok. 1980. *Speaking of Apes: A Critical Anthology of Two-Way Communication with Man*. New York: Plenum Press.

Sebeok, T. A., and R. Rosenthal, eds. 1981. *The Clever Hans Phenomenon: Communication with Horses, Whales, Apes, and People*. Annals of the New York Academy of Sciences, Vol. 364.

Smith, N. 1973. *The Acquisition of Phonology: A Case Study*. Cambridge, England: Cambridge University Press.

Terrace, H. S. 1979. *Nim: A Chimpanzee Who Learned Sign Language*. New York: Knopf.

Wanner, E., and L. Gleitman, eds. 1982. *Language Acquisition: The State of the Art*. Cambridge: Cambridge University Press.

White, L. 1989. *Universal Grammar and Second Language Acquisition*. Amsterdam/Philadelphia: John Benjamins.

≋ Exercises

1. *Baby talk* is a term used to label the word forms that many adults use when speaking to children. Examples in English are *choo-choo* for "train" and *bow-wow* for "dog." Baby talk seems to exist in every language and culture. At least two things seem to be universal about baby talk: The words that have baby-talk forms fall into certain semantic categories (e.g., food and animals), and the words are phonetically simpler than the adult forms (e.g.,tummy /tʌmi/ for "stomach" /stʌmɪk/). List all the baby-talk words you can think of in your native language; then (1) separate them into semantic categories, and (2) try to state general rules for the kinds of phonological reductions or simplifications that occur.

2. In this chapter we discussed the way children acquire rules of question formation. The following examples of children's early questions are from a stage that is later than those discussed in the chapter. Formulate a generalization to describe this stage.

Can I go?	Can I can't go?
Why do you have one tooth?	Why you don't have a tongue?
What do frogs eat?	What do you don't like?
Do you like chips?	Do you don't like bananas?

3. Find a child between two and four years old and play with the child for about thirty minutes. Keep a list of all words and/or "sentences" that are used inappropriately. Describe what the child's meanings for these words probably are. Describe the syntactic or morphological errors (including omissions). If the child is producing multiword sentences, write a grammar that could account for the data you have collected.

4. Noam Chomsky has been quoted as saying:

    It's about as likely that an ape will prove to have a language ability as that there is an island somewhere with a species of flightless birds waiting for human beings to teach them to fly.

In the light of evidence presented in this chapter, comment on Chomsky's remark. Do you agree or disagree, or do you think the evidence is inconclusive?

5. Roger Brown and his coworkers at Harvard University (see References in this chapter) studied the language development of three children, referred to in the literature as Adam, Eve, and Sarah. The following are samples of their utterances during the "two-word stage."

see boy	push it
see sock	move it
pretty boat	mommy sleep
pretty fan	bye-bye melon
more taxi	bye-bye hot
more melon	

A. Assume that the above utterances are grammatical sentences in the children's grammars.

(1) Write a minigrammar that would account for these sentences.

Example: One rule might be: VP → V N

(2) Draw phrase structure trees for each utterance. *Example:*

B. One observation made by Brown was that many of the sentences and phrases produced by the children were ungrammatical from the point of view of the adult grammar. The research group concluded, based on utterances such as those below, that a rule in the children's grammar for a noun phrase was:

NP → M N (where M = any modifier)

A coat	My stool	Poor man
A celery	That knee	Little top
A Becky	More coffee	Dirty knee
A hands	More nut	That Adam
My mummy	Two tinker-toy	Big boot

(3) Mark with an asterisk any of the above NPs that are ungrammatical in the adult grammar of English.

(4) State the "violation" for each starred item.

For example, if one of the utterances were *Lotsa book* you might say: "The modifier *lotsa* must be followed by a plural noun."

6. In the holophrastic (one-word) stage of child language acquisition, the child's phonological system differs in systematic ways from that in the adult grammar. The inventory of sounds and the phonemic contrasts are smaller, and there are greater constraints on phonotactic rules. (See chapter 7 for discussion on these aspects of phonology.)

A. For each of the following words produced by a child, state what the substitution is.

Example: spook (adult) [spuk]   substitution: initial cluster [sp] reduced
　　　　　(child) [pʰuk]   to single consonant; /p/ becomes aspirated, showing that child has acquired aspiration rule.

(1) don't　　[dot]
(2) skip　　[kʰɪp]
(3) shoe　　[su]
(4) that　　[dæt]
(5) play　　[pʰe]
(6) thump　　[dʌp]

(7) bath	[bæt]
(8) chop	[tʰap]
(9) kitty	[kɪdi]
(10) light	[wajt]
(11) dolly	[dawi]
(12) grow	[go]

B. State general rules that account for the children's deviations from the adult pronunciations.

7. Children learn demonstrative words such as *this, that, these, those;* temporal terms such as *now, then, tomorrow;* and spatial terms such as *here, there, right, behind* relatively late. What do all these words have in common? Why might that factor delay their acquisition?

8. We saw in this chapter how children overgeneralize rules such as the plural rule, producing forms such as *mans* or *mouses.* What might a child learning English use instead of the adult words given:

a. children

b. went

c. better

d. best

e. brought

f. sang

g. geese

h. worst

i. knives

j. worse

9. The following words are from the lexicons of two children ages 1 year 6 months (1;6) and 2 (2;0) years old. Compare the pronunciation of the words to adult pronunciation.[29]

Child 1 (1;6)

soap	[doʊp]	bib	[bɛ]
feet	[bit]	slide	[daɪ]
sock	[kak]	dog	[da]
goose	[gos]	cheese	[čis]
dish	[dɪč]	shoes	[dus]

Child 2 (2.0)

light	[wajt]	bead	[biː]
sock	[sʌk]	pig	[pɛk]
geese	[gis]	cheese	[tis]
fish	[fɪs]	biz	[bɪs]
sheep	[šip]	bib	[bɪp]

a. What happens to final consonants in the language of these two children? Formulate the rule(s) in words. Do all final consonants behave the same way? If not, which consonants undergo the rule(s)? Is this a natural class?

b. On the basis of these data, are there any pairs of words that allow you to identify any of the phonemes in the grammars of these children? What are they? Explain how you were able to determine your answer.

---

[29] These data are from M. Kehoe and C. Stoel Gammon. 2001. "The Development of Syllable Structure in English-Speaking Children with Particular Reference to Rhymes," *Journal of Child Language* 28(2):393–432.

10. Make up a "wug test" to test a child's knowledge of the following morphemes:

    comparative   -er   (as in *bigger*)

    superlative   -est   (as in *biggest*)

    progressive   -ing   (as in *I am dancing*)

    agentive   -er   (as in *writer*)

11. Children frequently produce sentences such as the following:

    Don't giggle me.

    I danced the clown.

    Yawny Baby – you can push her mouth open to drink her.

    Who deaded my kitty cat?

    Are you gonna nice yourself?

    a. How would you characterize the difference between the grammar or lexicon of children who produce such sentences and adult English?

    b. Can you think of similar, but well-formed, examples in adult English?

12. Many Arabic speakers tend to insert a vowel in their pronunciation of English words. The first column has examples from L2ers whose L1 is Egyptian Arabic and the second column from L2ers who speak Iraqi Arabic:[30]

L1 = Egyptian Arabic		L1 = Iraqi Arabic	
[bilastik]	plastic	[ifloor]	floor
[θirii]	three	[ibleen]	plane
[tiransilet]	translate	[čilidren]	children
[silayd]	slide	[iθrii]	three
[firɛd]	Fred	[istadi]	study
[čildiren]	children	[ifrɛd]	Fred

    a. What vowel do the Egyptian Arabic speakers insert and where?

    b. What vowel do the Iraqi Arabic speakers insert and where?

    c. Based on the position of the epenthetic vowel in the third example, can you guess which list, A or B, belongs to Egyptian Arabic and which belongs to Iraqi Arabic?

Arabic A		Arabic B	
kitabta	"I wrote him"	katabtu	"I wrote him"
kitabla	"He wrote to him"	katablu	"He wrote to him"
kitabɪtla	"I wrote to him"	katabtɪlu	"I wrote to him"

---

[30] This problem is based on E. Broselow. 1992. "Nonobvious Transfer: On Predicting Epenthesis Errors." In S. Gass and L. Selinker, eds. *Language Transfer in Language Learning*. Amsterdam: John Benjamins.

CHAPTER

Language Processing: Humans and Computer

No doubt a reasonable model of language use will incorporate, as a basic component, the generative grammar that expresses the speaker-hearer's knowledge of the language; but this generative grammar does not, in itself, prescribe the character or functioning of a perceptual model or a model of speech production.

Noam Chomsky, *Aspects of a Theory of Syntax*

The Human Mind at Work: Human Language Processing

Psycholinguistics is the area of linguistics that is concerned with linguistic performance — how we use our linguistic competence — in speech (or sign) production and comprehension. The human brain is able not only to acquire and store the mental lexicon and grammar, but also to access that linguistic storehouse to speak and understand language in real time.

How we process knowledge depends largely on the nature of that knowledge. If, for example, language were not open-ended, and were merely a finite store of fixed phrases and sentences in the memory, then speaking might simply consist of finding a sentence that expresses a thought we wished to convey. Comprehension could be the reverse — matching the sounds to a stored string that has been memorized with its meaning. Of course this is ridiculous! It is not possible because of the creativity of language. In chapter 8, we saw that children do not learn language by imitating and storing sentences, but by constructing a grammar. When we speak, we access our lexicon to find the words, and we use the rules of grammar to construct novel sentences and to produce the sounds

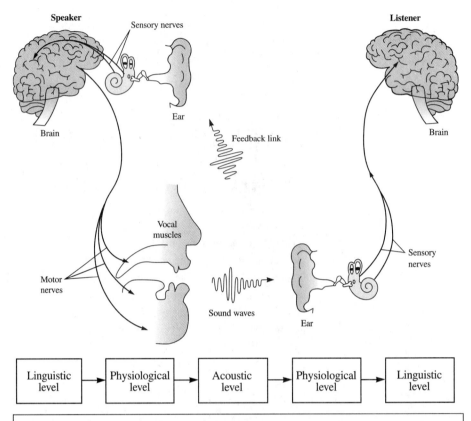

A spoken utterance starts as a message in the speaker's brain/mind. It is put into linguistic form and interpreted as articulation commands, emerging as an acoustic signal. The signal is processed by the listener's ear and sent to the brain/mind, where it is interpreted.

Figure 9.1   The Speech Chain.[1]

that express the message we wish to convey. When we listen to speech and understand what is being said, we also access the lexicon and grammar to assign a structure and meaning to the sounds we hear.

Speaking and comprehending speech can be viewed as a speech chain, a kind of "brain-to-brain" linking, as shown in Figure 9.1.

The grammar relates sounds and meanings, and contains the units and rules of the language that make speech production and comprehension possible. However, other psychological processes are used to produce and understand utterances. There are mechanisms that enable us to break the continuous stream of speech sounds into linguistic units such as phonemes, syllables, and words in order to comprehend, and to compose

[1] The figure is taken from P. B. Denes and E. N. Pinson, eds. 1963. *The Speech Chain*. Philadelphia, PA: Williams & Wilkins, p. 4.

sounds into words in order to produce meaningful speech. Other mechanisms determine how we pull words from the mental lexicon, and still others explain how we construct a phrase structure representation of the words we retrieve.

We usually have no difficulty understanding or producing sentences in our language. We do it without effort or conscious awareness of the processes involved. However, we have all had the experience of making a speech error, of having a word on the "tip of our tongue," or of misunderstanding a perfectly grammatical sentence, such as sentence (1):

1. The horse raced past the barn fell.

Conversely, there are ungrammatical sentences that are easily understandable such as sentence (2). This inconsistency between grammaticality and interpretability tells us that language processing involves more than grammar.

2. *The baby seems sleeping

A theory of linguistic performance tries to detail the psychological mechanisms that work with the grammar to permit language production and comprehension.

Comprehension

"I quite agree with you," said the Duchess; "and the moral of that is — 'Be what you would seem to be' — or, if you'd like it put more simply — 'Never imagine yourself not to be otherwise than what it might appear to others that what you were or might have been was not otherwise than what you had been would have appeared to them to be otherwise.'"

"I think I should understand that better," Alice said very politely, "if I had it written down: but I can't quite follow it as you say it."

Lewis Carroll, *Alice's Adventures in Wonderland*

The sentence uttered by the Duchess provides another example of a grammatical sentence that is difficult to understand. The sentence is very long and it contains several words that require additional resources to process, for example, multiple uses of negation and words like *otherwise*. Alice notes that if she had a pen and paper she could "unpack" this sentence more easily. One of the aims of psycholinguistics is to describe the processes people normally use in speaking and understanding language. The various "breakdowns" in performance such as "tip of the tongue" phenomena, speech errors, and failure to comprehend "tricky" sentences can tell us a great deal about how the language processor works, just as children's acquisition "errors" tell us a lot about the mechanisms involved in language development.

THE SPEECH SIGNAL

Understanding a sentence involves analysis at many levels. To begin with, we must comprehend the individual speech sounds we hear. We are not conscious of the complicated processes we use to understand speech any more than we are conscious of the complicated processes of digesting food and utilizing nutrients. We must study these processes deliberately and scientifically. One of the first questions of linguistic performance concerns segmentation of the acoustic signal. To understand this process, some knowledge of the signal itself can be helpful.

In chapter 6 we described speech sounds according to the ways in which they are produced. These involve the position of the tongue, the lips, and the velum; the state of the vocal cords; the airstream mechanisms; whether the articulators obstruct the free flow of air; and so on. All of these articulatory characteristics are reflected in the physical characteristics of the sounds produced.

Speech sounds can also be described in physical, or **acoustic,** terms. Physically, a sound is produced whenever there is a disturbance in the position of air molecules. The question asked by ancient philosophers as to whether a sound is produced if a tree falls in the middle of the forest with no one to hear it has been answered by the science of acoustics. Objectively, a sound is produced; subjectively, there is no sound. In fact, there are sounds we cannot hear because our ears are not sensitive to the full range of frequencies. *Acoustic phonetics* is concerned only with speech sounds, all of which can be heard by the normal human ear.

When we push air out of the lungs through the glottis, it causes the vocal cords to vibrate; this vibration in turn produces pulses of air that escape through the mouth (and sometimes also the nose). These pulses are actually small variations in the air pressure due to the wavelike motion of the air molecules.

The sounds we produce can be described in terms of how fast the variations of the air pressure occur, which determines the **fundamental frequency** of the sounds and is perceived by the hearer as *pitch.* We can also describe the magnitude, or **intensity,** of the variations, which determines the loudness of the sound. The quality of the speech sound — whether it's an [i] or an [a] or whatever — is determined by the shape of the vocal tract when air is flowing through it. This shape modulates the fundamental frequency into a spectrum of frequencies of greater or lesser intensity, and the particular combination of "greater or lesser" is heard as a particular sound.

An important tool in acoustic research is a computer program that decomposes the speech signal into its frequency components. When you speak into a microphone plugged into a computer (or when a tape recorder is plugged in), an image of the speech signal is displayed. The patterns produced are called **spectrograms** or, more vividly, **voiceprints.** A spectrogram of the words *heed, head, had,* and *who'd* is shown in Figure 9.2.

Time in milliseconds moves horizontally from left to right on the *x* axis; on the *y* axis the graph represents pitch (or, more technically, frequency). The intensity of each frequency component is indicated by the degree of darkness: the more intense, the darker. Each vowel is characterized by a number of dark bands that differ in their placement according to their frequency. They represent the strongest harmonics produced by the shape of the vocal tract and are called the **formants** of the vowels. (A harmonic is a special frequency that is a multiple (2, 3, etc.) of the fundamental frequency.) Because the tongue is in a different position for each vowel, the formant frequencies differ for each vowel. The frequencies of these formants account for the different vowel qualities you hear. The spectrogram also shows the pitch of the entire utterance (intonation contour) on the voicing bar marked P. When the striations are far apart, the vocal cords are vibrating slowly and the pitch is low; when the striations are close together, the vocal cords are vibrating rapidly and the pitch is high.

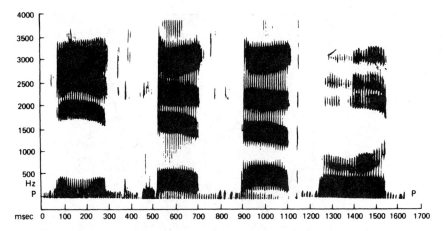

Figure 9.2   A spectrogram of the words *heed, head, had,* and *who'd,* spoken with a British accent (speaker: Peter Ladefoged, February 16, 1973). Courtesy of Peter Ladefoged.

By studying spectrograms of all speech sounds and many different utterances, acoustic phoneticians have learned a great deal about the basic acoustic components that reflect the articulatory features of speech sounds.

SPEECH PERCEPTION AND COMPREHENSION

Speech is a continuous signal. In natural speech, sounds overlap and influence each other, and yet the listener has the impression that he is hearing discrete units such as words, syllables, and phonemes. A central problem of speech perception is to explain how the listener carves up the continuous speech signal into meaningful units. This is referred to as the "segmentation problem."

Another question is, how does the listener manage to recognize particular speech sounds when they occur in different contexts and when they are spoken by different people? For example, how can a speaker tell that a [d] spoken by a man with a very deep voice is the same unit of sound as the [d] spoken in the high-pitched voice of a little child? Acoustically, they are very distinct. In addition, a [d] that occurs before the vowel [i] is somewhat different acoustically than a [d] that occurs before the vowel [u]. How does a listener know that two physically distinct instances of a sound are the same? This is referred to as the "invariance problem."

To address these complex problems, we must first try to understand the perceptual units involved in speech comprehension. Experiments show that perceptual units occur on different levels; we can segment the speech signal into strings of phonemes, syllables, morphemes, words, and phrases. There are also experimental results that show that the listener can calibrate her perceptions to control for differences in size and shape of the vocal tract of the speaker. These normalization procedures enable the listener to understand a [d] as a [d] regardless of the speaker, or the surrounding sounds.

As we might expect, the units we can perceive depend on the language we know. Speakers of English can perceive the difference between [l] and [r] because these phones

"I never let my kids watch this stuff. Too much Saxon violence."

"I Need Help" copyright © 1996 Vic Leo. Reprinted with special permission of King Features Syndicate, Inc.

represent distinct phonemes in the language. Speakers of Japanese have great difficulty in differentiating the two because they are allophones of one phoneme in their language. Recall from our discussion of language development in chapter 8 that these perceptual biases develop during the first year of life.

The context in which an utterance occurs also helps the segmentation task. One is more likely to discern the words *night rate* than the word *nitrate* if one is talking about the cost of parking or long-distance telephoning, but in a discussion of fertilizers or chemistry, perception would tend toward *nitrate*.

Spoken words are seldom surrounded by boundaries such as pauses. Nevertheless, words are obviously units of perception. The spaces between them in writing support this view. If we hear a word in isolation, we can analyze the acoustic signal, map it onto the phonemic representation, and find its meaning in the mental lexicon. When not in isolation, the perception of words is more difficult.

To see how complex speech processing is, suppose you heard someone say:

A sniggle blick is procking a slar

and you were able to perceive the sounds as

/ə s n ɪ g ə l b l ɪ k ɪ z p r a k ɪ ŋ ə s l a r/

You would still be unable to assign a meaning to the sounds, because the meaning of a sentence relies mainly on the meaning of its words, and the only English lexical items in this string are the morphemes *a, is,* and *-ing.* The sentence lacks any English content words. (However, you would accept it as grammatically well-formed because it conforms to the rules of English syntax.)

You can decide that the sentence has no meaning only if you attempt (unconsciously or consciously) a search of your mental lexicon for the phonological strings you decide are possible words. This process is called **lexical access.** In effect, it is word recognition. Finding that there are no entries for *sniggle, blick, prock,* and *slar,* you can conclude that the sentence includes *nonsense* strings.

If instead you heard someone say *The cat chased the rat,* through a similar lexical look-up process, you would conclude that an event concerning a cat, a rat, and the activity of chasing had occurred. You could only know this by segmenting the words in the continuous speech signal, analyzing them into their phonological word units, and matching these units to similar strings stored in your lexicon, which also includes the meanings attached to these phonological representations. This still would not enable you to tell who chased whom, since this is determined by syntactic processing. Processing speech to get at the meaning of what is said requires syntactic analysis as well as knowledge of *lexical semantics.*

Stress and intonation provide some clues to syntactic structure. We know, for example, that the different meanings of the sentences *He lives in the white house* and *He lives in the White House* can be signaled by differences in their stress patterns. Such prosodic aspects of speech also help to segment the speech signal into words and phrases. Syllables at the end of a phrase are longer in duration than at the beginning. Intonation contours mark boundaries of clauses. Relative loudness, pitch, and duration of syllables thus provide information in the comprehension process.

If you are traveling in Transylvania and a man in a black robe says "I vant to sock your blut," you would probably understand him. But, if he got the prosodics wrong and said "Ivan tsuckyour blut" his meaning might not be as clear. That is because understanding is as much a matter of timing and rhythm, as it is in the accurate perception of phones.

Speech comprehension is very fast and automatic. We understand an utterance as we hear it or read it. We don't wait for a pause and then say, "Hold on. I have to analyze the speech sounds, look the words up in my dictionary, and **parse** (provide a syntactic analysis of) your utterance." So, how do we understand a sentence?

Comprehension involves the ability to segment the continuous speech signal into phonemes, morphemes, words, phrases, and sentences; to construct a mental model of the discourse of which the sentence is a part; and to do all that more or less in parallel.

COMPREHENSION MODELS AND EXPERIMENTAL STUDIES

I have experimented and experimented until now I know that [water] never does run uphill, except in the dark. I know it does in the dark, because the pool never goes dry; which it would, of course, if the water didn't come back in the night. It is best to prove things by experiment; then you know; whereas if you depend on guessing and supposing and conjecturing, you will never get educated.

Mark Twain, *Eve's Diary*

In this laboratory the only one who is always right is the cat.

Motto in laboratory of Arturo Rosenblueth

The psychological stages and processes that a listener goes through in comprehending the meaning of an utterance are very complex. When we listen to a sentence we receive information sequentially (word-by-word from left to right). The listener attempts to construct a linguistic representation on-line as the words are spoken. He does not wait until the end of the sentence when all the information is available. Because of the sequential nature of the spoken (and written) language, there is a certain amount of guesswork involved in on-line comprehension. Alternative models of speech processing have been proposed in the attempt to clarify what information the listener uses in constructing the sentence and when. Some psycholinguists suggest that perception and comprehension involve both **top-down** and **bottom-up processing.**

Top-down processes proceed from semantic and syntactic information to the sensory input. Through use of such higher-level information, we can try to predict what is to follow in the signal. For example, upon hearing the determiner *the,* the speaker projects an NP and expects that the next word will be a noun, as in *the boy.* In this instance he would be using his knowledge of phrase structure.

Bottom-up processes move step-by-step from the incoming acoustic signal to semantic interpretation, building each part of the structure based on the sensory data alone. According to this model the speaker waits until he hears *the* and *boy* and then constructs an NP, and then waits for the next word, and so on.

Evidence for top-down processing is found in word identification experiments. Subjects make more errors when the words occur in isolation than when they occur in sentences. Moreover, they make more errors if the words occur in anomalous, or nonsense, sentences; and they make the most errors if the words occur in ungrammatical sentences. These results remain true even in the presence of noise. Apparently, subjects are using their knowledge of syntactic and semantic relations to help them identify words.

Top-down processing is also supported by a different kind of experiment. When subjects hear recorded sentences in which some part of the signal is removed and a cough substituted, they "hear" the sentence without a missing phoneme, and, in fact, are unable to say which phonemic segment the cough replaced. Context plays a major role in determining the sounds that the subjects replace. Thus, "[cough] eel" is heard as *wheel, heel, peel,* or *meal* depending on whether the sentence in which the distorted word occurs refers to an axle, shoe, orange, or food, respectively. We have also seen that context plays a role in word segmentation. If we heard [n a j t r e t] while checking into a motel, we would interpret it as *night rate,* whereas in a chemistry lab, we would think we heard *nitrate.* Similarly the phonetic string [w a j t š u z] would be heard as *white shoes,* rather than *why choose,* in a shoe store.

LEXICAL ACCESS AND WORD RECOGNITION

Psycholinguists have conducted a great deal of research on *lexical access* or *word recognition,* the process by which we obtain information about the meaning and syntactic category of a word from our mental lexicon. A number of experimental techniques have been used in studies of lexical access.

One technique asks subjects to decide whether a string of sounds (or letters if printed stimuli are used) is or is not a word. They must respond by pressing a button if the stimulus is an actual word. During these **lexical decision** experiments, measurements of **response time,** or **reaction time** (often referred to as RTs), are taken. The assumption is that the longer it takes to respond to a particular task, the more processing is involved. RT measurements show that lexical access depends to some extent on word *frequency;* the more commonly used words, both spoken and written, are responded to more quickly. This is evidence that comprehension involves both linguistic and nonlinguistic factors.

Reaction time is also measured in experiments using a **priming** technique. It has been found, for example, that if subjects hear a word such as *nurse,* their subsequent response to the written word *doctor* will be faster than to a semantically unrelated word such as *flower.* We say that the word *nurse primes* the word *doctor.* Words can be primed because semantically related words are located in the same part of the lexicon, and once the "path" to a priming word is taken, it is easier to travel that way a second time. It may also be because when we hear a priming word and look it up in our mental lexicon, semantically related, nearby words are "awakened" and more readily accessible for a few moments.

One of the most interesting facts about lexical access is that listeners retrieve all meanings of a word even when the sentence containing the word strongly biases towards one of the meanings. Priming experiments in which the lexically ambiguous word primes words related to both of its meanings show this. For example, suppose a subject hears the sentence:

The mouse ate the cheese.

Mouse primes the word *cat,* so in a lexical decision about *cat,* a shorter RT occurs than in a lexical decision about *cup,* say. However, a shorter RT also occurs for the word *computer.* The other meaning of *mouse* — a pointing device used with a computer — is apparently accessed even though that meaning is not a part of the meaning of the priming sentence.

In listening to speech, then, all the meanings represented by a phonological form will be triggered. This argues for at least some bottom-up processing because the individual word *mouse* is heard and processed somewhat independently of its context, and is thus capable of priming words related to all its lexical meanings, not just the lexical meaning in the particular sentence it occurs in.

Although the listener initially retrieves all meanings of the ambiguous word, she very quickly uses the disambiguating information in the sentence to discard the meanings that are not appropriate to the sentence. At this point she is using top-down information.

Another experimental technique, called the **naming task,** asks the subject to read aloud a printed word. (The naming task is also used in studies of aphasics, who are asked to name the object shown in a picture.) Subjects read real words faster than nonwords, and irregularly spelled, low-frequency words like *dough* and *bough* just slightly more slowly than regularly spelled words like *doe* and *bow,* but still faster than regularly spelled nonwords like *cluff.* This shows that the subjects first go to the lexicon to see if the word is there, access the phonological representation, and produce the word. They can use spelling-to-pronunciation rules if they cannot find the string of letters listed.

Frequency also has an effect in naming. That is, frequently occurring words are read more quickly than infrequent ones.

Syntactic Processing

British Left Waffles on Falkland Islands
Enraged Cow Injures Farmer with Ax
Killer Sentenced to Die for Second Time in 10 Years
Stolen Painting Found by Tree

Ambiguous Headlines

Psycholinguistic research has also focused on the more difficult problem of syntactic processing. In addition to recognizing words, the listener must figure out the syntactic and semantic relations among the words and phrases in a sentence, what we earlier referred to as "parsing." The parsing of a sentence is largely determined by the rules of the grammar, but it is also strongly influenced by the sequential nature of language.

The listener actively builds a phrase structure representation of the sentence as she hears it. She must therefore decide for each "incoming" word what its grammatical category is and how it attaches to the tree that is being constructed. Many sentences present "temporary" ambiguities. Some sentences contain a word or words that belong to more than one syntactic category. For example, the string *The warehouse fires....* could continue in one of two ways:

1. ... were set by an arsonist.
2. ... employees over sixty.

Fires is part of a compound noun in sentence (1) and a verb in sentence (2). Experimental studies of such sentences show that both meanings and categories are activated when the subject encounters the ambiguous word, similar to what was found in the priming experiments. The ambiguity is quickly resolved based on syntactic and semantic context, and on the frequency of the two uses of the word. So quick and seamless are the disambiguations that newspaper headlines such as those at the head of this section are scarcely noticeable except to linguists who collect them.

Another important type of temporary ambiguity concerns sentences in which the phrase structure rules allow two possible attachments of a constituent, as illustrated by the following example:

After the child visited the doctor prescribed a course of injections

Experiments that track eye movements of people when they read such sentences show that there are attachment preferences that operate independently of the context. When the mental syntactic processor, or parser, receives the word *doctor,* it attaches it as a direct object of the verb *visit.* For this reason subjects experience a strange perceptual effect when they encounter the verb *prescribed.* They must backtrack and attach *the doctor* as subject of the embedded clause. Sentences that induce this effect are called "garden path sentences." The sentence presented at the beginning of this chapter, *the horse raced past the barn fell* is also a garden path sentence. People will naturally interpret *raced* as the main verb, when in fact the main verb is *fell.*

These attachment preferences are due to the special procedures that the mental parser uses to construct trees. Two of these procedures are **the minimal attachment**

principle and **the late closure principle.** Minimal attachment says "Create the simplest structure consistent with the grammar of the language." In the string *the horse raced past the barn,* the simpler structure is the one in which *the horse* is the subject and *raced* the main verb; the complex subject is "the horse (that was) raced past the barn." In the string *after the child visited the doctor. . .,* the simplest structure is one in which *the child* is attached as the direct object of *visit.* This attachment becomes problematic when the mental parser subsequently encounters the verb *prescribed.*

Late closure says "Attach incoming material to the phrase that is currently being processed." Late closure is exemplified in the following sentence:

Jamie said he will leave this morning.

Listeners prefer to interpret *this morning* as modifying the embedded verb *leave* rather than the root verb *said.* By the time the processor gets to *this morning,* it is already parsing the embedded S so it will attach the adverb phrase to the lowest verb, namely *leave.*

The comprehension of sentences depends on syntactic processing that uses the grammar and special parsing procedures to construct trees. Garden path sentences suggest that the mental parser always pursues a single parse. Although this parse must sometimes be undone, a single parse strategy imposes less of a burden on the processor than attempting to conduct several parses in parallel.

There is also evidence that information about complement structure becomes available when the verb is encountered, and that this information is used to aid the parsing process.

Another striking example of processing difficulty is a rewording of a Mother Goose poem. In its original form we have:

This is the dog, that worried the cat, that killed the rat, that ate the malt, that lay in the house that Jack built.

No problem understanding that? Now try this paraphrase:

This is the malt that the rat that the cat that the dog worried killed ate.

No way, right?

Although the confusing "sentence" follows the rules of relative clause formation — you have no difficulty with *the cat that the dog worried killed the rat* — it seems that once is enough, and when you apply the same process twice, getting *the rat that the cat that the dog worried killed ate the malt,* it becomes difficult to process. (Put a comma after *killed* to see if that helps you.) If we apply the process three times, all the commas in *War and Peace* will not enable you to process it.

The difficulty with this kind of sentence is related to memory constraints. In processing the sentence you have to keep *the malt* in mind all the way until *ate,* but while doing that you have to keep *the rat* in mind all the way until *killed,* and while doing that . . . It's a form of structure juggling that is difficult to perform. Though we have the competence to create such sentences, just as we have the competence to make a sentence with 10,000 words in it, performance limitations prevent creation of such monsters.

Various experimental techniques are used to study sentence comprehension. In addition to the priming and reading tasks, there is a **shadowing** task in which subjects are asked to repeat what they hear as rapidly as possible. Exceptionally good shadowers can follow what is being said only about a syllable behind (300 milliseconds). Most of us, however, shadow with a delay of 500 to 800 milliseconds, which is still quite fast. More interesting than the speed, shadowers often correct speech errors or mispronunciations unconsciously, and even add inflectional endings if they are absent. Even when they are told that the speech they are to shadow includes errors and they should repeat the errors, they are unable to do so. Lexical corrections are more likely to occur when the target word is predictable from what has been said previously. These shadowing experiments provide further evidence that the syntactic parser makes use of context and lexical information.

The ability to understand and comprehend what is said to us is a complex psychological process involving the internal grammar, parsing procedures such as minimal attachment and late closure, frequency factors, memory, and both linguistic and nonlinguistic context.

Speech Production

As we saw, the speech chain starts with a speaker who, through some complicated set of neuromuscular processes, produces an acoustic signal that represents a thought, idea, or message to be conveyed to a listener, who must then decode the signal to arrive at a similar message. It is more difficult to devise experiments that provide information on how the speaker proceeds than to do so from the listener's side of the process. The best information has come from observing and analyzing spontaneous speech.

PLANNING UNITS

We might suppose that speakers' thoughts are simply translated into words one after the other via a semantic mapping process. Grammatical morphemes would be added as demanded by the syntactic rules of the language. The phonetic representation of each word in turn would then be mapped onto the neuromuscular commands to the articulators to produce the acoustic signal representing it.

We know, however, that this supposition is not a true picture of speech production. Although sounds within words, and words within sentences are linearly ordered, speech errors show that the pre-articulation stages involve units larger than the single phonemic segment or even the word, as illustrated by the "U.S. Acres" cartoon. Phrases and even whole sentences are constructed before the production of a single sound. Errors show that features, segments, and words can be anticipated, that is, produced earlier than intended, or reversed (as in typical spoonerisms), so the later words or phrases in which they occur must already be conceptualized. This point is illustrated in the following examples of speech errors (the intended utterance is to the left of the arrow, the actual utterance, including the error, is to the right of the arrow).

1. The *h*iring of minority faculty. → The *f*iring of minority faculty.
   (The intended *h* is replaced by the *f* of *faculty,* which occurs later in the intended utterance.)

2. *a*d hoc → *o*dd h*a*ck
   (The vowels /æ/ of the first word and /a/ of the second are exchanged or reversed.)

3. *b*ig and *f*at → *p*ig and *v*at
   (The values of a single feature are switched: [+ voiced] becomes [– voiced] in *big* and [– voiced] becomes [+ voiced] in *fat.*)

4. There are many ministers in our church. → There are many churches in our minister.
   (The stem morphemes *minister* and *church* are exchanged; the grammatical plural morpheme remains in its intended place in the phrase structure.)

5. Seymour sliced the salami with a knife. → Seymour sliced a knife with the salami.
   (The entire noun phrases — article + noun — were exchanged.)

In these errors, the intonation contour (primary stressed syllables and variations in pitch) remained the same as in the intended utterances, even when the words were disordered. In the intended utterance of (5), the highest pitch would be on *knife.* In the disordered sentence, the highest pitch occurred on the second syllable of *salami.* The pitch rise and increased loudness are thus determined by the syntactic structure of the sentence and are independent of the individual words. Thus syntactic structures also are units in linguistic performance.

Errors like those just cited are constrained in interesting ways. Phonological errors involving segments or features, as in (1), (2), and (3), primarily occur in content words, and not in grammatical morphemes, again showing the distinction between these lexical classes. In addition, while words and lexical morphemes may be interchanged, grammatical morphemes, free or bound inflectional affixes, may not be. As example (4) illustrates, the inflectional endings are left behind and subsequently attached, in their proper phonological form, to the moved lexical morpheme.

Such errors show that speech production involves different kinds of units — features, segments, morphemes, words, phrases, the very units that exist in the grammar. They also show that when we speak, words are structured into larger syntactic phrases that are stored in a kind of buffer memory before segments, features, or words are disordered. This storage must precede the articulatory stage. Thus, we do not select one word from our mental dictionary and say it, then select another word and say it. We organize an entire phrase and often an entire sentence.

The constraints on which units can be exchanged or moved also suggest that grammatical morphemes are added at a stage after the lexical morphemes are selected. This provides one of the motivations for a two-lexicon grammatical model, one containing lexical and derivational morphemes, and the other, grammatical morphemes.

LEXICAL SELECTION

> . . . Humpty Dumpty's theory, of two meanings packed into one word like a portmanteau, seems to me the right explanation for all. For instance, take the two words "fuming" and "furious." Make up your mind that you will say both words but leave it unsettled which you will say first. Now open your mouth and speak. If . . . you have that rarest of gifts, a perfectly balanced mind, you will say "frumious."
>
> Lewis Carroll, Preface to *The Hunting of the Snark*

In chapter 5, word substitution errors were used to illustrate the semantic properties of words. Such substitutions are seldom random; they show that in our attempt to express our thoughts by speaking words in the lexicon, we may make an incorrect lexical selection based on partial similarity or relatedness of meanings.

Blends, in which we produce part of one word and part of another, further illustrate the lexical selection process in speech production; we may select two or more words to express our thoughts and instead of deciding between them, produce them as "portmanteaus," as Humpty Dumpty calls them. Such blends are illustrated in the following errors:

1. splinters/blisters → splisters
2. edited/annotated → editated
3. a swinging/hip chick → a swip chick
4. frown/scowl → frowl

APPLICATION AND MISAPPLICATION OF RULES

> I thought . . . four rules would be enough, provided that I made a firm and constant resolution not to fail even once in the observance of them.
>
> René Descartes (1596–1650)

Spontaneous errors show that the rules of morphology and syntax, discussed in earlier chapters as part of competence, may also be applied (or misapplied) when we speak. It is hard to see this process in normal error-free speech, but when someone says *groupment* instead of *grouping, ambigual* instead of *ambiguous,* or *bloodent* instead of *bloody,* it shows that regular rules are applied to morphemes to form possible but nonexistent words.

Inflectional rules also surface. The UCLA professor who said **We swimmed in the pool* knows that the past tense of *swim* is *swam* but mistakenly applied the regular rule to an irregular form.

Morphophonemic rules also appear to be performance rules as well as rules of competence. Consider the *a/an* alternation rule in English. Errors such as *an istem* for the intended *a system* or *a burly bird* for the intended *an early bird* show that when segmental disordering changes a noun beginning with a consonant to a noun beginning with a vowel, or vice versa, the indefinite article is also changed so that it conforms to the grammatical rule.

Such utterances also reveal that in speech production, internal editing, or monitoring, attempts to prevent errors. When an error slips by the editor, such as the disordering of phonemes, the editor prevents a compounding of errors. Thus, when the /b/ of "bird" was anticipated and added to the beginning of "early" the result was not **an burly bird*. The editor applied (or reapplied) the a/an rule to produce *a burly bird*.

An examination of such data also tells us something about the stages in the production of an utterance. Disordering of phonemes must occur before the indefinite article is given its phonological form or the morphological rule must reapply after the initial error has occurred. An error such as *bin beg* for the intended *Big Ben* shows that phonemes are disordered before phonetic allophones are determined. That is, the intended *Big Ben* phonetically is [bɪg bẽn] with an oral [ɪ] before the [g], and a nasal [ẽ] before the [n].

In the utterance that was produced, however, the [ĩ] is nasalized because it now occurs before the disordered [n], whereas the [ɛ] is oral before the disordered [g]. If the disordering occurred after the phonemes had been replaced by phonetic allophones, the result would have been the phonetic utterance [bɪn bẽg].

Nonlinguistic Influences

The discussion on speech comprehension suggested that nonlinguistic factors are involved in and sometimes interfere with linguistic processing. They also affect speech production. The individual who said *He made hairlines* instead of *He made headlines* was referring to a barber. The fact that the two compound nouns both start with the same sound, are composed of two syllables, have the same stress pattern, and contain the identical second morphemes undoubtedly played a role in producing the error; but the relationship between hairlines and barbers may also have been a contributing factor. Similar comments apply to the congressional representative who said, "It can deliver a large *payroll*" instead of "It can deliver a large *payload*," in reference to a bill to fund the building of bomber aircraft.

Other errors show that thoughts unrelated structurally to the intended utterance may have an influence on what is said. One speaker said "I've never heard of classes *on April 9*" instead of the intended *on Good Friday*. Good Friday fell on April 9 that year. The two phrases are not similar phonologically or morphologically, yet the nonlinguistic association seems to have influenced what was said. A similar observation may apply to the earlier seen substitution of *firing* for *hiring* regarding minority faculty, or *payroll* for *payload* regarding the bomber contract. This influence is a further example of the distinction between linguistic competence and performance.

Both normal conversational data and experimentally elicited data provide the psycholinguist with evidence for the construction of models of both speech production and comprehension, the beginning and ending points of the speech chain of communication.

Computer Processing of Human Language

Man is still the most extraordinary computer of all.

John F. Kennedy

Until a few decades ago, language was strictly "humans only — others need not apply."
Today, it is common for computers to process language. **Computational linguistics** is
a subfield of linguistics and computer science that is concerned with the interactions of
human language and computers.

Computational linguistics includes the analysis of written texts and spoken discourse, the translation of text and speech from one language into another, the use of
human (not computer) languages for communication between computers and people,
and the modeling and testing of linguistic theories.

Text and Speech Analysis

[The professor had written] all the words of their language in their several moods, tenses and
declensions [on tiny blocks of wood, and had] emptied the whole vocabulary into his frame,
and made the strictest computation of the general proportion there is in books between the
numbers of particles, nouns, and verbs, and other parts of speech.

Jonathan Swift, *Gulliver's Travels*

FREQUENCY ANALYSIS, CONCORDANCES, AND COLLOCATIONS

Jonathan Swift prophesied one application of computers to language: statistical analysis. The relative frequencies (that is, the "general proportions") of letters and sounds, morphemes, words, word categories, types of phrases, and so on, may be swiftly and accurately computed for any textual or spoken input, or **corpus.**

A frequency analysis of one million words of written American English[2] reveals the ten most frequently occurring words: *the, of, and, to, a, in, that, is, was,* and *he.* These "little" words accounted for about 25 percent of the words in the corpus, with *the* leading the pack at 7 percent. A similar analysis of *spoken* American English produced somewhat different results.[3] The "winners" were *I, and, the, to, that, you, it, of, a,* and *know,* accounting for nearly 30 percent. This is but one of the differences between spoken and written language demonstrated by corpus analysis. All English prepositions except *to* occur more frequently in written than in spoken English, and not surprisingly, profane and taboo words (see chapter 10) were far more numerous in spoken than written language.

A **concordance** takes frequency analysis one step further by specifying the location within the text of each word, and its surrounding context. A concordance of the previous paragraph would not only show that the word *words* occurred five times, but would indicate in which line of the paragraph it appeared, and provide its context. If one chose a "window" of three words on either side for context, the concordance would look like this for *words:*

of one million	**words**	of written American
most frequently occurring	**words:**	*the, of, and,*
he. These "little"	**words**	accounted for about
percent of the	**words,**	in the corpus
profane and taboo	**words**	(see chapter 10)

A concordance, as you can see, might be of limited usefulness because of its "raw" nature. A way to refine a concordance is through **collocation analysis.** A collocation is the occurrence of two or more words within a short space of each other in a corpus. The point is to find evidence that the presence of one word in the text affects the occurrence of other words. Such an analysis must be statistical and involve large samples to show significant results. In the above concordance of *words,* there is not enough data to be significant. If we performed a concordance on this entire book, patterns would emerge that would show that *words* and *written, words* and *taboo,* and *words* and *of,* are more likely to occur close together than, say, *words* and *million.*

Such analyses can be conducted on existing texts (such as the works of Shakespeare or the Bible) or on any corpus of utterances gathered from spoken or written sources. Authorship attribution is one motivation for these studies. By analyzing the various books of the Bible, for instance, it is possible to get a sense of who wrote what passages.

---

[2] H. Kučera and W. N. Francis. 1967. *Computational Analysis of Present-Day American English.* Providence, RI: Brown University Press.

[3] H. Dahl. 1979. *Word Frequencies of Spoken American English.* Essex, CT: Verbatim

In a notable study of The Federalist Papers, the authorship of a disputed paper was attributed to James Madison rather than to Alexander Hamilton. This was accomplished by comparing the statistical analyses of the paper in question with those of known works by the two writers.

A concordance of sounds by computer may reveal patterns in poetry that would be nearly impossible for a human to detect. An analysis of the "Iliad" showed that many of the lines with an unusual number of etas (/i/) related to youth and lovemaking; the line with the most alphas (/a/) was interpreted as being an imitation of stamping feet, the marching of armies. The use of computers permits literary scholars to study poetic and prosaic features such as assonance, alliteration, meter, and rhythm. Today, computers can do the tedious mechanical work that once had to be done painstakingly with paper and pencil.

INFORMATION RETRIEVAL AND SUMMARIZATION

Hired
Tired
Fired

A career summary, source obscure

Many people use the search features of the Internet to find information. Typically, one enters a keyword, or perhaps several, and magically the computer returns the location of Web sites that contain information relating to that keyword. This process is an example of **information retrieval.** It may be as trivial as finding Web sites that contain the keyword exactly as it is entered, but usually some linguistic analysis is applied. Web sites are returned, and even ranked, according to the frequency of occurrence of the keyword, different morphological forms of the keyword, synonyms of the keyword, and concepts semantically related to the keyword. For example, the keyword *bird* might retrieve information based on *bird, birds, to bird, bird feeders, water birds, avian, sparrow, feathers, flight,* and so on.

In general, information retrieval is the use of computers to locate and display data gleaned from possibly very large databases. The input to an information retrieval system consists of words, statements, or questions, which the computer analyzes linguistically and then uses the results to sift through the database for pertinent information. Nowadays, highly refined and complex information retrieval systems identify useful patterns or relationships in corpuses or other computer repositories using highly complex linguistic and statistical analyses. The term **data mining** is used currently for the highly evolved information retrieval systems.

A keyword as general as *bird* may return far more information than could be read in a year if a large database such as an encyclopedia is queried. Much of the data would repeat itself, and some information would outweigh other information. Through **summarization** programs, computers can eliminate redundancy and identify the most salient features of a body of information. World leaders, corporate executives, and even university professors — all of whom may wish to digest large volumes of textual material such as reports, newspapers, and scholarly articles — can benefit through summarization processes providing the material is available in computer-readable form, which is increasingly the case in the first few years of the twenty-first century.

A typical scenario would be to use information retrieval to access, say, a hundred articles about birds. The articles may average 5,000 words. Summarization programs, which can be set to reduce an article by a certain amount, say 1/10 or 1/100, are applied. The human reads the final output. Thus 500,000 words can be reduced to 5,000 or 10,000 words containing the most pertinent information, which may then be read in 10 or 20 minutes. Former President Bill Clinton, a fast reader, could absorb the contents of relevant articles from upwards of 100 news sources from around the world with the help of aides using computer summarizations.

Summarization programs range from the simplistic "print the first sentence of every paragraph," to complex programs that analyze the document semantically to identify the important points, often using "concept vectors." A concept vector is a list of meaningful keywords whose presence in a paragraph is a measure of the paragraph's significance, and therefore an indication of whether the content of that paragraph should be included in a summarization. The summary document contains concepts from as many of the key paragraphs as possible, subject to length constraints.

SPELL CHECKERS

> Take care that you never spell a word wrong . . . It produces great praise to a lady to spell well.
>
> Thomas Jefferson

Spell checkers, and perhaps in the future, pronunciation checkers, are an application of computational linguistics that vary in sophistication from mindless, brute force lookups in a dictionary, to enough intelligence to flag *your* when it should be *you're,* or *bear* when *bare* is intended. One often finds spell checkers as front ends to information retrieval systems, checking the keywords to prevent misspellings from misleading the search. However, as the following poem reveals, spell checkers cannot replace careful editing:

> *I have a spelling checker*
> It came with my PC
> *It plane lee marks four my revue*
> miss steaks aye can knot see
>
> A checker is a blessing
> It freeze yew lodes of thyme
> It helps me right awl stiles to read
> *And aides me when eye rime*
>
> To rite with care is quite a feet
> Of witch won should bee proud
> And wee mussed dew the best wee can
> Sew flaws are not aloud
>
> Found on the Internet, source obscure

Machine Translation

Egad, I think the interpreter is the hardest to be understood of the two!

R. B. Sheridan, *The Critic*

. . . There exist extremely simple sentences in English — and . . . for any other natural
language — which would be uniquely . . . and unambiguously translated into any other
language by anyone with a sufficient knowledge of the two languages involved, though I
know of no program that would enable a machine to come up with this unique rendering. . . .

Yeshua Bar-Hillel

President Clinton required information from sources written in many languages, and
translators worked hard to fulfill the president's demand. Scholars and business personnel have a similar need, and that need has existed since the dawn of human writing (see
chapter 12).

The first use of computers for natural language processing began in the 1940s with
the attempt to develop **automatic machine translation.** During World War II, United
States' scientists, without the assistance of computers, deciphered coded Japanese military communications and proved their skill in coping with difficult language problems.
The idea of using deciphering techniques to translate from one language into another
was expressed in a letter written to cyberneticist Norbert Wiener by Warren Weaver, a
pioneer in the field of computational linguistics: "When I look at any article in Russian,
I say: 'This is really written in English, but it has been coded in some strange symbols.
I will now proceed to decode it.' "[4]

The aim in automatic translation is to input a written passage in the **source language** and to receive a grammatical passage of equivalent meaning in the **target language** (the output). In the early days of machine translation, it was believed that this
task could be accomplished by entering into the memory of a computer a dictionary of
a source language and a dictionary with the corresponding morphemes and words of a
target language. The translating program attempted to match the morphemes of the
input sentence with those of the target language. Unfortunately, what often happened
was a process that early experimenters with machine translation called "language in,
garbage out."

Translation is more than word-for-word replacement. Often there is no equivalent
word in the target language, and the order of words may differ, as in translating from a
SVO language like English to a SOV language like Japanese. There is also difficulty in
translating idioms, metaphors, jargon, and so on.

Human translators cope with these problems because they know the grammars of
the two languages and draw on general knowledge of the subject matter and the world
to arrive at the intended meaning. Machine translation is often impeded by lexical and
syntactic ambiguities, structural disparities between the two languages, morphological
complexities, and other cross-linguistic differences. It is often difficult to get good trans-

---

[4] W. N. Locke and A. D. Boothe, eds. 1955. *Machine Translation of Languages.* New York: Wiley.

lations even when humans do the translating, as is illustrated by some of the "garbage" printed on signs in non-English-speaking countries as "aids" to tourists:

> The lift is being fixed for the next day. During that time we regret that you will be unbearable. (Bucharest hotel lobby)
>
> The nuns harbor all diseases and have no respect for religion. (Swiss nunnery hospital)
>
> All the water has been passed by the manager. (German hotel)
>
> Because of the impropriety of entertaining guest of the opposite sex in the bedroom, it is suggested that the lobby be used for this purpose. (Hotel in Zurich)
>
> The government bans the smoking of children. (Turkey)

Similar problems are evident in this brief excerpt of the translation of an interview of the entertainer Madonna in the Hungarian newspaper *Blikk:*

> BLIKK: Madonna, let's cut toward the hunt: Are you a bold hussy-woman that feasts on men who are tops?
>
> MADONNA: Yes, yes, this is certainly something that brings to the surface my longings. In America it is not considered to be mentally ill when a woman advances on her prey in a discotheque setting with hardy cocktails present.

Such "translations" represent the difficulties of finding the right words, but word choice is not the only problem in automatic translation. There are challenges in morphology when translating between languages that are polymorphemic, such as English, and languages that tend to have less rich morphologies. A word like *ungentlemanliness* is certainly translatable into any language, but few languages are likely to have an exact word with that meaning, so a phrase of several words is needed. Similarly, *mbuki-mvuki* is a Swahili word that means "to shuck off one's clothes in order to dance." English does not have a word for that practice, but not for lack of need.

Syntactic problems are equally challenging. English is a language that allows possessive forms of varying syntactic complexity, such as *that man's son's dog's food dish,* or *the guy that my roommate is dating's cousin.* Translating these sentences without a loss of meaning into languages that prohibit such structures requires a great deal of sentence restructuring.

We have been implicitly discussing translation of written texts. What about the translation of speech from one language to another? On the one side, speech recognition is needed — or "speech-to-text." On the other side, "text-to-speech" is required. The most general machine translation scenario — that of speech-to-speech — encapsulates the areas of computational linguistics concerned with computers utilizing human grammars to communicate with humans, or to assist humans in communicating with each other. Diagrammatically, we have a progression like the flowchart in Figure 9.3.

Figure 9.3   Logic flow of machine translation of speech.

Computers That Talk and Listen

The first generations of computers had received their inputs through glorified typewriter keyboards, and had replied through high-speed printers and visual displays. Hal could do this when necessary, but most of his communication with his shipmates was by means of the spoken words. Poole and Bowman could talk to Hal as if he were a human being, and he would reply in the perfect idiomatic English he had learned during the fleeting weeks of his electronic childhood.

Arthur C. Clarke, *2001, A Space Odyssey*

The ideal computer is multilingual; it should "speak" computer languages such as FORTRAN and Java, and human languages such as French and Japanese. For many purposes it would be helpful if we could communicate with computers as we communicate with other humans, through our native language; but the computers portrayed in films and on television as capable of speaking and understanding human language do not yet exist.

The translation processes of Figure 9.3 summarize the areas of computational linguistics concerned with human-machine communication. Speech-to-text on the one end, and text-to-speech on the other end, are the chief concern of **computational phonetics and phonology.** The tasks of machine understanding and of language generation, whether for purposes of translation into a target language or as part of the human-machine communication process, encompasses **computational morphology, computational syntax, computational semantics,** and **computational pragmatics,** all of which are discussed below.

COMPUTATIONAL PHONETICS AND PHONOLOGY

Computational phonetics and phonology has two concerns. The first is with programming computers to analyze the speech signal into its component phones and phonemes. The second is to send the proper signals to an electronic speaker so that it enunciates the phones of the language and combines them into morphemes and words. The first of these is **speech recognition;** the second is **speech synthesis.**

Speech Recognition

When Frederic was a little lad he proved so brave and daring,
His father thought he'd 'prentice him to some career seafaring.
I was, alas! his nurs'rymaid, and so it fell to my lot
To take and bind the promising boy apprentice to a **pilot** —

"B.C." copyright © 1987 News America Syndicate. Reprinted by permission of Johnny Hart and Creators Syndicate, Inc.

A life not bad for a hardy lad, though surely not a high lot,
Though I'm a nurse, you might do worse than make your boy a pilot.
I was a stupid nurs'rymaid, on breakers always steering,
And I did not catch the word aright, through being hard of hearing;
Mistaking my instructions, which within my brain did gyrate
I took and bound this promising boy apprentice to a **pirate.**

The Pirates of Penzance, Gilbert and Sullivan, 1877

When you listen to someone speak a foreign language, you notice that it is continuous except for breath pauses, and that it is difficult to segment the speech into sounds and words. It's all run together. The computer faces this situation when it tries to do speech recognition.

Early speech recognizers did not even attempt to "hear" individual sounds. Programmers stored the acoustic patterns of words in the memory of the computer and programmed it to look for those patterns in the speech signal. The computer had a fixed, small vocabulary. Moreover, it best recognized the speech of the same person who provided the original word patterns. It would have trouble "understanding" a different speaker, and if a word outside the vocabulary was uttered, the computer was clueless. If the words were run together, recognition accuracy also fell, and if the words were not fully pronounced, say *missipi* for Mississippi, failure generally ensued. Coarticulation effects also muddied the waters. The computer might have [hɪz] as its representation of the word *his,* but in the sequence *his soap,* pronounced [hɪssop] the *his* is pronounced [hɪs] with a voiceless [s]. As well, the vocabulary best consisted of words that were not too similar phonetically, avoiding confusion between words like *pilot* and *pirate,* which might, as with the young lad in the song, have grave consequences.

Today, many interactive phone systems have a speech recognition component. They will invite you to "press 1 or say 'yes'; press 2 or say 'no,'" or something similar. These systems have very small vocabularies and so can search the speech signal for anything resembling a keyword's prestored acoustic patterns and generally get it right.

The more sophisticated speech recognizers that can be purchased for use on a personal computer have much larger vocabularies, upwards of 25,000 words. To be highly accurate they must be trained to the voice of a specific person, and they must be able to detect individual phones in the speech signal. The training consists in the user making multiple utterances known in advance to the computer, which extracts the acoustic patterns of each phone typical of that user. Later the computer uses those patterns to aid in the recognition process.

Because no two utterances are ever identical, and because there is generally noise (nonspeech sounds) in the signal, the matching process that underlies speech recognition is statistical. On the phonetic level, the computations may say [b] with 30 percent confidence, [p] with 35 percent confidence, and [pʰ] with 35 percent confidence. Other factors may be used to help the decision. For example, if the computer is confident that the preceding sound is [s], then [p] is the likely candidate, and the first two phonemes of the word are /sp/. The system takes advantage of its (i.e., the programmer's) knowledge of sequential constraints (see chapter 7). If, on the other hand, the sound occurs at the beginning of the word, it must be [pʰ] or [b] and further information is needed to determine whether it is the phoneme /p/ or /b/. If the following sounds are [ek} then /b/ is the one, since *bake* is a word but **pake* is not. If the computer is unable to decide, it may offer a list of choices such as *pack, back,* and ask the person using the system to decide.

Even these modern systems are brittle. They break when circumstances become unfavorable. If the user speaks rapidly with lots of coarticulation (*whatcha* for *what are you*), and there is a lot of background noise, recognition accuracy plummets. People do better. If someone mumbles, you can generally make out what they are saying because you have context to help you. In a noisy setting such as a party, you are able to converse with your dance partner despite the background noise because your brain has the ability to filter out irrelevant sounds. This effect is so striking it is given a name: **the cocktail party effect.** Computers are not nearly as capable of coping with noise as people, though research directed at the problem is beginning to show positive results.

Speech Synthesis

Machines which, with more or less success, imitate human speech, are the most difficult to construct, so many are the agencies engaged in uttering even a single word — so many are the inflections and variations of tone and articulation, that the mechanician finds his ingenuity taxed to the utmost to imitate them.

Scientific American (January 14, 1871)

Speak clearly, if you speak at all; carve every word before you let it fall.

Oliver Wendell Holmes, Sr.

Early efforts toward building "talking machines" were concerned with machines that could produce sounds that imitated human speech. In 1779, Christian Gottlieb Kratzenstein won a prize for building such a machine. It was "an instrument constructed like the vox humana pipes of an organ which . . . accurately express the sounds of the vowels." In building this machine he also answered a question posed by the Imperial Academy of St. Petersburg: "What is the nature and character of the sounds of the vowels *a, e, i, o, u* [that make them] different from one another?" Kratzenstein constructed a set of "acoustic resonators" similar to the shapes of the mouth when these vowels are articulated and set them resonating by a vibrating reed that produced pulses of air similar to those coming from the lungs through the vibrating vocal cords.

Twelve years later, Wolfgang von Kempelen of Vienna constructed a more elaborate machine with bellows to produce a stream of air to simulate the lungs, and with other mechanical devices to simulate the different parts of the vocal tract. Von Kempelen's machine so impressed the young Alexander Graham Bell, who saw a replica of the machine in Edinburgh in 1850, that he, with his brother Melville, attempted to construct a "talking head," making a cast from a human skull. They used various materials to form the velum, palate, teeth, lips, tongue, cheeks, and so on, and installed a metal larynx with vocal cords made by stretching a slotted piece of rubber. They used a keyboard control system to manipulate all the parts with an intricate set of levers. This ingenious machine produced vowel sounds, some nasal sounds, and even a few short combinations of sounds.

With the advances in the acoustic theory of speech production, and the technological developments in electronics, machine production of speech sounds has made great progress. We no longer have to build physical models of the speech-producing mechanism; we can now imitate the process by producing the physical signals electronically.

Research on speech has shown that all speech sounds can be reduced to a small number of acoustic components. One way to produce synthetic speech is to mix these important parts together in the proper proportions, depending on the speech sounds to be imitated. It is rather like following a recipe for making soup, which might read: "Take two quarts of water, add one onion, three carrots, a potato, a teaspoon of salt, a pinch of pepper, and stir it all together."

This method of producing synthetic speech would include a "recipe" that might read:

1. Start with a tone at the same frequency as vibrating vocal cords (higher if a woman's or child's voice is being synthesized, lower for a man's).
2. Emphasize the harmonics corresponding to the formants required for a particular vowel quality.
3. Add hissing or buzzing for fricatives.
4. Add nasal resonances for nasal sounds.
5. Temporarily cut off sound to produce stops and affricates.
6. and so on. . . .

All these "ingredients" are blended electronically, using computers to produce highly intelligible, more or less natural-sounding speech.

Most synthetic speech still has a machinelike quality or "accent," due to small inaccuracies in simulation, and because suprasegmental factors such as changing intonation and stress patterns are not yet fully understood. If not correct, such factors may be more confusing than mispronounced phonemes. Currently, the chief area of research in speech synthesis is concerned precisely with discovering and programming the rules of rhythm and timing that native speakers apply.

Still, speech synthesizers today are no harder to understand than a person speaking a dialect slightly different from one's own, and when the context is sufficiently narrow, as in a synthetic voice reading a telephone number, there are no problems.

A speech synthesizer has two components. One is the electronic device we have been describing that converts a phonetic symbol to an electronic representation which, when played through a speaker, resembles human speech. The other component is a text-to-speech system that translates the input text into a phonetic representation. This task is like the several exercises at the end of chapter 6 where we asked you for a phonetic transcription of written words.

The difficulties of text-to-speech are legion. We will mention two. The first is the heteronym problem: words spelled alike but pronounced differently (see chapter 5 for a fuller discussion).

Read may be pronounced like *red* in *She has read the book,* but like *reed* in *She will read the book.* How does the text-to-speech system know which is which? Make no mistake about the answer. The machine must have structural knowledge of the sentence to make the correct choice, just as humans do. Unstructured, linear knowledge will not suffice. For example, we might program the text-to-speech system to pronounce *read* as *red* when the previous word is a form of *have.* But this fails in a number of ways. First, the *have* governs the pronunciation at a distance, both from the left and the right, as in *Has the girl with the flaxen hair read the book?* and *Oh, the girl read the book, has she!* It's the underlying structure that needs to be known, namely that *has* is an auxiliary verb for the main verb *to read.* If we try the ploy of pronouncing *read* as *red* whenever *have* is "in the vicinity," we run into sentences like *The teacher said to have the girl read the book by tomorrow,* where this version of *read* gets the *reed pronunciation.* Even worse for the linear analysis are sentences like *It's the girl that you must have read the book,* where the words *have read* occur next to each other. Of course you know that this occurrence of *read* is of the *reed* type, because you know English and therefore know English syntactic structures. Only through structural knowledge can the heteronym problem be approached effectively. More discussion of this takes place in the section on computational syntax later in this chapter.

The second difficulty is inconsistent spelling, well illustrated by the first two lines of a longer poem:

> I take it you already know
> Of *tough* and *bough* and *cough* and *dough*

Each of the *ough* words is phonetically different, but it is difficult to find rules that dictate when *gh* should be [f] and when it is silent. Modern computers have sufficient storage capacity to store every word in the language, its alternative spellings, and its likely pronunciations. This list may include acronyms, abbreviations, foreign words, proper names, numbers including fractions, and special symbols such as #, whose pronunciation is "pound sign." Such a list is helpful — it is like memorizing rather than figuring out the pronunciations — and encompasses a large percentage of items, including the *ough* words. However, the list can never be complete. New words, new word forms, proper names, abbreviations, and acronyms are constantly being added to the language and cannot be anticipated. The text-to-speech system requires letter-to-phone conversion rules for items not in its dictionary. The challenges here are similar to those faced when learning to read, which are considerable and, when it comes to the pronunciation of proper names, which may be of foreign origin, are utterly daunting.

Speech synthesis has important applications. It benefits visually impaired persons in the form of "reading machines," now commercially available. Mute patients with laryngectomies or other medical conditions that prevent normal speech can use synthesizers to express themselves. For example, researchers at North Carolina State University developed a communication system for an individual with so severe a form of multiple sclerosis that he could utter no sound and was totally paralyzed except for nodding his head. Using a head movement for "yes" and its absence as "no," this individual could select words displayed on a computer screen and assemble sentences to express his thoughts, which were then spoken by a synthesizer.

Most of us these days hear synthesized speech when we call our bank and an "automated bank clerk" tells us our bank balance, or when a telephone information "operator" gives us a requested phone number. Most airlines offer up-to-the-minute arrival and departure information via automatic processing using a synthetic voice. Many information services are automated and deliver timely information, such as stock prices, over the telephone via synthesized speech. Although some people find the speech unpleasant, and even unnerving, it makes information that is accurate and current available to millions of people over the telephone.

COMPUTATIONAL MORPHOLOGY

If we wish our computers to speak and understand grammatical English, we must teach them morphology (see chapter 3). We can't have machines going around saying, "*The cat is sit on the mat," or "*My five horse be in the barn." Similarly, if computers are to understand English they need to know that *sitting* contains two morphemes, *sit+ing*,

"Tumbleweeds" copyright © 1991. Reprinted with special permission of North America Syndicate, Inc.

where as *spring* is one morpheme, and *earring* is two but they are *ear+ring*, not *earr+ing.*

The processing of word structures by computers is computational morphology. The computer needs to understand the structure of words both to understand the words and to use the words in a grammatically correct way. To process words the computer is programmed to look for roots and affixes. In some cases this is straightforward. *Books* is easily broken into *book+s, walking* into *walk+ing, fondness* into *fond+ness,* and *unhappy* into *un+happy.* These cases, and many like them, are the easy ones, because the spelling is well behaved, and the morphological processes are general. Other words are more difficult, such as *profundity = profound+ity, galactic = galaxy+ic,* and *democracy = democrat+y.*

One approach is to place all the morphological forms of all the words in the language in the computer's dictionary. Although today's computers can handle such a high computational load — many millions of forms — there would still be problems because of the generality of the processes. As soon as a new word enters the language, as *fax* did some years ago, a whole family of words is possible: *faxes, fax's, faxing, faxed, refax,* and *faxable;* and many others are not possible: **faxify, *exfax, *disfax,* and so on. The dictionary would be continually out of date.

Moreover, not all forms are predictable. Although *uglify* is not a dictionary word, if you hear it you know, and the computer should know, that it means "to make ugly." Likewise, compounding is a general process, and it would be impossible to predict all possible compounds of English. When *skybox* was coined from *sky+box,* no computer could have had it in its dictionary.

The computer needs to have the ability to break words correctly into their component morphemes, and to understand each morpheme and its affect on the word's meaning, and where the word can be placed in a sentence. Computational morphology, then, is a host of interwoven rules, exceptions, and word/morpheme forms, all with the purpose of comprehending the internal structure of words.

Always, difficult problems remain. If the computer sees *resent,* how does it know if it's the monomorphemic *resent* (with a /z/), or *re + sent?* A broader context is needed, and that is the topic of the next section.

COMPUTATIONAL SYNTAX

In the beginning, there was ELIZA.

PATIENT: Men are all alike.
ELIZA: In what way?
PATIENT: They're always bugging me about something or other.
ELIZA: Can you think of a specific example?
PATIENT: Well, my boyfriend made me come here.
ELIZA: Your boyfriend made you come here?
PATIENT: He says I'm depressed much of the time.
ELIZA: I am sorry to hear you are depressed.

ELIZA is a computer program designed to simulate a nondirective psychiatrist talking to a patient. ELIZA has a collection of prepared phrases stored in memory such as "In what way?" or "Tell me more" that help keep the conversation going when it doesn't "understand" the patient. When ELIZA recognizes certain syntactic patterns, however, it turns them around to make a sensible response, as when it echoes "Your boyfriend made you come here?" ELIZA was programmed with a small bit of syntactic knowledge, which allowed it to make grammatical utterances based on the patient's statements, but no semantic knowledge at all. If a patient says "My sniggle is untherible," ELIZA would respond with "How long has your sniggle been untherible?" ELIZA was designed by the MIT scientist Joseph Weizenbaum in the 1960s. Though its syntactic sophistication is low by today's standards, ELIZA is one of the earliest attempts at human-machine communication that took the syntax of English into account.

Twenty-five years after ELIZA, computer scientists at Duke University and North Carolina State University programmed the "Circuit Fix-It Shop," a system designed to help a technician repair a faulty circuit. Unlike ELIZA, which accepted only typed input and produced printed output, the Circuit Fix-It Shop accepted speech input and spoke its responses. It had its own syntax and was capable both of understanding and speaking syntactically complex utterances, as the following excerpt from a repair session shows:

COMPUTER: This is the circuit fix-it shop. How may I help you?
TECHNICIAN: I need to fix the RS111 circuit.
COMPUTER: I am familiar with that circuit. The LED is supposed to be displaying alternately blinking one and seven.
TECHNICIAN: Where is the LED?
COMPUTER: In the middle right of the blue region is the LED.
TECHNICIAN: No light.
COMPUTER: What is the switch at when the LED is off?
TECHNICIAN: The switch is down.
COMPUTER: You put up the switch.

Once the computer has understood the technician's utterance, it uses rules of semantics and syntax, together with a lexicon of words and morphemes, to formulate a grammatical, sensible response, which its synthesizer program then speaks. The rules in many cases are similar to the phrase structure rules seen in chapter 4, such as form a noun phrase from an article followed by a noun. It also has semantic rules that tells it to use *the* with the word *switch* since its "world knowledge" tells it that there is only one switch in that particular circuit.

To understand a sentence, you must know its syntactic structure. If you didn't know the structure of *dogs that chase cats chase birds,* you wouldn't know whether dogs or cats chase birds. Similarly, machines that understand language must also determine syntactic structure. A **parser** is a computer program that attempts to replicate what we have been calling the "mental parser." Like the mental parser, the parser in a computer uses a grammar to assign a phrase structure to a string of words. Parsers may use a phrase structure grammar and lexicon similar to those discussed in chapter 4.

For example, a parser may use a grammar containing the following rules: S → NP VP, NP → Det N, and so forth. Suppose the machine is asked to parse *The child found the kittens.* A top-down parser proceeds by first consulting the grammar rules and then examining the input string to see if the first word could begin an S. If the input string begins with a Det, as in the example, the search is successful, and the parser continues by looking for an N, and then a VP. If the input string happened to be *child found the kittens,* the parser would be unable to assign it a structure because it doesn't begin with a Determiner, which is required by this grammar to begin an S.

A bottom-up parser takes the opposite tack. It looks first at the input string and finds a Det (*the*) followed by an N (*child*). The rules tell it that this phrase is an NP. It would continue to process *found, the,* and *kittens* to construct a VP, and would finally combine the NP and VP to make an S.

Parsers may run into difficulties with words that belong to several syntactic categories. In a sentence like *The little orange rabbit hopped,* the parser might mistakenly assume *orange* is a noun. Later, when the error is apparent, the parser *backtracks* to the decision point, and retries with *orange* as an adjective. Such a strategy works on confusing but grammatical sentences like *The old man the boats,* and *The Russian women loved died.*

Another way to handle situations that may require backtracking is to make every parse that the grammar allows in parallel. Only parses that finish are accepted as valid. In such a strategy, the two parses of *The Russian women loved died* would have *Russian* as an adjective, and Russian as a noun. The first parse would get as far as *The Russian women loved* but then fail since *died* cannot occur in that position of a verb phrase. The parser must not allow ungrammatical sentences such as **The young women loved died.* The second parse, when it sees the two nouns *Russian women* together, deduces a relative clause (with a missing *that*) and is able to assign the category of noun phrase to *The Russian women loved.* The sentence is completed with the verb *died,* and that parse is successful. A backtracking parser would accomplish the same end by serially processing each possibility, succeeding on one, failing on the other.

In general, humans are far more capable of understanding sentences than computers. But there are some interesting cases where computers outperform humans. For example, try to figure out what the sentence *Buffalo buffalo buffalo buffalo* means. (*Hint:* One occurrence of *buffalo* is a verb meaning "to fool.") Most people have trouble determining its sentence structure, and are thus unable to understand it. A parser, with four simple rules and a lexicon in which *buffalo* has three entries (noun, verb, and adjective) will easily parse this sentence as follows:

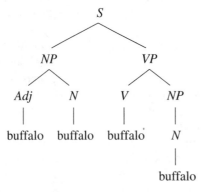

It means "Bison from the city of Buffalo deceive bison."

To produce a sentence it is also necessary to follow the syntactic rules of the grammar. This may be done simplistically. For example, a computer program to generate insults in the style of Shakespeare takes three columns of words, where the first column is a list of simple adjectives, the second a list of hyphenated adjectives, and the third a list of nouns. For example:

Simple Adjectives	**Hyphenated Adjectives**	**Nouns**
bawdy	beetle-headed	baggage
churlish	clay-brained	bladder
goatish	fly-bitten	codpiece
lumpish	milk-livered	hedge-pig
mewling	pox-marked	lout
rank	rump-fed	miscreant
villainous	toad-spotted	varlet

The program chooses a word from each column at random, to produce an adjective phrase insult. Instantaneous insults guaranteed, you goatish, pox-marked bladder, you lumpish, milk-livered hedge-pig.

In less simplistic language generation, the computer is given the meaning of what is to be said, which may be the output part of a translation system, or simply the computer's turn to give information, as in the Circuit-Fix-It-Shop.

The generation system first assigns lexical items to the ideas and concepts to be expressed. These, then, must be fit into phrases and sentences that comply with the syntax of the output language. As in parsing, there are two approaches: top-down and bottom-up. In the top-down approach, the system begins with the highest-level categories such as S(entence). Lower levels are filled in progressively, beginning with noun phrases and verb phrases, and descending to determiners, nouns, verbs, and other sentence parts, always conforming to the syntactic rules. The bottom-up approach begins with the lexical items needed to express the desired meaning, and proceeds to combine them to form the higher-level categories.

A **transition network** is a convenient way to visualize and program the use of a grammar to ensure proper syntactic output. A transition network is a complex of **nodes** (circles) and **arcs** (arrows). A network equivalent to the phrase structure rule S → NP VP is illustrated in Figure 9.4.

The nodes are numbered to distinguish them; the double circle is the "final" node. The object of the generation is to traverse the arcs from the first to the final node.

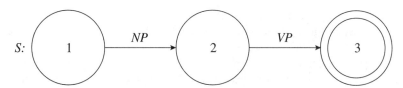

Figure 9.4   Transition network for S → NP VP.

The generator would start at node 1 and realize that a noun phrase is necessary to begin the output. The appropriate concept is assigned to that noun phrase. Other transition networks, in particular, one for NP, determine the structure of the noun phrase. For example, one part of a transition network for a noun phrase would state that an NP may be a pronoun, corresponding to the phrase structure rule NP → Pronoun. It would look like Figure 9.5.

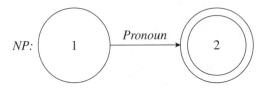

Figure 9.5   Transition network for NP → Pronoun.

To satisfy the NP *arc* in the S network, the *entire NP network* is traversed. In this case, the NP is to be a Pronoun, as determined by the concept needed. The NP arc is then traversed in the S network, and the system is at node 2. To finish, an appropriate verb phrase must be constructed according to the concept to be communicated. That concept is made to comply with the structure of the VP, which is also expressed as a transition network. To get past the VP arc in the S network, the entire VP network is traversed. Figure 9.6 shows one part of the VP complex of transition networks, corresponding to VP → V NP:

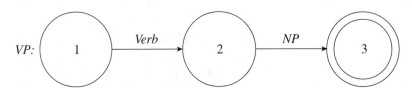

Figure 9.6   Transition network for VP → V NP.

Once the VP network is completed, the VP arc in the S network is traversed to the final node, and the system sends the sentence out to be spoken or printed.

The final sentence of the Circuit-Fix-It-Shop dialogue is *you put up the switch.* The concept is a command to the user (*you*) to move the switch to the up position. It chooses the verb *put up* to represent this concept, and the noun phrase *the switch* to represent the switch that the computer knows the user is already familiar with. The syntax begins in the S network, moves to the NP network which is finished and produces the subject of the sentence, the pronoun *you*. The NP arc is traversed to node 2 in the S network. Now the syntax requires a VP. The scene of action moves to the VP network. The first arc is traversed and gives the verb *put up*. An NP network is again required so that the VP can finish up. This network (not shown) indicates that an NP may be a determiner followed by a noun, in this case, *the* and *switch*. When that network is finished, the NP arc in the VP network is traversed, the VP network is finished, the VP arc in the S network is traversed, the S network is finished, and the final output is the sentence *you put up the switch.*

Since a reference to any network may occur in any other network, or even in the same network itself (thus capturing the recursive property of the syntax), a relatively small number of networks can generate the large number of sentences that may be needed by a natural language system. The networks must be designed so that they characterize only grammatical, never ungrammatical, utterances.

COMPUTATIONAL SEMANTICS

The question of how to represent meaning is one that has been debated for thousands of years, and it continues to engender much research in linguistics, philosophy, psychology, cognitive science, and computer science. In chapter 5 we discussed many of the semantic concepts that a natural language system would incorporate into its operation. For simplicity's sake, we consider computational semantics to be the representation of the meaning of words and morphemes in the computer, as well as the meanings derived from their combinations.

"ZITS" copyright © 2001 ZITS Partnership. Reprinted with special permission of King Features Syndicate, Inc.

Computational semantics has two chief concerns. One is to produce a semantic representation in the computer of language input; the other is to take a semantic representation and produce natural language output that conveys the meaning. These two concerns dovetail in a machine translation system. Ideally — and systems today are *not* ideal — the computer takes input from the source language, creates a semantic representation of its meaning, and from that semantic representation produces output in the target language. Meaning (ideally) remains constant across the entire process. In a dialogue system such as the Circuit-Fix-It-Shop, the computer must create a semantic representation of the user's input, act on it thus producing another semantic representation, and output it to the user in ordinary language.

To generate sentences, the computer tries to find words that fit the concepts incorporated in its semantic representation. In the Circuit-Fix-It-Shop system, the computer had to decide what it wanted to talk about next: the switch, the user, the light, wire 134, or whatever. It needed to choose words corresponding to whether it wanted to declare the state of an object, ask about the state of an object, make a request of the user, tell the user what to do next, and so forth. If the query involved the user, the pronoun *you* would be chosen; if the state of the switch were the chief concern, the words *the switch,* or *a switch above the blue light,* would be chosen. When the components of meaning are assembled, the syntactic rules that we have seen already are called upon to produce grammatical output.

To achieve **speech understanding** the computer tries to find concepts in its semantic representation capabilities that fit the words and structures of the input. When the technician says *I need to fix the RS111 circuit,* the system recognizes that *I* means the user, that *need* represents something that the user lacks and the computer must provide. It further knows that if fixing is what is needed, it has to provide information about the workings of something. It recognizes *the RS111 circuit* as a circuit with certain properties that are contained in certain of its files. It infers that the workings of that particular circuit will be central to the ensuing dialogue.

A computer can represent concepts in numerous ways, none of them perfect or preferable over others. All methods share one commonality: a lexicon of words and morphemes that it is prepared to speak or understand. Such a lexicon would contain morphological, syntactic, and semantic information, as discussed in chapters 3, 4, and 5. Exactly how that information is structured depends on the particular applications it is to be suited for.

On a higher level, the relationships between words are conveniently represented in networks similar (but different in objective) to the transition networks we saw previously. The nodes represent words, and the arcs represent thematic relations (see chapter 5) between the words. *You put up the switch,* then, might have the representation in Figure 9.7.

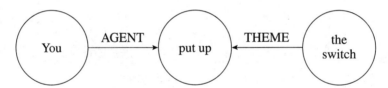

Figure 9.7   Semantic Network for *You put up the switch.*

This means that the user (*you*) is the agent, or doer, and *put up* is what is to be done, and it is to be done to the THEME, which is *the switch.*

Some systems draw on formal logic for semantic representations. *You put up the switch* would be represented in a function/argument form:

PUT UP(YOU, THE SWITCH)

where PUT UP is a "two-place predicate" in the jargon of logicians, and the arguments are YOU and THE SWITCH. The lexicon indicates the appropriate relationships between the arguments of the predicate PUT UP.

Two well-known natural language processing systems from the 1970s used this logical approach of semantic representation. One, named SHRDLU by its developer Terry Winograd, demonstrated a number of abilities, such as being able to interpret questions, draw inferences, learn new words, and even explain its actions. It operated in the context of a "blocks world," consisting of a table, blocks of various shapes, sizes, and colors, and a robot arm for moving the blocks. Using simple sentences, one could ask questions about the blocks and give commands to have blocks moved from one location to another.

The second system, LUNAR developed by William Woods, was capable of answering questions phrased in simple English about the lunar rock samples brought back from the Moon by the astronauts. LUNAR translated English questions into a logical representation, which it then used to query a database of information about the lunar samples.

COMPUTATIONAL PRAGMATICS

Pragmatics, as discussed in chapter 5, is the interaction of the "real world" with the language system. In the Circuit-Fix-It-Shop the computer knows that there is only one switch, that there is no other switch in (its) the universe, and that the determiner *the* is correct for this item. If the human mentioned *a wire,* however, the computer would ask *which wire* because it knows that there are several wires in the circuit. This is simple, computational pragmatics in action.

"Baby Blues" copyright © 1996 Baby Blues Partnership. Reprinted with special permission of King Features Syndicate, Inc.

When a sentence is structurally ambiguous, such as *He sells synthetic buffalo hides,* the parser will compute each structure. Semantic processing may eliminate some of the structures if they are anomalous, but often some ambiguity remains. For example, the structurally ambiguous sentence *John found a book on the Oregon Trail* is semantically acceptable in both its meanings. To decide which meaning is intended, situational knowledge is needed. If John is in the library researching history, the "book *about* the Oregon Trail" meaning is most likely; if John is on a two-week hike to Oregon, the "book *upon* the Oregon Trail" meaning is more plausible.

Many natural language processing systems have a knowledge base of contextual and world knowledge. The semantic processing routines can refer to the knowledge base in cases of ambiguity. For example, the syntactic component of the Circuit-Fix-It-Shop will have two structures for *The LED is in the middle of the blue region at the top.* The sentence is ambiguous. Both meanings are semantically well formed and conceivable. However, the Circuit-Fix-It-Shop's knowledge base "knows" that the LED is in the middle of the blue region, and the blue region is at the top of the work area, rather than that the LED is in the middle, top of the blue region. It uses pragmatic knowledge, knowledge of the world, to disambiguate the sentence.

To conclude this section we return to the subject of machine translation. All of the computational *X*'s (phonology, morphology, syntax, etc.) bear on the ability of computers to translate from a source language to a target language. The greater recognition of the role of syntax, and the application of the linguistic principles of semantics and pragmatics that have evolved over the past fifty years, have made it possible to use computers to translate simple texts — ones in a constrained context such as a mathematical proof — grammatically and accurately between well-studied languages such as English and Russian. More complex texts require human intervention if the translation is to be grammatical and semantically faithful. The use of computers to aid the human translator can improve efficiency by a factor of ten or more, but the day when travelers can whip out a "pocket translator," hold it up to the mouth of a native speaker, and receive a translation in their own language is as yet beyond the horizon.

Computer Models of Grammar

I am never content until I have constructed a . . . model of the subject I am studying. If I succeed in making one, I understand; otherwise I do not.

William Thomson (Lord Kelvin), *Molecular Dynamics and the Wave Theory of Light*

A theory has only the alternative of being right or wrong. A model has a third possibility: it may be right, but irrelevant.

Manfred Eigen, *The Physicist's Conception of Nature*

The grammars used by computers for parsing may not be the same as the grammars linguists construct for human languages, which are models of linguistic competence; nor are they similar, for the most part, to models of linguistic performance. Computers and people are different, and they achieve similar ends differently. Just as an efficient flying machine is not a replica of any bird, efficient grammars for computers do not resemble human language grammars in every detail.

Computers are often used to model physical or biological systems, which allows researchers to study those systems safely and sometimes even cheaply. For example, the performance of a new aircraft can be simulated and the test pilot informed as to safe limits in advance of actual flight.

Computers can also be programmed to model the grammar of a language. An accurate grammar — one that is a true model of a speaker's mental grammar — should be able to generate all and only the sentences of the language. Failure to generate a grammatical sentence indicates an error in the grammar, because the human mental grammar has the capacity to generate all possible grammatical sentences — an infinite set. In addition, if the grammar produces a string that speakers consider ungrammatical, that too indicates a defect in the grammar; although in actual speech performance we often produce ungrammatical strings — sentence fragments, slips of the tongue, word substitutions and blends, and so on — we will judge them to be ill-formed if we notice them. Our grammars cannot generate these strings.

One computer model of a grammar was developed in the 1960s by the computer scientist Joyce Friedman to test a generative grammar of English written by syntacticians at UCLA. More recently, computational linguists are developing computer programs to generate the sentences of a language and to simulate human parsing of these sentences using the rules included in various current linguistic theories. The computational models developed by Ed Stabler, Robert Berwick, Amy Weinberg, and Mark Johnson, among other computational linguists, show that it is possible, in principle, to use a transformational grammar, for example, in speech and comprehension, but it is still controversial whether human language processing works in this way. That is, even if we can get a computer program to produce sentences as output and to parse sentences fed into the machine as input, we still need psycholinguistic evidence that this is the way the human mind stores and processes language.

It is because linguistic competence and performance are so complex that computers are being used as a tool in the attempt to understand human language and its use. We have emphasized some of the differences in the ways human beings and computers process language. For example, humans appear to do speech recognition, parsing, semantic interpretation, and contextual disambiguation more or less simultaneously and smoothly while hearing and comprehending speech. Computers, on the other hand, usually have different components, loosely connected, and perform these functions individually.

One reason for this is that, typically, computers have only a single, powerful processor, capable of performing a single task at a time. Currently, computers are being designed with multiple processors, albeit less powerful ones, which are interconnected. The power of these computers lies both in the individual processors and in the connections. Such computers are capable of **parallel processing,** or carrying out several tasks simultaneously.

With a parallel architecture, computational linguists may be better able to program machine understanding in ways that blend all the stages of processing, from speech recognition through contextual interpretation, and hence approach more closely the way humans process language.

Summary

Psycholinguistics is concerned with **linguistic performance** or processing, the use of linguistic knowledge (competence) in speech production and comprehension.

Comprehension, the process of understanding an utterance, requires the ability to access the mental lexicon to match the words in the utterance to their meanings. Comprehension starts with the perception of the **acoustic speech signal.** The speech signal can be described in terms of the **fundamental frequency,** perceived as **pitch;** the **intensity,** perceived as loudness; and the **quality,** perceived as differences in speech sounds, such as an [i] from an [a]. The speech wave can be displayed visually as a **spectrogram,** sometimes called a **voiceprint.** In a spectrogram, vowels exhibit dark bands where frequency intensity is greatest. These are called **formants** and result from the emphasis of certain *harmonics* of the fundamental frequency, as determined by the shape of the vocal tract. Each vowel has a unique formant pattern.

The speech signal is a continuous stream of sounds. Listeners have the ability to segment the stream into linguistic units and to recognize acoustically distinct sounds as the same linguistic unit.

The perception of the speech signal is necessary but not sufficient for the comprehension of speech. To get the full meaning of an utterance, we must **parse** the string into syntactic structures, since meaning depends on word order and constituent structure in addition to the meaning of words. Some psycholinguists believe we use both **top-down** and **bottom-up** processes during comprehension. Top-down processing uses semantic and syntactic information in addition to the incoming acoustic signal; bottom-up processes use only information contained in the sensory input.

Psycholinguistic experimental studies are aimed at uncovering the units, stages, and processes involved in linguistic performance. A number of experimental techniques have proved to be very helpful. In a **lexical decision** task, subjects are asked to respond to spoken or written stimuli by pressing a button if they consider the stimulus to be a word. In **naming** tasks, subjects read from printed stimuli. The measurement of **response times, RTs,** in naming and other lexical decision tasks shows that it takes longer to comprehend ambiguous utterances versus unambiguous ones, ungrammatical utterances compared to grammatical sentences, and nonsense forms as opposed to real words.

A word may **prime** another word if the words are related in some way such as semantically, phonetically, or even through similar spelling. The priming effect is shown by experiments in which a word such as *nurse* is spoken in a sentence, and it is found that words related to *nurse* such as *doctor* have lower RTs in lexical decision tasks. If an ambiguous word like *mouse* is used in an unambiguous context such as *the mouse ran up the clock,* words related to both meanings of mouse are primed, for example, *cat* and *computer.*

Eye tracking techniques can determine the points of a sentence at which readers have difficulty and have to backtrack to an earlier point of the sentence. These experiments provide strong evidence that the parser has preferences in how it constructs trees and that it pursues a single parse consistent with the grammatical options, which may give rise to garden path effects.

Another technique is **shadowing,** in which subjects repeat as fast as possible what is being said to them. Subjects often correct errors in the stimulus sentence, suggesting that they use linguistic knowledge rather than simply echo the sounds they hear. Other experiments reveal the processes involved in accessing the mental grammar and the influence of nonlinguistic factors in comprehension.

The units and stages in speech production have been studied by analyzing spontaneously produced speech errors. Anticipation errors, in which a sound is produced earlier than in the intended utterance, and **spoonerisms,** in which sounds or words are exchanged or reversed, show that we do not produce one sound or one word or even one phrase at a time. Rather, we construct and store larger units with their syntactic structures specified.

Word substitutions and **blends** show that words are connected to other words phonologically and semantically. The production of ungrammatical utterances also shows that morphological, inflectional, and syntactic rules may be wrongly applied or fail to apply when we speak, but at the same time show that such rules are actually involved in speech production.

Computational linguistics is the study of how computers can process language. Computers aid scholars in analyzing literature and language, translate between languages, and communicate in natural language with human users.

To analyze a **corpus,** or body of data, a computer can do a frequency analysis of words, compute a **concordance,** which locates words in the corpus and gives their immediate context, and compute a **collocation,** which measures how the occurrence of one word affects the probability of the occurrence of other words. Computers are also useful for **information retrieval** based on **keywords,** automatic **summarization,** and **spell checking.**

Soon after their invention, computers were used to try to translate from one language to another. This is a difficult, complex task, and the results are often humorous as the computer struggles to translate text (or speech) in the **source language** into the **target language,** without loss of meaning or grammaticality.

Whether translating from one language to another, or communicating with a human being, computers must be capable of **speech recognition,** processing the speech signal into phonemes, morphemes, and words. They also must be able to speak its output. **Speech synthesis** is a two-step process in which text is first converted to phones, and the phones are simulated electronically to produce speech.

To recognize speech is not to understand speech, and to speak a text does not necessarily mean that the computer knows what it is saying. To understand or generate speech, the computer must process phonemes, morphemes, words, phrases, and sentences, and it must be aware of the meanings of these units (except for phonemes). The computational linguistics of speech understanding and speech generation has the subfields of **computational phonology, computational morphology, computational syntax, computational semantics,** and **computational pragmatics.**

Computational phonology relates phonemes to the acoustic signal of speech. It is statistical in nature because the acoustic signal of a phoneme varies from person to person, and may be degraded by noise. Computational morphology deals with the structure of words, so it tells the computer that the meaning of *bird* applies as well to *birds,* which has in addition the meaning of plural. Computational syntax is concerned with the syntactic categories of words, and with the larger syntactic units of phrases and sentences. It is further concerned with analyzing a sentence into these components for speech understanding, or assembling these components into larger units for speech generation. A formal device called a **transition network** may be used to model the actions of syntactic processing.

Computational semantics is concerned with representing meaning inside the computer, or **semantic representation.** To communicate with a person, the computer creates a semantic representation of what the person says to it, and another semantic representation of what it wants to say back. In a machine translation environment, the computer produces a semantic representation of the source language input, and outputs that meaning in the target language.

Semantic representations may be based on logical expressions involving predicates and arguments, on **semantic networks,** or on other formal devices to represent meaning.

Computational pragmatics may influence the understanding or the response of the computer by taking into account knowledge that the computer system has about the real world, for example, that there is a unique element in the environment, so the determiner *the* can be used appropriately to refer to it.

Computers may be programmed to model a grammar of a human language and thus rapidly and thoroughly test that grammar. Modern computer architectures include **parallel processing** machines that can be programmed to process language more as humans do insofar as carrying out many linguistic tasks simultaneously.

≈ References for Further Reading

Allen, J. 1987. *Natural Language Understanding.* Menlo Park, CA: Benjamin/Cummings.

Barr, A., and E. A. Feigenbaum, eds. 1981. *The Handbook of Artificial Intelligence.* Los Altos, CA: William Kaufmann.

Berwick, R. C., and A. S. Weinberg. 1984. *The Grammatical Basis of Linguistic Performance: Language Use and Acquisition.* Cambridge, MA: MIT Press.

Barnbrook, G. 1996. *Language and Computers: A Practical Introduction to the Computer Analysis of Language.* Edinburgh, Scotland: Edinburgh University Press.

Carlson, G. N., and M. K. Tanenhaus, eds. 1989. *Linguistic Structure in Language Processing.* Dordrecht, The Netherlands: Kluwer Academic Publishers.

Caron, J. 1992. *An Introduction to Psycholinguistics.* Tim Pownall, trans. Toronto, Canada: University of Toronto Press.

Carroll, D. W. 1994. *Psychology of Language.* Pacific Grove, CA: Brooks/Cole.

Clark, H., and E. Clark. 1977. *Psychology and Language: An Introduction to Psycholinguistics.* New York: Harcourt Brace Jovanovich.

Fodor, J. A., M. Garrett, and T. G. Bever. 1986. *The Psychology of Language.* New York: McGraw-Hill.

Foss, D., and D. Hakes. 1978. *Psycholinguistics.* Englewood Cliffs, NJ: Prentice-Hall.

Fromkin, V. A., ed. 1980. *Errors in Linguistic Performance.* New York: Academic Press.

Garman, M. 1990. *Psycholinguistics.* Cambridge, England: Cambridge University Press.

Garnham, A. 1985. *Psycholinguistics: Central Topics.* London and New York: Methuen.

Garrett, M. F. 1988. "Processes in Sentence Production." In F. Newmeyer, ed., *The Cambridge Linguistic Survey, Volume 3.* Cambridge, England: Cambridge University Press.

Gazdar, G., and C. Mellish. 1989. *Natural Language Processing in PROLOG: An Introduction to Computational Linguistics.* Reading, MA: Addison-Wesley.

Gleason, J. B., and N. B. Ratner, eds. 1993. *Psycholinguistics.* Orlando, FL: Harcourt Brace.

Hockey, S. 1980. *A Guide to Computer Applications in the Humanities.* London, England: Duckworth.

Johnson, M. 1989. "Parsing as Deduction: The Use of Knowledge in Language," *Journal of Psycholinguistic Research* 18(1):105–28.

Jurafsky, D., and J. H. Martin. 2000. *Speech and Language Processing.* Upper Saddle River, NJ: Prentice-Hall (Pearson Higher Education).

Ladefoged, P. 1996. *Elements of Acoustic Phonetics, 2d ed.* Chicago, IL: University of Chicago Press.

Lea, W. A. 1980. *Trends in Speech Recognition.* Englewood Cliffs, NJ: Prentice-Hall.

Levelt, W. J. M. 1993. *Speaking: From Intention to Articulation.* Cambridge, MA: MIT Press.

Marcus, M. P. 1980. *A Theory of Syntactic Recognition for Natural Language.* Cambridge, MA: MIT Press.

Miller, G., and P. Johnson-Laird. 1976. *Language and Perception.* Cambridge, MA: Harvard University Press.

Osherson, D., and H. Lasnik, eds. 1990. *Language: An Invitation to Cognitive Science, Volume 1.* Cambridge, MA: MIT Press.

Slocum, J. 1985. "A Survey of Machine Translation: Its History, Current Status, and Future Prospects." *Computational Linguistics* 11(1).

Smith, R., and R. Hipp. 1994. *Spoken Natural Language Dialog Systems.* New York: Oxford University Press.

Sowa, J., ed. 1991. *Principles of Semantic Networks.* San Mateo, CA: Morgan Kaufmann.

Stabler, E. P., Jr. 1992. *The Logical Approach to Syntax: Foundations, Specifications and Implementations of Theories of Government and Binding.* Cambridge, MA: MIT Press.

Weizenbaum, J. 1976. *Computer Power and Human Reason.* San Francisco: W. H. Freeman.

Winograd, T. 1972. *Understanding Natural Language.* New York: Academic Press.

_____. 1983. *Language as a Cognitive Process.* Reading, MA: Addison-Wesley.

Witten, I. H. 1986. *Making Computers Talk.* Englewood Cliffs, NJ: Prentice-Hall.

Exercises

1. Speech errors (e.g., "slips of the tongue" or "bloopers") illustrate a difference between linguistic competence and performance since our very recognition of them as errors shows that we have knowledge of well-formed sentences. Furthermore, errors provide information about the grammar. The following utterances are part of the UCLA corpus of over 15,000 speech errors. Most of them were actually observed. A few are attributed to Dr. Spooner.

   a. For each speech error, state what kind of linguistic unit or rule is involved, that is, phonological, morphological, syntactic, lexical, or semantic.

   b. State, to the best of your ability, the nature of the error, or the mechanisms which produced it.

   (*Note:* The intended utterance is to the left of the arrow; the actual utterance to the right.)

   Example: ad hoc → odd hack

   a. phonological vowel segment   b. reversal or exchange of segments

   Example: she gave it away → she gived it away

   a. inflectional morphology   b. incorrect application of regular past-tense rule to exceptional verb

   Example: When will you leave? → When you will leave?

   a. syntactic rule   b. failure to move the auxiliary to form a question

   (1) brake fluid → blake fruid

   (2) drink is the curse of the working classes → work is the curse of the drinking classes (Spooner)

   (3) we have many ministers in our church → . . . many churches in our minister

(4) untactful → distactful

(5) an eating marathon → a meeting arathon

(6) executive committee → executor committee

(7) lady with the dachshund → lady with the Volkswagen

(8) stick in the mud → smuck in the tid

(9) he broke the crystal on my watch → he broke the whistle on my crotch

(10) a phonological rule → a phonological fool

(11) pitch and stress → piss and stretch

(12) big and fat → pig and vat

(13) speech production → preach seduction

(14) he's a New Yorker → he's a New Yorkan

(15) I'd forgotten about that → I'd forgot abouten that

2. The use of spectrograms for speaker identification is based on the fact that no two speakers have exactly the same speech characteristics. List some differences you have noticed in the speech of several individuals. Can you think of any reasons for such differences?

3. Using a bilingual dictionary of a language you do not know, attempt to translate the following English sentences by looking up each word.

The children will eat the fish.

Send the professor a letter from your new school.

The fish will be eaten by the children.

Who is the person that is hugging that dog?

The spirit is willing, but the flesh is weak.

A. Using your own knowledge, or someone else's, give a grammatically correct translation of each sentence. What difficulties are brought to light by comparing the two translations? Mention five of them.

B. Have a person who knows the target language translate the grammatical translation back into English. What problems do you observe? Are they related to any of the difficulties you mentioned in part A?

4. Suppose you were given a manuscript of a play and were told that it is either by Christopher Marlowe or William Shakespeare (both born in 1564). Suppose further that this work, and all works by Marlowe and Shakespeare, were in a computer. Describe how you would use the computer to help determine the true authorship of the mysterious play.

5. Speech synthesis is useful because it allows computers to convey information without requiring the user to be sighted. Think of five other uses for speech synthesis in our society.

6. Some advantages of speech recognition are similar to those of speech synthesis. A computer that understands speech does not require a person to use hands or eyes to convey information to the computer. Think of five other possible uses for speech recognition in our society.

7. Consider the following ambiguous sentences. Explain the ambiguity, give the most likely interpretation, and state what a computer would have to have in its knowledge base to achieve that interpretation.

   Example: A cheesecake was on the table. It was delicious and was soon eaten.

   a. Ambiguity: "It" can refer to the cheesecake or the table.

   b. Likely: "It" refers to the cheesecake.

   c. Knowledge: Tables are not usually eaten.

   (1) For those of you who have children and don't know it, we have a nursery downstairs. (Sign in a church)

   (2) The police were asked to stop drinking in public places.

   (3) Our bikinis are exciting; they are simply the tops. (Bathing suit ad in newspaper)

   (4) It's time we made smoking history. (Antismoking campaign slogan)

   (5) Do you know the time? (*Hint:* This is a pragmatic ambiguity.)

   (6) Concerned with spreading violence, the president called a press conference.

   (7) The ladies of the church have cast off clothing of every kind and they may be seen in the church basement Friday. (Announcement in a church bulletin)

   The following three items are newspaper headlines:

   (8) Red Tape Holds Up New Bridge

   (9) Kids Make Nutritious Snacks

   (10) Sex Education Delayed, Teachers Request Training

8. Here is a transition network for the Noun Phrase (NP) rule given in chapter 4:

   NP → (Det) (AP) N (PP)

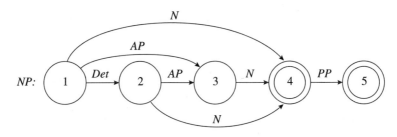

   Using this as a model, draw a transition network for the Verb Phrase Rules:

   VP → V (NP) (PP)

   (*Hint:* Recall from chapter 4 that the above rule abbreviates four rules.)

9. **A.** Here are some sentences along with a possible representation in predicate logic notation. Based on the examples in the text, and those in part B of this exercise, give a *semantic network* representation for each example.

   (1) Birds fly. FLY (BIRDS)

   (2) The student understands the question. UNDERSTAND (THE STUDENT, THE QUESTION)

(3) Penguins do not fly. NOT (FLY [PENGUINS])

(4) The wind is in the willows. IN (THE WIND, THE WILLOWS)

(5) Kathy loves her cat. LOVE (KATHY, [POSSESSIVE (KATHY, CAT)])

B. Here are five more sentences and a semantic network representation for each. Give a representation of each of them using the *predicate logic* notation.

(6) Seals swim swiftly.

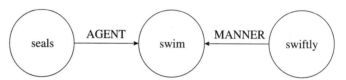

(7) The student doesn't understand the question.

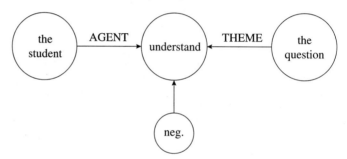

(8) The pen is on the table.

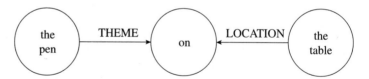

(9) My dog eats bones.

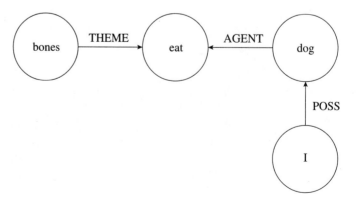

(10) Emily gives money to charity. (*Hint:* Give is a three-place predicate.)

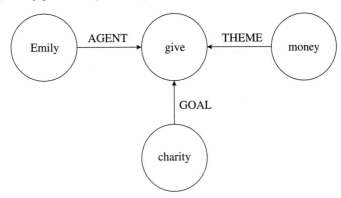

10. Let's play "torment the computer." Imagine a fairly good morphological parser. Give it *kindness,* it returns *kind + ness;* give it *upchuck,* it returns *up + chuck;* but if you give it *catsup* and it returns *cat + s + up,* you will scold it. Think of ten more words that are likely to lead to false analyses.

11. A major problem with text-to-speech is pronouncing proper names. Oh, how the telephone companies would like to solve this one! But it is difficult. Open a telephone directory at random, point at random, and try to pronounce surnames one after another, as they occur alphabetically. How far do you get before you are unsure — not clueless, which you may be if you ran across Duke University's basketball coach *Mike Krzyzewski* — but merely unsure. As we write this exercise, we are doing it. Here is what we got:

Honeycutt
Honeywell
Hong
Hongtong
Honig
Honkanen
Honnigford
Honorato
Honore
Honour
Honrine
Hontz

We think we could do the first four correctly, but there is some doubt regarding the first vowel in *Honig:* is it [o], [ɔ], [a], or even the [ʌ] of *honey?* We also are unsure where to place the primary stress in *Honkanen,* and is the last letter in *Honore* pronounced as in Balzac's first name, and is *Honrine* pronounced to rhyme with *carbine* or *hemline?* Oh, and are all those *h*'s pronounced, or are some silent, as in *honor?* Do this exercise ten times to see the average number of surnames you can pronounce with confidence before becoming unsure. This gives some measure of the vast difficulty facing computers that have to read names from phone directories.

Language and Society

Language is not an abstract construction of the learned, or of dictionary-makers, but is something arising out of the work, needs, ties, joys, affections, tastes, of long generations of humanity, and and has its bases broad and low, close to the ground.

Walt Whitman

CHAPTER 10

Language in Society

Language is a city to the building of which every human
being brought a stone.

Ralph Waldo Emerson, *Letters and Social Aims*

Dialects

A language is a dialect with an army and a navy.

Max Weinreich

All speakers of English can talk to each other and pretty much understand each other. Yet, no two speak exactly alike. Some differences are due to age, sex, size, speech rates, emotional state, state of health, and whether English is a first language. Other differences come from word choices, the pronunciation of words, and grammatical rules. The unique characteristics of the language of an individual speaker are referred to as the speaker's **idiolect.** English may then be said to consist of more than 450,000,000 idiolects, or the number equal to the number of speakers of English (which seems to be growing every day).

Like individuals, different groups of people that speak the "same" language speak it differently. Bostonians, New Yorkers, Blacks in Chicago, Whites in Denver, and Hispanics in Albuquerque all exhibit systematic variation in the way they speak English. When there are systematic differences in the way different groups speak a language, we say that each group speaks a **dialect** of that language. Dialects are mutually intelligible forms of a language that differ in systematic ways. *Every* group, whether rich or poor, regardless of region or racial origin, speaks a dialect, just as each individual speaks an idiolect. A dialect is *not* an inferior or degraded form of a language, and logically could not be so since a language is a collection of dialects.

It is not always easy to decide whether the systematic differences between two speech communities reflect two dialects or two languages. A rule-of-thumb definition

445

can be used: When dialects become mutually unintelligible — when the speakers of one dialect group can no longer understand the speakers of another dialect group — these "dialects" become different languages. However, to define "mutually intelligible" is itself a difficult task. Danes speaking Danish and Norwegians speaking Norwegian and Swedes speaking Swedish can converse with each other. Nevertheless, Danish and Norwegian and Swedish are considered separate languages because they are spoken in separate countries and because there are regular differences in their grammars. Similarly, Hindi and Urdu are mutually intelligible "languages" spoken in Pakistan and India, although the differences between them are not much greater than those between the English spoken in America and Australia. On the other hand, the various languages spoken in China, such as Mandarin and Cantonese, although mutually unintelligible, have been referred to as dialects of Chinese because they are spoken within a single country and have a common writing system.

Because neither mutual intelligibility nor the existence of political boundaries is decisive, it is not surprising that a clear-cut distinction between language and dialects has evaded linguistic scholars. We shall, however, use the rule-of-thumb definition and refer to dialects of one language as mutually intelligible versions of the same basic grammar, with systematic differences among them.

Regional Dialects

Phonetics . . . the science of speech. That's my profession. . . . (I) can spot an Irishman or a Yorkshireman by his brogue. I can place any man within six miles. I can place him within two miles in London. Sometimes within two streets.

George Bernard Shaw, *Pygmalion*

Dialectal diversity develops when people are separated geographically and socially. The changes that occur in the language spoken in one area or group do not necessarily spread to another. Within a single group of speakers who are in regular contact with one another, the changes are spread among the group and "relearned" by their children. When some communication barrier separates groups of speakers — be it a physical barrier such as an ocean or a mountain range, or social barriers of a political, racial, class, or religious kind — linguistic changes do not spread easily and dialectal differences are reinforced.

Dialect differences tend to increase proportionately to the degree of communicative isolation of the groups. *Communicative isolation* refers to a situation such as existed between America, Australia, and England in the eighteenth century. There was some contact through commerce and emigration, but an Australian was much less likely to talk to an Englishman than to another Australian. Today the isolation is less pronounced because of the mass media and air travel, but even within one country, regionalisms persist.

Dialect leveling is movement toward greater uniformity and less variation among dialects. Though one might expect dialect leveling to occur due to the mass media, there is little evidence that such is the case. Dialect variation in the United Kingdom is maintained despite the fact that only a few major dialects are spoken on national radio and television. Indeed, there may actually be an increase in dialects in urban areas, where different groups attempt to maintain their distinctness. On the other hand, dialects die out, and do so for a number of reasons. This is discussed in chapter 11 in the section on extinct and endangered languages.

Changes in the grammar do not take place all at once in a speech community. They take place gradually, often originating in one region and spreading slowly to others, and often taking place throughout the lives of several generations of speakers.

A change that occurs in one region and fails to spread to other regions of the language community gives rise to dialect differences. When enough such differences accumulate in a particular region (e.g., the city of Boston or the southern area of the United States), the language spoken has its own "character," and that version of the language is referred to as a **regional dialect.**

Accents

Regional phonological or phonetic distinctions are often referred to as different **accents.** A person is said to have a Boston accent, a southern accent, a Brooklyn accent, a midwestern drawl, and so on. Thus, *accent* refers to the characteristics of speech that convey information about the speaker's dialect, which may reveal in what country or what part of the country the speaker grew up or to which sociolinguistic group the speaker belongs. People in the United States often refer to someone as having a British accent or an Australian accent; in Britain they refer to an American accent.

The term *accent* is also used to refer to the speech of someone who speaks a language nonnatively. For example, a French person speaking English is described as having a French accent. In this sense, *accent* refers to phonological differences or "interference" from a different language spoken elsewhere. Unlike the regional dialectal accents, such foreign accents do not reflect differences in the language of the community where the language was acquired.

Dialects of English

> The educated Southerner has no use for an r except at the beginning of a word.
>
> Mark Twain, *Life on the Mississippi*

In 1950 a radio comedian remarked that "the Mason-Dixon line is the dividing line between *you-all* and *youse-guys*," pointing to the varieties of English in the United States. Regional dialects tell us a great deal about how languages change, which is discussed in the next chapter. The origins of many regional dialects of American English can be traced to the people who settled in North America in the seventeenth and eighteenth centuries. The early settlers came from different parts of England, speaking different dialects. Regional dialect differences existed in the first colonies.

By the time of the American Revolution, there were three major dialect areas in the British colonies: the Northern dialect spoken in New England and around the Hudson River; the Midland dialect spoken in Pennsylvania; and the Southern dialect. These dialects differed from each other, and from the English spoken in England, in systematic ways. Some of the changes that occurred in British English spread to the colonies; others did not.

How regional dialects developed is illustrated by changes in the pronunciation of words with an *r*. The British in southern England were already dropping their *r* 's before consonants and at the ends of words as early as the eighteenth century. Words such as *farm, farther,* and *father* were pronounced as [fa:m], [fa:ðə], and [fa:ðə], respectively. By the end of the eighteenth century, this practice was a general rule among the early settlers in New England and the southern Atlantic seaboard. Close commercial ties were maintained between the New England colonies and London, and Southerners sent their children to England to be educated, which reinforced the "*r*-dropping" rule. The "*r*-less" dialect still spoken today in Boston, New York, and Savannah maintained this characteristic. Later settlers, however, came from northern England, where the *r* had been retained; as the frontier moved westward, so did the *r*.

Pioneers from all three dialect areas spread westward. The mingling of their dialects leveled many of their dialectal differences, which is why the English used in large sections of the Midwest and the West is similar.

Other waves of immigration brought speakers of other dialects and other languages to different regions. Each group left its imprint on the language of the communities in which they settled. For example, the settlers in various regions developed different dialects — the Germans in the southeastern section, the Welsh west of Philadelphia, the Germans and Scotch-Irish in the Midlands area of Pennsylvania.

The last half of the twentieth century brought hundreds of thousands of Spanish-speaking immigrants from Cuba, Puerto Rico, Central America, and Mexico to both the east and west coasts of the United States. In addition, English is being enriched by the languages spoken by the large numbers of new residents coming from the Pacific Rim countries of Japan, China, Korea, Samoa, Malaysia, Vietnam, Thailand, the Philippines, and Indonesia. Large new groups of Russian and Armenian speakers also contribute to the richness of the vocabulary and culture of American cities.

The language of the regions where the new immigrants settle may thus be differentially affected by the native languages of the settlers, further adding to the varieties of American English.

English is the most widely spoken language in the world if one counts all those who use it as a native language or as a second or third language. It is the national language of a number of countries, such as the United States, large parts of Canada, the British Isles, Australia, and New Zealand. For many years it was the official language in countries that were once colonies of Britain, including India, Nigeria, Ghana, Kenya, and the other "anglophone" countries of Africa. Dialects of English are spoken in these countries for the reasons just discussed. It is likely that upwards of one billion human beings can speak English with useful fluency.

Phonological Differences

I have noticed in traveling about the country a good many differences in the pronunciation of common words. . . . Now what I want to know is whether there is any right or wrong about this matter. . . . If one way is right, why don't we all pronounce that way and compel the other fellow to do the same? If there isn't any right or wrong, why do some persons make so much fuss about it?

Letter quoted in "The Standard American," in J. V. Williamson and V. M. Burke, eds., *A Various Language*

A comparison of the "*r*-less" and other dialects illustrates phonological differences among dialects. There are many such differences among the dialects of American English, and they created difficulties in writing chapter 6, where we wished to illustrate the different sounds of English by reference to words in which the sounds occur. As mentioned, some students pronounce *caught* /kɔt/ with the vowel /ɔ/ and *cot* /kat/ with /a/, whereas other students pronounce them both /kat/. Some readers pronounce *Mary, marry,* and *merry* the same; others pronounce the three words differently as /meri/, /mæri/, and /mɛri/; and still others pronounce two of them the same. In the southern area of the country, *creek* is pronounced with a tense /i/ as /krik/, and in the north Midlands, it is pronounced with a lax /ɪ/ as /krɪk/. Many speakers of American English pronounce *pin* and *pen* identically, whereas others pronounce the first /pɪn/ and the second /pɛn/. If variety is the spice of life, then American English dialects add zest to our existence.

The pronunciation of British English (or many dialects of it) differs in systematic ways from pronunciations in many dialects of American English. In a survey of hundreds of American and British speakers conducted via the Internet, 48 percent of the Americans pronounced the mid consonants in *luxury* as voiceless [lʌkʃəri], whereas 96 percent of the British pronounced them as voiced [lʌgʒəri]. Sixty-four percent of the Americans pronounced the first vowel in *data* as [e] and 35 percent as [æ] as opposed to 92 percent of the British pronouncing it with an [e] and only 2 percent with [æ]. The most consistent difference occurred in the placement of primary stress, with most Americans putting stress on the first syllable and most British on the second or third in multisyllabic words like *cigarette, applicable, formidable, kilometer,* and *laboratory.*

Britain also has many regional dialects. The British vowels described in the phonetics chapter are used by speakers of the most prestigious British dialect.[1] In this dialect, /h/ is pronounced at the beginning of both *head* and *herb,* whereas in American English dialects it is not pronounced in the second word. In some English dialects, the /h/ is regularly dropped from most words in which it is pronounced in American, such as *house,* pronounced /aws/, and *hero,* pronounced /iro/.

There are many other phonological differences in the many dialects of English used around the world.

Lexical Differences

Regional dialects may differ in the words people use for the same object, as well as in phonology. Hans Kurath, an eminent dialectologist, in his paper "What Do You Call It?" asked:

> Do you call it a *pail* or a *bucket?* Do you draw water from a *faucet* or from a *spigot?* Do you pull down the *blinds,* the *shades,* or the *curtains* when it gets dark? Do you *wheel* the baby, or do you *ride* it or *roll* it? In a *baby carriage,* a *buggy,* a *coach,* or a *cab?*[2]

---

[1] This dialect is often referred to as R.P., standing for "received pronunciation," because it was once considered to be the dialect used in court and "received by" the British king and queen.

[2] H. Kurath. 1971. "What Do You Call It?" In J. V. Williamson and V. M. Burke, eds. *A Various Language: Perspective on American Dialects.* New York: Holt, Rinehart, and Winston.

"Liberty Meadows" copyright © 1998. By permission of Frank Cho and Creators Syndicate, Inc.

People take a *lift* to the *first floor* (our *second floor*) in England, but an *elevator* in the United States; they get five gallons of *petrol* (not *gas*) in London; in Britain a *public school* is "private" (you have to pay), and if a student showed up there wearing *pants* ("underpants") instead of *trousers* ("pants"), he would be sent home to get dressed.

If you ask for a *tonic* in Boston, you will get a drink called *soda* or *soda-pop* in Los Angeles; and a *freeway* in Los Angeles is a *thruway* in New York, a *parkway* in New Jersey, a *motorway* in England, and an *expressway* or *turnpike* in other dialect areas.

Dialect Atlases

Kurath published **dialect maps** and **dialect atlases** of a region (see Figure 10.1), on which dialect differences are geographically plotted. The dialectologists who created the map noted the places where speakers use one word or another word for the same item. For example, the area where the term *Dutch cheese* is used is not contiguous; there is a small pocket mostly in West Virginia where speakers use that term for what other speakers call *smearcase.*

In similar maps, areas were differentiated based on the variation in pronunciation of the same word, such as [krik] and [krɪk] for *creek.*

The concentrations defined by different word usage and varying pronunciations, among other linguistic differences, form **dialect areas.**

A line drawn on the map to separate the areas is called an **isogloss.** When you cross an isogloss, you are passing from one dialect area to another. Sometimes several isoglosses coincide, often at a political boundary or at a natural boundary such as a river or mountain range. Linguists call these groupings a *bundle* of isoglosses. Such a bundle can define a regional dialect.

DARE is the acronym for the *Dictionary of American Regional English,* whose chief editor is the distinguished American dialectologist Frederick G. Cassidy who "passed away" (see the section on *euphemisms* below) on June 14, 2000, at the age of 92. This work represents decades of research and scholarship by Cassidy and other

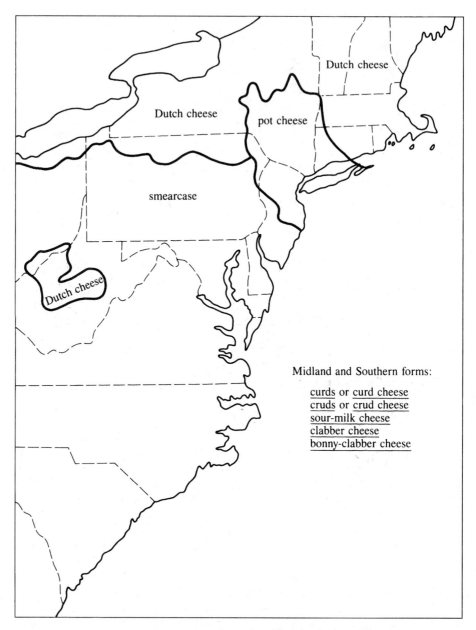

Figure 10.1   A dialect map showing the isoglosses separating the use of different words that refer to the same cheese. Kurath, Hans. *A Word Geography of the Eastern United States.* Ann Arbor. MI: University of Michigan Press, copyright © 1949. Reprinted with permission of University of Michigan Press.

American dialectologists and is a major resource for those interested in American English dialectal differences. Its first three volumes, covering *A* through *O* are published; volume 4, covering *P* through *S,* is due out in 2002. Its purpose is described on its World Wide Web page:

> The *Dictionary of American Regional English (DARE)* is a reference tool unlike any other. Its aim is not to prescribe how Americans should speak, or even to describe the language we use generally, the "standard" language. Instead, it seeks to document the varieties of English that are **not** found everywhere in the United States — those words, pronunciations, and phrases that vary from one region to another, that we learn at home rather than at school, or that are part of our oral rather than our written culture. Although American English is remarkably homogeneous considering the tremendous size of the country, there are still many thousands of differences that characterize the various dialect regions of the United States. It is these differences that *DARE* records.

Syntactic Differences

Systematic syntactic differences also distinguish dialects. In most American dialects, sentences may be conjoined as follows:

John will eat and Mary will eat → John and Mary will eat.

In the Ozark dialect the following conjunction is also possible:

John will eat and Mary will eat → John will eat and Mary.

Both shortened conjoined sentences are the result of deletion transformations similar to the ones discussed in Exercise 19 of chapter 4. It was shown there that the ambiguous sentence *George wants the presidency more than Martha* may be derived from two possible deep structures:

1. George wants the presidency more than he wants Martha.
2. George wants the presidency more than Martha wants the presidency.

A deletion transformation either deletes *he wants* from the structure of (1), or *wants the presidency* from the structure of (2). A similar transformation derives *John and Mary will eat* by deleting the first occurrence of the VP *will eat.* Most dialects of English, however, do not have a rule that deletes the second VP in conjoined sentences, and in those dialects *John will eat and Mary* is ungrammatical. The Ozark dialect differs in allowing the second VP deletion rule.

Speakers of some American dialects say *Have them come early!* where others would say *Have them to come early!* Some American speakers use *gotten* in a sentence such as *He should have gotten to school on time;* in British English, only the form *got* occurs. In a number of American English dialects, the pronoun *I* occurs when *me* would be used in other dialects. This difference is a syntactically conditioned morphological difference.

Dialect 1	Dialect 2
between you and I	between you and me
Won't he let you and I swim?	Won't he let you and me swim?
*Won't he let I swim?	

The use of *I* in these structures is only permitted in a conjoined NP as the starred (ungrammatical) sentence shows. *Won't he let me swim?* is used in both dialects. Dialect 1 is growing and these forms are becoming Standard English, used by TV announcers, governors of states, and university professors, although language purists still frown on this usage.

In British English the pronoun *it* in the sentence *I could have done it* can be deleted. British speakers say *I could have done,* which is not in accordance with the syntactic rules in the American English grammar. American English, however, permits the deletion of *done it,* and Americans say *I could have,* which does not accord with the British syntactic rules.

Despite such differences, we are still able to understand speakers of other dialects. Although regional dialects differ in pronunciation, vocabulary, and syntactic rules, they are minor differences when compared with the totality of the grammar.

For the most part, dialects share rules and vocabulary to a large extent, which explains why dialects of one language are mutually intelligible.

The "Standard"

> We don't talk fancy grammar and eat anchovy toast. But to live under the kitchen doesn't say we aren't educated.
>
> Mary Norton, *The Borrowers*

> Standard English is the customary use of a community when it is recognized and accepted as the customary use of the community. Beyond this is the larger field of good English, any English that justifies itself by accomplishing its end, by hitting the mark.
>
> George Philip Krapp, *Modern English: Its Growth and Present Use*

Even though every language is a composite of dialects, many people talk and think about a language as if it were a well-defined fixed system with various dialects diverging from this norm. This is false, though it is a falsehood that is widespread. One writer of books on language accused the editors of *Webster's Third New International Dictionary,* published in 1961, of confusing "to the point of obliteration the older distinction between standard, substandard, colloquial, vulgar, and slang," attributing to them the view that "good and bad, right and wrong, correct and incorrect no longer exist."[3] In the next section we argue that such criticisms are ill founded.

---

[3] M. Pei. 1964. "A Loss for Words," *Saturday Review* Nov. 14:82–84.

Language Purists

> A woman who utters such depressing and disgusting sounds has no right to be anywhere —
> no right to live. Remember that you are a human being with a soul and the divine gift of
> articulate speech: that your native language is the language of Shakespeare and Milton and
> The Bible; and don't sit there crooning like a bilious pigeon.
>
> George Bernard Shaw, *Pygmalion*

Prescriptive grammarians, or language purists, usually consider the dialect used by political leaders and national newscasters as the correct form of the language. This is the dialect taught in "English" or "grammar" classes in school, and it is closer to the written form of the language than many other dialects, which also lends it an air of superiority (see chapter 12 on writing).

"Rose Is Rose" copyright © 2001 United Feature Syndicate, Inc. Reprinted by permission.

Otto Jespersen, the great Danish linguist, ridiculed the view that a particular dialect is better than any other when he wrote: "We set up as the best language that which is found in the best writers, and count as the best writers those that best write the language. We are therefore no further advanced than before."[4]

The dominant, or **prestige,** dialect is often called the standard dialect. **Standard American English (SAE)** is a dialect of English that many Americans almost speak; divergences from this "norm" are labeled "Philadelphia dialect," "Chicago dialect," "African American English," and so on.

SAE is an idealization. Nobody speaks this dialect; and if somebody did, we would not know it, because SAE is not defined precisely. Teachers and linguists held a conference in the 1990s that attempted to come up with a precise definition of SAE. This meeting did not succeed in satisfying everyone as to what SAE should be. It used to be the case that the language used by national news broadcasters represented SAE, but today many of these people speak a regional dialect, or themselves violate the English preferred by the purists. Similarly, the British Broadcasting Corporation (BBC) once used mostly speakers of RP English, but today speakers of Irish, Welsh, Scottish, and

[4] O. Jespersen. 1925 (reprinted 1964). *Mankind, Nation, and Individual.* Bloomington, IN: Indiana University Press.

other regional dialects of English are commonly heard on BBC programs. The BBC it-self describes its English as "the speech of educated professionals."

Deviations from the indefinable Standard are a language crisis according to some writers. Edwin Newman, in his best seller *Strictly Speaking,* asks, "Will Americans be the death of English?" and answers, "My mature, considered opinion is that they will." All this fuss is reminiscent of Mark Twain's cable to the Associated Press, after reading his obituary: "The reports of my death are greatly exaggerated."

The idea that language change equals corruption goes back at least as far as the Greek grammarians at Alexandria, of 200–100 B.C.E. They were concerned that the Greek spoken in their time was different from the Greek of Homer, and they believed that the earlier forms were purer. They tried to correct the imperfections but failed as miserably as do any modern counterparts. Similarly, the Muslim Arabic grammarians working at Basra in the eighth and ninth centuries C.E. attempted to purify Arabic to re-store it to the "perfection" of the Arabic in the Koran.

For many years after the American Revolution, British writers and journalists railed against American English. Thomas Jefferson was an early target in a commentary on his *Notes on the State of Virginia,* which appeared in the *London Review:*

> For shame, Mr. Jefferson! Why, after trampling upon the honour of our country, and representing it as little better than a land of barbarism — why, we say, per-petually trample also upon the very grammar of our language. . . . Freely, good sir, we will forgive all your attacks, impotent as they are illiberal, upon our *na-tional character;* but for the future spare — O spare, we beseech you, our mother-tongue!

The fears of the British journalists in 1787 proved unfounded, and so will the fears of modern-day purists. From a linguistic point of view, one dialect is neither better nor worse than another, nor purer nor more corrupt, nor more or less logical, nor more or less expressive. It is simply different.

No academy and no guardians of language purity can stem language change, nor should anyone attempt to do so since such change does not mean corruption. The fact that for the great majority of American English speakers *criteria* and *data* are now mass nouns like *information* is no cause for concern. Information can include one fact or many facts, but one would still say "The information is." For some speakers it is equally cor-rect to say "The criteria is" or "The criteria are." Those who say "The data are" would or could say "The datum (singular) is."

A standard dialect (or prestige dialect) of a particular language may have social functions. Its use in a group may serve to bind people together or to provide a common written form for multidialectal speakers. If it is the dialect of the wealthy, influential, and powerful members of society, it derives significance from that state of affairs that may have important implications for the entire society.

In 1954 the English scholar Alan Ross published *Linguistic Class-Indicators in Present-Day English,* in which he compared the speech habits of the English upper class whom he labeled "U," with the speech habits of "non-U" speakers. Ross concluded that although the upper class had words and pronunciations peculiar to it, the main charac-teristic of U speech is the avoidance of non-U speech; and the main characteristic of non-U speech is, ironically, the effort to sound U. "They've a lovely home," for example, is pure non-U, because it is an attempt to be refined. Non-U speakers say "wealthy" and "ever so"; U speakers say "rich" and "very." Non-U speakers "recall"; U-speakers simply "remember."

No dialect, however, is more expressive, more logical, more complex, or more regular than any other dialect or language. Any judgments, therefore, as to the superiority or inferiority of a particular dialect or language are social judgments.

Banned Languages

Language purists wish to stem change in language or dialect differentiation because of their false belief that some languages are better than others, or that change leads to corruption. Languages and dialects have also been banned as a means of political control. Russian was the only legal language permitted by the Russian tsars who banned the use of Ukrainian, Lithuanian, Georgian, Armenian, Azeri, and all the other languages spoken by national groups under the rule of Russia.

Cajun English and French were banned in southern Louisiana by practice if not by law until about twenty years ago. Individuals over the age of fifty years report that they were often punished in school if they spoke French even though many of them had never heard English before attending school.

For many years, American Indian languages were banned in federal and state schools on reservations. Speaking Faroese was formerly forbidden in the Faroe Islands. A proscription against speaking Korean was imposed by the Japanese during their occupation of Korea between 1910 and 1945, and in retaliation, Japanese movies and songs were once banned in Korea. In a recent discussion among linguists via a computer network called Linguist Net, various degrees of the banning of languages and dialects were reported to exist or to have existed in many countries throughout history.

As recently as 2001 the *New York Times* reported that "Singapore's leaders want English, not Singlish." Although Standard English is the common language of Singapore's multi-ethnic population, many who do not learn English as their native language speak *Singlish*, a form of English with elements of Malay, Tamil, Mandarin Chinese, and other Chinese dialects (languages). They are the target of Singapore's "Speak Good English Movement."

In France, a notion of the "standard" as the only correct form of the language is propagated by an official academy of "scholars" who determine what usage constitutes the "official French language." A number of years ago, this academy enacted a law forbidding the use of "Franglais," which are words of English origin like *le parking, le weekend,* and *le hotdog.* The French, of course, continue to use them, and since such words are notorious, they are widely used in advertising, where being noticed is more important than being "correct." Only in government documents can these proscriptions be enforced.

The academy also disapproves of the use of the hundreds of local village dialects, or *patois* [patwa], despite the fact that some of them are actually separate languages, derived from Latin (as are French, Spanish, and Italian). This diverse, rich collection of dialects and languages of France have one thing in common: they are not officially approved French. There are political as well as misguided linguistic motivations behind the efforts to maintain only one official language.

In the past (and to some extent in the present), a French citizen from the provinces who wished to succeed in French society nearly always had to learn the Parisian French dialect. Then, several decades ago, members of regional autonomy movements demanded the right to use their own languages in their schools and for official business. In the section of France known as l'Occitanie, the popular singers sing in Langue d'oc, a romance language of the region, both as a protest against the official language policy and as part of the cultural revival movement. Here is the final chorus of a popular song in Langue d'oc (shown below with its French and English translations):

Langue d'oc	French	English
Mas perqué, perqué	Mais pourquoi, pourquoi	But why, why
M'an pas dit à l'escóla	Ne m'a-t-on pas dit à l'école	Did they not speak to me at school
La lega de mon pais?	La langue de mon pays?	The language of my country?

In the province of Brittany, there has also been a strong movement for the use of Breton in the schools, as opposed to the "standard" French. Breton is not a Romance language like French; it is a Celtic language in the same family as Irish, Gaelic, and Welsh. (We will discuss such family groupings in chapter 11.) It is not, however, the structure of the language or the genetic family grouping that has led to the Breton movement. It is rather the pride of a people who speak a language not considered as good as the "standard," and who wish to preserve it by opposing the political view of language use.

These efforts have proved successful. In 1982, the newly elected French government decreed that the languages and cultures of Brittany (Breton), the southern Languedoc region, and other areas would be promoted through schooling, exhibitions, and festivals. No longer would schoolchildren who spoke Breton be punished by having to wear a wooden shoe tied around their necks, as had been the custom.

In many places in the world (including the United States), the use of sign languages of the deaf was banned. Children in schools for the deaf, where the aim was to teach them to read lips and to communicate through sound, were often punished if they used any gestures at all. This view prevented early exposure to language. It was mistakenly thought that children, if exposed to sign, would not learn to read lips or produce sounds. Individuals who become deaf after learning a spoken language are often able to use their knowledge to learn to read lips and continue to speak. This is, however, very difficult if one has never heard speech sounds. Furthermore, even the best lip readers can comprehend only about one-third of the sounds of spoken language. Imagine trying to decide whether *lid* or *led* was said by reading the speaker's lips. Mute the sound on a TV set and see what percentage of a news broadcast you can understand, even with video to help.

There is no reference to a national language in the U. S. Constitution. John Adams proposed that a national academy be established, similar to the French Academy, to standardize American English, but this view was roundly rejected as not in keeping with the goals of "liberty and justice for all."

In recent years in the United States, a movement has arisen in the attempt to establish English as an official language by amending the Constitution. An "Official English" initiative was passed by the electorate in California in 1986; in Colorado, Florida, and Arizona in 1988; and in Alabama in 1990. Such measures have also been adopted by seventeen state legislatures. This kind of linguistic chauvinism is opposed by civil-rights minority-group advocates, who point out that such a measure could be used to prevent large numbers of non-English-speaking citizens from participating in civil activities such as voting, and from receiving the benefits of a public education, for which they pay through taxes. Fortunately, as of this writing, the movement appears to have lost momentum.

The Revival of Languages

The attempts to ban certain languages and dialects are countered by the efforts on the part of certain peoples to preserve their languages and cultures. This attempt to slow down or reverse the dying out of a language is illustrated by the French in Quebec. Gaelic, or Irish, is being taught again in hundreds of schools in Ireland and Northern Ireland, and there are numerous first language learners of this once moribund language. But such "antilinguicide" movements should not include the banning of any use of a language.

A dramatic example of the revival of a dormant language occurred in Israel. The Academy of the Hebrew Language in Israel undertook a task that had never been done in the history of humanity — to resuscitate an ancient written language to serve the daily colloquial needs of the people. Twenty-three lexicologists worked with the Bible and the Talmud to add new words to the language. While there is some attempt to keep the language "pure," the academy has given way to popular pressure. Thus, a bank check is called a *check* /ček/ in the singular and pluralized by adding the Hebrew suffix to form *check-im,* although the Hebrew word *hamcha'ah* was proposed. Similarly, *lipstick* has triumphed over *s'faton* and *pajama* over *chalifat-sheinah.*

African American English

> The language, only the language. . . It is the thing that black people love so much — the saying of words, holding them on the tongue, experimenting with them, playing with them. It's a love, a passion. Its function is like a preacher's: to make you stand up out of your seat, make you lose yourself and hear yourself. The worst of all possible things that could happen would be to lose that language.
>
> Toni Morrison, interview in *The New Republic,* March 21, 1981

The majority of regional dialects of the United States are largely free from stigma. Some regional dialects, like the *r*-less Brooklynese, are the victims of so-called humor, and speakers of one dialect may deride the "drawl" of southerners or the "nasal twang" of Texans (even though all speakers of southern dialects do not drawl, nor do all Texans twang).

There is one dialect of North American English, however, that has been a victim of prejudicial ignorance. This dialect, **African American English (AAE),** is spoken by a large population of Americans of African descent.[5] The distinguishing features of this

---

[5] AAE is actually a group of closely related dialects also called African American Vernacular English (AAVE), Black English (BE), Inner City English (ICE), and Ebonics.

English dialect persist for social, educational, and economic reasons. The historical discrimination against African Americans has created social isolation in which dialect differences are intensified. In addition, particularly in recent years, many blacks have embraced their dialects as a means of positive identification.

Since the onset of the civil rights movement in the 1960s, AAE has been the focus of national attention. There are critics who attempt to equate its use with inferior genetic intelligence and cultural deprivation, justifying these incorrect notions by stating that AAE is a "deficient, illogical, and incomplete" language. Such epithets cannot be applied to any language, and they are as unscientific in reference to AAE as to Russian, Chinese, or Standard American English. The cultural-deprivation myth is as false as the idea that some dialects or languages are inferior. A person may be "deprived" of one cultural background, but be rich in another.

Some people, white and black, think they can identify the race of a person by speech alone, believing that different races inherently speak differently. This belief is patently false. A black child raised in an upper-class British household will speak that dialect of English. A white child raised in an environment where AAE is spoken will speak AAE. Children construct grammars based on the language they hear.

AAE is discussed here more extensively than other American dialects because it provides an informative illustration of the regularities of a dialect of a major language, and the systematic differences from the so-called standard dialects of that language. A vast body of research shows that there are the same kinds of linguistic differences between AAE and SAE as occur between many of the world's major dialects.

Phonology of African American English

Some of the differences between AAE and SAE phonology are discussed in this section.

R-Deletion

Like a number of dialects of both British and American English, AAE includes a rule of *r-deletion* that deletes /r/ everywhere except before a vowel. Pairs of words like *guard* and *god, nor* and *gnaw, sore* and *saw, poor* and *pa, fort* and *fought,* and *court* and *caught* are pronounced identically in AAE because of this phonological rule.

L-Deletion

There is also an *l-deletion* rule for some speakers of AAE, creating identically pronounced pairs like *toll* and *toe, all* and *awe, help* and *hep.*

Consonant Cluster Simplification

A *consonant cluster simplification* rule in AAE simplifies consonant clusters, particularly at the ends of words and when one of the two consonants is an alveolar (/t/, /d/, /s/, /z/). The application of this rule may delete the past-tense morpheme so that *meant* and *mend* are both pronounced as *men* and *past* and *passed* (*pass* + *ed*) may both be pronounced like *pass.* When speakers of this dialect say *I pass the test yesterday,* they are not showing an ignorance of past and present, but are pronouncing the past tense according to this rule in their grammar.

The deletion rule is optional; it does not always apply, and studies have shown that it is more likely to apply when the final [t] or [d] does not represent the past-tense morpheme, as in nouns like *paste* [pes] as opposed to verbs like *chased* [čest], where the final past tense [t] will not always be deleted. This has also been observed with final [s] or [z], which will be retained more often by speakers of AAE in words like *seats* /sit + s/, where the /s/ represents plural, than in words like *Keats* /kit/, where it is more likely to be deleted.

Consonant cluster simplification is not unique to AAE. It exists optionally for many speakers of other dialects including SAE. For example, the medial [d] in *didn't* is often deleted producing [dɪnt]. Furthermore, nasals are commonly deleted before final voiceless stops, to result in [hīt] versus [hīnt].

NEUTRALIZATION OF [I] AND [ε] BEFORE NASALS

AAE shares with many regional dialects a lack of distinction between /ɪ/ and /ε/ before nasal consonants, producing identical pronunciations of *pin* and *pen, bin* and *Ben, tin* and *ten,* and so on. The vowel sound in these words is roughly between the [ɪ] of *pit* and the [ε] of *pet.*

DIPHTHONG REDUCTION

AAE has a rule

$$/ɔj/ \rightarrow /ɔ/$$

that reduces the diphthong /ɔj/ (particularly before /l/) to the simple vowel [ɔ] without the glide, so that *boil* and *boy* are pronounced [bɔ].

LOSS OF INTERDENTAL FRICATIVES

A regular feature is the change of a /θ/ to /f/ and /ð/ to /v/ so that *Ruth* is pronounced [ruf] and *brother* is pronounced [brʌvɛr]. This [θ]-[f] correspondence also is true of some dialects of British English, where /θ/ is not even a phoneme in the language. *Think* is regularly [fɪnk] in Cockney English.

Initial /ð/ in such words as *this, that, these,* and *those* are pronounced as [d]. This is again not unique to AAE, but a common characteristic of many nonstandard, nonethnic dialects of English.

All these differences are systematic and rule-governed and similar to sound changes that have taken place in languages all over the world, including Standard English.

Syntactic Differences between AAE and SAE

And of his port as meeke as is a mayde
He nevere yet no vileynye ne sayde

Geoffrey Chaucer, *The Canterbury Tales, Prologue,* 69–70

Syntactic differences also exist between dialects. They have often been used to illustrate the illogic of AAE, and yet these very differences are evidence that AAE is as syntactically complex and as logical as SAE.

DOUBLE NEGATIVES

Following the lead of early prescriptive grammarians, some "scholars" and teachers conclude that it is illogical to say *he don't know nothing* because two negatives make a positive.

Since such negative constructions occur in AAE, it has been concluded by some "educators" that speakers of AAE are deficient because they use language illogically. However, double negatives are part of many current dialects of all races in the English-speaking world. Multiple negations were standard in an earlier stage of English, as the triple negation in the second line of the quotation from the *Canterbury Tales* illustrates. Double negations are standard in many highly respected languages of the world such as French and Italian.

DELETION OF THE VERB "BE"

In most cases, if in Standard English the verb can be contracted, in African American English sentences it is deleted; where it can't be contracted in SAE, it can't be deleted in AAE, as shown in the following sentences:[6]

SAE	AAE
He is nice/He's nice.	He nice.
They are mine/They're mine.	They mine.
I am going to do it/I'm gonna do it.	I gonna do it.
He is/he's as nice as he says he is.	He as nice as he say he is.
*He's as nice as he says he's.	*He as nice as he say he.
How beautiful you are.	How beautiful you are.
*How beautiful you're	*How beautiful you
Here I am.	Here I am.
*Here I'm	*Here I

These examples show that syntactic rules operate in both dialects although they show slight systematic differences.

HABITUAL "BE"

In SAE, the sentence *John is happy* can be interpreted to mean *John is happy* now or *John is generally happy*. One can make the distinction clear in SAE only by lexical means, that is, the addition of words. One would have to say *John is generally happy* or *John is a happy person* to disambiguate the meaning from *John is presently happy*.

---

[6] Sentences from W. Labov. 1969. *The Logic of Nonstandard English.* Georgetown University Round Table, No. 22.

In AAE, this distinction is made syntactically; an uninflected form of *be* is used if the speaker is referring to *habitual* state.

John be happy.	"John is always happy."
John happy.	"John is happy now."
He be late.	"He is habitually late."
He late.	"He is late this time."
Do you be tired?	"Are you generally tired?"
You tired?	"Are you tired now?"

This syntactic distinction between habitual and nonhabitual aspect occurs in languages other than AAE, but it does not occur in SAE. It has been suggested that the uninflected *be* is the result of a convergence of similar rules in African, Creole, and Irish English sources.[7]

History of African American English

It is simple to date the beginning of AAE — the first black people were brought in chains to Virginia in 1619. There are, however, different theories as to the factors that led to the systematic differences between AAE and other American English dialects.

One view suggests that African American English originated when the African slaves learned English from their colonial masters as a second language. Although the basic grammar was learned, many surface differences persisted, which were reflected in the grammars constructed by the children of the slaves, who heard English primarily from their parents. Had the children been exposed to the English spoken by the whites, their grammars would have been more similar if not identical to the general Southern dialect. The dialect differences persisted and grew because social and racial barriers isolated blacks in America. The proponents of this theory point to the fact that the grammars of AAE and Standard American English are identical except for a few syntactic and phonological rules that produce surface differences.

Another view that is receiving increasing support is that many of the unique features of AAE are traceable to influences of the African languages spoken by the slaves. During the seventeenth and eighteenth centuries, Africans who spoke different languages were purposefully grouped together to discourage communication and to prevent slave revolts. In order to communicate, the slaves were forced to use the one common language all had access to, namely English. They invented a simplified form — called a pidgin (discussed below) — that incorporated many features from West African languages. According to this view, the differences between AAE and other dialects are due more to deep syntactic differences than to surface distinctions.

It is apparent that AAE is closer to Southern dialects of American English than to other dialects. The theory that suggests that the Negro slaves learned the English of white Southerners as a second language explains these similarities. They might also be explained by the fact that for many decades a large number of Southern white children were raised by black women and played with black children. It is possible that many of

---

[7] J. Holm. 1988–1989. *Pidgins and Creoles,* Vols. 1 & 2. Cambridge, England: Cambridge University Press.

the distinguishing features of Southern dialects were acquired from African American English in this way. A publication of the American Dialect Society in 1908–1909 makes this point clearly:

> For my part, after a somewhat careful study of east Alabama dialect, I am convinced that the speech of the white people, the dialect I have spoken all my life and the one I tried to record here, is more largely colored by the language of the negroes [*sic*] than by any other single influence.[8]

The two-way interchange still goes on. Standard American English is constantly enriched by words, phrases, and usage originating in AAE; and AAE, whatever its origins, is influenced by the changes that go on in the many other dialects of English.

Latino (Hispanic) English

A major group of American English dialects is spoken by native Spanish speakers or their descendants. The Southwest was once part of Mexico, and for more than a century large numbers of immigrants from Spanish-speaking countries of South and Central America have been enriching the country with their language and culture. Among these groups are native speakers of Spanish who have learned or are learning English as a second language. There are also those born in Spanish-speaking homes whose native language is English, some of whom are monolingual, and others who speak Spanish as a second language.

One cannot speak of a homogeneous Latino dialect. In addition to the differences between bilingual and monolingual speakers, the dialects spoken by Puerto Rican, Cuban, Guatemalan, and El Salvadoran immigrants or their children are somewhat different from each other and also from those spoken by Mexican Americans in the Southwest and California, called Chicano English (ChE).

A description of the Latino dialects of English is complicated by historical and social factors. While many Latinos are bilingual speakers, it has been suggested that close to 20 percent of Chicanos are monolingual English speakers.[9] Recent studies also show that the shift to monolingual English is growing rapidly. Furthermore, the bilingual speakers are not a homogeneous group; native Spanish speakers' knowledge of English ranges from passive to full competence. The Spanish influence on both immigrant and native English speakers is reinforced by border contact between the United States and Mexico and the social cohesion of a large segment of this population.

Bilingual Latinos, when speaking English, may insert a Spanish word or phrase into a single sentence or move back and forth between Spanish and English, a process called *code-switching*. This is a universal language-contact phenomenon that reflects the

---

[8] L. W. Payne. 1901. "A Word-List from East Alabama," *Dialect News* 3:279–328, 343–91.

[9] O. A. Santa Ana. 1993. "Chicano English and the Nature of the Chicano Language Setting, *Hispanic Journal of Behavioral Sciences* 15(1):3–35.

grammars of both languages working simultaneously. Québecois in Canada switch from French to English and vice versa; the Swiss switch between French and German. Code-switching occurs wherever there are groups of bilinguals who speak the same two languages. Furthermore, code-switching occurs in specific social situations, enriching the repertoire of the speakers.

Because of the ignorance of code-switching, there is a common misconception that bilingual Latinos speak a sort of "broken" English, sometimes called Spanglish or Tex-Mex. This is not the case. In fact, the phrases inserted into a sentence are always in keeping with the syntactic rules of that language. For example, in a Spanish noun phrase, the adjective usually follows the noun, as opposed to the English NP in which it precedes, as shown by the following:

> English: My mom fixes **green tamales.**   Adj N
> Spanish: Mi mamá hace **tamales verdes.**   N Adj

A bilingual Spanish-English speaker might, in a code-switching situation, say:

> My mom fixes **tamales verdes.**
> or   Mi mamá hace **green tamales**

but would not produce the sentences

> *My mom fixes verdes **tamales.**
> or   *Mi mamá hace tamales green

because the Spanish word order was reversed in the inserted Spanish NP and the English word order was reversed in the English NP.

What monolingual speakers of English should realize is that these are individuals who know not one, but two languages.

Chicano English (ChE)

We have seen that there is no one form of Latino English, just as there is no single dialect of SAE or American English. Nor is the Chicano English dialect, spoken by a major group of descendants of Mexican Americans, homogeneous. With this in mind, we can still recognize it as a distinct dialect of American English, one that is acquired as a first language by many children and that is the native language of hundreds of thousands, if not millions of Americans. It is not English with a Spanish accent nor an incorrect version of SAE but, like African American English, a mutually intelligible dialect that differs systematically from SAE. Many of the differences, however, represent variables that may or may not occur in the speech of a ChE speaker. The use of the nonstandard forms by native speakers of English is often associated with pride of ethnicity.

PHONOLOGICAL VARIABLES OF ChE

ChE is, like other dialects, the result of many factors, a major one being the influence of Spanish. Phonological differences between ChE and SAE reveal this influence.

Here are some systematic differences:[10]

1. Chapters 6 and 7 discussed the fact that English has eleven stressed vowel phonemes (not counting the three diphthongs): /i, ɪ, e, ɛ, æ, u, ʊ, o, ɔ, a, ʌ/. Spanish, however, has only five: /i, e, u, o, a/. Chicano speakers whose native language is Spanish may substitute the Spanish vowel system for the English. When this is done, a number of homonyms result that have distinct pronunciations in SAE. Thus *ship* and *sheep* are both pronounced like *sheep* /šip/, *rid* is pronounced like *read* /rid/, and so on. Chicano speakers whose native language is English may make these substitutions but have the full set of American English vowels.

2. Alternation of *ch* /č/ and *sh* /š/; *show* is pronounced as if spelled with a *ch* /čo/ and *check* as if spelled with an *sh* /šɛk/.

3. Devoicing of some consonants, such as /z/ in *easy* /isi/ and *guys* /gajs/.

4. The substitution of /t/ for /θ/ and /d/ for /ð/ word initially, as in /tin/ for *thin* and /de/ for *they*.

5. Word-final consonant cluster simplification. *War* and *ward* are both pronounced /war/; *star* and *start* are /star/. This process may also delete past-tense suffixes (*poked* becomes /pok/) and third-person singular agreement (*He loves her* becomes *he love her*), by a process similar to that in AAE. Alveolar-cluster simplification has become widespread among all dialects of English, even among SAE speakers, and although it is a process often singled out for ChE and AAE speakers, this is really no longer dialect specific.

6. Prosodic aspects of speech in ChE, such as stress and intonation, also differ from SAE. Stress, for example, may occur on a different syllable in ChE than in SAE.

7. The Spanish sequential constraint, which does not permit a word to begin with an /s/ cluster, is sometimes carried over to ChE. Thus *scare* may be pronounced as if it were spelled *escare* /ɛsker/, and *school* as if it were spelled *eschool*.

SYNTACTIC VARIABLES IN ChE

There are also regular syntactic differences between ChE and SAE. In Spanish, a negative sentence includes a negative morpheme before the verb even if another negative appears; thus negative concord ("double negatives") is a regular rule of ChE syntax:

SAE	ChE
I don't have any money.	I don have no money.
I don't want anything.	I no want nothin.

Another regular difference between ChE and SAE is in the use of the comparative *more* to mean *more often* and the preposition *out from* to mean *away from,* as in the following:

---

[10] J. Penfield and J. L. Ornstein-Galicia. 1985. *Chicano English: An Ethnic Contact.* Philadelphia: John Benjamins. Information on ChE was also provided by Otto Santa Ana.

SAE	ChE
I use English more often.	I use English more.
They use Spanish more often.	They use more Spanish.
They hope to get away from their problems.	They hope to get out from their problems.

Lexical differences also occur, such as the use of *borrow* in ChE for *lend* in SAE (*Borrow me a pencil*) as well as many other substitutions.

As noted, many Chicano speakers (and speakers of AAE) are bidialectal; they can use either ChE (or AAE) or SAE, depending on the social situation.

Lingua Francas

Language is a steed that carries one into a far country.

Arab proverb

Many areas of the world are populated by people who speak diverse languages. In such areas, where groups desire social or commercial communication, one language is often used by common agreement. Such a language is called a **lingua franca.**

In medieval times, a trade language based largely on the languages that became modern Italian and Provençal came into use in the Mediterranean ports. That language was called Lingua Franca, "Frankish language." The term *lingua franca* was generalized to other languages similarly used. Thus, any language can be a lingua franca.

English has been called "the lingua franca of the whole world." French, at one time, was "the lingua franca of diplomacy." Latin was a lingua franca of the Roman Empire and of western Christendom for a millennium, just as Greek served eastern Christendom as its lingua franca. Among Jews, Yiddish has long served as a lingua franca.

More frequently, lingua francas serve as trade languages. East Africa is populated by hundreds of villages, each speaking its own language, but most Africans of this area learn at least some Swahili as a second language, and this lingua franca is used and understood in nearly every marketplace. A similar situation exists in Nigeria, where Hausa is the lingua franca.

Hindi and Urdu are the lingua francas of India and Pakistan. The linguistic situation of this area of the world is so complex that there are often regional lingua francas — usually a local language surrounding a commercial center. Thus the Dravidian language Kannada is a lingua franca for the area surrounding the southwestern Indian city of Mysore. The same situation existed in Imperial China.

In modern China, the Chinese language as a whole is often referred to as *Zhongwen,* which technically refers to the written language, whereas *Zhongguo hua* refers to the spoken language. Ninety-four percent of the people living in the People's Republic of China are said to speak Han languages, which can be divided into eight major dialects (or language groups) that for the most part are mutually unintelligible. Within each group there are hundreds of dialects. In addition to these Han languages, there are more than fifty "national minority" languages, including the five principal ones: Mongolian, Uighur, Tibetan, Zhuang, and Korean. The situation is complex, and for this reason an extensive language reform policy was inaugurated to spread a standard language, called *Putonghua,* which embodies the pronunciation of the Beijing dialect, the grammar of northern Chinese dialects, and the vocabulary of modern colloquial Chinese. The native languages and dialects are not considered inferior. Rather, the approach is to spread the "common speech" (the literal meaning of Putonghua) so that all may communicate with each other in this lingua franca.

Certain lingua francas arise naturally; others are developed by government policy and intervention. In many places of the world, however, people still cannot speak with neighbors only a few miles away.

Pidgins and Creoles

Padi dɛm; kɔntri; una ɔl we de na Rom.
Mɛk una ɔl kak una yes. A kam bɛr Siza,
a nɔ kam prez am.

William Shakespeare, *Julius Caesar*, 3.2, translated to Krio by Thomas Decker

Pidgins

I include 'pidgin-English' . . . even though I am referred to in that splendid language as 'Fella belong Mrs. Queen.

Prince Philip, Husband of Queen Elizabeth II

A lingua franca is typically a language with a broad base of native speakers, likely to be used and learned by persons whose native language is in the same language family. Often in history, however, traders and missionaries from one part of the world have visited and attempted to communicate with peoples residing in another distant part. In such cases, the contact is too specialized, and the cultures too widely separated, for the usual kind of lingua franca to arise. Instead, the two (or possibly more) groups use their native languages as a basis for a rudimentary language of few lexical items and less complex grammatical rules. Such a "marginal language" is called a **pidgin.**

There are a number pidgins in the world, including many based on English. Tok Pisin is an English-based pidgin that is widely used in Papua New Guinea. Like most pidgins, many of its lexical items and much of its structure are based on only one language of the two or more contact languages, in this case English. The variety of Tok Pisin used as a primary language in urban centers is more highly developed and more complex than the Tok Pisin used as a lingua franca in remote areas. Papers in (not *on!*) Tok Pisin have been presented at linguistics conferences in Papua New Guinea, and it is commonly used for debates in the parliament of the country.

Although pidgins are in some sense rudimentary, they are not devoid of grammar. The phonological system is rule-governed, as in any human language. The inventory of phonemes is generally small, and each phoneme may have many allophonic pronunciations. In Tok Pisin, for example, [č], [š], and [s] are all possible pronunciations of the phoneme /s/; [masin], [mašin], and [mačin] all mean "machine."

Tok Pisin has its own writing system, its own literature, and its own newspapers and radio programs; it has even been used to address a United Nations meeting.

With their small vocabularies, however, pidgins are not good at expressing fine distinctions of meaning. Many lexical items bear a heavy semantic burden, with context relied on to remove ambiguity. Much circumlocution and metaphorical extension is necessary. All of these factors combine to give pidgins a unique flavor. What could be a friendlier definition of "friend" than the Australian aborigine's *him brother belong me,* or more poetic than this description of the sun: *lamp belong Jesus?* A policeman is *gubmint catchum-fella,* whiskers are *grass belong face,* and when a man is thirsty *him belly allatime burn.*

Pidgin has come to have negative connotations, perhaps because the best-known pidgins are all associated with European colonial empires. The *Encyclopedia Britannica* once described Pidgin English as "an unruly bastard jargon, filled with nursery imbecilities, vulgarisms and corruptions." It no longer uses such a definition. In recent times there is greater recognition that pidgins reflect human creative linguistic ability, as is beautifully revealed by the Chinese servant asking whether his master's prize sow had given birth to a litter: *Him cow pig have kittens?* as well as the description of Prince Philip, the husband of Queen Elizabeth of England, quoted in the epigraph to this section.

Some people would like to eradicate pidgins. Through massive education, English replaced a pidgin spoken on New Zealand by the Maoris. The government of China at the time forbade the use of Chinese Pidgin English. It died out by the end of the nineteenth century because the Chinese gained access to English, which proved to be more useful in communicating with non-Chinese speakers.

Pidgins have been unjustly maligned; they may serve a useful function.[11] For example, a New Guinean can learn Tok Pisin well enough in six months to begin many kinds of semiprofessional training. To learn English for the same purpose might require ten times as long. In an area with more than eight hundred mutually unintelligible languages, Tok Pisin plays a vital role in unifying similar cultures.

During the seventeenth, eighteenth, and nineteenth centuries, many pidgins sprang up along the coasts of China, Africa, and the New World to accommodate the Europeans. Chinook Jargon was a pidgin combining features from Nootka, Chinook, various Salishan languages, French, and English. Various tribes used it among themselves for commercial purposes, as well as with the European traders who had come to the Pacific Northwest of the United States.

Some linguists have suggested that Proto-Germanic (the earliest form of the Germanic languages) was originally a pidgin, arguing that ordinary linguistic change cannot explain certain striking differences between the Germanic tongues and other Indo-European languages. They theorized that in the first millennium B.C.E. the primitive Germanic tribes that resided along the Baltic Sea traded with the more sophisticated, seagoing cultures. The two peoples communicated by means of a pidgin, which either

---

[11] R. A. Hall. 1955. *Hands Off Pidgin English.* New South Wales: Pacific Publications.

grossly affected Proto-Germanic, or actually became Proto-Germanic. If this is true, English, German, Dutch, and Yiddish had humble beginnings as a pidgin.

Case, tense, mood, and voice are generally absent from pidgins. One cannot, however, speak an English pidgin by merely using English without inflecting verbs or declining pronouns. Pidgins are not "baby talk" or Hollywood's version of American Indians talking English. *Me Tarzan, you Jane* may be understood, but it is not pidgin as it is used in West Africa.

Pidgins are rule-governed. If they were not, no one could learn them. In Tok Pisin, most verbs that take a direct object must have the suffix *-m* or *-im,* even if the direct object is absent. Here are some examples of the application of this rule of the language:

Tok Pisin:	Mi driman long kilim wanpela snek.
English:	I dream of killing a snake.
Tok Pisin:	Bandarap i bin kukim.
English:	Bandarap cooked (it).

Other rules determine word order, which, as in English, is usually quite strict in pidgins because of the lack of case endings on nouns.

The set of pronouns is often simpler in pidgins. In Cameroonian Pidgin (CP), which is also an English-based pidgin, the pronoun system does not show gender or all the case differences that exist in Standard English (SE).[12]

CP			**SE**		
a	mi	ma	I	me	my
yu	yu	yu	you	you	your
i	i/am	i	he	him	his
i	i/am	i	she	her	her
wi	wi	wi	we	us	our
wuna	wuna	wuna	you	you	your
dɛm	dɛm/am	dɛm	they	them	their

Pidgins also may have fewer prepositions than the languages on which they are based. In CP, for example, *fɔ* means "to," "at," "in," "for," and "from," as shown in the following examples:

Gif di buk fɔ mi.	"Give the book to me."
I dei fɔ fam.	"She is at the farm."
Dɛm dei fɔ chɔs.	"They are in the church."
Du dis wan fɔ mi, a bɛg.	"Do this for me, please."
Di mɔni dei fɔ tebul.	"The money is on the table."
You fit muf tɛn frank fɔ ma kwa.	"You can take ten francs from my bag."

Characteristics of pidgins differ in detail from one pidgin to another, and often vary depending on the native language of the pidgin speaker. Thus the verb generally comes

---

[12] The data from CP are from L. Todd. 1984. *Modern Englishes: Pidgins & Creoles.* Oxford, England: Basil Blackwell.

at the end of a sentence for a Japanese speaker of Hawaiian Pidgin English (as in *The poor people all potato eat*), whereas a Filipino speaker of this pidgin puts it before the subject (*Work hard these people*).

Creoles

One distinguishing characteristic of pidgin languages is that no one learns them as native speakers. When a pidgin comes to be adopted by a community as its native tongue, and children learn it as a first language, that language is called a **creole;** the pidgin has become **creolized.**

The term *creole* is Portuguese and originally meant "a white man of European descent born and raised in a tropical or semitropical colony" The meaning shifted and "subsequently applied to certain languages spoken . . . in and around the Caribbean and in West Africa, and then more generally to other similar languages."[13]

Creoles often arose on slave plantations in certain areas where Africans of many different tribes could communicate only via the plantation pidgin. Haitian Creole, based on French, developed in this way, as did the "English" spoken in parts of Jamaica. Gullah is an English-based creole spoken by the descendants of African slaves on islands off the coast of Georgia and South Carolina. Louisiana Creole, related to Haitian Creole, is spoken by large numbers of blacks and whites in Louisiana. Krio, the language spoken by as many as a million Sierra Leoneans, developed, at least in part, from an English-based pidgin.

Creoles become fully developed languages, having more lexical items and a broader array of grammatical distinctions than pidgins. In time, they become languages as complete in every way as other languages.

The study of pidgins and creoles has contributed a great deal to our understanding of the nature of human language and the genetically determined constraints on grammars.

Styles, Slang, and Jargon

Slang is language which takes off its coat, spits on its hands — and goes to work.

Carl Sandburg

Styles

Most speakers of a language speak one way with friends, another on a job interview or presenting a report in class, another talking to small children, another with their parents, and so on. These "situation dialects" are called **styles,** or **registers.**

Nearly everybody has at least an informal and a formal style. In an informal style

---

[13] S. Romaine. 1988. *Pidgin and Creole Languages.* London/New York: Longman, p. 38.

the rules of contraction are used more often, the syntactic rules of negation and agreement may be altered, and many words are used that do not occur in the formal style.

Informal styles, although permitting certain abbreviations and deletions not permitted in formal speech, are also rule-governed. For example, questions are often shortened with the subject *you* and the auxiliary verb deleted. One can ask *Running the marathon?* or *You running the marathon?* instead of the more formal *Are you running the marathon?* but you cannot shorten the question *to *Are running the marathon?* Similarly, *Are you going to take the Linguistics 1 course?* can be abbreviated *to You gonna take the Ling 1 course?* or simply *Gonna take Ling 1?* but not to **Are gonna take Ling 1?* Informal talk is not anarchy, but the rules are more liberal with regard to deletion, contraction, word choice, and so on, than the grammar rules of the formal language.

It is common for speakers to have competence in a number of styles, ranging between the two extremes of formal and informal. Speakers of minority dialects sometimes display virtuosic ability to slide back and forth along a continuum of styles that range from the informal patterns of street talk to formal standard classroom talk. When William Labov was studying African American English used by Harlem youths, he encountered difficulties because the youths (subconsciously) adopted a different style in the presence of strangers. It took time and effort to gain their confidence to the point where they would forget that their conversations were being recorded and so use their less formal style.

Many cultures have rules of social behavior that govern style. In some Indo-European languages there is the distinction between "you (familiar)" and "you (polite)." German *du* and French *tu* are to be used only with "intimates"; *Sie* and *vous* are more formal and used with nonintimates. French even has a verb *tutoyer,* which means "to use the *tu* form," and German uses the verb *duzen* to refer to the informal or less honorific style of speaking.

Other languages have a much more elaborate code of style usage. Speakers of Thai use *kin,* "eat," to their intimates, to show contempt for people such as criminals, or when talking about animals. *Thaan,* "eat," is used informally with nonintimates, whereas *rabprathaan,* "eat," is used on formal occasions or when conversing with dignitaries or esteemed persons (such as grandparents). *Chan,* "eat," is used exclusively when referring to Buddhist monks. Japanese and Javanese are also languages with elaborate styles that must be adhered to in certain social situations.

Slang

One mark of an informal style is the frequent occurrence of **slang.** Almost everyone uses slang on some occasions, but it is not easy to define the word. Slang has been defined as "one of those things that everybody can recognize and nobody can define."[14] The use of slang, or colloquial language, introduces many new words into the language by recombining old words into new meanings. *Spaced out, right on, hang-up,* and *rip-off* have all gained a degree of acceptance. Slang also introduces entirely new words such as *barf, flub,* and *pooped.* Finally, slang often consists of ascribing entirely new meanings to old

---

[14] P. Roberts. 1958. *Understanding English.* New York: Harper & Row, p. 342.

"Jump Start" copyright © 2001 United Feature Syndicate, Inc. Reprinted by permission.

words. *Rave* has broadened its meaning to "an all-night dance party," where *ecstasy* (slang for a kind of drug) is taken to provoke wakefulness. *Grass* and *pot* widened their meaning to "marijuana"; *pig* and *fuzz* are derogatory terms for "police officer"; *rap, cool, dig, stoned, bread, split,* and *suck* have all extended their semantic domains.

The words we have cited may sound "slangy" because they have not gained total acceptability. Words such as *dwindle, freshman, glib,* and *mob* are former slang words that in time overcame their "unsavory" origin. It is not always easy to know where to draw the line between slang words and regular words. This confusion seems always to have been around. In 1890, John S. Farmer, coeditor with W. E. Henley of *Slang and Its Analogues,* remarked: "The borderland between slang and the 'Queen's English' is an ill-defined territory, the limits of which have never been clearly mapped out."

Earlier, in 1792, Friedrich Christian Laukhard wrote: "It is common knowledge that students have a language that is quite peculiar to them and that is not understood very well outside student society." The situation has not changed. Many college campuses publish a slang dictionary that gives college students the hip words they need to be cizool ("cool"), many of them for drinking and sex.

One generation's slang is another generation's standard vocabulary. *Fan* (as in "Dodger fan") was once a slang term, short for *fanatic. Phone,* too, was once a slangy, clipped version of *telephone,* as *TV* was of *television.* In Shakespeare's time, *fretful* and *dwindle* were slang, and more recently *blimp* and *hot dog* were both "hard-core" slang.

The use of slang varies from region to region, so slang in New York and slang in Los Angeles differ. The word *slang* itself is slang in British English for "scold."

Slang words and phrases are often "invented" in keeping with new ideas and customs. They may represent "in" attitudes better than the more conservative items of the vocabulary. Their importance is shown by the fact that it was thought necessary to give the returning Vietnam prisoners of war a glossary of eighty-six new slang words and phrases, from *acid* to *zonked.* The words on this list — prepared by the Air Force — had come into use during only five years. Furthermore, by the time this book was published, many of these terms may have passed out of the language, and many new ones added.

A number of slang words have entered English from the underworld, such as *crack* for a special form of *cocaine, payola, C-note, G-man, to hang paper* ("to write 'bum' checks"), *sawbuck,* and so forth. Prison slang has given us *con* ("a convicted prisoner"), *brek* ("young offender, from *breakfast*), *burn* (tobacco or cigarettes), *peter* ("cell"), and *screw* (prison officer).

Slang even emanates from the White House of the U.S. Capitol. Writers are called *pencils,* newspaper photographers are *stills,* TV camera operators are *sticks* (a reference to their tripods), and the *football* refers to the black box of national security secrets that the president's *mil aide* carries everywhere.

The now ordinary French word meaning "head," *tête,* was once a slang word derived from the Latin *testa,* which meant "earthen pot." Some slang words persist in the language, though, never changing their status from slang to "respectable." Shakespeare used the expression *beat it* to mean "scram" (or more politely, "leave!"), and most English speakers would still consider *beat it* a slang expression. Similarly, the use of the word *pig* for "policeman" goes back at least as far as 1785, when a writer of the time called a Bow Street police officer a "China Street pig."

Jargon and Argot

Police are notorious for creating new words by shortening existing ones, such as *perp* for perpetrator, *ped* for pedestrian and *wit* for witness. More baffling to court reporters is the gang member who . . . might testify that he was in his *hoopty* around *dimday* when some *mud duck* with a *tray-eight* tried to take him *out of the box.* Translation: The man was in his car about dusk when a woman armed with a .38 caliber gun tried to kill him.

Los Angeles Times, August 11, 1986

Practically every conceivable science, profession, trade, and occupation has its own set of words, some of which are considered "slang" and others "technical," depending on the status of the people using these "in" words. Such words are sometimes called **jargon,** or **argot.** Linguistic jargon, some of which is used in this book, consists of terms such as *phoneme, morpheme, case, lexicon, phrase structure rule,* and so on.

The existence of argots or jargons is illustrated by the story of a seaman witness being cross-examined at a trial, who was asked if he knew the plaintiff. Indicating that he did not know what *plaintiff* meant brought a chide from the attorney: "You mean you came into this court as a witness and don't know what 'plaintiff' means?" Later the sailor was asked where he was standing when the boat lurched. "Abaft the binnacle," was the reply, and to the attorney's questioning stare he responded: "You mean you came into this court and don't know where abaft the binnacle is?"

Because the jargon used by different professional groups is so extensive (and so obscure in meaning), court reporters in the Los Angeles Criminal Courts Building have a library that includes books on medical terms, guns, trade names, and computer jargon, as well as street slang.

The computer age not only ushered in a technological revolution, it also introduced a huge jargon of "computerese" used by computer "hackers" and others. So vast is this specialized vocabulary that *Webster's New World Computer Dictionary* has 400 pages and contains thousands of computer terms as entries. A few such words that are familiar to most people are *modem* (from **mod**ulator-**dem**odulator); *bit* (from **bi**nary digi**t**); and *byte* (eight *bits*). Acronyms are rampant in computer jargon. *ROM* (read-only memory), *RAM* (random-access memory), *CPU* (central processing unit), and CD (compact disk) are a small fraction of what's out there.

Many jargon terms pass into the standard language. Jargon, like slang, spreads from a narrow group until it is used and understood by a large segment of the population.

Taboo or Not Taboo?

Sex is a four-letter word.

Bumper sticker slogan

An item in a newspaper once included the following paragraph:

> "This is not a Sunday school, but it is a school of law," the judge said in warning the defendants he would not tolerate the "use of expletives during jury selection." "I'm not going to have my fellow citizens and prospective jurors subjected to filthy language," the judge added.

How can language be filthy? In fact, how can it be clean? The filth or beauty of language must be in the ear of the listener, or in the collective ear of society. The writer Paul Theroux points this out:

> A foreign swear-word is practically inoffensive except to the person who has learned it early in life and knows its social limits.

Nothing about a particular string of sounds makes it intrinsically clean or dirty, ugly or beautiful. If you say that you pricked your finger when sewing, no one would raise an eyebrow; but if you refer to your professor as a prick, the judge quoted above would undoubtedly censure this "dirty" word.

Words that are not acceptable in America are acceptable in England and vice versa. And the acceptance changes over time. In the 1830s, a British visitor to America, Fanny Trollope, remarked:

> Hardly a day passed in which I did not discover something or other which I had been taught to consider as natural as eating, was held in abhorrence by those around me; many words to which I had never heard an objectionable meaning attached, were totally interdicted, and the strangest paraphrastic phrases substituted.

Some of the words that were taboo at that time in America but not in England were *corset, shirt, leg,* and *woman.* Fanny Trollope remarked:

> The ladies here have an extreme aversion to being called women . . . Their idea is, that that term designates only the lower or less-refined classes of female human-kind. This is a mistake which I wonder they should fall into, for in all countries in the world, queens, duchesses, and countesses, are called women.

Certain words in all societies are considered **taboo** — they are not to be used, or at least, not in "polite company." The word *taboo* was borrowed from Tongan, a Polynesian language, in which it refers to acts that are forbidden or to be avoided. When an act is taboo, reference to this act may also become taboo. That is, first you are forbidden to do something; then you are forbidden to talk about it.

Forbidden acts or words reflect the particular customs and views of the society. Some words may be used in certain circumstances and not in others. Among the Zuni In-

"There are some words I will not tolerate in this house—and 'awesome' is one of them."

dians, it is improper to use the word *takka,* meaning "frogs," during a religious ceremony; a complex compound word must be used instead, which literally translated would be "several-are-sitting-in-a-shallow-basin-where-they-are-in-liquid."[15]

In the world of Harry Potter, the evil Voldemort is not to be named, but is referred to as "You-Know-Who." In certain societies, words that have religious connotations are considered profane if used outside of formal or religious ceremonies. Christians are forbidden to "take the Lord's name in vain," and this prohibition has been extended to the use of curses, which are believed to have magical powers. Thus *hell* and *damn* are changed to *heck* and *darn,* perhaps with the belief or hope that this change will fool the "powers that be." Imagine the last two lines of Act II, Scene 1, of *Macbeth* if they were "cleaned up:"

> Hear it not, Duncan; for it is a knell
> That summons thee to heaven, or to heck

Loses a little something, wouldn't you say?

---

[15] P. Farb. 1975. *Word Play.* New York: Bantam.

In England the word *bloody* is, or perhaps was, a taboo word. In Shaw's *Pygmalion* the following lines "startled London and indeed, flustered the whole Empire," according to the British scholar Eric Partridge,[16] when the play was first produced in London in 1910.

"Are you walking across the Park, Miss Doolittle?"
"Walk! Not bloody likely. I am going in a taxi."

Partridge adds, "Much of the interest in the play was due to the heroine's utterance of this banned word. It was waited for with trembling, heard shudderingly."

The *Oxford English Dictionary* states that *bloody* has been in general colloquial use from the Restoration and is "now constantly in the mouths of the lowest classes, but by respectable people considered 'a horrid word' on a par with obscene or profane language, and usually printed in the newspapers 'b_____y.' " The origin of the term is not quite certain. One view is that the word is derived from an oath involving the "blood of Christ"; another that it relates to menstruation. The scholars do not agree and the public has no idea. This uncertainty itself gives us a clue about "dirty" words: People who use them often do not know why they are taboo, only that they are, and to some extent they remain in the language to give vent to strong emotion.

Words relating to sex, sex organs, and natural bodily functions make up a large part of the set of taboo words of many cultures. Some languages have no native words to mean "sexual intercourse" but do borrow such words from neighboring people. Other languages have many words for this common and universal act, most of which are taboo.

Two or more words or expressions can have the same linguistic meaning, with one acceptable and the others the cause of embarrassment or horror. In English, words borrowed from Latin sound "scientific" and therefore appear to be technical and "clean," whereas native Anglo-Saxon counterparts are taboo. This fact reflects the opinion that the vocabulary used by the upper classes was superior to that used by the lower classes, a distinction going back at least to the Norman Conquest in 1066, when "a duchess perspired and expectorated and menstruated — while a kitchen maid sweated and spat and bled."[17] Such pairs of words are illustrated below:

Anglo-Saxon Taboo Words	Latinate Acceptable Words
cunt	vagina
cock	penis
prick	penis
tits	breasts
shit	feces

There is no linguistic reason why the word *vagina* is "clean" whereas *cunt* is "dirty" or why *prick* or *cock* is taboo but *penis* is acknowledged as referring to part of the male

---

[16] As quoted in "The History of Some 'Dirty' Words" by Falk Johnson. 1950. In *The American Mercury*, Vol. 71, pp. 538–45.
[17] P. Farb. 1975. *Word Play*. New York: Bantam.

anatomy, or why everyone *defecates* but only vulgar people *shit*. Many people even avoid words like *breasts, intercourse,* and *testicles* as much as words like *tits, fuck,* and *balls.* There is no linguistic basis for such views, but pointing this fact out does not imply advocating the use or nonuse of any words.

Euphemisms

Banish the use of the four-letter words
Whose meaning is never obscure.
The Anglos, the Saxons, those bawdy old birds
Were vulgar, obscene, and impure.
But cherish the use of the weaseling phrase
That never quite says what it means;
You'd better be known for your hypocrite ways
Than vulgar, impure, and obscene.

Folk song attributed to Wartime Royal Air Force of Great Britain.

The existence of taboo words and ideas stimulates the creation of **euphemisms.** A euphemism is a word or phrase that replaces a taboo word or serves to avoid frightening or unpleasant subjects. In many societies, because death is feared, there are a number of euphemisms related to this subject. People are less apt to *die* and more apt to *pass on* or *pass away.* Those who take care of your loved ones who have passed away are more likely to be *funeral directors* than *morticians* or *undertakers.*

The use of euphemisms is not new. It is reported that the Greek historian Plutarch in the first century C.E. wrote that "the ancient Athenians . . . used to cover up the ugliness of things with auspicious and kindly terms, giving them polite and endearing names. Thus they called harlots *companions,* taxes *contributions,* and prison a *chamber.*"

The poem, quoted above, exhorts against such euphemisms, as another verse demonstrates:

When in calling, plain speaking is out;
When the ladies (God bless 'em) are milling about,
You may wet, make water, or empty the glass;
You can powder your nose, or the "johnny" will pass.
It's a drain for the lily, or man about dog
When everyone's drunk, it's condensing the fog;
But sure as the devil, that word with a hiss,
It's only in Shakespeare that characters _____.

Some scholars are bemused with the attitudes revealed by the use of euphemisms. A journal, *Maledicta,* subtitled *The International Journal of Verbal Aggression* and edited by Reinhold Aman, "specializes in uncensored glossaries and studies of all offensive and negatively valued words and expressions, in all languages and from all cultures, past and present." A review of this journal by Bill Katz in the *Library Journal* (November 1977) points out, "The history of the dirty word or phrase is the focus of this substantial . . . journal [whose articles] are written in a scholarly yet entertaining fashion by professors . . . as well as by a few outsiders."

A scholarly study of Australian English euphemisms shows the considerable creativity involved:[18]

urinate:	drain the dragon
	syphon the python
	water the horse
	squeeze the lemon
	drain the spuds
	wring the rattlesnake
	shake hands with the wife's best friend
	point Percy at the porcelain
	train Terence on the terracotta
have intercourse:	shag
	root
	crack a fat
	dip the wick
	play hospital
	hide the ferret
	play cars and garages
	hide the egg roll (sausage, salami)
	boil bangers
	slip a length
	go off like a beltfed motor
	go like a rat up a rhododendron
	go like a rat up a drain pipe
	have a northwest cocktail

---

[18] J. Powell. 1972. Paper delivered at the Western Conference of Linguistics, University of Oregon.

These euphemisms, as well as the difference between the accepted Latinate "genteel" terms and the "dirty" Anglo-Saxon terms, show that a word or phrase not only has a linguistic **denotative meaning** but also has a **connotative meaning** that reflects attitudes, emotions, value judgments, and so on. In learning a language, children learn which words are taboo, and these taboo words differ from one child to another, depending on the value system accepted in the family or group in which the child grows up.

Racial and National Epithets

The use of epithets for people of different religions, nationalities, or races tells us something about the users of these words. The word *boy* is not a taboo word when used generally, but when a twenty-year-old white man calls a forty-year-old African American man "boy," the word takes on an additional meaning; it reflects the racist attitude of the speaker. So also, words like *kike* (for Jew), *wop* (for Italian), *nigger* or *coon* (for African American), *slant* (for Asian), *towelhead* (for Middle Eastern Arab), and so forth express racist and chauvinist views of society.

Such epithets are found under surprising circumstances. The chairman of the Raleigh Convention and Visitors Bureau in North Carolina was quoted in the newspaper[19] as saying: "If we had a shabby-looking place, we wouldn't have a Chinaman's chance of attracting the people we need to do business with." One is tempted to observe that the chances of attracting any of the 1.2 billion potential Chinese tourists might be lessened by such statements.

Even words that sound like epithets are probably to be avoided. An administrator in Washington, D.C., described a fund he administers as "niggardly," meaning stingy. He resigned his position under fire for using a word "so close to a degrading word."

The use of the verbs to *jew* or to *gyp/jip* also reflect the stereotypical views of Jews and Gypsies. Most people do not realize that *gyp*, which is used to mean "cheat," comes from the view that Gypsies are duplicitous. In time these words would either disappear or lose their racist connotations if bigotry and oppression ceased to exist, but since they show no signs of doing so, the use of such words perpetuates stereotypes, separates one people from another, and reflects racism.

Language, however, is creative, malleable, and ever changing. The very epithets used by a majority to demean a minority may be reclaimed as terms of bonding and friendship among members of the minority. Thus for some — we emphasize *some* — African Americans, the word *nigger* is used to show affection. Similarly, the ordinarily degrading word *queer* is used among *some* gay persons as a term of endearment, as is *cripple* among *some* individuals who share a disability.

---

[19] *Raleigh News and Observer,* February 22, 1999.

Language, Sex, and Gender

doctor, n. . . . a man of great learning.

The American College Dictionary, 1947

A businessman is aggressive; a businesswoman is pushy. A businessman is good on details; she's picky. . . . He follows through; she doesn't know when to quit. He stands firm; she's hard. . . . His judgments are her prejudices. He is a man of the world; she's been around. He isn't afraid to say what is on his mind; she's mouthy. He exercises authority diligently; she's power mad. He's closemouthed; she's secretive. He climbed the ladder of success; she slept her way to the top.

From "How to Tell a Businessman from a Businesswoman,"
Graduate School of Management, UCLA, *The Balloon* XXII, (6).

The discussion of obscenities, blasphemies, taboo words, and euphemisms showed that words of a language are not intrinsically good or bad, but reflect individual or societal values. In addition, one speaker may use a word with positive connotations while another may select a different word with negative connotations to refer to the same person. For example, a person may be called a *terrorist* or a *freedom fighter* depending on who is doing the calling. A woman may be a *castrating female* (or *ballsy women's libber*) or may be a *courageous feminist advocate,* again depending on who is talking. The words we use to refer to certain individuals or groups reflect our individual nonlinguistic attitudes and may reflect the culture and views of society.

Language reflects sexism in society. Language itself is not sexist, just as it is not obscene; but it can connote sexist attitudes as well attitudes about social taboos or racism.

Dictionaries often give clues to social attitudes. In the 1969 edition of *the American Heritage Dictionary,* examples used to illustrate the meaning of words include "manly courage" and "masculine charm." Women do not fare as well, as exemplified by "womanish tears" and "feminine wiles." In *Webster's New World Dictionary of the American Language* (1961), *honorarium* is defined as "a payment to a professional man for services on which no fee is set or legally obtainable." Attempts to deflect the inherent sexism in such definitions by claiming that *man* actually means "human" was deftly parried in 1973:

> If a woman is swept off a ship into the water, the cry is *Man overboard.* If she is killed by a hit-and-run driver, the charge is *manslaughter.* If she is injured on the job, the coverage is *workmen's compensation.* But if she arrives at the threshold marked *Men Only,* she knows the admonition is not intended to bar animals or plants or inanimate objects. It is meant for her.[20]

Until 1972, at Columbia University, the women's faculty toilet doors were labeled "Women," whereas the men's doors were labeled "Officers of Instruction." Yet, linguistically, the word *officer* is not marked semantically for gender. There were apparently few women professors at Columbia at that time, which was reflected in these

---

[20] A. Graham. "How to Make Troubles: The Making of a Nonsexist Dictionary." *Ms.,* December 1973.

designations. This shows that nonlinguistic aspects of society may influence our interpretation of the meaning of words. Thus, at least until recently, most people hearing *My cousin is a professor* (or a *doctor,* or *the Chancellor of the University,* or a *steel worker*) would assume that the cousin is a man. This assumption has nothing to do with the English language but a great deal to do with the fact that, historically, women have not been prominent in these positions. This is beginning to change, as more women become professors, doctors, chancellors, and political leaders.

On the other hand, if you heard someone say *My cousin is a nurse* (or *elementary school teacher,* or *clerk-typist,* or *house worker*), you would probably conclude that the speaker's cousin is a woman. It is less evident why the sentence *My neighbor is a blond* is understood as referring to a woman. It may be that hair color is a primary category of classification for women. If this is so, it is a linguistic fact and suggests, as discussed in chapter 4, that *blond* has a [+ female] feature associated with it in the lexicon.

Studies analyzing the language used by men in reference to women, which often has derogatory or sexual connotations, indicate that such terms go far back into history, and sometimes enter the language with no pejorative implications but gradually gain them. Thus, from Old English *huswif,* "housewife," the word *hussy* was derived. In their original employment, "a laundress made beds, a needlewoman came to sew, a spinster tended the spinning wheel, and a nurse cared for the sick. But all apparently acquired secondary duties in some households, because all became euphemisms for a mistress or a prostitute at some time during their existence."[21]

Words for women — all with abusive or sexual overtones — abound: *dish, tomato, piece, piece of ass, chick, piece of tail, bunny, pussy, pussycat, bitch, doll, slut, cow* — to name just a few. Far fewer such pejorative terms exist for men.

Marked and Unmarked Forms

Long afterward, Oedipus, old and blinded, walked the
roads. He smelled a familiar smell. It was
the Sphinx. Oedipus said, "I want to ask one question.
Why didn't I recognize my mother?" "You gave the
wrong answer," said the Sphinx. "But that was what
made everything possible," said Oedipus. "No," she said.
"When I asked, 'What walks on four legs in the morning,
two at noon, and three in the evening,' you answered,
'Man.' You didn't say anything about woman."
"When you say Man," said Oedipus, "you include women
too. Everyone knows that." She said, "That's what
you think."

Muriel Rukeyser, *Myth*[22]

---

[21] M. R. Schultz. 1975. "The Semantic Derogation of Woman," in B. Thorne and N. Henley, eds. *Language and Sex.* Rowley, MA: Newbury House Publishers, pp. 66–67.

[22] *A Muriel Rukeyser Reader.* 1994. J. H. Levi, ed. New York: W. W. Norton, p. 252. Reprinted with permission of International Creative Management, Inc. Copyright © 1994 Muriel Rukeyser.

One striking fact about the asymmetry between male and female terms in many languages is that when there are male/female pairs, the male form for the most part is unmarked and the female term is created by adding a bound morpheme or by compounding. We have many such examples in English:

Male	Female
prince	princess
author	authoress
count	countess
actor	actress
host	hostess
poet	poetess
heir	heiress
hero	heroine
Paul	Pauline

Since the advent of the feminist movement, many of the marked female forms have been replaced by the male forms, which are used to refer to either sex. Thus women, as well as men, are authors, actors, poets, heroes, and heirs. Women, however, remain countesses, if they are among this small group of female aristocrats.

Given these asymmetries, **folk etymologies** arise that misinterpret a number of non-sexist words. Folk etymology is the process, normally unconscious, whereby words or their origins are changed through nonscientific speculations or false analogies with other words. When we borrowed the French word *crevisse,* for example, it became *crayfish.* The English-speaking borrowers did not know that *-isse* was a feminine suffix. *Female* is not the feminine form of *male,* which some people claim, but came into English from the Latin word *femina,* with the same morpheme *fe* that occurs in the Latin *fecundus* meaning "fertile" (originally derived from an Indo-European word meaning "to give suck to"). It entered English through the Old French word *femme* and its diminutive form *femelle,* "little woman."

Other male/female gender pairs have interesting meaning differences. Although a governor governs a state, a governess takes care of children; a mistress, in its most widely used meaning, is not a female master, nor is a majorette a woman major. We talk of "unwed mothers" but not "unwed fathers," of "career women" but not "career men," because there has been historically no stigma for a bachelor to father a child, and men are supposed to have careers. It is only recently that the term *househusband* has come into being, again reflecting changes in social customs.

Possibly as a protest against the reference to new and important ideas as *seminal* (from *semen*), Clare Booth Luce updated Ibsen's drama *A Doll's House* by having Nora tell her husband that she is pregnant "in the way only men are supposed to get pregnant." When he asks, "Men pregnant?" she replies, "With ideas. Pregnancies there (she taps her head) are masculine. And a very superior form of labor. Pregnancies here (she taps her stomach) are feminine — a very inferior form of labor."

Other linguistic asymmetries exist, such as the fact that most women continue to adopt their husbands' names in marriage. This name change can be traced back to early legal practices, some of which are perpetuated currently. Thus we often refer to a woman as Mrs. Jack Fromkin, but seldom refer to a man as Mr. Vicki Fromkin, except in an insulting sense. This convention, however, is not true in other cultures.

We talk of Professor and Mrs. John Smith but seldom, if ever, of Mr. and Dr. Philippa Kerr. At a UCLA alumni association dinner, place cards designated where "Dr. Fromkin" and "Mrs. Fromkin" were to sit, although both individuals have doctoral degrees.

It is insulting to a woman to be called a *spinster* or an *old maid,* but it is not insulting to a man to be called a *bachelor.* There is nothing inherently pejorative about the word *spinster.* The connotations reflect the different views society has about an unmarried woman as opposed to an unmarried man. It is not the language that is sexist; it is society.

The Generic "He"

E, hesh, po, tey, co, jhe, ve, xe, he'er, thon, and *na*

Words that have been suggested replacements for *he.*[23]

The unmarked, or male, nouns also serve as general terms, as do the male pronouns. *The brotherhood of man* includes women, but *sisterhood* does not include men.

When Thomas Jefferson wrote in the Declaration of Independence that "all *men* are created equal" and "governments are instituted among *men* deriving their just powers from the consent of the governed," he was not using *men* as a general term to include women. His use of the word *men* was precise at the time that women could not vote. In the sixteenth and seventeenth centuries, masculine pronouns were not used as the generic terms; the various forms of *he* were used when referring to males, and of *she* when referring to females. The pronoun *they* was used to refer to people of either sex even if the referent was a singular noun, as shown by Lord Chesterfield's statement in 1759: "If a person is born of a gloomy temper . . . they cannot help it."

By the eighteenth century, grammarians (males to be sure) created the rule designating the male pronouns as the general term, and it wasn't until the nineteenth century that the rule was applied widely, after an act of Britain's Parliament in 1850 sanctioned its use. But this generic use of *he* was ignored. In 1879, women doctors were barred from membership in the all-male Massachusetts Medical Society on the basis that the bylaws of the organization referred to members by the pronoun *he.*

Changes in English are taking place that reflect the feminist movement and the growing awareness on the part of both men and women that language may reflect attitudes of society and reinforce stereotypes and bias. More and more, the word *people* is replacing *mankind, personnel* is used instead of *manpower, nurturing* instead of *mothering,* and to *operate* instead of *to man. Chair* or *moderator* is used instead of *chairman* (particularly by those who do not like the "clumsiness" of *chairperson*) and terms like *postal worker, firefighter,* and *public safety officer* or *police officer* are replacing *mailman, fireman,* and *policeman.*

---

[23] Pinker, S. *The Language Instinct.* New York: HarperCollins, p. 46.

A. A. Milne summed up the difficulty in *The Christopher Robin Birthday Book* where he wrote:

> If the English language had been properly organized . . . then there would be a word which meant both 'he' and 'she', and I could write, 'If John or Mary comes, heesh will want to play tennis,' which would save a lot of trouble.

Language and Gender

Beginning in 1973, when the first article specifically concerned with women and language was published in a major linguistics journal, an increasing number of scholars have been conducting research on language, gender, and sexism. Robin Lakoff's study suggested that women's insecurity due to sexism in society resulted in more "proper" use of the rules of SAE grammar than was found in the speech of men. Differences between male and female speech were investigated.[24]

"The Wizard of Id" copyright © 1990. Reprinted by permission of Johnny Hart and Creators Syndicate, Inc.

Variations in the dialects of men and women occur in America and in other countries. In Japanese, women may choose to speak a distinct dialect although they are fully aware of the standard dialect used by both men and women. It has been said that guide and helper dogs in Japan are trained in English, because the sex of the owner is not known in advance, and it is easier for an impaired person to use English than to train the dog in both language styles.

In the Muskogean language Koasati, spoken in Louisiana, words that end in an /s/ when spoken by men, end in /l/ or /n/ when used by women; for example, the word meaning "lift it" is *lakawhol* for women and *lakawhos* for men. Early explorers reported that the men and women of the Carib Indians used different dialects. In Chiquita, a Bolivian language, the grammar of male language includes a noun-class gender distinction, with names for males and supernatural beings morphologically marked in one way, and nouns referring to females marked in another.

One characteristic of female speech is the higher pitch used by women, due largely to shorter vocal tracts. Nevertheless, studies conducted by the phonetician Caroline

---

[24] R. Lakoff. 1973. "Language and Woman's Place," *Language in Society* 2:45–80.

Henton showed that the difference in pitch between male and female voices was, on the average, greater than could be accounted for by physiology alone, suggesting that some social factor must be involved during the acquisition period.

This chapter has stressed the fact that language itself is beyond good and evil, but its use may be one or the other. If we view women or Africans or Hispanics as inferior, then we are likely to regard their special speech characteristics as inferior. Furthermore, when society itself institutionalizes such attitudes, the language reflects it. When everyone in society is truly equal, and treated as such, there will be little concern for the asymmetries that exist in language.

Secret Languages and Language Games

Throughout the world and throughout history, people have invented secret languages and language games. They have used these special languages either as a means of identifying with a special group, for fun as with the Elfish language from "Lord of the Rings," or to prevent others from knowing what is being said. When the aim is secrecy, a number of methods are used; immigrant parents sometimes use their native language when they do not want their children to understand what they are saying, or parents may spell out words. American slaves developed an elaborate code that could not be

"MR. WILSON TOLD ME TO AM-SCRAY! I DON'T KNOW WHAT THAT MEANS, BUT I DIDN'T LIKE THE WAY HE SAID IT....SO I LEFT."

"Dennis the Menace®" used by permission of Hank Ketcham Enterprises and copyright © by North America Syndicate.

understood by the slave owners. References to "the promised land" or the "flight of the Israelites from Egypt" sung in spirituals were codes for the north and the Underground Railroad.

One special language is Cockney rhyming slang. No one is completely sure of how it first arose. One view is that it began as a secret language among the criminals of the underworld in London in the mid-nineteenth century to confuse the "peelers," that is, the police. Another view is that during the building of the London docks at the beginning of the century, the Irish immigrant workers invented rhyming slang to confuse the non-Irish workers. Still another view is that it was spread by street chanters who went from market to market in England telling tales, reporting the news, and reciting ballads.

The way to play this language game is to create a rhyme as a substitute for a specific word. Thus, for *table* the rhymed slang may be *Cain and Abel; missus* is called *cows and kisses; stairs* are *apples and pears; head* is *loaf of bread,* often shortened to *loaf* as in "use yer loaf." Several cockney rhyming slang terms have crossed the ocean to America. *Bread* meaning *money* in American slang comes from cockney *bread and honey;* and *brass tacks* — those things that Americans love to get down to — is derived from the cockney rhyming slang for *facts.*

Other language games, such as Pig Latin (see the " Dennis the Menace " cartoon), are used for amusement by and of children and adults. They exist in all the world's languages, and take a wide variety of forms. In some, a suffix is added to each word; in others a syllable is inserted after each vowel; there are rhyming games and games in which phonemes are reversed. A game in Brazil substitutes an /i/ for all the vowels; Indian children learn a Bengali language game in which the syllables are reversed, as in pronouncing *bisri,* "ugly," as *sribi.*

A language game based on writing disguises a forbidden word by adding strokes to alter letters. Thus FUCK becomes ENOR by altering its four letters; CUNT becomes OOMF, and now the innocent sounding nonsense words are codes for the vulgarities.

The Walbiri, natives of central Australia, play a language game in which the meanings of words are distorted. In this play language, all nouns, verbs, pronouns, and adjectives are replaced by a semantically contrastive word. Thus, the sentence *Those men are small* means *This woman is big.*

These language games provide evidence for the phonemes, words, morphemes, semantic features, and so on that are posited by linguists for descriptive grammars. They also illustrate the boundless creativity of human language and human speakers.

≋ Summary

Every person has a unique way of speaking, called an **idiolect.** The language used by a group of speakers is its **dialect.** The dialects of a language are the mutually intelligible forms of that language that differ in systematic ways from each other. Dialects develop because languages change, and the changes that occur in one group or area may differ from those that occur in another. **Regional dialects** and **social dialects** develop for this reason. Some differences in U.S. regional dialects may be traced to the dialects spoken by colonial settlers from England. Those from southern England spoke one dialect and those from the north spoke another. In addition, the colonists who maintained close contact with England reflected the changes occurring in British English while earlier forms were preserved among Americans who spread westward and broke communication with the Atlantic coast. The study of regional dialects has produced **dialect atlases** with **dialect maps** showing the areas where specific dialectal characteristics occur in the speech of the region. A boundary line called an **isogloss** delineates each area.

Dialect differences include phonological or pronunciation differences (often called **accents**), vocabulary distinctions, and syntactic rule differences. The grammar differences among dialects are not as great as the similarities, thus permitting speakers of different dialects to communicate.

In many countries, one dialect or dialect group is viewed as the **standard,** such as **Standard American English (SAE).** Although this particular dialect is not linguistically superior, some language purists consider it the only correct form of the language. Such a view has led to the idea that some nonstandard dialects are deficient, as is erroneously suggested regarding **African American English** (sometimes referred to as **Ebonics**), a dialect used by some African Americans. A study of African American English shows it to be as logical, complete, rule-governed, and expressive as any other dialect. This is also true of the dialects spoken by Latino Americans whose native language or those of their parents is Spanish. There are bilingual and monolingual Latino speakers of English. One Latino dialect spoken in the Southwest, referred to as **Chicano English (ChE),** shows systematic phonological and syntactic differences from SAE that stem from the influence of Spanish. Other differences are shared with many nonstandard ethnic and nonethnic dialects. **Code-switching** is when bilingual persons switch from one language to another, possibly within a single sentence. It reflects both grammars working simultaneously and does not represent a form of "broken" English or Spanish or whatever.

Attempts to legislate the use of a particular dialect or language have been made throughout history and exist today, even extending to banning the use of languages other than the preferred one.

In areas where many languages are spoken, one language may become a **lingua franca** to ease communication among the people. In other cases, where traders, missionaries, or travelers need to communicate with people who speak a language unknown to them, a **pidgin** based on one language may develop, which is simplified lexically, phonologically, and syntactically. When a pidgin is widely used, and is learned by children as their first language, it is **creolized.** The grammars of **creole** languages are similar to those of other languages, and languages of creole origin now exist in many parts of the world.

Besides regional and social dialects, speakers may use different **styles,** or **registers,** depending on the context. **Slang** is not often used in formal situations or writing, but is widely used in speech; **argot** and **jargon** refer to the unique vocabulary used by professional or trade groups.

In all societies certain acts or behaviors are frowned on, forbidden, or considered **taboo.** The words or expressions referring to these taboo acts are then also avoided, or considered "dirty." Language itself cannot be obscene or clean; the views toward specific words or linguistic expressions reflect the attitudes of a culture or society toward the behaviors and actions of the language users. At times, slang words may be taboo where scientific or standard terms with the same meaning are acceptable in "polite society." Taboo words and acts give rise to **euphemisms,** which are words or phrases that replace the expressions to be avoided. Thus, *powder room* is a euphemism for *toilet,* which itself started as a euphemism for *lavatory,* which is now more acceptable than its replacement.

Just as the use of some words may reflect society's views toward sex or natural bodily functions or religious beliefs, so also some words may reflect racist, chauvinist, and sexist attitudes. Language itself is not racist or sexist but reflects the views of various sectors of a society. Such terms, however, may perpetuate and reinforce biased views, and be demeaning and insulting to those addressed. Popular movements and changes in the institutions of society may then be reflected in changes in the language.

The invention or construction of secret languages and language games like Pig Latin attest to human creativity with language and the unconscious knowledge that speakers have of the phonological, morphological, and semantic rules of their language.

 # References for Further Reading

Allan, K., and K. Burridge. 1991. *Euphemism and Dysphemism.* New York: Oxford University Press.

Andersson, L., and P. Trudgill. 1990. *Bad Language.* Oxford, England: Basil Blackwell.

Ayto, J. 1993. *Euphemisms: Over 3000 Ways to Avoid Being Rude or Giving Offence.* London: Bloomsbury.

Baugh, J. 1983. *Black Street Speech.* Austin, TX: University of Texas Press.

Bickerton, D. 1981. *Roots of Language.* Ann Arbor, MI: Karoma.

Cameron, D. 1992. *Feminism and Linguistic Theory, 2nd ed.* London: Macmillan.

Carver, C. M. 1987. *American Regional Dialects: A Word Geography.* Ann Arbor, MI: University of Michigan Press.

Cassidy, F. G. (chief ed.). 1985, 1991, 1996. *Dictionary of American Regional English, Volumes 1, 2, 3.* Cambridge, MA: Harvard University Press.

Coates, J. 1986. *Women, Men and Language: A Sociolinguistic Account of Sex Differences in Language.* London and New York: Longman.

Dillard, J. L. 1972. *African American English: Its History and Usage in the United States.* New York: Random House.

Fasold, R. 1990. *Sociolinguistics of Language.* London: Blackwell Publishers.

Ferguson, C., and S. B. Health, eds. 1981. *Language in the USA.* Cambridge, England: Cambridge University Press.

Folb, E. 1980. *Runnin' Down Some Lines: The Language and Culture of Black Teenagers.* Cambridge, MA: Harvard University Press.

Frank, F., and F. Ashen. 1983. *Language and the Sexes.* Albany, NY: State University of New York Press.

Holm, J. 1988–1989. *Pidgins and Creoles, Vols. 1, 2.* Cambridge, England: Cambridge University Press.

Jay, T. 1992. *Cursing in America: A Psycholinguistic Study of Dirty Language in the Courts, in the Movies, in the Schoolyards and on the Streets.* Amsterdam: John Benjamins.

King, R. 1991. *Talking Gender: A Guide to Nonsexist Communication.* Toronto: Copp Clark Pitman.

Labov, W. 1969. *The Logic of Nonstandard English.* Georgetown University 20th Annual Round Table, Monograph Series on Languages and Linguistics, No. 22.

Michaels, L., and C. Ricks, eds. 1980. *The State of the Language.* Berkeley, CA: University of California Press.

Lakoff, R. 1990. *Talking Power: The Politics of Language.* New York: Basic Books.

Miller, C., and K. Swift. 1980. *The Handbook of Nonsexist Writing.* New York: Barnes & Noble.

Mulhausler, P. 1986. *Pidgin and Creole Linguistics.* Oxford, England: Basil Blackwell.

Munro, P. 1990. *Slang U: The Official Dictionary of College Slang.* New York: Harmony Books.

Newmeyer, F. J., ed. 1988. *Linguistics: The Cambridge Survey, Vol. 4. Language: The Socio-Cultural Context.* Cambridge, England: Cambridge University Press.

Penfield, J., and J. L. Ornstein-Galicia. 1985. *Chicano English: An Ethnic Contact Dialect.* Amsterdam/Philadelphia: John Benjamins.

Reed, C. E. 1977. *Dialects of American English, rev. ed.* Amherst, MA: University of Massachusetts Press.

Romaine, S. 1988. *Pidgin and Creole Languages.* London/New York: Longman.

Shopen, T., and J. M. Williams, eds. 1981. *Style and Variables in English.* Cambridge, MA: Winthrop.

Smith, P. M. 1985. *Language, the Sexes and Society.* Oxford: Basil Blackwell.

Spears, R. A. 1981. *Slang and Euphemism: A Dictionary of Oaths, Curses, Insults, Sexual Slang and Metaphor, Racial Slurs, Drug Talk, Homosexual Lingo, and Related Matter.* New York: Jonathan David Publishers.

Tannen, D. 1990. *You Just Don't Understand: Women and Men in Conversation.* New York: Ballantine.

Thorne, B., C. Kramarae, and N. Henley, eds. 1983. *Language, Gender, and Society.* Rowley, MA: Newbury House.

Todd, L. 1984. *Modern Englishes: Pidgins and Creoles.* Oxford, England: Basil Blackwell.

Trudgill, P. 1977. *Sociolinguistics.* Middlesex, England: Penguin Books.

Williams, G. 1992. *Sociolinguistics.* London/New York: Routledge.

Williamson, J. V., and V. M. Burke. 1971. *A Various Language: Perspectives on American Dialects.* New York: Holt, Rinehart and Winston.

Wolfram, W., and N. Schilling-Estes. 1998. *American English Dialects and Variation.* London: Blackwell Publishers.

≋ Exercises

1. Each pair of words is pronounced as shown phonetically in at least one American English dialect. Write in phonetic transcription your pronunciation of each word that you pronounce differently.

a. horse	[hɔrs]	hoarse	[hors]
b. morning	[mɔrnɪŋ]	mourning	[mornɪŋ]
c. for	[fɔr]	four	[for]
d. ice	[ʌjs]	eyes	[ajz]

e. knife	[nʌjf]	knives	[najvz]
f. mute	[mjut]	nude	[njud]
g. din	[dĭn]	den	[dɛ̃n]
h. hog	[hɔg]	hot	[hat]
i. marry	[mæri]	Mary	[meri]
j. merry	[mɛri]	marry	[mæri]
k. rot	[rat]	wrought	[rɔt]
l. lease	[lis]	grease (v.)	[griz]
m. what	[ʌ̃at]	watt	[wat]
n. ant	[æ̃nt]	aunt	[ãnt]
o. creek	[kʰrɪk]	creak	[kʰrik]

2. Below is a passage from *The Gospel According to St. Mark* in Cameroon English Pidgin. See how much you can understand before consulting the English translation given below. State some of the similarities and differences between CEP and SAE.

   a. Di fos tok fo di gud nuus fo Jesus Christ God yi Pikin.

   b. I bi sem as i di tok fo di buk fo Isaiah, God yi nchinda (Prophet), "Lukam, mi a di sen man nchinda fo bifo yoa fes weh yi go fix yoa rud fan."

   c. Di vos fo som man di krai fo bush: "Fix di ples weh Papa God di go, mek yi rud tret."

   Translation:

   a. The beginning of the gospel of Jesus Christ, the Son of God.

   b. As it is written in the book of Isaiah the prophet, "Behold, I send my messenger before thy face, which shall prepare thy way before thee."

   c. The voice of one crying in the wilderness, "Prepare ye the way of the Lord, make his paths straight."

3. In the period from 1890 to 1904, *Slang and Its Analogues* by J. S. Farmer and W. E. Henley was published in seven volumes. The following entries are included in this dictionary. For each item (1) state whether the word or phrase still exists; (2) if not, state what the modern slang term would be; and (3) if the word remains but its meaning has changed, provide the modern meaning.

   all out: completely, as in "All out the best." (The expression goes back to as early as 1300.)

   to have apartments to let: be an idiot; one who is empty-headed.

   been there: in "Oh, yes, I've been there." Applied to a man who is shrewd and who has had many experiences.

   belly-button: the navel.

   berkeleys: a woman's breasts.

   bitch: most offensive appellation that can be given to a woman, even more provoking than that of *whore.*

   once in a blue moon: seldom.

   boss: master; one who directs.

   bread: employment. (1785 – "out of bread" = "out of work.")

   claim: to steal.

   cut dirt: to escape.

dog cheap: of little worth. (Used in 1616 by Dekker: "Three things there are dog-cheap, learning, poorman's sweat, and oathes.")

funeral: as in "It's not my funeral." "It's no business of mine."

to get over: to seduce, to fascinate.

groovy: settled in habit; limited in mind.

grub: food.

head: toilet (nautical use only).

hook: to marry.

hump: to spoil.

hush money: money paid for silence; blackmail.

itch: to be sexually excited.

jam: a sweetheart or a mistress.

leg bags: stockings.

to lie low: to keep quiet; to bide one's time.

to lift a leg on: to have sexual intercourse.

looby: a fool.

malady of France: syphilis (used by Shakespeare in 1599).

nix: nothing.

noddle: the head.

old: money. (1900 – "Perhaps it's somebody you owe a bit of the old to, Jack.")

to pill: talk platitudes.

pipe layer: a political intriguer; a schemer.

poky: cramped, stuffy, stupid.

pot: a quart; a large sum; a prize; a urinal; to excel.

puny: a freshman.

puss-gentleman: an effeminate.

4. Suppose someone asked you to help compile items for a new dictionary of slang. List ten slang words, and provide a short definition for each.

5. Below are some words used in British English for which different words are usually used in American English. See if you can match the British and American equivalents.

British		**American**	
a. clothes peg	**k.** biscuits	**A.** candy	**K.** baby buggy
b. braces	**l.** queue	**B.** truck	**L.** elevator
c. lift	**m.** torch	**C.** line	**M.** can
d. pram	**n.** underground	**D.** main street	**N.** cop
e. waistcoat	**o.** high street	**E.** crackers	**O.** wake up
f. shop assistant	**p.** crisps	**F.** suspenders	**P.** trunk
g. sweets	**q.** lorry	**G.** wrench	**Q.** vest
h. boot (of car)	**r.** holiday	**H.** flashlight	**R.** subway
i. bobby	**s.** tin	**I.** potato chips	**S.** clothes pin
j. spanner	**t.** knock up	**J.** vacation	**T.** clerk

6. Pig Latin is a common language game of English; but even Pig Latin has dialects, forms of the "language game" with different rules.

   A. Consider the following data from three dialects of Pig Latin, each with its own rule applied to words beginning with vowels:

	Dialect 1	**Dialect 2**	**Dialect 3**
"eat"	[itme]	[ithe]	[ite]
"arc"	[arkme]	[arkhe]	[arke]

   (1) State the rule that accounts for the Pig Latin forms in each dialect.

   (2) How would you say *honest*, *admire*, and *illegal* in each dialect? Give the phonetic transcription of the Pig Latin forms.

   B. In one dialect of Pig Latin, the word "strike" is pronounced [ajkstre], and in another dialect it is pronounced [trajkse]. In the first dialect "slot" is pronounced [atsle] and in the second dialect, it is pronounced [latse].

   (1) State the rules for each of these dialects that account for these different Pig Latin forms of the same words.

   (2) Give the phonetic transcriptions for *spot*, *crisis*, and *scratch* in both dialects.

7. Below are some sentences representing different English language games. Write each sentence in its undistorted form; state the language-game "rule."

   a. /aj-o tʊk-o maj-o dag-o awt-o sajd-o/

   b. /hirli ɪzli əli mɔrli kamliplɪlikelitədli gemli/

   c. Mary-shmary can-shman talk-shmalk in-shmin rhyme-shmyme.

   d. Bepeterper latepate thanpan nepeverper.

   e. thop-e fop-oot bop-all stop-a dop-i op-um blop-ew dop-own /ðapə fapʊt

   bapɔl stape dapi apəm blapu dapawn/

   f. /kʌbæn jʌbu spʌbik ðʌbɪs kʌbajnd ʌbəv ʌbɪŋglʌbɪš/ (This sentence is in "Ubby Dubby" from a children's television program popular in the 1970s.)

8. Below are sentences that might be spoken between two friends chatting informally. For each, state what the nonabbreviated full sentence in SAE would be. In addition, state in your own words (or formally if you wish) the rule or rules that derived the informal sentences from the formal ones.

   a. Where've ya been today?

   b. Watcha gonna do for fun?

   c. Him go to church?

   d. There's four books there.

   e. Who ya wanna go with?

9. Compile a list of argot (or jargon) terms from some profession or trade (e.g., lawyer, musician, doctor, longshoreman, etc.). Give a definition for each term in nonjargon terms.

10. "Translate" the first paragraph of any well-known document or speech — such as the Declaration of Independence, the Gettysburg Address, or the Preamble to the Constitution — into informal, colloquial language.

11. In Column A are Cockney rhyming slang expressions. Match these to the items in Column B to which they refer.

A	B
a. drip dry	(1) balls (testicles)
b. In the mood	(2) bread
c. Insects and ants	(3) ale
d. orchestra stalls	(4) cry
e. Oxford scholar	(5) food
f. strike me dead	(6) dollar
g. ship in full sail	(7) pants

Now construct your own version of Cockney rhyming slang for the following words:

h. chair

i. house

j. coat

k. eggs

l. pencil

12. Column A lists euphemisms for words in Column B. Match each item in A with its appropriate B word.

A	B
a. Montezuma's revenge	(1) condom
b. joy stick	(2) genocide
c. friggin'	(3) fire
d. ethnic cleansing	(4) diarrhea
e. French letter (old)	(5) masturbate
f. diddle oneself	(6) kill
g. holy of holies	(7) urinate
h. spend a penny (British)	(8) penis
i. ladies' cloak room	(9) die
j. knock off (from 1919)	(10) waging war
k. vertically challenged	(11) vagina
l. hand in one's dinner pail	(12) women's toilet
m. sanitation engineer	(13) short
n. downsize	(14) fuckin'
o. peace keeping	(15) garbage collector

13. Defend or criticize the following statement in a short essay.

A person who uses the word *niggardly* in a public hearing should be censured for being insensitive and using a word that resembles a degrading, racist word.

14. The words *waitron* and *waitperson* are currently fighting it out to see which, if either, will replace *waitress* as a gender-neutral term. Using dictionaries, the Internet, and whatever other resources you can think of, predict the winner, or the failure of both candidates. Give reasons for your answers.

15. If you have access to the Internet, search for Tok Pisin. You will very quickly find Web sites where it is possible to hear Tok Pisin spoken. Listen to a passage several times. How much of it can you understand without looking at the text or the translation? Then follow along with the text (generally provided) until you can hear the individual words. Now try a new passage. Does your comprehension improve? How much practice do you think you would need before you could understand roughly half of what is being said the first time you heard it?

16. A language game so popular it has appeared in the *Washington Post* is to take a word or (well-known) expression and alter it by adding, subtracting, or changing one letter, and supplying a new (clever) definition. Read the following examples, try to figure out the expression from which they are derived, and then try to produce 10 on your own. (*Hint:* lots of Latin).

Cogito eggo sum	I think, therefore I am a waffle.
Foreploy	A misrepresentation about yourself for the purpose of getting laid
Veni, vipi, vici	I came, I am important, I conquered
Giraffiti	Dirty words sprayed very, very high
Ignoranus	A person who is both stupid and an asshole
Rigor Morris	The cat is dead
Felix navidad	Our cat has a boat
Veni, vidi, vice	I came, I saw, I smoked
Glibido	All talk, no action
Haste cuisine	Fast French food
L'état, c'est moo	I'm bossy around here
Intaxication	The euphoria that accompanies a tax refund
Ex post fucto	"Lost in the mail"

17. In his original, highly influential novel, *1984,* George Orwell introduces Newspeak, a government-enforced language designed to keep the masses subjugated. He writes:

Its vocabulary was so constructed as to give exact and often very subtle expression to every meaning that a Party member could properly wish to express, while excluding all other meanings and also the possibility of arriving at them by indirect methods. This was done partly by the invention of new words, but chiefly by eliminating undesirable words and by stripping such words as remained of unorthodox meanings, and so far as possible of all secondary meanings whatever. To give a single example. The word *free* still existed in Newspeak, but it could only be used in such statements as "This dog is free from lice" or "This field is free from weeds." It could not be used in its old sense of "politically free" or "intellectually free," since political and intellectual freedom no longer existed even as concepts, and were therefore of necessity nameless.

Critique Newspeak. Will it achieve its goal? Why or why not? (*Hint:* You may want to review concepts such as language creativity and arbitrariness as discussed in the first few pages of chapter 1.)

18. In *1984* Orwell proposed that if a concept does not exist, it is nameless. In the passage quoted below, he suggests that if a crime were nameless, it would be unimaginable, hence impossible to commit:

> A person growing up with Newspeak as his sole language would no more know that . . . *free* had once meant "intellectually free," than, for instance, a person who had never heard of chess would be aware of the secondary meanings attaching to *queen* and *rook*. There would be many crimes and errors which it would be beyond his power to commit, simply because they were nameless and therefore unimaginable.

Critique this notion.

CHAPTER 11

Language Change: The Syllables of Time

No language as depending on arbitrary use and custom
can ever be permanently the same, but will always be
in a mutable and fluctuating state; and what is deem'd
polite and elegant in one age, may be accounted
uncouth and barbarous in another.

Benjamin Martin, Lexicographer

All living languages change with time. It is fortunate that they do so rather slowly compared to the human life span. It would be inconvenient to have to relearn our native language every twenty years. Stargazers find a similar situation. Because of the movement of individual stars, the constellations are continuously changing their shape. Fifty thousand years from now we would hardly recognize Orion or the Big Dipper, but from season to season the changes are imperceptible. Linguistic change is also slow, in human — if not astronomical — terms. As years pass we hardly notice any change. Yet if we were to turn on a radio and miraculously receive a broadcast in our "native language" from the year 3000, we would probably think we had tuned in a foreign language station. Many language changes are revealed in written records. We know a great deal of the history of English because it has been written for about 1,000 years. Old English, spoken in England around the end of the first millennium, is scarcely recognizable as English. (Of course, our linguistic ancestors did not call their language Old English!) A speaker of Modern English would find the language unintelligible. There are college courses in which Old English is studied as a foreign language.

A line from *Beowulf* illustrates why Old English must be translated.[1]

> Wolde guman findan þone þe him on sweofote sare geteode.
> He wanted to find the man who harmed him while he slept.

Approximately five hundred years after *Beowulf,* Chaucer wrote *The Canterbury Tales* in what is now called Middle English, spoken from around 1100 to 1500. It is more easily understood by present-day readers, as seen by looking at the opening of the *Tales.*

> Whan that Aprille with his shoures soote
> The droght of March hath perced to the roote . . .
> When April with its sweet showers
> The drought of March has pierced to the root . . .

Two hundred years after Chaucer, in a language that can be considered an earlier form of Modern English, Shakespeare's Hamlet says:

> A man may fish with the worm that hath eat of a king, and eat of the fish
> that hath fed of that worm.

The stages of English are Old English (449–1100 C.E.), Middle English (1100–1500), and Modern English (1500–present). This division is somewhat arbitrary, being marked by dates of events in English history, such as the Norman Conquest of 1066, the results of which profoundly influenced the English language. Thus the history of English and the changes in the language reflect nonlinguistic history to some extent, as suggested by the following dates:

449 – 1066 Old English	449	Saxons invade Britain
	6th century	Religious literature
	8th century	*Beowulf*
	1066	Norman Conquest
1066 – 1500 Middle English	1387	*Canterbury Tales*
	1476	Caxton's printing press
	1500	Great Vowel Shift
1500 – Modern English	1564	Birth of Shakespeare

Changes in a language are changes in the grammars of those who speak the language, and are perpetuated when new generations of children learn the language by acquiring the altered grammar. This is true of sign languages as well as spoken languages. Like all living languages, American Sign Language continues to change. Not only have new signs entered the language over the past 200 years, but also the forms of the signs have changed in ways similar to the historical changes in spoken languages.

An examination of the past 1,500 years of English shows changes in the lexicon as well as to the phonological, morphological, syntactic, and semantic components of the

---

[1] The letter þ is called *thorn* and is pronounced [θ] in this example.

grammar. No part of the grammar remains the same over the course of history. Although most of the examples in this chapter are from English, the histories of all languages show similar changes.

The Regularity of Sound Change

That's not a regular rule: you invented it just now.

Lewis Carroll, *Alice's Adventures in Wonderland*

The southern United States represents a major dialect area of American English. For example, words pronounced with the diphthong [aj] in non-Southern English will usually be pronounced with the monophthong [a:] in the South. Local radio and TV announcers at the 1996 Olympics in Atlanta called athletes to the [ha:] "high" jump, and local natives invited visitors to try Georgia's famous pecan [pa:] "pie." The [aj]-[a:] correspondence of these two dialects is an example of a **regular sound correspondence.** When [aj] occurs in a word in non-Southern dialects, [a:] occurs in the Southern dialect, and *this is true for all such words.*

The different pronunciations of *I, my, high, pie,* and such did not always exist in English. This chapter will discuss how such dialect differences arose and why the sound differences are usually regular and not confined to just a few words.

Sound Correspondences

In Middle English a mouse [maws] was called a *mūs* [mu:s], and this *mūs* may have lived in someone's *hūs* [hu:s], the way *house* [haws] was pronounced at that time. In general, Middle English speakers pronounced [u:] where we now pronounce [aw]. This is a regular correspondence like the one between [aj] and [a:]. Thus *out* [awt] was pronounced [u:t], *south* [sawθ] was pronounced [su:θ], and so on. Many such regular correspondences show the relation of older and newer forms of English.

The regular sound correspondences we observe between older and modern forms of a language are due to phonological changes that affect certain sounds, or classes of sounds, rather than individual words. Centuries ago English underwent a phonological change called a **sound shift** in which [u:] became [aw].

Phonological changes can also account for dialect differences. At an earlier stage of American English a sound shift of [aj] to [a:] took place among certain speakers in the southern region of the United States. The change did not spread beyond the South because the region was somewhat isolated. Many dialect differences in pronunciation result from a sound shift whose spread is limited.

Regional dialect differences may also arise when innovative changes occur everywhere but in a particular region. The regional dialect may be conservative relative to other dialects. The pronunciation of *it* as *hit*, found in the Appalachian region of the United States, was standard in older forms of English. The dropping of the [h] was the innovation.

Ancestral Protolanguages

Many modern languages were first regional dialects that became widely spoken and highly differentiated, finally becoming separate languages. The Romance languages — French, Spanish, and so on — were once dialects of Latin spoken in the Roman Empire. There is nothing degenerate about regional pronunciations. They result from natural sound change that occurs wherever human language is spoken.

In a sense, the Romance languages are offspring of Latin, their metaphorical parent. Because of their common ancestry, the Romance languages are **genetically related.** Early forms of English and German, too, were once dialects of a common ancestor called **Proto-Germanic.** A **protolanguage** is the ancestral language from which related languages have developed. Both Latin and Proto-Germanic were themselves descendants of an older language called **Indo-European.**[2] Thus, Germanic languages such as English and German are genetically related to the Romance languages such as French and Spanish. All these important national languages were once regional dialects.

How do we know that the Germanic and Romance languages have a common ancestor? One clue is the large number of sound correspondences. If you have studied a Romance language such as French or Spanish, you may have noticed that where an English word begins with *f,* the corresponding word in a Romance language often begins with *p,* as shown in the following examples.

English /f/	French /p/	Spanish /p/
father	père	padre
fish	poisson	pescado

This /f/-/p/ correspondence is another example of a regular sound correspondence. There are many between the Germanic and Romance languages. The prevalence of such regular sound correspondences cannot be explained by chance. What then accounts for them? A reasonable guess is that a common ancestor language used a *p* in words for *fish, father,* and so on. We posit a /p/ rather than an /f/ since more languages show a /p/ in these words. At some point speakers of this language separated into two groups that lost contact. In one of the groups a sound change of *p* → *f* took place. The language spoken by this group eventually became the ancestor of the Germanic languages. This ancient sound change left its trace in the *f-p* sound correspondence that we observe today, as illustrated in the diagram.

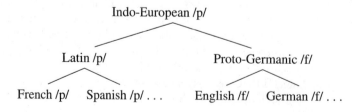

---

[2] It may also be called Proto-Indo-European.

Phonological Change

Etymologists . . . for whom vowels did not matter and who cared not a jot for consonants.

Voltaire

Regular sound correspondences illustrate changes in the phonological system. In earlier chapters we discussed speakers' knowledge of their phonological system, including knowledge of the phonemes and phonological rules of the language. Any of these aspects of the phonology is subject to change.

The velar fricative /x/ is no longer part of the phonemic inventory of most Modern English dialects. *Night* used to be pronounced [nɪxt] and *drought* was pronounced [druxt]. This phonological change — the loss of /x/ — took place between the times of Chaucer and Shakespeare. All words once pronounced with an /x/ no longer include this sound. In some cases it disappeared altogether, as in *night* and *light*. In other cases the /x/ became a /k/, as in *elk* (Old English *eolh* [ɛɔlx]). In yet other cases it disappeared to be replaced by a vowel, as in *hollow* (Old English *holh* [hɔlx]). Dialects of Modern English spoken in Scotland have retained the /x/ sound in some words, such as *loch* [lɔx] meaning "lake."

These examples show that the inventory of sounds can change by the loss of phonemes. The inventory can also change through the addition of phonemes. Old English did not have the phoneme /ž/ of *leisure* [ližər]. Through a process of palatalization — a change in place of articulation to the palatal region — certain occurrences of /z/ were pronounced [ž]. Eventually the [ž] sound became a phoneme in its own right, reinforced by the fact that it occurs in French words familiar to many English speakers such as *azure* [æžər].

An allophone of a phoneme may, through sound change, become a phoneme in its own right. Old English lacked a /v/ phoneme. The phoneme /f/, however, had the allophone [v] when it occurred between vowels. Thus *ofer* /ofer/ meaning "over" was pronounced [ɔvər] in Old English.

Old English also had a geminate phoneme /f:/ that contrasted with /f/, and was pronounced as a long [f:] between vowels. The name *Offa* /of:a/ was pronounced [ɔf:a]. A sound change occurred in which the pronunciation of /f:/ was simplified to [f]. Now /f:/ was pronounced [f] between vowels so it contrasted with [v]. This made it possible for English to have minimal pairs involving [f] and [v]. Speakers therefore perceived the two sounds as separate phonemes, in effect, creating a new phoneme /v/.

Similar changes occur in the history of all languages. Neither /č/ nor /š/ were phonemes of Latin, but /č/ is a phoneme of modern Italian and /š/ a phoneme of modern French, both of which evolved from Latin. In American Sign Language many signs that were originally formed at the waist or chest level are now produced at a higher level near the neck or upper chest, a reflection of changes in the "phonology."

Phonemes thus may be lost (/x/), or added (/ž/), or result from a change in the status of allophones (the [v] allophone of /f/ becoming /v/).

Phonological Rules

An interaction of phonological rules may result in changes in the lexicon. The nouns *house* and *bath* were once differentiated from the verbs *house* and *bathe* by the fact that the verbs ended with a short vowel sound. Furthermore, the same rule that realized /f/ as [v] between vowels, also realized /s/ and /θ/ as the allophones [z] and [ð] between vowels. This was a general rule that voiced intervocalic fricatives. Thus the /s/ in the verb *house,* was pronounced [z], and the /θ/ in the verb *bathe* was pronounced [ð].

Later a rule was added to the grammar of English deleting unstressed short vowels at the end of words. A contrast between the voiced and voiceless fricatives resulted, and the new phonemes /z/ and /ð/ were added to the phonemic inventory. The verbs *house* and *bathe* were now represented in the mental lexicon with final voiced consonants.

Eventually, both the unstressed vowel deletion rule and the intervocalic-voicing rule were lost from the grammar of English. The set of phonological rules can change both by addition and loss of rules.

Changes in phonological rules can, and often do, result in dialect differences. In the previous chapter we discussed the addition of an *r*-dropping rule in English (/r/ is not pronounced unless followed by a vowel) that did not spread throughout the language. Today, we see the effect of that rule in the *r*-less pronunciation of British English and of American English dialects spoken in the Boston area and the southern United States.

From the standpoint of the language as a whole, phonological changes occur gradually over the course of many generations of speakers, although a given speaker's grammar may or may not reflect the change. The changes are not planned any more than we are presently planning what changes will take place in English by the year 2300. Speakers are aware of the changes only through dialect differences.

The Great Vowel Shift

A major change in English that resulted in new phonemic representations of words and morphemes took place approximately between 1400 and 1600. It is known as the **Great Vowel Shift.** The seven long, or tense, vowels of Middle English underwent the following change:

Shift		Example		
Middle English	**Modern English**	**Middle English**	**Modern English**	
[i:] →	[aj]	[mi:s] →	[majs]	*mice*
[u:] →	[aw]	[mu:s] →	[maws]	*mouse*
[e:] →	[i:]	[ge:s] →	[gi:s]	*geese*
[o:] →	[u:]	[go:s] →	[gu:s]	*goose*
[ɛ:] →	[e:]	[brɛ:ken] →	[bre:k]	*break*
[ɔ:] →	[o:]	[brɔ:ken] →	[bro:k]	*broke*
[a:] →	[e:]	[na:mə] →	[ne:m]	*name*

By diagramming the Great Vowel Shift on a vowel chart (Figure 11.1), we can see that the high vowels [i:] and [u:] became the diphthongs [aj] and [aw], while the long vowels underwent an increase in tongue height, as if to fill in the space vacated by the high vowels. In addition, [a:] was fronted to become [e:].

These changes are among the most dramatic examples of regular sound shift. The phonemic representation of many thousands of words changed. Today, some reflection

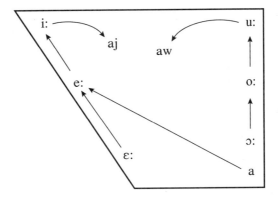

Figure 11.1 The Great Vowel Shift.

of this vowel shift is seen in the alternating forms of morphemes in English: *please — pleasant; serene — serenity; sane — sanity; crime — criminal; sign — signal;* and so on. Before the Great Vowel Shift, the vowels in each pair were the same. Then the vowels in the second word of each pair were shortened by the **Early Middle English Vowel Shortening** rule. As a result the Great Vowel Shift, which occurred later, affected only

The sniffles in 14ᵗʰ-century England

the first word in each pair. The second word, with its short vowel, was unaffected. This is why the vowels in the morphologically related words are pronounced differently today, as shown in Table 11.1.

Table 11.1   Effect of the Vowel Shift on Modern English

Middle English Vowel	Shifted Vowel	Short Counterpart	Word with Shifted Vowel	Word with Short Vowel
ī	aj	ɪ	divine	divinity
ū	aw	ʊ	profound	profundity
ē	i	ɛ	serene	serenity
ō	u	a	fool	folly
ā	e	æ	sane	sanity

The Great Vowel Shift is a primary source of many spelling inconsistencies of English because our spelling system still reflects the way words were pronounced before the Great Vowel Shift.

Morphological Change

Like phonological rules, rules of morphology may be lost, added, or changed. We can observe some of these changes by comparing older and newer forms of the language or by looking at different dialects.

Extensive changes in rules of morphology have occurred in the history of the Indo-European languages. Latin had **case endings,** suffixes on the noun based on its grammatical relationship to the verb. These are no longer found in the Romance languages. (See chapter 5 for a more extensive discussion of grammatical case.) The following is a **declension,** or list of cases, for the Latin noun *lupus,* "wolf":

Noun	Noun Stem	Case Ending	Case	Example
lupus	lup	+ us	nominative	The *wolf* runs.
lupī	lup	+ ī	genitive	A sheep in *wolf's* clothing.
lupō	lup	+ ō	dative	Give food to *the wolf.*
lupum	lup	+ um	accusative	I love *the wolf.*
lupe	lup	+ e	vocative	*Wolf,* come here!

In *Alice's Adventures in Wonderland,* Lewis Carroll has Alice give us a brief lesson in grammatical case. Alice has become very small and is swimming around in a pool of her own tears with a mouse that she wishes to befriend:

"Would it be of any use, now," thought Alice, "to speak to this mouse? Everything is so out-of-the-way down here, that I should think very likely it can talk: at any rate, there's no harm in trying." So she began: "O Mouse, do you know

cornū	cornua
cornūs	cornuum
cornū	cornibus
cornū	cornua
cornū	cornibus

You are now entering another declension, a declension not of adjectives, not of articles, but of nouns...

the way out of this pool? I am very tired of swimming about here, O Mouse!" (Alice thought this must be the right way of speaking to a mouse: she had never done such a thing before, but she remembered having seen in her brother's Latin Grammar, "A mouse-of a mouse-to a mouse- a mouse-O mouse!")

Alice gives the English corresponding to the nominative, genitive, dative, accusative, and vocative cases.

Ancient Greek and Sanskrit also had extensive case systems expressed morphologically through noun suffixing, as did Old English, as illustrated by the following noun forms:

Case	OE Singular		OE Plural	
nominative	stān	"stone"	stānas	"stones"
genitive	stānes	"stone's"	stāna	"stones'"
dative	stāne	"stone"	stānum	"stones"
accusative	stān	"stone"	stānas	"stones"

Lithuanian and Russian retain much of the early Indo-European case system, but changes have all but obliterated it in most modern Indo-European languages. In English, phonological changes over the centuries resulted in the loss of many case endings.

English retains the genitive case, which is written with an apostrophe *s*, as in *Robert's dog,* but that's all that remains as far as nouns are concerned. Pronouns retain a few more traces: *he/she* are nominative, *him/her* accusative and dative, and *his/hers* genitive.

English has replaced its depleted case system with an equally expressive system of prepositions. For example the dative case is often indicated by the preposition *to* and the genitive case by the preposition *of.* A noun occurring after a verb with no intervening preposition is often, but not always, in the accusative case.

English and most of the Indo-European languages, then, have undergone extensive morphological changes over the past 1,000 years, many of them induced by changes that took place in the phonological rules of the language.

Syntactic Change

All things change except the love of change.

Anonymous, *Madrigal* (1601)

The loss of case endings in English occurred together with changes in the rules of syntax governing word order. In Old English, word order was freer because the case endings on nouns indicated the meaning relations in a sentence.

Additionally, Modern English is an SVO (Subject-Verb-Object) language. Old English was both an SVO and an SOV language.[3] Sentences like *Se man þone kyning sloh,* literally *the man the king slew,* were grammatical. Thus the phrase structure rules that determine the word order of basic sentences changed in the history of English.

The syntactic rules relating to the English negative construction also underwent a number of changes from Old English to the present. In Modern English, negation is expressed by adding *not* or *do not*. We may also express negation by adding words like *never* or *no:*

I am going → I am not going
I went → I did not go
I go to school → I never go to school
I want food → I don't want any food; I want no food

In Old English the main negation element was *ne*. It usually occurred before a verbal element:[4]

---

[3] A later section in this chapter entitled "Types of Languages" explains this in more detail.
[4] From E. C. Traugott. 1972. *The History of English Syntax.* New York: Holt, Rinehart, and Winston.

> þæt he *na*   siþþan geboren   *ne*   wurde
> that he never after   born   not   would-be
> that he should never be born after that

> ac hie   *ne* dorston þær   on cuman
> but they not dared   there on come
> but they dared not land there

In the first example, the word order is different from that of Modern English, and there are two negatives: *na* (a contraction of *ne* + *a,* "not" + "ever" = "never") and *ne.* As shown, a double negative was grammatical in Old English. Although double negatives are ungrammatical in Modern Standard American English, they are grammatical in some English dialects.

In addition to the contraction of *ne* + *a* → *na*, other negative contractions occurred in Old English: *ne* could be attached to *habb-* "have," *wes-* "be," *wit-* "know," and *will-* "will" to form *nabb-, nes-, nyt-,* and *nyll-,* respectively.

Modern English also has contraction rules that change *do* + *not* into *don't, will* + *not* into *won't,* and so on. In these contractions the phonetic form of the negation element always comes at the *end* of the word because Modern English word order puts the *not* after the auxiliary verb. In Old English, the negative element occurred at the beginning of the contraction because it preceded the auxiliary verb. The rules determining the placement of the negative morpheme have changed. Such syntactic changes may take centuries to be completed, and there are often intermediate stages.

Another syntactic change in English affected the rules of comparative and superlative constructions. Today we form the comparative by adding *-er* to the adjective or by inserting *more* before it; the superlative is formed by adding *-est* or by inserting *most.* In Malory's *Tales of King Arthur,* written in 1470, double comparatives and double superlatives occur, which today are ungrammatical: *more gladder, more lower, moost royallest, moost shamefullest.*

When we study a language solely from written records, which is necessarily the case with nonmodern languages such as Elizabethan English (sixteenth century), we see only sentences that are grammatical unless ungrammatical sentences are used deliberately. Without native speakers of Elizabethan English to query, we can only infer what was ungrammatical. Such inference leads us to believe that expressions like *the Queen of England's crown* were ungrammatical in former versions of English. The title *The Wife's Tale of Bath* (rather than *The Wife of Bath's Tale*) in *The Canterbury Tales* supports this inference. Modern English, on the other hand, allows some rather complex constructions that involve the possessive marker. An English speaker can use possessive constructions such as

> The girl whose sister I'm dating's roommate is pretty.
> The man from Boston's hat fell off.

Older versions of English had to resort to an *of* construction to express the same thought (*The hat of the man from Boston fell off*). A syntactic change took place that accounts for the extended use of the possessive morpheme *'s.*

Lexical Change

Changes in the lexicon also occur. Among them are changes in the lexical category in which a word may function.

The word *menu* is ordinarily used only as a noun, but the waiter in the *New Yorker* cartoon uses it as a verb. If speakers adopt the usage, *menu* will take on the additional lexical category of verb in their mental lexicons. Such changes are common and are often put into effect in special usage situations. The noun *window* is used as a verb by carpenters as in, "Tomorrow we have to window the upper story," where *to window* means "put window frames in a house under construction." Recently, a radio announcer said that Congress was "to-ing and fro-ing" on a certain issue, to mean "wavering." This strange compound verb is derived from the adverb *to and fro*. In British English, *hoover* is a verb meaning "to vacuum up," derived from the proper noun *Hoover,* the name of a vacuum cleaner manufacturer. American police *Mirandize* arrested persons, meaning to read them their rights according to the Miranda rule. Since the judicial ruling was made in 1966, we have a complete history on how a proper name became a verb.

The word *telephone* was coined exclusively as a noun in 1844 and meant "acoustic apparatus." Alexander Graham Bell appropriated the word for his invention in 1876, and

"Have you folks been menued yet?"

in 1877 the word was first used as a verb, meaning "to speak by telephone." In languages where verbs have a specific morphological form such as the *-er* ending in French (*parler,* to speak), or the *-en* ending in German (*sprechen,* to speak), such changes are less common than in English. Thus the French noun *téléphone* cannot be a verb, but becomes the different word *téléphoner* as a verb.

Other categorical changes may occur historically. The word *remote* was once only an adjective, but with the invention of control-at-a-distance devices, the compound *remote control* came into usage, which ultimately was shortened to *remote,* which now functions as a noun; witness the half dozen remotes every modern household loses track of.

A recent announcement at North Carolina State University invited "all faculty to sandwich in the Watauga Seminar." We were not invited to squeeze together, rather to bring our lunches. Although the verb *to sandwich* exists, the new verbal usage is derived from the noun *sandwich* rather than the verb.

Addition of New Words

And to bring in a new word by the head and shoulders, they leave out the old one.

Montaigne

In chapter 3 we discussed ways in which new words can enter the language. These included deriving words from names (*sandwich*), blends (*smog*), back-formations (*edit*), acronyms (*NATO*), and abbreviations or clippings (*ad*). We also saw that new words may be formed by derivational processes, as in *uglification, finalize,* and *finalization.*

Compounding is a particularly productive means of creating words. Thousands of common English words have entered the language by this process, including *afternoon, bigmouth, cyberspace, egghead, force feed, global warming, icecap, jet set, laptop, moreover, nursemaid, offshore, pothole, railroad, skybox, takeover, undergo, water cooler, X-ray,* and *zookeeper.*

Other methods for enlarging the vocabulary that were discussed include word coinage. Societies often require new words to describe changes in technology, sports, entertainment, and so on. Languages are accommodating and inventive in meeting these needs. The words may be entirely new, as *steganography,* the concealment of information in an electronic document, or *micropolitan,* a city of less than 10,000 people. Even new bound morphemes may enter the language. The prefix *e-* as in *e-commerce, e-mail, e-trade,* meaning "electronic," is barely two decades old. The suffix *-gate,* meaning "scandal," derived from the Watergate scandal of the 1970s, may now be suffixed to a word to convey that meaning. Thus *Irangate* meant a scandal involving Iran, and *Dianagate,* a British usage, referred to a scandal involving wiretapped conversations of the late Princess of Wales, Diana. A change currently underway is the use of *-peat* to mean "win a championship so many years in succession," as in *threepeat* and *fourpeat,* which we have observed in the newspaper.

A word so new that its spelling is still in doubt is *dot com,* also seen in magazines as *.com,* and *dot.com.* It means "a company whose primary business centers on the Internet." The expression written 24/7, and pronounced *twenty-four seven,* meaning "all the time," also appears to be a new entry not yet found in dictionaries, but seen in newspapers and heard during news broadcasts.

Borrowings or Loan Words

Neither a borrow, nor a lender be.

William Shakespeare, *Hamlet,* I. iii

Languages ignore the "precept" of Polonius quoted above. Many of them are avid borrowers. **Borrowing** words from other languages is an important source of new words. Borrowing occurs when one language adds a word or morpheme from another language to its own lexicon. The pronunciation of the borrowed item is often altered to fit the phonological rules of the borrowing language. The borrowed word, of course, remains in the source language, so there is no need for its return. Languages are as much lenders and borrowers, and why shouldn't they be since they lose nothing in the transaction? Most languages are borrowers, so their lexicon can be divided into native and nonnative, or **loan words.** A native word is one whose history or **etymology** can be traced back to the earliest known stages of the language.

"Sally Forth" Copyright © 1996 Greg Howard. Distributed by King Features Syndicate.

A language may borrow a word directly or indirectly. A direct borrowing means that the borrowed item is a native word in the language from which it is borrowed. *Feast* was borrowed directly from French and can be traced back to Latin *festum.* On the other hand, the word *algebra* was borrowed from Spanish, which in turn had borrowed it from Arabic. Thus *algebra* was indirectly borrowed from Arabic, with Spanish as an intermediary.

Some languages are heavy borrowers. Albanian has borrowed so heavily that few native words are retained. On the other hand, most Native American languages borrowed little from their neighbors.

English has borrowed extensively. Of the 20,000 or so words in common use, about three-fifths are borrowed. Of the 500 most frequently used words, however, only two-sevenths are borrowed, and since these words are used repeatedly in sentences, the actual frequency of appearance of native words is about 80 percent. *And, be, have, it, of, the, to, will, you, on, that,* and *is* are all native to English.

HISTORY THROUGH LOAN WORDS

A morsel of genuine history is a thing so rare as to be always valuable.

Thomas Jefferson

We may trace the history of the English-speaking peoples by studying the kinds of loan words in their language, their source, and when they were borrowed. Until the Norman Conquest in 1066, the Angles, the Saxons, and the Jutes inhabited England. They were of Germanic origin when they came to Britain in the fifth century to eventually become the English.[5] Originally, they spoke Germanic dialects, from which Old English developed directly. These dialects contained a number of Latin borrowings but few foreign elements beyond that. These Germanic tribes had displaced the earlier Celtic inhabitants, whose influence on Old English was confined to a few Celtic place-names. (The modern languages Welsh, Irish, and Scots Gaelic are descended from the Celtic dialects.)

The Normans spoke French and for three centuries after the Conquest, French was the language used for all affairs of state and for most commercial, social, and cultural matters. The West Saxon literary language was abandoned, but regional varieties of English continued to be used in homes, in the churches, and in the marketplace. During these three centuries, vast numbers of French words entered English, of which the following are representative:

government	crown	prince	estate	parliament
nation	jury	judge	crime	sue
attorney	saint	miracle	charity	court
lechery	virgin	value	pray	mercy
religion	value	royal	money	society

Until the Normans came, when an Englishman slaughtered an ox for food, he ate *ox*. If it was a pig, he ate *pig*. If it was a sheep, he ate *sheep*. However, "ox" served at the Norman tables was *beef* (*boeuf*), "pig" was *pork* (*porc*), and "sheep" was *mutton* (*mouton*). These words were borrowed from French into English, as were the food-preparation words *boil, fry, stew,* and *roast*. Indeed, over the years French foods have given English a flood of borrowed words for menu preparers:

aspic	bisque	bouillon	brie	brioche
canapé	caviar	consommé	coq au vin	coupe
crêpe	croissant	croquette	crouton	escargot
fondue	mousse	pâté	quiche	ragout

English borrowed many "learned" words from foreign sources during the Renaissance. In 1475 William Caxton introduced the printing press in England. By 1640, 55,000 books had been printed in English. The authors of these books used many Greek and Latin words, and as a result, many words of ancient Greek and Latin entered the language.

From Greek came *drama, comedy, tragedy, scene, botany, physics, zoology,* and *atomic*.

Latin loan words in English are numerous. They include:

bonus	scientific	exit	alumnus	quorum	describe

---

[5] The word *England* is derived from *Anglaland,* "Land of the Angles."

During the ninth and tenth centuries, Scandinavian raiders, who eventually settled in the British Isles, left their traces in the English language. The pronouns *they, their,* and *them* are loan words from Old Norse, the predecessor of modern Danish, Norwegian, and Swedish. This period is the only time that English ever borrowed pronouns.

Bin, flannel, clan, slogan, and *whisky* are all words of Celtic origin, borrowed at various times from Welsh, Scots Gaelic, or Irish.

Dutch was a source of borrowed words, too, many of which are related to shipping: *buoy, freight, leak, pump, yacht.*

From German came *quartz, cobalt,* and — as we might guess — *sauerkraut.*

From Italian, many musical terms, including words describing opera houses, have been borrowed: *opera, piano, virtuoso, balcony,* and *mezzanine.* Italian also gave us *influenza,* which was derived from the Italian word for "influence" because the Italians were convinced that the disease was *influenced* by the stars.

Many scientific words were borrowed indirectly from Arabic, because early Arab scholarship in these fields was quite advanced. *Alcohol, algebra, cipher,* and *zero* are a small sample.

Spanish has loaned us (directly) *barbecue, cockroach,* and *ranch,* as well as *California,* literally "hot furnace."

In America, the English-speaking colonists borrowed from Native American languages. They provided us with *hickory, chipmunk, opossum,* and *squash,* to mention only a few. Nearly half the names of U.S. states are borrowed from one American Indian language or another.

English has borrowed from Yiddish. Many non-Jews as well as non-Yiddish-speaking Jews use Yiddish words. There was once even a bumper sticker proclaiming: "Marcel Proust is a yenta." *Yenta* is a Yiddish word meaning "gossipy woman" or "shrew." *Lox,* "smoked salmon," and *bagel,* "a hard roll resembling a doughnut," now belong to English, as well as Yiddish expressions like *chutzpah, schmaltz, schlemiel, schmuck, schmo,* and *kibitz.*

English is also a lender of copious numbers of words to other languages, especially in the areas of technology, sports, and entertainment. Words and expressions such as *jazz, whisky, blue jeans, rock music, supermarket, baseball, picnic,* and *computer* have been borrowed by languages as diverse as Twi, Hungarian, Russian, and Japanese.

Loan translations are compound words or expressions whose parts are translated literally into the borrowing language. *Marriage of convenience* is a loan translation borrowed from French *mariage de convenance.* Spanish speakers eat *perros calientes,* a loan translation of *hot dogs* with an adjustment reversing the order of the adjective and noun, as required by the rules of Spanish syntax.

Loss of Words

Pease porridge hot
Pease porridge cold
Pease porridge in the pot nine days old

Nursery Rhyme

Words also can be lost from a language, though an old word's departure is never as striking as a new word's arrival. When a new word comes into vogue, its unusual presence draws attention; but a word is lost through inattention — nobody thinks of it; nobody uses it; and it fades away.

A reading of Shakespeare's works shows that English has lost many words, such as these taken from *Romeo and Juliet: beseem,* "to be suitable," *mammet,* "a doll or puppet," *wot,* "to know," *gyve,* "a fetter," *fain,* "gladly," and *wherefore,* "why."

More recently, it appears that the expression *two bits,* meaning "twenty-five cents," is no longer used by the younger generation and is in the process of being lost (along with *four bits, six bits,* etc.). The word *stile,* meaning "steps crossing a fence or gate," is no longer widely understood. Other similar words for describing rural objects are fading out of the language due to urbanization. *Pease,* from which *pea* is a back formation, is gone, and *porridge,* meaning "boiled cereal grain," is falling out of usage, though it is sustained by a discussion of its ideal serving temperature in the childen's story *Goldilocks and the Three Bears.*

Technological change may also be the cause for the loss of words. *Acutiator* once meant "sharpener of weapons" and *tormentum* once meant "siege engine." Advances in warfare have put these terms out of business. Although one still finds the words *buckboard, buggy, dogcart, hansom, surrey,* and *tumbrel* in the dictionary — all of them referring to subtly different kinds of horse-drawn carriages — progress in transportation is likely to render these terms obsolete and eventually they will be lost.

Semantic Change

> The language of this country being always upon the flux, the Struldbruggs of one age do not understand those of another, neither are they able after two hundred years to hold any conversation (farther than by a few general words) with their neighbors the mortals, and thus they lie under the disadvantage of living like foreigners in their own country.
>
> Jonathan Swift, *Gulliver's Travels*

We have seen that a language may gain or lose lexical items. Additionally, the meaning or semantic representation of words may change, by becoming broader or narrower, or by shifting.

Broadening

When the meaning of a word becomes broader, that word means everything it used to mean, and more. The Middle English word *dogge* meant a specific breed of dog, but it was eventually **broadened** to encompass all members of the species *canis familiaris.* The word *holiday* originally meant a day of religious significance, from "holy day." Today the word signifies any day on which we do not have to work. *Picture* used to mean "painted representation," but today you can take a picture with a camera. *Quarantine* once had the restricted meaning of "forty days' isolation."

More recent broadenings, spurred by the computer age, are *computer* itself, *mouse, cookie, cache, virus,* and *bundle,* to name but a few.

NARROWING

In the King James Version of the Bible (1611 C. E.), God says of the herbs and trees, "to you they shall be for meat" (Genesis 1:29). To a speaker of seventeenth-century English, *meat* meant "food," and *flesh* meant "meat." Since that time, semantic change has narrowed the meaning of *meat* to what it is in Modern English. The word *deer* once meant "beast" or "animal," as its German cognate *Tier* still does. The meaning of *deer* has been narrowed to a particular kind of animal. Similarly, the word *hound* used to be the general term for "dog," like the German *Hund*. Today *hound* means a special kind of dog, one used for hunting. The word *davenport* once meant "sofa" or "small writing desk." Today, in American English, its meaning has narrowed to "sofa" alone.

MEANING SHIFTS

The third kind of semantic change that a lexical item may undergo is a shift in meaning. The word *knight* once meant "youth" but shifted to "mounted man-at-arms." *Lust* used to mean simply "pleasure," with no negative or sexual overtones. *Lewd* was merely "ignorant," and *immoral* meant "not customary." *Silly* used to mean "happy" in Old English. By the Middle English period it had come to mean "naive," and only in Modern English does it mean "foolish." The overworked Modern English word *nice* meant "ignorant" a thousand years ago. When Juliet tells Romeo, "I am too *fond*," she is not claiming she likes Romeo too much. She means "I am too *foolish*."

Reconstructing "Dead" Languages

The branch of linguistics that deals with how languages change, what kinds of changes occur, and why they occurred is called **historical and comparative linguistics.** It is

"historical" because it deals with the history of particular languages; it is "comparative" because it deals with relations among languages.

The Nineteenth-Century Comparativists

When agreement is found in words in two languages, and so frequently that rules may be drawn up for the shift in letters from one to the other, then there is a fundamental relationship between the two languages.

Rasmus Rask

The nineteenth-century historical and comparative linguists based their theories on observations of regular sound correspondences among certain languages, and that languages displaying systematic similarities and differences must have descended from a common source language — that is, were genetically related.

The chief goal of these linguists was to develop and elucidate the genetic relationships that exist among the world's languages. They aimed to establish the major language families of the world and to define principles for the classification of languages. Their work grew out of earlier research.

As a child, Sir William Jones had an astounding propensity for learning languages, including so-called dead ones such as Ancient Greek and Latin. As an adult he found it best to reside in India because of his sympathy for the rebellious American colonists. There he distinguished himself both as a jurist, holding a position on the Bengal Supreme Court, and as an "Orientalist," as certain linguists were then called.

In Calcutta he took up the study of Sanskrit, just for fun, mind you, and in 1786 delivered a paper in which he observed that Sanskrit bore to Greek and Latin "a stronger affinity . . . than could possibly have been produced by accident." Jones suggested that these three languages had "sprung from a common source" and that probably Germanic and Celtic had the same origin.

About thirty years after Jones delivered his important paper, the German linguist Franz Bopp pointed out the relationships among Sanskrit, Latin, Greek, Persian, and Germanic. At the same time, a young Danish scholar named Rasmus Rask corroborated these results, and brought Lithuanian and Armenian into the relationship as well. Rask was the first scholar to describe formally the regularity of certain phonological differences of related languages.

Rask's investigation of these regularities inspired the German linguist Jakob Grimm (of fairy-tale fame), who published a four-volume treatise (1819–1822) that specified the regular sound correspondences among Sanskrit, Greek, Latin, and the Germanic languages. It was not only the similarities that intrigued Grimm and the other linguists, but the systematic nature of the differences. Where Latin has a [p], English often has an [f]; where Latin has a [t], English often has a [θ]; where Latin has a [k], English often has an [h].

Grimm pointed out that certain phonological changes that did not take place in Sanskrit, Greek, or Latin must have occurred early in the history of the Germanic languages. Because the changes were so strikingly regular, they became known as **Grimm's law,** which is illustrated in Figure 11.2.

Grimm's Law can be expressed in terms of natural classes of speech sounds: Voiced aspirates become unaspirated; voiced stops become voiceless; voiceless stops become fricatives.

Earlier stage:[a]	bh	dh	gh	b	d	g	p	t	k
	↓	↓	↓	↓	↓	↓	↓	↓	↓
Later stage:	b	d	g	p	t	k	f	θ	x (or h)

[a] This "earlier stage" is Indo-European. The symbols bh, dh, and gh are breathy voiced stop consonants. These phonemes are often called "voiced aspirates."

Figure 11.2   Grimm's Law, an early Germanic sound shift.

COGNATES

Cognates are words in related languages that developed from the same ancestral root, such as English *horn* and Latin *cornū*. Cognates often, but not always, have the same meaning in the different languages. From cognates we can observe sound correspondences and from them deduce sound changes. In Figure 11.3 the regular correspondence *p-p-f* of cognates from Sanskrit, Latin, and Germanic (represented by English) indicates that the languages are genetically related. Indo-European **p* is posited as the origin of the *p-p-f* correspondence.[6]

"Shouldn't a unicorn be called a uniHORN?"

"Family Circus" copyright © 1992 Bil Keane. Reprinted with special permission of King Features Syndicate, Inc.

---

[6] The asterisk before a letter indicates a reconstructed sound, not an unacceptable form. This use of asterisk occurs only in this chapter.

Indo-European	Sanskrit	Latin	English
*p	p	p	f
	pitar-	pater	father
	pad-	ped-	foot
	No cognate	piscis	fish
	paśu[a]	pecu	fee

[a] ś is a sibilant pronounced differently than s was pronounced.

Figure 11.3   Cognates of Indo-European *p.

Figure 11.4 is a more detailed chart of correspondences, where a single representative example of each regular correspondence is presented. In most cases cognate sets exhibit the same correspondence, which leads to the reconstruction of the Indo-European sound shown in the first column.

Indo-European	Sanskrit		Latin		English	
*p	p	pitar-	p	pater	f	father
*t	t	trayas	t	trēs	θ	three
*k	ś	śun	k	canis	h	hound
*b	b	No cognate	b	labium	p	lip
*d	d	dva-	d	duo	t	two
*g	j	ajras	g	ager	k	acre
*bh	bh	bhrātar-	f	frāter	b	brother
*dh	dh	dhā	f	fē-ci	d	do
*gh	h	vah-	h	veh-ō	g	wagon

Figure 11.4   Some Indo-European sound correspondences.

Sanskrit underwent the fewest consonant changes, while Latin underwent somewhat more, and Germanic (under Grimm's Law) underwent almost a complete restructuring. Still, the fact that the phonemes and phonological rules, not individual words, changed has resulted in the remarkably regular correspondences that allow us to reconstruct much of the Indo-European sound system.

Exceptions can be found to these regular correspondences, as Grimm was aware. He stated: "The sound shift is a general tendency; it is not followed in every case." Karl Verner explained some of the exceptions to Grimm's Law in 1875. He formulated **Verner's Law** to show why Indo-European *p*, *t*, and *k* failed to correspond to *f*, θ, and *x* in certain cases:

Verner's Law: When the preceding vowel was unstressed, *f*, θ, and x underwent a further change to *b*, *d*, and *g*.

A group of young linguists known as the **Neo-Grammarians** went beyond the idea that such sound shifts represented only a tendency, and claimed that sound laws have no exception. They viewed linguistics as a natural science and therefore believed that laws of sound change were unexceptionable natural laws. The "laws" they put forth often had exceptions, however, which could not always be explained as dramatically as Verner's Law explained the exceptions to Grimm's Law. Still, the work of these linguists provides important data and insights into language change and why such changes occur.

The linguistic work of the early nineteenth century had some influence on Charles Darwin, and in turn, Darwin's theory of evolution had a profound influence on linguistics and on all science. Some linguists thought that languages had a "life cycle" and developed according to evolutionary laws. In addition, it was believed that every language could be traced to a common ancestor. This theory of biological naturalism has an element of truth to it, but it is an oversimplification of how languages change and evolve into other languages.

Comparative Reconstruction

. . . Philologists who chase
A panting syllable through time and space
Start it at home, and hunt it in the dark,
To Gaul, to Greece, and into 'Noah's Ark.

Cowper, "Retirement"

When languages resemble one another in ways not attributable to chance or borrowing, we may conclude they are related. That is, they evolved via linguistic change from an ancestral protolanguage.

The similarity of the basic vocabulary of languages such as English, German, Danish, Dutch, Norwegian, and Swedish is too pervasive for chance or borrowing. We therefore conclude that these languages have a common parent, Proto-Germanic. There are no written records of Proto-Germanic, and certainly no native speakers alive today. Proto-Germanic is a hypothetical language whose properties have been deduced based on its descendants.

In addition to similar vocabulary, the Germanic languages share grammatical properties such as irregularity in the verb *to be,* and similar irregular past-tense forms of verbs, further supporting their relatedness.

Once we know or suspect that several languages are related, their protolanguage may be partially determined by **comparative reconstruction.** One proceeds by applying the **comparative method,** which we illustrate with the following brief example.

Restricting ourselves to English, German, and Swedish, we find the word for "man" is *man, Mann,* and *man,* respectively. This is one of many word sets in which we can observe the regular sound correspondence [m]-[m]-[m] and [n]-[n]-[n] in the three languages. Based on this evidence the comparative method has us reconstruct *mVn as the word for "man" in Proto-Germanic. The *V* indicates a vowel whose quality we are unsure of since, despite the similar spelling, the vowel is phonetically different in the various Germanic languages, and it is unclear how to reconstruct it without further evidence.

Although we are confident that we can reconstruct much of Proto-Germanic with relative accuracy, we can never be sure, and many details remain obscure. To build confidence in the comparative method, we can apply it to Romance languages such as French, Italian, Spanish, and Portuguese. Their protolanguage is the well-known Latin, so we can verify the method. Consider the following data, focusing on the initial consonant of each word. In these data, *ch* in French is [š] and *c* in the other languages is [k].[7]

French	Italian	Spanish	Portuguese	English
cher	**c**aro	**c**aro	**c**aro	"dear"
champ	**c**ampo	**c**ampo	**c**ampo	"field"
chandelle	**c**andela	**c**andela	**c**andeia	"candle"

The French [š] corresponds to [k] in the three other languages. This regular sound correspondence, [š]-[k]-[k]-[k], supports the view that French, Italian, Spanish, and Portuguese descended from a common language. The comparative method leads to the reconstruction of [k] in "dear," "field," and "candle" of the parent language, and shows that [k] underwent a change to [š] in French, but not in Italian, Spanish, or Portuguese, which retained the original [k] of the parent language, Latin.

To use the comparative method, analysts identify regular sound correspondences in the cognates of potentially related languages. For each correspondence, they deduce the most likely sound in the parent language. In this way, much of the sound system of the parent may be reconstructed. The various phonological changes in the development of each daughter language as it descended and changed from the parent are then identified. Sometimes the sound that analysts choose in their reconstruction of the parent language will be the sound that appears most frequently in the correspondence. This approach was just illustrated with the four Romance languages.

Other considerations may outweigh the "majority rules" principle. The likelihood of certain phonological changes may persuade the analyst to reconstruct a less frequently occurring sound, or even a sound that does not occur in the correspondence. Consider the data in these four hypothetical languages:

Language A	Language B	Language C	Language D
hono	hono	fono	vono
hari	hari	fari	veli
rahima	rahima	rafima	levima
hor	hor	for	vol

Wherever Languages A and B have an *h*, Language C has an *f* and Language D has a *v*. Therefore we have the sound correspondence *h-h-f-v*. Using the comparative method, we might first consider reconstructing the sound *h* in the parent language; but from other data on historical change, and from phonetic research, we know that *h* seldom becomes *v*. The reverse, /f/ and /v/ becoming [h], occurs both historically and as a phonological rule and has an acoustic explanation. Therefore linguists reconstruct an **f* in the parent, and posit the sound change "*f* becomes *h*" in Languages A and B, and "*f* becomes *v*" in Language D. One obviously needs experience and knowledge to conclude this.

---

[7] Data are taken from Lehmann, 1973.

The other correspondences are not problematic insofar as these data are concerned. They are:

o-o-o-o   n-n-n-n   a-a-a-e   r-r-r-l   m-m-m-m

They lead to the reconstructed forms *o, *n, *a, *r, and *m for the parent language, and the sound changes "a becomes e" and "r becomes l" in Language D. These are natural sound changes found in many of the world's languages.

It is now possible to reconstruct the words of the protolanguage. They are *fono, *fari, *rafima, and *for. Language D, in this example, is the most innovative of the three languages, because it has undergone three sound changes. Language C is the most conservative, being identical to the protolanguage insofar as these data are concerned.

The sound changes seen in the previous illustrations are examples of **unconditioned sound change.** The changes occurred irrespective of phonetic context. Below is an example of **conditioned sound change,** taken from three dialects of Italian:

Standard	Northern	Lombard	
fisso	fiso	fis	"fixed"
kassa	kasa	kasǝ	"cabinet"

The correspondence sets are:

f-f-f   i-i-i   o-o-<>[8]   k-k-k   a-a-a   a-a-ǝ   s:-s-s

It is straightforward to reconstruct *f, *i, and *k. Knowing that a geminate like s: commonly becomes s (recall Old English f: became f), we reconstruct *s: for the s:-s-s correspondence. A shortening change took place in the Northern and Lombard dialects.

There is evidence in these (very limited) data for a weakening of word-final vowels, again a change we discussed earlier for English. We reconstruct *o for o-o-<> and *a for a-a-ǝ. In Lombard, conditioned sound changes took place. The sound o was deleted in *word-final position,* but remained o elsewhere. The sound a became ǝ in word-final position and remained a elsewhere. The conditioning factor is word-final position as far as we can tell from the data presented. Vowels in other position do not undergo change.

We reconstruct the protodialect as having had the words *fisso meaning "fixed" and *kassa meaning "cabinet."

It is by means of the comparative method that nineteenth-century linguists were able to initiate the reconstruction of the long-lost ancestral language so aptly conceived by Jones, Bopp, Rask, and Grimm, a language that flourished about 6,000 years ago, the language that we have been calling Indo-European.

Historical Evidence

You know my method. It is founded upon the observance of trifles.

Sir Arthur Conan Doyle, "The Boscombe Valley Mystery,"
The Memoirs of Sherlock Holmes

---

[8] The empty angled brackets indicate a loss of the sound.

How do we discover phonological changes? How do we know how Shakespeare or Chaucer or the author of *Beowulf* pronounced their versions of English? We have no recordings that give us direct knowledge.

For many languages, written records go back more than a thousand years. Linguists study these records to find out how languages were once pronounced. The spelling in early manuscripts tells us a great deal about the sound systems of older forms of modern languages. Two words spelled differently were probably pronounced differently. Once a number of orthographic contrasts are identified, good guesses can be made as to actual pronunciation. These guesses are supplemented by common words that show up in all stages of the language, allowing their pronunciation to be traced from the present stepwise into the past.

Another clue to earlier pronunciation is provided by non-English words that appear in English manuscripts. Suppose a French word known to contain the vowel [o:] is borrowed into English. The way the borrowed word is spelled reveals a particular letter-sound correspondence.

Other documents can be examined for evidence. Private letters are an excellent source of data. Linguists prefer letters written by naive spellers, who will misspell words according to the way they pronounce them. For instance, at one point in English history all words spelled with *er* in their stems were pronounced as if they were spelled with *ar*, just as in modern British English *clerk* and *derby* are pronounced "clark" and "darby." Some poor speller kept writing *parfet* for *perfect*, which helped linguists to discover the older pronunciation.

Clues are also provided by the writings of the prescriptive grammarians of the period. Between 1550 and 1750 a group of prescriptivists in England known as orthoepists attempted to preserve the "purity" of English. In prescribing how people should speak, they told us how people actually spoke. An orthoepist alive in the United States today might write in a manual: "It is incorrect to pronounce *Cuba* with a final *r*." Future scholars would know that there were speakers of English who pronounced it that way.

Some of the best clues to earlier pronunciation are provided by puns and rhymes in literature. Two words rhyme if the vowels and final consonants are the same. When a poet rhymes the verb *found* with the noun *wound*, it strongly suggests that the vowels of these two words were identical:

BENVOLIO: . . . 'tis in vain to seek him here that means not to be found.
ROMEO: He jests at scars that never felt a wound.

Shakespeare's rhymes are helpful in reconstructing the sound system of Elizabethan English. The rhyming of *convert* with *depart* in Sonnet XI strengthens the conclusion that *er* was pronounced as *ar*.

Dialect differences may provide clues as to what earlier stages of a language were like. Many dialects of English are spoken throughout the world. By comparing the pronunciation of various words in several dialects, we can draw conclusions about earlier forms and see what changes took place in the inventory of sounds and in the phonological rules.

For example, since some speakers of English pronounce *Mary, merry,* and *marry* with three different vowels ([meri], [mɛri], and [mæri]), we may conclude that at one time all speakers of English did so. (The different spellings are also a clue.) For some dialects, however, only one of these sounds can occur before /r/, namely the sound [ɛ]. Those dialects underwent a sound shift in which both /e/ and /æ/ shifted to /ɛ/ when followed immediately by /r/. This is another instance of a conditioned sound shift.

The historical-comparativists working on languages with written records have a difficult job, but not nearly as difficult as scholars who are attempting to discover genetic relationships among languages with no written history.

Linguists must first transcribe large amounts of language data from all the languages, analyze them phonologically, morphologically, and syntactically, and establish a basis for relatedness such as similarities in basic vocabulary, and regular sound correspondences not due to chance or borrowing. Only then can the comparative method be applied to reconstruct the extinct protolanguage.

Linguists proceeding in this manner have discovered many relationships among Native American languages and have successfully reconstructed Amerindian protolanguages. Similar achievements have been made with the numerous languages spoken in Africa. Linguists have been able to group the large number of languages of Africa into four overarching families: Afroasiatic, Nilo-Saharan, Niger-Congo, and Khoisan. For example, Somali is in the Afroasiatic family; Zulu is in the Niger-Congo family; Hottentot, spoken in South Africa, is in the Khoisan family. These familial divisions are subject to revision if new discoveries or analyses deem it necessary.

Extinct and Endangered Languages

Any language is the supreme achievement of a uniquely human collective genius, as divine and unfathomable a mystery as a living organism.

Michael Krauss

I am always sorry when any language is lost, because languages are the pedigree of nations.

Samuel Johnson

A language dies and becomes extinct when no children learn it. Linguists have identified four primary types of language death.

Sudden language death occurs when all of the speakers of the language die or are killed. Such was the case with Tasmanian and Nicoleño, a Native American Indian language once spoken in California.

Radical language death is similar to sudden language death in its abruptness. Rather than the speakers dying, however, they all stop speaking the language. Often, the reason for this is survival under the threat of political repression or even genocide. Indigenous languages embedded in other cultures suffer death this way. Speakers, to avoid being identified as "natives," simply stop speaking their native language. Children are unable to learn a language not spoken in their environment, and when the last speaker dies, the language dies.

Gradual language death is the most common way for a language to become extinct. It happens to minority languages that are in contact with a dominant language,

"Was Latin a dead language when you
were little, Daddy, or was it still alive?"

"Family Circus" copyright © 2001 Bil Keane, Inc. Reprinted with
special permission of King Features Syndicate, Inc.

much as American Indian languages are in contact with English. In each generation, fewer and fewer children learn the language until there are no new learners. The language is said to be dead when the last generation of speakers dies out. Cornish suffered this fate in Britain in the eighteenth century, as have many Native American languages in both the North and South continents.

Bottom-to-top language death is the term that describes a language that survives only in specific contexts, such as a liturgical language. Latin, and at one time, Hebrew, are such languages. It contrasts with gradual language death, which in its dying throes is spoken casually and informally in homes and villages. People stopped speaking Latin in daily situations centuries ago, and its usage is confined to scholarly and religious contexts.

Language death has befallen, and is befalling, many Native American languages. According to the linguist Michael Krauss, children are learning only 20 percent of the remaining native languages in the United States. Already, hundreds have been lost. Once widely spoken American Indian languages such as Comanche, Apache, and Cherokee have fewer native speakers every generation.

Doomed languages have existed throughout time. The Indo-European languages Hittite and Tocharian no longer exist. Hittite passed away 3,500 years ago, and both dialects of Tocharian gave up the ghost in the first century of the last millennium.

Linguists have placed many languages on an endangered list. They attempt to preserve these languages by studying and documenting their grammars — the phonetics, phonology, and so on — and by recording for posterity the speech of the last few speakers. Through its grammar, each language provides new evidence on the nature of human cognition. In its literature, poetry, ritual speech, and word structure, each language stores the collective intellectual achievements of a culture, offering unique perspectives on the human condition. The disappearance of a language is tragic; not only are these insights lost, but the major medium through which a culture maintains and renews itself is gone as well.

Dialects, too, may become extinct. Many dialects spoken in the United States are considered endangered by linguists. For example, the sociolinguist Walt Wolfram is studying the dialect spoken on Ocracoke Island off the coast of North Carolina. One reason for the study is to preserve the dialect, which is in danger of extinction because so many young Ocracokers leave the island and raise their children elsewhere, a case of gradual *dialect* death. Vacationers and retirees are diluting the dialect-speaking population, attracted to the island by its unique character, including, ironically, the quaint speech of the islanders.

Linguists are not alone in their preservation efforts. Under the sponsorship of language clubs, and occasionally even governments, adults and children learn an endangered language as a symbol of the culture. Gael Linn is a private organization in Ireland that runs language classes in Irish (Gaelic) for adults. Hundreds of public schools in Ireland and Northern Ireland are conducted entirely in Gaelic. In the state of Hawaii a movement is underway to preserve and teach Hawaiian, the native language of the island.

The United Nations, too, is concerned. In 1991, UNESCO (United Nations Educational, Scientific, and Cultural Organization) passed a resolution that states:

> As the disappearance of any one language constitutes an irretrievable loss to mankind, it is for UNESCO a task of great urgency to respond to this situation by promoting . . . the description — in the form of grammars, dictionaries, and texts — of endangered and dying languages.

Occasionally a language is resurrected from written records. For centuries classical Hebrew was used only in religious ceremonies, but today, with some modernization, and through a great desire among Jews to speak the language of their forefathers, it has become the national language of Israel.

The preservation of dying languages and dialects is essential to the study of Universal Grammar, an attempt to define linguistic properties shared by all languages. This in turn will help linguists develop a comprehensive theory of language that will include a specific description of the innate human capacity for language.

The Genetic Classification of Languages

The Sanskrit language, whatever be its antiquity, is of a wonderful structure, more perfect than the Greek, more copious than the Latin, and more exquisitely refined than either, yet bearing to both of them a stronger affinity, both in the roots of verbs and in the forms of grammar, than could possibly have been produced by accident; so strong, indeed, that no philologer could examine all three, without believing that they have sprung from some common source, which, perhaps, no longer exists. . . .

Sir William Jones (1786)

We have discussed how different languages evolve from one language and how historical and comparative linguists classify languages into families such as Germanic or Romance and reconstruct earlier forms of the ancestral language. When we examine the languages of the world, we perceive similarities and differences among them that provide evidence for degrees of relatedness or for non-relatedness.

Counting to five in English, German, and Vietnamese shows similarities between English and German not shared by Vietnamese.

English	German	Vietnamese[9]
one	eins	mot
two	zwei	hai
three	drei	ba
four	vier	bon
five	fünf	nam

The similarity between English and German is pervasive. Sometimes it is extremely obvious (*man/Mann*), at other times a little less obvious (*child/Kind*). No regular similarities or differences apart from those due to chance are found between them and Vietnamese.

Pursuing the metaphor of human genealogy, we say that English, German, Norwegian, Danish, Swedish, Icelandic, and so on are sisters in that they descended from one parent and are more closely related to one another than any of them are to non-Germanic languages such as French or Russian.

The Romance languages are also sister languages whose parent is Latin. If we carry the family metaphor to an extreme, we might describe the Germanic languages and the Romance languages as cousins, since their respective parents, Proto-Germanic and early forms of Latin were siblings.

As anyone from a large family knows, there are cousins, and then there are "distant" cousins, encompassing nearly anyone with a claim to family bloodlines. This is true of the Indo-European family of languages. If the Germanic and Romance languages are truly cousins, then languages such as Greek, Armenian, Albanian, and even the extinct Hittite and Tocharian are distant cousins. So are Irish, Scots Gaelic, Welsh, and Breton, whose protolanguage, Celtic, was once widespread throughout Europe and the British Isles. Breton is spoken in Brittany in the northwest coastal regions of France. It was brought there by Celts fleeing from Britain in the seventh century.

Russian is also a distant cousin, as are its sisters, Bulgarian, Serbo-Croatian, Polish, Czech, and Slovak. The Baltic language Lithuanian is related to English, as is its sister language, Latvian. A neighboring language, Estonian, however, is not a relative. Sanskrit, as pointed out by Sir William Jones, though far removed geographically, is nonetheless a relative. Its offspring, Hindi and Bengali, spoken primarily in South Asia, are distantly related to English. Persian (or Farsi), spoken in modern Iran, is a distant cousin of English, as is Kurdish, spoken in Iran, Iraq, and Turkey, and Pashto spoken in Afghanistan and Pakistan.

All the languages mentioned in the last paragraph, except for Estonian, are related, more or less distantly, to one another because they all descended from Indo-European.

---

[9] Tones are omitted for simplicity.

Figure 11.5 is an abbreviated family tree of the Indo-European languages that gives a genealogical and historical classification of the languages shown. This diagram is somewhat simplified. For example, it appears that all the Slavic languages are sisters. This suggests the comical scenario of speakers of Proto-Slavic dividing themselves into nine clans one fine morning, with each going its separate way. In fact the nine languages shown can be organized hierarchically, showing some more closely related than others. In other words, the various separations that resulted in the nine languages we see today occurred several times over a long stretch of time. Similar remarks apply to the other families, including Indo-European.

Another simplification is that the "dead ends" — languages that evolved and died leaving no offspring — are not included. We have already mentioned Hittite and Tocharian as two such Indo-European languages.

The family tree also fails to show a number of intermediate stages that must have existed in the evolution of modern languages. Languages do not evolve abruptly, which is why comparisons with the genealogical trees of biology have limited usefulness.

Finally, the diagram fails to show a number of Indo-European languages because of lack of space.

Languages of the World

And the whole earth was of one language, and of one speech.

Genesis 11:1

Let us go down, and there confound their language, that they may not understand one another's speech.

Genesis 11:7

Most of the world's languages do not belong to the Indo-European family. Linguists have also attempted to classify the non-Indo-European languages according to their genetic relationships. The task is to identify the languages that constitute a family and the relationships that exist among them.

The two most common questions asked of linguists are: "How many languages do you speak?" and "How many languages are there in the world?" Both are difficult to answer precisely. Most linguists have varying degrees of familiarity with several languages, and many are **polyglots,** persons who speak and understand several languages. Charles V, the Holy Roman Emperor from 1500 to1558 was a polyglot, for he proclaimed: "I speak Spanish to God, Italian to women, French to men, and German to my horse."

As to the second question, it's hard to ascertain the number of languages in the world because of disagreement as to what comprises a language as opposed to a dialect.

A difficulty with both these questions is that the answers rely on a sliding scale. Familiarity with a language is not an all-or-nothing affair, so how much of a language do you have to know before you can be said to "speak and understand" that language? And how different must two dialects be before they become separate languages? One criterion is that of mutual intelligibility. As long as two dialects remain mutually intelligible, it is generally believed that they cannot be considered separate languages. But mutual

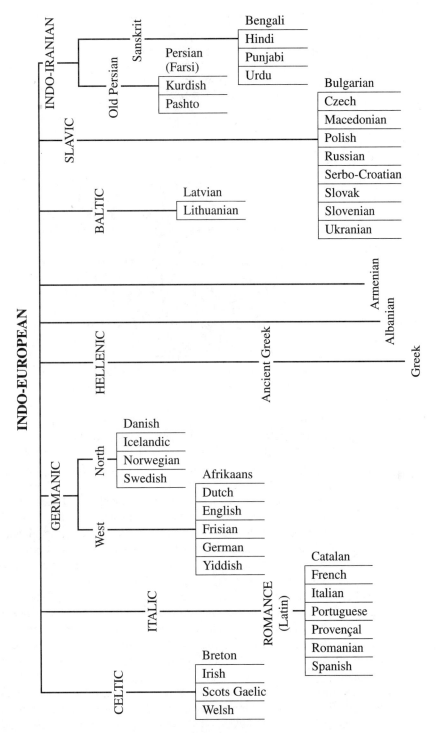

Figure 11.5   The Indo-European family of languages.

"Bizarro" copyright © 1994 by Dan Piraro. Reprinted with permission of Universal Press Syndicate. All rights reserved.

intelligibility itself lies on a sliding scale, as all of us know who have conversed with persons speaking dialects of our native language that we do not understand completely.

The Indo-Iranian languages Hindi and Urdu are listed as separate languages in Figure 11.5, yet they are mutually intelligible in their spoken form and are arguably dialects of one language. However, each uses a different writing system and each is spoken in communities of differing religious beliefs and nationalities. (Hindi, for the most part, is spoken in India by Hindus; Urdu is spoken in Pakistan by Muslims.) So what constitutes a separate language is not always determined by linguistic factors alone.

On the other hand, mutually unintelligible languages spoken in China are often thought of as dialects because they have a common writing system and culture, and are spoken within a single political boundary.

Estimates of the number of languages in the world vary widely. The minimum has been set at 4,000 and the maximum at 8,000. In the city of Los Angeles alone, more than 80 languages are spoken. Students at Hollywood High School go home to hear their parents speak Amharic, Armenian, Arabic, Marshallese, Urdu, Sinhalese, Ibo, Gujarati, Hmong, Afrikaans, Khmer, Ukrainian, Cambodian, Spanish, Tagalog, Russian, and more.

It is often surprising to discover what languages are genetically related and which ones aren't. Nepali, the language of remote Nepal is an Indo-European language, whereas Hungarian, surrounded on all sides by Indo-European languages, is not.

It is not possible in an introductory text to give an exhaustive table of families, subfamilies, and individual languages. Besides, a number of genetic relationships have not yet been firmly established. For example, linguists are divided as to whether Japanese and Turkish are related. We'll simply mention several language families with a few of their members. These language families appear not to be related to one another or to Indo-European. This, however, may be an artifact of being unable to delve into the past far enough to see common features that time has erased. We cannot eliminate the possibility that all the world's languages spring ultimately from a single source, an "ur-language" that some have termed **Nostratic,** buried, if not concealed, in the depths of the past. Readers interested in this fascinating topic may wish to read the writings of Professor Johanna Nichols of the University of California at Berkeley.

Uralic is the other major family of languages, besides Indo-European, spoken on the European continent. Hungarian, Finnish, and Estonian are the major representatives of this group.

Afro-Asiatic languages comprise a large family spoken in northern Africa and the Middle East. They include the modern *Semitic* languages of Hebrew and Arabic, as well as languages spoken in biblical times such as Aramaic, Babylonian, Canaanite, and Moabite.

The *Sino-Tibetan* family includes Mandarin, the most populous language in the world, spoken by around one billion Chinese. This family also includes all of the Chinese "dialects," as well as Burmese and Tibetan.

Most of the languages of Africa belong to the *Niger-Congo* family. These include over nine hundred languages grouped into a number of subfamilies such as Kordofanian and Atlantic-Congo. The latter includes individual languages such as Swahili and Zulu.

Equally numerous, the *Austronesian* family contains about nine hundred languages, spoken over a wide expanse of the globe, from Madagascar, off the coast of Africa, to Hawaii. Hawaiian itself, of course, is an Austronesian language, as are Maori, spoken in New Zealand; Tagalog, spoken in the Philippine Islands; and Malay, spoken in Malaysia and Singapore, to mention just a few.

Dozens of families and hundreds of languages are, or were, spoken in North and South America. Knowledge of the genetic relationships among these families of languages is often tenuous, and because so many of the languages are approaching extinction, there may be little hope for as thorough an understanding of the Amerindian language families as linguists have achieved for Indo-European.

Types of Languages

All the Oriental nations jam tongue and words together in the throat, like the Hebrews and Syrians. All the Mediterranean peoples push their enunciation forward to the palate, like the Greeks and the Asians. All the Occidentals break their words on the teeth, like the Italians and Spaniards. . . .

Isidore of Seville, seventh century C.E.

There are many ways to classify languages. One way already discussed in this chapter is according to the language "family." This method would be like classifying people

"We get a lot of foreign visitors."

"Herman" ® is reprinted with permission from Laughing Stock Licensing Inc., Ottowa, Canada.

according to whether they were related by blood. Another way of classifying languages is by certain linguistic traits, regardless of family. With people, this method would be like classifying them according to height and weight, or hair and eye color.

Every language has sentences that include a subject (S),[10] an object (O), and a verb (V), although some sentences lack all three elements. Languages have been classified according to the basic or most common order in which these occur in sentences.

There are six possible orders — SOV (subject, object, verb), SVO, VSO, VOS, OVS, OSV — permitting six possible language types. Here are examples of some of the languages in these classes.[11]

SVO: English, French, Swahili, Hausa, Thai
VSO: Tagalog, Irish, (Classical) Arabic, (Biblical) Hebrew
SOV: Turkish, Japanese, Persian, Georgian
OVS: Apalai (Brazil), Barasano (Colombia), Panare (Venezuela)
OSV: Apurina and Xavante (Brazil)
VOS: Cakchiquel (Guatemala), Huave (Mexico)

The most frequent word orders in languages of the world are SVO, VSO, and SOV. The basic VSO and SOV sentences may be illustrated as follows:

---

[10] In this section *only,* S will abbreviate *subject* not *sentence.*

[11] The examples of VOS, OVS, and OSV languages are from Pullum, 1981.

VSO (Tagalog):　　Sumagot　siya　sa　propesor
　　　　　　　　　answered　he　　the　professor
　　　　　　　　　"He answered the professor."

SOV (Turkish):　　Romalilar　barbarlari　yendiler
　　　　　　　　　Romans　　barbarians　defeated
　　　　　　　　　"The Romans defeated the Barbarians."

Languages with OVS, OSV, and VOS basic word order are much rarer.

The order of other sentence components in a language is most frequently correlated with the language type. If a language is of a type in which the verb precedes the object — a VO language, which includes SVO, VSO, or VQS — then the auxiliary verb tends to precede the verb; adverbs tend to follow the verb; and the language use *pre*positions, which precede the noun, among other such ordering relationships. English exhibits all these tendencies.

In OV languages, most of which are SOV, the opposite tendency occurs: Auxiliary verbs tend to follow the verb; adverbs tend to precede the verb; and there are *post*positions, which function similarly to prepositions but follow the noun. Japanese is an SOV language. It has postpositions, so to say "from Tokyo" in Japanese you say *Tokyo kara,* "Tokyo from." Also in Japanese, the auxiliary verb follows the verb, as illustrated by the following sentence:

Akiko　wa　　　　　　　sakana　o　　　　　　　tabete　iru
Akiko　*topic marker*　fish　　*object marker*　eating　is
"Akiko is eating fish."

The correlations between language type and the word order of syntactic categories in sentences are *preferred* word orders, and for the most part are violable tendencies. Different languages follow them to a greater or lesser degree.

The knowledge that speakers of various languages have about word order is captured in the phrase structure rules of the language. In English, an SVO language, the V precedes its NP Object, so the grammar contains the rule VP → V NP. In the SOV languages Turkish and Japanese, the NP Object precedes the Verb and the corresponding phrase structure rule is VP → NP V. Similarly, the rule PP → P NP occurs in SVO languages, whereas the rule PP → NP P is the correlate occurring in SOV languages.

That a language is SVO does not mean that SVO is the only possible word order. When a famous comedian said, "Believe you me" on network TV, he was understood and imitated despite the VSO word order. Yoda, the Jedi Master from the motion picture *Return of the Jedi,* speaks a strange but perfectly understandable style of English that achieves its eccentricity by being OSV. (Objects may be complements other than Noun Phrases.) Some of Yoda's utterances are:

Sick I've become.
Strong with the Force you are.
Your father he is.
When nine hundred years you reach, look as good you will not.

For linguists, the many languages and language families provide essential data for the study of universal grammar. Although these languages are diverse in many ways, they are also remarkably similar in many ways. We find that the languages of the "wretched Greenlanders," the Maoris of New Zealand, the Zulus of Africa, and the native peoples of North and South America all have similar sounds, similar phonological and syntactic rules, and similar semantic systems.

Why Do Languages Change?

Some method should be thought on for ascertaining and fixing our language forever. . . . I see no absolute necessity why any language should be perpetually changing.

Jonathan Swift (1712)

Stability in language is synonymous with rigor mortis.

Ernest Weekley

No one knows exactly how or why languages change. As we have shown, linguistic changes do not happen suddenly. Speakers of English did not wake up one morning and decide to use the word *beef* for "ox meat," nor do all the children of one particular generation grow up to adopt a new word. Changes are more gradual, particularly changes in the phonological and syntactic system.

Of course, certain changes may occur instantaneously for any one speaker. When someone acquires a new word, it is not acquired gradually, although full appreciation for all of its possible uses may come slowly. When a new rule enters a speaker's grammar, it is either in or not in the grammar. It may at first be an optional rule, so that sometimes it is used and sometimes it is not, possibly determined by social context or other external factors, but the rule is either there and available for use or not. What is gradual about language change is the spread of certain changes through an entire speech community.

A basic cause of change is the way children acquire the language. No one teaches a child the rules of the grammar. Each child constructs a personal grammar alone, generalizing rules from the linguistic input received. As discussed in chapter 8, the child's language develops in stages until it approximates the adult grammar. The child's grammar is never exactly like that of the adult community, because children receive diverse linguistic input. Certain rules may be simplified or overgeneralized, and vocabularies may show small differences that accumulate over several generations.

The older generation may be using certain rules optionally. For example, at certain times they may say "It's I" and at other times "It's me." The less formal style is usually used with children, who as the next generation may use only the "me" form of the pronoun in this construction. In such cases the grammar will have changed.

The reasons for some changes are relatively easy to understand. Before television there was no such word as *television*. It soon became a common lexical item. Borrowed words, too, generally serve a useful purpose, and their entry into the language is not mysterious. Other changes are more difficult to explain, such as the Great Vowel Shift in English.

One plausible source of change is *assimilation,* a kind of **ease of articulation** process in which one sound influences the pronunciation of an adjacent or nearby sound. Due to assimilation, vowels are frequently nasalized before nasal consonants because it is easiest to lower the velum to produce nasality in advance of the actual consonant articulation. This results in the preceding vowel being nasalized. Once the vowel is nasalized, the contrast that the nasal consonant provided can be equally well provided by the nasalized vowel alone, and the redundant consonant may be deleted. The contrast between oral and nasal vowels that exists in many languages of the world today resulted from just such a historical sound change.

In reconstructing older versions of French it has been hypothesized that *bol,* "basin," *botte,* "high boot," *bog,* "a card game," *bock,* "Bock beer," and *bon,* "good," were pronounced [bɔl], [bɔt], [bɔg], [bɔk], and [bɔ̃n], respectively. The nasalized vowel in *bon* was due to the final nasal consonant. Owing to a conditioned sound change that deleted nasal consonants in word-final position, *bon* is pronounced [bɔ̃] in modern French. The nasal vowel alone maintains the contrast with the other words.

Another example from English illustrates how such assimilative processes can change a language. In Old English, word initial [kʲ] (like the initial sound of *cute*), when followed by /i/, was further palatalized to become our modern palatal affricate /č/, as illustrated by the following words:

Old English (c = [kʲ])	Modern English (ch = [č])
ciese	cheese
cinn	chin
cild	child

The process of palatalization is found in the history of many languages. In Twi, the word meaning "to hate" was once pronounced [ki]. The [k] became first [kʲ] and then finally [č], so that today "to hate" is [či].

Ease of articulation processes, which make sounds more alike, are countered by the need to maintain contrast. Thus sound change also occurs when two sounds are acoustically similar, with risk of confusion. We saw a sound change of /f/ to /h/ in an earlier example that can be explained by the acoustic similarity of [f] to other sounds.

Analogic change is an "economy of memory" change that results in a reduction of the number of exceptional or irregular morphemes that must be individually learned and remembered. It may be by analogy to *foe/foes* and *dog/dogs* that speakers started saying *cows* as the plural of *cow* instead of the earlier plural *kine.* By analogy to *reap/reaped, seem/seemed,* and *ignite/ignited,* children and adults are presently saying *I sweeped the floor* (instead of *swept*), *I waked last night* (instead of *woke*), and *She lighted the bonfire* (instead of *lit*).

The same kind of analogic change is exemplified by our regularization of exceptional plural forms. We have borrowed words like *datum/data, agendum/agenda, curriculum/curricula, memorandum/memoranda, medium/media, criterion/criteria,* and *virtuoso/virtuosi,* to name just a few. The irregular plurals of these nouns have been replaced by regular plurals among many speakers: *agendas, curriculums, memorandums, criterias,* and *virtuosos.* In some cases the borrowed original plural forms were considered to be the singular (as in *agenda* and *criteria*) and the new plural (e.g., *agendas*) is therefore a "plural-plural." In addition, many speakers now regard *data* and *media* as nouns that do not have plural forms, like *information*. All these changes lessen the number of irregular forms that must be remembered.

Assimilation and analogic change account for some linguistic changes, but they cannot account for others. Simplification and regularization of grammars occur, but so does elaboration or complication. Old English rules of syntax became more complex, imposing a stricter word order on the language, at the same time that case endings were being simplified. A tendency toward simplification is counteracted by the need to limit potential ambiguity. Much of language change is a balance between the two.

Many factors contribute to linguistic change: simplification of grammars, elaboration to maintain intelligibility, borrowing, and so on. Changes are actualized by children learning the language, who incorporate them into their grammar. The exact reasons for linguistic change are still elusive, though it is clear that the imperfect learning of the adult dialects by children is a contributing factor. Perhaps language changes for the same reason all things change: it is the nature of things to change. As Heraclitus pointed out centuries ago, "All is flux, nothing stays still. Nothing endures but change."

 # Summary

Languages change. Linguistic change such as **sound shift** is found in the history of all languages, as evidenced by the **regular sound correspondences** that exist between different stages of the same language, different dialects of the same language, and different languages. Languages that evolve from a common source are **genetically related.** Genetically related languages were once dialects of the same language. For example, English, German, and Swedish were dialects of an earlier form of Germanic called **Proto-Germanic,** while earlier forms of Romance languages, such as Spanish, French, and Italian were dialects of Latin. Going back even further in time, earlier forms of Proto-Germanic, Latin, and other languages were dialects of **Indo-European.**

All components of the grammar may change. Phonological, morphological, syntactic, lexical, and semantic changes occur. Words, morphemes, phonemes, and rules of all types may be added, lost, or altered. The meaning of words and morphemes may **broaden, narrow,** or shift. The lexicon may expand by **borrowing,** which results in **loan words** in the vocabulary. It also grows through word **coinage, blends, acronyms,** and other processes of word formation. On the other hand, the lexicon may shrink as certain words are no longer used and become obsolete.

No one knows all the causes of linguistic change. Change comes about through the restructuring of the grammar by children learning the language. Grammars may appear to change in the direction of simplicity and regularity, as in the loss of the Indo-European case morphology, but such simplifications may be compensated for by other complexities, such as stricter word order. A balance is always present between simplicity — languages must be learnable — and complexity — languages must be expressive and relatively unambiguous.

Some sound changes result from **assimilation,** a fundamentally physiological process of **ease of articulation.** Others, like the **Great Vowel Shift,** are more difficult to explain. Some grammatical changes are **analogic changes,** generalizations that lead to more regularity, such as *sweeped* instead of *swept.*

The study of linguistic change is called **historical and comparative linguistics.** Linguists use the **comparative method** to identify regular sound correspondences among the **cognates** of related languages and systematically reconstruct an earlier **protolanguage.** This **comparative reconstruction** allows linguists to peer backward in time and determine the linguistic history of a language family, which may then be represented in a tree diagram similar to Figure 11.5.

Linguists estimate that there are 4,000 to 8,000 languages spoken in the world today (2002). These languages are grouped into families, subfamilies, and so on, based on their genetic relationships. A vast number of these languages are dying out because in each generation fewer children learn them. However, attempts are being made to preserve dying languages and dialects for the knowledge they bring to the study of Universal Grammar and the culture in which they are spoken.

References for Further Reading

Aitchison, J. 1985. *Language Change: Progress or Decay.* New York: Universe Books.

Anttila, R. 1989. *Historical and Comparative Linguistics.* New York: John Benjamins.

Baugh, A. C. 1978. *A History of the English Language,* 3rd ed. Englewood Cliffs, NJ: Prentice-Hall.

Cassidy, F. G., ed. 1986. *Dictionary of American Regional English.* Cambridge, MA: The Belknap Press of Harvard University Press.

Comrie, B., ed. 1990. *The World's Major Languages.* New York: Oxford University Press.

Hock, H. H. 1986. *Principles of Historical Linguistics.* New York: Mouton de Gruyter.

Jeffers, R. J., and I. Lehiste. 1979. *Principles and Methods for Historical Linguistics.* Cambridge, MA: MIT Press.

Lehmann, W. P. 1973. *Historical Linguistics: An Introduction,* 2d ed. New York: Holt, Rinehart and Winston.

Lyovin, A. V. 1997. *An Introduction to Languages of the World.* New York: Oxford University Press.

Nichols, J. 1992. *Linguistic Diversity in Space and Time.* Chicago: University of Chicago Press.

Pullum, G. K. 1981. "Languages with Object before Subject: A Comment and a Catalogue," *Linguistics* 19:147–55.

Pyles, T. 1993. *The Origins and Development of the English Language,* 4th ed. New York: Harcourt Brace.

Renfrew, C. 1989. "The Origins of the Indo-European Languages." *Scientific American* 261.4: 106–114.

Ruhlen, M. 1994. *On the Origin of Languages.* Stanford, CA: Stanford University Press.

Traugott, E. C. 1972. *A History of English Syntax.* New York: Holt, Rinehart and Winston.

Voegelin, C. F., and F. M. Voegelin. 1977. *Classification and Index of the World's Languages.* New York: Elsevier.

Wolfram, W. 2001. "Language Death and Dying," In *The Handbook on Language Variation and Change,* Chambers, J. K., Trudgill, P., and Schilling-Estes, N. (eds.) Oxford, UK: Basil Blackwell.

≋ Exercises

1. Many changes in the phonological system have occurred in English since 449 C.E. Below are some Old English words (given in their spelling and phonetic forms), and the same words as we pronounce them today. They are typical of regular sound changes that took place in English. What sound changes have occurred in each case?

   Example: OE hlud [xlu:d] → Mod. Eng. loud

              Changes: (1) The [x] was lost.

                       (2) The long vowel [u:] became [aw].

OE	Mod E

   a. crabba [kraba] → crab
      Changes:

   b. fisc [fɪsk] → fish
      Changes:

   c. fūl [fu:l] → foul
      Changes:

   d. gāt [ga:t] → goat
      Changes:

   e. lǣfan [læ:van] → leave
      Changes:

   f. tēþ [te:θ] → teeth
      Changes:

2. **A.** The Great Vowel Shift left its traces in Modern English in such meaning-related pairs as:

   (1) serene/serenity [i]/[ɛ]

   (2) divine/divinity [aj]/[ɪ]

   (3) sane/sanity [e]/[æ]

   List five such meaning-related pairs that relate [i] and [ɛ] as in example 1, five that relate [aj] and [ɪ] as in example 2, and five that relate [e] and [æ] as in example 3.

	[i]/[ɛ]	[aj]/[ɪ]	[e]/[æ]
(1)			
(2)			
(3)			
(4)			
(5)			

   B. In the section entitled "The Great Vowel Shift" is a cartoon of a woman sneezing. Explain the humor of the cartoon in terms of the Great Vowel Shift.

3. Below are given some sentences taken from Old English, Middle English, and early Modern English texts, illustrating some changes that have occurred in the syntactic

rules of English grammar. (*Note:* In the sentences, the earlier spelling forms and words have been changed to conform to Modern English. That is, the OE sentence *His suna twegen mon brohte to þæm cynige* would be written as *His sons two one brought to that king,* which in Modern English would be *His two sons were brought to the king.*) Underline the parts of each sentence that differ from Modern English. Rewrite the sentence in Modern English. State, if you can, what changes must have occurred.

Example: It *not* belongs to you. (Shakespeare, *Henry IV*)

> Mod. Eng.: It does not belong to you.

> Change: At one time, a negative sentence simply had a *not* before the verb. Today, the word *do,* in its proper morphological form, must appear before the *not.*

a. It nothing pleased his master.
   Mod. Eng.:
   Change:

b. He hath said that we would lift them whom that him please.
   Mod. Eng.:
   Change:

c. I have a brother is condemned to die.
   Mod. Eng.:
   Change:

d. I bade them take away you.
   Mod. Eng.:
   Change:

e. I wish you was still more a Tartar.
   Mod. Eng.:
   Change:

f. Christ slept and his apostles.
   Mod. Eng.:
   Change:

g. Me was told.
   Mod. Eng.:
   Change:

4. Yearbooks and almanacs often publish a new word list. In the 1980s and 1990s several new words, such as *Teflon* and *e-business,* entered the English language. From the computer field, we have new words such as *byte* and *modem.* Other words have been expanded in meaning, such as *memory* to refer to the storage part of a computer and *crack* meaning a form of cocaine. Sports-related new words include *threepeat, skybox,* as well as other compounds such as *air ball, contact hitter,* and *nose guard.*

   A. Think of five other words or compound words that have entered the language in the last ten years. Describe briefly the source of the word.

   B. Think of three words that might be on the way out. (*Hint:* Consider *flapper, groovy,* and *slay/slew.* Dictionary entries that say "archaic" are a good source.)

C. Think of three words whose dictionary entries do not say they are verbs, but which you've heard or seen used as verbs. *Example:* "He went to piano over at the club," meaning (of course) "He went to play the piano at the club."

D. Think of three words that have become, or are becoming, obsolete due to changes in technology. *Example: Mimeograph,* a method of reproduction, is on the way out due to advances in xerographic duplication technology.

5. Here is a table showing, in phonemic form, the Latin ancestors of ten words in modern French (given in phonetic form):

Latin	French	Gloss
kor	kœr[12]	heart
kantāre	šāte	to sing
klārus	klɛr	clear
kervus	sɛr	deer
karbō	šarbɔ̃	coal
kwandō	kã	when
kentum	sã	hundred
kawsa	šoz	thing
kinis	sãdrə	ashes
kawda/koda[13]	kø[12]	tail

Are the following statements true or false?

	True	**False**
a. The modern French word for "thing" shows that a /k/, which occurred before the vowel /o/ in Latin, became [š] in French.	_____	_____
b. The French word for "tail" probably derived from the Latin word /koda/ rather than from /kawda/.	_____	_____
c. One historical change illustrated by these data is that [s] became an allophone of the phoneme /k/ in French.	_____	_____
d. If there were a Latin word *kertus,* the modern French word would probably be [sɛr]. (Consider only the initial consonant.)	_____	_____

6. Here is how to count to five in a dozen languages, using standard Roman alphabet transcriptions. Six of these languages are Indo-European and six are not. Which are Indo-European?

---

[12] œ and ø are front, rounded vowels.
[13] /kawda/ and /koda/ are the word for "tail" in two Latin dialects.

	L1	L2	L3	L4	L5	L6
1	en	jedyn	i	eka	ichi	echad
2	twene	dwaj	liang	dvau	ni	shnayim
3	thria	tři	san	trayas	san	shlosha
4	fiuwar	štyri	ssu	catur	shi	arbaʔa
5	fif	pjeć	wu	pañca	go	chamishsha

	L7	L8	L9	L10	L11	L12
1	mot	ün	hana	yaw	uno	nigen
2	hai	duos	tul	daw	dos	khoyar
3	ba	trais	set	dree	tres	ghorban
4	bon	quatter	net	tsaloor	cuatro	durben
5	nam	tschinch	tasŏt	pindze	cinco	tabon

7. Recommend three ways in which society can act to preserve linguistic diversity. Be realistic and concrete. For example, "encourage children of endangered languages to learn the language" is *not* a good answer, being neither sufficiently realistic (why should they want to?), nor sufficiently concrete (what is meant by "encourage"?).

8. The vocabulary of English consists of native words as well as thousands of loan words. Look up the following words in a dictionary that provides their etymologies. Speculate how each word came to be borrowed from the particular language.

   Example: Skunk was a Native American term for an animal unfamiliar to the European colonists, so they borrowed that word into their vocabulary so they could refer to the creature.

a. size	h. robot	o. skunk	v. pagoda
b. royal	i. check	p. catfish	w. khaki
c. aquatic	j. banana	q. hoodlum	x. shampoo
d. heavenly	k. keel	r. filibuster	y. kangaroo
e. skill	l. fact	s. astronaut	z. bulldoze
f. ranch	m. potato	t. emerald	
g. blouse	n. muskrat	u. sugar	

9. Analogic change refers to a tendency to generalize the rules of language, a major cause of language change. We mentioned two instances, the generalization of the plural rule (*cow/kine* becoming *cow/cows*) and the generalization of the past-tense formation rule (*light/lit* becoming *light/lighted*). Think of at least three other instances of nonstandard usage that are analogic; they are indicators of possible future changes in the language. (*Hint:* Consider fairly general rules and see if you know of dialects or styles that overgeneralize them, for example, comparative formation by adding *-er*.)

10. Study the following passage from Shakespeare's *Hamlet,* Act IV, Scene iii, and identify every difference in expression between Elizabethan and current Modern English that is evident (e.g., in line 3, *thou* is now *you.*).

    HAMLET: A man may fish with the worm that hath eat of a king, and eat of the fish that hath fed of that worm.

    KING: What dost thou mean by this?

HAMLET: Nothing but to show you how a king may go a progress through the guts of a beggar.

KING: Where is Polonius?

HAMLET: In heaven. Send thither to see. If your messenger find him not there, seek him i' the other place yourself. But indeed, if you find him not within this month, you shall nose him as you go up the stairs into the lobby.

11. Here are some data from four Polynesian languages.

Maori	Hawaiian	Samoan	Fijian	Gloss	Proto-Polynesian (See Part C)
pou	pou	pou	bou	"post"	
tapu	kapu	tapu	tabu	"forbidden"	
taŋi	kani	taŋi	taŋi	"cry"	
takere	kaʔele	taʔele	takele	"keel"	
hono	hono	fono	vono	"stay, sit"	
marama	malama	malama	malama	"light, moon"	
kaho	ʔaho	ʔaso	kaso	"thatch"	

A. Find the correspondence sets. (*Hint:* There are 14. For example: o–o–o–o, p–p–p–b.)

B. For each correspondence set, reconstruct a proto-sound. Mention any sound changes that you observe. For example:

o–o–o–o   *o

p–p–p–b   *p   p → b in Fijian.

C. Complete the table by filling in the reconstructed words in Proto-Polynesian.

12. Consider these data from two American Indian languages:

Yerington Paviotso = YP	Northfork Monachi = NM	Gloss
mupi	mupi	"nose"
tama	tawa	"tooth"
piwɨ	piwɨ	"heart"
sawaʔpono	sawaʔpono	"a feminine name"
nɨmɨ	nɨwɨ	"liver"
tamano	tawano	"springtime"
pahwa	pahwa	"aunt"
kuma	kuwa	"husband"
wowaʔa	wowaʔa	"Indians living to the west"
mɨhɨ	mɨhɨ	"porcupine"
noto	noto	"throat"
tapa	tape	"sun"
ʔatapɨ	ʔatapɨ	"jaw"
papiʔi	papiʔi	"older brother"
patɨ	peti	"daughter"
nana	nana	"man"
ʔatɨ	ʔeti	"bow," "gun"

A. Identify each sound correspondence. (*Hint:* There are ten correspondence sets of consonants and six correspondence sets of vowels: for example, *p–p, m–w, a–a,* and *a–e.*)

B. (1) For each correspondence you identified in A not containing an *m* or *w,* reconstruct a proto-sound (e.g., for *h–h, *h; o–o, *o.*).

   (2) If the proto-sound underwent a change, indicate what the change is and in which language it took place.

C. (1) Whenever a *w* appears in YP, what appears in the corresponding position in NM?

   (2) Whenever an *m* occurs in YP, what two sounds may correspond to it in NM?

   (3) On the basis of the position of *m* in YP words, can you predict which sound it will correspond to in NM words? How?

D. (1) For the three correspondences you discovered in A involving *m* and *w,* should you reconstruct two or three proto-sounds?

   (2) If you chose three proto-sounds, what are they and what did they become in the two daughter languages, YP and NM?

   (3) If you chose two proto-sounds, what are they and what did they become in the daughter languages? What further statement do you need to make about the sound changes? (*Hint:* One proto-sound will become two different pairs, depending on its phonetic environment. It is an example of a conditioned sound change.)

E. Based on the above, reconstruct all the words given in the common ancestor from which both YP and NM descended (e.g., "porcupine" is reconstructed as **mihi.*).

13. The people of the Isle of Eggland once lived in harmony on a diet of soft-boiled eggs. They spoke proto-Egglish. Contention arose over which end of the egg should be opened first for eating, the big end or the little end. Each side retreated to its end of the island, and spoke no more to the other. Today, Big-End Egglish and Little-End Egglish are spoken in Eggland. Below are data from these languages.

   A. Find the correspondence sets for each pair of cognates, and reconstruct the proto-Egglish word from which the cognates descended.

   B. Identify the sound changes that have affected each language. Use <u>classes</u> of sounds to express the change when possible. (*Hint:* There are three conditioned sounds changes.)

Big-End Egglish	Little-End Egglish	Gloss	Proto-Egglish (To be completed)
šur	kul	omelet	*
ve	vet	yoke	*
rɔ	rɔk	egg	*
ver	vel	egg shell	*
žu	gup	soufflé	*
vel	vel	egg white	*
pe	pe	hard-boiled (obscene)	*

12

Writing:
The ABCs of Language

The Moving Finger writes; and, having writ,
Moves on: nor all thy Piety nor Wit
Shall lure it back to cancel half a Line,
Nor all thy Tears wash out a Word of it.

Omar Khayyám, Rubáiyát

The palest ink is better than the sharpest memory.

Chinese proverb

"Peanuts" copyright © 1986 United Feature Syndicate, Inc. Reprinted by permission.

Throughout this book we have emphasized the spoken form of language. The grammar, which represents one's linguistic knowledge, was viewed as the system for relating the sounds and meanings of one's language. The ability to acquire and use language represents a dramatic evolutionary development. No individual or peoples discovered or created language. The human language faculty appears to be biologically and genetically determined.

This is not true of the written form of human languages. Children learn to speak naturally through exposure to language, without formal teaching. To become literate, to learn to read and write, one must make a conscious effort and receive instruction.

Before the invention of writing, useful knowledge had to be memorized. Messengers carried information in their heads. Crucial lore passed from the older to the newer generation through speaking. Even in today's world many spoken languages lack a writing system, and oral literature still abounds. However, human memory is short-lived, and the brain's storage capacity is limited.

Writing overcomes such problems and allows communication across space and through time. Writing permits a society to permanently record its literature, its history and science, and its technology. The creation and development of writing systems is therefore one of the greatest of human achievements.

By *writing* we mean any of the many visual (nongestural) systems for representing language, including handwriting, printing, and electronic displays of these written forms. It might be argued that today we have electronic means of recording sound and cameras to produce films and television, so writing is becoming obsolete. If writing became extinct, however, there would be no knowledge of electronics for engineers to study; there would be, in fact, little technology in years to come. There would be no film or TV scripts, no literature, no books, no mail, no newspapers. There would be some advantages — no junk mail, poison-pen letters, or "fine print" — but the losses would far outweigh the gains.

The History of Writing

An Egyptian legend relates that when the god Thoth revealed his discovery of the art of writing to King Thamos, the good King denounced it as an enemy of civilization. "Children and young people," protested the monarch, "who had hitherto been forced to apply themselves diligently to learn and retain whatever was taught them, would cease to apply themselves, and would neglect to exercise their memories."

Will Durant, *The Story of Civilization 1*

There are many legends and stories about the invention of writing. Greek legend has it that Cadmus, Prince of Phoenicia and founder of the city of Thebes, invented the alphabet and brought it with him to Greece. In one Chinese fable, the four-eyed dragon-god Cang Jie invented writing, but in another, writing first appeared as markings on the back of the chi-lin, a white unicorn of Chinese legend. In other myths, the Babylonian god Nebo and the Egyptian god Thoth gave humans writing as well as speech. The Talmudic scholar Rabbi Akiba believed that the alphabet existed before humans were created; and according to Islamic teaching, the alphabet was created by Allah himself, who presented it to humans but not to the angels.

Although these are delightful stories, it is evident that before a single word was written, uncountable billions were spoken. The invention of writing comes relatively late in human history, and its development was gradual. It is highly unlikely that a particularly gifted ancestor awoke one morning and decided, "Today I'll invent a writing system."

Pictograms and Ideograms

One picture is worth a thousand words.

Chinese Proverb

The seeds out of which writing developed were probably the early drawings made by ancient humans. Cave drawings, called **petroglyphs,** such as those found in the Altamira cave in northern Spain, drawn by humans living over twenty thousand years ago, can be "read" today. They are literal portrayals of life at that time. We don't know why they were produced; they may be aesthetic expressions rather than pictorial communications. Later drawings, however, are clearly "picture writings," or **pictograms.** Unlike modern writing systems, each picture or pictogram is a direct image of the object it represents. There is a nonarbitrary relationship between the form and meaning of the symbol. Comic strips minus captions are pictographic — literal representations of the ideas to be communicated. This early form of writing represented objects in the world directly rather than through the linguistic names given to these objects. Thus they did not represent the words and sounds of spoken language.

Pictographic writing has been found throughout the world, ancient and modern: among Africans, Native Americans including the Inuits of Alaska and Canada, the Incas of Peru, the Yukagirians of Siberia, and the people of Oceania. Pictograms are used today in international road signs where the native language of the region might not be understood by all travelers. Such symbols can be understood by anyone because they do not depend on the words of any language. To understand the signs used by the National Park Service, for example, a visitor does not need to know English. (See Figure 12.1.)

Once a pictogram was accepted as the representation of an object, its meaning was extended to attributes of that object, or concepts associated with it. A picture of the sun could represent warmth, heat, light, daytime, and so on. Pictograms thus began to represent ideas rather than objects. Such generalized pictograms are called **ideograms** ("idea pictures" or "idea writing").

The difference between pictograms and ideograms is not always clear. Ideograms tend to be less direct representations, and one may have to learn what a particular

Figure 12.1   Six of seventy-seven symbols developed by the National Park Service for use as signs indicating activities and facilities in parks and recreation areas. These symbols denote, from left to right: environmental study area, grocery store, men's restroom, women's restroom, fishing, and amphitheater. Certain symbols are available with a prohibiting slash — a diagonal red bar across the symbol that means that the activity is forbidden. (National Park Service, U.S. Department of the Interior)

ideogram means. Pictograms tend to be more literal. For example, the no parking symbol consisting of a black circle with a slanting red line through it is an ideogram. It represents the idea of no parking abstractly. A no parking symbol showing an automobile being towed away is more literal, more like a pictogram.

Inevitably, pictograms and ideograms became stylized and formulaic so that the masses of people could read them. The simplifying conventions that developed so distorted the literal representations that it was no longer easy to interpret symbols without learning the system. The ideograms became linguistic symbols as they came also to stand for the sounds that represented the ideas — that is, for the words of the language. This stage represented a revolutionary step in the development of writing systems.

Cuneiform Writing

Bridegroom, let me caress you,
My precious caress is more savory than honey,
In the bed chamber, honey-filled,
Let me enjoy your goodly beauty,
Lion let me caress you

Translation of a Sumerian poem written in Cuneiform

Much of what we know about writing stems from the records left by the Sumerians, an ancient people of unknown origin, who built a civilization in southern Mesopotamia (modern Iraq) more than six thousand years ago. They left innumerable clay tablets containing business documents, epics, prayers, poems, proverbs, and so on. So copious are these written records that scholars studying the Sumerians are publishing a seventeen-volume dictionary of their written language. The first of these volumes appeared in 1984.

The writing system of the Sumerians is the oldest one known. They were a commercially oriented people, and as their business deals became increasingly complex, the need for permanent records arose. An elaborate pictography was developed, along with a system of tallies. Some examples are shown here:

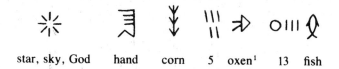

| star, sky, God | hand | corn | 5 | oxen[1] | 13 | fish |

Over the centuries the Sumerians simplified and conventionalized their pictography. They began to produce the symbols of their written language by using a wedge-shaped stylus that was pressed into soft clay tablets. The tablets hardened in the desert sun to produce permanent records far hardier than modern paper or electronic documents. Had the original American Declaration of Independence been written this way, it would not be in need of restoration and preservation. This form of writing is called **cuneiform** — literally, "wedge-shaped" (from Latin *cuneus,* "wedge"). Here is an illustration of the evolution of Sumerian pictograms to cuneiform:

---

[1] The pictograph for "ox" evolved, much later, into the letter *A*.

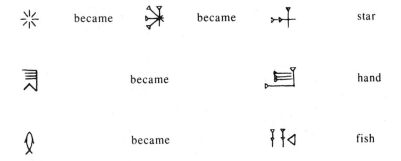

The cuneiform symbols in the right-most column do little to remind us (or the Sumerians) of the meaning represented. As cuneiform evolved, its users began to think of the symbols more in terms of the name of the thing represented than of the thing itself. Eventually cuneiform script came to represent words of the language. Such a system is called **logographic,** or **word writing.** In this oldest type of writing system, the symbol stands for both the word and the concept, which it may still resemble, however abstractly. Thus **logograms,** the symbols of a word-writing system, are ideograms that represent in addition to the concept, the word or morpheme in the language for that concept.

The cuneiform writing system spread throughout the Middle East and Asia Minor. The Babylonians, Assyrians, and Persians borrowed it. In adopting cuneiform characters, the borrowers often used them to represent the sounds of the syllables in their own languages. In this way cuneiform evolved into a **syllabic writing** system.

In a syllabic writing system, each syllable in the language is represented by its own symbol, and words are written syllable by syllable. Cuneiform writing was never purely syllabic. A large residue of symbols remained that stood for whole words. The Assyrians retained a large number of word symbols, even though every word in their language could be written out syllabically if it were desired. Thus they could write $matu$ "country" as:

ma	+	a	+	tu

The Persians (ca. 600–400 B.C.E.) devised a greatly simplified syllabic alphabet for their language, which made little use of word symbols. By the reign of Darius I (522–468 B.C.E.) this writing system was in wide use. The following characters illustrate it:

da   ma

di   tu

fa

Emoticons are strings of text characters which, when viewed sideways, form a face expressing a particular emotion. They are used mostly in e-mail and newsgroup messages to express a feeling about the text. They are a modern, pictographic system similar to cuneiform in that the same symbols are combined in different manners to convey different concepts. Most everyone who uses e-mail recognizes the smiley face **:-)** to mean "not serious" or "just joking." Several less common emoticons, and their generally accepted meanings, are shown here.

:'–(	"crying"
:–S	"bizarre"
:^D	"love it!"
:–)~	"drooling"

The invention, use, and acceptance of emoticons reflect on a small scale how a writing system such as cuneiform might have spread throughout a country.

The Rebus Principle

When a graphic sign no longer has a visual relationship to the word it represents, it becomes a **phonographic** symbol, standing for the sounds that represent the word. A single sign can then be used to represent all words with the same sounds—the homophones of the language. If, for example, the symbol ⊙ stood for *sun* in English, it could then be used in a sentence like *My* ⊙ *is a doctor.* This sentence is an example of the **rebus principle.**

A rebus is a representation of words by pictures of objects whose names sound like the word. Thus 👁 might represent *eye* or the pronoun *I.* The sounds of the two words are identical, even though the meanings are not. Similarly, 🐝🍃 could represent *belief* (*be* + *lief* = *bee* + *leaf* = /bi/ + /lif/), and 🐝🍃🍃 could be *believes.*

Proper names can also be written in such a way. If the symbol **|** is used to represent *rod* and the symbol 🧍 represents *man*, then **|** 🧍 could represent *Rodman,*

re·bus

GET BACK ON THE [bus]

WILEY'S DICTIONARY

WILEY'S DICTIONARY

© News America Syndicate, 1985   5-20

"B.C." copyright © 1985 News Service Syndicate. By permission of Johnny Hart and Creators Syndicate, Inc.

although nowadays the name is unrelated to either rods or men. Such combinations often become stylized or shortened so as to be more easily written. *Rodman,* for example, might be written in such a system as |⋆ or even ⺅.

Jokes, riddles, and advertising make use of the rebus principle. A well-known ice-cream company advertises "31derful flavors."

This is not an efficient system because in many languages words cannot be divided into sequences of sounds that have meaning by themselves. It would be difficult, for example, to represent the word *English* (/ɪŋ/ + /glɪš/) in English according to the rebus principle. *Eng* by itself does not mean anything, nor does *glish.*

From Hieroglyphics to the Alphabet

At the time that Sumerian pictography was flourishing (around 4000 B.C.E.), a similar system was being used by the Egyptians, which the Greeks later called hieroglyphics (*hiero,* "sacred," + *glyphikos,* "carvings"). These sacred carvings originated as pictography as shown by the following:

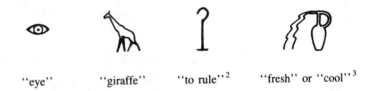

"eye" "giraffe" "to rule"[2] "fresh" or "cool"[3]

Eventually, these pictograms came to represent both the concept and the word for the concept. Once this happened, hieroglyphics became a bona fide logographic writing system. Through the rebus principle, hieroglyphics also became a syllabic writing system.

The Phoenicians, a Semitic people who lived in what is today Lebanon, were aware of hieroglyphics as well as the offshoots of Sumerian writing. By 1500 B.C.E.. they had developed a writing system of twenty-two characters, the West Semitic Syllabary. Mostly, the characters stood for consonants alone. The reader provided the vowels, and hence the rest of the syllable, through knowledge of the language. (Cn y rd ths?) Thus the West Semitic Syllabary was both a **syllabary** and a **consonantal alphabet.**

The ancient Greeks tried to borrow the Phoenician writing system, but it was unsatisfactory as a syllabary because Greek has too complex a syllable structure. In Greek, unlike Phoenician, vowels cannot be determined by grammatical context, so a writing system for Greek required that vowels have their own independent representations. Fortuitously, Phoenician had more consonants than Greek, so when the Greeks borrowed the system they used the leftover symbols to represent vowel sounds. The result was **alphabetic writing,** a system in which both consonants and vowels are symbolized. (The word *alphabet* is derived from *alpha* and *beta,* the first two letters of the Greek alphabet.)

---

[2] The symbol portrays the Pharaoh's staff.

[3] Water trickling out of a vase.

"You'd better phrase that more politely. We no longer use the [hand symbol] word."

A majority of alphabetic systems in use today derive from the Greek system. The Etruscans knew this alphabet and through them it became known to the Romans, who used it for Latin. The alphabet spread with Western civilization, and eventually most nations of the world were exposed to, and had the option of using, alphabetic writing.

According to one view, the alphabet was not invented, it was discovered. If language did not include discrete individual sounds, no one could have invented alphabetic letters to represent such sounds. When humans started to use one symbol for one phoneme, they merely brought their intuitive knowledge of the language sound system to consciousness: They discovered what they already "knew." Furthermore, children (and adults) can learn an alphabetic system only if each separate sound has some psychological reality.

Modern Writing Systems

. . . but their manner of writing is very peculiar, being neither from the left to the right, like the Europeans; nor from the right to the left, like the Arabians; nor from up to down, like the Chinese; nor from down to up, like the Cascagians, but aslant from one corner of the paper to the other, like ladies in England.

Jonathan Swift, *Gulliver's Travels*

We have already mentioned the various types of writing systems used in the world: word or logographic writing, syllabic writing, consonantal alphabet writing, and alphabetic writing. Most of the world's written languages use alphabetic writing. Even Chinese and Japanese, whose native writing systems are not alphabetic, have adopted alphabetic transcription systems for special purposes such as communicating with foreigners, computers, and over the Internet.

Word Writing

In a word-writing, or logographic writing system, a written character represents both the meaning and pronunciation of each word or morpheme. Such systems are cumbersome, containing thousands of different characters. On the other hand, the editors of *Webster's Third New International Dictionary* claim more than 450,000 entries. All these words may be written using only twenty-six alphabetic symbols, a dot, a hyphen, an apostrophe, and a space. It is understandable why, historically, word writing gave way to alphabetic systems in most places in the world.

"Peanuts" copyright © United Feature Syndicate, Inc. Reprinted by permission.

The major exceptions are the writing systems used in China and Japan. The Chinese writing system has an uninterrupted history that goes back more than thirty-five hundred years. For the most part it is a word-writing system, each character representing an individual word or morpheme. Longer words may be formed by combining two words or morphemes, as shown by the word meaning "business," mǎimai, which is formed by combining the words meaning "buy" and "sell." This is similar to compounding in English.

A word-writing system would be awkward for English and other Indo-European languages because of the pervasiveness of inflectional morphemes such as the *in-, im-,* and *iŋ-* of *intolerant, impossible,* and *incontinent,* inflected verb forms such as *take, takes, taken, took,* and *taking,* and inflected noun forms such as *cat, cats,* and *cat's.* These are difficult to represent without a huge proliferation of characters. Chinese, on the other hand, has little inflection.

Even without the need to represent inflectional forms, Chinese dictionaries contain tens of thousands of characters. A person need know "only" about five thousand, however, to read a newspaper. To promote literacy, the Chinese governments undertake character simplification programs from time to time. This process was first tried in 213 B.C.E., when the scholar Li Si published an official list of over three thousand characters whose written forms he had simplified by omitting unneeded strokes. This would be analogous to dictionary writers simplifying *amoeba* to *ameba,* eliminating the superfluous *o.*

Since that time successive generations of Chinese scholars have added new characters and modified old ones, creating redundancy, ambiguity, and complexity. Recent character-simplification efforts continue the ages old tradition of trying to make the system learnable and usable, while retaining its basic form.

The Chinese government has adopted a spelling system using the Roman alphabet, called **Pinyin,** which is now used for certain purposes along with the regular system of characters. Many city street signs are printed in both systems, which is helpful to foreign visitors. It is not the government's intent to replace the traditional writing, which is viewed as an integral part of Chinese culture. To the Chinese, writing is an art — **calligraphy** — and thousands of years of poetry, literature, and history are preserved in the old system.

An additional reason for keeping the traditional system is that it permits all literate Chinese to communicate even though their spoken languages are mutually unintelligible. Thus writing has served as a unifying factor throughout Chinese history, in an area where hundreds of languages and dialects coexist. A Chinese proverb states "people separated by a blade of grass cannot understand each other." The unified writing system is a scythe that cuts across linguistic differences and allows the people to communicate.

This use of written Chinese characters is similar to the use of Arabic numerals, which mean the same in many countries. The character 5, for example, stands for a different sequence of sounds in English, French, and Finnish. In English it is *five* /fajv/, in French it is *cinq* /sɛ̃k/, and in Finnish *viisi* /vi:si/, but in all these languages, 5, whatever its phonological form, means "five." Similarly, the spoken word for "rice" is different in the various Chinese languages, but the written character is the same. If the writing system in China were to become alphabetic, each language would be as different in writing as in speaking, and written communication would no longer be possible among the various language communities.

Syllabic Writing

Syllabic writing systems are more efficient than word-writing systems, and they are certainly less taxing on the memory. However, languages with a rich structure of syllables containing many consonant clusters (such as *tr* or *spl*) cannot be efficiently written with a syllabary. To see this difficulty, consider the syllable structures of English.

I	/aj/	V	ant	/ænt/	VCC
key	/ki/	CV	pant	/pænt/	CVCC
ski	/ski/	CCV	stump	/stʌmp/	CCVCC
spree	/spri/	CCCV	striped	/strajpt/	CCCVCC
an	/æn/	VC	ants	/ænts/	VCCC
seek	/sik/	CVC	pants	/pænts/	CVCCC
speak	/spik/	CCVC	sports	/spɔrts/	CCVCCC
scram	/skræm/	CCCVC	splints	/splɪnts/	CCCVCCC

Even this table is not exhaustive; there are syllables whose codas may contain four consonants such as *strengths* /strɛnkθs/ and *triumphs* /trajəmpfs/. With more than thirty consonants and over twelve vowels, the number of different possible syllables is astronomical, which is why English, and Indo-European languages in general, are unsuitable for syllabic writing systems.

The Japanese language, on the other hand, is more suited for syllabic writing, because all words in Japanese can be phonologically represented by about one hundred syllables, mostly of the consonant-vowel (CV) type, and there are no underlying consonant clusters. To write these syllables the Japanese have two syllabaries, each containing forty-six characters, called **kana.** The entire Japanese language can be written using kana. One syllabary, **katakana,** is used for loan words and for special effects similar to italics in European writing. The other syllabary, **hiragana,** is used for native words. Hiragana characters may occur in the same word as ideographic characters, which are called **kanji,** and are borrowed Chinese characters. Thus Japanese writing is part word writing, part syllable writing.

During the first millennium, the Japanese tried to use Chinese characters to write their language. However, spoken Japanese is unlike spoken Chinese. (They are genetically unrelated languages.) A word-writing system alone was not suitable for Japanese, which is a highly inflected language in which verbs may occur in thirty or more different forms. Scholars devised syllabic characters, based on modified Chinese characters, to represent the inflectional endings and other grammatical morphemes. Thus, in Japanese writing, kanji is commonly used for the verb roots, and hiragana symbols for the inflectional markings.

For example, 行 is the character meaning "go," pronounced [i]. The word for "went" in formal speech is *ikimashita,* written 行きました, where the hiragana symbols き ま し た represent the syllables *ki, ma, shi, ta.* Nouns, on the other hand, are not inflected in Japanese, and they can generally be written using Chinese characters alone.

In theory, all of Japanese could be written in hiragana. However in Japanese there are many homographs (like *lead* in "lead pipe" or "lead astray"), and the use of kanji disambiguates a word that might be ambiguous if written syllabically, similar to the ambiguity of *can* in "He saw that gasoline can explode." In addition, kanji writing is an integral part of Japanese culture, and it is unlikely to be abandoned.

In America in 1821, the Cherokee Sequoyah invented a syllabic writing system for his native language. Sequoyah's script, which survives today essentially unchanged, proved useful to the Cherokee people and is justifiably a point of great pride for them. The syllabary contains eighty-five symbols, many of them derived from Latin characters, which efficiently transcribe spoken Cherokee. A few symbols are shown here:

J	gu
ſ	hu
ℯℯ	we
W	ta
H	mi

In some languages, an alphabetic character can be used in certain words to write a syllable. In a word such as bar-b-q, the single letters represent syllables (*b* for [bi] or [bə], *q* for [kju]).

Consonantal Alphabet Writing

Semitic languages, such as Hebrew and Arabic, are written with alphabets that consist only of consonants. Such an alphabet works for these languages because consonants form the root of most words. For example, the consonants *ktb* in Arabic form the root of words associated with "write." Thus *katab* means "to write," *aktib* means "I write," *kitab* means "a book," and so on. Inflectional and derivational processes can be expressed by different vowels inserted into the triconsonantal roots.

Because of this structure, vowels can sometimes be figured out by a person who knows the spoken language, jst lk y cn rd ths phrs, prvdng y knw nglsh. English, however, is unrelated to the Semitic languages, and its structure is such that vowels are usually crucial for reading and writing. The English phrase *I like to eat out* would be incomprehensible without vowels, viz. *lk t t t.*

Semitic alphabets provide a way to use diacritic marks to express vowels. This is partly out of the desire to preserve the true pronunciations of religious writings, and partly out of deference to children and foreigners learning to read and write. In Hebrew, dots or other small figures are placed under, above, or even in the center of the consonantal letter to indicate the accompanying vowel. For example, ל represents an l-sound in Hebrew writing. Unadorned, the vowel that follows would be determined by context. However, לֶ indicates that the vowel that follows is [ɛ], so in effect לֶ represents the syllable [lɛ].

These systems are called consonantal alphabets because only the consonants are fully developed symbols. Sometimes they are considered syllabaries because once the reader or writer perceives the vowel, the consonantal letter *seems* to stand for a syllable. With a true syllabary, however, a person need know only the phonetic value of each symbol to pronounce it correctly and unambiguously. Once you learn a Japanese syllabary, you can read Japanese in a (more or less) phonetically correct way without any idea of what you are saying. (The syllabic text doesn't always show word boundaries, and there is no indication of prosodic features such as intonation.) This would be impossible for Arabic or Hebrew.

Alphabetic Writing

Alphabetic writing systems are easy to learn, convenient to use, and maximally efficient for transcribing any human language.

The term **sound writing** is sometimes used in place of *alphabetic writing,* but it does not truly represent the principle involved in the use of alphabets. One-sound ↔ one-letter is inefficient and unintuitive, because we do not need to represent the [pʰ] in *pit* and the [p] in *spit* by two different letters. It is confusing to represent nonphonemic differences in writing because the sounds are seldom perceptible to speakers. Except for the phonetic alphabets, whose function is to record the sounds of all languages for descriptive purposes, most, if not all, alphabets have been devised on the **phonemic principle.**

In the twelfth century, an Icelandic scholar developed an orthography derived from the Latin alphabet for the writing of the Icelandic language of his day. Other scholars in this period were also interested in orthographic reform, but the Icelander, who came to be known as "the First Grammarian" (because his anonymous paper was the first entry in a collection of grammatical essays), was the only one of the time who left a record of his principles. The orthography he developed was clearly based on the phonemic principle. He used minimal pairs to show the distinctive contrasts. He did not suggest different symbols for voiced and unvoiced [θ] and [ð], nor for [f] or [v], nor for velar [k] and palatal [č], because these pairs, according to him, represented allophones of the phonemes /θ/, /f/, and /k/, respectively. He did not use these modern technical terms, but the letters of this alphabet represent the distinctive phonemes of Icelandic of that century.

King Seijong of Korea (1397–1450) realized that the same principles held true for Korean when, with the assistance of scholars, he designed a phonemic alphabet. The king was an avid reader and realized that the over thirty thousand Chinese characters used to write Korean discouraged literacy. The fruit of the king's labor was the Korean alphabet called **Hangul,** which had seventeen consonants and eleven vowels.

The Hangul alphabet was designed on the phonemic principle. Although Korean has the sounds [l] and [r], Seijong represented them by a single letter because they are allophonic variants of the same phoneme. (See exercise 3, chapter 7.) The same is true for the sounds [s] and [š], and [ts] and [tš].

Seijong showed further ingenuity in the design of the characters themselves. The consonants are drawn so as to depict the place and manner of articulation. Thus the letter for /g/ is ㄱ to suggest the raising of the back of the tongue to the velum. The letter for /m/ is the closed figure ㅁ to suggest the closing of the lips. Vowels are drawn as long vertical or horizontal lines, sometimes with smaller marks attached to them. Thus ㅣ represent /i/, ㅜ represents /u/, and ㅏ represents /a/. They are easily distinguishable from the blockier consonants.

In Korean writing, the Hangul characters are grouped into squarish blocks, each corresponding to a syllable. The syllabic blocks, though they consist of alphabetic characters, make Korean look as if it were written in a syllabary. If English were written that way, "Now is the winter of our discontent" would have this appearance:

No	i	th	wi	te	o	ou	di	co	te
w	s	e	n	r	f	r	s	n	nt

The space between letters is less than the space between syllables, which is less than the space between words. An example of Korean writing can be found in exercise 9, item 10 at the end of the chapter.

These characteristics make Korean writing unique in the world, unlike that of the Europeans, the Arabians, the Chinese, the Cascagians, or even "ladies in England."

Many languages have their own alphabet, and each has developed certain conventions for converting strings of alphabetic characters into sequences of sound (reading), and converting sequences of sounds into strings of alphabetic characters (writing). As we have illustrated with English, Icelandic, and Korean, the rules governing the sound system of the language play an important role in the relation between sound and character.

Most European alphabets use Latin (Roman) letters, adding diacritic marks to accommodate individual characteristics of a particular language. For example, Spanish uses /ñ/ to represent the palatalized nasal phoneme of *señor,* and German has added an umlaut for certain of its vowel sounds that did not exist in Latin (for example, in *über).* Diacritic marks supplement the forty-six kana of the Japanese syllabaries to enable them to represent the one hundred-plus syllables of the language. Diacritic marks are also used in writing systems of tone languages such as Thai to indicate the tone of a syllable.

Some languages use two letters together — called a **digraph** — to represent a single sound. English has many digraphs, such as *sh* /š/ as in *she, ch* /č/ as in *chop, ng* as in *sing* (/siŋ/), and *oa* as in *loaf* /lof/.

Besides the European languages, languages such as Turkish, Indonesian, Swahili, and Vietnamese have adopted the Latin alphabet. Other languages that have more recently developed a writing system use some of the IPA phonetic symbols in their alphabet. Twi, for example, uses ɔ, ɛ, and ŋ.

Many Slavic languages including Russian use the Cyrillic alphabet, named for St. Cyril. It is derived directly from the Greek alphabet without Latin mediation.

Many contemporary alphabets, such as those used for Arabic, Farsi (spoken in Iran), Urdu (spoken in Pakistan), and many languages of the Indian subcontinent including Hindi, are ultimately derived from the ancient Semitic syllabaries.

Figure 12.2 shows a coarse time line of the development of the Roman alphabet.

15000 B.C.E. — Cave drawings as pictograms

4000 B.C.E.   — Sumerian cuneiform

3000 B.C.E.   — Hieroglyphics

1500 B.C.E.   — West Semitic Syllabary of the Phoenicians

1000 B.C.E.   — Ancient Greeks borrow the Phoenician consonantal alphabet
750 B.C.E.   — Etruscans borrow the Greek alphabet
500 B.C.E.   — Romans adapt the Etruscan/Greco alphabet to Latin

---

Figure 12.2   Time line of the development of the Roman alphabet.

Reading, Writing, and Speech

> . . . Ther is so great diversite
> In English, and in wryting of oure tonge,
> So prey I god that non myswrite thee . . .
>
> Geoffrey Chaucer, *Troilus and Cressida*

The development of writing freed us from the limitations of time and geography, but spoken language still has primacy, and is the principle concern of most linguists. Nevertheless, writing systems are of interest for their own sake.

The written language reflects, to a certain extent, the elements and rules that together constitute the grammar of the language. The letters of the alphabet represent the system of phonemes, although not necessarily in a direct way. The independence of words is revealed by the spaces between them in most writing systems. Japanese and Thai do not require spaces between words, although speakers and writers are aware of the individual words. On the other hand, no writing system shows the individual morphemes within a word in this way, even though speakers know what they are.

Many languages use punctuation, including capitalization, to indicate sentences, phrases, questions, intonation, stress, and contrast, but the written forms of other languages do not make use of punctuation.

Consider the difference in meaning between (1) and (2):

1. The Greeks, who were philosophers, loved to talk a lot.
2. The Greeks who were philosophers loved to talk a lot.

The relative clause in (1), set off by commas, is nonrestrictive because it means that all the Greeks were philosophers. It may be paraphrased as (1′):

1′. The Greeks were philosophers, and they loved to talk a lot.

The meaning of the second sentence, without the commas, can be paraphrased as:

2′. Among the Greeks, it was the philosophers who loved to talk a lot.

Similarly, by using an exclamation point or a question mark, the intention of the writer can be made clearer.

3. The children are going to bed at eight o'clock. (a simple statement)
4. The children are going to bed at eight o'clock! (an order)
5. The children are going to bed at eight o'clock? (a question)

These punctuation marks reflect the pauses and the intonations that would be used in the spoken language.

In sentence 6 *he* can refer to either John or someone else, but in sentence 7 the pronoun must refer to someone other than John:

6. John said he's going.
7. John said, "He's going."

The apostrophe used in contractions and possessives also provides syntactic information not always available in the spoken utterance.

8. My cousin's friends (one cousin)
9. My cousins' friends (two or more cousins)

Writing, then, somewhat reflects the spoken language, and punctuation may even distinguish between two meanings not revealed in the spoken forms, as shown in sentences 8 and 9.

In the normal written version of sentence 10,

10. John whispered the message to Bill and then he whispered it to Mary

he can refer to either John or Bill. In the spoken sentence, if *he* receives extra stress (called **contrastive stress**), it must refer to Bill; if *he* receives normal stress, it refers to John.

A speaker can usually emphasize any word in a sentence by using contrastive stress. Writers sometimes attempt to show emphasis by using all capital letters, italics, or underlining the emphasized word. This is nicely illustrated by the Garfield cartoon below.

In the first panel we understand Garfield as meaning, "I didn't do it, someone else did." In the second panel the meaning is "I didn't do it, even though you think I did." In the third, the contrastive stress conveys the meaning "I didn't do it, it just happened

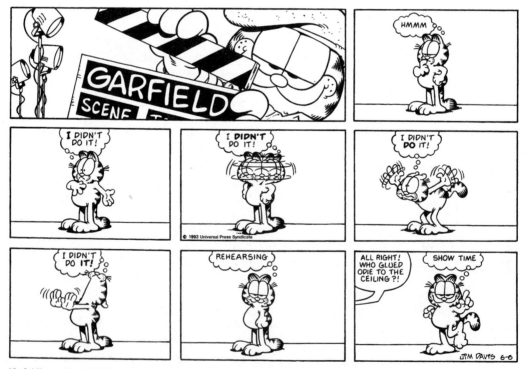

somehow." In the fourth panel Garfield means, "I didn't do it, though I may be guilty of other things." In each case the boldfaced word is contrasted with something else.

Although such visual devices can help in English, it is not clear that they can be used in a language such as Chinese. In Japanese, however, this kind of emphasis can be achieved by writing a word in katakana.

The use of italics has many functions in written language. One use is to indicate reference to the italicized word itself, as in "*the dog* is a noun article." A children's riddle, which is sung aloud, plays on this distinction:

> Railroad crossing, watch out for cars
> How do you spell it without any *r*'s?

The answer is "i-t." The joke is that the second line, were it written, would be:

> How do you spell *it* without any *r*'s?

Written language is more conservative than spoken language. When we write we are more apt to obey the prescriptive rules taught in school than when we speak. We may write "it is I" but we say "it's me." Such informalities abound in spoken language, but may be "corrected" by copy editors, diligent English teachers, and careful writers. A linguist wishing to describe the language that people regularly use therefore cannot depend on written records alone.

Reading

Children learn to speak instinctively without being taught. Learning to read and write is not like learning to speak. Recently, however, the Whole Language approach to reading has suggested that children can learn to read just as they learn to talk, through "constant interaction with family and friends, teachers and classmates." This view is given in a National Council of Teachers of English brochure that appears on the World Wide Web. It opposes the view that children be taught to segment speech into individual sounds and relate these sounds to the letters of the alphabet, which is sometimes referred to as *teaching phonics.*

As we have seen in this chapter, most written languages are based on oral language. The Whole Language advocates do not understand the way that children acquire language. They deny the fact that the ability to learn language is an innate, biologically determined aspect of the human brain, whereas reading and writing are not. Otherwise, one would not find so many people who speak so many languages that have no written form.

Many studies have shown that deaf children who have fully acquired a sign language have difficulty learning to read. This is understandable since the alphabetic principle in a system like English requires an understanding of sound-symbol regularities. Hearing children should therefore not be deprived of the advantage they would have if their unconscious knowledge of phonemes is made conscious.

In developing teaching methods for reading and writing, it is important to understand the interactions of speech, reading, and writing. Whatever methods are adopted, however, it should take advantage of the child's innate linguistic knowledge, and include helping the child relate sounds to letters.

Spelling

"Do you spell it with a 'v' or a 'w'?" inquired the judge.
"That depends upon the taste and fancy of the speller, my Lord," replied Sam.

Charles Dickens, The Pickwick Papers

If writing represented the spoken language perfectly, spelling reforms would never have arisen. In chapter 6 we discussed some of the problems in the English orthographic system. These problems prompted George Bernard Shaw to write:

> . . . It was as a reading and writing animal that Man achieved his human eminence above those who are called beasts. Well, it is I and my like who have to do the writing. I have done it professionally for the last sixty years as well as it can be done with a hopelessly inadequate alphabet devised centuries before the English language existed to record another and very different language. Even this alphabet is reduced to absurdity by a foolish orthography based on the notion that the business of spelling is to represent the origin and history of a word instead of its sound and meaning. Thus an intelligent child who is bidden to spell *debt,* and very properly spells it *d-e-t,* is caned for not spelling it with a *b* because Julius Caesar spelt the Latin word for it with a *b*.[4]

The irregularities between graphemes (letters) and phonemes have been cited as one reason "why Johnny can't read. "Homographs such as *lead* /lid/ and *lead* /lɛd/ have fueled the flames of spelling reform movements. Different spellings for the same sound, silent letters, and missing letters also are cited as reasons that English needs a new orthographic system. The following examples illustrate the discrepancies between spelling and sounds in English:

Same Sound, Different Spelling	Different Sound, Same Spelling		Silent Letters	Missing Letters
/aj/	thought	/θ/	listen	use/juz/
	though	/ð/	debt	fuse/fjuz/
aye	Thomas	/t/	gnome	
buy			know	
by	ate	/e/	psychology	
die	at	/æ/	right	
hi	father	/a/	mnemonic	
Thai	many	/ɛ/	science	
height			talk	
guide			honest	
			sword	
			bomb	
			clue	
			Wednesday	

---

[4] G. B. Shaw. 1948. Preface to R. A. Wilson, *The Miraculous Birth of Language,* New York: Philosophical Library.

The spelling of most English words today is based on English as spoken in the fourteenth, fifteenth, and sixteenth centuries. Spellers in those times saw no need to spell the same word consistently. Shakespeare spelled his own name in several ways. In his plays, he spelled the first person singular pronoun variously as *I, ay,* and *aye.*

When the printing press was introduced in the fifteenth century, archaic and idiosyncratic spellings became widespread and more permanent. Words in print were frequently misspelled outright because many of the early printers were not native speakers of English.

Spelling reformers saw the need for consistent spelling that correctly reflected the pronunciation of words. To that extent, spelling reform was necessary. But many scholars became overzealous. Because of their reverence for Classical Greek and Latin, these scholars changed the spelling of English words to conform to their etymologies. Where Latin had a *b,* they added a *b* even if it was not pronounced. Where the original spelling had a *c* or *p* or *h,* these letters were added, as shown by these few examples:

Middle English Spelling		Reformed Spelling
indite	→	indict
dette	→	debt
receit	→	receipt
oure	→	hour

Such spelling habits inspired Robert N. Feinstein to compose the following poem, entitled *Gnormal Pspelling:*[5]

> Gnus and gnomes and gnats and such —
> Gnouns with just one G too much.
> Pseudonym and psychedelic —
> P becomes a psurplus relic.
> Knit and knack and knife and knocked —
> Kneedless Ks are overstocked.
> Rhubarb, rhetoric and rhyme
> Should lose an H from thyme to time.

Even today spelling reform is an issue. Advertisers often spell *though* as *tho, through* as *thru,* and *night* as *nite.* The *Chicago Tribune* once used such spellings, but it gave up the practice in 1975. Spelling habits are hard to change, and many people regard revised spelling as substandard.

The current English spelling system is based primarily on the earlier pronunciations of words. The many changes that have occurred in the sound system of English since then are not reflected in the current spelling, which was frozen due to widespread printed material and scholastic conservatism.

For these reasons, modern English orthography does not always represent what we know about the phonology of the language. The disadvantage is partially offset by the fact that the writing system allows us to read and understand what people wrote hundreds of years ago without the need for translations. If there were a one-to-one correspondence between our spelling and the sounds of our language, we would have difficulty reading the *U.S. Constitution* or the *Declaration of Independence,* let alone the works of Shakespeare and Dickens.

Languages change. It is not possible to maintain a perfect correspondence between pronunciation and spelling, nor is it 100 percent desirable. For instance, in the case of homophones, it is helpful at times to have different spellings for the same sounds, as in the following pair:

The book was red. The book was read.

Lewis Carroll makes the point with humor:

> "And how many hours a day did you do lessons?" said Alice.
> "Ten hours the first day," said the Mock Turtle, "nine the next, and so on."
> "What a curious plan!" exclaimed Alice.
> "That's the reason they're called lessons," the Gryphon remarked, "because they lessen from day to day."

There are also reasons for using the same spelling for different pronunciations. A morpheme may be pronounced differently when it occurs in different contexts. The

---

[5] "Gnormal Pspelling" by Robert N. Feinstein from *National Forum: The Phi Kappa Phi Journal,* Summer, 1986. Reprinted with permission.

identical spelling reflects the fact that the different pronunciations represent the same morpheme. This is the case with the plural morpheme. It is always spelled with an *s* despite being pronounced [s] in *cats* and [z] in *dogs*. The sound of the morpheme is determined by rules, in this case and elsewhere.

Similarly, the phonetic realizations of the vowels in the following forms follow a regular pattern:

aj/ɪ	i/ɛ	e/æ
divine/divinity	serene/serenity	sane/sanity
sublime/sublimate	obscene/obscenity	profane/profanity
sign/signature	hygiene/hygienic	humane/humanity

These considerations have led some scholars to suggest that in addition to being phonemic, English has a **morphophonemic orthography.** To read English correctly morphophonemic knowledge is required. This contrasts with a language such as Spanish, whose orthography is almost purely phonemic.

Other examples provide further motivation for spelling irregularities. The *b* in "*debt*" may remind us of the related word *debit*, in which the *b* is pronounced. The same principle is true of pairs such as *sign/signal, bomb/bombardier,* and *gnosis/ prognosis/ agnostic.*

There are also different spellings that represent the different pronunciations of a morpheme when confusion would arise from using the same spelling. For example, there is a rule in English phonology that changes a /t/ to an /s/ in certain cases:

democrat → democracy

The different spellings are due in part to the fact that this rule does not apply to all morphemes, so that *art + y* is *arty*, not **arcy*. Regular phoneme-to-grapheme rules determine in many cases when a morpheme is to be spelled identically and when it is to be changed.

Other subregularities are apparent. A *c* always represents the /s/ sound when it is followed by a *y, i,* or *e,* as in *cynic, citizen,* and *censure.* Because it is always pronounced [k] when it is the final letter in a word or when it is followed by any other vowel (*coat, cat, cut,* and so on), no confusion results. The *th* spelling is usually pronounced voiced [ð] between vowels (the result of an historical intervocalic voicing rule), and in function words such as *the, they, this,* and *there.* Elsewhere it is the voiceless [θ].

There is another important reason why spelling should not always be tied to the phonetic pronunciation of words. Different dialects of English have divergent pronunciations. Cockneys drop their "(h)aitches" and Bostonians and southerners drop their *r*'s; *neither* is pronounced [niðər], [najðər], and [niðə] by Americans, [najðə] by the British, and [neðər] by the Irish; some Scots pronounce *night* [nɪxt]; people say "Chicago" and "Chicawgo," "hog" and "hawg," "bird" and "boyd"; *four* is pronounced [f:ɔ] by the British, [fɔr] in the Midwest, and [foə] in the South; *orange* is pronounced in at least two ways in the United States: [arənʤ] and [ɔrənʤ].

While dialectal pronunciations differ, the common spellings indicate the intended word. It is necessary for the written language to transcend local dialects. With a uniform spelling system, a native of Atlanta and a native of Glasgow can communicate through writing. If each dialect were spelled according to its pronunciation, written communication among the English-speaking peoples of the world would suffer.

Spelling Pronunciations

> For pronunciation, the best general rule is to consider those as the most elegant speakers who deviate least from written words.
>
> Samuel Johnson (1755)

Despite the primacy of the spoken over the written language, the written word is often regarded with excessive reverence. The stability, permanency, and graphic nature of writing cause some people to favor it over ephemeral and elusive speech. Humpty Dumpty expressed a rather typical attitude: "I'd rather see that done on paper."

Writing has affected speech only marginally, however, most notably in the phenomenon of **spelling pronunciation.** Since the sixteenth century, we find that spelling has to some extent influenced standard pronunciation. The most important of such changes stem from the eighteenth century under the influence and decrees of the dictionary-makers and the schoolteachers. The struggle between those who demanded that words be pronounced according to the spelling, and those who demanded that words be spelled according to their pronunciation, generated great heat in that century. The preferred pronunciations were given in the many dictionaries printed in the eighteenth century, and the "supreme authority" of the dictionaries influenced pronunciation in this way.

Spelling also has influenced pronunciation of words that are infrequently used in normal daily speech. In many words that were spelled with an initial *h,* the *h* was silent as recently as the eighteenth century. Then, no [h] was pronounced in *honest, hour, habit, heretic, hotel, hospital,* and *herb.* Common words like *honest* and *hour* continued *h*-less, despite the spelling. The other less frequently used words were given a "spelling pronunciation," and the *h* is sounded today. *Herb* is currently undergoing this change. In British English the *h* is pronounced, whereas in American English it generally is not.

Similarly, the *th* in the spelling of many words was once pronounced like the /t/ in *Thomas.* Later most of these words underwent a change in pronunciation from /t/ to /θ/, as in *anthem, author,* and *theater.* Nicknames may reflect the earlier pronunciations: "Kate" for "Ca*th*erine," "Be*tt*y" for "Eliza*beth,*" "Ar*t*" for "Ar*th*ur." *Often* is often pronounced with the *t* sounded, though historically it is silent, and up-to-date dictionaries now indicate this pronunciation as an alternative.

The clear influence of spelling on pronunciation is observable in the way place-names are pronounced. *Berkeley* is pronounced [bɜrkli] in California, although it stems from the British [baːkli]; *Worcester* [wʊstər] or [wʊstə] in Massachusetts is often pronounced [wʊrčɛstər] in other parts of the country. *Salmon* is pronounced [sæmən] in most parts of the United States, but many southern speakers pronounce the [l] and say [sælmən].

Although the written language has some influence on the spoken, it does not change the basic system—the grammar—of the language. The writing system, conversely, reflects, in a more or less direct way, the grammar that every speaker knows.

Summary

Writing is a basic tool of civilization. Without it, the world as we know it could not exist.

The precursor of writing was "picture writing," which used **pictograms** to represent objects directly and literally. Pictograms are called **ideograms** when the drawing becomes less literal, and the meaning extends to concepts associated with the object originally pictured. When ideograms become associated with the words for the concepts they signify, they are called **logograms.** Logographic systems are true writing systems in the sense that the symbols stand for words of a language.

The Sumerians first developed a pictographic writing system to keep track of commercial transactions. It was later expanded for other uses and eventually evolved into the highly stylized (and stylus-ized) **cuneiform writing.** Cuneiform was generalized to other writing systems by application of the **rebus principle,** which uses the symbol of one word or syllable to represent another word or syllable pronounced the same.

The Egyptians also developed a pictographic system known as **hieroglyphics.** This system influenced many peoples, including the Phoenicians, who developed the West Semitic Syllabary. The Greeks borrowed the Phoenician system, and in adapting it to their own language they used the symbols to represent both consonant and vowel sound segments, thus inventing the first alphabet.

There are four types of writing systems: **logographic** (word writing), where every symbol or character represents a word or morpheme (as in Chinese); **syllabic,** where each symbol represents a syllable (as in Japanese); **consonantal alphabetic,** where each symbol represents a consonant and vowels may be represented by diacritical marks (as in Hebrew); and **alphabetic,** where each symbol represents (for the most part) a vowel or consonant (as in English).

The writing system may have some small effect on the spoken language. Languages change in time, but writing systems tend to be more conservative. Thus spelling no longer accurately reflects pronunciation. Also, when the spoken and written forms of the language become divergent, some words may be pronounced as they are spelled, sometimes due to the efforts of pronunciation reformers.

There are advantages to a conservative spelling system. A common spelling permits speakers whose dialects have diverged to communicate through writing, as is best exemplified in China, where the "dialects" are mutually unintelligible. We are also able to read and understand the language as it was written centuries ago. In addition, despite a certain lack of correspondences between sound and spelling, the spelling often reflects speakers' morphological and phonological knowledge.

References for Further Reading

Adams, M. J. 1996. *Beginning to Read.* Cambridge, MA: MIT Press.

Biber, D. 1988. *Variation across Speech and Writing.* Cambridge, England: Cambridge University Press.

Coulmas, F. 1989. *The Writing Systems of the World.* Cambridge, MA: Blackwell Publishers.

Cummings, D. W. 1988. *American English Spelling*. Baltimore, MD: The Johns Hopkins University Press.

Daniels, P. T., and W. Bright, eds. 1996. *The World's Writing Systems*. New York: Oxford University Press.

DeFrancis, J. 1989. *Visible Speech: The Diverse Oneness of Writing Systems*. Honolulu: University of Hawaii Press.

Gaur, A. 1984. *A History of Writing*. London, England: The British Library.

Sampson, G. 1985. *Writing Systems: A Linguistic Introduction*. Stanford, CA: Stanford University Press.

Senner, W. M., ed. 1989. *The Origins of Writing*. Lincoln, NE: University of Nebraska Press

≋ Exercises

1. **A.** "Write" the following words and phrases, using pictograms that you invent:

   a. eye

   b. a boy

   c. two boys

   d. library

   e. tree

   f. forest

   g. war

   h. honesty

   i. ugly

   j. run

   k. Scotch tape

   l. smoke

   B. Which words are most difficult to symbolize in this way? Why?

   C. How does the following sentence reveal the problems in pictographic writing? "A grammar represents the unconscious, internalized linguistic competence of a native speaker."

2. A *rebus* is a written representation of words or syllables that uses pictures of objects whose names resemble the sounds of the intended words or syllables. For example, ◉ might be the symbol for "eye" or "I" or the first syllable in "idea."

   A. Using the rebus principle, "write" the following words:

   a. tearing

   b. icicle

   c. bareback

   d. cookies

   B. Why would such a system be a difficult system in which to represent all words in English? Illustrate with an example.

3. **A.** Construct non-Roman alphabetic letters to replace the letters used to represent the following sounds in English:

   t   r   s   k   w   č   i   æ   f   n

B. Use these symbols plus the regular alphabet symbols for the other sounds to write the following words in your "new orthography."

    a. character

    b. guest

    c. cough

    d. photo

    e. cheat

    f. rang

    g. psychotic

    h. tree

4. Suppose the English writing system were a *syllabic* system instead of an *alphabetic* system. Use capital letters to symbolize the necessary syllabic units for the following words, and list your "syllabary." *Example:* Given the words *mate, inmate, intake,* and *elfin,* you might use: A = mate, B = in, C = take, and D = elf. In addition, write the words using your syllabary. *Example: inmate* — BA; *elfin* — DB; *intake* — BC; *mate* — A. (Do not use more syllable symbols than you absolutely need.)

    a. childishness

    b. childlike

    c. Jesuit

    d. lifelessness

    e. likely

    f. zoo

    g. witness

    h. lethal

    i. jealous

    j. witless

    k. lesson

5. In the following pairs of English words the bold-faced portions are pronounced the same but spelled differently. Can you think of any reason why the spelling should remain distinct? (*Hint: Reel* and *real* are pronounced the same, but *reality* shows the presence of a phonemic /æ/ in *real.*)

A	B	Reason
a. I **am**	**iamb**	
b. g**oo**se	pr**o**duce	
c. fa**sh**ion	compli**c**ation	
d. New**ton**	org**an**	
e. **no**	**kn**ow	
f. hym**n**	hi**m**	

6. In the following pairs of words the bold-faced portions are spelled the same but pronounced differently. Try to state some reasons why the spelling of the words in column B should not be changed.

	A	B	Reason
a.	mingle	long	The *g* is pronounced in *longer*.
b.	line	children	
c.	sonar	resound	
d.	cent	mystic	
e.	crumble	bom**b**	
f.	cats	dogs	
g.	sta**gn**ant	desi**gn**	
h.	serene	obscenity	

7. Each of the following sentences is ambiguous in the written form. How can these sentences be made unambiguous when they are spoken?

   Example: John hugged Bill and then he kissed him.

   For the meaning "John hugged and kissed Bill," use normal stress (*kissed* receives stress). For the meaning "Bill kissed John," contrastive stress is needed on both *he* and *him*.

   a. What are we having for dinner, Mother?

   b. She's a German language teacher.

   c. They formed a student grievance committee.

   d. Charles kissed his wife and George kissed his wife too.

8. In the written form, the following sentences are not ambiguous, but they would be if spoken. State the devices used in writing that make the meanings explicit.

   a. They're my brothers' keepers.

   b. He said, "He will take the garbage out."

   c. The red book was read.

   d. The flower was on the table.

9. Match the ten samples of writing and the ten languages. There are enough hints in this chapter to get most of them. (The source of these examples, and many others, is *Languages of the World* by Kenneth Katzner, 1975, New York: Funk & Wagnalls.)

   a. _____ Cherokee

   b. _____ Chinese

   c. _____ German (Gothic style)

   d. _____ Greek

   e. _____ Hebrew

   f. _____ Icelandic

   g. _____ Japanese

   h. _____ Korean

   i. _____ Russian

   j. _____ Twi

   1. 仮に勝手に変えるようなことをすれば.

   2. Κι ὁ νοῦς του ἀγκάλιασε ποιητικὰ τὴν Κρήτη.

   3. «Что это? я падаю? у меня ноги подкашиваются»,

   4. וְהָיָה ׀ בְּאַחֲרִית הַיָּמִים נָכוֹן יִהְיֶה הַר

   5. Saá sáre yi bɛŋ atɛkyé bí â mpɔtorɔ áhyɛ

   6. 既然必须和新的群众的时代相结合.

   7. *ᎢᏯ ᎠᏣ ᏣᏍᏖᏓ ᏟᏫᎩ ᏉᎵᏆ.*

   8. Þótt þú langförull legðir sérhvert land undir fót,

   9. Pharao's Anblick war wunderbar.

   10. 스위스는 독특한 체계

10. The following appeared on the safety card of a Spanish airline. Identify each language. (You will probably have to spend some time in the library and/or visit various departments of foreign languages.)

1. **Para su seguridad**
2. **For your safety**
3. **Pour votre sécurité**
4. **Für ihre Sicherheit**
5. **Per la Vostra sicurezza**
6. **Para sua segurança**
7. **あなたの安全のために**
8. **Для Вашей безопасности**
9. **Dla bezpieczeństwa pasażerów**
10. **Za vašu sigurnost**
11. **Γιά τήν ἀσφάλειά σας**
12. **Kendi emniyetiniz için**
13. **من أجـل سـلامتك**

11. Diderot and D'Alembert, the French "Encyclopedists," wrote:

> The Chinese have no alphabet; their very language is incompatible with one, since it is made up of an extremely limited number of sounds. It would be impossible to convey the sound of Chinese through our alphabet or any other alphabet.

Comment on this.

12. Here are several emoticons. See if you can assign a meaning to each one. There is no one correct answer because they haven't been in the language long enough to become conventionalized. One possible set of answers is printed upside down in the footnote.[6]

   a. >:–(

   b. :–#

   c. 8:--(

   d. :D

   e. :-(o)

   f. :–(O)

   g. |–)

   h. :/)

---

[6] **a.** Annoyance. **b.** My lips are sealed. **c.** Condescension **d.** Ha, ha. **e.** Surprise. **f.** I'm yelling. **g.** See no evil. **h.** Not that funny.

13. Just as words may be synonyms (*sad, unhappy*), so may emoticons. Thus :–> and :–) are both used to mean "just kidding."

   A. If you are a user of electronic communication, try to think of three instances where different emoticons have approximately the same meaning.

   B. Emoticons may also be ambiguous, that is, subject to different interpretations. You may have discovered that in the previous exercise. Cite three instances where a single emoticon may be given two different interpretations.

14. Make up five or ten emoticons along with their meaning. Don't just look them up somewhere. Be creative! For example, **3:>8** to mean "bull!"

Glossary

AAE   Abbreviates **African American English.**[1] Cf. **Ebonics.**

abbreviation   Shortened form of a word, e.g., *prof* from *professor.* Cf. **clipping.**

accent   (1) Prominence. Cf. **stressed syllable;** (2) the phonology or pronunciation of a specific regional dialect, e.g., southern accent; (3) the pronunciation of a language by a nonnative speaker, e.g., French accent.

accidental gap   Phonological or morphological form that constitutes possible but nonoccurring lexical items, e.g., *blick, unsad.*

acoustic   Pertaining to physical aspects of sound.

acoustic phonetics   The study of the physical characteristics of speech sounds.

acoustic signal   The sound waves produced by any sound source, including speech.

acquired dyslexia   Loss of ability to read correctly following brain damage of persons who were previously literate.

acronym   Word composed of the initials of several words, e.g., *PET* scan from *positron-emission tomography* scan.

active sentence   A sentence in which the noun phrase subject in deep structure is also the noun phrase subject in surface structure, e.g., *The dog chased the car.* Cf. **passive sentence.**

adjective (Adj)   The syntactic category, also lexical category, of words that function as the head of an **adjective phrase**, and that have the semantic effect of qualifying or describing the referents of nouns, e.g., *tall, bright, intelligent.* Cf. **adjective phrase.**

adjective phrase (AP)   A syntactic category, also phrasal category whose head is an adjective possibly accompanied by modifiers, that occurs inside noun phrases and as complements of the verb *to be,* e.g., *worthy of praise, several miles high, green, more difficult.*

adverb (Adv)   The syntactic category, also lexical category, of words that qualify the verb such as manner adverbs like *quickly* and time adverbs like *soon.* The position of the adverb in the sentence depends on its semantic type, e.g., *John will soon eat lunch, John eats lunch quickly.*

affix   Bound morpheme attached to a stem or root. Cf. **prefix, suffix, infix, circumfix, stem, root.**

---

[1] Bold words in definitions have a separate entry in this glossary, regardless of whether the bold word or term is preceded by the expression *Cf.*

affricate   A sound produced by a stop closure followed immediately by a slow release characteristic of a fricative; phonetically a sequence of stop + fricative, e.g., the *ch* in *chip*, which is [č] and like [š] + [t].

African American English (AAE)   Dialects of English spoken by some Americans of African descent, or by any person raised from infancy in a place where AAE is spoken. Cf. **Ebonics.**

agent   The thematic role of the noun phrase whose referent does the action described by the verb, e.g., *George* in *George hugged Martha.*

agrammatism   Language disorder usually resulting from damage to Broca's region in which the patient has difficulty with certain aspects of syntax, especially functional categories. Cf. **Broca's area.**

agreement   The process by which one word in a sentence is altered depending on a property of another word in that sentence, such as gender or number, e.g., the addition of *s* to a regular verb when the subject is third-person singular (in English).

airstream mechanisms   The various processes in which air from the lungs or mouth is moved to produce speech sounds, e.g., **pulmonic egressive.** Cf., **egressive airstream mechanism, ingressive airstream mechanism.**

allomorph   Alternative phonetic form of a morpheme; e.g., the /-s/, /-z/, and /-əz/ forms of the plural morpheme in *cats, dogs,* and *kisses.*

allophone   A predictable phonetic realization of a phoneme, e.g., [p] and [pʰ] are allophones of the phoneme /p/ in English.

alphabetic writing   A writing system in which each symbol typically represents one sound segment.

alveolar ridge   The part of the hard palate directly behind the top front teeth.

alveolar   A sound produced by raising the tongue to the alveolar ridge, e.g., [s], [t], [n].

alveopalatal   A sound whose place of articulation is the hard palate immediately behind the alveolar ridge, e.g. [š] when it occurs before a front vowel.

ambiguous, ambiguity   The terms used to describe a word, phrase, or sentence with multiple meanings.

American Sign Language (ASL)   The sign language used by the deaf community in the United States. Cf. **sign languages.**

analogic change   A language change in which a rule spreads to previously unaffected forms, e.g., the plural of *cow* changed from the earlier *kine* to *cows* by the generalization of the plural formation rule or by analogy to regular plural forms. Also called **internal borrowing.**

analogy   The use of one form as an exemplar by which other forms can be similarly constructed, e.g., based on *bow/bows, sow/sows,* etc., English speakers began to say *cows* instead of the older *kine.* Analogy also leads speakers to say **brung* as a past tense of *bring* based on *sing/sang/sung, ring/rang/rung,* and so on.

analytic   Describes a sentence that is true by virtue of its meaning alone, irrespective of context, e.g., *Kings are male.* Cf. **contradictory.**

anomalous   Semantically ill-formed, e.g., *Colorless green ideas sleep furiously.*

anomaly   A violation of semantic rules resulting in expressions that seem nonsensical, e.g., *The verb crumpled the milk.*

anomia   A form of **aphasia** in which patients have word-finding difficulties.

antecedent   A noun phrase with which a pronoun is coreferential, e.g., *the man who is eating* is the antecedent of the pronoun *himself* in the sentence *The man who is eating bit himself.*

anterior   A phonetic feature of consonants whose place of articulation is in front of the palato-alveolar area, including **labials, interdentals,** and **alveolars.**

antonymic pair   Two words that are pronounced the same (i.e., are homonyms) but spelled differently and whose meanings are opposite, e.g., *raise* and *raze.* Cf. **autoantonym.**

antonyms   Words that are opposite with respect to one of their semantic properties, e.g., *tall/short* are both alike in that they describe height, but opposite in regard to the extent of the height. Cf. **gradable pair, complementary pair, relational opposites.**

aphasia   Language loss or disorders following brain damage.

arbitrary   Describes the property of language, including sign language, whereby there is no natural or intrinsic relationship between the way a word is pronounced (or signed) and its meaning.

arc   Part of the graphical depiction of a transition network represented as an arrow, often labeled, connecting two nodes. Cf. **node, transition network.**

argot   The specialized words used by a particular group, such as pilots or linguists, e.g., *morphophonemics* in linguistics.

article (Art)   One of several subclasses of determiners, e.g., *the, a.*

articulators   The tongue, lips, and velum, which change the shape of the vocal tract to produce different speech sounds.

articulatory phonetics   The study of how the vocal tract produces speech sounds; the physiological characteristics of speech sounds.

aspirated   Describes a voiceless stop produced with a puff of air that results when the vocal cords remain open for a brief period after the release of the stop, e.g., the [p^h] in *pit*. Cf. **unaspirated.**

assimilation rules/assimilation   A phonological process that changes feature values of segments to make them more similar, e.g., a vowel becomes [+nasal] when followed by [+ nasal] consonant. Also called **feature spreading rules.**

asterisk   The symbol [*] used to indicate ungrammatical or anomalous examples, e.g., *cried the baby, *sincerity dances.* Also used in historical and comparative linguistics to represent a reconstructed form.

audio-lingual method   The teaching of a second language through imitation, repetition, and reinforcement. It is more similar to the **grammar translation method** than to the **direct method.**

autoantonym   A word that has two opposite meanings, e.g., *cleave,* "to split apart" or "to cling together." Cf. **antonymic pair.**

auditory phonetics   The study of the perception of speech sounds.

automatic machine translation   The use of computers to translate from one language to another. Cf. **source language, target language.**

aux   A syntactic category containing auxiliary verbs and abstract tense morphemes. It is also called **INFL** and functions as the **head** of a **sentence.**

auxiliary verb   Verbal elements, traditionally called "helping verbs," that co-occur with, and qualify, the main verb in a verb phrase with regard to such properties as tense, e.g., *have, be, will.*

babbling   Sounds produced in the first few months after birth that gradually come to include only sounds that occur in the language of the household. Deaf children babble with hand gestures.

baby talk   A certain **style** of speech that many adults use when speaking to children that includes among other things exaggerated intonation. Cf. **motherese, child directed speech (CDS).**

back-formation   Creation of a new word by removing an affix from an old word, e.g., *donate* from *donation;* or by removing what is mistakenly considered an affix, e.g., *edit* from *editor.*

backtracking   The process of undoing an analysis — usually a top-down analysis — when sensory data indicates it has gone awry, and beginning again at a point where the analysis is consistent with the data, e.g., in the syntactic analysis of *The little orange car sped,* analyzing *orange* as a noun, and later reanalyzing it as an adjective. Cf. **top-down processing.**

bilabial   A sound articulated by bringing both lips together.

bilingual language acquisition   The (more or less) simultaneous acquisition of two or more languages before the age of three years such that each language is acquired with native competency.

birdcall   One or more short notes that convey messages associated with the immediate environment, such as danger, feeding, nesting, and flocking.

bird song   Complex pattern of notes used to mark territory and to attract mates.

blend   A word composed of the parts of more than one word, e.g., *smog* from *smoke* + *fog.*

bootstrapping   See **syntactic bootstrapping.**

borrowing   The incorporating of a loan word from one language into another, e.g., English borrowed *buoy* from Dutch. Cf. **loan word.**

bottom-to-top language death   The cessation of use of a language except in special circumstances, e.g., a liturgical language like Latin. Cf. **sudden language death, radical language death, gradual language death.**

bottom-up processing   Data-driven analysis of linguistic input that begins with the small units like phones and proceeds stepwise to increasingly larger units like words and phrases until the entire input is processed, often ending in a complete sentence and semantic interpretation. Cf. **top-down processing.**

bound pronoun   A pronoun (or more generally, a **pro-form**) whose antecedent is explicitly mentioned in the discourse. Cf. **unbound, free pronoun.**

bound morpheme   Morpheme that must be attached to other morphemes, e.g., *-ly, -ed, non-.* Bound morphemes are **prefixes, suffixes, infixes, circumfixes,** and some **roots** such as *cran* in *cranberry.* Cf. **free morpheme.**

broadening   A semantic change in which the meaning of a word changes over time to become more encompassing, e.g., *dog* once meant a particular breed of *dog.*

Broca, Paul   A French neurologist of the nineteenth century who identified a particular area of the left side of the brain as a language center.

Broca's aphasia   See **agrammatism.**

Broca's area   A front part of the left hemisphere of the brain, damage to which causes **agrammatism** or **Broca's aphasia.** Also called Broca's region.

calligraphy   The art of writing or drawing Chinese characters.

case   A characteristic of nouns and pronouns, and in some languages articles and adjectives, determined by the function in the sentence, and generally indicated by the morphological form of the word, e.g., *I* is in the nominative case of the first-person singular pronoun in English and functions as a subject; *me* is in the accusative case and functions as an object.

case endings   Suffixes on the noun based on its grammatical function, such as *'s* of the English genitive case indicating possession, e.g., Robert*'s* sheepdog.

case theory   The study of thematic roles and grammatical case in languages of the world.

cause/causative   The thematic role of the noun phrase whose referent is a natural force that is responsible for a change, e.g., *the wind* in *The wind damaged the roof.*

cerebral hemispheres   The left and right halves of the brain, joined by the **corpus callosum.**

characters (Chinese)   The units of Chinese writing, each of which represents a morpheme or word. Cf. **ideogram, ideograph, logogram.**

Chicano English (ChE)   A dialect of English spoken by some bilingual Mexican Americans in the western and southwestern United States.

child directed speech (CDS)   The special intonationally exaggerated speech that some adults sometimes use to speak with small children, sometimes called **baby talk.** Cf. **motherese.**

circumfix   Bound morpheme, parts of which occur in a word both before and after the root, e.g., *ge - - - t* in German *geliebt*, "loved," from the root *lieb.*

classifier   A grammatical morpheme that marks the semantic class of a noun, e.g., in Swahili, nouns that refer to human artifacts such as beds and chairs are prefixed with the classifiers *ki* if singular and *vi* if plural; *kiti*, "chair" and *viti*, "chairs."

click   A speech sound with an **ingressive airstream mechanism** that produces sounds by sucking air into the mouth and forcing it between articulators to produce a sharp sound, e.g., the sound often spelled *tsk.*

clipping   The deletion of some part of a longer word to give a shorter word with the same meaning, e.g., *phone* from *telephone.* Cf. **abbreviation.**

closed class   A category, generally a **functional category,** that rarely has new words added to it, e.g., prepositions, conjunctions. Cf. **open class.**

coarticulation   The transfer of phonetic features to adjoining segments to make them more alike, e.g., vowels become [+ nasal] when followed by consonants that are [+ nasal].

cocktail party effect   An informal term that describes the ability to filter out background noise and focus on a particular sound source or on a particular person's speech.

coda   One or more phonological segments that follow the **nucleus** of a syllable, e.g., the /st/ in /prist/ *priest.*

code-switching   The movement back and forth between two languages or dialects within the same sentence or discourse.

cognates   Words in related languages that developed from the same ancestral root, such as English *man* and German *Mann.*

coinage   The construction and/or invention of new words that then become part of the lexicon, e.g., *e-commerce.*

collocation analysis   Textual analysis that reveals the extent to which the presence of one word influences the occurrence of nearby words.

comparative linguistics   The branch of historical linguistics that explores language change by comparing related languages.

comparative method   The technique linguists use to deduce forms in an ancestral language by examining corresponding forms in several of its descendant languages.

comparative reconstruction   The deducing of forms in an ancestral language of genetically related languages by application of the **comparative method.**

competence, linguistic   The knowledge of a language represented by the mental grammar that accounts for speakers' linguistic ability and creativity. For the most part, linguistic competence is unconscious knowledge.

complement   The constituent(s) in a phrase other than the head that complete(s) the meaning of the phrase. In the verb phrase *found a puppy,* the noun phrase *a puppy* is a complement of the head verb *found.*

complementary distribution   The situation in which phones never occur in the same phonetic environment, e.g., [p] and [pʰ] in English. Cf. **allophones.**

complementary pair   Two **antonyms** related in such a way that the negation of one is the meaning of the other, e.g., *alive* means not *dead.* Cf. **gradable pair, relational opposites.**

complementizer (Comp)   A syntactic category, also functional category, of words, including *that, if, whether,* that introduce an embedded sentence, e.g., *his belief that sheepdogs can swim,* or, *I wonder if* sheepdogs can swim. The complementizer has the effect of turning a sentence into a complement.

compound   A word composed of two or more words, e.g., *washcloth, childproof cap.*

computational linguistics   A subfield of linguistics and computer science that is concerned with computer processing of human language.

computational morphology   The programming of computers to analyze the structure of words.

computational phonetics and phonology   The programming of computers to analyze the speech signal into phones and phonemes.

computational pragmatics   The programming of computers to take context and situation into account when determining the meaning of expressions.

computational semantics   The programming of computers to determine the meaning of words, phrases, sentences, and discourse.

computational syntax   The programming of computers to analyze the structure of sentences. Cf. **parse, bottom-up processing, top-down processing.**

concordance   An alphabetical index of the words in a text that gives the frequency of each word, its location in the text, and its surrounding context.

conditioned sound change   Historical phonological change that occurs in specific phonetic contexts, e.g., the voicing of /f/ to [v] when it occurs between vowels.

connectionism   Modeling grammars through the use of networks consisting of simple neuron-like units connected in complex ways so that different connections vary in strength, and can be strengthened or weakened through exposure to linguistic data. For example, in phonology there would be stronger connections among /p/, /t/, and /k (the voiceless stops and a natural class) than among /p/, /n/, and /i/. In morphology there would be stronger connections between *play/played,* and *dance/danced,* than between *play* and *danced.* Semantically, there would be stronger connections between *melody* and *music* than between *melody* and *sheepdog.* Syntactically there would be stronger connections between *John loves Mary* and *Mary is loved by John* than between *John loves Mary* and *Mary knows John.*

connotative meaning/connotation   The evocative or affective meaning associated with a word. Two words or expressions may have the same **denotative meaning** but different connotations, e.g., *president* and *commander-in-chief.*

consonant   A speech sound produced with some constriction of the airstream. Cf. **vowel.**

consonantal   Phonetic feature distinguishing the class of obstruents, liquids, and nasals, which are [+ consonantal], from other sounds (vowels and glides), which are [– consonantal].

consonantal alphabet   The symbols of a **consonantal writing** system.

consonantal writing   A writing system of symbols that represent only consonants; vowels are inferred from context , e.g., Arabic.

constituent   A syntactic unit in a **phrase structure tree**, e.g., *the girl* is a noun phrase constituent in the sentence *the boy loves the girl.*

constituent structure   The hierarchically arranged syntactic units such as noun phrase and verb phrase that underlie every sentence.

constituent structure tree   See **phrase structure tree.**

content words   The nouns, verbs, adjectives, and adverbs that constitute the major part of the vocabulary. Cf. **open class.**

context   The discourse preceding an utterance together with the real-world knowledge of speakers and listeners. Cf. **linguistic context, situational context.**

continuant   A speech sound in which the airstream flows continually through the mouth; all speech sounds except stops and affricates.

contour tones   Tones in which the pitch glides from one level to another, e.g., from low to high as in a rising tone.

contradiction   Negative entailment: the truth of one sentence necessarily implies the falseness of another sentence, e.g., *He opened the door* and *The door is closed.* Cf. **entailment.**

contradictory   Describes a sentence that is false by virtue of its meaning alone, irrespective of context, e.g., *Kings are female.* Cf. **analytic.**

contralateral   Refers to stimuli that travel between one side of the body (left/right) and the opposite **cerebral hemisphere** (right/left).

contrast   Different sounds contrast when their presence alone distinguishes between otherwise identical forms, e.g., [f] and [v] in *fine* and *vine,* but not [p] and [pʰ] in [spik] and [spʰik] (two variant ways of saying *speak*). Cf. **minimal pair.**

contrasting tones   In tone languages, different tones that make different words, e.g., in Nupe, *bá* with a high tone, and *bà* with a low tone mean "be sour" and "count," respectively.

contrastive stress   Additional stress placed on a word to highlight it or to clarify the referent of a pronoun, e.g., in *Joe hired Bill and he hired Sam,* with contrastive stress on *he,* it is usually understood that Bill rather than Joe hired Sam.

convention, conventional   The agreed-on, though generally arbitrary relationship between the form and meaning of words.

cooperative principle   A broad principle within whose scope fall the various **maxims of conversation.** It states that in order to communicate effectively, speakers should agree to be informative and relevant.

coordinate structure   A syntactic structure in which two or more constituents of the same syntactic category are joined by a conjunction such as *and* and *or*, e.g., *bread and butter, the big dog or the small cat, huffing and puffing.*

coordinate structure constraint   A constraint of Universal Grammar, and therefore applicable to all languages, that prohibits the movement of constituents out of a coordinate structure.

coreference   The relation between two noun phrases that refer to the same entity.

coreferential   Describes noun phrases (including pronouns) that refer to the same entity.

coronals   The class of sounds articulated by raising the tip or blade of the tongue, including **alveolars** and **palatals,** e.g., [t], [š].

corpus   A collection of language data gathered from spoken or written sources used for linguistic research and analysis.

corpus callosum   The nerve fibers connecting the right and left **cerebral hemispheres.**

cortex   The approximately ten billion neurons that form the outside surface of the brain; also referred to as gray matter.

count nouns   Nouns that can be enumerated, e.g., *one potato, two potatoes.* Cf. **mass nouns.**

cover symbol   A symbol that represents a class of sounds, e.g., C for consonants, V for vowels.

creativity of language, creative aspect of linguistic knowledge   Speakers' ability to combine the finite number of linguistic units of their language to produce and understand an infinite range of novel sentences.

creole   A language that begins as a **pidgin** and eventually becomes the first language of a speech community through its being learned by children.

critical age hypothesis   The theory that states that there is a window of time between early childhood and puberty for learning a first language, and beyond which first language acquisition is almost always incomplete.

critical period   The time between early childhood and puberty during which a child can acquire language easily, swiftly, and without external intervention. After this period, the acquisition of the grammar is difficult and, for some individuals, never fully achieved.

cuneiform   A form of writing in which the characters are produced using a wedge-shaped stylus.

data mining   Complex methods of retrieving and using information from immense and varied sources of data through the use of advanced statistical tools.

declension   A list of the inflections or cases of nouns, pronouns, adjectives, and determiners in categories such as grammatical relationship, number, and gender.

deep structure   Any phrase structure tree generated by the phrase structure rules of a transformational grammar. The basic syntactic structures of the grammar.

definite   Describes a noun phrase that refers to a unique object known to the speaker and listener.

deictic/deixis   Refers to words or expressions whose reference relies entirely on context and the orientation of the speaker in space and time, e.g., *I, yesterday, there, this cat.*

demonstrative articles, demonstratives   Words such as *this, that, those,* and *these* that function syntactically as articles but are semantically **deictic** because context is needed to determine the referent of the noun phrase in which they occur.

denotative meaning   The referential meaning of a word or expression.

dental   A place-of-articulation term for consonants articulated with the tongue against, or nearly against, the front teeth. Cf. **interdental.**

derivation   The steps in the application of rules to an underlying form that results in a surface representation, e.g., in deriving a syntactic surface structure from a deep structure, or in deriving a phonetic form from a phonemic form.

derivational morpheme   Morpheme added to a stem or root to form a new stem or word, possibly, but not necessarily, resulting in a change in syntactic category, e.g., *-er* added to a verb like *kick* to give the noun *kicker.*

derived structure   Any structure resulting from the application of transformational rules.

derived word   The form that results from the addition of a derivational morpheme, e.g., *firm + ly = firmly* is a derived word.

descriptive grammar   A linguist's description or model of the mental grammar, including the units, structures, and rules. An explicit statement of what speakers know about their language. Cf. **prescriptive grammar, teaching grammar.**

determiner (Det)   The syntactic category, also functional category, of words and expressions which when combined with a noun form a noun phrase. Includes the articles *the* and *a,* **demonstratives** such as *this* and *that,* quantifiers such as *each* and *every,* expressions such as *William's,* etc.

diacritics   Additional markings on written symbols to specify various phonetic properties such as **length, tone, stress, nasalization;** extra marks on a written character that change its usual value, e.g., the tilde [~] drawn over the letter *n* in Spanish represents a palatalized nasal rather than an alveolar nasal.

dialect   A variety of a language whose grammar differs in systematic ways from other varieties. Differences may be lexical, phonological, syntactic, and semantic. Cf. **regional dialect, social dialect, prestige dialect.**

dialect area   A geographic area defined by the predominant use of a particular language variety, or a particular characteristic of a language variety, e.g., an area where *bucket* is used rather than *pail.* Cf. **dialect, dialect atlas, isogloss.**

dialect atlas   A book of **dialect maps** showing the areas where specific dialectal characteristics occur in the speech of the region.

dialect leveling   Movement toward greater uniformity or decrease in variations among dialects.

dialect map   A map showing the areas where specific dialectal characteristics occur in the speech of the region.

dichotic listening   Experimental methods for brain research in which subjects hear different auditory signals in the left and right ears.

digraph   Two letters used to represent a single sound, e.g., *gh* represents [f] in *enough.*

diphthong   Vowel + glide, e.g., [*aj, aw, ɔj*] as in *bite, bout, boy.* Cf. **monophthong.**

direct method   The learning of a second language by "total immersion." The native language is never (or rarely) used in the classroom, and the students supposedly acquire the second language in a way similar to the way they acquired their first language. Cf. **grammar translation, audio-lingual method.**

direct object   The grammatical relation of a noun phrase when it appears immediately below the verb phrase (VP) and next to the verb in deep structure; the noun phrase complement of a transitive verb, e.g., *the puppy* in *the boy found the puppy.*

discontinuous dependency   The relationship of two words separated in surface structure that are linked, or dependent on each other, in deep structure, e.g., the verb *pull* and the verbal particle *over* in *the police pulled the speeder over* (from the deep structure *the police pulled over the speeder).*

discontinuous morpheme   A morpheme with multiple parts that occur in more than one place in a word or sentence, e.g., *ge* and *t* in German *geliebt,* "loved." Cf. **circumfix.**

discourse   A linguistic unit that comprises more than one sentence.

discourse analysis   The study of discourse.

discreteness   A fundamental property of human language in which larger linguistic units are perceived to be composed of smaller linguistic units, e.g., *cat* is perceived as the phonemes /k/, /æ/, /t/; *the cat* is perceived as *the* and *cat.*

dissimilation rules   Phonological rules that change feature values of segments to make them less similar, e.g., a fricative dissimilation rule: /θ/ is pronounced [t] following another fricative. In English dialects with this rule, *sixth* /sɪks + θ/ is pronounced [sɪkst].

distinctive   Describes linguistic elements that contrast, e.g., [f] and [v] are distinctive segments; voice is a distinctive phonetic feature of consonants.

distinctive features   Phonetic properties of phonemes that account for their ability to contrast meanings of words, e.g., *voice, tense.*

ditransitive verb   A verb that appears to take two noun-phrase objects, e.g., *give* in *he gave Sally his cat.* Ditransitive verb phrases often have an alternative form with a prepositional phrase in place of the first noun phrase, as in *he gave his cat to Sally.*

dominate   In a **phrase structure tree,** when a continuous downward path can be traced from a node labeled A to a node labeled B, then A dominates B.

downdrift   The gradual lowering of the absolute pitch of tones during an utterance in a tone language. During downdrift, tones retain their *relative* values to one another.

Early Middle English Vowel Shortening   A sound change that shortened vowels such as the first *i* in *criminal.* As a result *criminal* was unaffected by the **Great Vowel Shift,** leading to word pairs such as *crime/criminal.*

ease of articulation   The tendency of speakers to adjust their pronunciation to make it easier, or more efficient, to move the articulators. Phonetic and phonological rules are often the result of ease of articulation, e.g., the rule of English that nasalizes vowels when they precede a nasal consonant.

Ebonics   An alternative term, first used in 1997, for the various dialects of **African American English.**

egressive airstream mechanism   The articulation of speech sounds in which air is pushed out of the mouth.

egressive sound   Sound produced with an **egressive airstream mechanism,** including all of the speech sounds of English.

ejective   A speech sound produced when air in the mouth is pressurized by an upward movement of the closed glottis, and then released suddenly.

embedded sentence   A sentence that occurs within a sentence in a phrase structure tree, e.g., *You know that **sheepdogs cannot read.***

emoticon   A string of text characters which, when viewed sideways, forms a face expressing a particular emotion, e.g., [8<\ to express "dismay." Frequently used in e-mail.

entailment   The relationship between two sentences where the truth of one infers the truth of the other, e.g., *Corday assassinated Marat* and *Marat is dead;* if the first is true, the second must be true.

entails   One sentence entails another if the truth of the first necessarily implies the truth of the second, e.g., *The sun melted the ice* entails *The ice melted* since if the first is true, the second must be true.

epenthesis   The insertion of one or more phones in a word, e.g., the insertion of [ə] in *children* to produce [čɪlədrən] instead of [čɪldrən].

eponym   A word taken from a proper name, such as *Hertz* for "unit of frequency."

etymology   The history of words; the study of the history of words.

euphemism   A word or phrase that replaces a taboo word or is used to avoid reference to certain acts or subjects, e.g., *powder room* for *toilet.*

event-related brain potentials (ERP)   The electrical signals emitted from different areas of the brain in response to different kinds of stimuli.

event/eventive   A type of sentence that describes activities such as *John kissed Mary,* as opposed to describing states such as *John knows Mary.* Cf. **state/stative.**

experiencer   The thematic role of the noun phrase whose referent perceives something, e.g., *Helen* in *Helen heard Robert playing the piano.*

extension   The referential part of the meaning of an expression; the referent of a noun phrase. Cf. **reference, referent.**

feature matrix   A representation of phonological segments in which the columns represent segments and the rows represent features, each cell being marked with a + or – to designate the value of the feature for that segment.

feature-changing rules   Phonological rules that change feature values of segments, either to make them more similar (Cf. **assimilation rules**), or less similar (Cf. **dissimilation rules**).

feature-spreading rules   Cf. assimilation rules.

finger spelling   In signing, hand gestures that represent letters of the alphabet used to spell words for which there is no sign.

flap   Sound in which the tongue quickly touches the alveolar ridge and withdraws. It is often an allophone of /t/ and /d/ in words such as *latter* and *ladder.* Also called **tap.**

folk etymology   The process whereby the history of a word is derived from nonscientific speculation or false analogy with another word, e.g., *hooker* for "prostitute" is falsely believed to be derived from the name of the U.S. Civil War general Joseph Hooker.

fossilization   A characteristic of second language learning in which the learner reaches a plateau and seems unable to acquire some property of the L2 grammar.

form   Phonological or gestural representation of a morpheme or word.

formant   In the frequency analysis of speech, a band of frequencies of higher intensity than surrounding frequencies, which appears as a dark line on a **spectrogram.** Individual vowels display different formant patterns.

free pronoun   A pronoun that refers to some object not explicitly mentioned in the sentence, e.g., *it* in *Everyone saw it.* Also called **unbound.** Cf. **bound.**

free morpheme   A single morpheme that constitutes a word.

free variation   Alternative pronunciations of a word in which one sound is substituted for another without changing the word's meaning, e.g., pronunciation of *bottle* as [batəl] or [baʔəl].

fricative   Consonant sound produced with so narrow a constriction in the vocal tract as to create sound through friction.

front vowels   Vowel sounds in which the tongue is positioned forward in the mouth, e.g., /i, æ/

function word   A word that does not have clear lexical meaning but has a grammatical function; function words include **conjunctions, prepositions, articles, auxiliaries, complementizers,** and **pronouns.** Cf. **closed class.**

functional category   One of the categories of function words, including **determiner, aux, complementizer,** and **preposition.** These categories are not lexical or phrasal categories. Cf. **lexical categories, phrasal categories.**

fundamental difference hypothesis   Second language acquisition (L2) differs fundamentally from first language acquisition (L1).

fundamental frequency   In speech, the rate at which the vocal cords vibrate, symbolized as F_0, called F-zero, perceived by the listener as **pitch.**

gapping   The syntactic process of deletion in which subsequent occurrences of a verb are omitted in similar contexts, e.g., *Bill washed the grapes and Mary, the cherries.*

geminate   A sequence of two identical sounds; a long vowel or long consonant denoted either by writing the phonetic symbol twice as in [biiru], [sakki] or by use of a colon [bi:ru], [sak:i].

generic term   A word that applies to a whole class, such as *dog* in *the dog is found throughout the world.* A word that ordinarily has the semantic feature [+ male] when used to refer to both sexes, e.g., *mankind* meaning "the human race"; the masculine pronoun when used as a neutral form, as in *Everyone should do **his** duty.*

genetically related   Describes two or more languages that developed from a common, earlier language, e.g., French, Italian, and Spanish, which all developed from Latin.

glide   A sound produced with little or no obstruction of the airstream that is always preceded or followed by a vowel, e.g., /w/ in *we*, /j/in *you.*

gloss   A word in one language given to express the meaning of a word in another language, e.g., "house" is the English gloss for the French word *maison.*

glottal/glottal stop   Sound produced with constriction at the glottis; when the air is stopped completely at the glottis by tightly closed vocal cords, a glottal stop is produced.

glottis   The opening between the vocal cords.

goal   The thematic role of the noun phrase toward whose referent the action of the verb is directed, e.g., *the theater* in *The kids went to the theater.*

gradable pair   Two antonyms related in such a way that more of one is less of the other, e.g., *warm* and *cool;* more warm is less cool, and vice versa. Cf. **complementary pair, relational opposites.**

gradual language death   The disappearance of a language over a period of several generations, each of which has fewer speakers of the language until finally no speakers remain. Cf. **sudden language death, radical language death, bottom-to-top language death.**

grammar   The mental representation of a speaker's linguistic competence; what a speaker knows about a language, including its phonology, morphology, syntax, semantics, and lexicon. A linguistic description of a speaker's mental grammar.

grammar translation   A method of second language learning in which the student memorizes words and syntactic rules and translates them between the native language and target language. Cf. **direct method, audio-lingual method.**

grammatical, grammaticality   Describes a well-formed sequence of words, one conforming to rules of syntax.

grammatical case   See **case.**

grammatical categories   Traditionally called "parts of speech"; also called **syntactic categories;** expressions of the same grammatical category can generally substitute for one another without loss of grammaticality, e.g., **noun phrase, verb phrase.**

grammatical morpheme   Function word or bound morpheme required by the syntactic rules, e.g., *to* and *s* in *he wants **to** go.* Cf. **inflectional morpheme.**

grammatical relation   Any of several structural positions that a noun phrase may assume in a sentence. Cf. **subject, direct object.**

graphemes   The symbols of an alphabetic writing system; the letters of an alphabet.

Great Vowel Shift   A sound change that took place in English sometime between 1400 and 1600 C.E. in which seven long vowel phonemes were changed.

Grimm's Law   The description of a phonological change in the sound system of an early ancestor of the Germanic languages formulated by Jakob Grimm.

Hangul   An alphabet based on the phonemic principle for writing the Korean language designed in the fifteenth century.

head (of a compound)   The rightmost word, e.g., *house* in *doghouse.* It generally indicates the category and general meaning of the compound.

head (of a phrase)   The central word of a phrase whose lexical category defines the type of phrase, e.g., the noun *man* is the head of the noun phrase *the man who came to dinner;* the verb *wrote* is the head of the verb phrase *wrote a letter to his mother;* the adjective *red* is the head of the adjective phrase *very bright red.*

hemiplegic   An individual (child or adult) with acquired unilateral lesions of the brain who retains both hemispheres (one normal and one diseased).

heteronyms   Different words spelled the same (i.e., **homographs**) but pronounced differently, e.g. *bass,* meaning either "low tone" [bes] or "a kind of fish" [bæs].

hierarchical structure   The groupings and subgroupings of the parts of a sentence into syntactic categories, e.g., *the bird sang* [[[the] [bird]] [sang]]; the groupings and subgroupings of morphemes in a word, e.g., *unlockable* [[un] [[lock][able]]]. Hierarchical structure is generally depicted in a **tree diagram.**

hieroglyphics   A pictographic writing system used by the Egyptians around 4000 B.C.E.

hiragana   A Japanese syllabary used to write native words of the language, most often together with ideographic characters. Cf. **kanji.**

historical and comparative linguistics   The branch of linguistics that deals with how languages change, what kinds of changes occur, and why they occur.

historical linguistics   See **historical and comparative linguistics.**

holophrastic   The stage of child language acquisition in which one word conveys a complex message similar to that of a phrase or sentence.

homographs   Words spelled identically, and possibly pronounced the same, e.g., *bear* meaning "to tolerate," and *bear* the animal; or *lead* the metal and *lead,* what leaders do.

homonyms/homophones   Words pronounced, and possibly spelled, the same, e.g., *to, too, two;* or *bat* the animal, *bat* the stick, and *bat* meaning "to flutter" as in "bat the eyelashes."

homorganic consonants   Two sounds produced at the same place of articulation, e.g., [m] and [p]; [t], [d], [n]. Cf. **assimilation rules.**

homorganic nasal rule   A phonological assimilation rule that changes the place of articulation feature of a nasal consonant to agree with that of a following consonant, e.g., /n/ becomes [m] when preceding /p/ as in *impossible.*

hyponyms   Words whose meanings are specific instances of a more general word, e.g., *red, white,* and *blue* are hyponyms of the word *color; triangle* is a hyponym of *polygon.*

iconic, iconicity   A nonarbitrary relationship between form and meaning in which the form bears a resemblance to its meaning, e.g., the male and female symbols on (some) toilet doors.

ideogram, ideograph   A character of a word-writing system, often highly stylized, that represents a concept, or the pronunciation of the word representing that concept.

idiolect   An individual's way of speaking, reflecting that person's grammar.

idiom/idiomatic phrase   An expression whose meaning does not conform to the **principle of compositionality,** that is, may be unrelated to the meaning of its parts, e.g., *kick the bucket* meaning "to die."

ill-formed   Describes an ungrammatical or anomalous sequence of words.

illocutionary force   The effect of a speech act, such as a warning, a promise, a threat, and a bet, e.g., the illocutionary force of *I resign!* is the act of resignation.

imitation   A proposed mechanism of child language acquisition according to which children learn their language by imitating adult speech.

immediately dominate   If a node labeled A is directly above a node labeled B in a phrase structure tree, then A immediately dominates B.

implication   Some linguists describe presupposition in terms of implication. Thus *John wants more coffee* carries the implication or **entails** that John has already had some coffee. Cf. **entailment, presupposition.**

implosive   Sounds produced with an **ingressive airstream** that involves movement of the glottis.

impoverished data   Refers to the incomplete, noisy, and unstructured utterances that children hear, including slips of the tongue, false starts, and ungrammatical and incomplete sentences, together with a lack of concrete evidence about abstract grammatical rules and structure. Also referred to as **poverty of the stimulus.**

Indo-European   The descriptive name given to the ancestor language of many modern language families, including Germanic, Slavic, and Romance. Also called **Proto-Indo-European.**

infinitive   An uninflected form of a verb, e.g., (to) *swim.*

infinitive sentence   An embedded sentence that does not have a tense and therefore is a "to" form, e.g. *sheepdogs to be fast readers* in the sentence *He believes sheepdogs to be fast readers.*

infix   A bound morpheme that is inserted in the middle of another morpheme.

INFL   Abbreviates "inflection," a term sometimes used in place of **Aux; the head of a sentence.**

inflectional morpheme   Bound grammatical morpheme that is affixed to a word according to rules of syntax, e.g. third-person singular verbal suffix -s.

information retrieval   The process of using a computer to search a database for items on a particular topic. Cf. **data mining.**

ingressive airstream mechanism   Method of producing speech sounds in which air is sucked into the vocal tract through the mouth.

innateness hypothesis   The theory that the human species is genetically equipped with a **Universal Grammar,** which provides the basic design for all human languages.

instrument   The thematic role of the noun phrase whose referent is the means by which an action is performed, e.g., *a paper clip* in *Houdini picked the lock with a paper clip.*

intension   The inherent, nonreferential part of the meaning of an expression, also called **sense.** Cf. **sense, extension.**

intensity   The magnitude of an acoustic signal, which is perceived as loudness.

interdental   A sound produced by inserting the tip of the tongue between the upper and lower teeth, e.g., the initial sounds of *thought* and *those.*

interlanguage grammars   The intermediate grammars that second language learners create on their way to acquiring the (more or less) complete grammar of the target language.

internal borrowing   Cf. **analogic change.**

International Phonetic Alphabet (IPA)   The phonetic alphabet designed by the International Phonetic Association to be used to represent the sounds found in all human languages.

International Phonetic Association (IPA)   The organization founded in 1888 to further phonetic research and develop the International Phonetic Alphabet.

intonation   Pitch contour of a phrase or sentence.

intransitive verb   A verb that must not have a direct object complement, e.g., *sleep.*

IP   Inflection Phrase. A term sometimes used in place of *Sentence.* A phrasal category whose head is **INFL.**

ipsilateral   Refers to stimuli that travel between one side of the body (left/right) and the same **cerebral hemisphere** (left/right). Cf. **contralateral.**

isogloss   A geographic boundary that separates areas with dialect differences, e.g., a line on a map on one side of which most people say *faucet* and on the other side of which most people say *spigot.*

jargon   Special words peculiar to the members of a profession or group, e.g., *airstream mechanism* for phoneticians. Cf. **argot.**

jargon aphasia   Form of aphasia in which phonemes are substituted, resulting in nonsense words; often produced by people who have **Wernicke's aphasia.**

kana   The characters of either of the two Japanese syllabaries, katakana and hiragana.

kanji   The Japanese term for the Chinese characters used in Japanese writing.

katakana   A Japanese syllabary generally used for writing loan words and to achieve the effect of italics.

L2 acquisition.   See **second language acquisition.**

labial   A sound articulated at the lips, e.g., [b], [f].

labiodental   A sound produced by touching the bottom lip to the upper teeth, e.g., [v].

labio-velar   A sound articulated by simultaneously raising the back of the tongue toward the velum and rounding the lips. The *w* of English is a labio-velar glide.

larynx   The structure of muscles and cartilage in the throat that contains the vocal cords and **glottis;** often called the "voice box."

late closure principle   A psycholinguistic principle of language comprehension that states: Attach incoming material to the phrase that was most recently processed, e.g., *he said that he slept yesterday* associates *yesterday* with *he slept* rather than with *he said*.

lateralization, lateralized   Term used to refer to cognitive functions localized to one or the other side of the brain.

lateral   A sound produced with air flowing past one or both sides of the tongue, e.g., [l].

lax vowel   Short vowel produced with little tension in the vocal cords, e.g., [ʊ] in *put,* [pʊt]. Cf. **tense/lax vowel.**

length   A prosodic feature referring to the duration of a segment. Two sounds may contrast in length, e.g., in Japanese the first vowel is [+ long} in /biiru/ "beer" but [– long], therefore short, in /biru/ "building."

level tones   Relatively stable (nongliding) pitch on syllables of tone languages. Also called **register tones.**

lexical access   The process of searching the mental lexicon for a phonological string to determine if it is an actual word.

lexical ambiguity   Multiple meanings of sentences due to words that have multiple meanings, e.g., *He was lying on a stack of Bibles.*

lexical category   A general term for the word-level syntactic categories of noun, verb, adjective, and adverb. These are the categories of content words like *man, run, large,* and *rapidly,* as opposed to functional category words such as *the* and *and.* Cf. **functional categories, phrasal categories, open class.**

lexical decision   Task of subjects in psycholinguistic experiments who on presentation of a spoken or printed stimulus must decide whether it is a word or not.

lexical gap   Possible but nonoccurring words; forms that obey the **phonotactic rules** of a language yet have no meaning, e.g., *blick* in English.

lexical paraphrases   Sentences that have the same meaning due to synonyms, e.g., *She lost her purse* and *She lost her handbag.*

lexical semantics   The subfield of semantics concerned with the meanings of words and the meaning relationships among words.

lexicographer   One who edits or works on a dictionary.

lexicography   The editing or making of a dictionary.

lexicon   The component of the grammar containing speakers' knowledge about morphemes and words; a speaker's mental dictionary.

lingua franca   A language common to speakers of diverse languages that can be used for communication and commerce, e.g., English is the lingua franca of international airline pilots.

linguistic context   The discourse that precedes a phrase or sentence that helps clarify meaning.

linguistic sign   Sounds or gestures, typically morphemes in spoken languages and signs in sign languages, that have a form bound to a meaning in a single unit, e.g., *dog* is a linguistic sign whose form is its pronunciation [dag] and whose meaning is *Canis familiaris* (or however we define "dog").

linguistic theory   A theory of the principles that characterize all human languages; the "laws of human language"; **Universal Grammar.**

liquids   A class of consonants including /l/ and /r/ and their variants that share vowel-like acoustic properties and may function as syllabic nuclei.

loan translations   Compound words or expressions whose parts are translated literally into the borrowing language, e.g. *marriage of convenience* from French *mariage de convenance.*

loan word   Word in one language whose origins are in another language, e.g., in Japanese *besiboru,* "baseball," is a loan word from English. Cf. **borrowing.**

localization   The hypothesis that different areas of the brain are responsible for distinct cognitive systems. Cf. **lateralization.**

location   The thematic role of the noun phrase whose referent is the place where the action of the verb occurs, e.g., *Oslo* in *It snows in Oslo.*

logograms   The symbols of a **word-writing** or **logographic writing** system.

logographic writing   See **word writing.**

machine translation   See **automatic machine translation.**

magnetic resonance imaging (MRI)   A technique to investigate the molecular structures in human organs including the brain, which may be used to identify sites of brain lesions.

main verb   The verb that functions as the head in the verb phrase, e.g., *save* in *Dagny will always save money for travel.* Cf. **head of a phrase.**

manner of articulation   The way the airstream is obstructed as it travels through the vocal tract. Stop, nasal, affricate, and fricative are some manners of articulation. Cf. **place of articulation.**

marked   In a gradable pair of antonyms, the word that is not used in questions of degree, e.g., *low* is the marked member of the pair *high/low* because we ordinarily ask *How high is the mountain?* not **How low is the mountain?*; in a masculine/feminine pair, the word that contains a derivational morpheme, usually the feminine word, e.g. *princess* is marked, whereas *prince* is unmarked. Cf. **unmarked.**

mass nouns   Nouns that cannot ordinarily be enumerated, e.g., *milk, water; *two milks* is ungrammatical except when interpreted to mean "two kinds of milk," "two containers of milk," and so on. Cf. **count nouns.**

maxim of manner   A conversational convention that a speaker's discourse should be brief and orderly, and should avoid ambiguity and obscurity.

maxim of quality   A conversational convention that a speaker should not lie or make unsupported claims.

maxim of quantity   A conversational convention that a speaker's contribution to the discourse should be as informative as is required, neither more nor less.

maxim of relevance   A conversational convention that a speaker's contribution to a discourse should always have a bearing on, and a connection with, the matter under discussion.

maxims of conversation   Conversational conventions such as the **maxim of quantity** that people appear to obey to give coherence to discourse.

mean length of utterances (MLU)   The average number of words or morphemes in a child's utterance. It is a more accurate measure of the acquisition stage of language than chronological age.

meaning   The conceptual or semantic aspect of a sign or utterance that permits us to comprehend the message being conveyed. Expressions in language generally have both form — pronunciation or gesture — and meaning. Cf. **extension, intension, sense, reference.**

mental grammar   The internalized grammar that a descriptive grammar attempts to model; Cf. **linguistic competence.**

metalinguistic awareness   A speaker's conscious awareness *about* language and the use of language, as opposed to linguistic *knowledge,* which is largely unconscious. This book is very much about metalinguistic awareness.

metaphor   Nonliteral, suggestive meaning in which an expression that designates one thing is used implicitly to mean something else, e.g., *The night has a thousand eyes,* to mean "One may be unknowingly observed at night."

metathesis   The phonological process that reorders segments, often by transposing two sequential sounds, e.g., the pronunciation of *ask* /æsk/ in some English dialects as [æks].

metonym, metonymy   A word substituted for another word or expression with which it is closely associated, e.g., *gridiron* to refer to the game of American football.

mimetic   Similar to imitating, acting out, or miming.

minimal attachment principle   The principle that in comprehending language, listeners create the simplest structure consistent with the grammar, e.g., *the horse raced past the barn* is interpreted as a complete sentence rather than a noun phrase containing a relative clause, as if it were *the horse* (that was) *raced past the barn.*

minimal pair (or set)   Two (or more) words that are identical except for one phoneme that occurs in the same position in each word, e.g., *pain* /pen/, *bane* /ben/, *main* /men/.

modal   An auxiliary verb other than *be, have,* and *do,* such as *can, could, will, would,* and *must.*

modularity   The organization of the brain and mind into distinct, independent, and autonomous parts that interact with each other.

monogenetic theory of language origin   The belief that all languages originated from a single language. Cf. **Nostratic.**

monomorphemic word   A word that consists of one morpheme.

monophthong   Simple vowel, e.g., *ɛ* in *bɛd.* Cf. **diphthong.**

monosyllabic   Having one syllable, e.g., *boy, through.*

morpheme   Smallest unit of linguistic meaning or function, e.g., *sheepdogs* contains three morphemes, *sheep, dog,* and the function morpheme for plural, *s.*

morphological parser   A process, often a computer program, that uses rules of word formation to decompose words into their component morphemes.

morphological rules   Rules for combining morphemes to form stems and words.

morphology   The study of the structure of words; the component of the grammar that includes the rules of word formation.

morphophonemic orthography   A writing system, such as that for English, in which morphological knowledge is needed to read correctly, e.g., in *please/pleasant* the *ea* represents [i]/[ɛ].

morphophonemic rules   Rules that specify the pronunciation of morphemes; a morpheme may have more than one pronunciation determined by such rules, e.g., the plural morpheme in English is regularly pronounced /s/, /z/, or /əz/.

motherese   See **child directed speech (CDS).**

naming task   An experimental technique that measures the response time between seeing a printed word and saying that word aloud.

narrowing   A semantic change in which the meaning of a word changes in time to become less encompassing, e.g., *deer* once meant "animal."

nasal (nasalized) sound   Speech sound produced with an open nasal passage (lowered velum) permitting air to pass through the nose as well as the mouth, e.g., /m/ Cf. **oral sound.**

nasal cavity   The passageways between the throat and the nose through which air passes during speech if the velum is open (lowered). Cf. **oral cavity.**

natural class   A class of sounds characterized by a phonetic property or feature that pertains to all members of the set, e.g., the class of stops. A natural class may be defined with a smaller feature set than that of any individual member of the class.

Neo-Grammarians   A group of nineteenth-century linguists who claimed that sound shifts (i.e., changes in phonological systems) took place without exceptions.

neurolinguistics   The branch of linguistics concerned with the brain mechanisms that underlie the acquisition and use of human language; the study of the neurobiology of language.

neutralization rules   Phonological rules that obliterate the contrast between two phonemes in certain environments, e.g., in some dialects of English /t/ and /d/ are both pronounced as voiced flaps between vowels as in *writer* and *rider,* thus neutralizing the voicing distinction so that the two words sound alike.

node   A labeled branch point in a phrase structure tree; part of the graphical depiction of a transition network represented as a circle, pairs of which are connected by arcs. Cf. **arc, phrase structure tree, transition network.**

noncontinuant   A sound in which air is blocked momentarily in the oral cavity as it passes through the vocal tract. Cf. **stops, affricates.**

nondistinctive features   Phonetic features of phones that are predictable by rule, e.g., aspiration in English.

nonphonemic features   Cf. **nondistinctive features.**

nonredundant   A phonetic feature that is distinctive, e.g., *stop, voice,* but not *aspiration* in English.

nonsense word   A permissible phonological form without meaning, e.g., *slithy.*

Nostratic   A hypothetical language that is postulated as the first human language.

noun (N)   The syntactic category, also lexical category, of words that can function as the head of a noun phrase, such as *book, Jean, sincerity.* In many languages nouns have grammatical alternations for number, case, and gender and occur with determiners.

noun phrase (NP)   The syntactic category, also phrasal category, of expressions containing some form of a noun or pronoun as its head, and which functions as the subject or as various objects in a sentence.

nucleus   That part of a syllable that has the greatest acoustic energy; the vowel portion of a syllable, e.g., /i/ in /mit/ *meet.*

obstruents   The class of sounds consisting of nonnasal stops, fricatives, and affricates. Cf. **sonorants.**

onomatopoeia/onomatopoeic   Words whose pronunciations suggest their meaning, e.g., *meow, buzz.*

onset   One or more phonemes that precede the syllable **nucleus,** e.g., /pr/ in /prist/ *priest.*

open class   The class of lexical content words; a category of words that commonly adds new words, e.g., nouns, verbs.

oral cavity   The mouth area through which air passes during the production of speech. Cf. **nasal cavity.**

oral sound   Nonnasal speech sound produced by raising the velum to close the nasal passage so that air can escape only through the mouth. Cf. **nasal sound.**

orthography   The written form of a language; spelling.

overgeneralization   Children's treatment of irregular verbs and nouns as if they were regular, e.g., *bringed, goed, foots, mouses,* for *brought, went, feet, mice.* This shows that the child has acquired the regular rules but has not yet learned that there are exceptions.

palatal   A sound produced by raising the front part of the tongue to the palate.

palate   The bony section of the roof of the mouth behind the **alveolar ridge.**

paradigm   A set of forms derived from a single root morpheme, e.g., *give, gives, given, gave, giving;* or *woman, women, woman's, women's.*

parallel processing   The ability of a computer to carry out several tasks simultaneously due to the presence of multiple central processors.

parameters   The small set of alternatives for a particular phenomenon made available by Universal Grammar. For example, Universal Grammar specifies that a phrase must have a head and possibly complements; a parameter states whether the complement(s) precedes or follows the head.

paraphrases   Sentences with the same truth conditions; sentences with the same meaning, except possibly for minor differences in emphasis, e.g., *He ran up a big bill* and *He ran a big bill up.*

parse   The act of determining the grammaticality of sequences of words according to rules of syntax, and assigning a linguistic structure to the grammatical ones.

parser   A computer program that determines the grammaticality of sequences of words according to whatever rules of syntax are stored in the computer's memory, and assigns a linguistic structure to the grammatical ones.

participle   The form of a verb that occurs after the auxiliary verbs *be* and *have,* e.g., *kissing* in *John is kissing Mary* is a present participle; *kissed* in *John has kissed many girls,* is a past participle; *kissed* in *Mary was kissed by John* is a passive participle.

passive sentence   A sentence in which the verbal complex contains a form of *to be* followed by a verb in its participle form, e.g., *The girl was kissed by the boy*; *The robbers must not have been seen.* In a passive sentence, the direct object of a transitive verb in deep structure functions as the subject in surface structure. Cf. **active sentence.**

performance, linguistic   The *use* of linguistic competence in the production and comprehension of language; behavior as distinguished from linguistic knowledge.

performative sentence   A sentence containing a performative verb used to accomplish some act. Performative sentences are affirmative and declarative, and are in first-person, present tense, e.g., *I now pronounce you husband and wife,* when spoken by a justice of the peace in the appropriate situation is an act of marrying.

performative verb   A verb, certain usages of which comprise a **speech act,** e.g., *resign* when the sentence *I resign!* is interpreted as an act of resignation.

person deixis   The use of terms to refer to persons whose reference relies entirely on context, e.g., pronouns such as *I, he, you* and expressions such as *this child.* Cf. **deictic, time deixis, place deixis, demonstrative articles.**

petroglyph   A drawing on rock made by prehistoric people.

pharynx   The tube or cavity in the vocal tract above the glottis through which the air passes during speech production.

phone   A phonetic realization of a **phoneme.**

phoneme   A contrastive phonological segment whose phonetic realizations are predictable by rule.

phonemic principle   The principle that underlies alphabetic writing systems in which one symbol typically represents one phoneme.

phonemic representation   The phonological representation of words and sentences prior to the application of phonological rules.

phonetic alphabet   Alphabetic symbols used to represent the phonetic segments of speech in which there is a one-to-one relationship between each symbol and each speech sound.

phonetic features   Phonetic properties of segments (e.g., voice, nasal, alveolar) that distinguish one segment from another.

phonetic representation   The representation of words and sentences after the application of phonological rules; symbolic transcription of the pronunciation of words and sentences.

phonetic similarity   Refers to sounds that share most phonetic features.

phonetics   The study of linguistic speech sounds, how they are produced (**articulatory phonetics),** how they are perceived (**auditory** or perceptual phonetics), and their physical aspects (**acoustic phonetics).**

phonographic symbol   A symbol in a writing system that stands for the sounds of a word.

phonological rules   Rules that apply to phonemic representations to derive phonetic representations or pronunciation.

phonology   The sound system of a language; the component of a grammar that includes the inventory of sounds (phonetic and phonemic units) and rules for their combination and pronunciation; the study of the sound systems of all languages.

phonotactics/phonotactic constraints Rules stating permissible strings of phonemes, e.g., a word-initial nasal consonant, may be followed only by a vowel (in English). Cf. **possible word, nonsense word, accidental gaps.**

phrasal category The class of syntactic categories that occur on the left side of phrase structure rules, and are therefore composed of other categories, including other phrasal categories, e.g., noun phrase. Cf. **lexical categories, functional categories.**

phrasal semantics See **sentential semantics.**

phrase structure rules Principles of grammar that specify the constituency of syntactic categories, e.g., NP → (Det) (AP) N (PP).

phrase structure tree A tree diagram with syntactic categories at each node that reveals both the linear and hierarchical structure of phrases and sentences.

phrenology A pseudoscience, the practice of which is determining personality traits and intellectual ability by examination of the bumps on the skull. Its contribution to neurolinguistics is that its methods were highly suggestive of the modular theory of brain structure.

pictogram A form of writing in which the symbols resemble the objects represented; a nonarbitrary form of writing.

pidgin A simple but rule-governed language developed for communication among speakers of mutually unintelligible languages, often based on one of those languages.

Pinyin An alphabetic writing system for Mandarin Chinese using a western-style alphabet to represent individual sounds.

pitch The **fundamental frequency** of sound perceived by the listener.

pitch contour Intonation of a sentence.

place deixis The use of terms to refer to places whose reference relies entirely on context, e.g., *here, there, behind, next door.* Cf. d**eictic, time deixis, person deixis, demonstrative articles.**

place of articulation The part of the vocal tract at which constriction occurs during the production of most consonants. Cf. **manner of articulation.**

plosives Oral, or nonnasal, stop consonants, so called because the air that is stopped explodes with the release of the closure.

polymorphemic word A word that consists of more than one morpheme.

polysemous/polysemy Describes a single word with several closely related but slightly different meanings, e.g., *face,* meaning "face of a person," "face of a clock," "face of a building."

positron-emission tomography (PET) Method to detect changes in brain activities and relate these changes to localized brain damage and cognitive tasks.

possessor The thematic role of the noun phrase to whose referent something belongs, e.g., *the dog* in *The dog's tail wagged furiously.*

possible word A string of sounds that obeys the **phonotactic constraints** of the language but has no meaning, e.g., *gimble.* Also called a **nonsense word.**

poverty of the stimulus See **impoverished data.**

pragmatics The study of how context and situation affect meaning.

predictable feature A nondistinctive, noncontrastive, redundant phonetic feature, e.g., aspiration in English voiceless stops, or nasalization in English vowels.

prefix An **affix** that is attached to the beginning of a morpheme or stem, e.g., *in-* in *inoperable.*

preposition (P) The syntactic category, also lexical category, that heads a prepositional phrase, e.g., *at, in, on, up.*

prepositional object The grammatical relation of the noun phrase that occurs immediately below a **prepositional phrase (PP)** in deep structure.

prepositional phrase (PP) The syntactic category, also phrasal category, consisting of a preposition and a noun phrase.

prescriptive grammar   Rules of grammar brought about by grammarians' attempts to legislate what speakers' grammatical rules should be, rather than what they are. Cf. **descriptive grammar, teaching grammar.**

prestige dialect   The dialect usually spoken by people in positions of power, and the one deemed correct by prescriptive grammarians, e.g., RP (*received pronunciation*) (British) English, the dialect spoken by the English royal family.

presupposition   Implicit assumptions about the world required to make an utterance meaningful or appropriate, e.g., "some tea has already been taken" is a presupposition of *Take some more tea!*

primes   The basic formal units of sign languages that correspond to phonological elements of spoken language.

priming   An experimental procedure that measures the response time from hearing to accessing a particular word as a function of whether the participant has heard a related word previously.

principle of compositionality   A principle of semantic interpretation that states that the meaning of a word, phrase, or sentence depends both on the meaning of its components (morphemes, words, phrases) and how they are combined structurally.

productive   Refers to morphological rules that can be used freely and apply to all forms to create new words, e.g., the addition to an adjective of *-ish* meaning "having somewhat of the quality," such as *newish, tallish, incredible-ish.*

pro-form   A word that replaces another word or expression found elsewhere in discourse, or understood from the situational context. Pronouns are the best known pro-forms, but words like *did* may function as "pro-verb phrases" as in *John washed three sheepdogs and Mary did too.*

proper name   Word that refers to a person, place, or other entity with a unique reference known to the speaker and listener. Usually capitalized in writing, e.g., Nina Hyams, New York, Atlantic Ocean.

prosodic feature   Duration (**length), pitch,** or loudness of speech sounds.

Proto-Germanic   The name given by linguists to the language that was an ancestor of English, German, and other Germanic languages.

Proto-Indo-European (PIE) See **Indo-European.**

protolanguage   The first identifiable language from which genetically related languages developed.

psycholinguistics   The branch of linguistics concerned with **linguistic performance,** language acquisition, and speech production and comprehension.

pulmonic egressive   Speech sounds produced by movement of air flowing out of the lungs through the vocal tract and out the mouth or nose. Cf. **ingressive airstream mechanism, ejective.**

radical language death   The disappearance of a language when all speakers of the language cease to speak the language. Cf. **sudden language death, gradual language death, bottom-to-top language death.**

rebus principle   In writing, the use of a **pictogram** for its phonetic value, e.g., using a picture of a bee to represent the verb *be* or the sound [b].

reduced vowel   A vowel that is unstressed and generally pronounced as schwa [ə] in English.

redundant   Describes a nondistinctive, nonphonemic feature that is predictable from other feature values of the segment, e.g., [+ voice] is redundant for any [+ nasal] phoneme in English since all nasals are voiced.

reduplication   A morphological process that repeats or copies all or part of a word to produce a new word, e.g., *wishy-washy, teensy-weensy, hurly-burly.*

reference   That part of the meaning of a noun phrase that associates it with some entity. That part of the meaning of a declarative sentence that associates it with a truth value, either true or false. Also called **extension.** Cf. **referent, sense.**

referent   The entity designated by an expression, e.g., the referent of *John* in *John knows Sue* is the actual person named John; the referent of *Raleigh is the capitol of California* is the truth value *false*. Also called **extension**.

reflexive pronoun   A pronoun ending with *-self* that generally requires a noun-phrase antecedent within the same S, e.g., *myself, herself, ourselves, itself*.

regional dialect   A dialect spoken in a specific geographic area that may arise from, and is reinforced by, that area's integrity. For example, a Boston dialect is maintained because large numbers of Bostonians and their descendants remain in the Boston area. Cf. **social dialect**.

register   A stylistic variant of a language appropriate to a particular social setting. Also called **style**.

register tones   Level tones; high, mid, or low tones.

regular sound correspondence   The occurrence of different sounds in the same position of the same word in different languages or dialects, with this parallel holding for a significant number of words, e.g., [aj] in non-Southern American English corresponds to [a:] in Southern American English. Also found between newer and older forms of the same language.

relational opposites   Pair of **antonyms** in which one describes a relationship between two objects and the other describes the same relationship when the two objects are reversed, e.g., *parent/child, teacher/pupil;* John is the parent of Susie describes the same relationship as Susie is the child of John. Cf. **gradable pair, complementary pair.**

retroflex sound   Sound produced by curling the tip of the tongue back behind the alveolar ridge, e.g., the pronunciation of /r/ by many speakers of English.

retronym   An expression that would once have been redundant, but which societal or technological changes have made nonredundant, e.g., *silent movie,* which was redundant before the advent of the "talkies."

rime   The **nucleus + coda** of a syllable, e.g., the /en/ of /ren/ *rain*.

root   The morpheme that remains when all affixes are stripped from a complex word, e.g., *system* from *un + system + atic + ally*.

rounded vowel   Vowel sound produced with pursed lips, e.g., [o].

rules of syntax   Principles of grammar that account for the grammaticality of sentences, their hierarchical structure, their word order, whether there is structural ambiguity, etc. Cf. **phrase structure rules, transformational rules.**

SAE   see **Standard American English.**

savant   Individual who shows special abilities in one cognitive area while being deficient in others. Linguistic savants have extraordinary language abilities but are deficient in general intelligence.

second language acquisition   The acquisition of another language or languages after first language acquisition is under way or completed. Also **L2 acquisition.**

segment   (1) An individual sound that occurs in a language; (2) the act of dividing utterances into sounds, morphemes, words, and phrases.

selection   A specification in the lexical entry of a word that determines the constituents required or permitted as complements when that word is the head of a phrase. For example, in a verb phrase, a transitive verb such as *find* requires a direct object complement, whereas a verb such as *eat* permits a direct object complement.

semantic features   A notational device for expressing the presence or absence of semantic properties by pluses and minuses, e.g., *baby* is [+ young], [+ human], [– abstract], etc.

semantic network   A network of **arcs** and **nodes** used to represent semantic information about sentences.

semantic properties   The components of meaning of a word, e.g., "young" is a semantic property of *baby, colt, puppy*.

semantics   The study of the linguistic meaning of morphemes, words, phrases, and sentences.

sense   The inherent part of an expression's meaning which, together with context, determines its referent. Also called **intension**. For example, knowing the sense or intension of a noun phrase such as *the president of the United States in 2002* allows one to determine that George W. Bush is the referent. Cf. **intension, reference.**

sentence (S)   A syntactic category of expressions consisting minimally of a **noun phrase (NP),** followed by an **auxiliary (Aux),** followed by a **verb phrase (VP)** in deep structure. Also called an **inflection phrase (IP),** whose head is **inflection (INFL).**

sentential semantics   The subfield of semantics concerned with the meaning of syntactic units larger than the word.

separate systems hypothesis   The bilingual child builds a distinct lexicon and grammar for each language being acquired.

shadowing task   An experiment in which subjects are asked to repeat what they hear as rapidly as possible as it is being spoken. During the task, subjects often unconsciously correct "errors" in the input.

sibilants   The class of sounds that includes affricates, and alveolar and palatal fricatives, characterized acoustically by an abundance of high frequencies perceived as "hissing," e.g., [s].

sign   A single gesture (possibly with complex meaning) in the sign languages used by the deaf.

sign languages   The languages used by deaf people in which linguistic units such as morphemes and words as well as grammatical relations are formed by manual and other body movements.

sisters   In a phrase structure tree, two categories that are directly under the same node, e.g., V and the direct object NP are sisters inside the verb phrase.

situational context   Knowledge of who is speaking, who is listening, what objects are being discussed, and general facts about the world we live in, used to aid in the interpretation of meaning.

slang   Words and phrases used in casual speech, often invented and spread by close-knit social or age groups, and fast-changing.

slip of the tongue   An involuntary deviation of an intended utterance. Cf. **spoonerism.** Also called **speech error.**

sluicing   The syntactic process in which material following a *wh* word is deleted when it is identical to previous material, e.g., *John is talking with* is deleted from the second clause in *John is talking with someone but nobody knows who _____.*

social dialect   A dialect spoken by a particular social class (e.g., Cockney English) that is perpetuated by the integrity of the social class. Cf. **regional dialect.**

sonorants   The class of sounds that includes vowels, glides, liquids, and nasals; nonobstruents. Cf. **obstruents.**

sound shift   Historical phonological change.

sound symbolism   The notion that certain sound combinations occur in semantically similar words, e.g., *gl* in *gleam, glisten, glitter,* which all relate to vision.

sound writing   A term sometimes used to mean a writing system in which one sound is represented by one letter. Sound-writing systems do not employ the phonemic principle and are similar to phonetic transcriptions.

source   The thematic role of the noun phrase whose referent is the place from which an action originates, e.g., *Mars* in *Mr. Wells just arrived from Mars.*

source language   In automatic machine translation, the language being translated. Cf. **target language, automatic machine translation.**

specific language impairment (SLI)   Difficulty in acquiring language faced by certain children with no other cognitive deficits.

spectrogram   A visual representation of speech decomposed into component frequencies, with time on the x axis, frequency on the y axis, and intensity portrayed on a gray scale — the darker, the more intense. Also called **voiceprint.**

speech act   The action or intent that a speaker accomplishes when using language in context, the meaning of which is inferred by hearers, e.g., *There is a bear behind you* may be intended as a warning in certain contexts, or may in other contexts merely be a statement of fact. Cf. **illocutionary force.**

speech error   An inadvertent deviation from an intended utterance that often results in ungrammaticality, nonsense words, anomaly, etc. Cf. **slip of the tongue, spoonerism.**

speech recognition   In computer processing, the ability to analyze speech sounds into phones, phonemes, morphemes and words.

speech synthesis   An electronic process that produces speech.

speech understanding   Computer processing for interpreting speech, one part of which is **speech recognition.**

spelling pronunciation   Pronouncing a word as it is spelled, irrespective of its actual pronunciation by native speakers, e.g., pronouncing *Wednesday* as "wed-ness-day."

split brain   The result of an operation for epilepsy in which the **corpus callosum** is severed, thus separating the brain into its two hemispheres; split-brain patients are studied to determine the role of each hemisphere in cognitive and language processing.

spoonerism   A speech error in which phonemic segments are reversed or exchanged, e.g., *you have hissed my mystery lecture* for the intended *you have missed my history lecture;* named after the Reverend William Archibald Spooner, a nineteenth-century Oxford University professor.

standard   The dialect (regional or social) considered to be the norm.

Standard American English (SAE)   An idealized dialect of English that some prescriptive grammarians consider the proper form of English.

states/statives   A type of sentence that describes states of being such as *Mary likes oysters,* as opposed to describing events such as *Mary ate oysters.* Cf. **events/eventives.**

stem   The base to which one or more affixes are attached to create a more complex form that may be another stem or a word. Cf. **root, affix.**

stops   [– Continuant] sounds in which the airflow is briefly but completely stopped in the oral cavity, e.g., /p, n, g/.

stress, stressed syllable   A syllable with relatively greater length, loudness, and/or higher pitch than other syllables in a word, and therefore perceived as prominent. Also called **accent.**

structural ambiguity   The phenomenon in which the same sequence of words has two or more meanings based on different phrase structure analyses, e.g., *He saw a boy with a telescope.*

structure dependent   (1) A principle of Universal Grammar that states that the application of **transformational rules** is determined by phrase structure properties, as opposed to structureless sequences of words or specific sentences; (2) the way children construct rules using their knowledge of syntactic structure irrespective of the specific words in the structure or their meaning.

style   Situation dialect, e.g., formal speech, casual speech; also called **register.**

subject   The grammatical relation of a noun phrase to a S(entence) when it appears immediately below that S in a phrase structure tree, e.g., *the zebra* in *The zebra has stripes.*

subject-verb agreement   The addition of an inflectional morpheme to the main verb depending on a property of the noun phrase subject, such as number or gender. In English, it is the addition of *s* to a verb when the subject is third-person singular present-tense, e.g., *A greyhound runs fast* versus *Greyhounds run fast.*

sudden language death   The disappearance of a language when all speakers of the language die or are killed in a short time period. Cf. **radical language death, gradual language death, bottom-to-top language death.**

suffix   An **affix** that is attached to the end of a morpheme or stem, e.g., *-er* in *Lew is taller than Bill.*

summarization   The computer scanning of a text and condensation to its most salient points.

suppletive forms   A term used to refer to inflected morphemes in which the regular rules do not apply, e.g., *went* as the past tense of *go*.

suprasegmentals   Prosodic features, e.g., length, tone.

surface structure   The structure that results from applying transformational rules to a deep structure. It is syntactically closest to actual utterances. Cf. **transformational rule.**

syllabary   The symbols of a syllabic writing system.

syllabic   A phonetic feature of those sounds that may constitute the nucleus of syllables; all vowels are syllabic, and liquids and nasals may be syllabic in such words as *towel, button, bottom.*

syllabic writing   A writing system in which each syllable in the language is represented by its own symbol, e.g., hiragana in Japanese.

syllable   A phonological unit composed of an **onset, nucleus,** and **coda**, e.g., *elevator* has four syllables: *el e va tor; man* has one syllable.

synonyms   Words with the same or nearly the same meaning, e.g., *pail* and *bucket.*

syntactic bootstrapping   Children's use of their knowledge of syntax to learn the meaning of words. Experiments have shown that knowing that a word is a verb or a noun informs them that it has a meaning referring to an action or to an object of some kind, respectively.

syntactic category/class   See **grammatical category.**

syntax   The rules of sentence formation; the component of the mental grammar that represents speakers' knowledge of the structure of phrases and sentences.

taboo   Words or activities that are considered inappropriate for "polite society," e.g., *cunt, prick, fuck* for "vagina, penis, sexual intercourse."

tap   Sound in which the tongue quickly touches the alveolar ridge, as in some British pronunciations of /r/. Also called **flap.**

target language   In automatic machine translation, the language into which the source language is translated. Cf. **source language, automatic machine translation.**

teaching grammar   A set of language rules written to help speakers learn a foreign language or a different dialect of their language. Cf. **descriptive grammar, prescriptive grammar.**

telegraphic speech   Utterances of children that may omit **grammatical morphemes** and/or **function words,** e.g., *He go out* instead of *He is going out.*

telegraphic stage   The period of child language acquisition that follows the two-word stage and consists primarily of **telegraphic speech.**

tense/lax   Features that divide vowels into two classes. Tense vowels are generally longer in duration and higher in tongue position and pitch than the corresponding lax vowels, e.g., in English [i, e, u, o] are tense vowels and carry the feature [+ tense], whereas the corresponding [ɪ, ɛ, ʊ, ɔ] are their lax counterparts and carry the feature [– tense]. Cf. **lax vowels.**

thematic role   The semantic relationship between the verb and the noun phrases of a sentence, such as **agent, theme, location, instrument, goal, source.**

theme   The thematic role of the noun phrase whose referent undergoes the action of the verb, e.g., *Martha* in *George hugged Martha.*

theta assignment   The process of assigning thematic roles to the subject and complements of a verb.

theta-criterion   A proposed universal principle stating that a particular thematic role (e.g., agent) may occur only once in a sentence.

time deixis   The use of terms to refer to time whose reference relies entirely on context, e.g., *now, then, tomorrow, next month.* Cf. **deictic, deixis, demonstrative articles, person deixis, place deixis.**

tip of the tongue; (TOT) phenomenon   The difficulty encountered from time to time in retrieving a particular word or expression from the mental lexicon. Anomic aphasics suffer from an extreme form of this problem. Cf. **anomia.**

tone   Contrastive pitch of syllables in **tone languages** in which two words may be identical except for such differences in pitch, e.g., in Thai [naa] with falling pitch means "face," but with a rising pitch means "thick." Cf. **register tones, contour tones.**

tone language   A language in which the tone or pitch on a syllable is phonemic, so that words with identical segments but different tones are different words, e.g., Mandarin Chinese, Thai. Cf. **tone.**

top-down processing   Expectation-driven analysis of linguistic input that begins with the assumption that a large syntactic unit such as a sentence is present, and then analyzes it into successively smaller constituents (phrases, words, morphemes, etc.), which are ultimately compared with the sensory or acoustic data to validate the analysis. If the analysis is not validated, the procedure backs up to the previously validated point and then resumes. Cf. **bottom-up processing, backtracking.**

topicalization   A transformation that moves a syntactic element to the front of a sentence, e.g., deriving *Dogs I love very much* from *I love dogs very much.*

transcription, phonemic   The phonemic representation of speech sounds using phonetic symbols, ignoring phonetic details that are predictable by rule, usually given between slashes, e.g., /pan/, /span/ for *pan, span* as opposed to the phonetic representation [pʰæn], [spæn]].

transcription, phonetic   The representation of speech sounds using phonetic symbols between square brackets. They may reflect nondistinctive predictable features such as aspiration and nasality, e.g., [pʰat] for *pot* and [mæn] for *man.*

transfer of grammatical rules   The application of rules from one's first language to a second language that one is attempting to acquire. The "accent" that second language learners have is a result of the transfer of first language phonetic and phonological rules.

transformational rule, transformation   A syntactic rule that applies to an underlying phrase structure tree of a sentence (either deep structure or an intermediate structure already affected by a transformation) and derives a new structure by moving or inserting elements, e.g., the transformational rules of *wh* movement and *do* insertion relate the deep structure sentence *John saw who* to the surface structure *Who did John see.*

transition network   A graphical representation that uses nodes connected by labeled arcs to depict syntactic and semantic relationships of grammar. Cf. **node, arc.**

transitive verb   A verb that selects an obligatory noun-phrase complement, e.g., *find.*

tree diagram   A graphical representation of the linear and hierarchical structure of a phrase or sentence. A **phrase structure tree.**

trill   Sound in which part of the tongue vibrates against some part of the roof of the mouth, e.g., the /r/ in Spanish *perro* is articulated by vibrating the tongue tip behind the alveolar ridge; the /r/ in French *rouge* is articulated by vibrations at the uvula.

truth condition   The circumstances that must be known to determine whether a sentence is true, and therefore part of the meaning, or **sense,** of declarative sentences.

unaspirated   Phonetically voiceless stops in which the vocal cords begin vibrating immediately upon release of the closure, e.g., [p] in *spot.* Cf. **aspirated.**

unbound   A pronoun or pro-form whose reference is determined from context rather than linguistic discourse. Cf. **free pronoun, bound pronoun.**

unconditioned sound change   Historical phonological change that occurs in all phonetic contexts, e.g., the **Great Vowel Shift** of English in which long vowels were modified wherever they occurred in a word.

ungrammatical   Structures that fail to conform to the rules of grammar.

uninterpretable   Describes an utterance whose meaning cannot be determined because of nonsense words, e.g., *All mimsy were the borogoves.*

unitary system hypothesis   A bilingual child initially constructs only one lexicon and one grammar for both (or all) languages being acquired.

Universal Grammar (UG)   The innate principles and properties that pertain to the grammars of all human languages.

unmarked   The term used to refer to that member of a gradable pair of antonyms used in questions of degree, e.g., *high* is the unmarked member of high/low; in a masculine/feminine pair, the word that does not contain a derivational morpheme, usually the masculine word, e.g., *prince* is unmarked, whereas *princess* is marked. Cf. **marked.**

uvula   The fleshy appendage hanging down from the end of the **velum,** or soft palate.

uvular   A sound produced by raising the back of the tongue to the **uvula.**

velar   A sound produced by raising the back of the tongue to the soft palate, or **velum.**

velum   The soft palate; the part of the roof of the mouth behind the hard palate.

verb (V)   The syntactic category, also lexical category, of words that can be the head of a verb phrase. Verbs denote actions, sensations, and states, e.g., *climb, hear, understand.*

verbal particle   A word identical in form to a preposition which, when paired with a verb, has a particular meaning. A particle, as opposed to a preposition, is characterized syntactically by its ability to occur next to the verb, or transposed to the right, e.g., *out,* in *spit out* as in *he spit out his words,* or *he spit his words out.* Compare with: *He ran out the door* versus **he ran the door out*, where *out* is a preposition.

verb phrase (VP)   The syntactic category of expressions that contains a verb as its head along with its complements such as noun phrases and prepositional phrases, e.g., *gave the book to the child.*

Verner's Law   The description of a conditioned phonological change in the sound system of certain Indo-European languages wherein voiceless fricatives were changed when the preceding vowel was unstressed.   It was formulated by Karl Verner as an explanation to some of the exceptions to Grimm's Law. Cf. **Grimm's Law.**

vocal tract   The oral and nasal cavities, together with the vocal cords, glottis, and pharynx, all of which may be involved in the production of speech sounds.

vocalic   Phonetic feature that distinguishes vowels and liquids, which are [+ vocalic], from other sounds (obstruents, glides, nasals) which are [– vocalic].

voiced sound   Speech sound produced with vibrating vocal cords.

voiceless sound   Speech sound produced with open, nonvibrating vocal cords.

voiceprint   A common term for a **spectrogram.**

vowel   A sound produced without significant constriction of the air flowing through the **oral cavity.**

well-formed   Describes a grammatical sequence of words, one conforming to rules of syntax. Cf. **grammatical, ill-formed.**

Wernicke, Carl   Neurologist who showed that damage to specific parts of the left cerebral hemisphere causes specific types of language disorders.

Wernicke's aphasia   The type of aphasia resulting from damage to Wernicke's area.

Wernicke's area   The back (posterior) part of the left brain that if damaged causes a specific type of aphasia. Also called Wernicke's region.

word writing   A system of writing in which each character represents a word or morpheme of the language, e.g., Chinese. Cf. **ideographic, logographic.**

Index

599